ONE MAN GAVE LOUISE LOVE

Pierre de Gand, godson of the Emperor himself, taught Louise Vernet what it was to love and be loved. But it was all destroyed in a shattering act of betrayal.

ONE MAN GAVE LOUISE HIS HAND

Robert Prestbury, an Englishman who claimed to be a gentleman, lured Louise into a Victorian marriage. It was a union that trapped her like a vise as he used her for his profit and tormented her for his pleasure.

ONE MAN GAVE LOUISE MONEY

Will Russell nurtured Louise's genius and offered her the financial backing that made her fortune. It wasn't long before her debt to him mounted beyond what she could pay without gambling her heart.

There were many men in Louise Vernet's life who fed her ambition and passion—but where was the one who could give her happiness. . . ?

BANNERS OF SILK

"An absorbing novel . . . an exciting journey through the world of silks and satins in the days of Prince Louis Napoleon."—CLEVELAND PRESS

BANNERS OF SILK

ROSALIND LAKER

A SIGNET BOOK
NEW AMERICAN LIBRARY
TIMES MIRROR

PUBLISHER'S NOTE

This novel is a work of fiction. Names, characters, places, and incidents are either the product of the author's imagination or are used fictitiously, and any resemblance to actual persons, living or dead, events, or locales is entirely coincidental.

This is an authorized reprint of a hardcover edition published by Doubleday and Company, Inc.

SIGNET TRADEMARK REG. U.S. PAT. OFF. AND FOREIGN COUNTRIES
REGISTERED TRADEMARK—MARCA REGISTRADA
HECHO EN CHICAGO, U.S.A.

SIGNET, SIGNET CLASSICS, MENTOR, PLUME, MERIDIAN AND NAL BOOKS are published by The New American Library, Inc., 1633 Broadway, New York, New York 10019

First Signet Printing, June, 1982

1 2 3 4 5 6 7 8 9

PRINTED IN THE UNITED STATES OF AMERICA

My most grateful acknowledgments to Monsieur Maurice Worth for factual details of the life of his great-grandfather, Charles Frederick Worth, and to Madame Ginette Spanier for her advice on the world of haute couture.

R.L.

1

She sat huddled in the darkness, young, afraid, and alone. It was quiet in the pauper's burial ground. Beyond the encompassing railings the lofty buildings that flanked the narrow street shut off all sound of the night-throb of Paris and the lights that went with it. Nothing showed of the flares illuminating entrances to the crowded theatres on the Boulevard du Temple. Oil-lamps spreading a glow over fashionable comings and goings in the Boulevard des Italiens did not penetrate the malodourous alleyways not far away. In the rue de Richelieu, which was no more than a stone's throw over the rooftops, no echo came of the clatter of the hooves on the cobbles by high-stepping carriage horses in the frosty January night. In that year of 1843 the dense labyrinth of ancient properties and the maze of crooked streets that made up most of the city were much the same as they had been over previous centuries.

Nothing disturbed the immediate stillness in the child's vicinity except the shiver of grass around the newly turned patch of earth, and sometimes the scuttling of rats in the garbage that littered the corners and gutters nearby. It was the fifth consecutive night that Louise Vernet had kept her vigil there. She was ten years old, and all she had to defend herself and the place she guarded was a rusty kitchen knife.

Fear kept her from tears. A blurring of her vision could prevent her from sighting any intruder before it was too late. She had braced herself in terror countless times during each of the previous nights, but those unidentifiable figures who took a shortcut along the path through the burial ground had not seen her in the velvet shadows, and whatever nefarious business had them abroad in the night hours, it was not for the purpose of disturbing the recently buried.

Others who passed by, unaware of her presence, at the earlier hour of eight o'clock, were the workers who came from a building farther down the unlit back street. These were a crowd of *grisettes,* the seamstresses who were employed by a certain Madame Camille, one of the leading couturières in Paris. Not that the child knew or understood anything more about them except that they earned their living with a needle, and at the end of their long working day she looked forward to their comfortable femininity surging out into her bleak surroundings and dispelling for a matter of minutes the dreadful solitude that possessed her. Eagerly she would listen for the opening of doors out of her range of vision, and then she would watch for the first rays of the little lanterns that they carried to shine palely across the walls of the buildings opposite in announcement of their coming. As they streamed past, thirty or more in number, their glow-worm light flickered between the railings in a bobbing pattern that touched weed and branch and sometimes the thin face of the child herself. In her desolation she yearned to be part of their company, to keep close to the skirts of the motherly older women while joining in the giggles and backchat of the younger ones, who never seemed quite so weary as the rest, always a livelier rhythm to their footsteps. She never saw them in the morning, being gone before an early hour brought them in to work again, but at night she was warmed and brightened by their passage, all fear banished until the last echo of their homeward trek faded and silence reigned once more.

Now, on this fifth night, they had come and gone. Nothing would relieve the quaking fear of the night-watch for her until dawn dispersed the danger that she dreaded. Suddenly she lifted her head. What was that? Another rat on the move? No, it was a faint screech of hinges. Somebody was coming through the far gate, but without an honest light to show the way. She swallowed hard, aware that even the muscles in her throat had become stiff with terror, and she rose slowly to her feet. The knife shook in her clasp. The drumming of her own heart filled her ears.

The grisette coming into the churchyard had a lantern, but not for the first time the flame had all but gone out, and she cursed it under her breath as she tried to coax the wick back into life. Moreover, she was hampered by the box of outwork, the *travail à façon,* that she carried over her arm, the packing of which had delayed her departure with the others. Normally neither she nor any of the other grisettes used the pauper's path, as it was called, not so much out of respect for those lying there, but for the more practical reason of it being muddier in winter and dustier in summer than the ill-kept street itself. But it provided a shortcut to a square on the far side when on one's own, and was safer than going through the narrow alleyways, where more than one murder had been committed in the past year. At least in the burial ground there was room to run if need be, and Catherine Allard, soft and round and buxom in her twenty-eighth year, could move swiftly enough when she wanted to, her leisurely air deceptive.

In order not to trip anywhere along the path in the darkness she moved at a snail's pace, feeling her way cautiously as she took one slow step and then another, unaware that she was increasing the rigid terror of one from whom she was hidden by bushes. Then at last the wick of the lantern flared high to Catherine's grunt of satisfaction. The glare momentarily dazzled her doll-like blue eyes, but she caught the gleam of a knife blade. Screaming involuntarily, she dropped the lantern in the very second that she registered the gaunt, half-demented visage of the child clutching the weapon. Rage exploded within her. She leapt forward, knocked the knife flying, and then snatched it up from the path to hold it with point angled aggressively. Grabbing the child by the collar, Catherine shook her with a violence that made her own auburn ringlets tumble about untidily.

"All right, you little vixen! Who put you up to this caper? Where are the others?"

"What others, mademoiselle?" Louise cried frantically, almost swung off her feet.

"The rest of the gang of young hooligans waiting to pounce on and rob an honest citizen! I know the tricks!" She raised her voice raucously and bawled into the darkness. "You've met your match in me! Come on out, or else your accomplice here will feel this blade between her ribs!"

Louise gave a screech of fright. "I'm alone! I swear it! And I wouldn't rob anyone."

Catherine cocked an alert ear and listened intently. There came no breath of movement, and she sensed the emptiness of the place. It seemed that the brat she held captive was on her own. Her frown became ferocious. "So! Playing pranks, are you? Take that! And that and that!"

The ringing blows sang in the night air. Drawing breath, Catherine released her captive with a thrust that sent the child reeling backwards to fall in a sprawl of skirt. Returning her attention to her lantern, she retrieved it and found to her relief that it was not broken. After settling the cord of her box more securely into the crook of her arm and tossing the knife into the bushes, the blade on inspection proving to be blunt, she fully expected the misdemeanant to have taken to her heels. Instead the child had risen to her feet where she had fallen, standing stubbornly and defensively in spite of narrow shoulders heaving with sobs and one palm pressed to a blow-reddened cheek, her clothes muddied, and battered bonnet awry. Catherine made a threatening gesture.

"Be off with you! Or else I'll call on the curé responsible for this burial ground *and* the law to decide fit punishment for you."

Still the child stood, her long-lashed amber eyes brilliant with tears in the half-starved face that was contorted in desperate appeal.

"Don't send me away from here." The strength of the sobs made it difficult to catch the words. "If the medical students come with spades there'll be nobody to raise the alarm."

Catherine gaped. Then comprehension dawned, and she raised her lantern, the rays leaping out across the new grave which was being indicated. Her anger and her sympathies were switched. Without doubt this *misérable* had been the victim of a cruel practical joke. "Who sent you to guard this place?" she demanded as before, wishing she could set about the culprit.

"No one. There is no one else and never has been. Just my *maman* and me. That's why I'm here to protect her from being taken away."

A gush of compassion overwhelmed Catherine. She was by nature intensely emotional, able to love and hate with equal ease, her origins stemming from the district of Les Halles where the market folk were renowned for their generosity and good humor as well as for their foul language and lusty appetites. Her own mother had been one of the *dames des Halles,* a warm-hearted, boisterous woman who had slapped fish about on her stall for the whole of her life, supplementing her husband's services with lovers among the biggest and strongest of the meat-porters, for she liked a muscular man with a good laugh and broad shoulders, and she had had plenty to choose from. It was from her that Catherine had inherited a giving heart, but not, unfortunately, the sound common sense that had enabled her mother to weather a tough life comparatively unscathed. Yet in her pity for the child she could have been her own mother, who had concerned herself in her lifetime with many a waif and stray.

"You poor lamb. To think I beat you when all the time you had only a dutiful purpose at heart." Catherine was filled with remorse. Putting aside both the box and the lantern she crouched down to bring her face on a level with the child's. "What's your name? Tell me what happened." With gentle hands she tucked the strands of tangled black hair back under the bonnet, and with the balls of her thumbs smoothed away the tears on the wet cheeks.

The sobs subsided, and amid sniffs and gulps the tale was told. Louise's widowed mother, Anne-Madeleine Vernet, one of the many weavers in Paris who used their own homes as work-shops, had fallen ill, a misfortune that had brought the most terrible hardships in its wake. Everything that could be sold went to raise funds, and then the loom itself had to go. Finally a pauper's funeral ended the sorry tale. Catherine filled in the details for herself of what had followed for Madame Vernet's daughter, with no food that could not be stolen or scrounged, and four terrible nights spent in a churchyard, which was something she would never have had the courage to do. It was said that medical students still helped themselves from new graves when allotted supplies ran short, but how much truth there was in it she did not know and did not want to think about. At least it was a danger safely removed from any grave more than twenty-four hours old. As tactfully and carefully as she could, Catherine managed to explain why the particular violation Louise feared could not and would not now take place.

"So you see, there's no need for you to remain here any longer," she concluded comfortingly.

Louise had absorbed what had been said. She nodded slowly, suddenly at a loss with all responsibility lifted and nothing left to occupy her will or distract her from the gnawing hunger in her stomach, which now seemed to overcome her, making her fold her arms and huddle into herself. Catherine recognised the child's state. The signs were common enough in a city where hundreds were out of work and destitute. She gave a sigh.

"You had better come home with me, Louise Vernet," she

said resignedly, beginning to gather up the lantern and the box again. "I'll find you a bit of supper." It was not really convenient to have a stranger in her quarters, but being the woman she was it was impossible for her not to make some amends for having treated a child with such unnecessary harshness. Moreover, she remembered how she had felt in losing her mother when she had been only a few years older than Louise, and it had been a harrowing time. "I dare say you can bed down in the warmth by the cooking stove for the night," she added generously.

Louise's face became radiant and she sprang into activity, scooping up a bundle of her own belongings and insisting on taking the parcel from her benefactress and carrying it. Miracle of miracles. She was to be given shelter by one of the most privileged beings who lived the life of a grisette. Blissfully she hurried along at the woman's side as together they followed the path that branched away to the distant street gates, the lantern showing the way.

Catherine was uncomfortably aware of Louise's rapt expression. Now that the puckering of fright and distress had been smoothed from the child's face, the arched brows emphasised a look of anticipatory delight as if all life's troubles had melted away. It was best to make the situation perfectly clear.

"I can't do with you under my roof for more than a night's rest." The statement was firm. "You must get yourself off early in the morning even if it is Sunday." She shook an admonishing finger. "And no begging at my door afterwards."

"No, mademoiselle."

There was further emphasis to drive the point home. "In Less Halles where I was brought up it has always been customary to help those in trouble, but anyone who comes back for a second hand-out is acknowledged to be a parasite, and given the boot. Understand?"

"Yes, mademoiselle." Acquiescent. Butter would not melt in the docile mouth.

Catherine graciously volunteered more personal information. "My name is Allard. Catherine Allard."

"It is a pleasure to make your acquaintance, Mademoiselle Allard."

"Hmm." Catherine eyed her again with a sideways glance. "Your mother taught you to be polite, I'll say that for her. It should stand you in good stead. If you tidy yourself up and present yourself at a convent door somewhere you'd stand a chance of being taken in as a future novice. Otherwise you had better try to get yourself into an orphanage, although I hear that the authorities have more children on their hands in these hard times than they know how to cope with."

They had reached the far gates into the square, and in hurrying across it to avoid a drunken brawl Catherine did not notice that there was no acknowledgement of her advice. Louise's mind was racing, and the idea that she should present herself at any institution, be it religious or otherwise, did not come into her budding plans. She had decided to be a grisette. From an early age she had been taught to sew, as were all female children with mothers worth their salt, a meticulous standard set and more than often achieved. She had had an exceptional flair with a needle almost from the start, taking to any kind of sewing and embroidery as readily as she had taken to playing with dolls, and it had been a foregone conclusion between her mother and her that one day she would earn a living by it. Watching the nightly procession of the grisettes go by had settled without question the direction of the course she should follow, and she saw Mademoiselle Catherine as a vital link with her dreams, a link that must be neither severed nor broken. Whatever happened, she must not be sent on her way in the morning.

After a while they reached the row of tall, half-timbered houses where the grisette lived on the rue du Fouarre. Like so many others who sewed for a living she had cheap garret accommodation, the wages earned even by those of her skill and experience being abysmally low. Her lantern showed the worn treads as she and Louise climbed the stairs, one floor after another. In the majority of properties in Paris the better-off people lived on the lower floors and the poorer ones on the upper floors, but this being a student district, and the dilapidated, half-timbered houses more ancient than anyone could estimate, there was little difference in the monetary status of anyone living there. Catherine's accommodation at the top of the house happened to be airier and roomier than average for the rent she paid, and for that reason she continued to live there. As always when she climbed the flight she wondered why she was not thin as a rake with the daily haul of it, but nothing made any difference to her figure, which even in lean times managed to stay more than amply curved, a pleasure to those men who had come in and out of her life over the past years and had broken her heart in the process more times than she cared to remember.

"Here we are." She set a key in the lock, but it was unfastened, and she gave a little moan of joyful surprise, pushing it open eagerly. Louise, following her, saw in the lantern rays that the rafters of the roof sloped sharply to form a large, wedge-shaped room that served as both kitchen and parlour. Expectantly Catherine darted across to the bedroom door and swung it wide, lamplight flooding out to silhouette her in the doorway.

"*Marcel, chéri!*" she exclaimed in loving breathlessness.

Louise, craning her neck, saw a man much younger than Catherine lower the newspaper that he was reading where he sat in his silken shirt sleeves at the end of the bed. There was a scowl on the boyish features, a sulky twist to the full-lipped mouth.

"You're late," he complained harshly in reply to the woman's greeting. "You're usually home long before this hour."

"Yes, yes, I know. I had the chance to bring home some outwork to sew tomorrow, and it created a series of delays." Catherine sounded flustered, her voice high-pitched with exultation. "If I had known you would be here—" She broke off, removing her bonnet and swirling aside her shawl as she spun around to address Louise in a whisper. "Light a candle and help yourself to something to eat. I'll be entertaining my gentleman friend until long after you'll be wanting to bed down. You'll find a coverlet in the cupboard." She swept into the bedroom, closing the door behind her. Its bolt was shot home.

Philosophically Louise set down the box that she now knew contained extra sewing and looked about her. Spotting a candle, she lit it and then doused the wick of the lantern, which she hung on a nail beside the peg where she put Catherine's shawl and bonnet. She soon found the food. It was in a cupboard containing a few cheap bottles of wine such as were sold by any commonplace *épicier*, together with some poor-quality coffee of the bitterest kind. She helped herself to a modest share of the bread, cheese, and cold meat, supposing that Catherine would wish to offer what victuals were available in her entertainment of the young gentleman. And he was a gentleman, in spite of his lack of mannerly address towards Catherine. Louise had seen enough of them around to know that elegance of speech did not necessarily go with politeness, or fine clothes with consideration, and she wondered why Catherine was so taken with him. At least now he appeared to have recovered from his displeasure at her tardiness, judging from the muffled sounds within the room.

Having lived in accommodation that had deteriorated sharply with each move in a reflection of her mother's declining health, Louise had acquired a broader knowledge of life than she would otherwise have for her age and upbringing. Alert and observant, she had seen more in the mean streets and in the hovel dwellings to which they were reduced than Anne-Madeleine Vernet in her sickness had been aware of, and she had learnt to use her wits and take care of herself with an inherent fierceness of pride and independence that had been a trait in both her parents. It had been this ability to look out for herself that had taken Louise back to their last home after the funeral to break in and gather what she could that would be of use before the landlord sold what was there against rent arrears. There was little enough, but when she had left the locked place by way of the window again, she had an old shawl, a small sewing-basket, a pair of woollen stockings, half a loaf from the cupboard, and the kitchen knife. She had sold the shawl and the stockings, eaten the loaf, and Catherine had thrown away the knife, but she still had the sewing-basket which she and her mother had used in sharing the linen-mending that had been their only means of livelihood after the loom had gone. On that sewing-basket Louise had thought always to build her future life. Now she was resolved that through it she would become a grisette.

With a moistened fingertip she took up all the crumbs on the table where she had been eating and popped them into her mouth. With hunger lessened if not abated she turned her attention to the box she had carried for Catherine and untied the cords to lift the lid, interested to see the sewing-work that it contained. She caught her breath at the sheen of yellow satin lying amid tissue paper. It seemed to radiate its own sunshine into the candlelit room. After wiping her fingers on her skirt to make sure that they were clean she raised a corner of the folded satin carefully, and found other layers underneath. A note fluttered free. She read it. There were a number of marks and figures, and a written sentence stated that the satin had to be turned up a certain number of millimetres. Simple hemming. She could do that. Thoughtfully she replaced the lid, certain she had found the means by which she could prove herself. In the morning she would offer to sew every stitch. Had she not been so tired, hardly able to keep her eyes open, she would have made a start now.

Unbuttoning her dress and stepping out of it, she turned to the corner of the stove where she had spread the coverlet. In her petticoat she tumbled down thankfully into its folds, pulling it over her. She was already drifting into sleep when she felt it being tucked more cosily around her. Catherine's bare feet padded away, and the chink of glasses and a wine bottle being taken from the shelf told of her purpose in coming out of the other room. Through a haze of lashes, lids too heavy to lift, Louise glimpsed Catherine in an aura of pale flesh, Junoesque and queenly, long, dark red hair rippling with golden lights over her shoulders and down her dimpled back. Then the door was closed and bolted again, leaving the kitchen in darkness, the candle snuffed.

Louise was up and dressed and had been stitching the yellow satin for more than two hours when the young man emerged from the bedroom in the early Sunday-morning light, thrusting his arms into a well-cut coat. He gave the child a sharp glance and without a word took his hat from a peg, arranging it at a modish angle before a looking-glass, smoothing his hair into place. About to depart, he paused and dived into his pocket to take out a key which he weighed contemplatively on his palm for a few seconds before tossing it onto a wooden dresser. The door closed behind him, and his footsteps faded quickly down the stairs as if he were suddenly eager to get away.

Louise, who had stilled her sewing to watch him with open curiosity, put aside the work with care and went to the bedroom door, which had been left ajar. Catherine lay sound asleep in the tangled bedclothes, sharing the pillow with an indentation that showed where the young man had recently lifted his head. Louise closed the door quietly and went back to her work.

It was past noon when Catherine emerged, roseate with sleep, in a robe made of multicoloured pieces of silks garnered from workshop scraps. Yawning and stretching luxuriously, she looked beatifically at Louise.

"Still here, are you? I thought you would have gone long—" Her voice trailed off in a gasp of horror as she saw how Louise had been occupying the time. "Dear God! What have you done?"

She leapt forward in a frenzy to snatch up one piece of

hemmed yellow satin after another, each being petal-shaped as Louise had discovered, and shrieked as if crazed, beside herself with panic and fury. For the second time in less than twenty-four hours she turned on Louise like a virago.

"You wicked, vindictive little wretch! One small scrap of that satin would cost more than your life is worth!"

Ashen with dismay, not knowing what she had done wrong, Louise managed to dodge the blows aimed at her. "I did it to help. To repay you. To show I can work for what I receive. My hemming is perfect. Maman always said that, and I washed my hands to keep it clean."

"But it wasn't to be turned up that way!" Catherine screamed. "Not a commonplace hem for the ballgown that the yellow satin is going to be. You've ruined it with your ham-fisted digging at the stuff!" In lunging at Louise again, she happened to catch her wide hip on the edge of the rickety dresser, which rocked wildly. A couple of plates danced loose and smashed to the floor, accompanied by the ringing clang of a key. Seeing it among the debris she seemed instantly to forget all else. Her hand went unsteadily to the base of her pulsating throat, and an unnatural calm took possession of her. "Where did that key come from?" she questioned in a half-strangled voice.

Louise, panting hard and trembling at this fresh disaster of the crockery, answered shakily. "The gentleman left it when he went away."

Catherine tilted back her head and closed her eyes, all colour draining from her face, and she spoke more to herself than to the child. "I should have known. He's been coming here less and less, but I believed all the reasons that he gave me." The calmness evaporated and she gave a dreadful groan, bending double and throwing her arms over her head as she collapsed on her knees to the floor. "I can't bear it. I love Marcel. How can I live without him? I'll die! I'm going to die, die, die."

Her grief was terrible to see, far more alarming to Louise than her rage, which had been bad enough. She swayed as she sobbed, all self-control gone in an orgy of desolation, her wailing coming from the depths of her heart. With a child's instinct to comfort, Louise went and put her arms around the woman, who turned blindly to cling to her. Half-smothered by fleshy weight and with her dress soon soaked at the shoulder by the grisette's tears, Louise endured the embrace stoically until at last she could ease Catherine up into a chair.

"I'll make you some coffee," she said consolingly. "It will do you good."

When she had poured a cup she carried it carefully across to where Catherine sat. It was taken from her by shaking hands, and the grisette sipped at it gratefully, her eyes shut, as if trying to draw back from the abyss of despair into which she had been plunged. Louise busied herself unpicking some stitches from a piece of the satin that had caused such trouble between them, and after a little while she brought it to Catherine for inspection.

"Do look at what I've done. It hardly shows where my hemming was. A gentle press with a flat-iron will put it completely right."

Catherine blinked red and swollen eyes at the result being displayed. There was no denying that properly unpicked the satin would be as good as new again. "You're quite the young needlewoman, aren't you?" she admitted warily, scarcely daring to accept that one calamity was being resolved.

"My mother taught me."

"Taught you to read other people's instruction notes too, did she?" There was an edge to Catherine's voice that was lost on the child.

"Yes, she did," Louise replied innocently. "My father taught her to read and she taught me. How did you learn?"

Catherine wiped her wet lashes with the back of her hand and sniffed heartily with some signs of revival. "One of my first gentlemen, the kindest of souls, paid for me to have reading and writing lessons. He missed me when he travelled far afield on business, and wanted me to write letters to him."

"He sounds agreeable."

Catherine heaved a deep sigh that was ashudder with the aftermath of tears. "I was really fond of him, although he was three times my age. I had a comfortable little apartment then on the rue de Soissons, but he died suddenly abroad, and I was turned out into the street by his wife's lawyers."

"Were you a grisette then?"

"Yes, but he didn't want me to work. Unbeknown to him, after a while I did take in outwork, not because I needed the extra money as I do nowadays, which is why I bring a boxful of sewing home sometimes, but simply to keep my hand in, and because it gave me an excuse to see the other girls. I missed the company, you see, the laughs and jokes and the pranks we younger ones played. The first two or three months I nearly went mad with loneliness. Believe me, there's nothing worse in the whole world than being on your own, waiting for the man you care about to slot you back into his life for an hour or two." She saw how starkly her listener was regarding her, and sought to cheer the child. "Don't look so upset. It needn't be like that for you when you're grown up. Keep out of bad ways that your late maman wouldn't like, and one day you'll find a nice young man to marry you."

Louise felt chilled to the marrow of her bones by the bleakness that had echoed in Catherine's voice in her talk of loneliness, the cause of the circumstances immaterial. She felt she had experienced its emptiness to the limits in the churchyard, and the ordeal had set its ice-cold mark on her for the rest of her life. "I don't want to be lonely ever again," she said tonelessly, her lips tremulous.

"Well, you won't be for the time being if the Sisters of Mercy take you in, or the orphanage claims you. In either place you'll have to work hard, but for all your skinniness you look strong enough."

"Why are you not married?"

Catherine thought it was like being questioned by a changeling, that strangely adult and articulate voice coming from a ragamuffin with a quaint face made even stranger by the blue-blackness of tousled locks that sprang back from the forehead as if designed to create a dark frame for the skin's pallor. At any other time Catherine knew she would have resented the inquisitive interrogation, but now it did her good to talk, although she sighed again, more heavily. "The men I would have liked to marry either had wives already, or didn't want to marry me." Recalled memories brought a bitter frown to her brow. "I've met some bastards in my time. My God! One of them walked out of here this morning." Anger grew in her, bringing the colour back into her face, and she straightened her shoulders away from the chair. "Good riddance to him! Not dry behind the ears yet and thought he was doing me favours. *Me!* I even lent him money that I'll never see again, the crafty devil. Why, I wouldn't let him have my key back in his pocket if he came on his bended knees and pleaded for it. I'd snap my fingers at him." She demonstrated somewhat theatrically, " 'Go to hell,' I'd say. 'I've no more time to waste on you.' " Her withering note faded and without warning her face crumpled, fresh tears awash in the violet-blue eyes. "No, I don't suppose I would. I'd probably fling my stupid arms about him and beg him to stay with me awhile longer."

Louise could see that more lamentations were about to begin, and hastily sought to divert her. "I'll get started on unpicking all the hems that I've done."

With thoughts dwelling on her faithless lover, Catherine answered almost automatically. "Take each stitch out with a needle point. No tugging or pulling or catching of threads."

Louise noticed the abstracted gaze, and her sharp urchin wits seized the chance presented. "It will take until midnight to do that. Hours and hours. I'll have to stay on till tomorrow."

A vague nod. "Very well. Just get things right." Catherine stirred on the realisation of the promise she had made and was drawn back into the moment, stroking fingertips across her forehead as if to clear it. She looked towards the stove. "Have you been cooking?" She sniffed the air, aware that it was a long time since she had last eaten. "Something smells good."

"I made some soup out of a few bits and pieces I found in the cupboard." Louise had learnt to make soup from all sorts of scraps, and although it was the beginning and end of her culinary achievements, she did have the gift of making it tasty with plenty of seasoning, herbs, and fried onions. Towards the end of her mother's life she had had to forage for any food she could find, stealing from stalls and begging at doors, and most of it was only suitable for a soup-pot. Sometimes she had had to fight other destitutes for possession of the bounty, and it was as well that Anne-Madeleine Vernet never knew that for her sake her daughter did not spare tooth or claw. Anxiously she watched Catherine go across to lift the lid of the pot and taste the contents with a spoon. There was a nod of approval.

"Fetch two bowls from the cupboard," Catherine said. "I'm sure you're as hungry as me."

They had an unexpectedly companionable meal. Before sitting down to it Catherine bathed her inflamed eyes, brushed her hair, and put on a clean dress. Normally she would have gone to church at that hour, but she had by no means recovered from the shock of her lover's desertion, and she said a pious grace instead, which comforted her. Then at Louise's prompting she talked readily about her work, rating her employer, Madame Camille, high among the renowned dressmakers of Paris. Mesdames Delatour, Vignon, and Palmyre held sway with her, there being no male of any consequence in the field, nor had there been for many years. Much of the work done was commonplace, the customers mostly deciding themselves on how a new garment should be, and sometimes for economy providing a discarded silk dress for lining. If their wishes were not carried out, they would go elsewhere, and such was the number of dressmakers in Paris that even those on the plane of Madame Camille competed fiercely in price. In contrast to the mundane *confection* work, as it was called, there was the grander and sought-after sewing of ball-gowns and wedding garments and all the handsome dresses that ladies had to have for countless changes in a day, together with the masses of petticoats needed to hold out the voluminous, dome-shaped skirts, although even for this elaborate work customers were only prepared to pay a low sum, and the couturières complied; thus no fortunes were made, and the grisette who sewed for a living was lucky to earn whatever came her way.

"We work twelve hours a day," Catherine said between spoonfuls of soup. "That's when trade is normal. Between seasons when it slumps we can be turned off at a moment's notice, which is hard, especially for those with families to support. Then there are times when we're too busy to think, and we have to work right through the night. Some customers are such bitches that for a big occasion they won't order a dress until the day before in case anyone else finds out what they're wearing. Them's the kind I really hate, because they never give a thought to the likes of us stitching away by lamplight until dawn to get it ready for them." She gave a sigh. "We get a miserable pittance per hour for that extra work over and above our regular wages, but it's no good complaining unless a body is looking to be booted out for good." She elaborated on her grievances. "We could do with more space in the workrooms, too. It gets hot and stuffy with the oil-lamps overhead, but at the same time the chill from the flagstones goes right up the thighs, which is why most of us have our own wooden slats in front of our chairs." She tilted her head proudly. "Others working in similar conditions might wear sabots, but not a grisette. We wouldn't be seen dead in them. A grisette, whether she be a seamstress like me or a milliner or makes artificial flowers or any similar dainty work, has her reputation to think of. We like to wear pretty caps, a clean silk apron, and give the men of Paris something to think about when we trip by." A complacent little smile touched her mouth. In spite of her plumpness she knew she walked light as a feather and was used to gathering men's glances wherever she went. But there was respect in those glances too. Grisettes were not prostitutes. Many were virgin when they wed, and others had their lovers, but their position in society was unique, and Catherine knew it had been said many a time that it was the grisettes of Paris who made it a city to see. Her thoughts came back to the moment, and she took another spoonful of soup. "I like the work I do, no matter if things aren't all they should be. I wouldn't want to do no other. Neither would the rest of us. Dedicated, that's what we are. I suppose the truth is that sewing lovely garments is the next best thing to wearing 'em."

Louise had made herself deaf to the more dismal aspects of being a seamstress that Catherine had mentioned. In her mind's eye the life held story-book colours. She could imagine the wonderful shades of the material that was sewn, the sparkle and gleam of the jewels and beads and pearls incorporated into the embroidery that Catherine had described to her, and the flurry of frills and ribbons and feathers as the final touches were added to the exquisite garments. She pictured the workrooms as one treasure trove opening into another, the image quite dazzling her.

"I'd want to wear those beautiful clothes," she burst out, still in something of a dream.

"*Wanting* to and being able to afford to are two different things, as you should have found out by now, young as you are. Only the rich can do what they want in this life."

Louise fixed her with entranced eyes. "Then I'll get rich. Someday I'll dress like the Queen of France."

"Huh." Catherine snorted derisively. "You'd do better to set your sights elsewhere. Queen Marie-Amélie has no taste in attire. She and Madame Adélaïde, her sister-in-law, have clothes dull as ditchwater. They spread their orders out among the leading couturières, and I've sewn seams in their outfits many a time."

"Then the fault must lie with Madame Camille and the other grand dressmakers." It seemed logical to the child.

Catherine frowned across the table at her. "Maybe it does and maybe it doesn't. You're getting a mite too impudent in my opinion. Your maman wouldn't like to hear you being impudent."

She had developed a respect for the late Madame Vernet, an honest, hardworking woman who had not deserved a pauper's grave. All the time the weaver's child was under her roof she would deal with her as the mother would have wished. A thought struck her. "How was it that nobody in your maman's family gave her a helping hand when she needed it?"

"She didn't have folks of her own any more, and she was too proud to ask the Vernet family. Maman had never met them, you see. She was a silkweaver in the city of Lyons when she met and married my father. There was trouble over it, but what sort she never told me. Then, before I was born, he died as Maman did a few days ago with consumption of the lungs."

"Hmm." Catherine peered in sudden self-concern across the table at her. "You don't have a cough, do you?"

"No. Just the stomach-ache when I'm hungry."

"That's all right, then." Catherine was relieved. "Madame Camille gets rid of anyone with a persistent cough, so it wouldn't do for me to go catching anything from you."

With the meal finished, Louise washed the dishes while Catherine looked over the satin pieces in the box. She gave the child a helping hand with the unpicking, not realising that her assistance was not welcomed. When early evening came, all but one piece still held by Louise was done. Catherine heated a pair of flat-irons on the stove and carefully pressed out the material. Then she sat down again, and with nimble fingers she began to fasten the hems as they should have been done in the first place. The opaque side of the satin was the right one and used uppermost, while the shiny surface was brought over into a hem to make a handsome edging to each petal piece, and fastened with an embroidery stitch. Happening to glance up, she saw that Louise was transfixed with fascination at what she was doing. As with the unaffected interest shown in her talk at table, it was balm to Catherine in her present heart-sore state, making her feel she was still a person of some importance, and she realised that the child's oddly old-fashioned presence had eased the terrible day for her. Without someone else to think about and talk to she would have still been lying for hours in sodden, pointless grief on the bed. She was moved to explain why the satin was being thus prepared.

"All these separate pieces will be put into layers on a skirt, making it look like a big, upside-down rose, but first each section must be stitched like this"—she leaned forward in order that the child could see better—"and then like that." Her needle caught the thread in three and then four different ways, leaving it fastened as a minuscule part of a pattern like trailing leaves.

Louise breathed out in awe. "That's clever. No wonder I did it wrong." She bent her head again over the careful unpicking of the final stretch. It was then that Catherine came to see that the child was spinning out the task and had been from the start. She voiced a niggling worry that had been plaguing her against her will.

"What shall you do if there's no getting into an orphanage?"

Louise looked up with a composed expression. "I could come back and sew for you."

"For me?"

"Doing other outwork. You've seen how I can sew. There must be simple stitching I could do, and you could pocket the payment for it."

Catherine stared. "What a sauce you've got! It would cost me my job tomorrow at Madame Camille's if anyone as much as suspected that the outwork I took home went into other hands." She tapped her chest importantly. "I'm privileged as it is. It's not every seamstress who's allowed to earn a little extra."

Louise shrugged her narrow shoulders, dismissing the argument. "You've nothing to worry about. You can check every stitch I do. All I ask in return is that you let me live here until I can get taken on as an apprentice at Madame Camille's."

Catherine threw back her head in a laugh. "You couldn't get the job of picking up pins in any dressmaking establishment of consequence until you're at least fourteen years old. Even I didn't start at Madame Camille's. I served an apprenticeship elsewhere and gained some experience first."

Louise was undeterred. "Then it appears I've lots of time to practise first. In the meantime I'll keep this place clean for you, collect firewood from the Bois, carry water supplies up from the nearest spout, and cook your meals. I'll also be at your bidding for any errands you wish to send me on. In short, everything I used to do for my mother when she was sick. All I want is that one day I'll be a seamstress just like you."

Catherine's soft heart could not harden itself against such flattering appeal. Moreover, the conditions were solely to her advantage. She could always bring home petticoat frills to be hemmed and understiffening that had to be sewn, as well as other straightforward items that normally she did not bother with, choosing the more complicated work that paid better. Nobody need ever know she had not done the work herself, and she would let nothing go by that was not perfectly executed. But outweighing the temptation of a few extra francs to ease her frugal standard of living was the thought of having the everyday household chores lifted from her shoulders, which she always found hard after the exacting work she did for Madame Camille. She decided that no harm could come from giving the suggested arrangement a trial.

"We'll see how it goes," she said cautiously. "In the meantime, you can forget about leaving tomorrow."

Louise gave a long sigh of thankfulness. Catherine searched her memory to try to discover why she should be reminded of something that had happened in the past. Then she remembered. Once she had taken pity on a stray cat, only to suspect later that it was the cat which had selected its new home. Well, she had liked that cat. There was no reason why she should like the weaver's daughter any the less.

2

It was not Catherine's intention to exploit Louise's willingness to work. Still pining over the faithless Marcel, she accepted without much thought the new leisure time that was given her. No more going to market unless it suited her convenience; no more carrying water buckets or scrubbing floors or preparing vegetables; her clothes were washed and ironed and left in neat piles; her shoes took on a daily shine, and her bed was always smoothly made. In addition, there was the extra money that Louise's outwork brought in. The girl had had plenty of practice in sewing at top speed when she had shared the linen-mending with her mother, and the payment for the poorly rated sewing tasks mounted up better than Catherine had anticipated.

Louise had been two months in her new home when Catherine awoke one night to see candlelight flickering under the door. Thinking that Louise must have fallen asleep before extinguishing it, she rose to make the economy of nipping the wick. The sight that met her was not what she expected. Instead of being tucked up under the coverlet in the corner, Louise sat, still fully dressed, at the table, bowed over her sewing and asleep. With consternation Catherine realised just how such an abundance of work had been completed, even allowing for a speedy needle, and it was then she stopped having the last foolish regrets about her lost love, and became herself again. She shook Louise gently by the shoulder.

"Wake up," she said in soft tones, nodding a smile into the sleep-heavy eyes that opened. "You can't sit in this chair all night. I don't suppose the floor is very comfortable either. I'll see about getting a truckle-bed in the market for you tomorrow."

Louise knew then that she had nothing more to fear. Catherine would never send her away. Only one cloud remained on her horizon. She had discovered during their talks about the life of a seamstress that a premium had to be paid for apprenticeships in dressmaking establishments of any standing. Catherine would never have obtained one if her mother had not still been alive at the time and secured one for her far below the usual rates. Madame Allard had seized the chance of placing her young daughter with a skilled dressmaker from the provinces, who had decided to open modestly in Paris. The unfortunate woman, being unused to Paris ways, had been dealt with ruthlessly on all sides, not least by Catherine's mother, who had taken advantage of her ignorance of city premiums. Bankruptcy finally closed the little business, but not, luckily for Catherine, before her training was completed. In the hope that fate might have some similar stroke of good fortune in store for her, Louise ignored all mention of sweat-dens that swallowed up unapprenticed sewing-hands, and rededicated herself to her needle. She found Catherine to be a patient and interested teacher, more than willing to pass on her own exceptional skills in the time ahead as each new stage of advancement was reached.

Slowly and steadily their relationship strengthened into the kind of bond that bridges the gap between an older and younger sister. Catherine liked companionship, being too garrulous and sociable to be content with her own company, and Louise, with the adaptability of the intelligent child, settled completely into her surroundings.

A year and more went by. During that time Louise discovered how easily and unwisely Catherine could fall in love in what was undoubtedly a search for a man who would give her the lasting devotion for which her affectionate nature craved. It began to dawn on Louise that most of Catherine's troubles stemmed from her inability to judge character in the opposite sex, love blinding her to faults and imperfections.

As Louise began to develop physically, Catherine talked about having a narrow space under the eaves made into a bedroom for her, there being a window on that side to give light, but even such a modest scheme would take more money than could be spared, and nothing was done about it. Instead, a patched and faded curtain was rigged up around the truckle-bed to give some degree of privacy, and Louise had no complaints.

Except when the seasonal rise and fall in trade brought Catherine close to dismissal through lack of orders or nigh to exhaustion through overwork, nothing other than the men in her life disrupted the day-to-day existence in the garret. Together she and Louise managed well enough on their meagre funds. There were few treats, but Catherine was childlike in her sense of fun and would choose occasions to celebrate, decorating the place from a store of paper flowers she kept in a box, and there would be a bottle of cheap wine from the épicier on the table, Louise's glass well watered down. For all her emotional instability and often foolhardy behaviour she was steadfast in looking after Louise. Her maternal instincts were strong, and had she been fulfilled in marriage, she would have done well with a large family to care for.

Every Sunday they attended church together. Catherine was a devout worshipper with a genuine piety of spirit that others might have found incongruous in view of her apparently questionable morals, but Louise did not hold to that opinion. She understood that Catherine was enthralled by love and, in loving, gave without stint with the whole of her heart. Had she not benefitted herself through Catherine's essential goodness in taking in a homeless starveling from a pauper's burial ground? If Louise had any complaint it was that Catherine paid too much thought to what she believed the late Anne-Madeleine Vernet would have wanted for her only child. Many a pithy reprimand and heavy clout had been delivered for any lapse of manners, or just for coming home late from an errand, giving cause for anxiety. It often seemed to Louise that had she been a novice in a nunnery she could not have been better protected or kept on a stricter path.

After church, whatever the weather, they would go for a walk, mingling with the crowds that made every Parisian Sunday a joyous escape for all from the long and heavy labours of the week. At times a sense of pure carnival prevailed, and always the people came into their own, making the city theirs, and were never refused admission to the royal gardens by the sentries at the gates of the Palace of the Tuileries unless a man was foolish enough to wear a working frock smock instead of some better attire, or there was a show of drunken behaviour from either sex. Catherine was always enlivened to a happy mood on these Sunday walks, even when a love affair was on the wane; it was as if for one day in the week all troubles must be put aside, and she would chat away to Louise as if her tongue never tired or her lungs needed breath. Often they would meet some of Catherine's friends or fellow workmates, when jokes and laughter and gossip were exchanged, most of which would have been lost on Louise if it had not been her way to listen and observe and learn whatever she could wherever she went. Talk among the men when they all sat on the grass in the gardens of the Luxembourg Palace or ambled in a group by the Seine was invariably political, a subject not normally shared with women, but Catherine with her Halles origins had decided opinions and did not hesitate to voice them, which resulted in lively discussion and argument. As a result Louise became aware at an early age of the tug and pull of politics, weighing up all she heard, and sometimes pausing to listen when out on an errand to soapbox speakers in the street, the cry invariably for political reform. She often felt she would have been better equipped for all kinds of discourse herself if she could have gone to school on a regular basis, her only attendance having been a span of sixteen weeks when Catherine had had one particular lover who had made her an allowance sufficient for her to do without Louise's outwork. There had been a clean pinafore for the first day at the charity school, a pair of good second-hand boots, and a dress cut down from one of Catherine's. Louise had not wasted a moment of her school time, avid for books and learning, and the day it came to an abrupt end she had her own reasons for being as terribly downcast as Catherine that the man, a suave, complacent fellow, should have been given a long prison sentence for embezzlement. Afterwards, when Catherine had recovered from the blow, she realised she could have persuaded him to give her a little extra to have the room made under the eaves for Louise, but by then it was too late.

If on their Sunday strolls they failed to join up with others there was still plenty to see and do, particularly on a fine day. The Bois de Boulogne made a leafy setting for thoroughbred horses and their riders, while the fashionable boulevards held a constant stream of elegant equipages bobbing with parasols and high silk hats. Everywhere of interest the people promenaded leisurely in their best clothes, Catherine and Louise among them. Under the bordering trees the professional entertainers gathered, the mountebanks and the jugglers, the beggar bards, the fortune-tellers, the strong men breaking chains, and those with dancing bears or performing monkeys or trained dogs. Louise liked the tragic actors most of all, enraptured by the short, highly dramatic playlets that were performed. Catherine, who had a respect for the nicety of things, tried always to set aside a sou out of her wages for their Sunday outings so that she was able to drop a contribution into at least one of the hats shaken under their noses as they moved from one source of amusement to another among other spectators.

Occasionally they caught a glimpse of King Louis-Philippe when the royal coach went bowling by. A few always waved and cheered their country's constitutional monarch, but he was not a popular figure, and over the years he had become the butt of ridicule and scorn. Lampoonists were particularly savage, depicting him as a dumpy figure looking more like a provincial shopkeeper than a royal personage, the umbrella he invariably carried exaggerated out of all proportion to emphasise his lack of personal fire in all things military. This matched the bourgeois dullness to which he had reduced the trappings of royalty from the splendour of the Empire days, even the royal fleur-de-lys having been removed by his orders long since from the panels of his carriages. A sword in place of an umbrella would have been much more to the liking of many Frenchmen, who yearned to see France restored to heights of power and glory. Plots and counterplots were discussed and schemed, with occasional attempts at assassination. The King himself continued to go about his duties without overconcern for his personal safety, leaving the uselessness of worrying to his wife and his sister, who made a point of sitting on either side of him in the coach to offer him some protection against an assassin's bullet. Louis-Philippe had more interest in restoring Paris from the neglect of previous decades, which was a tremendous task, but to him the city owed a considerable amount of embellishment as well as the improvement of some pavements and the widening of a few central boulevards. Staunch to the Napoleonic legend, which was entirely divorced from the pro-Bonaparte militarism that was rife, he had seen the Emperor's body brought home from St. Helena and had had the great man's statue reinstated on its column in the Place Vendôme. Old soldiers often gathered there on the anniversaries of the battle of Austerlitz and other splendid victories, all of which had been carved into the stone of the finally completed Arc de Triomphe. Catherine made her own laurel wreath every year to add to others that constantly adorned the railings at the base of the Emperor's statue, not so much in tribute to the past, but in hope for the future. Many people believed that Prince Louis Napoleon Bonaparte, in exile in England, was the Emperor's own son and not just his nephew, and Catherine was one among a host of others who held to the opinion that France would not be France again until a Bonaparte held the reins once more.

Thus, on principle, she never turned her head when the King rode by. Had the Queen and the King's sister been alone in the royal carriage with their bonnets nodding the familiar abundance of plumes, she still would not have looked, knowing that in relation to fashion they were nothing to see. Marie Duplessis, the famous courtesan, was another matter, being dressed by Madame Camille with far more style, but glimpses of the young, raven-haired beauty of declining health were rare, living as she did without show or flamboyance in the pattern of manners set by the royal court, which had changed much since the days when the Empress Joséphine had held sway.

A Sunday outing was never considered complete by Catherine unless she had done some gazing into shops. She liked best to visit the rue de Richelieu, where the most fashionable establishments were to be found. Once the Empress Joséphine's gowns had been made for her in the rue de Richelieu, and the tradition of fine merchandise fit for the grandest in the land was still firmly entrenched there. Although there was little contrived display for the common passer-by, Catherine and Louise, standing side by side, would peer through the glass to glimpse within the garments and fripperies that a grisette's wages for a whole lifetime would not be enough to buy. At number 87 beautiful bonnets created by Pinaud were to be seen, their plumes wafting in a slight draught, their clusters of roses and ribbons holding every hue of a flower garden, the lace within the brims delicate as cobwebs. Lachuitt sold furs of unbelieveable magnificence at number 104; chinchilla and ermine, lynx, musk, and Siberian sables, which always roused Catherine to a sensuous envy, making her shiver with delight as she imagined their softness against her skin. In the elegant premises of Verdier, the renowned cane-maker, parasols with ferrules of coral, jade, and carved ivory with handles to match, were suspended like vast butterflies from the ceiling by silken cords. La Maison de Caravanne lived up to its name in a profusion of jewel-coloured brocades and silks and gauzes from as far afield as India, China, and Japan, but Catherine, who was accustomed to sewing such materials in her daily work, always passed them by with no more than a cursory glance. Audot, the goldsmith, was more to her liking, specialising as he did in travelling cases that held gold-topped bottles and trinket boxes, while Fossin, jeweller to kings and princes and popes, displayed precious wares that sparkled on cushions of velvet in the gloom of the closed showrooms. One of the imposing entrances was to that of Maison Gagelin, which supplied materials to the leading couturières, one of whom, Madame Delatour, had premises almost next door. Madame Camille's establishment was no great distance away, the tastefully classic façade giving no indication that to the rear of the building was the cramped work-shop where her seamstresses sewed extravagant clothes to an outlook of a dismal alley where the rats scuttled in rubbish-strewn gutters.

Catherine and Louise had planned to take a walk to the rue de Richelieu on the first Sunday in April, which was to be a celebration of Louise's twelfth birthday, when a heavy shower sent them scurrying into shelter in the Louvre. Catherine, who was always overawed by so many pale statues and dark paintings, shook the raindrops from her shawl and stepped back to gape at a large sepulchral relief, not noticing the man close behind her who had also come in out of the rain. He could have avoided her bumping into him if he had stepped aside, but he had been eyeing her under the brim of his hat ever since she had entered the place, and seized the opportunity to make her acquaintance.

"La! Your pardon," she exclaimed upon contact, not knowing who it could be, and a firm hand steadied her elbow. Turning, she saw a stocky man of medium height with a squarish face, roguish eyes, a knowing mouth curled into a smile, and without doubt an engaging way with him. The coquette in her rose to meet the unmistakable invitation to flirtation.

"Who's taking up the most room?" she challenged archly. "You or me?"

"Not you, mademoiselle. It was my fault entirely. I should have seen how absorbed you were in that masterpiece. You obviously have a real taste for all this stuff." He gestured sweepingly to encompass the treasures around them. "Perhaps I could prevail upon you to explain the merits of that lump of sculpture to me." He caught his breath in affected apology. "Forgive me again. I have not presented myself. I'm Henri Berrichon and I've not been long in Paris. Just three months to be exact. And you, mademoiselle?"

Introductions took place. Louise half expected to be ignored, having observed that men favoured with Catherine's smiles rarely had eyes for anyone else, but he bowed to her and inquired after her health and was altogether a thoroughly pleasant man. In the exchange of talk that followed, neither he nor Catherine referred to the sepulchral relief or anything else in the Louvre again, interested only in each other, the opening pretext having been duly made use of and discarded. Before long the three of them were drinking hot chocolate, an unbelievable luxury to Louise, at a café on the Boulevard des Italiens. The sun had come out again, creating a rainbow over the city and striking the same colours from the drips that ran from the scalloped edge of the awning under which they sat at one of the small, round tables amid ball-shaped mulberry trees in tubs. This is what it is like to be rich, Louise thought, letting the nectar of the hot chocolate roll over her tongue. When she was rich and dressed grander than the Queen of France she would drink chocolate three—no, four!—times a day. *Mmm.* She drained out the last drops with a sucking noise that made Catherine kick her ankle in reproof under the table while her smiling attention appeared to remain on Henri Berrichon.

When they left the café he, having learned it was Louise's birthday, bought her a paper twist full of caramels from a street hawker, and then, shortly afterwards, he purchased a bunch of violets from a flower-seller for Catherine, saying that they matched her eyes. By the close of that momentous Sunday Catherine was in love again.

By trade he was a horse-dealer and, like so many to whom money is easy come, easy go, he was extremely good-natured and generous to the point of being extravagant, taking a pleasure in spoiling Catherine with little gifts to please her. Louise was never left out, receiving a hair-ribbon or a handkerchief trimmed with lace, and sometimes, after he had heard from Catherine how she liked to read, a leather-bound book from a market stall. He had a keen sense of humour and a huge belly-laugh to go with it, able to reduce them to helpless mirth with his endless quips, which suited Catherine, who liked nothing better than a jolly atmosphere. It was not long before Louise was certain that Catherine's feelings were reciprocated by Henri in full measure. There was a look that was warm and tender and cherishing in his eyes whenever he regarded Catherine, which Louise had never seen in the eyes of any other man who had professed to love her. All too often it had been a burning, somehow frightening look like hunger trapped behind glass that, with time, faded to no more than a glaze of boredom, heralding an end to the affair. With Henri, Louise was sure that things were to be different.

To her delight she was always included when he took Catherine on Sunday outings, and throughout the summer there were picnics and joy-rides in wagonettes and boat-trips on the Seine. Often they ate in *guinguettes* where the air was hot and rich from the roasting meat, and the three-piece orchestras played nonstop for the singing and dancing in which everyone joined robustly. Sometimes when they were homewards bound after an expedition Henri would dart into a *rôtisseur's* shop, and through the grease-spattered window Catherine and Louise would watch him pick out the best-looking chicken among those sizzling golden-brown on the spits above a blazing fire, and when he emerged with his purchase they would carry it home with all speed to enjoy a succulent supper. Apart from all the pleasure that Henri brought into their lives, best of all to Louise was to see how happy he and Catherine were together. She thought she had never witnessed anything more touching than the blissful way they held hands, the loving manner in which they cuddled, and the everlasting radiance in Catherine's face. Yet that radiance was like a candleflame beside a lamp after Henri had proposed to her and she had promised to be his wife. Overcome, she had put her arms around Louise and wept with joy.

When the last of the autumn horse-fairs had been held, signalling the start of the winter stagnation in Henri's trade, it seemed only sensible that they should continue to live in the garret for the time being. Henri gave the whole place a coat of whitewash and bought timber and mixed plaster to construct the long-awaited room under the eaves. He made it much larger than Catherine had envisaged possible, and built a good-sized bed, which made her decide that it should be their room, while Louise moved into her own smaller one when the day came. Although she and Henri had been lovers for a considerable time, Catherine with her romantic heart and that curiously puritan streak in her would not move into the new quarters with him until his ring should be on her finger. "I want to feel like a bride," she told him quite shyly. He, humouring her, kissed her fondly.

The wedding dress was sewn from a length of russet silk that he had bought her, and it lay in its shining folds over a chair beside the prettiest bonnet she had ever owned. One evening there came a demanding knock on the garret door. Catherine, tidying a stray curl back into a ringlet with one hand, opened the door to a tight-faced woman standing on the threshold.

"Yes?" Catherine asked, thinking she had never seen a visage more sour.

The woman looked her contemptuously up and down before replying. "So you're the latest," she observed scathingly in a Rouen dialect. "Where's my husband? I'm Madame Henri Berrichon."

The truth came out. Catherine sank into a chair where she sat completely stunned and could not speak for the shaking that possessed her whole body from her quivering jaw to her jerking fingers. Henri Berrichon had been through a bigamous marriage during the six years that had elapsed before his wife traced him to Catherine's door. Although the woman waited until midnight for his return and called again next morning, Henri did not appear. Whether he had glimpsed his wife on her way into the house from a distance, or had been alerted by some sixth sense, was never to be known. He had slipped from his wife's grasp once more. Neither Catherine nor Louise saw him again.

There followed a winter as gloomy and full of heartache as the summer had been carefree and joyous. Louise was still convinced that Henri had truly loved Catherine, that he had genuinely found the woman with whom he would have spent the rest of his life, but in her anguish and disillusionment Catherine clapped her hands over her ears and would not listen to any words of comfort. The russet silk dress and the bonnet were packed away and never worn, and with a histrionic gesture of despair that symbolized the end of all zest for life, Catherine turned the key on the new room and all that was in it.

3

The winter passed. In the spring of 1845 the key still remained turned in the door of the spare room. Louise had no objection to continuing to sleep behind the curtain on the truckle-bed, but she did think they should supplement their income by taking in a lodger. Catherine, who had not ceased to mope, refused to have the suggestion discussed. Louise, logical and clear-headed, feared that her friend would never recover her spirits and get on with living again if the room continued to be kept as a kind of shrine to the past as if Henri had died in it. Unbeknown to Catherine she kept it clean, having a dread of large spiders taking over in there, and as she aired the good straw mattress that Henri had bought and banished the dust she was irritated by the unused space. On all the other floors every available nook and cranny was rented and sublet, accommodation at a low rent always being in demand. For the first time she did her outwork with some resentment. It was not that she minded a stitch of it, but that Catherine should continue to set aside through mawkish and unhealthy sentiment a source of income that could add a piece of rabbit or some pig's brawn to the table now and again as a change from the eternal vegetable stockpot offended a stomach that in the past had known near-starvation and still did now and then when the dressmaker trade slumped. Not for the first time it grated on Louise that Catherine should be unnecessarily improvident.

The return of warmer days brought stuffiness to the garret, but with a window open wide Louise could sew in whatever breezes skimmed the rooftops. The sounds of Paris reached her as if carried by the sunlight in a hollowed rumble of wheels and a clatter of hooves on cobbles. She heard the shouts of street vendors blending with the noise of family living that came from lower floors and neighbouring buildings, a baby always crying in one direction or another, and with it all the twitter of birds that pecked among the garbage far below. Within the house there was the constant thud of banging doors and feet on stairs, but usually she worked undisturbed without any direct interruptions. On the day she heard somebody mounting the last section of the flight to the top landing she raised her head, her needle poised in her hand, wondering who it could be.

A knock came. She put aside her sewing and answered the door to a stranger. He was young and tall and lithely built, his top-coat well fitting, somewhat dusty from long travelling, and he had set down beside him a small, brass-cornered trunk, which he must have carried on one broad shoulder up the stairs. He was extremely personable, not far from being handsome, clean-shaven with crisp, dark hair. His forehead was broad with peaked brows over narrow, brown eyes that were very bright, alert, and intelligent, the nose splendidly shaped, the mouth firm-lipped, and the chin determined.

"Bonjour, mademoiselle." He was smiling at her in a friendly manner. She realized with some embarrassment that she was staring at him and was brought back to herself with a start by his pronunciation that told her at once her mother tongue was alien to him. Quickly she returned his greeting, inclining her head.

He had a book ready in his hand that was phrase-book and dictionary combined, and began to read a sentence haltingly from it. "Have—you—a room—to—rent?" he inquired in tortured French.

Then she knew him by his accent to be an Englishman.

She had heard his fellow countrymen imperiously ordering porters and cabbies about outside the Hôtel des Princes and other leading hotels, some of them with full command of the French language, but many more dragging it under heavy vowels. "You have come to the wrong door, monsieur," she replied. "It must be somewhere else in the house that a room is vacant. I did hear that a lodger on the floor below this one is leaving."

He looked at her blankly, and she realised he had not understood one word of what she had said. Recovering himself, he thrust the phrase-book forward for her to point out the translation of her reply. She found the negative answer that would have been adequate, but at the same time she had second thoughts about turning him away. Catherine would have to face up to the opening of the room sooner or later, and this seemed as good a time as any. Without further hesitation she indicated the sentence that stated a room was available by the month at reasonable terms. Then she found a currency table on the next page and showed him what the rent would be, basing it on what was paid for accommodation on the other floors. The young man nodded to show that the terms were acceptable if the room should suit him.

"Come in," she invited gravely, feeling the weight of the responsibility she had taken upon herself.

He thought her a quaint creature, neither child nor woman, but awkwardly in between, while having a distinctly sure and adult air about her. He reshouldered his trunk, made sure it was balanced, and then removed his hat politely with his free hand as he entered. Looking around, he was relieved to see the place clean, which was more than could be said for the gloomy staircase and the hall below. Personally fastidious, he could live in poverty, but not in squalor, and the simple furnishings of the combined living-room and kitchen did not offend him. In any case, with no more than five pounds left in his pocket he was in no position to be too selective.

The girl unlocked a recessed door and stood aside for him to enter first. He set down his trunk, and found himself in a typical attic room of ugly proportions, with barely enough space to get past the wide bed built under the eaves, but it was clean and smelt faintly and not unpleasantly of newish timber and whitewash. A narrow window with four panes gave light onto a small, round table and a chair which, with a chest of drawers and a chipped enamel basin on a rusty metal stand, made up the room's only other furniture. He put his hat on a peg by the door to show that he was satisfied with the accommodation and would take it. Oddly, the girl looked both pleased and scared by his decision, and he thought he had better make himself known to put her at her ease.

"My name is Worth," he said slowly and clearly. "Charles Frederick Worth, to be exact."

She comprehended and gave a quick bob. "Louise Vernet."

He thought the way she had spoken her name quite enchanting. On another scale he would have to master the Gallic inflexion that came hard to an Englishman, while at the same time learning the language as fast as he could, or else he would never find employment in the trade in which he was fully qualified.

"I'm honoured to make your acquaintance, Louise," he said, thinking that the seniority of his twenty years should give him the right to address by her Christian name a girl whom he judged to be about seven years younger than himself. She smiled in reply and shrugged sweetly to show that whatever he had said had gone beyond her understanding this time. When she held out her hand he would have taken her fingers to bow formally over them, had not her palm been turned uppermost to receive the first month's payment in advance.

When the door closed after her he took two swift strides to the window and flung it wide. Paris! He was here at last! Let others go to the New World to make a fortune. He had chosen a totally different sphere to conquer. The monotonous view of rooftops stretching away into the distance did not disappoint him. Nothing could disappoint him on this day of days. In any case, his artistic eye enabled him to appreciate the mellow russets and greenish-greys of the weathered tiles set at crazy angles amid crooked chimneypots against a high, clear sky.

He breathed the air in deeply, wanting to become a physical part of the city in which he had arrived less than two hours ago. How well the journey had gone. First boarding the Channel packet at London Bridge and then sailing away down the Thames in sunny weather. A good crossing to Boulogne, a few night hours spent snoozing on a bench until dawn while better-off passengers took hotel accommodation, and then an outside seat on a coach where he had cheerfully viewed the soft green flatness of the French countryside, not caring about the bone-shaking discomfort of the ride that continued throughout his second night in France, or the heavy shower of rain that had made water drip from the brim of his stovepipe hat. Then, with the coming of the dawn, the windmills on the hill of Montmartre were sighted, and not long afterwards, with a thunder of wheels over cobbles, he had been swept into Paris. He had wanted to shout his jubilation aloud. How eagerly he had twisted on his seat to look enthusiastically in one direction and then another as the city stirred in the rising sunlight that had blazed within the vivid yellow blossom of the drooping laburnum and was caught, dappled, in the foliage of the limes and poplars and shady chestnuts. On all sides wooden shutters, peeling paint on the tall houses cramped together, were thrown open in an endless staccato clatter as sleepers awoke, giving him glimpses of yawning faces and wallflowers in jars on windowsills and occasionally a stretching cat. In doorways, some studded like those of the forts that guarded the stout walls and defensive ditch around the city, the concierges were busy with their brooms, the dust billowing out in little clouds on the warm air.

As the coach lumbered on, the postillions urging the tired horses over the last lap with cracking whips, he smelt the true Paris in the blend of aromas that came and went from the numerous cafés and vine-adorned wine-shops, the malodorous back alleys from which beggars were appearing trailing their rags, in the fragrance of cigarshops, and the spit-and-polish of the glossy carriages taking home all-night revellers. Traffic was increasing, trade wagons with heavy wheels rolling out of archways and milk-carts jogging by in a clanking of cans and ladles. Fountains were being turned on, sparkling streams gushing from the mouths of iron fish and cupids and gargoyles to supply the city with water, some housewives already gathering with their buckets, and in other streets they were having it poured for them from water-casks or from the baskets suspended from yokes on the shoulders of individual water-carriers who kept up the persistent cry of *"Eau! Eau!"* Everywhere all kinds of hand-carts rumbled along as people arrived with produce for market, vegetables and fruit brimming the baskets. It seemed almost odd to him that so many folk could be stolidly starting their daily round in total ignorance of the dawning for him of one of the most momentous days in his life. *Paris!*

Not far from the Arc de Triomphe the mud-splashed and

dusty diligence had set down its passengers. Trying to appear as nonchalant as if he travelled abroad every day of his life, he was nevertheless extremely thankful when a fellow passenger gave him some advice about where to start looking for accommodation. And he had found it. One garret room to make his own domain in the rue du Fouarre and—here he leaned out of the window and looked down—the use of an outdoor privy in the courtyard below.

It did not take him long to unpack. He made up the bed with the linen and blankets he had brought with him, not having expected bedding to be provided at the small rent that he could afford. On the table he placed his Bible, which he was accustomed to reading from early every morning, giving deep thought to spiritual matters, although regular church-going had been given up with childhood. Beside it he arranged his sketching materials which he used to capture in a simple, untrained style whatever subject caught his interest. The last items to be unpacked from the trunk were his tools of trade, consisting of a tape measure and a large pair of sharp shears necessary to a draper's shop assistant, and he hoped it would not be long before they were needed. Louise had brought him a ewer of hot water, and after washing away the dust and tiredness of the journey he changed his clothes and brushed the outer garments he had discarded before hanging them on the row of pegs. Pulling his cuffs neatly into place under his sleeves he glanced about his new home with a satisfied, proprietory air. Now to settle the emptiness of his stomach at the cheapest café he could find, and afterwards, once he had got his bearings, he would start looking for work without further delay.

As he came from his room he saw that the girl was sitting by the window, hemming a length of cambric. He tried out the phrase he had rehearsed in readiness.

"I—am—going—out—to—luncheon." It rather dressed up the inexpensive repast he was planning, but it had been the nearest to what he had wanted to say. To his surprise she repeated the phrase, correcting his pronunciation, and gratefully he took note, saying it again and able to hear the difference himself.

"Merci," he said with a flourish, feeling a little like a pupil who had gone to the top of the class.

She nodded. *"Bon appétit, Monsieur Worth."*

He went out and down the rickety flight of twisting stairs,

swinging his new cane. Once outside, he felt a trifle conspicuous with his debonair accessory in such a poor area, several dubious-looking people pausing in whatever they were doing to stare after him. He hoped it was merely curiosity about a stranger in their midst that was prompting their unwelcome interest, because he had no wish to be set upon and robbed, or to be forced to defend himself with the blade that flicked out of the end of the cane when a button in the top was depressed. He would never have bought such a cane himself, but before he had left London, friends had clubbed together to present him with it as a memento, certain he would need it more for defence than for fashion in a foreign city where the unlit streets away from the boulevards were notoriously dangerous.

In the days when he and his brother, who was older by a number of years, had lived in the comfortable house at Bourne in Lincolnshire, he remembered that his father had had a collection of elegant canes, several having blades concealed. He could see them now in his mind's eye, each one polished and shining and taller than he was at the time, the tops made of gold and silver and ebony, engraved with feathery designs and initialled *W.W.* William Worth, lawyer and gentleman who, when Charles was still a young boy, had been brought down to ruin by a passion for the gambling-tables, the racecourse, the prize-ring, the cock-pit, and any other means of gambling by which a man might lose his head and empty his purse. The house at Bourne and its pleasant garden, the horses and carriages, the household staff, and all that had made up a secure family life gone, all gone. To Charles the shock and despair of his dear mother overshadowed the upheaval of everything else. He knew she had never recovered from the loss of his two sisters in infancy, and it went hard with his kindly nature to see her misfortunes increased as she was turned out of her home, humiliated and hurt at every turn. For himself he cared nothing, but no one deserved less to suffer than she. He knew he would never forgive his father for what had been done. Mrs. Worth in her turn, left deserted with her youngest child, was at a loss to know where to go and what to do. Her elder son had received his law training while there was still enough money to foot the bills, and as he had to make his way in the world she was determined not to make herself a burden to him. She sought refuge with a branch of the family who had no gaming ways and enjoyed the high standard of living to which she had been accustomed from birth, having been a Quincy of Quincy before her marriage, and they agreed to take her in, but they were hard-headed folk, lacking in compassion and generosity, and she was given the ignominious post of housekeeper in return for her keep and an annual pittance that was barely enough to keep her in working stockings. "But not the boy," her ill-graced benefactor said in tones that brooked no argument. "One charity mouth to feed is enough. Take him away from school and set him to work."

He was eleven years old. Intelligent, sensitive, and affectionate, he found himself sent away from all that was dear and familiar to him, in a printer's shop, his heart sinking at the grime and ugliness and sheer tedium of his new life. He worked from dawn until darkness, sleeping in exhaustion at night on sacks under one of the presses. Each day he awoke to a new loathing of the ink-mixing and the sweeping up and the turning of roller-handles that filled every minute of his day. Yet he did not spare himself. It was not in his nature to be slothful, and he did his best, but the prospect of spending his future years in a trade completely alien to his interests was dreadful to him. As time went by he toyed with the idea of running away to sea, but was abhorred no less by the thought of a seaman's life. His health began to be affected. From a strong-looking boy he became painfully thin, the smell of printer's ink nauseating him until he vomited up whatever food he had managed to force down. He had been a year in the printing trade when he faced his mother at breaking point.

"I'm not made to be a printer, Mamma." His whole expression was one of desperation. "Every day has been purgatory for me."

They were sitting on a seat in the park, Mrs. Worth not being encouraged to receive visitors, not even her own son, in the house she could never think of as home. She reached out restless fingertips and touched his pale cheek in loving concern.

"I know you've not been happy, my son. But we must be grateful to our cousin for helping me to secure employment for you when it was most needed."

He was deaf to what she was saying, bent only on his impassioned plea that the course of his life be changed. "Don't make me stay there any longer," he implored her. "You can set me free of my misery if only you say the word." He caught her hand as if he were drowning. "If I don't get away I'll die."

Suddenly she truly believed that he would. Since their last meeting there was much more than unhappiness in his young boy face. It seemed to her he was gaining that hollow-eyed, high-boned look that all too frequently heralded the dreaded consumption. She came close to panic. "You shall not stay. We will find something else for you to do." Then the breath was almost knocked from her body as he flung his arms about her in speechless relief, but as she cradled him to her she felt swamped by the very hopelessness of what she had promised. "What would you perfer? There is no point in saying again that you would like to be an artist, because I could not afford to support you for as much as a day during whatever instruction would be required."

He drew back and smiled seriously in reassurance as if he had become more adult than she. "I know that, Mamma. All I want is to work in surroundings as different as they could possibly be from a printer's shop, somewhere that has material finer to handle than paper and I can see what is going on in the world instead of reading about it in newsprint."

"But where?" she asked helplessly. "What kind of work would that be?"

He looked entirely confident, beaming at her. "In a draper's shop. Not a small, local business, but one of the renowned establishments in London where there would be the chance of promotion after finishing an apprenticeship." Eagerness flooded his voice. "Do this for me, Mamma. Secure be an apprenticeship. Say, oh, say you approve of my ambition."

She took his face between her hands, her gaze travelling fondly over him. "I do," she endorsed, thinking how he never failed to amaze her, always as practical as he was aesthetic in his tastes. There was nothing unmanly about her fine son. She felt obliged to offer a word of caution. "If we should manage to obtain such an opening for you, the work would be just as hard and tiring as in the printing trade, and the hours even longer."

Amusement danced in his eyes. "It's not hard work I detest, Mamma. Only printing presses."

Mrs. Worth did everything in her power for her son. She humbled herself completely in order to persuade her influential cousin to write letters to the Draper's Guild on Charles's behalf. With closed lips she endured the biting sarcasm directed towards her supposed indulgence of her offspring and did not flinch under the scathing reminders of her own dependence upon charity. She was shut out of a family consultation to discuss the matter, and possibly it was agreed between them that the sooner she was separated from her son the better it would be. With all maternal ties severed they themselves could look for even more concentrated service from her.

Whichever the way of it, Mrs. Worth cared only that the letters were duly forthcoming. Her dear Charles was to get the chance he wanted, and nothing else counted. A six-year apprenticeship at the esteemed linen-drapers Sawn and Edgar was to be his, and during that time he would serve a twelve-hour day, live on the premises, obey to the letter the rules laid down for good behaviour, and have little time off. At the end of it he would be a fully-fledged salesman with a trained knowledge of every branch and department of selling the merchandise concerned, able to deal with all types of customers, and ripe for advancement should he prove himself possessed of exceptional ability. On the day of his departure she went to see him off on the stagecoach with his brass-cornered black trunk. She embraced him, popped a guinea into his pocket that she had obtained through selling her best lace collar, and kept up a smile until a curve in the road took his still waving hand from her sight.

Charles arrived in a London that was just getting accustomed to having a new young Queen ascended to the throne. It was a larger and more confusing and exciting place than he had ever imagined possible, with streets crowded with traffic. The shop where he was to work was situated at the south end of Nash's elegant Regent Street at Piccadilly, the most fashionable as well as one of the busiest centres in the whole of the great capital. Somewhat overcome he presented himself at the premises numbers 45–51, and was at once absorbed into the drapery business.

He took to it like the proverbial duck to water. The dormitory and living-quarters that he shared with his fellow apprentices were spartan, furnished with only the barest necessities, but had he been attending the eminent public school where he would otherwise have been if the family fortunes had not changed, he would have found no better surroundings, and the food provided would have been of similar quality, ample and sustaining while giving no quarter to taste-buds. He was always too hungry to pay much attention to flavour, being ever active and never idle, and he took his meals with the rest of the young gentlemen of the establishment, the female sector being segregated into another dining-room as well as into their own sitting-room after working hours, which he thought was a pity. Such segregation added to the similarity to school, together with being addressed solely by his surname, whether by employers or workmates. He became so used to being called Worth that it was unusual for him to hear his Christian name, a pattern set for the rest of his life.

For the first year an apprentice was everyone's dogsbody, but Worth's interest and willingness as well as his quickness with bills and accounts were soon observed by Mr. Edgar, whose partner, Mr. Swan, had died many years before, and while Worth was still only thirteen he was advanced to the post of cashier. But he had not come to London to deal with coins and banknotes, and before long he asked to be assigned to selling the fine merchandise of materials, shawls, mantles and all else that the shop retailed. The rules of good salesmanship were drummed into all beginners, but having been reared in the manners of a gentleman it was natural for Worth to greet customers at all times, and other aspects of selling followed as a matter of course. He worked hard, and being of a companionable nature was never short of friends. Puberty had come early to him, and he soon became a tall, well-built youth. As for London, he came to know it better than any other place. It had, he thought, the most beautiful women in the world.

He loved women. Not lasciviously and not only with the natural desires of any healthy, growing youth, but with an eye to their shape and form that would have had him setting down their likeness on canvas or sculpting them in marble, had his earlier yearning to be an artist been fulfilled. He had always adored his mother and thought often of the sisters he had lost, and from an early age had sought to kiss the little girls in their frills and ribbons who had come to parties at the house at Bourne before all had gone down in a rattle of dice. He fell deeply in love with his pretty governess when he was seven years old, and when one day he stroked her bare forearm with reverent fingertips she was wise enough not to destroy his innocent passion by a show of shocked disapproval that would have instilled a sense of something shameful in him; instead she smiled kindly and kissed the top of his head, inadvertently cementing his belief that women lived to be admired. Now he found that in selling material by the yard, or capes or shawls or any of the accessories pleasing to women, he could judge exactly the colour and style best suited to an individual customer's complexion or her hair or her eyes, or even to enhance her appearance generally.

The ladies who shopped at leading stores expected and received the best of attention whether they made a purchase or not, nothing being too much trouble for the assistant who served them and who always maintained a perfect politeness however querulous their demands, and the handsome young apprentice-salesman at Swan and Edgar's was without equal in his service. His charm, his genuine interest, his way of looking at a woman as if she eclipsed all others, made them seek him out at whichever counter he happened to be. Inevitably temptations came his way, but those whom he advised on adornment were not necessarily the women he fancied. It was because on the whole he saw them more as the finished product of his creative sales, an image he might have brought into being with an artist's brush, and he was both wise and straightforward enough to turn a blind eye to subtle blandishments. He was not aware of having high principles, but the waywardness of his father's behaviour had set an aversion in him to all that was loose and callous and akin to greedy self-indulgence. Yet, being strongly sensual, it went hard with him to be deprived of female company in his own free time.

He received no wages as an apprentice, which barred him from theatres and concerts and even the humble pub. The small amount of money that his mother was able to send him twice a year went on such necessities as soap and shoe repairs. Yet, for no charge at all the whole panorama of London was his, and he had seen the young Queen on her way to her coronation and many other processions and sights of royal splendour. Every single morning the Life Guards rode in a brilliant splash of scarlet and gold down Regent Street to Whitehall and St. James's. During his training when orders were delivered to personages of importance he was often picked out through his good-looking apprearance to carry out the task, which gave him the opportunity to enjoy the hustle and bustle of the city at an hour when he would normally have been behind a counter. He happened to be in the Mall when the Queen and Prince Albert were setting out from Buckingham Palace on the first stage of a state visit to Paris.

As he stood amid the cheering crowds being acknowledged by the small, white-gloved hand within the carriage, he knew a spurt of envy for those of the entourage accompanying the royal couple. How grand to see Paris, the centre of fashion that influenced every piece of merchandise that passed through his hands. It left him feeling vaguely discontented as if somehow he could never reach the peak of his chosen career unless he had had some experience at the very core of French modes. Later, looking back, he knew it was that day when the seed of his great ambition was planted and began to grow.

Since his arrival in London he had made the most of every other kind of free entertainment, including the galleries of paintings and sculpture where there was no charge for admission and he could study works of art and make sketches of his own to store away for future reference. He had never forgotten one of his earliest visits, when he had come face to face with the famous portrait of Queen Elizabeth with her red-gold hair, her upstanding ruff high and wide and delicate as butterfly wings, wearing the flame-coloured gown with its design of eyes and ears that proclaimed her omnipotence as sovereign of the land. He had understood the quaint symbolism of the design that told of the Queen seeing and hearing everything, and the luxuriance of the heavy velvet outmatched anything he had ever seen. "If ever I'm rich enough," he had promised himself under his breath, "I'll have that copied. I'll have stuff with eyes and ears." Now that he was older the vow was becoming inextricably linked with a sense of destiny.

In the galleries he always found the women of the past no less beautiful than those of the present time, and from the day when he had viewed England's greatest queen he took careful note of the way they had adorned themselves throughout the centuries, his interest heightened by the wide knowledge of materials that he was gaining through his apprenticeship. It intrigued him to see how velvet of a softer quality was used as a provocative agent to enhance a creamy bosom, how silk was gathered to diminish a waist, the way merino was cut with style for an eighteenth-century riding habit, and the manner in which gauze and other gossamer fabrics were used, particularly by Gainsborough, for ethereal effect. It came to him how these ideas could be adapted to suit women of the present day, whose garments had lost the joyous enrichment of their charms and over the past decade had taken on a prim, almost defensive air. Even the low-cut ballgowns sewn by fashionable dressmakers out of the fabrics that he sold had such tight crossfolds and elaborate berthas that more was hidden than revealed, making chaste, unapproachable alabaster of fine shoulders and hiding glorious depths of cleavage.

Every time he emerged from a gallery his eyes were offended afresh by the daunting rigidity of silhouette in which every woman, rich or poor, was encased. The bonnet, the shawl or mantle, and the dome-shaped skirt made them as uniform as pawns on a chessboard. He did not wish for a return of the farthingale, ruff, and slashed sleeve, but he wished that the dressmakers who made clothes for those of their own sex would use more imagination. Until the middle of the previous century couturiers and corsetiers in France had always been men, and although Madame Rose Bertin had made those magnificent panniered gowns for Marie-Antoinette, it was high time that another Leroy came onto the scene. He had sewn for Parisian women those high-waisted gowns of Napoleonic times, emphasising the beauty of their breasts and the allure of their hips and thighs with diaphanous materials that had clung and floated with utmost seductiveness. Worth had come to the conclusion that fashion should both free and beautify women, not imprison them. On these thoughts and others more complex he would turn his steps in the direction of Piccadilly, his brief spell of liberty over for another week.

His apprenticeship drew to a close. He went to work for a short while at Lewis and Allenby, the silk mercers, also in Regent Street. Of all the fabrics, silk was the one he most favoured, and he was already an expert in judging its quality and origins. His intelligence and business acumen was noticed by Mr. Allenby, who took an interest in the new junior shopman, seeing that he stood out from the rest. Although promotion would soon have come Worth's way, the idea of going to Paris had laid such a hold on him that he could think of nothing else. He gave in his notice. Mr. Allenby, wishing him success, offered testimonials in French, a thoughtful suggestion that Worth appreciated. He wrote to his mother and told her of his decision. Would she lend him the money for the fare?

Mrs. Worth was dismayed at the thought of all he would be throwing away in London to go to a foreign city with only a few words of French that he had taught himself from a book. How did he know whether the status he had gained in England as a fully trained shop assistant would be acceptable in Paris? But she had not blocked his way before and she would not do it now. Swallowing her pride, still not inured to the slights and snubs she received daily in the household, she once more sought her cousin's aid. This time it was for money. She had none herself and had kept her son in ignorance of the miserly amount she received in her employ. After a certain amount of procrastination, which her unpleasant benefactor deemed necessary to keep a poor relation in her place, a reluctant purse was opened on condition that the sum was repaid to the last farthing. Mrs. Worth was able to send her son his fare, with just enough over to guarantee his keep for a short while until he found employment. It was as well that she was not informed as to the number of those without work in Paris, or she would not have slept at night.

Worth, swinging his cane as he came out of the back streets into the rue de Rivoli, was full of optimism. Opposite him across the street was the elegant shop of Luclère, where bonnets and cowls and shawls were displayed. That was as good as any place to start presenting himself for employment. But first of all he must satisfy the inner man. Ten minutes later he was enjoying his first taste of bouillabaisse from the steaming bowl that had been set before him.

When Catherine came home and heard that the room was let she flew into an hysterical rage, the thought of another man crossing the threshold of the room that was to have been her nuptial quarters with Henri Berrichon threatening to cause her a nervous collapse. Louise, white-faced, endured the tirade for as long as she could.

"Monsieur Worth is nice," she insisted stoutly. "He's homeless in a land that is strange to him and knows so little French that I doubt if he's been able to ask the way. He will make a good tenant, I'm sure of it. It's not as if he were one of our own countrymen to remind you of—someone else." She saw that she had struck the right note and Catherine, a little calmer now, was listening. "And he paid a month's rent in advance." She dived her hand into her apron pocket and held out the attractive display of money.

Catherine drew breath, looked at it, and then looked away again as if still unpersuaded, but in her heart she knew that a new source of income could not have come at a better time. The dressmaking business was in the doldrums due to the summer orders having been filled and it being far too soon for anyone to give a thought to autumn clothes. There was no more outwork to bring home to Louise for the time being; several grisettes had been crossed off the working list only that morning, and others would be out tomorrow. It was touch and go whether she would be among the senior seamstresses surplus to the amount of work left in hand. It would be madness to reject the money.

"Very well," she mumbled reluctantly. She took the francs and locked them away in the little box where they kept their funds. The high color remained in her cheeks, an angry defence against the pain behind her eyes. Anything remotely reminding her of Henri Berrichon was almost more than she could bear. The intruder's only saving grace was his being an Englishman. "I'll see how things go with this Monsieur Worth. If he drinks or whores he'll get thrown out on his ear." She emphasised her threat by rolling up her sleeves and setting her hands on her waist as if getting ready for the task. Louise could see that she was returning to normal and was more herself than she had been for a long time.

Shortly afterwards Worth came in. He had had a disappointing day as far as getting a post was concerned, but on the other hand he had become familiar with the city and gained his bearings. He bowed to Catherine as the introductions were made, but any attempt at conversation, even with the aid of Louise and the phrase-book, was too much for him at that point. He had the physical fatigue of two days' travel and two nights that were practically sleepless catching up on him, and he had walked the city for several hours since.

"Bonne nuit, mesdemoiselles," he said, and went off to his room.

Catherine glared after him. "Stand-offish, isn't he? He found time to exchange a few words with you earlier, so you said, but he had none for me. Who does he think he is? This is my home, and he's here on my sufferance."

"He looked very tired," Louise said placatingly. Privately she was warming herself on the little smile that he had given her.

Catherine sniffed, but said nothing. She was never to take to Charles Worth. Through no fault of his and none of her own he had appeared as an intruder to her, and in an oblique way she was never to forgive him for not being Henri Berrichon. Irrational though it was, a fact she partly recognised, she could never overcome a feeling of enmity towards him.

As it happened, Catherine was not put out of work during the falling-off of business, but was kept on to sew a wedding gown for stock. Normally nothing was made except to suit each customer's individual requirements, but bridal raiment was the occasional exception, it being necessary always to keep two or three in stock for those marriages that had to take place with undue haste. Adjustment could be made to suit the bride's particular taste or measurements, and there was nothing like an elaborate wedding gown that must have taken months of preparation in its making and ornamentation to quash any hint of scandal about the occasion. It was one such wedding dress that Catherine and those other senior grisettes retained worked on together, the rich satin skirt spread out over the large table, a thousand pin-tucks being exquisitely stitched by hand.

At home Louise, now quite accomplished, utilised her skills in some sewing work for a neighbour that came her way, and afterwards made a new dress for herself out of two old ones she had outgrown. She used the material of one to inset bands into the other that increased in width as they passed down from waist to hem in what was known as pyramid trimming. Daily she sewed, and daily Worth went out searching for employment. One look at his face when he returned told her he had had no luck.

"Never mind, Monsieur Worth," she would say, finding some remark to cheer him. "Tomorrow is another day."

They had fallen into the way of talking together every evening for an hour or more before Catherine came home, which was an invaluable aid to him in extending his vocabulary and improving his pronunciation. Without either of them referring to it, he usually made himself scarce before the hour of eight o'clock heralded Catherine's return, her dislike of him more than noticeable. He was puzzled as to why Mademoiselle Allard should be so hostile, not being used to it in any woman who had not been spurned, and for his part he found her Rubenesque appearance pleasing to the eye. Since to his knowledge he had done nothing to offend her he could only conclude that with her own livelihood always precariously in the balance and with so little employment available generally, she resented a stranger coming into the country to take work away from a Frenchman. Well, she had no need to worry so far. His stumbling attempts at the French language shut doors to him before they were opened, and on one occasion he had suffered the humiliation of being openly ridiculed for some error of speech that he had made. Each setback only strengthened his determination not to be driven out of Paris by failure, and once on his own in his room again he sat at his table studying and writing and memorising his French by candlelight far into the night.

He was hungry all the time. Energetic and vigorous, still at the age of needing plenty of sustaining food, he often had to make do for the day with a stale loaf from the local boulangerie and a small lump of cheese or an onion. He went out of his way to avoid passing restaurants and patisseries in his search for work, his mouth stinging with saliva and his empty stomach groaning as the delicious smell of food tormented him. It was bad enough in the garret in the evening when Louise prepared a meal for Catherine, but he used this time to eat whatever he had for the day, which lessened the additional pangs he would otherwise have suffered. And every morning he began again a search for the work for which he was suited. Sometimes he managed to get a few hours of menial work loading wagons or clearing drains, while his continued hope was that a shop employer somewhere would eventually recognise the quality of his references as being more than enough to outweigh his shortcomings in the French language.

Louise had long suspected he was getting little to eat, but with no outwork herself, and Catherine down to minimum wages, they could not spare any of their frugal fare. She would gladly have given him her portion anytime, but she knew that Catherine, being as protective towards her as a mother hen, would make sure it did not happen a second time by telling him to leave. In fact, Louise was certain that Catherine was watching and waiting for the first possible excuse to be rid of him. Nobody could have been quieter or less trouble under the same roof, but Catherine could not reconcile herself to his presence. When Louise questioned her as to the reason she would shrug off a definite reply.

"He'd be better off somewhere else among those of his own kind," or "Why he had to come to France in the first place I'll never know."

Louise, who could not endure the thought of Worth being told to leave, felt sometimes as if she herself were treading on glass. The slightest wrong move could bring disaster. Two or three times, out of the corner of her eye, she had observed Catherine's sharp scrutiny when she had done her hair in a new way. Normally she wore it hanging down her back as girls of her age did, but wanting now to appear more grown up in Worth's eyes she had taken to tying it up with one or other of the hair-ribbons that Henri Berrichon had given her. It was not as if she had not reached womanhood and had every right to appear more adult, she told herself, tilting her face critically to one side and then the other as she examined her reflection in a looking-glass. She had long since given up any hope of her sharp facial bones taking on the fleshy prettiness she admired in Catherine, but she found the analytical assessment of her appearance as fascinating and absorbing as did any other young girl awakening to her own allure and in love for the first time.

She was not aware of it being love at first. The sweet and tender emotion that welled up in her just on the thought of Worth was so utterly new and strange that she was bewildered by it. Catherine in love was a passionate creature, needing to touch and fondle constantly, forever leaning against the lover's shoulder, seeming to find it difficult to breathe, so rapidly did her voluptuous bosom rise and fall, and with it all there were those burning looks that spoke such volumes of what went on between a man and woman in their mating. With no other measure to judge love by, it had taken Louise some time to recognise the origin of her own feelings, which bore no resemblance in outlet to Catherine's amorous turmoil, but were on a gentle, almost nebulous level that did not look beyond a supreme contentment in the beloved's company.

She wondered how one said *je t'aime* in English. She picked up quite a smattering of English words and expressions from him during their conversation-times and stored them away in her retentive memory, but love had never been mentioned in any context to give her some clue as to how it might be expressed. She had no desire to confess her feelings, shying away from sharing even that intimacy with him, but for her own sake she would like to know how the most beautiful words in any language were expressed in the English tongue.

"You are looking very *élégante*," he said admiringly when she was wearing the finished dress with the pyramid trimming. He had seen her sewing it on many previous evenings.

She was overwhelmed by the compliment, smoothing the gathers over her lap where she sat and drawing her shabby boots back under her chair. The only things she hated in her life were her market-stall boots, it being so difficult to find cast-off footwear that was not well worn and uncomfortable. Out of a nervous embarrassment she sought to deprecate the garment she had made. "Do you really like it? It looks what it is, two old dresses made into one."

"But you have made such a charming *châle*." It was an incorrect word and he saw her puzzlement, but the true one evaded him. As he sought about in his mind for it he leaned forward on the bench where he was sitting and touched the drapery looped in scallops around the neckline. "This ornamentation here."

She swallowed hard. His fingertips had accidentally brushed her flesh and it was as if fire had shot through her. *"Collerette,"* she said.

He struck his forehead in exasperation with the heel of his hand. "Yes, yes, of course. I should have known that. The English word is basically the same. Why do I have to add stupidity to everything else?"

She was indignant, straightening her spine away from the back of the chair. "You're not stupid. I think you're very clever. Only a short time in France and already you're able to say so much that I can understand."

He chuckled ruefully. "Not everyone has your patience with me. I find it so much easier to converse with you than with strangers."

"You do?" She held her breath, suddenly unable to look at him, and lowering her lashes she concentrated on lacing her trembling fingers in her lap. She felt his eyes on her and feared with her whole being that he would become aware of the love for him that was emanating from her.

His face drew into a thoughtful expression, kindness in his eyes. He knew and understood and revered her youthful and ephemeral devotion, and with that inner eye of the artist that was his, which enabled him to draw back and view a woman as if she were a work of art, he could see beyond the hesitant girl that she was now to the woman she would become. Out of those brittle features, the bird-sharp cheekbones and the nipped chin, those huge, black-lashed eyes with their topaz depths, and the full-lipped, rosy mouth, there would bloom a rare handsomeness, combined with a power to fascinate. In her present trembling, vulnerable state she already possessed those indefinable depths of mystery that were an essential quality in any feminine woman, and without which beauty itself was a veneer that meant nothing. Such a creature could wear the clothes of any century to perfection. Even the simple dress that had disappointed her needed only a minor adjustment to enhance her graceful arms and hands.

"I'm sure I know what should be done to your dress," he said on a deepening note of enthusiasm. "Wait a moment." He jumped up and went into his room from which he returned almost at once with pencil and sketch-pad. With a few swift lines he captured the outline of her dress and changed its whole appearance by adding a loose falling cuff to the sleeves of the same pattern as the pyramid trimming. "*Voilà!* What do you think of that?"

All tension went from her as she appraised the simple innovation. "That's clever! Those cuffs would make all the difference."

He smiled, handing her the sketch to keep. "I can't take all the credit. I saw similar cuffs on a comtesse in a portrait in the Louvre."

She gave back a smile, unconsciously holding the sketch to her heart. "Then I'll be in grand company."

When she wanted to know more about his drawing skills he explained that he had plenty of ideas, but little ability to express them beyond a few sharp and telling lines that captured the essence of the subject. Had he been tutored in art it might have been different. He sometimes thought he should have been a sculptor, having discovered long ago that he could fold and drape materials to his will, much as he might have moulded clay or carved marble. The colours and textures of fabrics had become his palette and his chisel. Later when Louise looked at the sketch again, she was glad he had drawn in her face, the few dots and dashes somehow catching her likeness, and she felt it showed that he had looked closely at her. It was small comfort, but unrequited love garners every grain.

When Catherine saw the sketch she expressed dislike of the sleeves. She disapproved on principle of anything Worth said or did. Although Louise imagined that her secret love was her own, Catherine was well aware of it. And she was jealous. She could not help her jealousy any more than she could help the hostility she felt towards the young Englishman, simply because she was a woman who thrived on loving, and to be bereft of it while Louise's face was lost in romantic contemplation exacerbated her present unhappy state of mind. Her nerves were constantly at screaming pitch, and she would hurl herself into a quarrel with Louise on the slightest pretext. Afterwards she would be ashamed of her pettiness and weep tears of remorse.

"Forgive me," she would beg. "I don't know what's the matter with me these days."

But they both knew that the cause was the breaking of her heart by Henri Berrichon. Out of compassion Louise would always readily forgive the hurt Catherine had inflicted, and all would be well again until the next time.

With no regard to the disparaging remarks that her friend had expressed about Worth's sketch, Louise made up the sleeves that he had designed for her out of some leftover material. She was delighted with the result, able to see that they gave the dress considerable style, and she basked in his praise when he said how well she had carried out his idea. Every day he became dearer to her.

Before long Worth ran right out of money. He was behind with the rent, and each day he feared that Mademoiselle Allard would tell him to leave. In desperation he tried again as he had done before for other work to tide him over, willing to labour in the widening of two or three of the boulevards that was taking place, move crates, or sweep gutters, but with so many men increasingly frantic for work the tall young foreigner with the artistic hands was continually thrust aside.

Then miraculously his luck changed. Turned away with others from restoration work on a monument when the complement of workers for the day had been filled, he happened to notice a shop called La Ville de Lyons with quality goods in its windows. He straightened his hat, brushed a little dust from the restoration site from his coat, and marched in with an air of perfect confidence. In his much improved French he asked if there was a vacancy for an assistant.

"There might be." The proprietor himself came from behind the counter and looked him up and down. Smart young fellow, good-looking, and an English accent that could be cut with a knife, but that did not matter if he could serve well. "What made you come applying to me?"

"I simply saw your shop and thought I'd like to work in it," Worth replied with disarming honesty.

"Hmm. Do you have your indentures? Letters of reference?"

Worth, who went nowhere without them, brought his papers out of an inside pocket and presented them. The proprietor glanced over them. He had been to London buying woolen cloth many times and was familiar with Regent Street and St. James's and other shopping areas of distinction. Swan and Edgar's. Lewis and Allenby. The names stood out and he knew them to be businesses of high repute. He prided himself on a similar elegance and good taste in his merchandise although his shop was on a smaller scale. "Hmm," he said again. "You had better come into my office, Monsieur Worth. Yes, you may do that. We'll have a little talk."

It was soon settled. Within half an hour Worth had served his first customer at La Ville de Lyons and made a very successful sale. He was totally happy to be back at the work he enjoyed and knew so well, and he was convinced that at last he had taken the first rung of the ladder that would lead him to the top.

When the shop closed at eight o'clock he cheerfully tidied the stock on the shelves for the morning, and in his shirt sleeves he swept the floor. All the way home he walked with a buoyant step, beaming to himself with pride. As a bonus a lady had tipped him for putting her parcels into her carriage, and it was enough to buy him a little food and some coffee, which he was carrying in his arms.

He ran up the flights to the garret floor, and there he stopped in dismay. Outside the door was his trunk and a pile of his books. He hammered a fist on the door. Catherine's voice shouted from within.

"If that's Monsieur Worth, go away. Your rent is ten days overdue and your accommodation here is terminated. All your possessions are out there. I'm an honest woman and nothing is missing."

It was on the tip of his tongue to tell her he had work and would be paid at the end of the week, but his pride prevented him. He had never grovelled in his life and he was not going to begin now. His anger surged. "So be it. Whatever is owing shall be paid to you before long. Is Louise there?" He wanted to say farewell to the girl.

"No, I've sent her out. You've turned her head enough. Goodbye to you, Monsieur Worth."

He knelt and repacked some of his belongings, managing to get his purchases in the trunk and his books strapped to it. Then he shouldered his trunk and went down the stairs and away from the rue du Fouarre. Out of his first week's wages he sent the outstanding rent by messenger. Catherine accepted it and sent him back a receipt. She did not ask the messenger where he was. She did not want to know.

4

For a long time Louise looked for Worth wherever she went, but she never saw him. In a city of well over a million people it was not to be wondered at, but always she hoped to see him somewhere. Several times in the early days she mistook strangers for him, disappointment overwhelming her when heads turned and unfamiliar features were revealed. But gradually she became resigned to the state of things, thinking that he might even have returned to his native land, and the day came when she could go out on an errand without making it a search for him.

They had moved from their garret, Catherine having decided that they should make a fresh start in new surroundings, and taken a room with two sleeping alcoves on an upper floor above a warehouse in the rue St.-Martin. The accommodation was no less mean than before, but it did have an outside wooden staircase that gave easy access, and a view of the river from the windows that appealed to Louise, who never tired of leaning out to watch the traffic on the water. Catherine was more influenced by the lower rent, although they were soon aided in their financial situation by a state event in another country. There was to be a double wedding in the Spanish Royal Family, the young Queen Isabella of Spain and her sister, the Infanta, having decided that it should be a joint marriage ceremony. The Infanta's bridegroom was to be one of King Louis-Philippe's sons, the Duc de Montpensier, and so it was to be expected that French couturières should be entrusted with the making of all that would be required by the royal brides. Madame Camille was chosen to make Queen Isabella's wedding gown as well as over fifty dresses regal in style for the royal trousseau. Since it had all been arranged at extremely short notice for so important an event, the needlewomen of every established dressmaker of repute were soon working night and day to complete the other orders that poured in from ladies of the Spanish aristocracy as well as from others of the French and foreign courts who were invited guests. Needles flashed, scissors cut, and thousands of metres of silk chiné, satin broché, damasks, and taffetas and mousseline de laine were measured out, some by Worth at his counter, horizontal stripes and shot colours being the height of fashion as well as every shade of apricot and green and blue. All was made up into countless variations of the long established fashion of stiff, dagger-pointed corsage, sleeves cut with horseshoe openings to reveal a tight undersleeve, and huge skirts stiffened beneath with cumbersome bands of a horsehair material known as *crinoline*. Louise came in for the nail-breaking work of sewing the hateful crinoline onto underskirts, but she was thankful to have plenty of work again, and Catherine was working all through several nights on the royal wedding gowns.

When the feverish activity was done and those in the dressmaking profession drew breath again, Catherine and Louise went on a foray to the old-clothes stalls in the Rotonde at the Marché du Temple, a rare treat for them both. Dealers whom Catherine knew from the past had bargains to offer her that were kept back for special customers. As long as the quality of the material was good, the age and style of the garment itself was unimportant, because they would unpick the seams, dispense with any worn parts, wash and recut and sew it into something new again. In this manner they were able to have garments in materials that they could otherwise never afford, cheap cotton being the best they could have off the roll.

To complete the shopping expedition, piles of shoes and boots on other stalls were raked over to find a fairly good pair for Louise. She had never complained about having to wear cast-off shoes, not even when her heels had been chafed and her toes rubbed sore, because she knew that funds would not run to new shoes for her as well as Catherine, who had to be neatly shod to meet Madame Camille's rules, apart from anything else. But on this occasion she did remark on a smothered sigh that she wished she could cobble as well as sew, and then she could always have comfortable shoes on her feet. Catherine, who had never given the matter much thought, was stricken by conscience, and after recounting the money in her purse decided to make her own latest pair last longer and let Louise choose a new pair, saying that this time funds could run to the purchase. Overjoyed, Louise chose a pair of flash leather with waisted heels and did not tire of admiring her feet in them, thinking how the slimness of her ankles was enhanced by the fancy lacing.

Strangely, it was the boots that revived her yearning to see Charles Worth again. She felt that he, more than anyone else, would have approved her new elegance from head to toe. Her remodelled garments bore no resemblance to their original state when purchased, but had been cut to a considerable flair under Catherine's direction. The sleeves of the grey cloth coat were an adaption of those he had once designed for her dress, and with bindings of ochre velvet from somebody's cast-off waistcoat, Louise felt she looked elegant enough to call on the King at the Palace of the Tuileries. The new boots completed the ensemble. Surely if Charles could see her dressed so finely he would find an echo of more than friendship for her in his heart.

Her pining for him was to her an exquisite sensation, neither pain nor pleasure, but linked to the burgeoning of full maturation. She became quite dreamy at times, given to gazing into space with her needle idle in her hand. Where was he? Did he ever think of her? For the first time Catherine had to remind her constantly of chores that needed to be done.

The mood eventually dispersed. The boots split the first time she wore them in the rain, and she outgrew the garments, letting tucks out over the bosom and taking seams in at the waist. Again she concentrated on the more practical aspect of living, tender memories relegated once more to the back of her mind.

Worth had left La Ville de Lyons. It had served him as well as he had served its customers, enabling him to establish himself solidly in the French drapery trade while at the same time allowing him to exercise the language, which he now spoke fluently. His only regret was that he found it impossible to banish his English accent no matter how he tried to sound as if he were Parisian-born.

"Ah! You are English, monsieur," was the remark most forthcoming as soon as he opened his mouth, causing his smile to freeze slightly. Eventually he became accustomed to the comment and used his very Englishness to make himself remembered. With satisfaction he heard those customers who did not know his name ask to be served by "the Englishman." This acceptance of the situation did not lessen his determination to make French as much his own as his mother tongue, accent and all. Nightly he continued his studies by candlelight, much as he had done in the rue du Fouarre and again at his later lodgings. Now he had an attic room that was no improvement on accommodation he had had in the past, and it had similar views of variegated rooftops and lines of dingy washing.

He read as a matter of course the trade and fashion magazines, such as *Le Follet* and others, throughout his time at La Ville de Lyons, and kept abreast of the latest modes, which in his opinion continued to show a singular lack of imagination. Then the day came when he learned that there was a vacancy for a qualified assistant at number 83, rue de Richelieu. It was the exalted premises of Maison Gagelin. If he could get the post he would be plunged into the heart of the most fashionable street in the most fashionable city in the world. His hand shook slightly with eagerness that night when he wrote a letter applying for the post. A few days later a reply advised him on time and date when he should present himself for consideration.

In his black broadcloth frockcoat, well pressed but a trifle shabby after a deal of hard wear, his neat trousers encasing his long legs, and the same stovepipe hat that he had worn on the Channel packet from England, all of which he had purchased at a reduced price to staff at Swan and Edgar's out of delivery tips hoarded for it, he arrived at the grand establishment of Maison Gagelin. It was not the first time he had been there. It was another of the shops where he had tried to get work during his early days in Paris, but at that time with his impossible French he had barely crossed the threshold before the shaking head and patronising condescension of a very minor member of the managerial staff had sent him packing. Now it was different. He took the ornate entrance in his stride and knew a sense of intense satisfaction as the spread of Persian carpet, all tawny and russet like mingled wine, swallowed up his footsteps. Through high-flung arches he could see how one section of the shop opened into another like a procession of marble halls and no less imposing, each illumined by the shimmer of crystal chandeliers suspended by gilded chains from ceilings rich in plasterwork. Garlands and swags trailed from the encrustations overhead to frame looking-glasses recessed into the walls, alternating with damask panels the hue of decanted Burgundy. In contrast the impressive mahogany counters seemed a mundane reminder of the true purpose of such a grandiose setting, but as if to disperse the taint of commerce there were plentiful arrangements of hot-house flowers such as would be found in the salon of any customer of distinction. Display of the merchandise itself was limited to a tasteful glimpse here and there of the cashmere shawls and ready-made mantles and cloaks sold by Maison Gagelin, as well as swathes of the handsome materials for which it was renowned. Worth had long ago noted that opulence and luxury of any kind gave off a peculiarly sensuous aroma, and it hung in the air about him, soft and scented and heady like an exotic incense released solely for the benefit of the rich and élite.

"May I be of assistance, monsieur?" It was a senior assistant, a thin, impeccably groomed fellow, whose unctuousness was curtailed to a degree by a critical appraisal of the young man's well-cut but well-worn apparel.

"I have an appointment to see Monsieur Gagelin."

The assistant, guessing the purpose of that appointment, did not deign to show the candidate through to the office himself, but summoned with a snap of fingers one of the apprentices, who came with flying coat-tails to perform the errand. The proprietor's office proved to be no less grand than the rest of the premises, with crimson drapes at windows set with coloured glass, oil-lamps with fringed silken shades, and an abundance of dark, carved furniture dominated by a desk with a gold inkstand, an embossed leather folder for immediate papers, and an Indian elephant carved out of ivory with a cavity for pens. In a squat rotating chair behind the desk Monsieur Gagelin sat squarely, rigid and stern, with a gold watch-chain looped across his well-cut waistcoat, his moustache large as befitted his importance, his side-whiskers abundant. He gestured with the gleam of a ruby ring for Charles to be seated.

"Sit down, Monsieur Worth." He picked up the letter of application from the desk and glanced over it. "You are an Englishman, I see, and yet I will say that your command of the written word of my native language is not to be faulted. I congratulate you." The letter was laid down again, and Monsieur Gagelin folded his hands on the desk in front of him. "However, in spite of the comprehensive account you have given me of your time in the drapery business, I would like to hear from your own lips why you came to Paris in the first place, and also the reason why you should be considered as a worthy applicant."

Worth was well aware that his fluency in the spoken word of French was being tested as much as he was being judged on other attributes. He had no qualms, discoursing freely while pointing out that customers from the British Isles and the United States, as well as those from other English-speaking countries, would welcome the attention of an assistant able to deal with their requirements in their own tongue. To Monsieur Gagelin the appointment of the young man was almost a foregone conclusion. Good looks, a striking presence, and a sound command of the language backed by impeccable references both from La Ville de Lyons and earlier ones from London would secure him the post.

A quarter of an hour later Worth left the precincts of the shop in high good humour. He was to start working the following Monday at the material counters where he would cut lengths for the couturières, who favoured Maison Gagelin above all others for their supplies, as well as for individual customers choosing fabrics for themselves. It could be said, he thought, grinning to himself at his own little joke, that the premises of Maison Gagelin were right up his street. The dancing gleam in his eye was caught through the fringe of her parasol by a pretty woman in a passing carriage, and admiringly he held her gaze until the pavement slid him away from her line of vision, and the fragile contact was broken and lost. Whereupon a wave of loneliness engulfed him as if it had rolled from under the wheels of the disappearing equipage itself. He was reminded acutely that work and ambition and study and books had taken up almost every minute of his time since he had come to Paris. There was scarcely a day when he had not risen early and gone to bed late, asleep even as he extinguished the candle, and always his wages were barely enough to keep him in food and shelter. Admittedly, at Maison Gagelin there would be a small improvement in his financial status, and with the debt paid off at last to his mother's cousin, he should be marginally better off, but there still would not be a sou left over for anything more advanced than an extra book for his studies from a market stall. His jaw tightened. He could wait. He was set on making a success of his life, and nothing worth having ever came easily.

When Monday morning came he was waiting at the staff entrance before it was unlocked. After being fitted out with a new frockcoat and trousers in the cut and style required by the establishment, which would be paid for by an amount stopped weekly from his wages, he was taken as a newcomer on a round of the shop by one of his fellow assistants from the material counter, who had been relegated to the task. As always before shop doors opened to custom, a bustle of activity prevailed as shelves and counters were dusted and merchandise uncovered. There were a number of young women assistants, chosen, as female counter-hands always were, for brightness of smile and countenance and pleasant demeanour, and introductions took place with those with whom his own particular work would bring him into contact, he bowing his head to their nods and bobs. The tour continued on through the sewing-rooms where the seamstresses were already at work making up outdoor garments for stock or altering purchases to suit customers' requirements, and they glanced up to observe with curiosity the stranger being conducted through their domain.

In the stockrooms Worth was shown where various wares were stored, although for the present it was the one containing bales and bolts of every kind of material that was his particular concern. He eyed the heavily stacked shelves with satisfaction. It had never been his misfortune to handle shoddy goods, and now he would be dealing in the best merchandise to be had anywhere in the world.

In the weeks that followed he heaved and carried his stock, unrolled it, matched it, measured it, changed one fabric for another, and ran out the billowing, undulating metres yet again, often a couple of dozen times or more before he was able to take his shears to it. Long experience had taught him how to guide a customer into making up her mind, but there were always those who liked to run an assistant off his feet, or else were so indecisive that they did not know the right choice when it was staring them in the face. In these cases he would take a bolt of a particularly expensive cloth, often one that had been shown first and dismissed back to the shelves without consideration, which he knew to be right in quality and colour to suit the customer ideally as he had done originally. Instead of unrolling it he would hold it to him as though he had made an error in bringing it forward in the first place. Shaking his head as if at his own folly he would make a show of hesitancy, appearing to be making an excuse for keeping it intact.

"This exquisite material would be perfect for you, madame. However, the design and workmanship that have gone into it make it so costly that I cannot be sure that you would be willing to meet it."

Since price was never a barrier to those who chose to shop at Maison Gagelin, the customer immediately assumed that something exclusive was being withheld from her, perhaps reserved for someone else when she should have first right to it, and at once would demand to have it displayed in no uncertain terms. Invariably a sale resulted. The customer was more than satisfied at what she imagined to be a personal triumph in her selection, and Worth, equally well pleased, bowed her to the door before returning to tidy the counter in readiness for the next lady to be served. He often thought that women were like the books that he collected, all easy enough to read individually once the language had been mastered.

His skillful salesmanship did not go unnoticed by Monsieur Gagelin. He was summoned one morning, a few minutes before the shop was opened for the day's custom, to the proprietor's office.

"You have been promoted to the counter selling mantles and capes and so forth," Monsieur Gagelin informed him with a nod of approval. "Your salary will be adjusted accordingly. Go along to it at once. Your fellow assistant is a *demoiselle de maison* who has returned from leave of absence. Her name is Mademoiselle Vernet."

Worth closed the door of the office behind him and fingered his dark silk cravat thoughtfully. *Vernet!* Surely not Louise Vernet! At once he realised the folly of such speculation. Louise would never have reached so exalted a position out of her circumstances, *demoiselles de maison* in such an establishment being young women from good backgrounds and respectable homes, whose parents or guardians paid for the privilege of having them trained in business, together with board and lodging and chaperonage on the premises. As he hurried in the direction of his new counter he looked forward to meeting the young woman with whom he was to work.

He saw her before she saw him. In diffused sunshine streaming down from an opaque glass lantern in the ceiling, which touched the rich chestnut of her curly hair with golden lights, she was standing with her back to him, busily arranging the folds of an embroidered shawl that was draped on the counter's display stand. Then, as he came through the connecting archway, she was alerted to his presence as his reflection passed across a tilted cheval-glass near at hand. Instantly her shoulders stiffened, shifting the sheen of the black silk that covered them, and the vertical row of buttons fastening the back of the full-skirted dress went ramrod-straight. With some dismay he wondered if she resented having to work with a fresh partner. He covered the last stretch of floor between them.

"Mademoiselle Vernet? I'm Charles Worth. We are to serve at this counter together, I've been told. May I say that the profound honour is mine."

For a moment or two she hesitated before turning, making him fear he was right in thinking that there was some hostility on her part, but when she did move gracefully to face him he realised instantly that he was mistaken in his supposition. There was no pique in her expression, no animosity in her open gaze. With that keen perception he had towards women he sensed that she was an extremely shy young woman, her momentary tenseness and hesitancy having been caused by no more than a passing nervousness at meeting for the first time the foreigner with whom she was to work in close cooperation. Already she was composed again, dignified and gracious.

"It is a pleasure to become acquainted with you, Monsieur Worth." She had a quiet, melodious voice that matched her appearance. Her face was oval and sweet-mouthed, the lower lip full and generous, and her chin was rounded. Under the well-defined curve of her brows her eyes were a most unusual sapphire blue. Her nose was long and fractionally hooked in shape, but due to a delicate curve of nostril merely served to enhance her fine looks, and her skin was pale and softly gleaming. But it was her unconsciously arresting carriage that made the greatest impact on him. Few women had that indefinable poise that would have enabled them to wear sackcloth and still stand out in a magnificently clothed crowd of their own sex, but he recognised unequivocally that Mademoiselle Vernet was blessed with it whether she knew it or not. Her full-skirted dress was simple, being little different from those worn by the other young women assistants, all of whom were allowed to choose any pattern within reason in a good black silk to be made up in the sewing-room, but she made hers appear extraordinarily stylish.

"I'm sure we shall get on well together," he assured her agreeably, wanting to establish a complete rapport, which he never found difficult where women were concerned. "You have just returned after being away from Paris, I believe."

"I was allowed to go home to Clermont-Ferrand to help look after an ailing member of the family, who is now, I'm thankful to say, fully recovered." She was still an inestimable distance from him, withdrawn safely into herself beyond the power of his charm, which he was deliberately bringing into play, something which he did not normally have to do.

"You must be a splendid nurse."

Flattery did not work on her. "I was one of a household team under the direction of an excellent doctor."

He felt gently put in his place, but he persisted with the best of intentions. "Have you been long at Gagelin's?"

Her tranquil blue eyes regarded him steadily. "Five years."

Too late he realised that his question had been tantamount to asking her age since *demoiselles de maison* started their apprenticeships at the age of sixteen, and he was afraid he had appeared uncouth in his unintentional directness. Yet he digested the information he had received. So she was twenty-one. His age. The faint glaze of rose along her cheekbones had deepened its tint, but otherwise she still stood with that quality of calmness and serenity, co-ordinated, integrated, completely in charge of herself, her shyness springing from a natural modesty and not through any awkwardness. Without doubt a most unusual young woman.

"Then you must be more than familiar with this counter," he said in a more businesslike manner, deciding it might be better to get into a working routine and let matters sort themselves out. I'd be obliged if you would tell me about the stock we have to sell and where the items are located on the shelves and in the drawers."

She proved to be neat and quick and efficient in dealing with his request, and although on the surface he took note and absorbed it all, some part of an inner eye, linked to his innate appreciation of the female form, registered the unconscious grace of her every movement as if one of those new-fangled camera apparatus was changing shutters constantly in his mind. Her beautiful body flowed. Nothing was jerky or angular. She made the very gathers of her skirt sweep into undulating ripples, and it seemed to him that even the escaping tendrils of her curling hair wafted like feathers against the smoothness of her cheek.

She, all unknowing of the admiration lurking in his eye, was soon to observe his flair in selling when the first customer of the day came to the counter shortly after she had finished listing the goods for him. The lady in question wanted a short cape, and after he had displayed any number of them and she had tried them on, the choice was whittled down to two of similar style in different colours.

"Which is it to be?" the lady reiterated over and over again, holding one up against her and then the other with sighs and a puckered brow. She turned in melting appeal to Monsieur Worth. "Tell me what you think."

Marie Vernet felt sympathy for him. She knew from her own experience how difficult it was to pinpoint such dithering customers to a choice. Whichever was suggested, the customer would immediately imagine for a few moments that she preferred the other, and then the whole tedious performance would begin all over. But Monsieur Worth merely smiled and tilted the cheval-glass to recapture the lady's reflection at a better angle.

"Match your eyes, madame," he advised, his own right brow raised a little higher as if there could be no question about it. "In *your* case, whenever in doubt, always match your eyes."

The lady, taken by surprise, looked from him to her own wide-eyed reflection with every show of pleasure. "Yes, of course," she agreed, a trifle breathlessly, letting the olive-coloured cape slide from her hand onto the counter while retaining the dark-brown velvet. "Yes, indeed."

Marie hid her astonishment. The lady did have handsome eyes and obviously knew it, but Marie knew it would never have occurred to her or, she was sure, to any other assistant to compel a direct decision from the customer herself by the simple means of a subtle compliment. From anyone less self-assured, less smooth-mannered, it would have appeared to be an impertinent piece of flattery, but not from Monsieur Worth. He had merely spoken the truth as he had seen it, and in the most charming way. None could deny that dark brown should be the lady's colour above all others. Nothing could suit her better.

As the day went on, Marie's respect grew for the selling

talents of her new fellow assistant. She also detected a certain arrogance in him, but could see that it would be hard for him not to be a trifle high-handed in the consciousness he had of his power to sway and guide and direct the often seemingly intractable female sex. She herself, totally lacking in conceit, could only hope that she would prove herself an adequate partner at what was now his counter, and fully complement his salesmanship with her own. It would also be prudent, she thought, to guard herself against his apparently irresistable charm.

It took Worth a little while to discover her Christian name, and then it was not Marie herself but another young lady assistant who let it slip in conversation. He would have liked to call her by it whenever customers were not present, but she retained a polite formality which made the taking of such a liberty out of the question. They worked together in perfect harmony, but once the dust-covers were placed over the displayed goods for the night, communication was at an end. She was always quick to gather up her little reticule from its special niche under the counter and depart with all haste to join the other *demoiselles de maison* taking a rear staircase together to the quarters known jokingly as "the nunnery" among the male assistants, who were not allowed to venture there, all having lodgings away from the premises. Once he did set foot on the forbidden staircase. It was shortly after they had met, and she had forgotten her handkerchief in the niche, a folded wisp of fine linen with her initial in the corner. He hurried after her with it.

"Mademoiselle Vernet! One moment, please."

She had almost reached the head of the flight in conversation with some of her companions, and she turned her head quickly, giving a gasp of dismay as she saw that he had ascended a quarter of the flight. She gathered her full skirts and flew down to meet him, catching him by the arm and hastening him with her to the floor level.

"It's not permitted for any gentleman to set as much as a foot on the lowest tread," she explained hastily, looking about to make sure he had not been spotted by a shopwalker or anybody else in authority. "Surely you know that!"

"Not even to return property?" He held out the handkerchief to her.

She relaxed, the coast being clear and his recklessness having gone undetected. With one of her enchanting smiles, which brought her dimples into play, she took the handkerchief from him. "Thank you. I'll not be so forgetful again. I would never have forgiven myself if I had been the cause of bringing you into trouble."

He stood and watched her go up the flight again, hoping she would look back at him when she reached the top, but she did not. He was left feeling restless and bereft as he went to take his hat from the peg in the men's cloakroom and wend his way home to his garret lodgings.

In the morning he looked for some improvement in their relationship, a degree of interest that hitherto had been lacking on her part, but she was as polite and courteous as before and made no reference to the interlude on the stairs. It irked him increasingly that she should remain impervious to his overtures, there being no ulterior motive in his mind, and at times he showed his irritation in an uncharacteristic display of impatience towards her, which she accepted without retaliation, her face composed, her even disposition unriled. As the weeks went by, confirming daily that they made an efficient working team, he became more and more tantalised by the mental distance she retained between them, at a loss to get through to her. She must know that he liked and admired her. Every woman discerned those attitudes in a man. He searched his mind for anything he had overlooked in the acquaintanceship. He made another attempt to engage her interest by trying to form a link with her through Louise Vernet. He chose a time at the close of evening when there were few customers left in the shop and he was unlikely to be interrupted. Marie was kneeling to fold away some cashmere shawls into a bottom drawer, and he collected up the rest of a pile from the counter before crouching down to hold them for her.

"When I first came to Paris I stayed in a place where there was someone whose surname was Vernet."

"Oh?" She was busy at her task.

"Yes, a young girl called Louise Vernet, who had been more or less adopted by the seamstress whose home it was. I wonder if she could have been related to you in any way."

Her tapering fingers took the last shawl from him and smoothed it away. "My surname is not an uncommon one. There must be hundreds of Vernets in Paris." She closed the drawer and accepted the hand he offered to assist her to her feet.

"Yes, but you mentioned once that you came from Clermont-Ferrand. I seem to remember that Louise told me that her father was born there."

She was smoothing the creases from her skirt where she had knelt on it, but now she looked at him, her face showing surprise. "What was his name? He could have been a distant cousin, I suppose."

He had difficulty in remembering whether it had been Jacques or Jean, and he went on to tell Marie of his early days in Paris and about Louise, who had guarded her mother's grave at night until she had been taken in and given a home. Marie was deeply moved as she pictured the young girl's plight at the time.

"What a tragic situation. The mother was originally a Lyons silkweaver, you say?"

"Yes. Does that convey anything to you?"

She shook her head. "No, but it's an extremely sad story."

Unbeknown to him Marie wrote home to make enquiries about the father of Louise Vernet, whose Christian name was either Jacques or Jean. Confirmation came back that it had been Jacques, the son of a family bearing the same surname, but in no way related, who some years ago, while still a student, had run away with a silkweaver with whom he had become entangled during a sojourn in Lyons. Where they had gone and what had happened to them nobody knew, except that three years after their disappearance the woman, by then his wife, had written to inform his family of his death from consumption.

Marie's ever gentle heart was touched anew. She folded the letter away and half wished that some kinship to Louise Vernet had been proved, that would have given her the chance to befriend the girl who had had such an unhappy background and known so little of the parental love with which she herself had been cossetted during the most impressionable years of her life. It had made later hardships much easier to bear.

Marie and Worth had had a particularly busy morning at their counter when a certain customer, greatly esteemed by the proprietor, swept into the shop with bonnet plumes rearing imperiously, cape floating, and hands clasped in a sable muff, all amid the discreet fragrance of a new Guerlain perfume. She was Madame Marie-Thérèse de Gand, a rich and powerful widow, known to all the staff at Maison Gagelin with the exception of Worth who, being a comparative newcomer to the establishment, had not seen her before. She visited Paris at irregular intervals from her château in the Loire Valley to attend to matters of business and pleasure, the latter including the lavish replenishment of her wardrobe from the establishment of Madame Palmyre. On this occasion she had come to Paris to attend the passing-out parade at the Ecole Militaire of her only son, Pierre. The darting forward of the senior assistants at her approach, and the appearance of Monsieur Gagelin himself to take the forefront in the obeisance, sent vibrations throughout the premises like sparks running along wires. Whispers passed swiftly from counter to counter. "She's back! It's Madame de Gand. *Mon Dieu!* I hope I don't have to serve her this time. She'll want the whole stock laid out for her again. Watch it! Here she comes."

Madame de Gand had announced her requirements. She wanted an evening shawl of jewel-like brilliance to set off her new black-velvet Palmyre gown at the Opéra that evening.

"This way, madame."

She allowed them to bow and escort her through to one of the gilded chairs set conveniently by the appropriate counter. She sat down on the striped silk upholstery and withdrew her gloved hands from her sable muff, the shop being warm after the chill day outside. As she put it aside she looked disdainfully at the young *demoiselle de maison* who was to wait on her. Worth, already engaged in serving at the other end of the counter, took a glance at the formidable widow out of the corner of his eye. He recognised instantly the most dreaded of all customers, the woman set on being impossible to please.

Marie was tireless in her efforts to serve Madame de Gand. She displayed shawl after shawl in the colours requested, carmine and emerald and golden yellow, cobalt and acid pink and shimmering coral. The soft silk and lace mounds grew on the polished mahogany surface in her ardent willingness to find one to suit her customer, but it was in vain. Marie became paler and paler as Madame de Gand continued to shake her head disdainfully, hold up a hand in ridicule, and generally deride everything she was shown.

Worth, whose own satisfied customer had departed, observed the widow closely. She had the high bones, the concave cheeks, and the square jaw of the aristocratic Frenchwoman. Under thick brows her heavy-lidded eyes were more green than grey, and her black hair was arrestingly winged with perfectly balanced white streaks drawn back like ribbons under the horizontally shaped bonnet, its final arrangement in plaited coil or smooth knot hidden under the flounce known as a *bavolet,* which hung from all such feminine headgear to the shoulders. It was a mode that had been established over two decades or more, and Worth detested it, not only because it was representative of the static state of fashion, but also because it covered in a most ugly manner a woman's crowning glory. In his mind's eye he could picture the customer's dramatic hair as it would appear without that aberration when elaborately dressed for evening, and he formed his own opinion as to which shawl should be the customer's choice.

Deliberately he waited until Madame de Gand had reached saturation point with all she had been shown and had become bored, making it obvious that Marie was not going to make a sale. He could imagine Marie's anxious feelings. He knew as well as she did that Monsieur Gagelin would be far from pleased if his grand customer went from the shop without her requirement being fulfilled and in dissatisfaction. Quickly opening the drawer, Worth took from it a particularly beautiful, snow-white shawl, and he swept the rest aside to hold its silken spread before Madame de Gand. "The opera-house has colour enough, madame. Don't compete with it. Outshine it! Your gown is to be black velvet and your jewels are to be diamonds. So what could be more outstanding than the sophistication of pure white?"

She was no fool. She saw immediately that he was right. As well as the gilt of crimson of the opera-house and the splendour on the stage, her son and the rest of the gentlemen in the party were, without exception, in the military, and she had thought to dazzle against their brilliance. Instead, with a coloured shawl, however rare and vivid the shade, she would be swamped into the background.

"I am not sure," she declared spuriously, not ready yet on principle to be won over.

Worth turned to Marie. "Let me place this shawl around your shoulders for you to show Madame de Gand the effect it will have."

Marie was used to displaying shawl and capes behind the counter to customers, but she was dismayed when he drew her to the front of it and told her to walk up and down.

"Go a few yards this way and that," he instructed.

Her fine nostrils blanched, and inwardly she quaked, aware that not only were Madame de Gand's steely eyes glued on her, but other customers at the busy counters were turning their heads to look in her direction. All her life she had hated being the centre of attention, and usually managed to avoid it. Her earliest memories were of hiding behind her mother's skirts, clutching in panic at the folds again whenever her hands were plucked away in an effort to bring her forward to meet company. For years as a child she was haunted by nightmares of a particularly boisterous uncle who had clapped his hands in appreciation at her when she was only a toddler, his booming laugh and loud voice striking terror into her, no matter that he was praising her looks to her proud and loving mama. At school she had toiled diligently, prompted as much by the fear of being stood conspicuously in the corner as a dunce as by a natural interest in her studies, and it gave her no pleasure to be praised, standing by her desk with all the class looking at her while the teacher commented favourably on her work. Behind the shop counter she knew herself to be an impersonal pair of hands to most customers, which was a comfortable position, no different from the ordinary run of everyday life, but to parade up and down wearing one of Maison Gagelin's most costly shawls under the gaze of innumerable pairs of eyes almost paralysed her.

"Go on," Worth prompted gently, propelling her with the lightest of touches on her arm.

She began to walk. Her shyness was a deeply personal burden, and because she liked people individually while fearing their attention *en masse,* few if any suspected the great handicap it was to her. In no way did it show as she took one graceful step after another, nothing conscious or deliberate in her movements, her glorious poise of head coming from a straight spine and the good set of her prettily shaped shoulders. The shawl was Chinese, encrusted with silken embroidery that gave a shimmering opulence to its whiteness, the fringe swinging gently in undulating ripples, and on Marie's shoulders and against the black silk of her dress it took on an immeasurable splendour.

Worth, watching her, thought again that he had never seen a woman more born to set off clothes. As she traced the full length of the Persian runner and swung slowly about within the framework of the archway to retrace her steps, several ladies drifted away from counters to stare at her. Some assistants craned their necks. One gentleman, bored with waiting for his wife, wandered from a distant department to see why a crowd was gathering, and others in turn followed him.

Marie, not daring to glance right or left at those collecting about her, kept her gaze on Worth as if he were the anchor to stop her teetering away in her agonising embarrassment, and his eyes held hers in a compelling look of encouragement, admiration, and an indefinable spark of something that could have been speculation. Long afterwards she was to pinpoint the first stirrings of love for him in those interminable moments of walking to and fro along a million miles of Persian carpeting while being sustained as firmly by his gaze as if he were gripping her hands. He was seeing her not only as the lovely young female that she was, but also as the only one who could wear to full advantage all the wonderful clothes that he longed to transpose from the many sketches he had made into the fabrics he knew and understood so well.

"Once more," he said as she came within earshot. She obeyed, but with no lessening of her inner trepidation, and the shawl, slipping a little from one shoulder, was further enhanced by a deepening of its seductive folds.

Madame de Gand rose to her feet. "The white shawl will do well enough," she said imperiously, inwardly disconcerted at having experienced an unprecedented surge of avariciousness when another customer had stretched out to finger the fringe as it floated by. Thrusting her gloved hands back into her muff she added, "Send it to my suite at the Hôtel Dauphine in the rue de Rivoli to arrive not later than four o'clock."

Worth bowed as he always did whether a sale had been transacted or not, and escorted her to the door and out into her carriage. When he returned the little crowd had dispersed, the shawl was being packed by an apprentice, and there was no sign of Marie. Jubilant at the triumph of their shared sale he searched about and after a few minutes he found her leaning against the wall in one of the stockrooms, an arm raised across her eyes. He was alarmed, not knowing that she had needed the calm of solitude to recover from her ordeal, and he pulled the velvet curtain behind him across the doorway to give them privacy as he went to her.

"What's the matter? Are you feeling faint?"

She lowered her arm, resolutely shaking her head. "It's nothing. It will pass."

He saw she was trembling, her face open and vulnerable, her eyes magnified almost to violet in her duress. With a stab of barely controlled excitement he recognised that her guard was down and he was glimpsing her intimately in a way that she was powerless to withstand. In thoughtful consideration, having no wish to torment her, he reached for a carafe of water and a glass kept on a shelf for emergencies, and poured some for her. "Here. Drink this."

She did not think the water would be of any help to her, but she sipped it to please him, unwittingly setting the precedent of always considering his wishes before her own that she was to follow throughout time to come. "Thank you." She handed the glass back into his charge and he put it down. Bravely she managed a smile, thrusting off her inertia in a defence against any further probing, however well-intentioned, on his part. Her shyness to her was a shameful weakness, ever to be battled with alone, a secret foolishness with an extent that must never be known or suspected by others. She adopted a light note that was a trifle at variance with the tremor in her voice.

"All went well with the shawl in the end, due to your salesmanship. I would never have dared to show the lady a white one when she had asked to see the very opposite."

He regarded her with pride. "The credit is entirely yours. You sold it, not I. The customer viewed you in the shawl and thought she could look the same. But never in a thousand years could another woman match you for elegance."

Her cheeks glowed swiftly at his extravagant praise, the sparkle returning to her eyes. "You exaggerate beyond all reason, Monsieur Worth." She straightened away from the wall, putting up her hands to smooth unnecessarily her unruffled arrangement of curls, and her beautifully shaped breasts rose beneath the black silk of her bodice, making him feel a deep and boundless reverence for her sheer perfection.

"I've never been more sincere about anything in my whole life," he insisted quietly.

She could not doubt him. The intensity of his statement had throbbed in his throat. All the virile strength of him, his capacity for passion, the pent-up longing that coursed through his veins, became almost tangible to her within the confines of the narrow stockroom, making her aware of how close he was to putting his arms about her in the emotion of the moment. A delicious, slightly delirious panic seized her, and without the least thought of coquetry she took the seductive step of withdrawing just out of his reach. She took hold of the velvet curtain to go back into the counter area, and over her shoulder her sapphire gaze came to rest on him with a look of pure affection.

"I have never been paid a more moving compliment. It meant more to me than you could possibly know."

It did indeed. It had told her that her secret trial was still her own. She had faced some of the most critical stares that had ever come her way, and not even her working partner had guessed what torture it had been for her to make a public parade. The brass rings rattled noisily along the rail as she left him alone in the shadows of the stockroom. As if the floor were slipping away from beneath his feet he began to realise that he was falling in love with her.

5

For the first few weeks Worth made no headway with his courtship. It was hampered for him by Marie's inherent shyness that also made her so loath to parade in shawls and pelisses and mantles to customers, which he now made a regular practice, finding that nothing sold a piece of apparel quicker than when she displayed it on her person. Sales at their counter had risen, which was always a point of pride for him. He had become aware of her dislike of parading garments, something that was entirely new in the drapery business and anywhere else in the clothing trade, proving a great novelty to customers, but he was certain that with time she would become used to being admired and he merely loved her all the more for her modesty. He never noticed the unbridled envy and the glint of jealousy in feminine glances that were sometimes directed at her, but to Marie they were like daggers, adding to the private torment that she never revealed to outsiders by as much as a flicker of lash or tremble of hand.

Then a new development was destined to bring her still

further into the public eye. She needed another working dress, it being important to her personally as well as to the shop that she should always look her best. Knowing Worth was an expert on silk she asked his advice about which quality to choose, and he selected a ribbed one, which she approved, abiding by his choice. She purchased the required length the same day and took it to the sewing-room to await its turn in being made up. The next day being Sunday, she attended mass as usual at her church and emerged from the vast portals to find Worth waiting outside, heedless of the bitter cold day that blew his coat-tails about, a folder under his arm. He doffed his hat, and she was both surprised and pleased to see him.

"Monsieur Worth! What are you doing here?"

"I've been waiting to invite you to have coffee with me. I have some sketches to show you. I hope you'll be interested."

She was intrigued. Paris was full of aspiring artists, but she had not suspected that her fellow counter-hand was one. At a corner table in the gaudy gilt and mirrored interior of a café he ordered the coffee, and when it had been served he opened the folder for her. It contained brief but concise sketches of a dress viewed from the front, back, and sides.

"It's my design for your new dress," he explained tensely, always abhorring criticism and not at all sure what her reaction would be. "Not only do I think it would suit you well, but it will set off to full advantage the shawls and mantles that you display."

She gazed at it in awe. It was a beautiful dress, simple in line with the most intricate tucking that gave a sunray effect across the bodice, a discreet piping of velvet highlighting the standing collar and cuffs. She drew in a deep breath and raised shining eyes to his.

"It's a wonderful dress. I adore it. How clever you are! But the seamstresses at Gagelin's would be at loss with all those tucks."

His face had become suffused with pleasure at her unstinted praise. All tension went from him and he showed his enthusiasm for the project, sweeping aside her doubts. "There's no problem there. My apprenticeship included some instruction in tailoring and I have the pattern worked out for them to follow down to the last detail. And I'll supervise the fittings myself."

"Fittings?" she queried with a touch of embarrassment. "I never have more than one. Nobody does."

"Ah, but you will with my dress. It has to be perfect. Your shoulders are shapely, but I doubt very much if they are exactly the same both sides. Human beings are not geometrically formed, and from what I have observed, dressmakers make up garments as if they were."

"Yes, I think that's true," she agreed. "Tell me, did you have the design for my dress in mind when you selected the silk?"

"It came to me as I handled the fabric."

"Do you have other sketched designs that you have done?"

He grinned cheerily. "I jot them down all the time."

She hesitated bashfully. "May I see them? Not to choose another for myself," she assured him quickly, "because no dress could be better than the one you have designed for me. I'm just extremely interested."

He seized his chance. "Suppose we meet again at the same place and time next Sunday, and then I could show them to you. Afterwards we'll go for a walk and have luncheon somewhere."

She accepted. Then she had to leave, having friends to meet. He saw her on her way, wishing he could have accompanied her. Next morning, as soon as he arrived at the shop, he sought out the most accomplished seamstress and explained the workings of Marie's dress. She was dubious at first, but soon found that his pattern and instructions covered all points. It would be ready for a fitting in about ten days.

It was a momentous occasion for him when he met Marie the following Sunday as arranged. It was the first time he had revealed his collection of sketches to another's gaze. Once more he opened the folder, watching her face keenly. Her whole expression was instantly one of enchantment. She gave little involuntary gasps of sheer delight as she took up one design and then another. When she had seen them all she sat back on her chair, marvelling at the originality and grace of the dresses he had drawn.

"I've never seen anything like them," she declared reverently. "If only they could be made up, they would captivate all who saw them."

He smiled, closing the folder again and tying the cords. "I'm very glad you like my sketches. If the day should come when they or others like them take form, I would want you to be there to wear the best of them."

It was the first hint he had given of his serious intentions towards her and she blushed, conscious of the honour he had bestowed upon her in showing her the designs. He said no more about the possible future of their personal relationship then, and leaning an arm on the marble-topped table, he launched into his long-held ideas and opinions on the subject of fashion. He told her how he deplored its stalemate, declaring that it should be solely for the individual enhancement of women, the rigid bonds of present dictate broken once and for all in a great flowering of beauty. She was enthralled and entranced. She saw that he had the spark of genius in the field that she knew and understood. In wordless admiration she rested a hand lightly on his arm. Immediately he covered it with his own clasp, looking into her eyes. He was aware of having created a special bond between them.

When they left the café they took a stroll down the Boulevard des Italiens, mingling with the throng of other promenaders, and after they had eaten in a small restaurant they went to the Jardin des Plantes, where they sat on a park bench. It had snowed earlier in the day, but the sun had come out to melt it away on the concave roofs of the glass conservatories, making a chequered pattern of the panes and striking diamonds into the icicles that quite dazzled the eyes. In the sparkling air and with a sense of freedom they found they were able to talk now in a way that had never been possible within the confines of the shop. They called each other by their Christian names for the first time, and filled in the background of their lives to each other. She was particularly understanding towards all he had been through as a child in the separation of his parents and the loss of his home, having been through a similar experience, although older at the time, and it had been on a far less drastic scale. She told him all about it. Her childhood at the heart of a close-knit family had been happy and secure and, unlike the marriage of Mr. and Mrs. William Worth, the union of her parents had been a contented one. Her elder sister married well as befitted the Vernets' social position, the bridegroom being an architect renowned for his restoration work on several of the country's greatest cathedrals. Then Monsieur Vernet, who was a tax collector, fell on hard times. The desperate financial straits to which he was reduced meant that, contrary to all he and his wife had hoped for, their younger child, Marie, had to be sent out into the world among strangers to earn her own living. Marie in her recounting of this change of circumstances for herself made little of it, but Worth could guess at the traumatic ordeal it must have been for such a gently reared and intensely shy girl to come alone to Paris and enter the hard and competitive world of the drapery trade.

To both Worth and Marie their time together that Sunday was over far too quickly. He escorted her back to the employee's entrance of Maison Gagelin. "It's been a most enjoyable outing," she said warmly, her lovely smile enhanced by a myriad of dimples, and she gave him her hand.

Daringly he pressed her fingers lightly through the thin leather of her glove. "Say you'll come out with me again next Sunday."

"That would be most pleasurable."

He stood with hat in hand, watching her shadowy figure disappear beyond the panels of opaque glass. He did not know how he would have endured a refusal.

She had the first fitting of her dress in the deserted sewing-room after shop hours. The seamstress had left it for her on one of the work-tables, and when she had put it on she called in Worth, who was waiting. She herself was excited by the dress, turning one way and then the other to view her reflection in a long mirror, smoothing her hands in delight over the tiny tucks fanning out across the bodice.

"How splendid it looks! How elegant! Oh, I've never had such a dress—" Her voice trailed away and she stopped her twirling, seeing that his face was ravaged by angry disappointment.

"Those ham-fisted women haven't begun to get it right!" he stormed, forgetting all else in the lack of perfection he wanted in the garment. "Look at the set of that sleeve!" He ripped it away from its seam. "The collar is at least two millimetres askew, the darts at the back are too high, and some of the gathering at the waist is not even!" Snatching up a pair of scissors, he began snipping away at all that was offending him.

"No! Please don't!" she gasped, trying to hold together the pieces that were falling apart.

"It has to be repinned and retacked. I'll do it myself now." More stitches parted at a run. Gathers gave way to show her top petticoat.

"I beg you! No more!"

The desperation of her plea made him halt what he was doing. With a start he saw that he had exposed her creamy shoulder and she was clutching the front of the bodice to her in a vain attempt to hide her deep cleavage revealed by the low neckline of her lace-trimmed chemise. He did not politely avert his eyes. He stared at her. She was lovely beyond belief.

"The repinning won't take long," he said dazedly. "I've taken apart all that's necessary."

He went to work on the dress and gained the perfection of fit for which he had aimed. All the time she stood motionless with her lashes downcast, the colour coming and going in her cheeks. He longed to put his arms around her, to press his lips to the nape of her neck as he drew together the back fastening of buttons and loops. The self-control he was exerting made his brow glisten and he was in such a state of excitement that his fingers shook against her skin as he slid them under the cloth to protect her from the pins. When all was done she raised her head to look again into the mirror.

"Yes," she said faintly. "The dress is much improved. I can see now why you were not pleased with it in the first place."

He left her to change out of it. Marie in her petticoats had ignited in the man who loved her an adoring passion that was to last the rest of his life.

The next fitting went without a hitch. Nothing but a minuscule adjustment to the length of one cuff was needed. On the morning that Marie appeared in the dress for the first time she drew her fellow vendeuses to her from every quarter like bees to nectar, all of them exclaiming and complimenting her on it.

She was delighted to give the praise where it was due. "Monsieur Worth designed it. Yes, isn't he clever. I agree, it is most distinctive. I feel privileged to be wearing it. Oh, I'm so pleased you like it so much."

That was only the beginning of the day. As it continued, customers began to make enquiries as to the name of the dressmaker who had made the dress worn by the young saleswoman selling shawls, or had Maison Gagelin added ready-made dresses to their stock of capes and coats? Marie herself was approached for information, and many ladies were disappointed or annoyed to learn that such a garment of outstanding elegance was not available to them through any channel.

From that day forward the enquiries and comments continued. In contrast to displaying the shawls, it gave her pride and pleasure to be instrumental in showing off her Englishman's flair for designing, particularly since she could do it in the run of her daily work without making what she considered to be an unwarranted exhibition of herself.

Worth, seeing at last the opportunity he had long awaited

was presenting itself, went to his employer with a suggestion as to how this keen interest in his dress could be commercialised. Enthusiastically he made his point to Monsieur Gagelin and the new partner in the business, Monsieur Obigez. "You could have a collection of dresses made up from my designs for stock just as you have always had ready-made coats for sale. If they were fashioned first in muslin, customers could choose from the materials that you already sell wholesale and retail. I'm sure, from the countless enquiries that every assistant in this shop has to answer daily, that there would be a ready sale. In other words, expand the sewing-room and install a dressmaking department that would bring in the triple profit of wholesaling and retailing and the making of each garment."

There was a long silence as Monsieur Gagelin suffered the affront that had been dealt him, his outrage gathering force. "You would turn this distinguished house into a common dressmaker's!" His voice shook with a scandalised vehemence. The hierarchy in trade was as clearly defined as it was in social circles, and to slip down by one fraction could change the whole class of one's customers. "I will remind you that Maison Gagelin shines with a long tradition of good taste and refinement. I say no to your suggestion. More than that, I say never!" He recalled that he had a partner and turned to him in deference. "Do you not agree, M'sieur?"

Monsieur Obigez was not an imaginative man. Had he been, it was unlikely that Monsieur Gagelin, to whom he was related, would have allowed the partnership in the first place. "Let us hear no more of the matter," he endorsed inflexibly.

It was a bitter blow to Worth. He was both angered and exasperated by the short-sighted rejection of his idea. Marie soothed him, bade him be patient, and pointed out that not even Messieurs Gagelin and Obigez could withstand the customers' insistence forever.

She was his joy. They spent every Sunday together. She had shown him in countless small and innocent ways that she was aware of his feelings towards her, although he had not dared as yet to voice his longing.

It was a warm Sunday afternoon in May when they accepted seats on a hired equipage for an expedition with friends to the Palace of Versailles. There the picture and sculpture galleries had become an attraction since the recent restoration work on the building had been carried out as a direct result of the King's personal interest in his country's heritage. She had truly expected to go into the palace as soon as they arrived, but somehow, when their companions disappeared inside the vast edifice, she turned her steps with his by mutual, unspoken consent in the direction of the fountains and the gardens. The air was soft as a feathered fan, and their feet made no sound on the lush grass. A kind of magic had taken possession of the day. She could tell that he was set on fiinding somewhere for them to be on their own, his whole frame urgent and intense and seeking.

They came upon an ancient stone seat, its claw feet stained green by lichens, under a veritable canopy of purple lilac in a leafy grove. He drew her down on it beside him and took both her hands, threading her fingers into his. Raising them to his lips, he kissed each one. She could scarcely breathe, her heart hammering in her breast. As he looked at her she saw such loving in the stretched contours of his face, such tenderness in his gaze, that she knew the words he would say before he had uttered them.

"I love you, Marie. With all my heart and soul and for all eternity I'll love only you."

She melted into his arms. It was her first kiss, and her shyness gave way out of wonder and surprise to his unleashed ardour. When he withdrew his lips from hers, still holding her to him, she looped her arms about his neck, her voice holding a sweet huskiness.

"I love you, dearest Charles. This is truly the happiest day of my life."

He kissed her again, savouring the shape of her lips, but when he would have repeated the delicious experience a group of children came to play with a ball in the grove, and their time alone was at an end. They smiled at each other, and then, hand in hand, they left the seat to retrace their steps to the palace, and although they went dutifully through the galleries they saw only each other. Everything else was a haze. On the drive back to Paris they sat with his arm about her waist, each gazing at the other in a cocoon of blissful silence amid the rest of the chattering passengers, numbed by the knowledge of love reciprocated and knowing without a shadow of doubt that they had been destined for each other.

They could make no plans for the future. She knew that as well as he. Like thousands of other young couples in love in Paris on that May afternoon, circumstances and low wages prevented any talk of marriage. She had no money at all apart from her meagre salary. Worth on his earnings could not begin to keep a wife. For an unforseeable length of time their loving must remain in limbo. Their consolation was that unlike most other couples they had the enviable privilege of being in each other's company every day. Only one shadow was to mar their time together. No matter how hard she tried, she still could not overcome her dislike of being propelled into the public eye and avoided it whenever she could, which sometimes resulted in the loss of a sale. It was the only point about which they ever had a disagreement and, as time went on, the occasional quarrel. He could only see that the more they sold on their counter and the greater increase in profits for Gagelin's, the sooner his earnings would rise and make it possible for them to marry. He put this argument forward constantly. She kept from him the full depths of the abject misery that she suffered in that endless promenading up and down the Persian runner that she had come to loathe.

He designed another shop-dress for her with fluted inlets in the flow of the graceful skirt. Customers took one look at it and became rapacious in wanting a dress for themselves with such a skirt. When thwarted in their wishes, they made their displeasure known to the proprietors, who were at a loss to comprehend such avariciousness, particularly since some of their most esteemed ladies were numbered amongst those wanting dresses as worn by a lowly vendeuse! What was happening to all of them? Without doubt, Monsieur Worth was turning the long established régime of the house upside down.

Althought Marie was proud of her latest dress, just as she was to be of far more extravagant ones to come, she never forgot the very first one with the velvet piping that Worth had designed for her. It had held a secret that only the two of them had shared. All his soul had been in that design. He had created it for her out of the fathomless depths of his love.

* * *

It was during this time that many changes took place in Louise's life. On reaching the age of fifteen she realised to her relief that she had stopped growing. She was taller than average, but not as much as she had feared she would be, and she had developed a high-breasted figure with a slender waist and long, well-shaped legs that nobody saw but herself. Her face had changed little in her opinion; not even Catherine, who was always biased as far as she was concerned, was able to say that her looks were in any way remarkable. Only her eyes had any quality, having ever changed from golden brown to amber according to the variance of light as well as mood, and were palisaded by long dark lashes, of which she was more than a little conceited. Her hair was straight and heavy, a disappointment to her, because it was impossible for her to crimp it fashionably in any way. In the past she had tried to emulate Catherine's curly top with borrowed rag-papers, but the result had been so ludicrous that she had long since given up any attempts of that sort, wearing her hair coiled like a skein of blue-black silk at the nape of her long white neck.

Yet men looked at her. Not just boys of her own age, but gentlemen in carriages as well as ordinary men on the street. She had observed too much of life to cherish any illusions about what was behind those avid glances, but sometimes, for her own amusement, when a youth or boy she knew from the neighbourhood tried to engage her in talk, she would stare into his eyes, composed and sure of herself, making him the one to flush and stammer. Catherine, had she known of this game, would probably have boxed her ears, but Louise saw no reason why the male sex should not sometimes have a taste of its own medicine. She did not risk such pranks on older men, aware of the dangers involved, and as if Catherine had not drummed it into her every day she had been under the same roof, she used her own natural wisdom in avoiding any unpleasant encounters.

Over the past months she had presented herself with examples of her sewing work at various dressmaking establishments, but she was one of a countless army of females who applied daily at such doors, which were shut firmly in the faces of those without evidence of a fully completed apprenticeship. The inferior establishments could have their pick of workless women and reduced the wages shamelessly, most with workrooms no better than the dreaded sweat-dens where the majority of sewing-hands worked. Louise knew that at anything less than the best she would learn nothing, and earn less than she gathered in from her own sewing at home, making simple dresses for the wives and daughters of stall-holders and boatmen on the Seine and small tradesmen. She had brought in the first orders by the simple method of touting her needle and thread, sometimes sitting on a doorstep or at the end of a fish-barrow to patch or mend some torn garment on the spot, but again she was not alone when there was such an endless quest among so many merely trying to find the means by which to keep alive. The failure of the corn harvest and the blighting of the potato crop the previous year throughout most of Europe had made the price of bread and other foodstuffs soar, and she frequently sewed a whole dress for less than the price of half a loaf. The outwork that Catherine had brought home from Madame Camille's had come to an end long ago, not only because of a general decline in trade everywhere due to the economic crisis, but on a more human level when one of the seamstresses was discovered using it as a means to smuggle out materials she had stolen to sell, and the privilege of outwork had been withdrawn once and for all. For Louise it meant she no longer had any good-quality fabric to sew, and she was frustrated and restless, determined somehow to break the chains that presently bound her. She was sustained by a belief in herself and the certainty that sooner or later a chance would come and she would seize it with all her strength.

The summer ended on innumerable scuffles of political groups with the gendarmerie that told of the eruptive forces gathering out of the desperation of circumstances. Posters demanding work, food, and wider suffrage appeared overnight, only to be torn down by officialdom in the morning. Catherine, who normally took such interest in these matters, gave them no apparent thought or comment. She had become involved romantically again with a new man. He was the first of any importance to her for a long time. He was not quite forty, his name Jean-François Noiret, and he dealt in *passementerie,* as garment trimmings were called, on behalf of his employers, who also supplied ribbons and feathers and various haberdashery items to milliners and dressmakers as well as to customers in their shops. It was a minor business matter that took Jean-François to Madame Camille's work-shop, and it resulted in a fateful meeting with Catherine. She was quite overcome to emerge from work to find him waiting in a cab to take her home, his purpose being to secure a further meeting. He never repeated the courtesy of the cab-driver at that hour, although he did take her in a hired equipage to suit his own purpose on other occasions, but he had made the good impression necessary, and Catherine was awed and flattered.

He was lean and foxy in appearance, not unattractive, with sharply scooped cheeks and hollowed temples, his light-brown hair well groomed, his jaw adorned with wedge-shaped side-whiskers neatly trimmed. He had an ease of stance and bearing that gave him a dandified air, and his manners were positively silky, but more than anything else it was his eyes that chilled Louise towards him, their dapper glitter unable to shield a hardness that matched the restrained brutality of the fleshy mouth. She dreaded being in the same room with him, hating the way his glance stripped her clothes from her, every nerve in her body alert in abhorrence and defence. But Catherine, dazzled by his smooth attentions, was soon infatuated with him, and was ready in no time at all without thought or caution to commit herself once more to the shadows of a married man's life. It irritated her immeasurably that Louise did not share her high opinion of him.

"For goodness' sake, try not to be so button-lipped when Monsieur Noiret comes today," she admonished shortly, putting a final touch to her appearance before the looking-glass. "Just because you've never liked any of my gentleman friends as much as Henri Berrichon there's no need to make everybody else feel unwelcome."

"There hasn't been anyone else for you either since Henri Berrichon," Louise retorted sharply out of anxiety for her. "That's why I wish it weren't this Noiret man. He'll never care for you as Henri did." Instantly she regretted her hasty words, seeing such a stricken look crumple the woman's face. But it was too late to make amends then. Jean-François had knocked on the door with his silver-topped cane, and Catherine flew to answer it, knowing he did not like to be kept waiting.

After embracing her, making no bones about fondling her lasciviously in another's presence, he let her go fetch bonnet and shawl while he addressed Louise, letting his cane swing suspended between two fingers.

"How is our dainty young girl this evening then? Now, now. Haven't you a smile for me?"

How two-faced he is, Louise thought. Not in a cheerfully rapscallion way like Henri, but with a slyness and ingratiation that made her flesh creep. He knew she did not like him, and took a perverse pleasure in goading her. *Dainty*. How dare he call her that! It was a direct taunt about her height, which was on a level with his, and far from tall in a man.

"Good evening, Monsieur Noiret," she replied without expression, refusing to be drawn. Then Catherine appeared from the bedroom ready to depart, quite on tip-toe with excitement, and he turned to her.

"Come, my dear." He offered her his arm. Catherine took it like a lady born.

For a number of weeks he continued to be obliging to

Catherine, taking her into cheap theatre seats and to backstreet dance-halls and cafés where there was little chance of his meeting acquaintances or being recognised, but he begrudged spending money, and soon these small treats were denied her. He began to come and go with no more purpose than to assuage his sexual appetites, treating Catherine without affection or respect, and Louise's loathing of him grew. She noticed bruises on Catherine that were not explained, and it tore at her to see all sparkle and vivacity go from her good friend, who became more and more dispirited as fear of Jean-François began to take over.

"Tell him to leave you alone," Louise advised her fiercely. "Say he must stop coming here."

"I can't do that." There was frenzy in Catherine's quivering voice. "He would be upset, and I wouldn't like to be responsible for that."

"Wouldn't dare, don't you mean?" Louise retorted hotly, her anger directed against the man himself. "Would he strike you or would it be worse? What does he make you *do* that makes you so scared of him?"

Catherine looked as if she might faint at such unwarranted directness. "Don't you ever let me hear you ask questions like that again." She took refuge in her favourite adage, gaining control over herself again through it. "Your maman wouldn't have liked you to pry into grown-up matters."

Louise took Catherine's limp fingers into hers, shaking her head in fond despair. "My maman couldn't bear to see anyone she cared about unhappy any more than I can."

Catherine snatched her fingers free. "It's all right, I tell you. Nothing for you to worry your head about. He'll leave of his own accord one day, you'll see. My men always do, don't they?" Her tone was faintly bitter, her eyes full of Henri Berrichon, and then she dismissed the memory, her voice strengthening stoutly as she flapped her white hands in emphasis. "Until Jean-François goes let's keep the peace. That's all I ask of you. Just don't let us set his temper off." Her normally rosy colour receded on the prospect of such a dreadful occurrence. His minor displays of sadistic impatience with her had been worse than anything else she had ever known.

Louise noticed, but said no more. It would be up to her to find some means of breaking his hold on Catherine. She applied her mind to the problem with the same dedication of purpose that she applied to all matters of importance. Catherine would have been beside herself with panic if she had not been too agitated in her own thoughts to notice the all too familiar set of the girl's mouth and chin.

The first step, in Louise's opinion, was to find out where he lived. Jean-François had always been taciturn about his background, but she discovered it by the simple process of waiting outside the shop in the rue de Rivoli where he worked, and following him home. He went by carriage, which was surprising since he only held a mediocre post. If the traffic had not been so dense Louise would not have been able to keep up with the horses, but as it was, with running part of the way, she was able to spot the gates where he turned in. It was a large house of considerable grandeur, and she returned to it several times to observe the comings and goings there. On Jean-François's subsequent visits to Catherine he was unaware how keenly Louise was waiting for the chance to bring him down. She thought she knew the way it might be done, and all she had to do was to wait for the means to do it.

Every time he came he removed his outdoor clothing before going into Catherine's room, and each time Louise moved his cane or set his gloves in a slightly different place in the hope that he would forget them. He never did. Then one evening his white silk scarf slipped unnoticed from a pocket as he hung his coat on the peg. She pretended to be sewing, holding her breath in the hope that he would not notice it lying there and retrieve it. Luck was with her. As soon as he had gone into the bedroom she darted from her chair, snatched up the scarf, and concealed it. Then she went out for a walk until he was gone. She could not bear to hear Catherine's whimpering through the closed door.

The next day she took the scarf to his place of residence, timing her call for when he would be at business. From her observations of Madame Noiret's timetable she expected her to be at home, and asked to see her.

"Please tell Madame Noiret that I have some property of her husband's that I wish to return into her safekeeping," she stated with an air that suited her best clothes. The manservant looked her up and down. She had some style about her, and her footwear was polished to a shine in spite of having seen better days, but he decided to keep her on the doorstep.

"Wait here," he ordered, not committing himself. He came back a few moments later and showed her into Madame Noiret's presence.

Louise knew whom she would see from the vigil she had

kept on the house. She also knew that the Noirets had five daughters and two sons under the age of twelve, a governess, two nursemaids, two indoor servants, and three outdoor ones, not counting the coachman, groom, and stable-boy. Madame was writing at a rosewood escritoire in the ornate salon of ice-blue and gold. She put down her pen and twisted in her chair in a rustle of green moiré taffeta, a stern, powerful-looking woman with a commanding air and no charm. Louise was convinced that Jean-François had married for money, and from his miserliness there was every indication that his wife held the purse-strings.

"You have my husband's scarf, I see." Madame Noiret spoke in a deep, uncompromising voice and nodded at the monogrammed scarf that Louise had unfolded. "I was not aware that he had mislaid it. I suppose you are anticipating a reward." Her gaze took in the give-away boots and her eyes narrowed suspiciously. "How do I know you did not steal it in the first place?"

Louise's jaw clenched, but for the sake of what she had come to do she kept an outwardly composed expression. "No, madame, and I want no reward for returning it. I can tell you exactly where Monsieur Noiret left it and when."

"Indeed? Explain."

"He was visiting the grisette for whom I keep house, and I found it on the floor where he had dropped it. I'm not surprised he didn't notice it. He never has time for anything else but her when he comes, and no man could be blamed for that. She's a very comely woman."

Her words seemed to hang in the quiet salon. On the mantel the Sèvres clock chimed melodiously and sounded as loud as the bells of Notre Dame. In fascination Louise watched the crimson dye rise up Madame Noiret's solid throat to suffuse her heavy cheeks with a final explosion of colour. The woman swallowed hard, her face working.

"Where do you live?"

"On the rue St.-Martin." Louise laid the scarf carefully over the arm of a roll-ended sofa. "I must be getting back there." She made a polite bob and turned to leave.

"Wait!" Madame Noiret had stretched out a beringed hand, and she lowered it to clasp her fingers tensely together in her lap. "How long has your—er—grisette been acquainted with my husband?"

Louise's dark amber eyes in their fringe of black lashes were unblinking. "Since last October. Too long, madame. I hope that now I have returned his property we shall not have to see him again. I bid you good day."

She left the house, the quaking lessening in the pit of her stomach and her rapid pulse subsiding. It had been an excruciating ordeal not knowing how things would go, but she felt almost sure that Jean-François Noiret would not return again to the rooms in the rue St.-Martin. His wife would see to that. Softly and triumphantly she began to laugh as she hurried back along the street.

The evening came and went without a sign of him. Louise saw out of the corner of her eye how Catherine, thinking herself unobserved, closed her eyes in private thankfulness when the hour grew too late for him to come. One week followed another, and then, when more than a month had gone by, Catherine grew more confident, no longer giving a nervous start at every creak on the stair. Gradually there was a return to the old self that Louise knew so well, desperate shadows no longer haunting Catherine's eyes. Strangely, neither of them mentioned the man's disappearance to the other; Louise because the less said about it the better, and Catherine in superstitious dread that to speak of the devil was to summon him up. And Jean-François had been evil. Only she knew how vile the desires he had inflicted upon her, how sadistic his satisfaction in using her as he pleased while fully aware of her longing to be free of him. But now he was gone and she could live without fear again. Her laughter and her quick appreciation of a joke returned, her step grew light once more, and she changed her hairstyle to a more frivolous one of curls in a top-knot and bunches over each ear.

She was hurrying home from work and was no more than a few yards from her home on the night when a man loomed from the shadows to block her path in the darkness of the unlit passageway. She could not see his face, but she knew him. Her heart gave a sickening lurch of terror. Her low moan seemed to echo and re-echo against the curved brickwork that arched overhead. Before she could utter his name his first blow knocked her to the ground, and then he most savagely attacked and raped her.

Louise, beginning to get anxious because Catherine was late home, opened the door into the night to look for her. The moonlight showed her crawling up the outside flight of wooden stairs, her clothing torn, and her face so battered as to be almost unrecognisable.

"Oh, oh, oh." It was Louise who cried out for her friend's

condition, trying to help her rise to take the rest of the flight. Catherine clutched at her frantically.

"It was him," she managed to croak through cut and swollen lips. She had no need to say more.

Louise was distraught, blaming herself for it all. Jean-François must have held Catherine responsible for the *fait accompli* that had removed him so neatly from her life. The fact that he had sought vengeance in the darkness, not taking the risk of being seen and named to his spouse a second time, was an indication of the measure of unpleasantness that he must have been subjected to at home, but it was small satisfaction to Louise as she helped poor Catherine to bed.

The next morning when Catherine tried to get up, she kept fainting away. As she became more and more anxious about getting to work the swooning spells increased, making it impossible for her to move. Louise donned Catherine's cap and shawl.

"I'm going in your place," she said firmly. "After all you've taught me, I'll get by somehow."

"You mustn't!" Catherine was frantic. "You'll be spotted. The work will be beyond your capabilities. You'll make a mess of it." She groaned aloud, putting a hand to aching head. "I know I'll end up getting the boot."

"You'll get it anyway if you don't appear, according to what you were saying earlier," Louise replied crisply. "So it's worth a try. Wish me luck."

By the time Louise reached the back street where once she had hidden in the burial ground, she was already in the midst of the throng of grisettes making their way to work. She explained the circumstances to two of Catherine's workmates, Berthe and Aude, who soon spread the word among the others. This was a time when they could rally together. Too often there was a cut-throat competition for the better-paid work or a vying to be kept on during a seasonal slump, but by the very nature of their profession they were women of a certain temperament, having a profound respect for their fellow artists with a needle, and Catherine was well liked.

"You keep with us," said Berthe. "As long as there isn't an empty seat at the table we might get away with it."

Louise had been to the gates of the work-shop many times to meet Catherine, but it was the first time she had gone beyond the cobbled yard into the building itself. Keeping her head down she hurried hard on the heels of Berthe, with Aude close behind her. As it had been in her dreams, the workrooms opened one into another, but with less colour and romance than she had visualised, the smell of lamp-oil blending with the curiously acrid aroma of new material. She followed Berthe through the pattern-making room, the pressing-room where already the irons were being heated on hot stoves, the cutting-room for which shears were being sharpened in an outside porch on a grindstone, and the packing-room stacked with boxes, before she reached those set aside for the needlewomen. As with all the previous rooms, each sewing area had a vast table occupying the centre space, making a focal point for individual activities. All were scrubbed white, matching the cleanliness of the rest of the place, to ensure that no dust or dirt descended on the costly materials. After lining up to collect Catherine's allotted work for the day, Louise squeezed into the chair jammed between Berthe's and Aude's at the table.

"Thread your needle and get started," Aude advised sagely. "It don't do to look idle for a second, 'specially today when there's a rush of work on."

The work Louise had in hand was gauging seven breadths of shot taffeta onto a waistband, the secret being to keep a remarkable evenness, but she had no qualms about her sewing, only experiencing a certain amount of awe with regard to the splendour of the material itself. As she slipped on her thimble she caught the encouraging nods and smiles of the other seamstresses around the table, and then all heads bent over their work. Talk was discouraged by the supervisor, Madame Rousseau, a thin, energetic woman with a pale complexion and dyed red hair, whom Louise had glimpsed busily occupied in the embroiderers' room where some kind of crisis had arisen. However, when she was out of earshot, as she was now, low-voiced chatter buzzed around the table. Louise commented to Berthe on her right hand on the day's limited range of hues.

"Everybody's sewing such sombre shades. Not at all what I had expected."

Berthe snipped a thread with her scissors. "The court is still in mourning for the King's sister. It's only about a couple of months since she died, and for a while all the ladies' new clothes will be in these colours. If it had been King Louis-Philippe himself we would have been up to our necks in oceans of black material for a year. As it is, I hear that it's nigh impossible for the couturières to get another metre of anything more in purple or grey shades anywhere in Paris, there being such a run on these funereal hues out of respect for the lady."

It was soon afterwards that Louise glimpsed one of the vendeuses employed to attend customers in the showroom, a haughty-looking young woman who came somewhat bad-temperedly to collect a dress that had had the sleeves changed. Berthe at Louise's right hand gave her a nudge, nodding toward the retreating back of the vendeuse.

"She and the other bitch in the showroom think it's beneath their dignity to run errands to the workrooms. They like best just to take the garments for fitting and fetch the finished dresses from the racks in the *cabine* to the customers."

"I'd like to see the *cabine*. Catherine told me that there are often racks and racks of handsome dresses hanging there."

"Well, you won't get the chance today. The less you move from your chair, the safer you are from being nabbed."

It was advice that Louise did not intend to ignore. She had taken the precaution of pulling Catherine's cap well down with her hair tucked away under it, and it helped to give her anonymity among the rest, who were similarly adorned. There were a few uncomfortable moments of suspense when the fitter from the showroom, who seemed to spend her time darting between the workrooms and that more exalted sphere upstairs, came into the room where Louise was sewing. She was an anxious-eyed woman with a nose and chin as sharp as the pins held in the tiny velvet cushion strapped to her wrist, a tape-measure looped around her neck, and scissors swinging from a châtelaine. She wanted to know which seamstress had been responsible for altering a black foulard mourning dress for one of her special customers, and picked out Louise at random, probably associating that seat at the table with Catherine. "Was it you?"

Hastily Louise shook her head, keeping her face down, and to her relief a grisette at the far end of the table spoke up and the danger passed. The ding-dong of a handbell summoned everyone to the kitchens where they sat down at long tables and ate whatever food they had brought with them, some heating soup or making a hot drink on the range. It seemed to Louise that every employee in the whole workshop must be in on the secret, because heads turned on all sides to look across at her, some of the younger ones giggling behind their hands. After twenty minutes everyone was back at work.

Between five and six o'clock there was another interval, but a shorter one. When calls of nature had to be observed an absence of no more than a few minutes was permitted, including the time it took to reach the outdoor privies. Louise dreaded having to go there, knowing there was the danger of discovery as soon as she moved out of the general hive of activity, but yet again she escaped detection. On the way she passed a storeroom, and within Madame Camille herself was having a bolt of cloth unrolled for her inspection. Louise was left with a feeling of disappointment. The couturière had looked no different from any other quietly dressed lady of the day, nothing new or exciting in her appearance, which was what Louise had somehow expected from such a renowned high priestess of fine clothes. At the table she finished the last of the gauging and was satisfied with it, knowing it would spring out from the waist exactly as required when fastened to its bodice on which Aude was working. Berthe noticed that Louise had come to the end of her task and signalled to a woman who was a work-supplier, and she came with five widths of the same taffeta already cut to be made into ruffles on the skirt. Louise set to work again, feeling some sympathy for the eventual wearer of the garment, who with her many petticoats and underskirts stiffened with crinoline would have a not inconsiderable weight to carry around with her. Even the sleeves would constrict her movements, designed as so many were to make it impossible for her to lift her arms beyond a right angle. Decorative and passive in her role of cherished womanhood, ignorant of politics, dependent upon a lady's maid to lace in her stays and unfasten the simplest hook in the garment for her, she did not arouse envy in the girl who sat sewing the moiré taffeta skirt. Louise was thinking that to live a life without work of interest, something as enthralling as creating beautiful clothes for choice, would be stultifying for her. She also enjoyed expressing her opinions, owing much to the encouragement of Catherine, who never failed to boast that her own Halles upbringing had given her a natural right to best any man in talk. Only in love was Catherine fallible, and Louise was resolved that she would never fall into the same pitfall. She still thought of Worth with tender nostalgia, knowing she had seen the gentle face of love. If such a love should come to her again with time she would welcome it, but not for her a man's dominance with all the anguish and heartache and misery involved. In all things she would remain her own mistress, and in affairs of the heart most of all.

"Mademoiselle Allard! Are those ruffles finished?"

Louise came from her reverie with a start. Madame Rousseau had addressed her from a little distance away, not looking in her direction, but checking a list that she held.

"Almost," Louise mumbled, drawing back in her chair as Berthe and two or three other grisettes leaned forward obligingly to help block the woman's view of her.

"You're slow today. What has been the delay?"

Louise froze, hearing the clack of footsteps bent on investigation. Then there came a gasp of astonishment, and the cap was whipped from her head with a speed that jerked her black hair from its pins, sending it slithering down in a quickly unwinding coil into a flow across her back. Slowly she looked up into the incredulous face of the supervisor.

"Where have you come from?" the woman exploded. "How long have you been on these premises? Who *are* you?"

Louise gave the simple explanation of Catherine being attacked, giving no other or more intimate details. The inquisition did not end there. In the supervisor's office Louise's work was spread out and examined by both Madame Rousseau and a senior first hand for defects and faults, but none of any consequence were found. The first hand left the office with the garment pieces, and the supervisor sat down in her chair at the desk, facing Louise sternly.

"I do not know who is the most to blame, Mademoiselle Allard or you."

"I am. She didn't want me to come, but I hoped to save her from losing her job."

"I have never dismissed a seamstress yet for being genuinely indisposed, although naturally I have to suspend them from employment during any illness. However, being set upon is a different matter, as Mademoiselle Allard well knows. She is at fault in an extremely serious matter. Madame Camille expects her seamstresses to conduct themselves in a mannerly way and take care of their persons in all circumstances, keeping out of street brawls and political uprisings such as are particularly rife at the present time." Her eyes scrutinised Louise's face as if trying to probe out some grain of undisclosed truth. "Do you give me your word that the attack on Mademoiselle Allard was totally unprovoked?"

Louise answered with perfect truth. "Yes, I do."

The woman gave a nod of acceptance. "In that case I'll take no disciplinary action against her this time." There was a pause. "How old are you?"

"Almost sixteen."

The supervisor's long fingers beat a thoughtful tattoo on the desk. "You are remarkably young to have reached the standard of sewing that you have shown here today. Mademoiselle Allard has been teaching you, you say? She is to be commended there."

"Thank you, madame." Louise set her shoulders and came out boldly with her request. "Would Madame Camille take me as an apprentice on the merits of my work alone? I have no money to pay for the privilege."

Madame Rousseau raised her eyebrows at the audacious request and answered without hesitation. "Out of the question." She saw disappointment strike the girl's expressive face. "However," she added, knowing true sewing potential when she saw it, "all is not lost. Do you know what it means to be an improver?"

Louise blinked, hardly daring to hope. "Yes. Improvers are those who have served a dressmaking apprenticeship and are ready to take on more varied and extended work."

"Correct. I happen to think that you have reached that stage." Madame Rousseau took up a pen and dipped it in the inkwell to write on a sheet of paper that she had drawn towards her. "In view of your accomplishments, I feel justified in creating such a niche for you. Tell me your name again." She wrote it down. "You will inform Mademoiselle Allard that she may have one more day's respite to recover from her injuries, without pay, of course, and she is to bring you with her when she returns to work the following morning."

Louise set off to run all the way home, the little lantern that was Catherine's bobbing joyously in her clasp. She had not gone far before she realised that something serious was afoot in the city. The air was charged and electric, and several times she had to skirt throngs of men gathering at rallying points, their voices angry in their political discourse. She heard shouts of *Vive la réforme!* and down one street there came the sound of the singing of the "Marseillaise" that was forbidden on pain of imprisonment. When she reached the safety of her own door, Catherine fell upon her in relief.

"Thank God you're safely home. I heard neighbours in the street saying that the government has banned the rally that was to be held tomorrow as a demand for political reform, and heaven alone knows what will happen now."

All the anxiety and suspense could not quell Catherine's

reaction to the good news that Louise had to tell, and she insisted on opening a bottle of wine. They drank two toasts, the first to Louise's future, and the second to the future of France.

"May we see our country restored to the glory of the days of the Empire," Catherine said. As Louise raised her glass Catherine did likewise, but directed hers towards a tricolour pinned to the wall. "I couple the name of France with that of another Bonaparte, Prince Louis-Napoléon. Let his exile soon be over, and may whatever comes about in the next few days bring him into his own."

"Without bloodshed," Louise added before putting the wine to her lips.

By the evening of the following day thirty people had been killed and wounded, shot down by the National Guard in a demonstration outside the Prime Minister's house after a day of unrest when the thwarted marchers had overturned omnibuses, made bonfires of park seats, and smashed windows. The slaughter was the signal for a great uprising. The next morning, when Louise should have set off with Catherine for her first day at Madame Camille's, the city was in a state of armed mob rule, and it was not safe for any woman to venture out. Within a few yards of their quarters the paving stones of the street had been levered up, as had been done in many other parts of the city, to form one of the innumerable insurrectionary barricades, a red flag flying defiantly, and looted guns spat continuously while many public buildings burned, the thick smoke forming a pall over the city. Before the next day was over King Louis-Philippe and his Queen fled Paris ignominiously in a cab, but in the nick of time, more fortunate than certain royal ghosts of the past, and upon reaching the coast they took ship for England with only the clothes they stood up in. In Paris there was further sacking and rampage. One of the graceful windows at the Palace of the Tuileries smashed into a cascade of glittering shards as the royal throne was hurled through and afterwards burnt in the Place de la Bastille. A Second French Republic was declared under a provisional government.

As soon as it was safe to venture out again Catherine and Louise joined streams of people anxious to get back to work and normal routine. Picking their way over rubble and averting their eyes from bloodstains on the cobbles, the two of them hurried through streets bearing the scars of the short and violent overthrow, to reach Madame Camille's work-shop. They found the gates closed and padlocked, and took their turn with other silent and subdued grisettes to read the notice displayed. *February 25th, 1848. Madame Camille regrets that in the present uncertain circumstances this establishment will remain closed until further notice.*

Louise did not take her disappointment lightly. She grabbed the bars of the gates and shook them until they rattled noisily, such fury in her face that even Catherine did not dare to restrain her. When finally she calmed down and turned away from the gates she was very pale, her expression rigid. She spoke through clenched teeth.

"Madame Camille will have to open again before long. Women will always want dresses no matter how many monarchies and republics come and go."

As Louise swept away in the direction from which they had come, her head high, her back very straight, Catherine followed at a wary pace. There were times when Catherine felt she did not know this strong, sane, and ambitious girl any better now than when she had taken her in as a waif from the very burial ground that they were passing. From the start she had been aware of having a steel-willed young individualist in her care. She hoped that Louise would not lose the sweeter side of life through the folly of setting herself a course too hard.

It was not only Madame Camille who had put up her shutters. Stocks had fallen, there had been a run on the banks, and payment was being suspended. Foreigners, who normally crowded the city of pleasure, had departed, and as time went by with more political troubles brewing, they continued to stay away, causing many of the hotels to close. With a little money saved and a few things that could be bartered for food Catherine and Louise managed to exist, but they were among thousands deprived of a livelihood, and were soon in arrears with their rent. After a while Madame Camille did open again, but with such a reduced number of hands that not even Catherine was senior enough to be included.

In May further mob violence occurred. The Second French Republic had widely increased the franchise, but was failing to give promised work for which so many were desperate. Starvation was rife. In June a hundred thousand hungry, sullen men rose up in vengeful revolt, and once again Paris was a city of guns and flames and stone barricades. Troops were rushed in by road and by train on the single St.-Germain line, and were backed by a flow of reinforcements as for three terrible days the battle was fought with no mercy shown on either side. Women were among those caught in the cross-fire and mown down. The number of dead amounted to thousands, an archbishop attempting reconciliation and an army general in parley murdered with the rest. The gutters ran with blood. Catherine with Louise gave aid to the wounded who staggered from the fray to collapse across each other in the dreadful carnage. Over and over again the two of them prayed with the dying, getting a priest whenever they could find one of those giving succour tirelessly in all the uproar and confusion.

* * *

The aftermath of the quelled rebellion brought still greater hardships to the citizens of Paris. Businesses collapsed in bankruptcy and ruin, shops closed through lack of custom, and elegant carriages became a rare sight in the streets. Ladies made do with the dresses they had, and what little work came the couturières' way was mostly in the retrimming of garments and the shortening of hems by an inch or two to save wear and tear on precious fabrics. Yet, in spite of everything, there were still some with money they were not afraid to spend, and Maison Gagelin, being a firmly established business, weathered the storm as did many other similarly situated, but the slump in trade continued the downward slide at a devastating rate. Worth and Marie could not look for any improvement in their financial position until the situation improved generally, and were thankful to be in employment when so many were begging in the streets.

Neither Catherine nor Louise had work of any kind. Earlier they had both managed to earn a little by asking for sewing tasks at the doors of the normally well-to-do, but with so many other women similarly engaged the source soon dried up. Under cover of darkness they removed their belongings on a borrowed hand-cart to avoid confiscation for what they owed in rent. In the Place Maubert in the Latin Quarter they took one small room in a hovel near the bread market, and the squalor of their new home reminded Louise of the miserable conditions in which her mother had died. But this time she was older and no longer afraid. Like a lone wolf, at times gaunt and ruthless in the struggle for survival, Louise went back to her well-remembered methods of foraging for any food she could find, returning to the haunts of her childhood and her old tricks of snatching anything edible from stalls or passing carts. But it was a far more dangerous game than before, and twice she narrowly escaped arrest, which sent Catherine into a frenzy of concern whenever she went out on her sorties.

In all parts of the city the scrawled slogan *Liberté, égalité, et fraternité* met her eyes on every important building and monument, but starvation and despair fostered enmity and made mockery of the fine sentiments. Whenever the pangs of hunger allowed her to think of anything else, she paid more attention to other slogans concerned with the forthcoming elections and the posters advocating votes for Louis-Napoléon, whose name was registering as another Bonaparte for France among thousands who were to vote for the first time.

There were days when she was not able to beg or steal or find a morsel to eat. As a last resort she would join others like her in the bread market where armed gendarmerie gave protection to the bakers' wares, but also where someone more wily than the rest could occasionally make a grab and run for it. It was a hazardous chance to take, and she never let Catherine know where her spoils had come from. She hated returning empty-handed as she had to many times, and it was always a relief when Catherine had managed to obtain a little money from a charity fund. For a few days afterwards there would be food on the table honestly come by. Later, much, much later, Louise was to discover the origins of that fund. Catherine, for the first time in her life, had taken men whom she had not loved into her bed. The experience left its mark, all her sentimental nature and joyous self-esteem sullied and violated by it, and she was never as ebullient and heart-giving towards the opposite sex again. In time to come Louise was to pinpoint the serious turn in Catherine's character to those terrible months in the Place Maubert hovel in the same year that the December elections brought Louis-Napoléon into power. He was elected by universal suffrage President of the French Republic.

At the first opportunity Louise and Catherine went to see him on a triumphant ride through Paris, for he was making it clear after a curiously damp-squib start to his coming into power that he believed in being seen by the people. Not wanting to go without a token of loyal support, Louise picked some pale-green winter rosebuds on the way from the deserted garden of an empty house, and carefully removed every thorn from the stalks as she waited at Catherine's side at the forefront of those gathered near the Elysée Palace, which had become the new President's official residence. It was a crisp, sunny day, and not only was she comfortably well fed from what she still believed to be Catherine's benevolent charity fund, but she had managed to obtain a little sewing work from a shopkeeper's wife. Her spirits were high, her mood optimistic, and the winter nip in the air brought colour to her cheeks.

The drumming of regimental music heralded the coming of the Prince-President. What a sight to see pageantry on the streets of Paris! The older people in the crowd remembered it from the past, but for Louise and thousands of others it was the very first time. Along the rue de Faubourg St.-Honoré, already macadamised at the Prince-President's orders to deprive any unruly mob of the paving stones for barricades, there rode into view a splendid escort of cavalry, line after line almost as far as the eye could see. Among the most spectacular were the cuirassiers with the sun striking fire from the brass crests surmounting their white metal helmets, and from which black horsehair flowed magnificently. In a jingling of harness and accoutrements they trotted by, creating a searing burst after burst of scarlet and blue set off by white breeches and black kneeboots against the sheen of their uniformly dappled grey horses. The crowd pressed forward excitedly, those at the forefront being pushed almost into the path of the jogging cavalry. Louise, alarmed at being within touching distance of the horses, tried to draw back, and in the same instant a young officer's white-gauntleted hand swept down and snatched the winter rosebuds from her hand. She gasped, caught totally unawares, and saw the cuirassier's face directly above her as he leaned in the saddle. She had a full impression of a firm-jawed face of dashing looks, lean and intelligent and tanned by wind and weather to a brownish tint, with low-lidded, grey-green eyes at present lively with incipient laughter at his own action, and quite blatant with amatory invitation.

"Flowers for me?" he quipped wickedly. "Ever at your service, mademoiselle!"

Helplessly she watched him bear her rosebuds away in triumph, his glance sliding back recklessly to hold her gaze until he could look no longer, adhering rigidly once more to keeping eyes to the front and the spine straight in the saddle, lost from her view in an endless clatter of hooves as further lines of escorting cavalry blocked all sight of him, the horses' tails swirling like long, silken tassels. She released a long, pent-up breath at his audacity. Only then did she turn and pluck impatiently at Catherine's sleeve to gain her ear in the dense noise of cheering arising in crescendoes from the crowd as the man whom all had come to see approached at a steady pace.

"Did you see what happened to my flowers?" she exclaimed indignantly between amusement and outrage. But Catherine did not hear, straining to catch her first glimpse of the Bonaparte she had long awaited.

"There he is!" Catherine's cry burst exuberantly from her throat. *"Vive le Président!"*

Louise, her thoughts still full of the cuirassier, watched the new ruler of France's destiny ride into view, and was acutely conscious of being empty-handed with no roses to throw in his spectacular path. Mounted on a magnificent chestnut charger that he had brought with him from his sojourn in England, his uniform immaculate with gold epaulettes dancing, Prince-President Louis-Napoléon in his mid-forties bore a strong resemblance to his Emperor uncle whose statue he was shortly to pass in the Place Vendôme. He was a long-bodied, short-legged man of superb horsemanship, with a prominent forehead, a large nose, the wax-ended moustache and goatee beard that many Frenchmen were already emulating, and brilliant eyes which he kept fixed ahead of him as he rode, keeping up a spanking pace as if bringing about the recovery of France were a physical battle that he was engaged in. In himself he was not a particularly impressive figure, but there was about him the Bonaparte mystique and air of power that fired the enthusiasm of those who cheered and shouted without restraint. Louise joyfully joined in the cheers with the rest until he had gone by, continuing his path of acclaim through the city. She was convinced that the Prince-President's calm, inscrutable expression denoted a will to succeed that was as determined as her own. Like her, he was going to combat all odds. She wished him well with all her heart.

That same evening Lieutenant Pierre de Gand of the 6th Cuirassiers, off duty and no longer in uniform, returned to the rue du Faubourg St.-Honoré and reached the place along the route where he had snatched the rosebuds from a pair of reluctant hands. With his dark-brown hair worn down into thick sideburns, his lean build and his splendid height, he was well aware that his appearance was more than set off by his erect military bearing and air of virile health and vigour. As he sauntered along at a leisurely pace his cloak, to which one of the rosebuds was attached, swung from his strong shoulders over his evening clothes. His mouth, normally quick and mobile in its smiling, was unusually serious as if he more than realised the futility of the quest he had set himself. Yet there was a determined thrust to the indented chin as his trained soldier's eyes scrutinised the area in the faint hope that he might see the girl again somewhere in the vicinity.

Who was she? he pondered. Did she make bonnets for a milliner or sell bread in a boulangerie? Sewing-hand or shopgirl or cigar-maker? Not since his cadet days had he thought to consort with a pretty grisette, but it had been the magnetism emanating from her that had gripped the very core of him, sexual and tantalising and forceful, giving drama to those few extraordinary moments. Had he been of a fanciful turn of mind he would have imagined that fate had drawn him to the sight of her being jostled at the front of that surging crowd while he had been still a little distance away, only to have her practically thrust into his path.

There were a few passers-by in the street, but no figure that he recognised. What had made him suppose even remotely that she would have realised the effect she had had on him and come back in the shared hope of meeting again? He frowned impatiently at the compulsive whim that had brought him there, condemning himself for having set out on a fool's errand. He had better things to do with his time than waste it pointlessly. A hackney cab was coming along the street and he hailed it, giving the address of a married lady in affluent circumstances whose loneliness he consoled from time to time. But before the cab had gone far he changed his mind and gave the cabby another destination, his mood edgy and discontented. He was not used to being thwarted when his mind was made up to a purpose, and for this evening anyway, arms other than those of the elusive grisette lost any real power to entice him. Better the male company of his fellow officers in the drinking binge that would be in full swing in an upper room at the café to which he was driven at a spanking pace through the dark streets.

As week followed week the Prince-President's influence on the economy gradually made itself felt. Hotels reopened. Shutters were taken down from shops, and here and there a coat of fresh paint made an optimistic splash of colour. Nothing was easy, nothing could be hurried, but foreigners returned and were seen again, bent on commerce as well as pleasure. Trade began to revive, and once more Madame

Camille took on a full complement of sewing-hands, including the young improver named Louise Vernet who had been recommended by the supervisor before the start of all the troubles.

Catherine, happy to be back at the work she loved, sang softly to herself as she sewed with her fellow grisettes. At a table in another room Louise stitched away on some less complicated work, the bloom on her cheek caught by the light of the window behind her. Sometimes the memory returned to her of the impudent cuirassier who had claimed flowers intended for a president, and she had no doubt that she would know him if ever their paths should cross again. A secret smile played on her lips, but at the present time it had nothing to do with him. She was satisfied that her talents outstripped the work allotted to her, and it should not be long before she was moved to the lower end of Catherine's table. One day she would be at the head of it. Her horizons were widening and releasing such a renewed force of ambition that at times she almost caught her breath on the joy and wonder of it. Anything was possible if she could prove herself to be a better dressmaker than anyone else. Her needles hissed in and out of the silk she was sewing in a song of its own.

6

As Louise had anticipated, her time on the less complicated work at Madame Camille's had been comparatively short. By the time she was seventeen she had been promoted by way of a brief spell at Catherine's table to the embroiderers' room, where the perfection of her stitches was put to full glory. Leaves and flowers and classic motifs sprang forth from her multicoloured embroidery silks to garland and festoon and trail in abundance over ballgowns and day-dresses, wedding mantles and sweeping trains, and every kind of collar and cape. Madame Camille and the rest of the couturières made no distinctive changes in the fashion itself of long corsage and enormously full skirt, but vied with each other in the lavishness of ornamentation on the clothes that they produced.

Louise and Catherine had long ago left the hovel in the Place Maubert and moved back into quarters similar to those they had shared before, their frugal standard of living raised fractionally by Louise's wages. The seasonal rise and fall in trade still prevented the smallest extravagance, but Louise was able to buy herself new shoes whenever she needed replacement, and hoped never to have to wear anybody else's cast-off footwear again. Mercifully her small, well-shaped feet did not appear to have suffered any lasting damage from the variety of their past encasements, but that could have been due to her going barefoot indoors and on grass and anywhere else where it had been at all possible.

From the first day of her employment at Madame Camille's, Louise had absorbed everything that would stand her in good stead in her professional career, following the practice she had adopted early in life of listening and learning and tucking away all information of value like hoarded gold. It was a tradition among the grisettes that any helpful hint gained out of their own sewing experience be passed on, and although most of these tips had been learned already from Catherine, such as the commonplace trick of using a little of one's own spit to erase blood marks on fabric from a pricked finger, Louise gathered quite a lot from her fellow workers. Best of all she enjoyed instruction in new work from a senior hand, always eager to advance her talents. At the present time she was expanding the range of her dressmaking knowledge whenever she had some spare minutes, by taking impromptu lessons in pattern-making and cutting from the cutter at Madame Camille's. For the second time an Englishman had entered her life. His name was Will Russell.

His presence at the cutting-table was something of an innovation. Male cutters were not unusual, but dressmakers' establishments were not tailors' shops with the emphasis on the cut of a garment, and Madame Camille had been among those preferring female hands as cutters, holding to the opinion they produced feminine lines better suited to the air of gentility and helplessness necessary to a lady's garments. But those closely involved in fashion always keep an ear to the ground in politics and current affairs, and Madame Camille had become as intuitively aware as the rest of the couturières of the evolving trend towards cut lines of extreme smartness that alone were able to express the uncompromising assertion of Frenchwomen generally, that was the aftermath of the 1848 revolution. With this new emphasis in mind, she had decided that she needed an English cutter to interpret her clothes, because none could deny that the best tailoring in the world was lodged across the English Channel. She hoped to bring some of that skill into the new fit of her garments, and she had, surprisingly, ended up with Will Russell. With tailoring experience in a cloth mill behind him, he was already in Paris, working for the renowned court tailor Ebeling, whose premises were in the same building as the shop Gagelin in the rue de Richelieu. Will Russell was one of many drawn to the Mecca of fashion to widen their experience before returning to their own countries.

"I must point out," he informed her uncompromisingly in his excellent French, "that at Ebeling's I have already expended some of the time I allotted to being in Paris. I intend to go back to England as soon as my two years are up."

"I do not see any great problem there," she replied cautiously, her mouth neat as a purse. Knowing how the pendulum of fashion could swing, she did not expect to need him beyond the remainder of his time left, and it was not that point which made her hesitate to employ him. It was the effect that his extremely masculine presence would have on her needlewomen that concerned her. With his rebellious fair hair and head set arrogantly on the strong neck, the unmistakable ripple of muscle and obvious power of limb and loin, Will Russell was at the age of twenty-seven in his full and lusty prime. But there was no denying his professional skill. She came to the reluctant conclusion that her neddlewomen would have to look out for themselves, and any who showed the slightest distraction to the detriment of their work would be dismissed immediately. "Very well, Mr. Russell. The rest of your time in France shall be in my employ."

Will Russell moved into the cutting-room with all the dedicated upheaval of a new broom, turning out the feminine clutter that the two women cutters, now put to a sewing-table again, had gathered there. Unnecessary boxes and waste stacks were cleared away. He extended the two long tables with his own carpentry and put up sectioned shelves to hold the bolts of cloth waiting to be cut, which simplified selection and protected them from any damage. He rearranged the oil-lamps to give maximum light with reflectors he had made himself, being something of an inventor in his own time, and he had devised a number of small and handy gadgets to assist him in his work. From the start he made it clear that he considered the cutting-room at Madame Camille's to be his domain, and he kept very much to himself. It suited him that he had his own bench set apart in the kitchen where he could eat his food away from close contact with the chattering grisettes. Yet he was agreeable to them, and was more aware than they realised of the stir he created amid their concentrated femininity whenever he had cause to be in their workrooms for one reason or another. He was particularly courteous to Madame Rousseau, puzzling the grisettes, who considered her domineering, with the plainest of looks to match, but unbeknown to them, quite early on in his days at the work-shop he had come across the supervisor, made white-lipped and helpless by a shaft of pain before she could reach her office door, and had helped her there, seeing that she was struggling with an illness that she wanted no one to know about.

Whenever Madame Camille had reason to speak to him in the workroom, his attitude towards her was very much male to female, bold and free. Those grisettes working at tables within earshot gasped and whispered together at the manner in which he refused to give in over any point of work in which he believed himself to be right, and she, the *grande dame* whom the rest held in awe, always conceded to him, at the same time seeming to forget her middle years, never failing to be a little flustered and a trifle pink in the cheeks as if she were a girl again.

"I handle a fabric like a horse or a woman," he was once overheard saying to her quite blatantly. His words were repeated and flew like fire around the tables in the workrooms, heads gathering together, the grisettes either saucer-eyed or indignant or slyly titillated. Whatever the individual reaction, afterwards many a grisette shivered deliciously when she saw him smooth and stroke the unrolled materials into shape on his cutting-table in what was known as a *lay* of cloth with his firm, caressing fingertips.

Almost without exception the women liked him, and some were a little afraid of him. A good number, particularly those who liked to watch him at work, fancied him, but even the boldest who twitched their petticoats harder than most gained no more than a sharply appreciative grin and sometimes a glance that lingered speculatively and was then recalled as decisively as the shutting of a door. There was a great deal of speculation as to whether he had a wife that nobody knew about, or if he cohabited with a paramour somewhere, which was what many foreigners did for the time of their sojourn. In any case, it was easy to conclude that the old bachelor adage of never soiling one's own doorstep was the one that he had decided to live by.

They were not far from the truth. He had come to Paris to further his own plans, not to seduce or to deceive, which would be the outcome of a relationship with any of Madame Camille's grisettes, all of whom he admired generally for their exquisite workmanship and stout cheerfulness in rigid conditions for very little remuneration. But no young man could be lonely in the city that spread itself out in a carpet of pleasure to all who came with some money in their pockets, and he had suffered no deprivation before arriving at Madame Camille's, and none since through not accepting the unspoken invitations that continued to be issued in his direction.

Although he had been born in England, the son of a Portsmouth sea-captain, his mother was Welsh, and when she went to sea with his father, as many wives did, he spent most of his childhood holidays from school with his grandfather and uncles on a sizeable sheep farm in North Wales. It was from that side of the family that he inherited his rugged good looks, his deep singing voice, and his alert and watchful steel-grey eyes that came from generations of forebears inured to husbanding the reluctant soil of mining the belly of the earth for coal. At times he felt more Welsh than English, and just as the Prince-President had picked up a German accent during his education at Augsburg, never to lose it, so had the musical speech of Wales fastened itself on the tongue of Will Russell with the same steadfastness.

He had come into the making of clothing by chance, his interest awakened by the selling of the wool from his grandfather's sheep. More than once he travelled on a wagon carrying bales of it to a mill in Bradford, not far from the middle-class boarding school he had attended. There he had endured the rigours of a classical education instilled with the aid of prison-like conditions, corporal punishment for the smallest misdemeanour, and the most abominable diet, all of which was common to many other educational establishments of the day. No score was given to his interest in machinery and all things industrial, and when his grandfather died and with his parents unapproachable strangers whom he heard from rarely and saw even less, he walked out of the school at the age of fifteen and tramped all the way to Bradford, back to the power-looms he had seen clanking and wheezing many a time. There he obtained work for himself in the industry of producing woollen cloth. Before long he was on the looms, not working them, but in maintenance, together with other general repairs, which often brought out the best of his ingenuity and mechanical inventiveness. As a branch of the mill's output some ready-made clothes were made for men, the cutting done on the main premises, the wretched outworkers slaving away at the sewing in their own hovels. Will, quick-witted and adaptable, fast rising in authority, extended this field, and because he made it his business to know how and why and wherefore things were done, he learnt to cut cloth in order to be master of most of the skills involved in the particular trade he had chosen. He was always making various tools and aids to the work in hand, which he patented, and it was a new kind of shuttle that had brought in enough money to enable him to leave the mill and seek a widening of experience in the making of clothes in France.

When Louise first heard the rich cadences of his Welsh voice she thought he must be almost as newly come to her country as Worth had been at their first meeting, but she soon realised her mistake when she heard him cursing someone's error like a matelot born. It amused her to imitate his undulating foreign accent for the entertainment of the other grisettes at her table until one day they fell silent, choking back their giggles, and stared in embarrassed consternation towards the doorway. There he stood listening ominously with muscular arms folded, curly, straw-coloured hair in a full disorder that gave his hewn features the look of a Michelangelo head, his sweat-stained blue work-smock sticking to him, his stance aggressive. Louise lowered her needlework, not yet advanced to the embroiderers' table, and did not quail before his ferocious gaze, finding herself struggling not to laugh.

"La! Monsieur Russell! I didn't see you there."

He glowered afresh at the gurgle in her voice and shook an admonishing finger fiercely at her. "When you can speak English better than I can speak French you'll have the right to mock, but not before."

Her quick wits, which so often stood her in good stead, reacted instantly. She sprang up from her chair and faced him pertly, setting her hands on her small waist with arms akimbo.

"*Bon!*" Then she added in what little English she could summon up from what she had learnt from Worth, "You may teach me. Yes?"

For a second or two he looked dumbfounded, astonished as much by her impudence as by the snatch of English she had used. Then an answering glint danced in his narrowed eyes. "I'll teach you, Mademoiselle Whatever-Your-Name-Is. You could not have approached a better teacher, but perhaps you'll come to regret your request. I'm warning you that I'll tolerate nothing less than the best of results."

With a guffaw, running a hand through his thick hair, he returned to the cutting-room, and Louise collapsed back into her chair, convulsed with mirth, the rest of the women and girls around her table joining in and causing the room to resound like an aviary. Madame Rousseau came hot-foot to quell their merriment and restore order again. Shortly afterwards he began to sing, something he did spontaneously from time to time, his fine voice booming out an old English folk-song, and again she had to exert her authority to reduce him to silence, much to the regret of all the grisettes, who disagreed with Madame Camille's ruling that perfect quiet was essential to ensure the best work.

After that day Will Russell never saw Louise or passed her by without speaking some words of English to illustrate the occasion or their surroundings or the weather, anything at all that would make her familiar with a variety of words and phrases as well as accustom her ear to the sound and rhythm of the language. She bought a French-English phrase-book and dictionary from a market stall and would rehearse sentences to practise on him, and he was merciless in his corrections, sometimes bringing her to the point of tears, until she realised it amused him to taunt her pride, and after that she gave back as good as he gave her. Gradually she began to build solidly on the bare bones of the language she had gained from Worth, and eventually was able to converse with some fluency, her quick ear and retentive mind overcoming difficulties for her. Without either of them being aware of it,

Will set his mark on her, because for the rest of her life she was to speak English with a soft lilt in her voice as if she had learnt it in the heart of the Welsh mountains.

It was after she had been a while in the embroiderers' room that she began to feel all that was missing in her dress-making talents was an ability to cut a pattern with a masterly touch. Long, long ago Catherine had taught her how to make a garment pattern from any picture or design, but even Catherine, skilled as she was, did not have the ability to create the dashing style that Will Russell could fashion with his shears. Opinion about his work varied among her fellow grisettes. Many of them were against dresses being cut with the severity of a riding habit, no amount of the ornamentation of which Madame Camille was inordinately fond at all able to soften it, but others sided with Louise in appreciating the quality of his lines and the adept way he could adjust a pattern fractionally for further perfection of fit, which was what she wanted to acquire. He heard out her request, and then gave a contemplative nod.

"Yes. Very well. You'll have to be here a quarter of an hour earlier in the mornings, and I can spare you a short time during the midday break."

She proved to be as enthusiastic a pupil in the cutting-room as she had been with learning English. Madame Rousseau did not disallow the instruction since no time was taken for it from Madame Camille, and in her opinion it was all to the good. She saw Louise as her protégée, but how long she would be able to continue to encourage the girl was in the lap of the gods. She was terminally ill and knew it. Pain never left her. When she could no longer carry on she must leave Paris and spend whatever months were left to her with her sister in Provence. In the meantime she must try to keep hold on the discipline on which she had always prided herself, because without it standards slipped and the quality of work with it.

Louise had become used to being teased by the other grisettes about Will's instruction, and some, who made it a grievance, were less kind. But untouched and physically unawakened, she tripped in and out of his company without the least consideration towards the effect she might be having upon him. When she visualised an attractive man her thoughts drifted to Worth, whom she had loved, or to the never-to-be-forgotten face of the cuirassier about whom she had dreamt disturbingly on several occasions, always in reunion in the most unlikely places. In contrast Will's visage appeared as rocky and impersonal as the Welsh mountains about which he had talked to her in English among other subjects as part of teaching her his language. If at times she caught a look in those very aware eyes of his that made her feel singled out from the rest, she took it with all the arrogance of the young and beautiful as her right, well used to male admiration. And since he was such an enigmatic character to everyone else she preened over his being on closer terms with her than with any other person on the premises, her conceit causing Catherine displeasure. It brought about one of those maternal homilies on modesty in all things in which Catherine excelled.

"Why shouldn't I be proud?" Louise argued defiantly, scooping up her hair in front of the bedroom looking-glass to see if it would suit her plaited around her head. He had told her and nobody else of the sewing-machine he was putting together. One of the reasons he had come to France was to view for himself the machine that Monsieur Thimolier had made, one of many in the field, and Will believed that his own looping needle was a refinement towards smoother stitching. She had argued with him about such machines, not that she had ever seen one, and what he had said in their favour had impressed her, although they could never be used in fine dressmaking. She pursed her lips, eyeing her reflection as she twisted her hair another way, and pursued the theme. "Everybody else at Madame Camille's dances about Will as if they had been shut up in a convent all their lives. I wouldn't be like that for any man."

"That's half your attraction for him," Catherine muttered to herself. She had seen the way Will looked at Louise sometimes, and the minx had seen it herself whether she cared to admit it or not.

"What's that?" Louise twisted her head to look through the crook of her upraised arm.

"Nothing," Catherine replied on a sigh. In the past she might have fancied Will Russell along with the rest of them, but she had changed and knew it. In the end kindness in a man meant more than anything, and although it could be said that Will had been kind to Louise, all men fell over themselves to oblige a lovely young creature, while a plain one had to fend for herself.

Madame Rousseau announced her retirement, her face white and almost skeletal against her dyed, red hair. Most were sorry to see her go. Those who were not would have welcomed her back with open arms after her successor had been in authority for one day. Mademoiselle Nenette Deneuve, who was small, dark-haired, and youngish, proved to be a veritable martinet when it came to discipline, which had slackened over past weeks. She altered everything, rearranged the seating to separate talkers and old friends, unstuffed ventilators against protests of draughts across necks to which grisettes in their stationary positions were vulnerable, sacked two embroiderers who argued with her within the first week, and started a battle with Will that was to rage unceasingly. She tried to exercise her power over him as with the rest of the workers, and he stubbornly refused to alter his method of work by one iota. When she attempted to reorganise the cutting-room he ordered her out. She retaliated by having one of his lamps removed, saying it was needed elsewhere, and he merely replaced it with one from the corridor near her office, and there was nothing she could do about that except have another one brought from the stores. She resorted to being critical and scathing about his cutting, but it continued to leave his hands as faultless as ever, and never once was there the slightest delay in the making up. Louise had fallen an early victim to the battle, being ordered out of the cutting-room and forbidden re-entry on the old rule of segregation between the sexes that Madame Rousseau had chosen to overlook. Louise's instruction had reached a point where a request was to have been made to Madame Rousseau to allow her to make a full pattern from one of Madame Camille's designs and cut from it under Will's supervision, but that chance was snatched from her. She fumed and threw up her hands and stamped her foot, her Gallic blood aroused, but the dismissal of the embroiderers was a dire warning to the rest, and there was nothing to be done about it. She found it additionally galling that she received no sympathy from Catherine.

"You've learnt what you wanted to learn, so why all the fuss?"

Louise paced up and down across the floor of their living quarters. "That's not the point. I wanted to prove that I could do it without fault for my own satisfaction."

Catherine, who was resting with her slippered feet on a footstool, adjusted a cushion behind her shoulders. "It's just as well. You might have learnt more than you bargained for if you spent much more time with Will Russell."

Louise tossed her head impatiently. "I can take care of myself, and you know it. I'm neither gullible nor foolhardy."

No, she wasn't, Catherine thought. Life had been too hard on her for that, but it did no harm to give warning now and again. It was what the long departed Madame Vernet would have done, and Catherine never shirked her duty.

Louise spent a sleepless night, and by morning had decided to make a special request to Mademoiselle Deneuve. If the plain facts were put to the woman, surely she could not refuse? Shortly after the working day had gone into full swing Louise tapped on the office door and was told to enter. Mademoiselle Deneuve was seated at her desk, and without looking up she pointed briefly with the tip of her quill pen at the spot where she wanted Louise to stand. "Yes?"

Louise gave a full explanation to the woman's down-bent head. All she wanted was the chance to show she could qualify as a cutter attuned to the high standard Monsieur Russell had set her. She waited for a reply. It came without as much as an upward glance.

"Monsieur Russell is employed to cut cloth, not to indulge the whim of a seamstress out to usurp his position."

Louise flushed at the injustice of the accusation. "That's not the case at all. Monsieur Russell knows that, and so did Madame Rousseau, who encouraged my interest. If you would allow—"

The scratching of the nib continued as the woman cut her short in a bored tone. "You have a choice. Either you return to your embroidery this minute, or you collect whatever possessions you have in this establishment and leave without further ado."

Louise swallowed hard and left the room quickly. She slapped her palms against the sides of her skirts in frustration at the woman's intractable attitude. At the doorway of the cuting-room she halted to break the news, not caring that she was flouting the rules again.

"The supervisor has refused permission for me to cut a garment," she exclaimed indignantly. "She wouldn't hear of it."

Will straightened up from setting a pattern out on a lay. "Wouldn't she now? Well, don't you worry." He came strolling across to her and leaned a broad shoulder against the doorjam, his face relaxed into an amused and reassuring smile. "There's more ways of killing a cat than drowning it."

She gave a vexed little laugh. "What do you mean?"

He had no chance to tell her. Down the corridor from the office doorway a sharp voice echoed against the walls. "Mademoiselle Vernet! Why are you dawdling? You know the rules. Must I warn you again? Monsieur Russell! Back to work!"

Louise rolled up her eyes expressively and shot away to the embroiderers' room. She snatched up her work, ignoring the whispered questions from the others as to what was happening, and craned her neck to see across to the cutting-room. To her dismay Will had not moved from the doorway, but had merely folded his muscular arms, the tawny hairs glinting below the rolled-up sleeves of his smock. There came an angry clack of heels, and Mademoiselle Deneuve was facing him, her lips drawn tight, bristling with temper.

"Are you deaf as well as insolent?"

Very slightly his lids lowered at her tone, and without expression he began to sing under his breath. Her temper increased. She began to abuse him, unjustly accusing him of laziness, making threats as deadly as the invitation to dismissal that she had issued to Louise, and acidly criticising his work as she had done so often before. He heard none of it, and neither did anyone else, for he drowned her tirade in an old song of the Welsh valleys, seeming to make the rafters thunder in echo as he turned back to his table, completely ignoring her. Beside herself, she darted after him, becoming lost from Louise's sight, but those who could still see them described afterwards amid much hilarity how Mademoiselle Deneuve, her face contorted, had sprung about him like an enraged wasp, shaking her small fists, while her full-gathered skirt had swung to and fro. Finally she gave up, casting her head back on her neck as she stamped from the cutting-room. She slammed the door to shut out his musical disregard of her, and instantly he became silent, the shuddering growl that she was emitting in her fury being clearly heard by all those nearby. Her face became pierced through with still more heightened colour, and she drew breath shakily before she moved away from the door to stalk back down the passageway to her office, swiftly patting a few loosened wisps of her otherwise immaculately dressed hair into place. Her office door shut after her. In every workroom mirth exploded, and only fear of the consequences enabled the grisettes to keep a straight face when she reappeared later on her usual rounds of snapping and sarcastic fault-finding.

From that day forward Louise became the target of Mademoiselle Deneuve's most vicious criticism. It was as if, having been bested by Will, the woman did not care to show herself in open conflict with him a second time, and needed a whipping-boy to bear her chagrin. She still battled with him while keeping at a level that did not get out of her control, but with Louise, who had been the indirect cause of her humiliation, she could let fly the worst of her temper, daring the slightest murmur of retaliation. Throughout each verbal attack Louise seethed inwardly, her teeth gritted, her eyes fixed on her embroidery. There were evenings when she went home pale from her ordeal. Catherine was sympathetic as well as indignant on her behalf.

"I've met her sort before. Jealous women always try to belittle the skills of others and deride their achievements."

"Why should she be jealous of me?" Louise tossed at her.

"If you don't know, then I'm not telling you."

On one particular evening Louise had more to think about than Mademoiselle Deneuve's unpleasantness. On the way to work that morning Will had caught her up near the gates and told her she could come back after everyone else had gone, as that was when he was there alone to make a pile of work ready for the women to start on in the morning. All she had to do was to select an evening when it suited her. She was overjoyed, but said nothing to Catherine, who would only have presented argument and opposition.

The opportunity came when Catherine went out to supper with a beau, who was more old friend than lover these days. Louise took the path through the paupers' burial ground where she had less chance of being seen, set a small bunch of flowers on her mother's grave as she always did when she entered there, and climbed the wall with the aid of a stout wooden crate that Will had concealed in the long grass. On the other side she found another set ready for her, hidden by outbuildings from any chance sighting from the concierge's quarters, and she stepped down into the courtyard without difficulty. A quick, signalled tap on the shutters of the cutting-room, and then a darting round to the work-shop door where Will unlocked it to let her in.

"Isn't this fun!" she exclaimed excitedly, and sprang ahead of him through the barely illuminated workrooms, shedding shawl and bonnet and gloves like petals and tossing them over her shoulder into his arms as he followed her. In the corridor she bobbed an impudent curtsey towards the closed and deserted office of Mademoiselle Deneuve and then swept into the brightly lit cutting-room where she pirouetted gleefully between the two tables, one of which was spread with crimson velvet that he was cutting out. "Where do I start?"

He was putting her belongings down on a stool. "At the beginning, of course. Take the next design off the pattern pile, whatever it is, and set to work."

Her whole face sparkled and she clasped her hands together. "All on my own?"

He chuckled indulgently. "That's the whole point, isn't it?"

She took the top design from the shelf. It was for a grey silk carriage dress with the corsage tight to the shape and high to the neck, much trimmed with fancy buttons and tassels, the sleeves ending in small cuffs, the skirt having multiple flounces. She arched her eyebrows in mock-ruefulness, not quite hiding from him an initial nervousness. The design was not an easy one, but nothing that she had not practised before, and she resolved to complete it to perfection.

While he continued with his work she set to at the long table allotted to her, making the pattern according to the design and to the customer's measurements written on it. Neither spoke to the other. She was deft and accurate in what she was doing, but extremely tense due to the importance of the task in hand, a frown of concentration on her face. No pattern was needed for the skirt itself, which in this case consisted of six lengths of material cut at full width to be gathered onto a waistband, but every part of the bodice and sleeve needed the most careful charting, and she smiled over the completion of it.

"There! The pattern is done."

She extended her smile proudly to Will, brushing back a fallen strand of hair from her heat-dampened brow with the back of her hand. It was stifling in the room, the solid shutters being closed to avoid any chance sighting of her from outside, and the ventilators did not give enough air to cool the warmth of the oil-lamps. Her face held a silvery sheen, her long throat showing deep into the neckline of her dress, which she had unbuttoned a few inches. She was all unaware how often Will had glanced compulsively across at her and seen the sweet, pendulous suspension of her curving breasts within the shadows of her bodice as she bent over her work. He was also half dizzy with the bouquet of her presence, fragrant and elusive and seductively feminine. On many previous occasions her nearness brushing past him had wrenched his loins, but never more than this night of being totally alone with her for the first time.

"Congratulations," he answered automatically, his mind dwelling on the allure of her. "You did that first stage of the work in very good time."

"I must have a drink of water before I do any more." She shut her eyes against the room's heat, smoothing her fingertips down her neck as she stretched it in a seeking of some coolness.

"There's always some left in the buckets in the kitchen," he informed her quite brusquely. "Do you need a lamp?"

"No. I know the way like the back of my hand."

In the kitchen there was enough moonlight to show her the drinking buckets, and she sipped the coolness from a ladle with a thirst that had come as much from a nervous excitement over the whole venture as from the heat.

Back at her table she unrolled the bolt of grey silk for the carriage dress, the rich fabric shimmering out along the table. He did not help her spread it out into its lay and she did not expect him to, not knowing that he did not want to risk the slightest physical contact with her. As it was, it seemed to him that the room was charged electrically with her every movement. Now and again she emitted a little sigh over the snipping of her shears as one piece of silk and then another was cut to her satisfaction. All he could think about was to have her sighing blissfully in his arms for another reason, and he vowed to himself that whether she finished cutting out the whole pattern or not that night, he would not let her come on her own to his workroom a second time to inflict such heady purgatory.

"Louise."

She was jerked out of her concentration and turned her head towards him. "Yes?"

He had finished with the crimson velvet and was unrolling a flow of dark blue merino. "I'll cut the skirt lengths for you tomorrow. After all, that's no more than a draper's assistant could do, and you don't want to extend your time any longer than necessary, do you?"

"No, I don't. That is obliging of you." She put down her shears and made a move towards the door. "I think I'll take a look at the clock."

"Would you collect another work-tray at the same time?" he reminded her. "We'll need one for the carriage dress when you've finished cutting it."

She gave a nod and left a thread of light through a gap in the doorway to guide her as she hastened to view the clock face above the office door. It was not as late as she had feared, and now that Will had removed the tedious skirt-length cutting she could complete her task without worrying about Catherine returning home first to find her absent in the dead of night. She turned her attention to finding a spare tray, all of which were lined with lustrine like candy boxes to protect whatever costly materials were laid in them from being snagged. Back in the cutting-room she placed it in readiness and resumed her task.

Again they worked on in silence. When he had done all he needed to do that night he folded into a tray the last garment he had cut and cleared his table completely of all scraps in readiness for the morning. Last of all he swept up the floor, she being too absorbed to do more than move automatically as he took the broom near her feet. Finally she cut the last flounce and straightened up. She had lost all count of time, and blinked dazedly.

"It's after midnight," he said, extinguishing all the lamps but one. He wanted her gone.

She placed a hand on her spine at the waist and arched her tired back against it. "I've kept you late," she apologised contritely.

"No. On the contrary. I usually work to one or two o'clock. Now I'll escort you home and cut those skirt lengths in the morning. Leave everything just as it is."

Tired and deliriously happy at what she had achieved she swayed towards him and smiled up into his face, intending to thank him, but the words were never said. His senses snapped. He crushed her to him and dealt her a kiss that made his head reel, his mouth swamping hers, her moist lips forced apart under the press and violence with which he sought blindly to assuage the thwarted yearning that he thought he had subdued.

They fell apart, breathless. She stared at him like an awakening sleepwalker, putting uncertain fingertips to her lips as if to reassure herself that he had not burnt them away in the blaze of his amorous onslaught. He reached for her again, and as if she knew he would handle her more gently, she did not draw back or try to avoid the arm he curved about her waist. He put his hand softly at the side of her face and with his thumb he tilted her chin to meet his tenderly persuasive and no less ardent kiss. This time her lips responded deliciously, and again the fire within him flared almost beyond endurance, his embrace tightening about her as she leaned against him, her arms around his neck, her fingers buried convulsively in the curls that grew thick at the nape of his neck. Neither heard the distant jingle of a key-ring outside as the concierge opened the gates to a newcomer. No sound reached them of that person's passage across the courtyard. It was a trick of the draught through workrooms and corridor that made the door of the cutting-room creak and shiver as someone entered the building. For a few paralysed seconds they did not move, Louise's eyes dilating with disbelief and panic.

"I mustn't be found here!"

He collected his wits as he released her, listening intently. It was not the shuffling gait of the concierge that was echoing faintly in approach, but a lighter and far more purposeful step that was all too familiar to both of them.

"It's the Deneuve woman!" he exclaimed, grabbing a chair and thrusting it under the door handle, there being no lock. "Quick! The window!"

Louise snatched up her bonnet and shawl, forgetting her gloves, which he retrieved and thrust into her hands as he crossed to the window, jerking it open into the room and then throwing the outside shutters wide, making them clatter back on their hinges. Effortlessly he picked her up in his arms and propelled her through into the night air. She caught his sleeve for balance as her feet touched the ground, and then was off into the darkness, making for the wall by which she had come. He only had time to refasten the window before the door behind him strained against the chair. Nenette Deneuve's voice snapped at him from the corridor.

"Monsieur Russell. Open this door!"

He removed the chair leisurely and opened it. She glared at him from the threshold. "Are you nervous on your own in these premises at night that you bar the door?" she demanded sarcastically.

He shrugged and went to Louise's table, where he began to fold up the pieces of grey silk that lay there. "I don't care for uninvited visitors," he answered pointedly.

She had entered the room and her colour sharpened. Suspiciously her eyes were everywhere, and they came to rest on the window. "The shutters were closed when I came by them a minute or two ago. Why have they been opened at this late hour?"

"A breath of air, mam'selle."

She charged across, the silk floss fringe on her mantle swinging, and pulled open the window to look out for a few seconds before slamming it shut again. She swung about and once more her swift vixen gaze took in the disorder of the cutting-table that he was clearing, the shears left open and not closed, which was a safety precaution that every professional cutter took automatically, and there was not his usual neatness about the remainder of the roll from which, by the amount left, she could tell that the skirt had yet to be cut.

"Have you been alone here this evening?" she questioned acidly.

"Am I not always alone?"

She came and stood between the two tables, facing him across the one from which he had cleared the last of the carriage-dress pieces into the work-tray. "I've never seen you use this table except for an emergency cutting when the other was in use."

He closed the shears and set them in a rack he had made. "You haven't visited me in the night hours before."

In a burst of fury she hammered a fist on the table, making some left-over scraps flutter and rise like tiny birds. "Stop deceiving me! I heard the thud of the shutters and a scuffling as I drew near. You've had the effrontery to let one of my needlewomen into this place with you. Don't think I can't deduce who it was! That contrary baggage, Louise Vernet!"

He sat sideways on the edge of the table with the breadth of it between them, his expression impassive. "Are you sure your imagination isn't running away with you?"

She jerked up her chin, viciously, her lips made thin by temper. "Indeed it is not. In gross defiance of my instructions you have allowed her access to the cutting-table, and against my explicit order on pain of dismissal Vernet has tampered with costly material that has most surely been ruined. Madame Camille shall hear of this first thing in the morning."

"No she won't," he said, his quiet tone implacable, "and there are two good reasons why. Firstly, I don't expect any mistakes to be found in what has been cut. Secondly, you can't denounce anyone without involving me, and you don't want to run the risk of seeing me thrown out at the same time."

Her face was patchy. "I don't know what you're talking about."

His eyes held hers compellingly. "You're more angry about finding out that I haven't been alone here than about the flouting of your discipline."

Her neck was taut. "I only came to check that all was in order. There was pilfering in the past before I came to this establishment. I mean to ensure that it doesn't happen again, which is why I like to take a look around when the needlewomen are absent."

He raised an eyebrow. "At midnight? About the hour when you judged my work to be almost done?" He swung his long legs across the table and sat on the opposite edge facing her, hands resting on muscular thighs and elbows jutting.

She made a last, haughty retort, which was in itself a capitulation. "You are as conceited as you are uncouth."

He seized her by the buttocks through the thickness of her skirts and hauled her hard in to him between his thighs. "You've been ripe for me since the day you first came to this establishment," he told her brutally. "Now I'm going to find out if you're worth having."

At any other time and in any other place she might have been. She was exultant and utterly abandoned in what was to her a total surrender to long-denied sinfulness. He took her ruthlessly again and again in a variety of mindless couplings out of his own rage and frustration that she was who she was and not another to whom he would have given love in every sense of the word. He took vengeance on Nenette Deneuve for her untimely intrusion, and only succeeded in gratifying her most secret desires.

When dawn came into the room he stirred from the makeshift bed of multi-coloured remnants and looked across at her once as he gathered up his clothes. She lay pale-limbed with her face turned away from him, her long hair half tumbled across her face. He knew she was awake, but did not wonder that exhaustion still overcame her. In any case, there was still plenty of time before she need depart. He went through to the kitchen, where he raked the embers in the range, set on fresh wood, and then went out to the small inner courtyard. He doused himself at the fountain's spout, emptying a bucket over his head and gasping as the water poured from his gleaming body and ran in rivulets between the cobbles. Back in the kitchen he dried and dressed himself, set a battered coffeepot on the red-hot range, and when he returned to the cutting-room with two steaming cups she had dressed and gone. He shrugged and drank both cupfuls himself, ate a piece of bread left from the day before, and then stretched out on one of the tables with an arm beneath his head, where he slept until the gates clanged as the concierge opened them for the chattering arrival of the grisettes.

Louise, hollow-eyed and anxious, had no idea what to expect of the day ahead. Did trouble await her? Had someone sighted her climbing the wall and summoned Mademoiselle Deneuve to investigate? She had not dared a backward glance in order to see if Will had been right in his supposition as to the identity of the intruder at that late hour, there being nothing else in her head at the time but to get away as quickly as possible. She had managed to get home shortly before Catherine and had feigned sleep, being in no mood to talk. In the darkness she had given herself up to remembering all that passed between Will and her in those alarmingly passionate minutes, the taste of his wild, hot mouth lingering on hers, all her flesh aquiver as if it still cried out against the severance of contact between his long, hard body and hers. But in spite of being caught off guard by his first tempestuous embrace, she had lost neither her head nor her heart and had let him kiss her again out of her own sensual curiosity, experiencing sensations of pleasure that were entirely new to her, all liking for him brought to a fondness, all depths to her voluptuously stirred.

Yet this morning she did not want to see him or to meet his eyes. It was as if she wished to withdraw into herself again, recapturing from him the freedom of that kissing embrace she had allowed, and to her dismay, when she took her place at the embroiderers' table, the sound of his voice addressing somebody else sent such colour soaring into her face that she felt it must surely scorch the edge of her frilled linen cap. She bent her head low over her stitching and worked at double her normal pace.

For a while it seemed that it was to be a day like any other. Mademoiselle Deneuve went on her usual fault-finding rounds, but nothing untoward occurred. Louise's gratitude towards Will increased steadily. If it had been the supervisor on the premises last night, he had shielded her from discovery. By the midday break she had overcome her earlier disconcertion, and when he gave her a wry half-nod from where he sat in the kitchen, she gave him back a quick look of thankfulness before returning her attention to the food she had brought with her.

It was quite late in the afternoon when there appeared to be some confusion at Catherine's table in the sewing-room. The grisette sitting opposite Louise tilted her chair backwards in order to catch a glimpse of what was going on. "Looks like trouble with some grey silk," she said in an awed voice, and immediately the rest of the embroiderers were all agog to know more. "As far as I can tell, the pieces aren't matching up."

Louise went ice-cold. She could not conceive that anything might be wrong with the pattern she had cut. Out of the corner of her eye she saw Mademoiselle Deneuve come to the threshold of the embroiderers' room, the tray containing the grey-silk carriage dress, some of it tacked together, supported on her hip by one hand. Louise lifted her head. Without a word the woman beckoned her ominously. Louise rose from the table and, smoothing her apron nervously, she obeyed the summons, conscious of inquisitive stares following her.

"Come with me."

Mademoiselle Deneuve led the way, not to her office, which was what Louise had expected, realising that some investigation was about to take place, but through a door to an inner hallway and up a flight of stairs that led to Madame Camille's showroom, all without a word. In her wake Louise could contain herself no longer.

"What is it? What is wrong? Why are you bringing me up here?" She had never been in this part of the building before. To her knowledge no grisette had ever been beyond the door downstairs.

Mademoiselle Deneuve paused on the crimson-carpeted flight and glared penetratingly over a shoulder at her. "I happen to know that Monsieur Russell's first task today was to cut the skirt lengths of this carriage dress. Otherwise he is not responsible for any part of it. Do you deny that you are?"

Louise's hand tightened on the mahogany banister rail. "Why haven't you said anything to me before now?"

"I waited to see if your work was of the high standard that you professed it to be." Her mouth twisted. "I'm a fair-minded woman. If you were prepared to risk so much to be on these premises after hours and cut into such expensive silk with abandon, I decided that I would bide my time to see the results before taking any action. If your pattern-making and cutting had been comparable to the standard of your stitching, I would most probably have taken a charitable view of your trying to prove yourself, and merely penalised you with loss of wages for a month or two. However, since the reverse has been proved, the matter is out of my hands."

She continued ascending the flight, and Louise hastened after her. "I simply don't understand what is amiss."

They had reached a wide landing with ornate, recessed double doors. The supervisor opened them. "In here," she ordered.

Louise was left in an octagonal anteroom while the woman disappeared through a corridor leading off it, by which she could reach Madame Camille's office without going through the showroom. Silk drapes almost obscured that exclusive area from the anteroom, but Louise could see tall, graceful windows giving light to rich carpeting and gilded Louise XV furniture. One of the black-gowned vendeuses, wide skirt rustling, went past with a satin ballgown laid across her arms. Her self-assurance and confident air as she went to her customer seemed to emphasise Louise's own desperate and uncertain position. There was no doubt in her mind that something terrible and unforeseen had happened with regard to the carriage dress, and she clasped and unclasped her hands agitatedly, seeing herself reflected many times over in the looking-glasses that were set in the panels around her.

Mademoiselle Deneuve reappeared. "This way."

Louise drew breath and followed her once more. In a small but much ornamented salon she came face to face with Madame Camille, whose plumpish visage was irate, her shrewd eyes flashing. She shook the half-tacked bodice of the carriage dress at Louise.

"Did you cut this silk?"

Louise stood very still and straight. "Yes, madame."

"How *dare* you!" Madame Camille hurled what she held to the floor. "Mademoiselle Deneuve reported to me two or three weeks ago that she had had to stop you pestering Monsieur Russell with your presence in the cutting-room, and then you have the audacity to give him some falsified story of having received permission from her to cut a garment in full. You have ruined a length of an important customer's own silk which was brought home to France from abroad and cannot be replaced."

Louise scarcely knew what to say. In no way would she

deny Will his right to dissociate himself from her at this time, there being no reason why he should jeopardise his employment when all the persistence in pursuing the venture had been hers. Nevertheless, it was hard not to feel deserted and abandoned by his distortion of the truth. "What is wrong with the dress, madame?"

"Everything!" Madame Camille thundered her reply. "It was not cut according to the customer's measurements, it has been caused to fray, and every frill is uneven!"

Louise was aghast. "I can't believe it. I took such care."

Madame Camille seemed to find this statement particularly galling. "Any fool can take care!" she expostulated, the very flesh of her soft neck aquiver with her wrath. "It's a lack of professional skill that results in bungling and failure. The late Madame Rousseau must be turning in her grave. You have betrayed her trust in venturing beyond your sphere. What is more, you deliberately defied my supervisor's orders and, worst of all, there is little doubt that through your irresponsibility I shall lose one of my best customers." She seemed scarcely able to control her rage any longer. "You are dismissed! Never mention your time in my employ in any application you make for work elsewhere, because it will be my duty to warn anybody thinking to engage you of your destructive and inexcusable behaviour. Go!"

Throughout it all Nenette Deneuve had neither moved nor spoken. With lowered lids to hide the gleam of satisfaction in her eyes she bobbed to Madame Camille and once again led the way for Louise, who was as stunned by her own miscutting of the dress as by her dismissal. Where had she gone wrong? What miscalculations had she made? In despair at events she was thankful to bypass the workrooms. Within a matter of minutes she found herself outside the gates, completely rejected after two years of employment by the world into which she had gained an entrée with more hours of work and striving than could ever be estimated.

It was early evening, but she did not want to go home and wait for Catherine, who would have heard the news by now. She began to walk, taking no heed of direction, merely walking and walking in the daze of the shock she had suffered. Darkness fell, and the oil-lamps threw her shadow before and aft as she passed below them. Gradually she started to adjust to what had befallen her, and with it came a rallying of her indomitable spirit.

At the work-shop it was more than an hour before Will

heard of her dismissal. Working behind his closed doors, it was not until he emerged for a five-minute break that one of the grisettes told him that Louise had gone. He went straight to Nenette Deneuve's office and walked in.

"What has happened?" he demanded. "Why has Louise been dismissed?"

She sat back in her chair, turning a pencil between her fingers. She had been expecting him. "I did not hear you knock," she said coolly.

He was not surprised by her attitude. By day, for the sake of her own sensibilities, she would keep up a façade of nothing untoward having occurred between them. "Don't prevaricate. I want the truth of it."

She gave him a smile made thin and narrow by the jealousy within her. His expression was enough to confirm what she had suspected from the start. He had fancied that scheming little bitch, and it would take more than one night like last night to erase his thoughts of her. How often behind bale and door and pattern pile had the girl lifted her skirts to him? The cords in Nenette Deneuve's neck stood out as she kept a tight control over herself. Had they again been alone in the night hours she would have clawed his face in the jealous frenzy that made her want him here and now on the floor of her own office.

"It is perfectly simple. Louise Vernet did not cut the stuff as expertly as you appear to have imagined. It was so full of errors that nothing can be salvaged." That should teach him the folly of being bewitched by the persuasions of a young grisette into a situation that would have had dire consequences for him if she, Nenette Deneuve, had not used her remarkable wits for his sake and, undeniably, for her own.

"Why did Louise's dismissal take place without my being questioned about the carriage dress?" he said in a dangerous tone.

She raised her eyebrows questioningly. "What did it have to do with you? I explained to Madame Camille that it was no fault of yours that the girl took it upon herself to cut the silk." She looked at him under her lashes. "You should thank me. I stood between you and your dismissal."

He went quite white about the mouth, and the papers on her desk scattered as he leaned across and seized her by the shoulders, half lifting her from the chair. "You recut that silk! When I left you alone early this morning you took the shears and snipped off enough here and there to destroy the garment!"

A sudden fear of him made her answer sound convincing as she jerked herself free, the chair teetering under her weight as she sat back in it with a thud. "I did no such thing. You're making excuses for that girl."

His lids came close together in his despisal of her. "You heard Louise depart, and when you entered my room it was obvious instantly to you that Louise had barely put down the shears. You saw me fold away the pieces in the tray ready for the sewing-rooms as we talked, and then at dawn today you conceived a means to be rid of the girl who has long been a thorn in your flesh."

"Ouf!" She displayed contempt, rising from her chair. "These wild suppositions are too ridiculous."

He continued fiercely as if she had not spoken. "What you did not take into account was that I had checked it all except the last few pieces during the cutting." The corners of his mouth lifted derisively at her involuntarily startled glance. "That surprises you. You knew that Louise's one aim was to complete the whole exercise entirely on her own. That is what Louise believed that she did, but I could not let her risk her whole future by any miscalculation through nervousness, and when she went from the room a couple of times I went over the work she had done and found it perfect to the last millimetre."

Nenette Deneuve gripped the back of the chair by which she was standing, her face vicious. "Think what you like," she spat. "Say what you like. It will make no difference to me. I will deny everything, and in my position of trust I shall not be doubted. Go back to your workroom, Monsieur Russell. Too much of this day has been wasted already."

He took a step backwards away from the desk, his gaze on her cynical and derisive. "As you say, much time has been wasted."

He returned to his workroom, collected his shears and the various small gadgets he had set up to aid him in his work, and tied them all into a bundle with a piece of waste cloth. Then he put on his coat, took up the bundle and, heedless of the stares and gaping expressions of the grisettes that followed him, he made his way upstairs to find Madame Camille. She was amazed to see him in her own precincts, and was still more taken aback by what he had to say.

"I regret that I have to give you my immediate resignation, madame. I'm not leaving you in the lurch since you have two female cutters who were transferred to the sewing-room upon my arrival."

"But why this sudden decision?" she questioned in bewilderment. "Has the dismissal of that foolish seamstress made you feel responsible for the loss of the carriage dress? Mademoiselle Deneuve explained everything to me. You are in no way to blame for what happened."

"On the contrary, madame. I'm entirely responsible. I should have locked her work away when I knew it to be faultless, and given no chance for anyone else to interfere with it. Mademoiselle Vernet should be reinstated without delay."

Madame Camille held up her hand. "Do not try to shift the blame on her behalf. The matter is closed. I will not discuss it further." She was remembering her first doubts about employing him, and was coming to the conclusion that there could have been more in the liaison between the young seamstress and him than had met the guileless Mademoiselle Deneuve's eye. Perhaps it was as well that this Englishman was leaving. In any case there was no doubt in her mind that the trend of severity in garments was on the wane, keeping pace with the easing of the country's political situation, and she would soon have had to dispense with his style of cutting anyway. She decided that his departure was most timely. "I accept your resignation," she said to him, inclining her head. "Your work has always been of the highest standard. You may call upon this house for a reference whenever you should need it."

He would have preferred such an offer to have been made to Louise. "I doubt if I'll ever find it necessary. I have other plans. Goodbye, madame."

He did not leave the premises by the route by which he had come, but went through the showroom and descended the grand staircase used by Madame Camille's customers. An attendant opened the door for him to the fashionable street beyond.

When Louise came home the hour was late, and she was cold and shivering. She found that Catherine and Will had had supper together. They both sprang up at once to greet her, Catherine flying forward to embrace her, alternately weeping and raging over the injustice of her dismissal. When Louise had managed to calm her down she faced Will, who told her briefly that he had no doubt at all that Mademoiselle Deneuve had taken shears to the grey silk. Louise, overcome, sank into the chair he had pushed forward, shaking with relief at having it confirmed that the faults in the work had not been hers. It was also comfort to have the misunderstanding brought about by the supervisor's duplicity cleared away.

"You're out of work because of me, Will," she said remorsefully when he had finished all he had to say.

He smiled at her, an arm resting on the table by which they sat. "It was time I left anyway. I've gained some insight into French tailoring and Parisian fashion, which is what I wanted, and now I'm going home to start my own clothing business. On a small scale at first, naturally, but I've patented my version of the sewing-machine and I intend to train hands to use it and others that I'll have made. The machines won't eliminate hand-sewing by any manner of means, but they will accelerate production."

Catherine looked dubious. "Ladies wouldn't like anything that wasn't hand-sewn right through."

Louise answered her. "Will is thinking of ready-made clothes."

Will nodded endorsement, and Catherine looked a trifle supercilious. "Oh, that sort of thing," she remarked deprecatingly.

He regarded Louise steadily and assessingly. "What are you going to do now?"

She had had plenty of time to consider her immediate future while walking. "That's easy to answer. I'm going to get back into fine sewing somehow."

"How will you do that?" he asked.

"And where?" Catherine interposed. "No couturière will take you on without testimonials."

Louise tilted her head confidently. "If I re-establish myself through my own efforts, Madame Camille can't create barriers against my good name forever." Her eyes were brightly optimistic as she outlined her plan. Daringly she would apply for work by letting it be thought that she had only recently returned to France after working as an independent dressmaker in England. "I'll try to get into one of the shop sewing-rooms where garments are made up for stock. After a breathing space I'll be able to launch forth from there again with my reputation unsullied."

Catherine was not enthusiastic and showed it. Will, impressed by her initiative, gave his full support. "You speak

English well enough to convince anybody that you have spent the last two or three years in England. I think it's a capital plan."

She was grateful for his encouragement. "It's the only way I can make a fresh start without awkward questions being asked."

"I'll write a testimonial as to the high standard of your work," he offered. "If you like, I'll word it in such a way that you'll be able to decide yourself whether or not you want a future employer to assume you learned cutting from me in Paris or in England."

"That would be a great help to me." She rushed to fetch writing materials for him.

When the letter was signed he made his farewells. "Perhaps we shall meet again one day," he said to her.

"I hope so, Will," she replied sincerely.

Just for a second or two she thought by the long look he gave her that he was going to kiss her much as he had done the night when they had been alone together, but then she realised that in spite of his words he was only taking a full goodbye of her. She stood at the doorway to watch him leave, and he turned once to wave before he rounded the corner and disappeared from view.

As she closed the door Catherine spoke meditatively from where she still sat, chin in hand. "Do you know, I had the feeling that he would have liked to employ you in that new business of his."

Louise was faintly incredulous. "I'm sure you're mistaken."

Catherine eyed her penetratingly. "Would you have gone if he had asked you?"

"No," Louise answered forthrightly and without hesitation. "Paris is my city. There's nowhere else that can offer what I want from life."

But she knew she would miss Will. The roots of their relationship had gone deep. She had the curious feeling that he had been as instrumental in preparing her for love whenever it should come as Worth, all unknowingly, had been in another way. Through Worth she had been awakened to a realisation that there was more tenderness within her than she had ever dreamed possible, and with Will she had glimpsed the extent of her sensuality. She had yet to be shown how far her heart would go.

That same night Will departed by coach from Paris. For the first stage of the journey the interior of it was shared by only one other passenger, a fellow countryman who was also returning home. They exchanged a few conventional remarks, and then each set his feet on the opposite seat, tipped his hat over his eyes, and settled down to sleep as best he could. For a while Will almost dozed, but already his mind was set homewards with a feeling of extreme well-being, making him realise how much he had missed his own land without being aware of it. His thoughts dwelt in rising anticipation on his reunion with Ellen, to whom he had been betrothed for over two years, the greater part of it spent away from her. Lovely and chaste and faithful, she had put up no barriers about his going to Paris, innocent in her encouragement, wanting only what was best for him. In France he had certainly taken all the opportunities that had come his way, those in the business field having widened his knowledge of the background to fashion, and those of the other kind much enjoyed at the time, but now best forgotten. He felt secure in the step he was shortly to take. Ellen would continue to approve his efforts, although whether her domineering father would permit a marriage until he had proved himself well and truly successful was another matter. He had never kissed Ellen as he had kissed Louise in that rush of passion that had made him forget all he had resolved with regard to her. The cold light of reason told him that it was as well that fate had intervened in the shape of Nenette Deneuve, there being no telling what emotional complications would have arisen out of another two or three hours alone in Louise's company. Yet for the rest of his life he would feel that he had missed capturing the very essence of Paris in having her snatched from him on what he believed to have been the very brink of conquest.

Now Ellen awaited him. As English as roses and tea and the flag over the Empire. With her, Louise would soon become a distant memory. After such a long parting from each other, Ellen's prudery would surely melt away. Under the brim of his hat the corners of his wide mouth indented in the compression of a quiet smile to himself. There was always a first time for everything.

A week later he bought a copy of *The Times* again from a newspaper boy to read the latest news about Prince-President Louis-Napoléon's *coup d'état*, which had taken place with lightning speed the very night that Will had left Paris. While he had been jogged about on that interminable journey to Boulogne, Louis-Napoléon had solidified his position as France's supreme ruler in such a way that none could dislodge him. There had been hundreds of arrests and an aftermath of terrible carnage, but now it seemed that Paris was herself again.

Will handed the folded newspaper with his hat, cane, and gloves to the butler who had admitted him at the house in Bryanston Square. Adjusting his cravat and running a hand over his vigorous curls, he waited to be announced in the drawing-room. It was hard that his reunion with Ellen should take place in the presence of her parents. Then the double doors opened and he caught his first glimpse of her within the room, seated beside her mother, her father standing with his back to the fireplace. Her demure face was luminous in her welcoming, her sweet mouth smiling beautifully. He forgot all else. Even Paris and all he had left there.

7

In exasperation Louise tumbled her dresses about as she tried to decide what she should wear. Nothing she owned suited the purpose. Catherine, after watching her for a while, went to an old chest in the corner of the room and lifted the lid. With a rustling of yellowed tissue paper she drew out a russet silk dress and shook it free from its folds.

"Here you are," she said in an odd, cracked voice. "Alter it to the latest mode, and you'll look fresh out of a bandbox. The bonnet to go with it has never been worn either."

Louise saw what she was holding up, and felt a lump come into her throat. "Dear, dear Catherine. I can't take that from you. It was to be your wedding dress for your marriage to Henri Berrichon."

"It's high time some use was made of it." Catherine was blinking rapidly to hide the glistening of her eyes. "Henri paid a lot for the silk, and you'll appear the grand young lady that you want to be if you wear it." Resolutely she picked up a pair of scissors and applied them to part of the stitching. "If I give you a hand we should manage to have it ready for you to wear tomorrow. No sense in wasting time."

Louise threw her arms about her and hugged her hard, both of them deeply moved. Then, for the rest of that Sunday they unpicked and pressed and recut and stitched. The result dazzled both of them, Louise because she had never worn anything so fine, and the russet silk moulded her form and hugged her waist from which the gathers sprang out to accentuate its handspan. Catherine, lost in admiration, saw clearly that Louise was at the age of eighteen a handsome, striking creature fit to be the bride of the Prince-President if he were not double her age and more, apart from being a roué to boot. Not that Catherine held lustiness against any man, but in her opinion Louise deserved one of those rare and wonderful men who would love her forever.

"Now for the bonnet," Louise said eagerly, taking up the shovel-shaped straw, which they had relined with some lace that had been hoarded. She put it on, tied the ribbons, and swung around to present herself for Catherine's approval. "What do you think? Do I look like a high-class seamstress who has learnt her skills at home and abroad?"

Catherine felt compelled to be honest. "You look real nice, that's for sure. As to the rest of it, I don't know. That stuck-up Englishman, Monsieur Worth, never had luck going from shop to shop to get work on the strength of what he had done in England."

"But it was his French that was against him." Her voice rose on a rush of optimism. "It will be different for me, and in any case I have a fine story ready in my head."

Catherine's mouth pursed disapprovingly. "I brought you up to speak the truth. Your maman wouldn't have liked to think of you getting work on a pack of lies."

Louise's jaw tightened and her whole face flashed defiance. "I've worked too hard and too long to have my dearest ambition snatched from me now!"

Catherine became pious. "It's no good risking your soul for a few fine feathers. I know you've never forgotten your ambition to dress like a queen of France."

Still fierce, Louise tossed up her head and set her hands on her waist. "If that were all I wanted I could get them by parading myself this minute in the right quarter and before the right eyes." She saw Catherine shrink, and remorse overcame her. Her good friend had been irrevocably scarred by the dark and terrible times that had been endured. Somehow and somewhere she would make it all up to her. She set a gentle arm around Catherine's shoulders. "Don't let us quarrel. I can't bear it."

"You ought to wash your mouth out with soap," Catherine answered stubbornly with pain in her voice, not quite ready to be pacified. "Suggesting such a thing."

"Forget what I said and listen to me," Louise urged persuasively. "You know that whoever employs me won't be the loser just because I have had to embroider a tale to gain an *entrée*." She struck a mock-boastful attitude. "In fact, the only loss would be if I denied ladies of fashion my skill as a seamstress able to hold her own with any other in Paris or anywhere else for that matter." She had succeeded in coaxing a reluctant smile from Catherine, and then suddenly there was no longer any banter in her tone, and her face became set and resolute. "The time will come when I'll have my own dressmaking establishment, and you shall be in charge of my grisettes and we'll live in a grand residence in the Faubourg St.-Germain, where we'll rub shoulders with all my most aristocratic customers."

Catherine was made uncomfortable by the intensity of the girl's demeanour and took refuge in a lilt of levity, refusing to take all she had said quite seriously. "Then with those fancy aims that you've got worked out in your head you'll have to find a rich husband to back the whole spree."

Louise gave her a wide, level look. "Not necessarily," she replied crisply, adjusting a cuff fractionally to a more fashionable depth. "A woman can always make money with the right financial information. Will Russell taught me that. He gave me advice on how to go about investing any money I could spare, and at the time I had a few francs saved from all those extra working hours, which he managed to double for me. We reinvested, and every spare sou I have had since then has gone into that nest-egg." She shrugged. "It's still tiny yet, but it will grow. At the present time it is invested indirectly in Baron Haussmann's rebuilding programme. Nothing could be better than that. I'll never make a fortune with the little I have now, but eventually there should be enough to enable me to open up on my own with one room at a good address, which is important in establishing a business as one means to go on. I'll be a success in my own right one day, and not through selling myself through a wedding ring."

Slowly Catherine shook her head at such an incomprehensible enterprise, her curls bobbing about her unusually solemn face. Somehow she did not dare to ask if love entered into these grandiose plans anywhere.

The next morning Louise set out in a mood to conquer all bastions. Fortunately it was a bright and sunny day with no wind to ruffle her finery or sway her wide skirt. She was wearing all Catherine's petticoats as well as her own to hold it out to its full width, which made it extremely heavy. She thought it not surprising that many women fainted through a combination of tight stays and weighty dresses, but she was young and strong and light-hearted on this day of days, a dancing trip to her step, and an ambitious sparkle to her eyes. She was conscious of heads turning to watch her go by, her russet silk ashimmer in the sun, a pristine whiteness to the cotton gloves meant for a bride and never taken from the box before this day.

When she had no luck at the shops of her choice in the rue de Rivoli and the colonnaded rue de Castiglione, she turned in the direction of the rue de Richelieu. Upon entering number 83, she deliberately avoided being approached by an assistant, wanting to get her bearings and gain some idea of the full range of goods for sale. She took refuge among the materials, which particularly interested her, and gazed around at the velvets and silks draped like hangings in a potentate's palace, the brocades and damasks set taut like exotic sails, and the gauzes and tulles and muslins that were allowed to waft and billow enticingly. Long experience had taught her which of the fabrics on show would sew well and which would fray or split threads under a needle point or handle too stiffly for enchantment.

"Is anyone attending you, mademoiselle?"

For a matter of seconds her lids closed with quivering lashes on the voice that came to her across a span of five years. How was it possible to have lived in the same city and not known he was still there! She turned and looked into the face of Worth as he stood holding aside a drape of gold-tinted tulle. She saw his incredulous look.

"Louise!"

She knew then that first love could never be truly banished. The old familiar tenderness flooded through her veins as if the time between had never been. The only change she could see in him was that his features had hardened and strengthened from the youthful looks she remembered into those of a handsome man. "How are you, dear Worth?" she asked emotionally. "I can scarcely believe that it is you."

"Nor I that it is my little friend from my first days in Paris." He took her hands into his and at arms' length looked her up and down in admiration. "You've grown up into a beautiful young woman. And such elegance!"

She laughed happily, withdrawing her fingers from his clasp. "Fine feathers make fine birds. I know that this dress is a long way from the concocted garment for which you designed the sleeves, but it is donated finery which I remodelled after it was given to me by Catherine for my purpose in being here today. I'm hoping that Messieurs Gagelin and Obigez will employ me on the strength of it as an example of my professional skill."

"So you have continued with your sewing?" His glance ran over the seams of her dress and he touched the pleated edging to her cuff.

"Practically night and day." She listed the range of her accomplishments, but gave no details of where she had gained all the experience. "And what of you since you left the rue du Fouarre?"

"On the whole all has gone remarkably well, but more of that later. So you are hoping for work, are you? Come!" He took her by the elbow and drew her out into the centre of the floor where they stood. "Walk up and down for me. Let me see how well this dress of yours hangs and if it fits you as perfectly in motion as it appears to while you are standing still." As she hesitated he flapped his hands at her as if shooing geese. "Walk! Walk!"

Bewildered and not at all sure that he had not taken leave of his senses, she walked. When she had covered a short distance she looked back and saw that he was dealing with some query being put to him by another assistant while still keeping an eye on her. He gestured again that she should continue and, suppressing amusement, she obeyed.

When she retraced her steps he was standing directly in her path with feet apart and arms folded, his head at an angle as he observed her critically with narrowed eyes. Before she could reach him he had nodded over some other shop matter brought to his attention, and had directed two customers to a distant counter, never once taking his gaze fully from her.

"You are the *premier commis,*" she exclaimed with some

awe, dipping a bob of a curtsey in compliment. To be an assistant at Maison Gagelin and Obigez was grand enough, but to be head salesman was an extremely exalted position.

A flicker of surprise crossed his face as if he had forgotten she could not possibly know about it. "Yes. Yes, I am. A comparatively recent promotion, but a most welcome one. As a matter of fact, I have some voice now in connection with the sewing-room, and since I cannot fault your dress, except that I would have preferred a larger bow crushed more dramatically at the throat, you have obtained the employment you were looking for. All that remains is for Monsieur Gagelin or Monsieur Obigez to authorise your appointment."

She stared at him, her cheeks hollowing, seeing all she would gladly have obtained vanishing through her own rejection of it. "You can't recommend me," she burst out. "I won't let you. It could put you in a bad light if ever the truth came out. I came here today ready to let it be thought I had spent the last two or three years in England. I—"

He interrupted her, drawing her out of earshot of anyone who happened to be standing nearby. "Now," he said, "how could you make such a claim? And why?"

She told him everything, speaking in English to reduce further the chance of any snatch of what she was saying being overheard. When she had finished he stroked his chin thoughtfully as he digested all she had disclosed. He was not without compassion for Louise, understanding why she had felt compelled to play out a charade in order to re-establish herself. Her full strength had shown itself in her willingness to sacrifice everything he had offered her in order to save him from any adverse repercussions. He was glad that he had seen that side of her, because it endorsed what he felt was the right thing for him to do.

"Give me Mr. Russell's letter," he said. She took it from her drawstring purse, and he read it. "This is recommendation enough. Wait here."

He was back a few minutes later. "All is well," he informed her with satisfaction. "I gave my personal guarantee as to your character, and my request to take you on as a sewing-hand was granted immediately."

It gave her an inkling of the high regard in which the proprietors held their *premier commis*. She felt weak with relief and thankfulness. "I can't thank you enough. You'll never regret giving me this chance, I promise you. I'll work so hard."

His gaze on her was kindly. "You always did. I used to

think how industrious you were for a young girl. Now I had better put you in the charge of someone who can show you where you'll be working and tell you the rules that have to be observed in this shop, and so forth. As a matter of fact, she is your namesake."

Louise thought later that had she been wearing anything but the russet silk she would have felt as ill clad as a country wench before Marie Vernet's diminutive and *soignée* appearance. Yet the charming smile that was forthcoming, the spontaneous friendliness in Marie's eyes and her whole expression of welcoming interest took no heed of anything but a pleasure in their meeting.

"Charles has told me how he stayed at your home when he first came to Paris," Marie exclaimed, remembering what she had learnt of this girl's unfortunate beginnings in life and wanting to do what she could for her. "I hope we shall be good friends and that you will be happy working here."

"I'm sure I shall, Mademoiselle Vernet," Louise replied, smiling. "How strange that we should both have the same surname."

"Call me Marie, please. I intend to call you Louise on the strength of Charles's acquaintanceship with you. Do you mind?"

"No, of course not. Please do."

Worth had taken his place beside Marie at the counter, and he looked down at her fondly. "The surname should not be Vernet very much longer, at least not if I can help it." Shyness and joy mingled in Marie's face and she slipped her hand into his, he clasping it tightly. "We hope to marry before long if all continues to go as well as it is at present."

The colour had drained sharply from Louise's face as nebulous dreams and unformed longings that she had not realised still lingered within her were swept away. "Now it is my turn to wish you both happiness in the fulfillment of your hopes."

"Thank you, Louise." Normally Marie would have been the first to notice paleness in another's complexion, but she was full of what had happened in recent months to bring their chance of marrying much nearer. "You see, so many customers began wanting dresses like those that Charles designs for me that our employers were finally persuaded to let him have a few *toiles* on hand to satisfy the demand, muslin replicas of his designs of dresses and cloaks that could then be made up in the customer's choice of material from the shop." She gave an enchanting little laugh. "Far from satisfying the demand, the availability of the *toiles* only increased it. Now Charles has widened the range, and designs each garment with a particular fabric in mind. If it is wool, he uses one pattern, and if brocade another, and so on, which means that the garment will always handle exactly as he intended and not be ruined by a customer's wrong choice of material."

"How wise," Louise murmured, thankful to lose herself in admiration at Worth's initiative. Then Marie took her companionably by the arm and led her away to introduce her to those busy in the sewing-room and tell her all she needed to know about the rules and restrictions of the house for which she would be working. Worth, left at the counter, served a customer who wanted a mantle and refused to look at anything that was not of his design.

Once more Louise found herself at a sewing-table working twelve hours a day. Conditions were better than they had been at Madame Camille's and her wages fractionally higher. Moreover, there was no danger of being turned off in the presently unlikely case of trade going into a slump, because a stock of ready-made garments were always being made for retail. In addition, meals were provided for the staff, which Louise appreciated. She would have liked Catherine to come and work with her, extra hands being taken on at fairly regular intervals as more work-tables were added to cope with the making of an increasing number of *toiles*, but Catherine refused to consider it, able to be extremely stubborn when it suited her.

"Not me! I'm not going there. This Monsieur Worth of yours is no more than a flash in the pan as far as fashion is concerned. Those that rise fast in the world fall the harder, and he'll be one of them, mark my words. Then where would you and I be? Both out on our ears, most likely. No, I'm sticking to Madame Camille's, and when old Gagelin and Obigez decide that their toffee-nosed customers are getting a mite too rattled by all the common dressmaking talk going on behind their posh shopfront, I'll at least still be in work and able to keep us going until you find something else."

There was no moving her. Louise gave up trying to make her see that her prophecy of doom had no grounds to it except a dislike of the Englishman whose only fault had been in innocently occupying a room that Catherine was ever to associate with someone else. Then, as if to confirm Louise's certainty that Worth could only go from strength to strength, the proprietors decided that a limited number of his designs should be made up for a display of their merchandise on the stand that they were to have at the Great Industrial Exhibition at the Crystal Palace in London, which had been instigated by Prince Albert, Consort to the Queen of England. Louise was proud that much of the sewing that went into the dresses was hers. She thought she had never seen anything more beautiful and original than these designs, and for the first time she discovered Worth's preference for elusive colours that could shade from one into another like the depths of water, tantalising the eye with the question as to whether it was mulberry or mauve, grey or blue, and other such intriguing hues. She saw the garments being packed into the huge, specially made boxes for transport, disappearing amid forests of rustling tissue paper, and she wished she could have been in London to have a hand in arranging them in the vast crystal palace that had been erected to hold the thousands of exhibits.

* * *

On the twenty-first of June, just seven weeks after the opening of the Great Exhibition, Louise was one of the guests at the wedding of Marie Vernet and Charles Frederick Worth. It was a Roman Catholic ceremony, and although he held to being an Anglican and could never consider becoming a convert, he had agreed willingly that any children of the union should be brought up in the church of which his wife was a devout member. Though they were to quarrel many more times about her reluctance to parade before customers, and later, whenever she felt unhappily conspicuous in his more outstanding designs, their different religious paths were never to cause the slightest friction between them. They had a unique understanding of each other in that respect. He had his own way of gaining spiritual strength and guidance, avoiding organised worship, but never passing a church of any denomination out of service hours without going in for a while to sit in silent meditation. Marie, knowing him to be the good man that he was, never had the slightest doubts about the salvation of his soul.

He had loved her dearly before their marriage, but since their wedding night his adoration had reached new and glorious heights. Never before had any man possessed such a beautiful and loving wife. What a darling creature she was! He, who had always loved women for their feminine allure, had found one who was a queen above them all. Everything he was to design in the years ahead was in reality a paean in praise of Marie Worth.

By the time the Great Exhibition closed in October, the Worth dresses had commanded a tremendous amount of attention from people there from all corners of the world. The jurors of the exhibition were devastating in the severity of their criticism, sharing the opinion of many others that although the wide domed skirt had been adhered to, the dresses in themselves differed far too drastically from the current mode. Nevertheless, in all fairness the jurors could not deny a trophy, and Maison Gagelin won a gold medal for France. But long before that summer of 1851 had ended, buyers and businessmen of many nationalities came to Paris from London to see more of the clothes designed by this extraordinarily imaginative young Englishman and to place orders amounting to many hundreds of thousands of francs with a view to importing more examples of these startlingly new Parisian clothes into their own countries in the not too distant future.

The proprietors of Maison Gagelin finally bowed to the opening of a dressmaking department within their hallowed precincts. That they should lower the tone of their establishment so abysmally made them fear the censure of their long-established customers, and both of them endured hours of doubt and heart-searching that were not shared by Worth, who knew that at last he could unleash his genius upon the women of the world. Modesty had never been his failing, and as he came into his new power his inherent arrogance, natural to him by reason of his lineage and early upbringing, became more noticeable, but it was tempered as it had always been by his kindly nature and sense of justice. His theatrical instincts, which had ever given him that perfect sense of timing in bringing a customer to the point of a sale, also received full rein in the setting of the salon of the new dressmaking department, which had become the stage that he had long awaited.

The venture was an immediate success. Contrary to all that the proprietors had feared, no complaints were forthcoming, and far from losing the custom of those whom they most esteemed, dresses were ordered by the very names they had thought would vanish from their books. For Marie Worth it meant a drastic change. She was removed from the security of her counter behind which she had discreetly worn her husband's designs, and thrust completely into the public eye by being called upon to promenade in all his latest creations up and down and around the salon of the dressmaking department before the seated customers. She would have preferred all the garments to have been shown on the wicker frames pushed forward on wheels, which was the established method of display, but that would no longer have suited the customers of Maison Gagelin. Her belief in her husband's artistry and her joy in his personal triumph helped to ease the strain involved in displaying the beautiful clothes, making it less of an ordeal than the shawl- and mantle-wearing had been, but the old shyness still tortured her when he deemed it necessary for her to make a spectacular entrance through a sudden throw-back of curtains in those of his designs made up in the most breathtaking of all the marvellous fabrics that the house had for sale. Usually these were ballgowns, and since a décolletage was not acceptable in daytime hours, Marie had to wear an undertop of black silk to cover her arms, shoulders, and bosom, which looked odd, but did not deter customers from buying.

"Why can't I just come in as I usually do?" she would protest when ready. "The suspense of waiting behind the curtains for your signal is misery for me."

"Nonsense!" he would declare, not as unfeeling as she imagined him to be on such occasions, but determined to win yet another of their endless battles on this one particular issue. "The whole point is that you should burst upon the customers' vision like the sudden blossoming of a rose."

In the end he would get his way, but she also baulked when it came to wearing some of his more outlandish designs, convinced that she would simply look ridiculous, and their resulting quarrels were far from infrequent behind the scenes.

For Louise life had never been better. The weeks and months seemed to slip past with a speed that matched the pace of her needle. It was a tremendous day for her when Worth, who had observed her work closely, promoted her from a first sewing-hand to a fitter. He soon realised that she was in perfect harmony with his aims, having a unique understanding of what he wanted from the fit of a dress, and he raised her without further ado to be his *première* fitter. His only regret was that he had not done it sooner, and from the early summer of 1852 she became his right hand in the fitting-rooms. In a black silk dress with a small, white velvet pin-cushion fastened to a ribbon around her wrist, she became completely at home in a sphere where women ran the whole gamut of emotions from tantrums to ecstatic bliss over a dress. Over and over again she saw them change from discontented creatures in petticoats at the first fittings, disappointed at not seeing themselves transformed immediately in the full-length glass to the breathtaking image they had envisaged, a new dress in its incomplete stages being far from flattering, to satisfied and preening *précieuses* in the finished creation, knowing that they looked supreme. Worth, flouting convention by his male presence with women frequently in a state of half-undress, supervised all the fittings himself, and throughout the whole process he controlled the customers with his charm, his tact, and occasionally with drama when the situation demanded it. Louise found him a demanding master. In contrast to Madame Camille, who like the rest of the couturières had pandered to the customers' dislike of the rigours of a fitting and kept them to a minimum, Worth aimed for one or two, but did not hesitate to command as many as he deemed necessary. Each time he would make Louise repin a hundred times if need be to gain the perfection he demanded, his keen eye able to discern exactly when a dart or a seam needed to be changed by a degree that was almost infinitesimal. Yet it had been Louise's meticulous attention to detail that had made him promote her in the first place, and she revelled in his standards that so matched her own. After each fitting the whole garment was *mis à plat*, laid out in its reclining beauty on a large table to be unpicked and adjusted to whatever alterations had been deemed necessary before being resewn once again, a process that often took place three times or more. Worth's enthusiasm for perfection and nothing less than perfection reached out to the rest of those associated with the dressmaking department, none of whom ever begrudged him a minute of all the endless specialised work that was involved. He had known what he was going to be about when he had insisted upon choosing his own seamstresses and the rest of his dressmaking staff. Those of anything but a dedicated nature devoted to fine needlework would have fallen by the wayside long since.

It was a relief to Louise that Catherine was not jealous of her friendship with Marie Worth, but upon being introduced had taken a great liking to her, as almost everyone did. Catherine talked about her as "that nice Madame Worth," and it was in deference to that liking that she no longer spoke in derogatory tones of the lady's husband, although the old restraint towards him continued. Nevertheless, he was now "Monsieur Worth" anytime he happened to come into a conversation with Louise, and was no longer referred to as "that stuck-up Englishman." Catherine had paid Marie a compliment that she would never know about, and it made life easier for Louise.

November came damply to Paris that year, bringing early-morning mists that lay over the city like silvery gauze and lingered in hollows under the chestnut trees where split husks still held dulled brown nuts in the grass. Madame de Gand, making one of her visits to Paris, complained of the weather to her son when he arrived at her hotel to escort her on a drive, only to discover that she had decided to make it a shopping expedition instead.

"There's no point in driving about on a day like this, Pierre," she declared as they went out of the hotel to her waiting carriage. "You shall come with me to the rue de Richelieu. I have changed my mind about withholding my patronage from Gagelin and Obigez now that I have learned from my Parisian acquaintances that it is no ordinary dress-maker in sway there, but a couturier of exceptional ability. I have decided that he shall make me a gown before I leave for Fontainebleau tomorrow at the Prince-President's invitation." She sat down in the carriage, and as he took the seat beside her she thought as she always did how the uniform of the cuirassiers suited him, even the walking-out dress with the blue stripe down the scarlet trousers being particularly flattering to a handsome man. And her son was exceptionally handsome in her eyes, a credit in every way to the memory of his gallant father and to the family name in the long, unbroken military tradition of service to one's country.

"I suggest, Mother," he said as the carriage began to bowl along, "that since we are both going to this house-party at Fontainebleau we travel there together."

"That would be most agreeable."

Marie-Thérèse de Gand rarely accepted the invitations that were sent out automatically to state functions from the élite list in the Elysée Palace to her as well as to her son, but this invitation had been one of those on a personal level from the Prince-President, and she was looking forward to attending for her own particular reasons. When only a girl herself she had met the seven-year-old Louis-Napoléon and his mother, Hortense, ex-Queen of Holland, when her parents had given them shelter and hospitality on their flight from Paris. Hortense had then recently parted from Napoléon at Malmaison before he left France for the last time, knowing that from St. Helena he would never come again in his lifetime. Marie-Thérèse de Gand still remembered the tragic beauty of the woman who had arrived by night with her younger son, escorted by a single adjutant, her face strained and courageous, marked by all she had been through in losing her lover after the traumatic period of the Hundred Days and being deprived of her elder son by the King who had divorced her. Louis-Napoléon, who had been devoted to his mother, never forgot those who had befriended her in time of trouble, and throughout the years he had kept in touch with Marie-Thérèse de Gand when her own parents were no more. He was godfather to her son, having sent the gift of a gold-handled sword and a proxy to stand in for him at the baptism due to a matter of exile, and since he had become Prince-President she had been received by him several times, preferring the smaller and more intimate occasions of dinner parties for fewer than twenty people to the grand social events where there was little or no chance to converse with him. At every opportunity, and unbeknown to her son, she liked to bring Pierre's name forward and remind Louis-Napoléon indirectly of his obligations as a godfather, which should be lifelong. There was no better way for any young man to secure the advancement of a military career than to be favoured by the patronage of the illustrious ruler of France himself. One of those godfatherly obligations was to be fulfilled at Fontainebleau, a secret between Louis-Napoléon and her, of which Pierre was as yet ignorant. She gave the faintest start as he spoke to her again, uncomfortably aware that it was almost as if he had been following her train of thought to a certain extent.

"Did you know that the Prince-President rarely rides out these days without hearing shouts of *Vive l'Empereur* on all sides?"

She nodded and rolled up her eyes delightedly. "Yes. Is it not thrilling? Yet have we not always known that such a rich reward must be the final outcome for him? They say that the plebiscite at the end of this month is a foregone conclusion." She tapped his arm playfully with the tips of her gloved fingers. "That is why I'm most interested to see this young Spanish noblewoman who is to be among the guests at

Fontainebleau. I want to see for myself if she will make a suitable empress."

Pierre gave her a smiling look of indulgence under the peak of his cap. From what he had heard, it was not as a wife that his godfather wanted Eugénie de Montijo, but it seemed that the lady was resisting his advances. However, he saw no point in destroying his mother's romantic notions and spoiling the visit to Fountainebleau for her as a result of it.

As he entered Maison Gagelin at her side he was prepared for boredom, but since he was not often in her company these days a sense of filial duty had prevented him from getting out of the shopping expedition. He merely hoped that the whole business would not take too long. As Monsieur Obigez swept ahead in bowing obeisance to his mother he followed in her wake, taking a glance here and there whenever a pretty face and figure caught his eye. At least, as much as any man could see of a woman's figure in public. Were women never going to rid themselves of those voluminous tea-cosy skirts that hid the lower half of their delicious shape like vast and ungainly chastity belts?

In the salon a vendeuse showed them to gilded chairs. Worth came through a draped archway that led to the fitting-rooms and bowed out another customer. He then turned to the new arrivals with every courtesy. He and Madame de Gand recognized each other immediately, for he had waited on her several times in the serving of minor accessories since the occasion when he had sold her the white Chinese shawl.

"So you are the Monsieur Worth I have been hearing about," she exclaimed, not entirely pleased. He always seemed to know what suited her better than she did herself, and although the results always gratified her she did not care for any situation of which she was not entirely mistress. However, in the matter of a gown she did know where she stood. Had not Madame Palmyre invariably complimented her on her exquisite taste and made each one exactly to her directions, which was what one expected from a good couturière? "I have decided on a satin ballgown in rose red or a deep pink. My servant will be delivering one of my dresses shortly that will be a guide to you as to my measurements and the style I require. You may add some variation to the neckline in frills of a lighter shade. It must be finished and delivered to my hotel by tomorrow morning. All that remains is for you to show me a choice of satins in the range of colour that I mentioned."

It was not the first time that Worth had met with this established method of dealing with a maker of clothes, and he knew it would not be the last. It was going to be a long time before every customer became acquainted with the new gospel of fit and fashion that he was preaching, and this woman had a particularly difficult figure that would need more than the one or two fittings to meet his standard of perfection.

"Provided you do not object to fittings going late into the night," he answered easily, "there will be no problem in the making and delivery of a dress in such a limited time."

Her brows drew together ominously. "I do not need a fitting if you are as good a couturier as you are claimed to be. I have told you clearly enough what I want."

He smiled, his charm flowing, and was quite unruffled. "I would never rely on measurements from a garment that could not possibly fit as I would fit you, madame. I also suggest that a garnet red would enhance your alabaster skin far better than the shades you mentioned. Now Madame Worth will show you a range of dresses for you to choose from."

The curtains parted at his signal, and Marie emerged in a ballgown of blue-green satin in which the skirt appeared to consist entirely of latticed strips of the material in a lovely effect that Madame de Gand had never seen before. Anything she had been about to say in a crushing departure was lost in her throat. She even stayed leaning slightly forward in her chair where she had been making the first move in rising from it. Pierre, watching Marie appreciatively under his lashes and deploring the daytime necessity of the black silk covering of her arms and bosom, made the comment that further cemented his mother to the seat. He indulged her in a little flattery at times.

"Nobody would look at Eugénie de Montijo at Fontainebleau if you wore that dress, Mother. In garnet red, of course."

Marie displayed several more dresses. Although it was hard to choose, Madame de Gand decided on the first one, making a selection from a wide range of fabrics afterwards, all in shadings of the same garnet red. Worth showed her through a draped archway toward a fitting-room outside which the fitter waited. Pierre could see her. A young woman with raven-black hair and a lovely throat. Then she happened to turn her head and their eyes met. To each came instant recognition clouded with puzzlement as neither remembered at once where each had seen the other before. It came to her first. He saw her amber gaze clear vividly. Then he knew her. It was the girl of the winter rosebuds.

Swiftly she disappeared into the fitting-room in the wake of his mother. He hoped to see her when she came out again, but she remained out of sight even when his mother had rejoined him in readiness to leave. Whether the girl had evaded him deliberately or not he did not know. He would most certainly take steps to find out.

Madame de Gand thought her son was being unusually attentive when he returned that same afternoon with her to number 83, rue de Richelieu, for her first fitting, and again in the early evening for the second. As if that were not enough, he arrived at her hotel shortly before midnight to escort her there for the final one. Then Monsieur Worth allowed him into the fitting-room to see how fine she looked while the fitter and the first hand, who was in charge of the sewing under the young woman's directions, made some alteration of about a millimetre to the hem that was not deemed to be perfect. For herself, she had not been able to see any fault in it. Moreover, she thought it was quite wonderful how the bodice moulded her bosom, her right breast being larger than her left, and for the first time ever there was not the slightest shimmer of a pucker showing there.

"Good night, Pierre," she said contentedly when he handed her into her carriage, not accompanying her back to the hotel. "Until tomorrow then."

"Later today, as it happens," he corrected, speaking to her through the window.

"Yes, of course. Do not be late." She settled back in her seat and was driven away.

It was three in the morning when the activity in the dressmaking-room slowed to a tired halt. Worth was giving some special instructions on the final pressing of the finished dress as the rest made ready to go home. Louise followed the clattering footsteps of the seamstresses ahead of her down the corridor to the door that had been unlocked by the shop's concierge. Outside she paused to take a deep breath of the night air, thankful for its chill against her face. She had been in a state of turmoil and confusion ever since she had looked from the area of the fitting-rooms and seen the cuirassier officer once again. Pierre de Gand. She had soon heard his Christian name, because his imperious mother had used it often enough. It was a year or more now since she had last dreamt of meeting him again, and never once had it been in a couturier's salon, but always on a clifftop or a mountainside or in the bow of a ship, anywhere that was dangerous and where she stood on the brink of plunging down into the unknown. It was because he was a soldier, she supposed, linked in her mind with battle and war and the threat of death. The intervening space of time since he had whirled the nosegay away from her had not diminished his extreme attractiveness, or his boldness either, for that matter. During the final fitting, each time she had looked up his eyes had been waiting for hers, not always in direct contact, but reflected in the looking-glasses that lined the fitting-room, so that it was impossible not to have her glance caught and snared like a bird in a net. Her stupid heart had been hammering all the time, as if it mattered to her that a spoiled young man was whiling away a time of boredom by repeating flirtatious tricks that he must have played innumerable times before.

"Good evening—or should I say good day, Mademoiselle Louise."

She smothered her startled cry by clapping a hand over her mouth. The cuirassier had been waiting in the shadows, and now he moved into the light of the single lantern that showed the way out into the street. "You frightened me!"

"I apologise. That was not my intention. I'm leaving Paris later today for about a week, and I wanted to renew our acquaintanceship before I left."

"I was not aware that we shared one." She began to walk on purposefully, and he immediately fell into leisurely step at her side.

"I've looked for you ever since I took your roses," he said with considerable exaggeration. Admittedly he had scanned faces in the crowd on later occasions, but the memory of her had soon faded. Seeing her again he wondered how that could have been possible. There was a freshness and vitality and piquancy about her that he found as irresistible now as when that brief and tantalising encounter had taken him back to the rue de Faubourg Stl-Honoré in the night hours in the faint hope of finding her again.

She made no coy pretence of not remembering the occasion. "I make sure that I don't stand at the front of a crowd any more," she replied crisply. "I might get the flowers on my bonnet snatched away next time." She wanted to discourage him, to make him go away, but he showed no sign of being in any haste to leave her. Quite the reverse.

"Forgive me," he persisted, "and let us make a new beginning. I'm Pierre de Gand, as you know, having heard my name as I heard yours. I want to be sure that you will see me again when I return. Say you will." He was eyeing her sideways with a twinkling glance. "I swear never again to take tribute intended for another. Not even from your *chapeau,* however great the temptation."

She bit deep into her lower lip, forcing back the smile that quivered in the corners of her mouth. To let him see that she was in any way won over would be disastrous. "No, Lieutenant de Gand. The work I do extends to all hours under the sun, often without warning, and I never make promises that I can't be sure of keeping. Good night."

She broke into running steps to catch up with the seamstresses with whom she walked home. She did not have to turn her head to know that he was standing where she had left him, looking after her.

By next morning Louise had quite decided how she would deal with him when he returned to Paris. She had no doubt that he would seek her out again. It was a truth that many men were further incited to pursuit by a rebuff, and she judged him to be one of them. It was not in a soldier's nature to admit defeat. Fortunately the element of surprise, which had been to his advantage previously and which had so unnerved her in more ways than one, would be gone when he next appeared. She would be in full control of herself and the situation.

She had no illusions as to the purpose that he had in his mind. It was as clear to her as if it had been written down before her in black and white. The bait usually offered by well-bred young gentlemen who pursued grisettes was a silk petticoat or a pair of ear-bobs or sometimes a rope of pearls. Had she not seen enough girls brought to ruin by bulges some months later under those same silk petticoats? Where were the gallants then? Conspicuous by their absence, and the poor grisette turned off work to end up most likely putting her baby in the revolving box in the door of the Hospice des Enfants Trouvés where a stricken mother was spared the ignominy of being seen at her heart-rending dispossession. When Pierre came again Louise was resolved that any relationship that developed between them would be on her terms, keeping him at the distance that she decreed, and the old determination that no man should find means to dominate her heart to his own ends was as steadfast as ever.

Mid-morning found her as busy as usual in the fitting-rooms. She had collected up a dress carefully after a second fitting and had handed it into the charge of the chief sewing-hand to be taken to the dressmaking-room, when Worth returned from seeing the customer out.

"One moment, Mademoiselle Louise," he said, addressing her formally as he always did in hours of business, his expression and tone so unexpectedly severe that she looked at him in puzzlement as she approached.

"Yes, Monsieur Worth?" she inquired with equal formality, wondering what could possibly be amiss.

"Kindly inform your swain, whoever he is, not to have his tokens delivered to this house and—worse!—to my department!" He held out a bouquet of tight, cream rosebuds in a silver frill and dripping with satin ribbons.

Again Pierre had caught her off guard. No silk petticoat, no gew-gaws proclaiming an ulterior motive that could have been refused and hurled back with aplomb, but an offering beguiling as a Valentine, impossible to spurn. She held out both hands to take the bouquet, and inhaled the hothouse fragrance of the buds. Some part of her heart melted for the first time. She felt it go from her like snow in the sun, and did not know how to draw it back.

8

At the Palace of Fontainebleau, which was well situated for the hunting season in thousands of acres of forest encompassing ravines and gorges and heather-clad plains, Pierre was given comfortable rooms that looked down on the huge horseshoe staircase that gave access from the wide forecourt to the grand entrance. He could see the spot where Napoleon bade adieu to his guards before leaving for Elba and where he had received them again with such high hopes upon that fleeting and doomed return. Throughout the palace there were reminders everywhere of sad and dramatic times from the past, but for himself Pierre was looking forward to a pleasurable few days. There would be riding to hounds, which he enjoyed, and in the evenings there would be dancing and theatricals and cards and other entertainment, plenty in all to distract him from an impatience to return to Paris. He could not remember when he had been so smitten. He found it exciting, his blood racingly stirred, and there was a buoyancy to his mood that had pleased his mother, although it would not have if she had suspected the origins of it, and she had remarked more than once in the carriage that she was sure the visit to Fontainebleau would sustain his good humour in every way. He had barely refreshed himself and changed his clothes after the journey when a servant brought word that the Prince-President wished to see him without delay.

It was not his first visit to the palace, and he needed no directing to the salon where he was to await the Prince-President. Entering, he found he was not alone. The salon, a handsome room rich with painted panels and a silken, circular carpet, was graced by tall windows, and in front of them, her back to him, was a girl looking out at the fading November day. She wore a dark-blue dress that with the wintry gloom combined to make the white-gold fairness of her smooth hair shine with the brightness of a candle-flame. She started at the click of the double doors behind him, and swung about quickly to regard him steadily and assessingly with very fine, hazel eyes. Otherwise, apart from her fair complexion, which was flawless, her looks were no more than average. Her nose was a fraction too tip-tilted, her mouth a trifle wide, and her smile, dawning quirky and quizzical, showed teeth marred by a slight irregularity, which was—surprisingly—not unattractive, due to their pearly whiteness.

"You must be Pierre de Gand." Her voice was light and pleasing.

"You have me at a disadvantage, mademoiselle."

"Don't be alarmed. Your memory isn't failing you. We have never met, although we share the same godfather in the Prince-President. No, wait a moment." She had given her head a little shake. "I will rephrase what I have said since the restoration of the Empire is almost accomplished." Her fingertips were placed lightly together in a steeple under her chin. "You and I rejoice in the Emperor, Napoléon III, as our mutual godfather."

He took a few steps toward her. "But with all this imperial talk, you still haven't told me your name."

"I'm Stéphanie Casile. This is my first visit to this part of the country, you know. I've lived in Savoie for as long as I can remember. I haven't seen Paris yet. Isn't that a sad admission? To have reached the age of seventeen and never to have seen Paris."

He chuckled quietly. "Not necessarily. I would guess that you have been incarcerated within walls for the benefit of your education."

"Correct, m'sieur. Go to the top of the class." She composed her face into a passable impression of a nun's prime countenance, cupping her hands about her face like a coif. "Or," she added in the same pinched voice, "if your willfulness is comparable with that of Mademoiselle Stéphanie's, you had better go to the bottom of it."

He joined in her laughter readily, amused and entertained by her. "At least I have seen your part of the country. Too much of it, in fact. I spent nearly two years in Savoie with my regiment, patrolling the border. Are you to visit Paris while you are here?"

She let her shoulders rise and fall with a regretful sigh. "No, I must go back to school again until the summer. Then my darling godfather has promised that I shall come to court." She wagged a finger roguishly, her eyes sparkling. "That will be at the Palace of the Tuileries! Once again a royal home more than fitting for an all-powerful Emperor. What state occasions I shall see! What balls I shall attend!"

He chuckled again. "There has been no stint at the Elysée Palace, so it can be guaranteed that at the Tuileries you'll be able to make up for the social deprivation you have known throughout your schooldays."

Her toothy little smile was mischievous. "That is what I'm counting on." Then she swivelled around on her heel as the door opened again and Louis-Napoléon came into the room. Stocky and dapper, his hair smoothed into a curling side-quiff with Macassar oil, his moustache ends waxed to needle points and his goatee beard immaculately trimmed, he smiled benignly at seeing them together.

"So you have made each other's acquaintance." He spread his arms as if to encompass them both within his godfatherly benediction. "I felt this would be the only opportunity I should have for the next few days to spend a little time with my children of the church." He raised Stéphanie up from her curtsey and kissed her on both cheeks, complimenting her on her newly grown-up appearance and then asking questions and making enquiries that made it obvious to Pierre that Louis-Napoléon took his duties seriously towards the girl. Then it was Pierre's turn for greeting and attention. Some explanation about Stéphanie was forthcoming. "This charming young lady is the daughter of a good friend of mine, Joseph Casile, who stood by me in less happy days. Now, alas, he and his dear wife are no longer in this world, denied the chance to see the new dawning of France's greatness that has come upon us." Louis-Napoléon looked from one to the other of them, taking Stéphanie's hand into his left, and reaching up his right to place it in a fatherly manner on Pierre's tall shoulder. "But you two young people, Stéphanie, dear child, and you, Pierre, of my loyal cuirassiers, in all the splendour of your youth, symbolise the future of our country and represent all that those in past struggles hoped for and longed to achieve. I know you will both be a credit to France always, and to me."

Stéphanie was deeply moved. "You are too kind, monsiegneur."

Louis-Napoléon then led them to chairs to sit down with him, and there followed a convivial hour of conversation during which he and Pierre smoked cigars and Stéphanie nibbled sugared almonds from a silver bon-bon dish. He encouraged the two of them to talk about themselves, to relate various events, and more than once joined them in ready laughter. Both could see that he wished most sincerely to cement their friendship with each other, but Pierre was less than pleased, when Louis-Napoléon finally left them, to realise he had been inveigled into promising to look after Stéphanie during the sojourn at Fontainebleau. It was not hard to see his mother's matrimonial meddling in it all.

As always at such gatherings, there were plenty of opportunities for a good-looking young officer to engage in amorous dalliance, and although at the present time thoughts of Louise made all other women less attractive, he still felt encumbered at dinner that evening by having Stéphanie at his right hand, and again at his side when the dancing commenced. Dutifully he danced with her, and then was glad when other partners took her off his hands for a while. There was one woman present with whom he wanted to dance above all the rest. Not even Marie-Thérèse de Gand, regal in the garnet-red satin dress which caught every female eye, could detract from the evening that belonged undeniably to Eugénie de Montijo, Countess of Teba. Whether she was waltzing with Louis-Napoléon, taking supper with him, evading his limpet-like attentions to dance with someone else, or sitting quietly engaged in conversation, she illumined the gathering with her extraordinary beauty. Her features were classically moulded, her face a delicate oval with a high, clear brow, her eyes an exceptional hyacinth blue, and her complexion as pale and translucent as was usual to those fortunate enough to be blessed with such magnificent Titian hair, which she wore in thick coils around the crown of her head, needing little imagination on anyone's part to see it was an empress's red-gold diadem. She was twenty-five years old, the daughter of a Spanish grandee, and fiery and adventurous in her disposition for all the exquisite porcelain docility of her expression. She knew Louis-Napoléon was avid for her, but while trying to seduce her he was letting his eye reach out to the royal houses of Europe in a search for a lady more suited by rank than she to the glory of becoming an emperor's bride. For herself, she had considered marriage in the past, but had suffered two devastating disappointments in love, the second time even more excruciatingly heart-rending than the first, and in each case the man concerned had preferred her sister. This in no way lessened her abounding affection for her sister, Paca, who was the dearest and kindest creature, innocent of any intrigue, but all Eugénie had been through made her far less easy to win than she might otherwise have been. Everywhere her noble company was in great demand, and although she turned young men's heads wherever she went, her good name continued to be without a stain, her virginity still totally unassailed. When Pierre de Gand, whom she had met earlier that evening, asked her to dance with him, she accepted in her customary gracious manner, gliding onto the floor with him in a drifting of water-green tulle.

"Your godfather mentioned that you are in the cavalry," she remarked as they rotated around the shining floor amid the other dancers, her French perfect, as was her English, due to schooling in both countries. "Were you escorting him when he rode back into Paris after his triumphal tour of the country two weeks ago?"

"I was. You saw the procession, did you?"

"I watched from an apartment window along the route. Such a splendid sight! All those mounted generals paying homage, and every member of the Senate there to welcome him." Her thin and curiously oblique eyebrows, which gave such interest to her ravishing face, rose in marvel at what she had seen. "Yet France's new Emperor in all but final recognition rode completely alone at the head of the column and looked neither to one side nor the other."

"He never does. His gaze is always fixed ahead as a soldier's should be." Pierre chose to ignore the occasion of his own digression when he had snatched the flowers from Louise. As his senior officer had pointed out afterwards, scorching him with a virulent reprimand, only on processions of conquest was it allowed to take floral tribute from the belauding crowds.

"I have heard that your godfather made many enemies through the *coup d'état* two years ago," Eugénie continued.

"He did indeed."

"Then he must have known he was a perfect target for any assassin!"

"He never considers danger. I would say he does not know fear in any shape or form."

"How courageous," she breathed softly, her long lashes drooping to veil the limpid eyes and hiding whatever look lay in those azure depths.

Then Pierre remembered that her father, whose memory she was said to idolise, had been one of Spain's most revered heroes of recent years. He thought that on those grounds the future Emperor could rate his chances high, and in that he was to be envied. There was no doubt in Pierre's mind that Eugénie had the most exquisite looks and perfectly formed body that he had ever seen; even her shoulders sloped seductively, following the line of those enchanting eyebrows, as if created solely to be caressed by a man's hands and drawn to him by them. But when he danced with her again that evening, the topic of their conversation being on a lighter note and bringing twinkling smiles to her lips and eyes, he realised even more than the first time that he felt no sexual rapport with her, no normal awareness of the emanation of the senses to which he was accustomed when faced with a lovely woman to whom he knew himself to be pleasing by his attention. Intrigued, he came to the conclusion that she needed to be strongly and deeply awakened, and knowing his godfather's reputation with women, he thought she could not deliver herself into better hands. Except, of course, his own, and that was as much out of the question as having a third dance with her. Louis-Napoléon had looked most annoyed when he had captured her for the second time. Pierre decided it would be expedient to spend the rest of the evening with Stéphanie. He rescued her from his mother's company and danced with her until the festivities came to a close.

He was up early for the hunting next morning, and Stéphanie was there in the forecourt before him, mounted on a black mare, very neat and purposeful in a convent-governed riding habit that was as lacking in fit and style as the muslin dress she had worn the previous evening, but her face was merry and excited through the veil attached to her hard-crowned hat, and her breath hung before her in the frosty air.

"Do you ride as well as you have undoubtedly been taught to pray?" he chaffed irreverently, bringing his horse alongside.

She laughed and made a face at him. "You'll see, Lieutenant High-and-Mighty."

Even as she spoke Eugénie made her appearance. Stéphanie saw Pierre's eyes go from her to fasten on the Spanish noblewoman with a look that was reflected in the face of almost every other man present. She had to admit to herself that not even Venus stripped to the buff could have offered much competition that morning to the strikingly-clad horsewoman approaching on the most high-spirited of all the thoroughbreds in the stable.

Scorning a side-saddle, she rode astride with a full skirt covering grey trousers which were tucked, Spanish fashion, into her high-heeled leather boots. Her felt hat was shaped like those worn by matadors, a diamond brooch attaching the ostrich feather that wafted and curled against her flame-gold, plaited coils. Her face was animated and smiling, her eyes ashine with anticipation of the chase.

"Good morning, ladies. Good morning, gentlemen," she greeted the company, saluting them with her short, pearl-handed whip. She had a specially dazzling smile for Louis-Napoléon, who leaned forward in the saddle to say something to her that nobody else could catch, although it was not hard to guess the ardour of his compliment by the way she lowered her lashes bewitchingly. He was still talking only to her as together they led the rest of the hunting party into the forest.

Stéphanie had hoped to impress Pierre that day, because she rode exceedingly well and normally received more than a full share of praise, but none could compete with Eugénie, who eclipsed everyone else with her superb Spanish horsemanship. She took stone walls and ditches with a grace and ease that made her one radiant arc with her horse, her strength and skill breathtaking, and she crowned it all by being first in at the kill.

Stéphanie, who had reined in to the rear, not wanting to see the stag go down under the hounds, was joined almost immediately by Eugénie, who had wheeled away at once. It was obvious to Stéphanie that the Spanish lady, who held the bullfight high in her esteem, had no stomach when it came to the prolonged torment of gentler animals.

"What a display!" Pierre enthused to Stéphanie as he helped her down from her steaming horse amid the rest of the dismounting company. "Did you see how Eugénie de Montijo rode? I have never seen a woman handle a horse so magnificently before."

"Magnificent indeed," Stéphanie endorsed with a sigh that was lost on him. He put his arm about her slender waist to lead her into the palace, but his eyes were directed towards the horsewoman smilingly acknowledging the acclaim from all sides.

The following day, with a bouquet, Louis-Napoléon made a gift to Eugénie of the Andalusian thoroughbred that she had ridden so splendidly, causing gossip and speculation to reach new heights. Eugénie herself seemed a trifle embarrassed by the munificent gift, but later she went to the stables to give an apple and some sugar-pieces to her new acquisition. Louis-Napoléon's generosity did not end there. During a walk by the lake, Eugénie and Stéphanie and some other ladies were ahead of the gentlemen when the subject of the conversation turned to clothes and favourite colours.

"Coral in all its shades," Stéphanie said yearningly. She had never owned anything in the lovely colour, but she would before very long. At eighteen she would come into her inheritance, which was far from meagre.

"I like green myself," Eugénie remarked. "Not wishy-washy versions of it, but strong, clear shades—like this spread of clover leaves." She looked down at the lush spread underfoot and then stooped and picked a leaf. Louis-Napoléon, thinking she had found something of interest, detached himself from the gentlemen and came to her side.

"Look," she said in quiet wonder at the beauty of the simple leaf, holding it carefully against her gloved palm. "See how the dew hangs on it like a tear."

That evening she was wearing another gift from him, which had been brought from Paris by a messenger specially despatched. It was a spray of clover leaves fashioned in emeralds. Stéphanie was enchanted by the romantic gesture. She thought she would love a man for the rest of her life if ever she was the recipient of such an expression of passion. How long could Eugénie continue to resist his amorous pursuit?

On the last day of the sojourn at Fontainebleau the weather was poor, and the gentlemen in the party went riding off on their own, Pierre included. Stéphanie watched him go in disappointment. She had made no impression at all on the dashing young officer, whose splendid height and looks had quite dazzled her when she had turned from the windows in the salon and seen him standing there. Always there had been some idea in her head that at her first launching into society she would sweep innumerable young men off their feet, but nothing like that had happened. Quite the reverse, in fact. What was more, throughout the whole time she had been horribly self-conscious about her dreary clothes. Never again would she suffer the humiliation. When the inheritance was hers she would spend and spend, making sure that she had a change of dress for every hour of the day. Mesdames Palmyre, Camille, Delatour, and the rest of the well-known couturières should compete to provide her with the most elegant wardrobe in the whole of Paris. Dreams, dreams. Impatiently she tapped her foot, thinking how many months were left before they could be fulfilled.

For want of something better to do she joined Eugénie and some other ladies in exploration of some of the oldest parts of the palace, and they came after a while to one of the chapels. There, in the tinted light that came through the stained-glass windows, they tried to decipher inscriptions worn almost away by time, and whispered reverently among themselves as they admired the wall paintings executed three hundred years or more before any of them had been born. In the quietness they heard the distant sound of the huntsmen returning, and all of them went out onto a balcony from the chapel to see what bag was being brought back from the chase.

Tired, rain-drenched, and mud-splashed, the huntsmen

saluted with their whips the bevy of beauty clustered picturesquely at the stone balustrade. Louis-Napoléon brought his sweat-flecked horse forward.

"How can I get up there to you, dear ladies?" he questioned jokingly.

Impishly Stéphanie leaned over and offered a hand that was far above his upturned face. "Here! I'll help you climb up."

There was laughter. Another lady offered to let down her long, golden hair, the atmosphere becoming merry and flirtatious. Then Eugénie spoke, her expression guileless, the touch of a smile to lips.

"All I can perceive, Prince, is that you take the way through the chapel to reach me."

A little hush fell. Her meaning was clear. *Marriage or nothing, Louis-Napoléon.* His eyes narrowed slightly, not leaving those of the woman whom he was almost beside himself to possess. Among the ladies hands quickly covered smiles, and twinkling glances of comprehension were exchanged, some spiked with malice. Several of the huntsmen adjusted their reins or pulled their hats forward to conceal their grins, and in some cases laughter, Pierre himself swinging his horse around to hide his amusement. Stéphanie felt hot with embarrassment at the ultimatum that had been issued before so many witnesses, and did not want her godfather hurt by it.

"I know how to solve this dilemma," she exclaimed with her voice high-pitched, uncomfortably aware of sounding childish in that sophisticated company. "Let those of us on the balcony go downstairs and meet the huntsmen in the vestibule."

Eugénie did not follow the others there. She hurried away to her own rooms, dismayed that so many had interpreted accurately the double-edged remark she had made on the spur of the moment to Louis-Napoléon, having imagined only he would fully understand. Since she never showed emotion publicly she doubted that anyone suspected how violently in love she was with him. Although he was thirteen years older than she, it only added to his attraction in her eyes. He was like her dear father in character, courageous and brave and yet inestimably kind. With all her heart she adored Louis-Napoléon and had known there could be no other man for her from the day she had wtinessed his haughtily fearless ride into Paris. However, sex was another matter altogether. If it had to be endured, it must have the comfort and tenderness of marriage for the procreation of children. Bed for bed's sake was not for her. She shuddered at the thought. It never failed to amaze her that men were unable to love on an aesthetic level, but in their huge conceit imagined all women yearned to be subjected to their uncouth and bodily onslaughts. Whatever happened in the future, whether Louis-Napoléon asked her to marry him or made some European princess his wife, she would always treasure and wear every day of her life the clover spray of emeralds. It epitomised the pure romanticism of love, and would remind her of one of the happiest moments she had ever known when he had given it to her.

The next day the party broke up, and people went their separate ways, most of them back to Paris, but some had greater distances to travel. Madame de Gand said goodbye to her son, and would convey his regards to those old friends with whom she would be staying on her homeward journey to the de Gand château in the Loire Valley. In the vestibule he bade Stéphanie farewell. She was dressed for travelling in an ugly plaid cape, an outmoded bonnet hiding her hair and somehow taking the light from her face.

"It has been an honour to make your acquaintance," he said to her. "I wish you a safe journey back to the convent."

At that moment she knew despair at his conventional expression of goodwill and the uninterested surface to his eyes that showed his mind was on other matters and nothing about her was going to linger in his memory. She would *make* him remember her! Completely without warning she took a step forward and flung her arms about his neck, fastening her mouth on his in a kiss not to be expected of any well-brought-up young girl. But she had twice come across lovers locked in stolen embraces at Fontainebleau, and not all that long ago she and some of her fellow pupils had observed with wide-eyed curiosity the amorous writhings of a servant wench and a gardener's boy, who had imagined they were alone. She kissed Pierre as if she would eat him alive.

Sheer astonishment paralysed him for no more than a second, and then he took full advantage of her unexpected behaviour. A pretty girl was always a pretty girl. She was not to know that he liked her well enough; it was that his thoughts had been so centred on seeing Louise again that he had had difficulty in concentrating fully on anything else that morning. When he released her it was she who had been roundly kissed and it amused him to see she was abashed by the experience, scarcely able to look at him. Her embarrassment was increased by the titters from other guests on the point of departure, who had observed the whole incident.

"*Au revoir*, Pierre." She flung up her head, regaining her poise, extending her hand to him as she should have done originally. He found such a mannerly gesture quite comical after her previous exhibition, but, controlling his features, he took it and bowed conventionally.

"Until we meet again, Stéphanie."

She went out of the palace with a billowing of her plaid cloak. His gaze followed her with a glint of laughter still in his eyes. Now that he came to think about it she had contributed a great deal to his stay at Fontainebleau with her lively conversation and, once he had resigned himself to a brotherly care of her, never had he found her company boring. Brotherly? There had been nothing of that in the response he had shown her. Nor had he wanted there to be.

9

Louise edged her way through the thronging crowds. In her hand was a card of invitation allotting a seat for her on a stand at the Champ-de-Mars for a viewpoint of the military parade being held in honour of the bestowing of the title of emperor on Louis-Napoléon. All shops and businesses were closed for the fête-days, and Paris was a sight never to be forgotten. Bunting and flags adorned public buildings and private houses. The imperial eagle was everywhere, but nowhere more prominent than in the main boulevards where hundreds of banners whipped in the wintry air, making the gilded feathers shine as if truly made of gold on the billowing surfaces. The most ornamental of the fountains ran with wine, and garlands of evergreens entwined posts and made loops between them. Such great numbers of people had swarmed into the city from miles around that it was like every Sunday of a whole decade rolled into one.

She had not seen Pierre since the night she had left him near the shop, but his consideration in having an invitation sent to her showed that it was as she had supposed, and he had no intention of giving up his pursuit. It was doubtful whether she would be able to pick him out in the parade, because it was said that sixty thousand troops were to take part.

Her seat proved to be a grand one. She found herself in the centre of the front row in the stand next in importance to the one seating members of the Senate and distinguished foreign representatives. Before her lay the vast stretch of the sandy parade area with the background of cream stone military buildings, the only spot of colour so far in the swagged and crimson-carpeted dais where shortly Napoléon III would take his place. Yet it was not as brilliant in hue as the yellow silk flowers that she had made for her bonnet or the shawl in the same sharp colour, which Marie Worth had kindly loaned her. It would not be her fault if Pierre failed to see her, even if she was not able to spot him.

He did see her. As he rode in line with a number of his fellow officers amid the thunder of the vivid spectacle that had filled the whole arena with the might of France's military power in a moving carpet of scarlet and blue and green and gold, he could see her bright face in the midst of a collection of other visages that meant nothing to him. This time and on such an important state occasion there was nothing he could do to direct her attention towards him, his shining helmet newly emblazoned with the letter *N* surrounded by laurels and surmounted by the imperial crown, which now marked all cavalry and infantry alike in their service to the Emperor and to France.

Louise paid particular attention to the cuirassiers in the flashing steel breast- and backplates that gave them their name as line after line went riding by, but could not see Pierre. Yet she felt a certain reflected pride when it was the turn of his regiment to receive the imperial eagle, which Louis-Napoléon was handing out tirelessly to his loyal troops. Then a military band struck up "Partant pour la Syrie," which had been composed by Hortense Bonaparte, the Emperor's own mother, and spontaneously the spectators rose to their feet to join those at attention in honour of the Second Empire of France. The "Marseillaise," that song born of revolution, had been banned on pain of imprisonment in the new age of peace and prosperity that had dawned at last, and a thunderous cheer for the Emperor echoed over the Champ-de-Mars as the last notes of the new anthem faded away.

It was all over. Around Louise everyone moved away and gradually departed. Still she sat on until she was alone in the huge stand and soldiers in working overalls came to clear away the stamp of the cavalry and sweep up litter that had blown across the ground. She had no idea how long it took an officer to remove his helmet and sword, unbuckle the steel cuirass, and change into undress uniform, but she thought, allowing for the distance between the dismounting yard and private room somewhere in the vast spread of the barracks, that an hour should be plenty. If he had not appeared by then, she would go.

It took him half an hour to get out of the buildings and come striding across the Champ-de-Mars to the stand where she sat, neat and composed, holding her draw-string purse on her lap. She had not known that he would come. All she had known was that she hoped he would. He came to a halt as if again on parade, and saluted her smartly. Then, and only then, did he allow a grin to steal across his mouth.

"Thank God you waited," he said with intense satisfaction. "Otherwise how on earth should I have found you in all of Paris on this day of days?"

"Or I discover a means to thank you for the ticket to the parade, to say nothing of the beautiful rosebuds, Captain de Gand." She had noticed his promotion immediately in his insignia.

He was well pleased with his rise in rank. A good many honours and promotions had been handed out to coincide with the rise of another Bonaparte to imperial power, and it had been extremely gratifying to find he was listed. The compliment of her observance of his new status added to his pleasure in this reunion. He reached up a hand to take hers across the bunting-swagged balustrade, and gripped her fingers firmly as he walked level with her to the flight of three steps down, asking her at the same time whether she had enjoyed the parade, and she full of enthusiasm for the fine sight that had been presented. At the foot of the steps he offered her his arm.

"The rest of the day is ours, Mademoiselle Louise. There never was such a day as this one for celebrations and beginnings." His look was serious and eloquent despite the smile he was giving her, and his words struck deep, although she gave no sign of having absorbed them below her carapace of calm as she put her fingers into the crook of his elbow. Whatever was to be lay before her. She was confident and unafraid. He was welcome to the one small part of her heart that she had lost to him, but the remainder of it would stay closely guarded no matter what happened.

Thousands of the troops released from duties added the splendour of their uniforms to the colourful crowds that surged up and down the Champs-Elysées and the other boulevards, filled the cafés, watched the entertainers, and spent their money freely as if an emperor in the Tuileries was the guarantee of a permanently gold-filled purse for all. Louise was reminded of her first taste of luxury in the hot chocolate that Henri Berrichon had bought her when she found herself swept into an expensive café for some refreshment. The place was full as were all such establishments, high and low, that day, but miraculously, as soon as Pierre was sighted by the headwaiter, there appeared to be space after all.

"This way, Captain de Gand. I trust this table by the window will be to your satisfaction."

By the window! Louise caught her breath with excitement and peered out at the merry flow of humanity in the boulevard below. She felt no embarrassment in the opulent surroundings, and had the Worths to thank for that. She had dined with them and been to small gatherings at their modest apartment, and although their financial situation prevented lavish hospitality the occasions were always graciously conducted in a warm and welcoming atmosphere that put any guest at ease, and, without the Worths being aware of it, revealed their own mannerly upbringing as gentlefolk. Through taking notice of their behaviour and observing everything at their table she had learnt all the refinements of polite society. As Pierre asked her what she would like, she turned her gaze from the window.

"Hot chocolate with cream would be most pleasant."

He was mildly intrigued by her restrained request, having expected her to make the most of present opportunities. Whatever the hour he would not have been surprised if she had ordered some rich and extravagant delicacy. It was an old adage, based on a certain amount of truth, that a grisette could be won with a lobster salad, theatres, and a ride on a fairground switchback. He ordered coffee for himself and watched her contemplative enjoyment of the chocolate as they talked. She was unlike any other grisette he had ever known, neither cowed nor vulgarly emboldened by the flurry of waiters, taking her place at the table as if she came there every day, and completely lacking in the loudness that was an all too frequent ingredient in young women of her class. Her appearance pleased him greatly. Her dress was dark-brown wool with stitching that looked amazingly intricate, fitting the fullness of her breasts to a provocative perfection and enhancing the shape of her shoulders which, now that he came to think about it, were even more seductive than those of Eugénie de Montijo.

"Have you ever spoken to the Emperor?" she asked during the course of their conversation. She had told him about her background, how she had always wanted to be a seamstress, the good fortune she had had in meeting Monsieur Worth again on the day she had gone looking for work at Gagelin and Obigez's, and by a roundabout track had come back to comments on the day's parade.

He hesitated for a moment. "On occasion," he answered uncommittedly. "You may not know that the cuirassiers have always been amongst the most loyal of the Emperor's troops and have special favour with him. Now that we are forming part of the Imperial Guard at the Tuileries I don't doubt that seeing the Emperor will become a daily occurrence."

"Did you always want to go into the Army, just as I cherished my ambition from an early age?"

He leaned his arms on the table, looking across at her. "Yes, I did, which was lucky for me since I would have had little choice in the matter. There is a tradition of service with the Army in the de Gand family that I feel honoured to continue. As a boy I had whole regiments of tin soldiers and used to fight out the battles in which de Gands had taken part." He did not add that, like countless numbers of his fellow officers, he was impatient for experience in the field himself. It went against his intense personal pride that he did not have an Austerlitz or a Jena behind him. He had had a full share of bloody and terrible fighting in the restoration of law and order during the mob violence that had followed the flight of Louis-Philippe from France, but that was a different sphere altogether and had been abhorrent to him. "My home is in the countryside not far from Tours. That's where I grew up." His lips parted in that slow, white-toothed smile that women never failed to find attractive. "I was the youngest in a household of females. I have six sisters, all married now, and I believe my parents had begun to despair of ever begetting a soldier for France."

"La! You must have been spoilt!" she exclaimed on her soft laugh.

"So they say," he agreed amicably, his eyes crinkling.

Actually she was better informed about his background than he realized. She had gathered quite a few details from what was known about Madame de Gand at Gagelin and Obigez's, and although he had referred so lightly to his home, Louise knew it to be a château of grand dimensions commanding a great area of land. He had talked modestly of riding when he was home as if he had a choice of two horses at the most, but she could imagine the range of the stable at his disposal. She liked him for not trying to dazzle her with a metaphorical rope of pearls. Perhaps he had realised from the start that he could not win her that way.

When they left the café he managed to hail one of the fiacres that were in great demand, and they rode about the city seeing everything that was taking place and listening to the bands. Soon the early dusk brought the few recently installed gas-lamps into yellowish chains of light and, if anything, the crowds seemed to increase along the boulevards. He had taken her hand into his as soon as the carriage had begun to move, but without fuss she had withdrawn it after a few moments, and the classic advances he had planned were neatly nipped in the bud. He decided that since the evening ahead seemed unlikely to bring profitable advancement in the direction in which he wished to propel her, he would dismiss a candlelit supper for two and further their relationship in surroundings more suited to the mood of the fête-day. He retained the fiacre to drive them to the liveliest guinguette he knew, the Grande-Chaumière on the Boulevard du Montparnasse, a favourite haunt of his cadet days.

It was hot and crowded inside, with waiters in large white aprons darting hither and thither with trays held high over one shoulder, a band playing loudly for the dancing and competing against the clatter of knives and forks, the noisy laughter, and endless din of conversation. This time some francs changed hands between Pierre and the headwaiter, and they were guided through to an alcove where the cloth was whipped from the table and a clean one shaken from its crackling folds and spread across it. The atmosphere of the place was charged with good humour and jollity. Outside, the gardens were full of people braving the cold night air under Chinese lanterns as they danced riotously to a second band. White-hot braziers gave off plenty of heat by the seats encircling the trees, but since it was customary in such places for a man to dance wearing his hat and a woman her bonnet and shawl, the dancers appeared to be generating their own heat, their faces flushed as they whirled around in the popular polka that had first been danced in Paris on that very spot over a decade ago.

"Would you like to dance?" Pierre asked after wine had been brought and their order given.

Louise's eyes were sparkling in her enjoyment of everything. "Yes, I would," she replied happily. "Let's dance outside."

Under the lanterns she fastened the ends of her borrowed shawl securely to make sure it did not go flying off, and then he put his hand on the back of her waist and took her fingers into his. He looked down into her face as he drew her close to him, the brown cloth of her dress sliding a little over the stiffness of her stays, her breasts firm against his chest, the whole of her an invitation to his senses that he scarcely knew how to resist.

"The music," she prompted gaily, tilting her head to one side. "It's another polka."

They joined the swirling throng, feet flashing, her petticoats tossing, and it was the first of the many times they danced that night, taking to the floor between the courses of their meal, and then dancing again afterwards. They had come to a breathless halt at the final chord of a gallop when suddenly the sky was filled with bright-pink stars bathing the scene around them in a rosy glow that changed to a vivid green as one firework began to follow another in a splendid end to the fête-day. Those still dining poured out to watch, some men with napkins tucked under their chins, and roars of approbation greeted each new burst of colour against the darkness. Pierre put his arm around Louise as they watched, and felt her lean a little against him, but he could tell it had been done without thought, her rapt attention lost in the fireworks.

When they arrived at the tall house in the narrow street where she and Catherine lived on the third floor, she stopped in the hallway to part from him there.

"Never have I known such a fête-day," she declared out of her own serene contentment, resting her back in blissful weariness against the wall.

"Nor I." He propped his weight on a hand set on the wall beside her. They had already arranged to meet the following Saturday, which was the one day of the working week when Gagelin and Obigez's closed at five instead of eight o'clock. "I'll get tickets for the Conservatoire, if you would like that." He had earlier discovered that she enjoyed music, and in any case he would not suggest the theatre to her this first time, the seduction adage now distasteful to him in connection with her. There had been lobster salad on the menu at the Grande-Chaumière, and perhaps a trifle over-sensitively he had avoided any suggestion of it and, which was probably more important and not in any way coincidental, so had she.

"I should like to go to a concert very much." She smiled in anticipation. "Now I must bid you good night."

She found her way barred by the arm he stretched out to clasp the coiled end of the ancient, rusty balustrade. Without looking at him she tautened, her swan-like throat seeming to stretch a little, and under her lowered lashes her gaze ran along from the back of his hand, up his sleeve, to rise and meet his eyes, her own wary and alert, almost gold in the faint half-light that came from a single lamp in the narrow hallway.

"Not yet," he implored softly. "Not quite yet."

He leaned forward and kissed her very lightly, a smile in his eyes and on his lips. Almost in the same instant he caught her about the waist, hauling her in to him and there was no more lightness in his kissing, the mobile pressure of his mouth on hers hard and ardent. Her own arms wrapped themselves about his shoulders. He lifted his lips away once to look into her face, their eyes dwelling in each other's, and then her head dropped back as he retook her mouth in rapturous possession, and she felt her whole being yearn to him in a mind-spinning forgetfulness of all else. It was as if both of them had known from the hour he had come across the Champ-de-Mars to where she had waited for him that they had merely been passing time until this moment.

She drew away from him, breathless, sparkling, her eyes very bright. He was reluctant to let her go, regretfully aware of having no choice, and she paused on the lowest stair to kiss him as lightly and fleetingly as he had first kissed her. "Good night, Pierre. Good night."

His voice followed her up the flight, echoing hollowly in the stairwell. "Good night, *chérie*."

In her room she whirled exultantly around and around, her arms upflung, until she became dizzy and threw herself backwards onto the bed, merrily kicking off her shoes. He was the man for her and she the woman for him. Not on his terms, only on hers. Not when he wished to have her, only when she would be willing. No brief and shadowed *affaire*, only the exchange of true and lasting love. The old adage of all or nothing should be duly applied, or else he could go. Yes, let him go! Let him go! She laughed quietly, confident she would emerge unscathed anytime she wished it. Then her expression softened, gentleness in the slight parting of her moist lips. She would spin the web until he was enmeshed. A web of her own love. Surrender meant more to her than the giving of her body when the time came. It would mean the subjection of her will to another's. The prospect frightened her. She could not give herself easily, no matter how deeply her feelings ran. Pierre would have to show her first that he loved her above all others and that her freedom of spirit would never be shackled by his errant whims and thus destroyed.

She sat up abruptly and swung her stockinged feet to the floor. With a shiver, she rubbed her arms as if chilled. Subdued, she made herself ready for bed and slid down between the sheets. Shortly afterwards Catherine came home, her cheeks rosy with excitement and wine. She was full of the good time she had had as she unlaced her scarlet boots and wriggled her aching toes. She had danced nearly the whole evening, finally tripping all around the Place de la Concorde with arms linked with thirty others or more. Then she realised that Louise, deep in the pillow, had not said much. "How did you enjoy yourself with your soldier-boy?"

Louise had already decided to guard against such an enquiry, to give no hint of the true wonder of the day, because she remembered only too well Catherine's jealousy where Worth had been the object of her unrequited love. How could she be sure that Catherine would not react in the same way again if there was any sign given of a deeper relationship developing with Pierre de Gand? Better to keep matters on a superficial level. Later she could reconsider what to do.

"The parade was a sight I'll never forget." She made much of it and little of the rest that had happened. Catherine, yawning, was left supposing that the cuirassier meant no more to Louise than the other young men with whom she had been on outings from time to time. The next morning they both left the house at the same early hour to go to their respective places of work. As far as Catherine was concerned, the previous day had become just a pleasant memory.

Not able to talk to Catherine, Louise turned to Marie as a confidante. A firm friendship had grown up between them, although in character they were entirely different. Marie recognised in Louise the same driving ambition that spurred her own husband, and to both she was content to be staunch and encouraging in a secondary role, wanting only to help where she could.

Marie tried not to have misgivings about Louise and her officer. It was difficult to tell whether Louise realised that his distinguished origins and connections must bar any future for them. It was noticeable to Marie when the girl chatted happily about her evenings with him that each time, apart from the Conservatoire where the seats had been in a secluded gallery, he had taken her to places of entertainment where he would never have escorted a young woman of his own class. The venues were respectable enough, popular centres of wining and dining and dancing, much patronised by officers and others of good standing, but the distinction remained. No aristocratic female would be taken to them.

Louise was going to the theatre with him for the first time when Marie was called upon to see an alteration that Louise had made to her russet silk dress, which still had a place in her modest wardrobe. Louise had cut the neckline into a low décolletage, and sought Marie's aid in the final fastening on of the roses that had been made out of the piece of material discarded. It took place in one of the fitting-rooms after the shop was shut, Marie pinning the roses for first effect.

"I hope you enjoy the play." She had some doubt and it echoed in her tone. It was the subject matter and not the presentation that gave rise to her concern. She stood back to view Louise's full-length reflection in the looking-glass. "There! What do you think of that?"

Worth had appeared in the doorway. He was ready to go home and was looking for Marie. "What's this? Which play?" He did not wait for a reply. Shaking his head, he stepped forward and swivelled Louise abruptly about to face him. "Not *three* flowers on the décolletage in this case. Only one. That's enough for emphasis." Oblivious to the amused glances of supplication to a superior authority being exchanged between his wife and Louise, he unpinned two of the roses and held them trailing downwards against her skirt. "That's where they must be. As if they did not all dare to rival the splendour of your shoulders and bosom."

Louise had long become used to his extravagant comments, which made so many women preen and blush and simper. Yet she knew that nothing was said without truth. He would never praise falsely.

"Louise is going to see the play that we saw a while ago," Marie informed her husband, handing him the needle and thread that Louise had put ready and for which he had snapped his fingers, frowning over the adjustment of the top rose. *"La Dame aux Camélias."*

"It's still playing to packed houses, I believe," he muttered out of his concentration centred on the task in hand, nothing ever undertaken lightly or without the utmost care.

"I saw the real Marie Duplessis of the Camellias when I was a child," Louise reminisced, her thoughts far away in the Sundays of her childhood. "A pale, dark-haired lady going past in her carriage. I didn't realise then how young she was, only two or three years older than I am now."

Worth's fingers brushing against her skin as he stitched the rose into place no longer held the effect that once they had had when he had reached out to touch the *collerette* of her dress. She was barely aware of them as she stood patiently as women always did when he was putting a final masterly touch to a garment. She hoped Pierre would think it was a new dress since she had not worn it for him before.

"That's done." Worth handed back the needle to Marie, and Louise thanked him. As he made to leave he gave her a long look. "The play is a sad one. Most of the women in the audience weep, and my dear wife was no exception. So go prepared, Louise."

She did not weep. Splendid though the acting was in the classic theme of woman's sacrifice for love, Louise found it impossible to reconcile the golden-haired, bosomy actress to the frail beauty that she remembered. Moreoever, she understood that Worth had wanted her to draw a comparison between the courtesan barred by class and status from marrying the man she loved and her own relationship with Pierre. But she was no Marie Duplessis doomed to go down under pressure from outside influences. All her life she had had to fight for everything she had attained, and was no stranger to opposition. She appreciated the concern of her dear friends the Worths, but her star was in the ascendant and she was resolved that it should not fall.

Pierre had never been more attentive than that evening. Louise felt that he looked more at her than at the stage, and so probably the significance of the social incompatibility of the two main characters in the play in relation to themselves went unnoticed by him. He certainly did not appear to have been aware of it at supper afterwards, although he made the comment that the acting had been praiseworthy. He also had other matters on his mind.

"During the next few weeks it may be difficult for me to see you as often as I would wish. It seems almost certain from all I've been hearing at the Tuileries today that an official announcement of the betrothal of the Emperor to Mademoiselle de Montijo will be given out any moment now. From dawn extra guards are to be in force, and the duties of officers doubled and trebled in some cases. It is at such times that assassins attempt their cowardly plots in order to bring more notice to their cause."

She had felt a deep pang at being deprived of his company, although she never let the power to govern any situation between them slip away from her. If he suspected the glorious explosion of mind and heart that was hers every time he held her in his arms, he would gain an advantage over her that would be difficult to combat.

Always now when he took her home he would see her to her door, although she had never asked him in. On this night when she inserted the key in the lock, he put his hand over hers.

"Let me see where you live, Louise. It plagues me not to be able to picture you in your home surroundings when you are away from me."

She had no choice but to let him across the threshold. She slipped off her shawl and lit a lamp, the pearly light filling the opaque globe and rising up over her face as she adjusted the wick. He looked about him with a lively interest, noticing the simple furnishings, the neatness. Then he looked again at her standing by the lamp, her throat and shoulders and the swell of her breasts holding an aura in the pale glow. Never had he desired any woman more than he desired her.

"Louise—"

Like an echo another voice called sleepily from beyond the door leading off the room. "Louise? Is that you?"

Louise moved across to open the door by a narrow gap and peep through. "Yes, it is. Good night, Catherine. I'll tell you all about the play in the morning." She closed the door again quietly and saw that there was annoyance in Pierre's expression. She supposed he had believed that they were alone. "Catherine is mother and sister and guardian to me," she emphasised. "She always likes to know that I'm safely home."

"Don't you find that oppressive from someone who, with it all, is not of your kin?"

"Sometimes," she admitted, "but I owe everything to her. If she had not taken me into her safekeeping as I described to you, my life would not be as it is today." A wry smile compressed her lips. "Not that I shouldn't have survived. Some of my earliest memories are of fighting tooth and nail for a crust of bread. Does that surprise you?"

"It saddens me to think you should have known such hardship." He took her face between his palms, his fingers sliding into the soft luxuriance of her hair. "I would like to make up to you for all the deprivation of the past. To give you everything you have always wanted. To make you happier than you ever imagined possible."

She jerked from his grasp, fiercely defensive, able to tell what would be forthcoming if she did not halt the words. Swiftly she pressed the fingertips of both hands against his lips, shaking her head, her eyes angry. "No more. Say no more. Never speak of making such amends to me!"

She did not blame him for trying to proposition her, realising that sooner or later by his very nature and the situation between them he would attempt it, but she felt if she actually heard him offer the equivalent to the proverbial silk petticoat or the rope of pearls, some part of her would die in terrible despair. She could never be another Catherine, never be content to wait for whatever time a man could spare her out of his life, no matter how much she loved, and if he left her now for reason of what she had said, he would have to go. Her pride would never let her call him back.

He did not leave. Although he was greatly put out by the rebuff, he was worldly enough not to show it. Every grisette had her price; he had only to bide his time and he would discover it. In the meantime he would continue to move towards his goal by persuasions that would be delectable to her and provide no small pleasure to himself. He drew her fingertips away and lowered his head to kiss the length of her throat and the curve of her shoulders and every enticing part of her that was exposed. She quivered sensuously under the passage of his lips, able to hear the clangour of her own heart, and when his lips found its wild beating he pressed deeper into the contour of her breast. Her arms, as if of their own volition, lifted and she held his head to her. When at last his mouth took hers she kissed him with a loving passion that he could tell was taking all her power to restrain. Only the presence of another person in the neighbouring room with the danger of intrusion stayed him from further amorous advancement.

As he went down the dark stairway and made his way out of the house into the street he decided on the course of action he should take. He had given thought before to getting a place of his own in Paris where he could spend time away from duty, and now he would see about obtaining one without delay. Above all he needed somewhere to be alone with Louise. He thought he knew her price now. It was love. Her kiss had given that away. The crazy thing was that she had already won that from him. He had never been more in love, which was why he had treated her from the start with a consideration that he would never normally have shown to a girl of her station in life. Louise, Louise. Her very name made him crave her with every nerve and fibre of his being. Louise. Whom he loved.

The next day, as Pierre had assumed from the alerting of the Palace Guard, Louis-Napoléon announced his forthcoming marriage to Eugénie de Montijo, and startled everyone with the information that the civil ceremony would take place a week later, and the religious ceremony with full pomp the day after. Many thought such haste unseemly in an imperial bridegroom, but others who knew him were aware that his passion for the lady concerned was almost at breaking point.

For those who had to organise the procession and refurbish the state coaches, many yet to have the imperial arms gilded upon the doors, seven days was a perilously short span of time in which to get everything completed, and forces of saddlers and upholsterers and embroiderers and other craftsmen were called in. For the dressmakers and the suppliers of fine fabrics the announcement meant a rush of business even greater than anyone had anticipated. Maison Gagelin was overwhelmed with customers, and Worth took orders solidly, a customer barely measured before the fabric of her choice for her selected design was in the hands of the cutters. It was the impetus needed to make Worth's employers capitulate to his insistence that the dressmaking department should be hugely expanded, and in the meantime he and Marie, with Louise and the rest of the sewing team, worked around the clock to get the orders completed. Throughout Paris the same hectic speed was maintained in every workroom. Louise, in a rare moment of liberty, went to see the dresses made for Mademoiselle de Montijo's trousseau, that had been set up for public display almost as the last thread was snipped from the stitches. Her keen eye took in every detail of the forty-four gowns created by Mesdames Palmyre and Vignon, and magnificent though they were, from the rose moiré fringed with lace to the feather-trimmed emerald taffeta, she did not see one to eclipse anything that Worth had designed.

The civil marriage was a private affair, but the religious ceremony at the Cathedral of Notre-Dame, being held on a Sunday, brought vast crowds to pack themselves behind the hedge of blue-coated infantrymen that lined the route from the Tuileries. There was strong sunshine unseasonable to the close of January, and the sky a bright gentian blue above the city that was ashimmer with banners and streamers. Louise and Catherine had secured a good viewing place, and it was Pierre whom Louise wanted to see even more than the new Empress. He had written to her, although, as he had feared, there had been no chance to meet.

Yet luck was with her that day. As the cavalry of the Imperial Guard clattered past in a jingling of harness, she spotted him riding alone beside a fellow officer of the same rank. He faced rigidly ahead, the sunshine flashing on the chin scales that fastened the fine helmet, but his eyes slid to the right and to the left as he looked for her, knowing she would be somewhere in the vicinity. She waved frantically and stood on tiptoe, but he failed to see her as he rode by, controlling his caracoling horse made nervous by the noise of the crowd.

Soon afterwards came the red-and-gold-glass coach in which the Emperor and the Empress sat side by side acknowledging the crescendoes of cheering and the endless shouts of *"Vive l'Empereur! Vive l'Impératrice!"* Louise thought how nervous and strained the beautiful woman looked, her face white as her velvet gown beneath its misty covering of dark-violet lace. In the magnificent red-gold hair the diamond coronet, which had once adorned the Empress Joséphine, flashed multi-coloured fire that seared the gaze of onlookers and made it impossible to discern the expression in the long-lashed eyes. But already she was loved. The path she intended to tread had revealed itself in her donation of Paris's own wedding gift to the founding of a home for young children and a hospital for the incurable. Tales of her kindnesses were legion. She had been the first to give aid to a workman who fell from a scaffold. Believing herself to be unnoticed she had once given her own cloak to a beggar woman, and was more than generous to the poor. Eugénie was being taken to the heart of France. No emperor ever had a more worthy bride.

When dawn touched the silken drapes of the windows of the bridal chamber at the country palace of St.-Cloud where they had travelled from Paris incognito the previous evening, Eugénie lay beside her sleeping husband and gazed unseeingly at the swagged canopy overhead. If she had not loved him, and it had not been her duty to bear an heir, she would have risen from this bed, covered her nakedness, and gone away to another part of the house, never to share a marital bed again. She was shocked, dismayed, and faintly disgusted that a princely nobleman should be no less demanding than a humble peasant in such matters. Yet her love was strong enough to rise above the distasteful side of marriage, and her devotion to him was no less than before. On a spiritual level she would always be close to him.

He was not quite asleep. Haunting him was a dull disappointment. Where was the fire and passion he had anticipated in the lovely creature whose physical charms had stunned him with their perfection? Where the Andalusian sensuality he had been certain to arouse? Never could any man have been more tender and patient and ardent than he had been. Out of his intense love his arm tightened involuntarily about her, and sadly he felt her resign herself submissively to his embrace.

10

Marie had known for some time that she was expecting a baby, and her husband's cup of happiness was overflowing. Throughout a difficult pregnancy she managed to maintain her service and efficiency in the shop, keeping at her post with no reduction in her hours allowed by her employers, in spite of Worth's request on the matter, until she reached a state of collapse and was advised by her doctor to rest for the remainder of her time. Messieurs Gagelin and Obigez, who seemed to have expected her to go on serving at her counter like an automaton until the last minute, reluctantly agreed to a leave of absence prior to the event while stipulating that she must return to work afterwards with the least possible delay.

The Worths' firstborn proved to be a fine boy, and they rejoiced in their blessing, naming him Gaston. Marie, conscientious to a degree, returned to the shop as soon as she could, although it was hard for her to leave her baby to another's care for the entire span of every working day. She thought how wonderful it would be to live close at hand, but nothing was available to suit the modest income that she and her husband earned between them.

It took Pierre longer than he had expected to find the house of his choice, which had to be within reasonable distance of the Tuileries and of a size suited to a bachelor with military commitments that could necessitate the premises being closed up for periods at a time. When he did find a small residence of some elegance it turned out to be on one of the lists for street demolition by Baron Haussmann, who had been commissioned by the Emperor to create a Paris that was to be to all other cities what the Empress was in surpassing beauty to all womankind. What Napoleon I had started his imperial successor had decided to finish, but on a scale beyond anything that had been previously visualised.

It had become customary for the Emperor and Empress to include the officer in charge of the Guard in their dinner parties, but it was not only on these occasions that Pierre heard the grandiose plans discussed, because his godfather would occasionally invite him to spend an hour or two in conversation over a drink and a cigar, or to join him for luncheon with two or three other gentlemen.

"I admit to it being one of two long-held dreams of mine," the Emperor confided on one occasion when he and Pierre were alone. "The other is to free Italy from its bondage. In the days when my adored mother was hounded from France with my brother and myself, the Italian revolutionaries showed us a comradeship and a purpose that I have never forgotten, but that dream must remain a dream for the time being and perhaps forever, who knows? It is the rebuilding of Paris that concerns me now. It was reading of Voltaire's demands for it many years ago that first implanted the idea in my mind that when I came into my own it should be one of the first actions to take. Moreover, it will supply work for hundreds of thousands of men, and eliminate one of the main causes of previous unrest." His eyes shone with enthusiasm through the smoke rising lazily from his cigarette. "Down will come the ugly and dilapidated property where dens of trouble-makers have festered, and up will go houses of grace and dignity to face boulevards with carriageways wide enough for whole battalions to manoeuvre if need be. Along the avenues will be strategically placed military barracks to ensure law and order. I tell you that the day of the barricades will be gone forever. There'll be no more insurrection in the capital of capitals, where shade trees are to be planted as copiously as flowers. My Empire stands for peace, and never will the world have seen such a city as shall come in this new and golden time on which we have embarked."

All splendid talk, but to an officer seeking to find accommodation with some haste in which to cohabit with the girl he loved, it was more than irritating to see row after row of quite suitable property go down in rubble as boulevards were widened to breathtaking dimensions, and avenues sliced through the city like wire through cheese. Louise had done nothing to show she had changed her mind since she had deliberately silenced the proposition he had been on the point of making to her the night he was in her home for the first time, but he was not discouraged. He had made her more than aware of his feelings for her, and although he had not yet mentioned love in so many words, it was simply because he was awaiting the right moment in which to win her completely. He would not risk a second false move. The prize was too great to lose. In the meantime she was his to escort constantly, and together they dined and danced, attended places of entertainment, took refreshment at small tables set out under awnings at the *cafés chantants* on the Champs-Elysées, sometimes joining in the singing, sometimes just talking as they held hands. Before the colder weather set in again they took drives in the soft, autumnal evenings, often through the Bois de Boulogne, which the Emperor had given to the city of Paris to be turned into a park covering its vast acreage. Pierre sometimes thought that he would never again recall the summer of '53 without associating it with Louise's intense happiness, which emanated from her like her own personal bouquet. He did not doubt that she was falling deeper and deeper in love with him as he was with her, and the anticipation of conquest when she was caught beyond recall spiced erotically his every outing with her.

It was by sheer chance that he happened to hear of an apartment in a building being retained for its architectural value, and upon inspection it proved to have good-sized rooms and was altogether suitable. Obtaining craftsmen of some standard to do the necessary redecorating and refurbishing was difficult, all being in full employment under the direction of Baron Haussmann, but thousands of others were flocking in from the provinces to take advantage of the labor demand, and several of these were secured to undertake his work before embarking on municipal tasks. When all was near completion he sent for some fine pieces of his own from the château to complete the furnishings, and eagerly awaited their delivery. He had told Louise nothing about his acquisition, but since the house where she was living was in a street listed for demolition, it was more than providential that he would have a place for her when the time came.

Life had rarely been more agreeable. His hours of duty at the Tuileries were anything but tedious, and often extremely pleasant. The Empress had thought it fitting that her husband's godson should benefit from certain privileges, and one of them was to be her personal escort, riding beside her carriage when she took her regular afternoon drives. Like the Emperor, she believed in being seen by the people, who never failed to respond to her bewitching smile with cheers and applause and holding up of babies to see the fairest woman in the land drive by. She adored children, always giving them special acknowledgement, and frequently visited the home for little ones that she had founded. Pierre knew these visits must be particularly poignant for her since the miscarriage she had suffered in the early months of her marriage. Often there were tears in her eyes when she returned to the carriage. Whether she ever shed tears over her husband's unfaithfulness to her was not known, but they had been married only a short while when it became common knoweldge in court circles that he had returned to his insatiable indulgences with the opposite sex.

Yet in spite of an embitterment that at times manifested itself in her attitude, she and the Emperor were in complete harmony over many points and in many ways ideally suited to each other. She took a keen interest in political matters, which the two of them discussed at the same highly intellectual level, and he consulted her frequently on governmental problems that arose. They both held to the belief that the imperial court should bring forth in a great renaissance all that belonged to France's glory in the past, and by its very scintillation remove doubts about its solidarity to the rest of the world. As a result, the state balls at the Tuileries to which thousands were invited, as well as the banquets and receptions and other splendid functions that were held on a grand scale, were giving rise to the imperial court being spoken of as the most brilliant in Europe, set to out-glitter even that of St. Petersburg. Nowhere else was there an emperor devoted so wholeheartedly to the promotion of all that was elegant, or an empress whose presence at any gathering delighted all who looked upon her, her appearance always supreme whether in the elaborate crinolines she wore with such grace, or in the simple dresses she chose for informal wear. Moreover, as if she had begun to revel in the feminine perfection of looks with which she had been blessed, she now surrounded herself constantly with lovely women, each one a complement to her own beauty as well as to each other's, and she was never happier than when in their company. To see her approach in the midst of them was a sight that many found beyond description, although a Greek diplomat declared they looked like goddesses descending from Mount Olympus, and the billowing of their huge skirts the tinted clouds that bore them.

Some of Pierre's fellow officers had begun to place wagers on who among them could take to any Tuileries function a partner pretty enough to outshine any one of the Empress's ladies. Since the rules laid down applied only to the presentation of new faces, great competition arose, and many a sister or the best-looking of her friends was invited up from the country to Paris under chaperonage to attend an imperial occasion on a young officer's arm. The judging committee consisted of half a dozen married officers, who could only take their wives to such gatherings, and were therefore to be relied upon to adjudicate with an unbiased eye. The stakes sometimes accumulated to many thousands of francs when function after function went by without a winner until someone was lucky enough to be awarded the jackpot, allowing the proceedings to start all over again.

Pierre began to think of taking Louise as his partner and making a try for the stakes. Many of those who attended the enormous state balls were of little consequence in society, being invited through the Emperor's aim to extend the aura of his glittering court far and wide, and Pierre knew it would be easy enough to get her name on one of the guest lists. The more he toyed with the idea, the more determined he was that it should come about. The only problem was how to go about giving her the dress she would need for the occasion. A direct gift was out of the question. He had glimpsed her fierce independence more than once, and did not doubt that such an extravagant donation on his part would be refused. In the end he overcame the difficulty by enlisting the aid of a woman whose favours were always at his disposal. She was about the same height and build as Louise, and after they had passed an hour or two between her silken sheets he further elaborated the plan he had outlined to her upon his arrival.

"But I've never been to Gagelin's for a dress," she pouted

moistly from the depths of her lace-trimmed pillow. "I always patronize Palmyre or Camille."

He was leaning over her, propped on his elbows, his muscular body ribbed by the slatted light that came through the closed shutters. "What does it matter?" he cajoled. "You're not going to wear it anyway. Say you will do what I ask, Elyanne."

She looked at him through her curling lashes. "Have I not always done everything you have wanted of me, you wicked man?" Her perfumed arms slid about him like pale snakes and delayed his departure a while longer.

Worth recognised Elyanne Valmont as a courtesan as soon as she came into the dressmaking department. She was a slender, sharp-faced woman in her twenties, with hair dyed to the reddish gold that the Empress had made so fashionable with her own natural locks. The morals of the customers of Maison Gagelin and Obigez were not his concern, but nevertheless he believed it boded ill for many marriages that such women, who had previously kept discreetly in the background, had begun to emerge flamboyantly in the new and extravagant mood that was taking possession of Paris on its wave of prosperity. They were creating a half-world of their own on the fringe of society that was becoming disturbingly obtrusive and exuberant in its own dubious right.

Elyanne was more impressed by Worth and his surroundings than she cared to show. Although she had heard that Maison Gagelin had extended the dressmaking department lavishly she had not expected to find salons larger than the premises of the other dressmakers she had patronised. Even the couturières who boasted of the Empress's patronage did not have so much space at their disposal. She took the seat she was offered and sat back to watch Madame Worth display a range of some of the most beautiful dresses she had ever seen. She found it almost impossible to make a choice, even for someone else, and at last decided upon one with a low-cut silk bodice that extended into a many-pointed, tasselled peplum spreading out over a flowing tulle skirt in a lighter shade spangled with gold.

"I'll have it in corn-yellow silk with the tulle in a paler shade." It was a colour she would not normally wear herself, but Pierre had told her that Louise had raven-black hair and sometimes wore a yellow silk shawl that suited her admirably.

"Allow me to suggest jade for your colouring, madame,

with the skirt floating in layers of blues and greens shot with silver and pale as mist."

She almost swooned at the image Worth had conjured up. How such a dress would suit her! But she was not here to choose for herself. She shook her head firmly, and then deftly countered all his persuasion that almost any other colour would suit her better than gold. Inwardly she marvelled at the skill of his compliments designed to sway her. Knowing the male sex as well as she did, she could tell he was a man used to felling opposition and getting his own way. She found it interesting to hold a momentary upper hand over this attractive man of twenty-seven or -eight, who had gone a trifle pink with annoyance about his handsome ears at what he took to be her stubbornness. At any other time she would not have been able to resist him, and made her own private judgement that he would be a commendable lover. Dispassionately she watched him reach boiling point.

"Do you *want* to look like a field of barley in the setting sun, madame?" he expostulated, throwing his arms wide in a lifting of the shoulders that was entirely French for all that his accent proclaimed him an Englishman.

She met his gaze coolly. "One of my favourite sights, Monsieur Worth. You have completely decided me."

He was quite furious, his mouth compressed tightly, and every gesture crisp with controlled temper as he showed her into a fitting-room. There was no doubt in her mind that had the premises been his he would have ordered her out and refused to make anything for her. A few moments later she guessed immediately from the description Pierre had given her that the striking-looking girl with the quick, precise movements and vivacious step who came to measure her was Louise Vernet. She checked to make sure.

"Have you worked here long?" she asked as an opening gambit when the tape measure was run around her waist. Then—"Do you do all the fitting? Oh, under Monsieur Worth's direction. What is your name?"

Elyanne did battle with Worth at every fitting. It was easy, since she looked positively plain to her own eyes in the colour that drained from her skin and hair, and it always irritated her not to look her best. She found fault with everything, but when the dress was completed there was nothing to complain about except the colour, which she put to good use as planned.

"You were right, Monsieur Worth," she submitted tearfully. "The gold is quite wrong for me. I *do* look like a field of barley." In the looking-glass she saw his face grow taut, and Louise, who was standing patiently in the background, looked concerned. Did they imagine that she would refuse to pay for it? All the better! "Nothing would induce me to appear beyond this fitting-room in it."

He cleared his throat. "Madame—"

She interrupted him, dabbing with a dainty handkerchief at the tears that long experience had enabled her to conjure up at will. "I know, I know. You told me and I wouldn't listen. Well, I intend to settle the bill at once for my mistake, and then we shall start all over again." She smiled at him in the coquettish ploy of sunshine through the rain, having looked forward to this moment all along since Pierre had promised her a dress for herself for her time and trouble. Any thought she had had of going anywhere else for it had long since gone. "This time you shall advise me on everything." It amused her to see that Worth looked positively triumphant at her apparent capitulation.

When he had left the fitting-room Elyanne was helped out of the dress by Louise, who said it would be packed and delivered that day.

"No!" Elyanne threw up her hands and shook her head wildly. "I never, never want to see the wretched garment again. It will be a reminder in my wardrobe of a foolish mistake." Although the dress was lying across Louise's arms she half picked it up and flung it against her. "You can have it! Take it! A gift for your endless patience throughout those tiresome fittings."

Louise had gone white to the lips. "Madame! I couldn't accept it."

"Indeed you shall. Summon Monsieur Worth. I insist that you have it."

The matter was soon settled. Louise was in a daze for the rest of the day. Every time she had a spare second she peeped into the room where sold dresses were hung to await packing. Worth had promised that it should have whatever alterations were necessary, it being against his pride and principles that any garment of his creation should not fit the wearer to perfection. She was resolved to appear in it at the next outing of any style to which Pierre invited her. So often she had wished for a dress more in the mode than the russet silk to match the toilettes of other women present.

How Pierre had opened Paris up to her over the past months! She had seen a side of the city that she had only ever glimpsed from the shadows before. At times she dined at restaurants or drank an apéritif at cafés where once she had begged for food at the doors or salvaged from the gutter a roll that had fallen from an outside table. There were still beggars and many poor people, but few went hungry any more with such an abundance of work available, and the increasing extravagances of the rich promoted employment in every kind of luxury trade and craft. Fashion was on the crest of the wave of this prosperity, and the dresses she fitted had crinoline skirts spreading wider and wider over pads and frames and petticoats so stiffened by horsehair that they could stand alone. Her own new dress was designed to be worn over such a petticoat which, like all those Worth had made for his dresses, was both lined and covered with a satin to match the top layers.

She could hardly wait to show her acquisition to Catherine, with whom she still shared wholeheartedly all mutual pleasures and sorrows, with the one marked exception of her own private feelings for Pierre. It was hard not to give herself away with one who knew her so well, especially when at times there was such joy in her that she felt she could hardly speak without singing or walk without dancing. Fortunately Catherine put it down to her having the kind of work she truly enjoyed with the Worths, of whom she was so fond, but when she would have confided that love had come to her at last, Catherine again fell victim to amorous disappointment with all its attendant depression. Apart from any other repercussions, Louise felt it would have been cruel to rub salt into such a wound, and she continued to keep up the pretence that Pierre was no more to her than agreeable company. At Madame Camille's the seamstresses were kept working longer and longer hours in the present crescendoes of work, and Catherine welcomed the chance of slaving with her needle until she was too exhausted either to think or to lie awake weeping. For Louise herself there was only one small cloud on the horizon. The newspapers were full of Turkey's declaration of war on Russia over a religious bone of contention and Pierre held to the general belief that it might not be long before France was drawn into the conflict in support of Turkey if the hostilities were not soon settled. In a Paris so carefree and lavish in the pursuit of pleasure it seemed impossible that war could overtake its Imperial Guard, and she tried to put the matter from her mind with the fervent hope that those far-away, foreign countries would soon sign a peace treaty. The days flashed by as she worked hard and tirelessly fitting the dresses ordered endlessly for state balls and other great social events, and she had no idea as she pinned and adjusted Worth's creations on other women how near she had come to wearing her own Worth dress to the Tuileries. But all Pierre's well-laid plans in that direction were brought to naught on the day he was sent for by his godfather.

He found the Emperor reading state papers, and at first he wondered if he was to hear about a possible military posting in a general alert in the present touchy international situation. For himself, he was spoiling for battle. Much as he enjoyed Paris and all that went with it, his whole training had geared him for war with the enemies of France, and he had no wish to grow soft in a handsome and unbloodied uniform. But the matter that the Emperor wished to discuss proved to be as far removed from war as it could be. Being on duty, Pierre stood in front of the desk at attention.

"At ease, my boy," his godfather said, smiling benignly. "No need to stand on ceremony today. Sit down in that chair where I can look at you without having to crane my neck. That's better." Louis-Napoléon sat back in his chair and with the habit he had developed whenever he talked he twirled one end of his waxed moustache, which he had recently grown to exaggerated proportions. "Now you will remember my goddaughter, the wholly delightful Stéphanie Casile, I know." His eyes twinkled. "From what reached my ears at the time, it appeared that the two of you became remarkably well acquainted during that sojourn last year at Fontainebleau. You far exceeded propriety in the passion of your farewell to her."

Pierre frowned uncomfortably. He could not reveal the truth of Stéphanie's behaviour. "I should have restrained the incident," he admitted.

"No doubt you should have, but it did not displease me to hear of such budding affection between two young people in whom I take a truly paternal interest. Well, now Stéphanie is in Paris." The Emperor raised his eyebrows high to reflect the pleased surprise he imagined he had imparted with such news. "She arrived four weeks ago, and has been staying with the Duchess of Bassano, who has been preparing her for life at court. The Empress is quite taken with my goddaughter and has decided to appoint her to be in personal attendance."

"An honour indeed," Pierre murmured. The duchess was one of the loveliest companions in the Empress's entourage, well able to instruct the newcomer. It seemed that in the absorbing of Stéphanie into the élite circle, a little gosling was to appear among the swans.

"The duchess is bringing Stéphanie to the next state ball, and I want you to meet the girl upon her arrival at the palace and partner her for the evening. Now that's not an arduous task, is it?"

"No, Sire," he replied stiffly. Thank God he had not already invited Louise! Well, his wager would be lost again, and he had set a large amount this time on his certainty of winning with her. He rose smartly to his feet as his godfather got up to come around the desk. A fatherly hand was clapped on Pierre's shoulder.

"I am going to rely on you to see that Stéphanie is not lonely or unprotected during her new life in Paris. She will continue to reside in the duchess's household and take up her duties at allotted hours of certain days at the palace as the other ladies-in-waiting do. Now I'll keep you from your duty no longer."

Pierre went angrily from that part of the great building. He had been clearly directed to dance attendance on Stéphanie for the next two or three months at least, and there was nothing he could do to go against that order. And it had been an order, no matter how thick the sugar coating of the pill.

On the evening of the state ball his temper had worsened. In the marquee set up as a first vestibule in front of the entrance he moved restlessly on a section of the rich carpeting as he awaited the arrival of the Bassano carriage. Lights streamed out into the Paris night from every window of the palace, making it a glowing edifice that could be seen from afar, the gently floating tricolour held in its aura over the dome of the Pavillon de l'Horloge, wherein the Emperor's own apartments were situated. In the gardens thousands of gas-lit globes made garlands amid the trees where cascading fountains alone were touched by colour, the whole fairytale scene not at all in keeping with Pierre's mood. A customary five thousand or more guests had been invited, and the rue de Rivoli and the Quai des Tuileries had been blocked with slowly moving equipages lining up to take their place in the forecourt for the past hour and more. A never-ending stream of richly dressed people was flowing through the marquee. Waiting lackeys in powdered wigs opened door after door as each fresh carriage arrived. Diplomats, senators, high-ranking military personnel, and many other distinguished guests both French and foreign passed through, the men as adorned with decorations and ribbons of honour as the women were bejewelled. Then at last the Bassanos arrived. He stepped forward, greeted the lady and her husband, and then turned to speak to Stéphanie as she emerged from the carriage. He barely recognised her.

"We meet again, Pierre."

A broad grin spread across his face. He was going to win that damned wager after all! She had positively bloomed since their last meeting, the small irregularities to her features giving interest and a curious charm to her face framed by the white-gold of her hair, which was worn *à l'Impératrice*, drawn back from her fine brow into a huge coil at the nape of her neck, an inverted horseshoe-shaped circlet of flowers appearing to hold it in place. He could tell that the duchess had not been idle in the grooming of the girl put into her charge. The gaucheness was gone. The brashness had melted away. She had even manipulated her wide skirt over the carriage steps with more grace than most women had managed upon their arrival.

"I'm honoured, Stéphanie. So you have come as you promised to conquer Paris."

The smiling corners of her mouth indented impishly in the way he remembered. "Yes, I have, so let this city beware."

With her heart beating so wildly with excitement that she could scarcely breathe, she went with him into the palace itself. The duchess had been merciless in the drumming in of instructions on how to walk, sit, smile, and conduct herself generally, and Madame Palmyre had produced a wardrobe to cover every occasion, but throughout the lessons and the endless fittings Stephanie had known that it had all been building up to this moment when she would see Pierre again. She had wanted to do everything right for *him*. She wanted to look her best for *him*. The honour the Empress had bestowed upon her took second place beside the joy of his escorting her on this evening of evenings.

They passed through an anteroom where footmen in braided coats stood stiff as ramrods, and came to the long staircase which was flanked at the foot by trumpeters, their gleaming instruments set at an angle on their hips, the gold pennants hanging motionless. Guards resplendent in helmets and breastplates made a double rank on each step, and at the head of the flight Pierre handed over their invitations to two ushers in full dress uniform.

At her first sight of the Salle des Maréchaux, Stéphanie caught her breath with incredulous awe at the magnificent scene. The whole ceiling seemed composed of waterfalls of crystal, thousands of candles glowing in the huge chandeliers. In the wonderful light the vast assemblage sparkled and glittered, all the men not in uniform wearing formal court dress, every woman with a skirt shaped like an extended rose, which gave the huge salon the look of a living garden.

She was introduced to many people and caused a great deal of attention. A new and lovely face was always a matter of speculation at a court where the Empress had established so firmly the cult of beauty. Several of Pierre's fellow officers made a point of being presented, and in their flirtatious admiration she coquetted with them, keeping within the bounds that her instructress had laid down, while at the same time exulting in the power to attract that had come alive within her. She hoped that Pierre noticed, and it appeared that he did, especially since two or three of the officers gave him surreptitiously what seemed to be a congratulatory slap on the back at being with her. At half past nine exactly the Emperor and Empress made their spectacular entry, becoming the focus of all eyes, and the whole gathering took on the appearance of an undulating sea in the dips and bows that accompanied their progress to an endless whispering of silks and satins and the occasional clinking of decorations. He was in the scarlet tunic and white breeches of a general, black hair shining and waxed moustache ends gleaming, and she wore azure taffeta the colour of her eyes, sapphires in her hair and around her neck, her glorious shoulders exposed, and in her hand she wafted an ivory fan with a grace that was peculiarly Spanish.

They opened the dancing, and as soon as it became general Pierre took the floor with Stéphanie. He lost her to several partners afterwards, but claimed the supper dance. They did not take supper with the majority of the guests, having been invited to join the Emperor and Empress with selected personages including the Bassanos in another salon. Both Pierre and Stéphanie were singled out for special attention. First their godfather chatted with them, and then Eugénie bade them sit by her. Since she was a brilliant conversationalist, entertaining and witty, it was quite the best group to be with. Had it not been for the prospect of dancing again with Pierre, Stéphanie would have been quite content to spend the rest of the evening there, but the Emperor and Empress led the way to rejoin the rest of the company, with whom they mingled, speaking to as many people as was possible. They left the gathering at midnight, Eugénie half turning once more to give that gracious sweep of the hand that was characteristically hers, and then the two of them vanished from sight. The festivities would continue until the early morning, but the Bassanos were ready to leave, and Stéphanie had to go with them, not at all pleased at being taken away, although she did not dare show it except to Pierre as he accompanied them to the point of departure.

"I feel the night has only just begun," she whispered indignantly.

He thought the same, but consoled her. "There'll be plenty of other times ahead for you now. Try to persuade the duchess to allow you a chaperone prepared to stay up to all hours."

Her eyes gleamed determinedly. "I will. I haven't come to Paris at long last to go to bed before dawn."

The Bassanos' carriage departed. Pierre stood in the marquee that was deserted except for the lackeys, and wondered where to pass the next few hours. He did not particularly want to return to the dancing, and yet none of the diversions that lay around him in the light-spattered darkness of the city held out any special invitation to him. It was only Louise he wanted to see and be with. This should have been her evening, and although Stéphanie's company had been comparatively beguiling, he had felt bereft and denied the whole time, obsessed with the feeling he had been tricked out of what should have been his that night. He became consumed by an aching for her akin to hunger, and almost without further thought he had a hackney cab summoned for him and directed the cabby to her address. In the mean and narrow street he alighted and looked up at the building with its crumbling plasterwork where she lived. A candle showed behind curtains at one of her windows. He entered the house and took the turns in the flight of stairs at a run. At her door he rapped with his knuckles. Louise's voice answered cautiously.

"Who's there?"

"I! Pierre!"

"Wait a moment." He heard the bolt drawn back and the key turned. Then the door opened and she stood there with the candlestick in her hand, a shawl draped around her shoulders over her white nightgown, her hair flowing down. "Whatever is the matter?" she asked anxiously, her eyes wide.

His heart almost stopped with love at the sight of her. Not one woman who had displayed her finery at the Tuileries that evening could have outshone Louise in her simple and intimate attire, her face moulded into beautiful planes by the candle's glow. He had never seen her with her hair loose before, and although it hung straight and heavy as silk almost to her waist, the ends curled upwards into half-crescents of their own accord. He stepped into the room and closed the door behind him.

"I had to see you. Are you alone?" His swift glance had taken in the door standing open to Catherine's darkened room, and he noted that Louise had not lowered her voice.

"Yes," she replied unthinkingly. "Catherine is still at work and will be until morning." All that possessed her was an anxiety for his safekeeping that was increasing to unbearable proportions, tautening her face, and she reached out an uncertain hand to touch his sleeve, never having seen him in the splendour of his dress uniform reserved for imperial functions of a social nature. "Are you going away?" she questioned tremulously, mistaking the reason for such attire. "Is that why you're here at this late hour?"

Then he remembered mentioning to her that the conflict between Russia and Turkey might soon involve France, and he had not realised that he had instilled a fear of their separation in her. He saw she was caught completely off guard for the first time, open and vulnerable, all the barriers she had kept up against him momentarily breached. Suddenly he knew that, all unwittingly, he had created the very time for which he had watched and long waited with a patience of which he had never previously deemed himself capable. "No. Not yet. Maybe very soon." He put aside onto a chair the cocked hat he had been carrying, military fashion, under one arm. "But that's not why I've come. Suddenly I had to see you. If you had been asleep I would have awakened the whole house if need be. I knew I could not go another hour, another day, or another night without telling you what I should have told you long ago."

She took a step backwards, her feet bare on the rough

boards, and the candle dripped pearly wax as the flame quivered in her hold. He took it from her, and the two of them were captured in its nimbus as he set it down on the table beside them. The silk lining of his jacket slithered as he removed it and tossed it aside. She felt she was drowning in the candleglow and in the elated, entranced look on his face as he pulled her into his arms and held her hard against him, smoothing back the sweep of her hair. A shivering racked her from the icy shock she had experienced in thinking he had come to say goodbye.

His talk of war never failed to awaken dread in her as to the danger he would face, and now she clung to him, needing the physical comfort of his immediate presence to dispel the nightmare that had come upon her, wanting to be held protectively against his warm and living body, to be reassured that time was still theirs and not to be ended yet by a call to some foreign battlefield. She met his mouth with her own in a loving wildness that she had never known before, and their kiss seemed to go on forever in the passionate ferocity with which he reacted. When their lips did part, he leaned from the waist to reach for the key to the door. Too late she realised how far along the path to seduction she had gone, and she feared surrender as never before.

"No!" She tried to catch his arm, but he merely crushed her tighter to him and she felt his muscles flex as he turned the key in the lock. Gasping, feeling that her ribs must snap, she struggled again as he reached upwards for the bolt at the top of the door in a double precaution against intrusion, a thrust of his fingertips sending it home. His mouth swooped down on hers in kisses of even more demanding passion.

"I love you," he whispered into her lips, their breath mingling. He was set on adoring ravishment and nothing could stop him now. Keeping her mouth captive with his own, he swept her up in his arms and carried her through to the bed, her nightgown billowing. There he explored the lovely shape of her beneath its rumpled folds, and passed his hands over her breasts in sensitive touch that made her shiver with a voluptuousness she could not control. Yet still she strained away from him, whatever she would have said lost in the loving ferociousness of his inescapable kisses. He tugged free the tie of ribbons at her throat and the soft garment was easy to pull away, revealing her in her ivory nakedness, her tresses swirling like black silk over her face as instinctively she tangled herself against him. But her struggle was of short duration. She could not fight her love, her own awakened passion, and the inexorable tenderness of his caresses. Suddenly and gloriously she found herself lost and ardently submissive.

Only then did he strip and take his place beside her, sweeping away the last traces of her modesty with the cherishing homage of his lips and hands and body. She understood at last what it meant to be made for each other, exulting in his obsessive adoration of her. It was as if he were uncovering treasure in every part of her and together they shared in rapturous discoveries. For herself she found him beautiful. There was beauty in the fire of his mouth, in the muscles that rippled across his back under the sensuous spread of her fingers, and in the vigour and power of his whole frame. When he brought her with him at last to the final assailment of love there was no world, no time, no night, no day. Only his arms holding her that she might not die of ecstasy. Only Pierre.

Throughout the rising light of dawn he held her curled softly against him while they murmured and whispered to each other. "We'll be together forever," he pledged, kissing her eyes. "Nothing exists that can come between us now, and in no time at all we'll be able to let it be known that you are mine and only mine for as long as we live."

It had become clear to him that somehow from their first meeting he had known she could be all women and one woman to him, and he saw his future stretching immeasurably ahead through the image of her as an integral part of his life. The depths of his love for her had stirred him to a desire to cherish and protect with an unselfishness that he had never experienced before. All this he told her and more.

She had difficulty in persuading him to leave before Catherine came home, but eventually and with reluctance he dressed ready to depart. Yet still he lingered at the door, holding her to him.

"It will be days before I see you again," he sighed. Never had his duties appeared more burdensome, and he resented the hours she had to spend at work when they might otherwise have met. "Tell me I may stay a little longer."

"You must go now," she chided fondly.

He did manage to linger a few more minutes before he finally left. It came as a complete surprise to him that same evening when the jackpot for the wager was handed to him with due ceremony in the officers' mess, where he had to buy champagne and cognac for all. He had forgotten all about it in that other, far more valuable prize that he had won.

11

In her bedroom Marie regarded herself in the tilted cheval-glass with complete dismay. She and Worth were to attend a Halles ball being held in honour of the Empress and her court, one of innumerable city events following the pattern set by the Tuileries, and he had designed an outstanding dress for her to wear. It was of pink tulle trimmed with toning purple ribbons, startling in its simplicity, its crinoline wider than ever. And she hated it. Everything in her shy and retiring nature rebelled against it. It was the kind of dress she most dreaded to wear, knowing that there would be gasps and stares and endless whispering about it, and it mattered not one iota to her that half the women present would be envying her the garment, when a good many others might titter. Why did he always have to put her in something so *new* and *different* whenever they went anywhere? It was bad enough in the shop at times when she felt she looked as ridiculous as a jester in garments that suited other women well enough, and she was certain that the day would come sooner or later when she would just curl up and die in the midst of some vast gathering under the sheer pressure of thousands of probing and derisive eyes.

She heard him coming up the stairs and steeled herself to requesting that she be allowed to wear one of her more conventional ballgowns. They had been anything but commonplace when she had first worn them, but fashion had been led by them, and she could comfortably expect to see many other women clad in the same style. The door burst open and in he came, handsome in his evening clothes with white shirtfront gleaming, and in his hand he held high a small, flat posy with floating ribbons.

"The final touch, my darling!"

"Charles—" she began to protest, making a little fluttering movement with her hands to prevent him from pinning the posy of silk and velvet pansies to the dress.

He did not listen, and neither was the posy destined for adornment of the dress. To her complete horror he slipped it on its concealed comb into her curls, and its ribbons settled in loops from it to drift down to one shoulder. Her eyes dilated enormously, and her voice and her tears burst forth in the same instant.

"I will not go to the ball with that tree in my hair!"

He threw up his arms dramatically in wrathful exasperation that she should fail to see how enchanting she looked. Although he had long since lost count of how often they had quarrelled in similar circumstances he never failed to be keenly hurt that she of all people should dislike what he had created, the hurt exacerbating his anger, his sensitivity towards criticism deepening each time.

"It's not in the least like a tree! A simple cluster of the most superbly fashioned pansies that one of the shop flowermakers has been working on for hours."

"*Pansies!*" Marie stamped her foot, her fists clenched, her tears gushing. "I'm supposed to dance this evening, not push a country plough or milk a cow. Nobody has ever worn huge bunches of pansies all over their hair to a Paris ball. Why don't you make it a daisy chain with sticks of straw and be done with it!"

"You're being ridiculous and making your eyes red!"

"Ridiculous!" she echoed shrilly, flinging her head back as if appealing for patience to contend with him. "It is due to you that I look ridiculous. The dress is bare as a nun's garb, and my head like the Bois de Boulogne." She suddenly dropped her face into her hands, sobbing helplessly. "Why can't you see that I would be the laughing-stock of everyone present?"

His anger ebbed. He enfolded her into his arms and laid her head against his shoulder, stroking her hair and kissing her brow. He spoke softly to her in his cajoling. "I decided on pansies for the very reason that they have never been worn before. The simplicity of them is in harmony with the dress. Amid all the other women in their elaborate toilettes you are going to stand out as an example of how beautiful a woman can look in a dress relying entirely on line to achieve a dazzling elegance. If I had used roses or jasmine there would have been no unusual emphasis as a final touch."

He won her round eventually as he always did. Almost without realising exactly when she gave in, she found herself persuaded into wearing not only the hateful dress, but the posy as well with the ribbons unaltered. She dried her eyes and blew her nose on the clean linen handkerchief he had drawn from his sleeve to hand her, allowing herself to be kissed and comforted and told that she was the dearest wife in all the world. Yet she was convinced that she knew exactly how Marie-Antoinette had felt in the tumbril on the way to the guillotine as she took his arm to set forth to attend the festivities. If only she had been allowed a few conventional frills on the skirt!

It was as Worth had predicted. Her dress drew admiring attention; even those hostile to its lack of adornment could not keep their eyes from it, and more and more at any public function that she attended the women present made a point of seeing what she was wearing. As always she made herself appear smiling and unconcerned by such critical scrutiny; none suspected her vulnerability, and it was some consolation for her torment when Worth whispered to her that by the end of the week the dressmaking department would be getting orders for dresses exactly like the one she was displaying with such graceful aplomb. "*And* with pansies for the hair," he added, unable to resist proving to her that he had been right after all. It was one of the rare times when, much as she loved him, she found his complacency insufferable, and then he whispered to her again. "But not one will compare with you in them, my darling." She melted before the worship in his eyes. Not for the first time she thought it was no wonder that other women envied her, and not just for the clothes that she wore on her back.

The municipal ballroom echoed the opulence of the Tuileries in the velvet hangings of deepest blue with garlands of flowers intertwined amid the silk-fringed swags and tassels, the whole scene lit by chandeliers and reflected in mirrors that multiplied the vast gathering into endless crowds spreading away into inestimable distances. Acquaintances greeted the Worths on all sides. They had come to know many people in Paris, and invitations flowed their way, but far more were politely declined than were ever accepted. Worth always insisted that he was far too busy to give his valuable time to events and people in whom he had little or no interest, which was true enough, but Marie could see signs that he was becoming as imperialistic in his own realm as the Emperor was in another sphere. Without doubt her husband was fast making his attendance in social as well as dressmaking circles an honour to bestow how and when it solely suited him. Yet with their own close circle of friends he was relaxed and jovial and marvellous company. It was no wonder that Louise, a credit to him in the new gold-spangled dress, had shown pleasure in being invited to join the Worth party that evening with her escort, Pierre de Gand, whom Marie found more agreeable than his autocratic and alarming mother.

At last the Empress arrived with her ladies, the moment for which all the gathering had been waiting. As always, she did not disappoint in a dress of silvery gauze with a diadem of emeralds. As she drew near with her entourage, Pierre saw that Stéphanie was in the group. He was surprised and annoyed that she should be there, supposing it to be a last-minute substitution in another's place, and his enjoyment of the evening ended when he saw that she had spotted him.

In the dancing that followed, he took Louise on to the floor, the other couples in the Worth party swinging out around them in the rotating steps of a waltz. He was uncomfortably aware of being duty-bound to pay Stéphanie the usual courtesies, but he had no wish that she and Louise should meet. The chance came to go to her on his own when Louise danced with Worth himself. He threaded his way through the assemblage to where the imperial party was gathered under a specially erected canopy. He had decided to attend the occasion in the first place to give Louise the chance to see at close hand the Empress in all her finery, which he knew would be a grand sight for her. He could no longer consider taking her to any event at the Tuileries, where he was hampered by his allotted duties to Stéphanie, but the city of Paris glittered with other social occasions that she would enjoy, and this evening had been one of them. He did not foresee any difficulties in presenting her once she was his wife. After all, with a self-acknowledged *parvenu* on the imperial throne, the social barriers of France were more flexible than those in long-established courts. Nevertheless, he still had not given Louise the full truth of the elevated status of his own connections, and maybe the time was ripe for it at last.

Stéphanie must have been watching out for him. As he approached her she spun about with alacrity from those to whom she was talking, and held out her hand to him. "What a surprise! What fun! How clever of you to find out that I would be here this evening. I did not know myself until the last minute when one of the Empress's ladies was indisposed. Yes, I would love to dance." He spun her into a Strauss waltz, and she went chattering on as they rotated around the floor in the midst of a thousand or more other couples. "You have rescued me from what promised to be a most tedious evening." Her eyes were sparkling, her exuberance joyful. "How the Empress manages to look charmingly interested in all the boring company presented to her I just do not know."

"I'm afraid I can't be your knight to the rescue," he replied seriously. "Not on this occasion."

She pouted merrily, not believing him since he often jested with her. "Don't tease. You don't deserve to be promised every dance with me, but I'm prepared to forgive you."

"Stéphanie." His tone changed and hardened as he pressed her fingers to make her accept what he had said. "I'm not here on my own."

Her reaction dismayed him. As she stared at him her cheeks flooded with scarlet and her eyes became very bright and angry. "The devil take your arrogance, Pierre de Gand! You let me make a fool of myself. Don't think I care whom you are with, but I do care that you let me think you had come specially to find me." There was no logic in her accusation, which he was prepared to suffer, but when she would have flung herself away to leave him on the floor, his grip about her waist tightened and he almost crushed her hand in his, his anger equal to hers.

"No one leaves me in the middle of a ballroom floor! You'll finish this waltz with me if it goes on for the rest of the night."

She would still have escaped him if she had not been indirectly reminded by what he had said of the gossip such behaviour would cause. At all cost she must do nothing to jeopardise her position at court. The Duchess of Bassano had warned her that the Empress was a strict moralist who would not tolerate a breath of scandal surrounding any member of her entourage. Perhaps Eugénie had enough to bear in the whispered tales of her husband's indiscretions, which did most surely reach her ears.

On the final chord from the orchestra Pierre returned Stéphanie to the Empress's company. Eugénie spoke to him, something he had hoped to avoid that evening, and nearby Louise put a hand to the base of her throat in an involuntary gesture of amazement.

"The Empress is speaking to Pierre," she exclaimed.

Somebody in the party, catching her words, threw a remark over a shoulder at her. "Why should she not, since he is the Emperor's godson, after all?"

Louise looked in sharp distress at Marie for confirmation. "Is that true?"

Marie smiled and patted Louise's arm, trying to look reassuring. "The captain obviously thinks it can make no difference if he hasn't yet mentioned it. After all, he's not a man to boast about such a matter, is he?"

"No," Louise agreed in a subdued tone. "He is not."

The music was taking everyone back onto the floor again when Pierre returned to her. Stéphanie, pretending otherwise, tried to follow him with her gaze to catch a glimpse of the unknown partner who had aroused such painful jealousy in her, but he was lost from her sight completely as a great host of couples swept into a gavotte. Behind her one female voice asked another about the identity of the wearer of a pink tulle dress. The reply came promptly.

"That is Madame Worth, wife of the couturier at Maison Gagelin."

"Would he have designed that dress, do you think?" Avidly curious.

"She only ever wears his creations." Enviously.

"How interesting." A pause of contemplation. "Those pansies are quite enchanting."

Stéphanie was roused out of her despondency to look at this Madame Worth dancing past. There was no doubt that in the unusual simplicity of her lovely gown she made everyone else look absurdly overdressed. Even the Empress.

The Empress left at her usual hour of midnight, much to Worth's relief. He had had enough of the festivities, pleasant though they had been, and with thoughts in his head of another busy working day only a few hours away he bade friends good night and departed with Marie, who removed the pansies from her hair as soon as she was seated in the hackney cab. Worth, who had immediately slumped into a doze with his legs crossed at the ankles on the opposite seat, had his top hat tilted over his eyes and would not have seen in any case the little grimace she made at the flowers lying on her lap.

While travelling across the city in another direction, Pierre was giving Louise what was in her view a long overdue explanation. "I should have told you before that my family became acquainted with the Emperor and his mother, Queen Hortense, long before I was born. Years later, while in exile in England, a prince denied the right to step into his own country, he honoured my parents and me by becoming my godfather. Perhaps you wonder why I've waited until now to tell you all this, but although in any case I'm not one to make pretentious claims, the chief reason was that I didn't want to alarm you unduly by it all. Now that you know me, you can understand that it was a simple family matter that grew to proportions that neither he nor my parents could have anticipated at the time. Admittedly some social privileges come my way, but for the rest of the time my life is the same as that of any other cuirassier officer attached to the Tuileries." His arm tightened about her in the darkness of the carriage, and he brought his face close to hers. "Now I have no more to tell you about myself that you don't already know." His voice became amused. "Do you want to hear it all again? About my six sisters? My childhood? My horses? My years at the Ecole Militaire?"

The fact was that she never tired of hearing anything about him, no matter if it was something new or some addition to what she had already heard before, but she made a light, noncommittal reply, and with the matter apparently settled to his satisfaction, he began to peer through the window in an impatience to reach their destination. For the first time she noticed that they were not near her home, but in a different district altogether.

"Where are we?" she asked in bewilderment.

"You'll soon see. It's a surprise."

As they alighted she looked up at the creamy-stoned rank of elegant, terraced houses and recognised that they were in the rue de Lenoir. The concierge admitted them and went ahead across the vestibule and up the stairs to light the way. On the first floor Pierre took from his pocket the key that had become his, and quickly opened the double-doored entrance into the apartment he had rented. No servants were yet in residence, and there was a hollow ring to his footsteps on the polished floors as he put a lighted taper in one lamp and then another. She followed him as the glowing wicks rose to banish wave after wave of darkness. Finally, in a high-ceilinged drawing-room with three tall windows giving a view of the lights of Paris beyond one of the newly laid-out parks, he stooped to put flame to the fire of logs in the marble fireplace, and then stood with his back to it, facing her.

"Well? What do you think of it?"

The furnishings were rich and comfortable, in hues of green and gold and blue amid the gleam of rosewood and marquetry. Through opened doors she had caught glimpses of other rooms, which were no doubt as sumptuous as the one around which her gaze travelled. Letting her silken shawl slip from her shoulders she trailed it in her hand as she went across to one of the windows to look out. Light from a lamp, reflected in a pier-glass, slid the gleam of polished ivory onto her shoulders exposed by the décolletage of the handsome dress.

"Whose view is this?" she ventured huskily, having guessed easily enough, but deeply moved by the loving surprise of it that he had arranged.

"Does it please you?"

"Almost any aspect of Paris pleases me, but this particular view must be even more magnificent by day than it is by night."

He came and stood behind her, taking her by the shoulders and drawing her back against him. "It's yours and mine." His voice was vibrant against her ear. "Ours for as long as we wish." He turned her about, and with gentle fingertips under her chin he raised her face to his, his own expression serious and ardent. "The first home of our marriage."

She nodded, overcome almost beyond words. "It must be the most splendid accommodation in all of Paris. I know we'll be happy here."

"All that remains now is to hear when a marriage furlough will be granted to me, and how long a leave of absence it will be. As soon as I know, we'll fix the wedding date, and nobody shall deem it otherwise." He drew her with him to a wing-chair where he sat down and took her onto his knees. Her head came blissfully to rest against his shoulder, and her wide skirt settled like a huge coverlet about them. He was full of plans for the honeymoon journey they would make.

He wanted to take her by a long and picturesque route home to the Loire Valley to see the fortified mansion that would one day be theirs, telling her how it stood atop some of the most beautiful countryside in the whole of France, and that there were so many places around there that he wanted to show her. He would teach her to ride. All his sisters would love her. And when they left the château their love-journey would continue by the most leisurely means all the way back to Paris. She noted, but did not remark on it, that although he mentioned his mother, he did not name her among those who would be ready to welcome her into the de Gand fold, but she would face whatever came from that direction when the day arrived. In the meantime she had much to look forward to, and it was decided that she should move into the apartment with Catherine with the least possible delay.

She straightened her back and sat up. "Don't ask me to say that it will be tomorrow or the day after that. I must choose the right moment to tell Catherine that we are to be wed. After I've told her I must ask Worth's permission for time away from the dressmaking department."

He looked incredulous. "Time away? What do you mean by that? You won't be going back there once we are married."

She stared at him. "Surely you're not asking me to give up all I've been aiming for in the fashion world?"

He gave her waist an indulgent squeeze. "As my wife you'll have no time—"

She broke in. "Nearly all the leading couturières are married."

"No doubt they are. But they are women who have to earn their living. You will no longer be in that position. Quite the reverse, in fact."

"That's beside the point. As I have told you, I enjoy everything to do with the making of beautiful clothes, and in any case, to work hard is natural to me. I couldn't idle my time away all day in an apartment where there are servants to do the housework and a chef to cook the meals." She made an uncharacteristically lost and helpless gesture with a spread of her hands to emphasise her argument.

He did not believe she could ever be idle, but he fully expected that energy to be channeled into the pastimes enjoyed by women of his class, who never seemed to have a spare minute between the social events of any given day. She had yet to realise how totally different her new life was going to be, and she had to be won over to it with much of the patience and restraint he had shown in previous months.

"I want you to be happy, and if it makes you happy to remain involved in the world of fashion, so be it. But I'll not have you kneeling to pin the hems to dresses of women not fit to tie your shoe. You must have some advancement. Some authoritative post where you can direct instead of partaking in the tasks."

She lowered her head to kiss his brow. How dear he was, and how little he understood. There was no more disgrace in pinning a hem on one's knees than in a painter kneeling to put a final brush stroke to a masterpiece or a sculptor lying flat on the floor to give a finishing touch to the base of a plinth. She shared Worth's attitude in seeing a lovely dress as an artistic creation that was as important in its own way as any picture hanging in the Louvre.

"Let everything stay as it is for a while longer," she persuaded gently. "I know I will have to adjust to many changes in my life when we are married, and although I can never relinquish that long-held dream of mine to own a dressmaking salon, you and our love for each other will always come first with me."

He did not doubt it. Louise would never make a promise that she did not intend to keep. His love for her knew no bounds, and lurking in the back of his mind was the knowledge of the one sure way he could remove her from her dressmaking environs once and for all when it suited him. A woman was unable to divide her time with anything else when it came to the bearing of children. He pulled her close to him again, his lips finding hers in a kiss that shut out all else but the immediate present. She pressed herself passionately to him, and felt him begin to pull the pins from her hair with an amorous intent that she welcomed with all her heart.

Later, when they were ready to leave the apartment, he took up her shawl and draped it around her shoulders, embracing her cherishingly at the same time. Impulsively she caught his hand and kissed it devotedly before laying it against her cheek. "To think that only a matter of hours ago I was so afraid," she told him, her eyes deeply ashine with emotion.

He smiled at her questioningly, stroking back a drifting tendril of hair from her face. "Afraid? What could you possibly have been afraid of? Not of me, I trust."

She shook her head. "No. It was when I learned that you were the Emperor's godson. I thought that you might hold some élite position in the palace that you had not told me about, one that would mean imperial permission to marry me, which I saw as a great danger. Instead, all is well."

"Indeed it is, *chérie*." He took her face between his hands. "Put all your fears away. I'm the one who must go in peril of losing you until my ring is on your finger."

"To me, it is there already," she said softly.

When he left her at her door he impressed upon her again that she break the news to Catherine and remove with her as soon as possible into the apartment. She understood that the betrothed of a palace officer should reside at an address of some distinction, suitably chaperoned, and promised that it should be accomplished with the least possible delay. What he had not told her was that he was withholding his application to become betrothed to her until he could give that very address, simply to avoid awkward questions that could jeopardise their union. He had no reason to believe that anything would go amiss with the required application that he intended to place before his commanding officer, with a corresponding request for leave of absence upon marriage, which was normally granted immediately. To spare her feelings he had thought it best to avoid pointing out the impossibility of giving her present address which, if not exactly a slum, was in a far from savoury area of Paris. Admittedly it was preferred that officers did not marry before the age of thirty, but over the age of twenty-five it was allowed and, provided the lady in question was beyond reproach, permission to become betrothed was given and no difficulty incurred.

By the time he had reached his military quarters he had decided that he could allow Louise no longer than a week to deal with Catherine. At the end of that time he would have to break the reason for urgency to her. It was a task he hoped to avoid. He saw it as an affront to a lovely woman that anyone should belittle her either by her means of an honest livelihood or by a humble abode.

Louise did not know that Catherine had already deduced that she had taken the irrevocable step into full womanhood. Intuitively Catherine was certain of it, although she was keeping her suspicions to herself, unable to decide when and where it could have happened. At first she was enraged and would mercilessly have slain the seducer responsible, having no doubt in her mind as to who he was, but then knew a kind of absolution of her own weakness as far as men were concerned when even a female as strong and intelligent and independent as Louise could succumb to a male's carnal blandishments. It made her realise that for a long time she had been in awe of Louise, and she was ashamed that somehow she should rejoice in the erring since it showed that Louise was as human and vulnerable and as prone to love as she always hoped she would be. It was not how Louise's mother would have felt about it, she told herself strictly, but suddenly that rule did not seem to apply any more, and all that remained was a frantic anxiety that there should be no unwanted outcome of what had taken place between Louise and the officer.

All appeared to be well. The one day of the month when Louise was always particularly pale and suffered from cramps came and went as usual. Catherine decided that some stern and sensible warning should now be given to ensure against any mishap in the future. She gave it, choosing the time when she was helping Louise re-press the seemingly endless spread of tulle in the Worth dress that had been donated by a customer. She kept busy with the flat-iron all the time she was talking, the primness that warred so constantly with her sensual nature taking over and making gushes of embarrassed colour fill her cheeks. Her listener, with head tilted attentively, regarded her steadily and with increasing compassion. Finally Louise could keep silent no longer.

"Oh, my sweet Catherine! You have been worrying yourself about me and I wasn't aware of it." She pulled the flat-iron away from Catherine's hand to dispense with distraction, and set it back on the stove. "I haven't known how to tell you, but Pierre and I love each other and we're to be married just as soon as a furlough is granted to him. Give me your blessing, I beg you. I never knew it was possible to achieve such happiness."

There followed the kind of emotional scene in which Catherine revelled. She laughed and cried and hugged Louise, exclaiming over her good fortune, saying untruthfully that she had been able to tell all along that the captain was too much of a gentleman to be anything but honourable. "I could see you were in love," she admitted, wiping her eyes. "Shouldn't I of all people know the signs? Maybe for a while I didn't want you to tell me; maybe—yes, I confess it—I was a mite uncertain about letting you go. That doesn't mean that the day you marry won't be the happiest time in your old Catherine's life. It's what I've hoped for ever since the night I took you in like a half-starved kitten from the paupers' graveyard."

"Say nothing to anyone else yet about the betrothal," Louise requested, thankful that the good-heartedness in Catherine's nature had overcome all else. "Perhaps I'm a little nervous about being so much in love. I just want the date set before the rest of the world is let into the secret."

"Was it him suggested it be kept quiet?" Catherine asked with doubts revived.

"No, no. I think he would shout it from the gallery of the Arc de Triomphe if it were possible," Louise said with a little laugh, "but such behaviour would not be suited to a palace cuirassier. His regiment with all its tradition is very formal about these matters. Now I have more news for you. You and I are to move at once into the apartment where I'm soon to be Madame de Gand. Pierre is most anxious that everything of the best shall be mine." She saw the change of expression in Catherine's face and sought to reassure her. "Pierre will not be living there, so don't fret about that. He'll be remaining in his military quarters until the wedding day."

"Where is this apartment?" Uncertainly.

"In the rue de Lenoir."

"What! That posh street! A fine fool I'd look going in and out of there to work!"

"I'll be doing the same. After I'm married, too. I'm learning so much from Worth every single day. He's such a genius with materials, and to my mind he has only just begun to show what he can do. I can't leave him yet."

Catherine was barely listening, not knowing how she could cope with the envy and jealousy and perhaps the ridicule of some of her workmates when they heard of her new abode. "I must have time to think about moving from here. I can't promise anything yet."

On that decision she remained adamant. Often with the other grisettes around the sewing-tables talk was exchanged about what each would do if a fortune fell in their laps, and a dream place in which to live came high on each woman's list, but being faced with the realisation of such a residence, with the presence of disdainful servants, and neighbours who probably patronised Madame Camille's, was an alarming prospect. The dream became a nightmare. Catherine had to find the courage to face it, and perhaps her inner self at the same time.

Pierre, impatient with the delay, found himself committed in an official capacity more and more to Stéphanie's company. By chance they had come face to face the morning after they had clashed at the municipal ball, she on her way to the Empress's apartment in the company of the mistress of the ladies-in-waiting, the Princess d'Essling, which prevented any conversation even if he had wished it. Stéphanie, very pink in the cheeks, nodded haughtily in acknowledgement of his salute, and kept her nose high as she swept past him. He was not to know that no sooner was she out of his sight than a wave of misery engulfed her. Why hadn't she smiled or looked amiable to show she bore him no malice over what she knew to have been in all honesty her own foolish jealousy?

Entering the rose salon of the Empress's apartment she struggled to keep back tears. Deliberately she dropped a step or two behind the Princess as they went on through the blue salon where receptions took place. Normally it was a room that never failed to delight her eye with its white silk curtains and blue gauze blinds, its Sèvres porcelain and superb bronzes, but this morning she kept her gaze lowered and did not look up until the change of pattern in the carpet told her she was in her imperial patroness's study, a room of gracious size with purple-tinted drapes, where Eugénie wrote letters, made a collection of papers that she considered to be of historical importance that would otherwise have been thrown away, and continually added souvenirs and other small items she treasured to those already amassed there. On the walls of pale-green striped satin were portraits of the Emperor, her sister, Paca, and the ladies of her entourage who were particularly dear to her. Drawing close to the foot of the Emperor's likeness Stéphanie pretended to be studying it as if from a fresh angle, and surreptitiously wiped her eyes. Behind her in the room the Princess was complaining about some correspondence not being in its place, and when she went bustling out to see about it, Stéphanie sank down in the low, sloping chair by the fire where the Empress always sat while writing on her knees, and gave way to her pent-up despair. She did not know she was no longer alone until she felt a hand on her shoulder.

"Whatever is amiss, my child?" It was Eugénie, who had

come through the intervening rooms from her bedroom, clad as she always was at that hour in a simple dress that happened to be in one of her favourite shades of blue. Stéphanie sprang to her feet in confusion, dipped a hasty curtsey, and gabbled an apology, but Eugénie was not going to let the matter slip aside so lightly. "Come now," she insisted kindly. "I told you when you came here that I would be like a mother to you whenever you had problems or difficulties that you did not know how to face. Why are you crying? Are you ill? Has someone been cruel to you?" A slight frown of exasperation puckered the beautiful brow. "Surely you are not weeping over a man?" When Stéphanie's nod confirmed this state of affairs Eugénie gave a heavy sigh and put her arm about the girl's shoulders. "Never waste your tears over any man, I implore you. Not one is worth a single tear from a woman's eye. Who is the rogue who has caused you such distress?"

"He's not a rogue," Stephanie protested vehemently. "It is I who have been foolish in alienating him by my own behaviour."

"Let us sit down and you can tell me all about it."

Protected from the full heat in the marble fireplace by a green silken screen, Stéphanie sat on a stool by the Empress and poured out the whole tale, from falling in love with Pierre at the first meeting at Fontainebleau when, she confessed, she turned around from the window to see a young man so handsome that he seemed to have materialised out of her wildest dreams, through to her snubbing of him in the corridor a matter of minutes ago. Eugénie, always practical, and knowing the Emperor's purpose in having brought his two godchildren together in the first place, declared that she had the perfect solution for healing the breach.

"You shall come with me on my daily drive this afternoon. Pierre will be escorting my carriage. That should give you ample opportunity to make amends."

It happened as Eugénie promised. Pierre, bearing no grudge against Stéphanie, responded quickly enough to her first tentative smile, not wholly ignorant of how his own turned her heart over, and later, when the drive came to an end, they conversed for a few minutes before she hurried away in the wake of the Empress. From that day onwards he resumed his attendance on her as if nothing had happened, dancing with her at various social functions or sitting with her at concerts and plays, always under the eye of one chaperone or another. There were times when he found the duty of escort to her decidedly pleasurable, but nevertheless he was looking forward to when she selected a beau of her own choice, which would return to him his freedom to come and go on any given occasion without considering her wishes. With some natural conceit he imagined it was her doing that she was now included frequently on drives with Eugénie when he was riding as escort, his male ego only flattered by her innocent subterfuge, and he saw no threat in it. Moreover, he found it more noticeable than ever that her comely looks more than outshone the loveliest of the Empress's companions, and yet it did not cross his mind that he was observing a beauty maturing through the effect of an all-encompassing love.

Stéphanie lived for the sight of him, and any glance, word, or smile that appeared to have any special significance was hoarded and mulled over blissfully in what she now took to be his serious courtship. She could have had her choice of any number of young men showing an interest in her, but she wanted none of them. None was so dashing in uniform, so straight in the saddle, so smiling or so quick to share her sense of humour, or had sometimes such a dancing, wicked glint in his gaze, when she was made to feel gloriously naked and utterly sinful in a way that she did not dare to try to comprehend. There were times when she read more into his naturally courteous attitude towards her than was there, such as when he tactfully tried to dissuade the Empress from including her in a party that was to visit La Petite Roquette, a children's prison that had a grim reputation.

"Nonsense!" Eugénie retorted. "Mademoiselle Casile has a Christian duty to involve herself in works of charity. Your concern for her sensibilities is commendable, but misplaced."

He said no more, but fell into step beside Stéphanie to follow the Empress and other members of the party who were to be shown around the sombre building by the governor himself. Eugénie, who had been prepared for the worst, found conditions more horrifying than she had imagined possible. Stéphanie became quite ashen almost as soon as the tour had started, but she stoically kept pace with the others, and was deeply grateful when Pierre took hold of her arm by the elbow to give her some support. Five hundred children were confined within these terrible walls, convicted mostly for theft, although some had more serious crimes laid at their door. The young prisoners, some of whom seemed scarcely old enough to know why they were there, presented a pitiable sight, huddled in abject misery in individual, sparsely furnished cells, which prevented them from seeing each other or having any comfort of human contact even when allowed into the walks separated by high walls for a limited period of exercise each day, all whom the visitors saw shuffling along listlessly with their heads hanging. Many of the ladies in the party became faint and had to retreat. But Eugénie, loving children as she did, thought only of their plight and, paying no heed to the fetid stench or the chance of any unpleasantness being directed towards herself, she insisted on being allowed into the cells to talk to some of the youthful inmates. Stéphanie fought down her qualms and followed suit. She forgot the revulsion she had felt in overwhelming pity as some of the younger ones held out their arms to her in pathetic appeal, and heedless of her own finery she knelt to gather them to her. With patience she attempted to communicate with many who were stunned almost to imbecility by the dreadful conditions in which they were incarcerated, and did not flinch when others shrieked obscenities at her out of the frantic outrage from which they were suffering. When it was time to leave she felt in a state of complete exhaustion. She noticed that the Empress had a pallor that she guessed to be equal to her own, and there was strain and distress in the lovely features. Yet as always, Eugénie was not thinking of herself, although her voice was faint from the ordeal.

"You did well, my dear. I'm proud of you. We shall come here again, you and I, and in the meantime I intend to do everything in my power to improve the lot of those unfortunate children."

It was praise indeed, and Stéphanie valued it, but the Empress's words faded into insignificance by the compliment Pierre paid her later.

"You have courage, Stéphanie. A remarkable courage. You knew well enough that any one of those young prisoners could have attacked you without warning. I salute you."

The rest of that day she felt as if she were walking on air. It soon became known that the Empress was set on reforming conditions at La Petite Roquette, and while many supported her, there were always those who grumbled about her interference in matters not strictly her concern. Stéphanie could not help drawing a comparison with Marie-Antoinette, in whom Eugénie was extraordinarily interested, avidly collecting relics connected with her, and even on honeymoon had visited Versailles and the Petit Trianon. It seemed to Stéphanie that Eugénie had the same unfortunate knack as Marie-Antoinette of making enemies where it was least intended, but she consoled herself with the thought that circumstances were very different now from the days of that tragic queen.

Daily the newspapers gave news of the conflict between Turkey and Russia. The Turks won the battle of Citate, but three days later Russian troops invaded the Dobruja. Catherine did not share Louise's renewed anxiety, seeing only glory for France should their country become involved in the war, and she remained as stubborn as ever about removing to the apartment.

"Let him marry you first, and then none can point a finger at you," she advised doggedly with a wisdom she had never applied to her own affairs of the heart. There was also a far more personal reason why she did not want to move that outweighed anything else, a reason she did not care to acknowledge even to herself.

Louise sighed, tired of the argument for the moment. Nobody could be more pig-headed than Catherine.

Unbeknown to Louise, Pierre had come to the limit of his patience. He handed in his prepared application to become betrothed, giving the apartment in the rue de Lenoir as her address, and hoped it would not be long before permission was granted. It was now tacitly accepted in military circles that it was simply a question of time before France went to war with Russia, and although he welcomed the prospect of being able to prove himself in the field, he wanted as much time as was left to spend as husband to his bride. The following day an interview with his colonel appeared to go without a hitch. Pierre made no mention of Louise's work, and therefore the subject did not come up. If it had, it might have been an end to everything, but to all intents and purposes he wished to marry a young lady of good address, an orphan who had always been closely chaperoned, with nothing to tarnish a good name. Just when he expected the colonel to pick up a pen and put a signature to the paper, it was folded and set aside.

"I'll see that your request is laid before His Majesty later today."

"Is that necessary, sir?" Pierre asked stiffly, considerably alarmed. "The fact that I'm the Emperor's godson has never been officially recognised in my army life. Why should this matter be an exception?"

The colonel looked well pleased. "Because of a special appointment that has come through. It is my pleasant duty to inform you, Captain de Gand, that you are one of a number of officers specially selected to take up command in the Escadron des Cent-Gardes à Cheval that is being formed."

At any other time Pierre would have welcomed such extraordinary good fortune. The Cent-Gardes were to be a specially created élite cavalry corps with duties confined to providing a bodyguard to the Emperor and carrying out ceremonial guard and duties that would entitle them to a military and social precedence over all other troops in the French Army. He had known that he fitted the physical requirements in being well built and over six feet tall, but had never expected that such promotion would come his way. He heard himself make some appreciative reply to the news he had received.

"Yes. I congratulate you," the colonel continued. "Now you know why the Emperor himself must approve your request to become betrothed."

There was nothing to do but to hope for the best. Pierre felt furiously angry with Catherine, whose stupid dallying over the move to the apartment had prevented his request going through while it could still have escaped the imperial eye. He was of the opinion that Louise gave far too much consideration to the woman, and he would see to it that she did not stay under their roof any longer than was absolutely necessary after the marriage.

When the Emperor picked up Pierre's application from his desk he smiled, stroking his goatee beard in his hand, until his eye alighted on the name of the bride-to-be. He was an even-tempered man and did not fall easily into a rage, but there was a frozen look of intense displeasure on his countenance when he gave one of his own equerries certain instructions. The application went into a drawer. It remained there until a report was delivered into his hands a few days later. Only then did he send for his godson.

"This betrothal is out of the question." The Emperor's intractable expression was matched by the severity of his voice. "It is a match so unsuitable as to be beyond discussion."

There was no informality about the occasion, which was an indication in itself of the imperial mood. Pierre stood as straight as if he were on the parade ground, although his chin began to jut. "I beg permission to argue that point, Sire. I love the lady and want no other to be my wife."

Deliberately Louis-Napoléon picked up the report on his desk and selected a few salient points. "There is some doubt as to whether the parents of this particular young female were ever married. She has lived with a woman of questionable morals for many years, and has worked in the dressmaker trade since she was fourteen. The rent of the apartment given as her address is paid by a certain Captain de Gand." He tossed the application form contemptuously down on the desk again. "Do you deny that she is already your mistress?"

The reply came stubbornly. "I wish to see her acknowledged as my betrothed."

"Is she *enceinte*? Is that why you feel you must act honourably in marrying her?"

Pierre's eyes blazed. "No, she is not. I want to marry her because I love her."

Louis-Napoléon's attitude became more sympathetic. "I do not doubt that you love her. We have all loved women in our time who have meant much to us, but whom we could never honour with our name or the privilege of bearing our legitimate heirs. Such a marriage as you have requested would put an end to your professional career and to your life in society." He observed his young officer closely. "Would you really be prepared to turn your back not only on the Army, with the new position in the Cent-Gardes to which you have been raised, but on your duty at the very hour when your country stands on the brink of war?"

Pierre's jaw clenched, the skin straining white over the cheekbones. "No, Sire, but I'm asking only to be allowed to marry. My loyalty to my Emperor and to France is not on trial."

"I happen to believe that it is. Should you go against my wishes in this matter it would be tantamount to treason."

"Sire!" It was an exclamation of vehement protest.

Louis-Napoléon shrugged, getting up from his green plush chair to stand by his desk. "A strong statement, I agree, but how else could I view such insubordination? By such a match you would degrade yourself, the de Gand family, and above all your association with me and all that I represent. That cannot be allowed. I totally forbid the marriage that you have requested."

It had been a short, sharp tussle, but the outcome had been

decreed from the start. His godson stood pale and stricken, the white-gloved hand gripping involuntarily the hilt of the sheathed sabre in the acuteness of stress. A lessening of tension was now necessary. Louis-Napoléon adopted a kindlier tone that was entirely genuine.

"Don't think that your little grisette won't understand the situation. She will. Much better than you, I dare say. Such women prove to be just as accommodating without a ring as ever they would have been with one. After all, you've already prepared a little love-nest for her, and I'm the last one to quarrel with that kind of sensible arrangement." He hoped his words were taking full effect. He had no wish to be at loggerheads on a personal level with his godson, and he repressed a sigh. Maybe he should have made it clear to Pierre long since that Stéphanie Casile had been selected as a suitable wife for him, but when it had appeared that events were following their desired course it seemed better not to let any outside guidance make itself known. Had Stéphanie not been willing it would have been a different matter, but according to Eugénie the girl was deeply in love with Pierre and more than ready to marry him, while he—the headstrong young fool!—had been entangled in a classic situation from which he was now far from the first or the last to be extricated by one older and wiser and considerably more experienced in such matters. At least the little *affaire* had been put into proper perspective with no harm done. Louis-Napoléon decided that the time was more than opportune to enlighten his godson as to the correct choice of a wife that he was expected to make. "Be at ease now, Pierre," he urged. "The difficult business is over and done with. Be assured that I shall never refer to it again, although I must continue to speak for the moment on the subject of marriage. Believe me, I fully understand the feelings of any man without a son when war looms large on the horizon, but you do not have to look far to find a young woman of whom I know you to be extremely fond, and where you would find your affection more than reciprocated."

Pierre, numbed by the blow he had suffered, looked at him stonily. "I'm not sure that I understand you, Sire."

Louis-Napoléon paced leisurely about the room, twirling one end of his moustache. "I refer to Stéphanie. From the start I have been committed to finding her a suitable husband, one I could trust to give her a fulfilled life in every sense of the word, and it was only to be expected that I should have had you in mind some long time ago." He did not add that Madame de Gand had been of the same opinion that it would be a good match, not knowing that Pierre had been made aware of her view at the outset. Coming again to his desk, Louis-Napoléon stood with his back to the huge map of Paris that showed Baron Haussmann's steady transformation of the city and faced his godson squarely. "I'm exerting no pressure on you, particularly at this time when you are in the throes of a disappointment. I'm simply making my desire known. A gentleman must invariably make a marriage of convenience to ensure the health, wealth, and breeding of the woman who is to bear his children, and in Stéphanie you would have the joy of love as well."

"Perhaps the Empress would not wish one so young in her entourage to marry yet," Pierre answered gratingly.

His godfather smiled reassuringly, the waxed ends of the wide moustache tilting upwards. "The Empress would be overjoyed. You would have her blessing and mine."

Pierre's resolve was unchanged. Whatever happened, he would not let Louise go, no matter that the few words of a marriage ceremony were to be withheld from their union. He loved her. She was his. And he would take steps to ensure that she remained his.

Four days after the decree that brought the Cent-Gardes into being, France and Britain made the expected declaration of war on Russia. All furlough was automatically cancelled, and those regiments that had not already sailed for the battle zone were put on the alert throughout the country. It meant that matters such as requests for betrothals by officers were shelved for the time being, and Pierre was given a reprieve in which to continue to keep Louise in ignorance of what had taken place. She was able to tell he was depressed, and misunderstood the reason, trying to cheer him by saying that a little delay in the wedding ceremony was not important when eventually they would be spending the rest of their lives together. Her loving reassurance only twisted the knife in the wound and aroused him to a despairing passion fed on the fear of losing her.

Louise tried not to show that she lived in dread of his going to the war. At the present time the Cent-Gardes were settling into their new duties, and Pierre took his turn with the other officers in sleeping outside the Emperor's door at night, as well as riding in constant escort to the Emperor at all times. Since it was not conceivable that the new pride of the

French Army should not achieve first distinction in the war, and without either of them discussing it, Louise knew as well as Pierre did that it was only a question of time before the sky-blue tunics of the Cent-Gardes were seen in array on the battlefield. She did not let her anxiety spoil any of their time together, was as quick as ever to appreciate any quip he made with her ready laughter, and in every way became dearer to him with every meeting.

Stéphanie was less reticent. She went to the Emperor as soon as she heard that there was the possibility of the detachment of Cent-Gardes being sent to the war. He received her in the Empress's study where he liked to sit talking to his wife as he smoked the cigarettes of which he was inordinately fond. They both made her welcome, and Eugénie bade her take a seat facing them on the chaise-longue. After a short conversation on other subjects the purpose of the visit became known.

"I beg you not to let Pierre go to the war, Sire," she implored her godfather. "I would rather go myself as one of the *cantinières* than that any harm should befall him."

Louis-Napoléon hid a smile. "Charming though you would look in the females' enchanting uniform while nursing wounded soldiers or taking victuals to the front line, I fear the exchange you request is not feasible. In any case, I suggest you say no more. Pierre would not thank you for trying to shield him from his duty."

Her eyes were wide with fright. "But he is your godson! He could be killed or wounded."

Louis-Napoléon was unmoved. "He is also a very fine soldier. He would acquit himself with valour."

Stéphanie flung out her hands in desperate appeal to Eugénie. "Madame! I beg you."

Eugénie's face was stern. "If he were my own son and wished to fight for France I would move heaven and earth to pave the way for him."

Stéphanie's hands sank slowly back into her lap where she clasped them tightly, her head bowing on her neck as she tried to regain her self-control. "If he died, I should die, too," she whispered croakingly.

After she had left them Eugénie raised her oblique eyebrows inquiringly at her husband. "Is Pierre's name down to go?"

Louis-Napoléon nodded as he took another cigarette from the gold box on the table at his side. "I happen to know he has been straining at the leash for such an opportunity for a long time. It will do no harm either to get him away from Paris for a while. Young men with time on their hands have an uncanny knack of complicating their lives. A spell of fighting the Russians will help him sort out the true values of life."

March became April, chill and unusually blustery. Louise took every day that came as a bonus in which she could still see Pierre. For his part, he crowded their time together as if neither of them must have the chance to talk seriously or even think about the future. They had a box at the grand Opéra and the Opéra-Comique, went to every playhouse from the Théâtre Français to the Bouffes Parisiennes, danced the night away at the Café Anglais, and took late suppers, which were the gayest and most exotic of all repasts for well-to-do Parisians, at the famed Véfour's or the exotic Maison Dorée. For Pierre his flaunting of her in places where he would be seen and recognised was an act of defiance against all the pressures that had been brought to bear on him. Outrage burned as fiercely in him as his passion for her. With her fine looks and her figure she caught glances and held attention wherever they went, and he had never been more proud of her or known a greater satisfaction in his exclusive possession of her.

Involved in such a round of pleasure, Louise used her ingenuity to vary her limited wardrobe, and was in luck when Worth let her have a black silk net overtop and skirt that a customer had rejected because of its trimming. Bored with conventional adornment, he had seized upon the idea of creating glitter with black jet, which had never been used before. Unfortunately it was proving too bizarre to women accustomed to ribbons and feathers, but Louise had no qualms about it and rejoiced in her good fortune. When she danced with Pierre the jet sparkled and swung like a flow of black diamonds, which was exactly the effect that Worth had wanted to achieve. For daytime outings she retrimmed her bonnets frequently, having access to scraps of silk that would otherwise have been thrown away, and on her birthday Pierre arrived at the apartment with a red-and-white-striped bandbox bearing the name of Madame Virot, milliner to the Empress herself. Inside Louise found a concoction in the latest style, a hat with a wide and flattering brim, made in coral silk and trimmed with curly cream feathers and floating velvet ribbons. She gave an excited cry and put it on at once, tissue paper flying in all directions, while Pierre grinned at her delight. Joyously she twirled about before the looking-glass, tilting her head this way and that to view the hat from every angle until she flung herself against him to thank him with a kiss. She sometimes thought that these must be the happiest days of her whole life, a time forever sprinkled with the lights of Paris in gasflares and candleglow, the glitter of jet and the sparkle of champagne, a time fragrant with the perfume that he gave her in crystal bottles, a time of passion and tenderness and the sweetest words of love that any woman could ever have heard.

She was alone at home, not long returned from work, when he arrived one evening unexpectedly. Knowing that it was rare for him to have duties changed, she felt a sudden sickening stab of premonition. One look at his face was enough to confirm her fears.

"I have some important news," he said gravely.

She stood quite still, one hand pressed against her heart, the other covering it. When he would have spoken again, she shook her head and helped him off with his coat. Only then did she take him by the arm and draw him into the room. She pushed him gently down into a chair and then sank down on to the floor at his feet, her skirt billowing out around her before settling in its silken folds. There she folded her hands and rested her arms on his knees, looking up into his face.

"Now tell me," she said bravely. "I'm ready now."

He traced the side of her cheek gently with his knuckles. "I'm leaving tomorrow for the battlefield. This is our last meeting for a long time."

She closed her eyes tightly on the awful impact of his words. It was what she had dreaded to hear, but she had hoped all along that somehow, when the time came, she would be comforted and strengthened by being his wife. Time had run out too quickly.

"When did you hear?" she asked tremulously.

"Orders came through early today. I came as soon as I could get away."

"How long have we?"

"A very little while. Two hours at the most."

Her head lowered as she struggled with her anguish. She must not spoil the time that was left to them in useless tears. "I'm thankful for every moment granted to us."

"We have much to talk about. If anything should happen to me—"

She looked up swiftly, her eyes dilating. "Don't say that!"

He smiled seriously at her. "I'll put it another way. Nobody knows how long this war will last. Should you need anything at any time my banker has instructions to let you have whatever you require. In the event of my death you will be provided for until the end of your days."

A sob broke from her, and she buried her face against his knee. He stroked her hair, and then, getting up from the chair, he raised her to her feet with him. Holding her in the curve of one arm, he delved into his waistcoat pocket and brought out a tiny, velvet-covered box. He snapped it open for her, and inside on the crimson satin was a gold wedding ring and a diamond-set keeper to be worn with it. It was what he had bought her for the day that had not come. She could hardly speak, her voice coming in a barely audible whisper.

"I'll wear the keeper until you come home again."

"Wear them both for me now. Let me put them on your finger. I want to remember seeing them there. I want to know that you belong only to me."

She could not refuse him. They stood facing each other, the lamplight throwing their shadows across the room. He took her hand, and she watched him slide the gold band onto her finger. Raising her eyes, she met such ardour in his that she felt her whole being was absorbed by him.

"I love you, my darling Louise. My own for evermore."

The diamond keeper followed, a seal of love upon the ring of vows. He kissed her with tenderness, and they clung to each other long and lovingly. They kissed again in fierce desire when they lay together in her narrow bed. He made love to her more sensitively than ever before, and the imminence of their parting gave a new and exquisite fire to their passion, the complete abandonment of her loving destined to haunt him through many seemingly endless nights of war.

They took a last farewell of each other after he had shrugged on his coat. Once more he crushed her to him, kissing her insatiably as if in that final embrace he hoped somehow to assuage the hunger for her that would never leave him. With a supreme effort he tore himself away, and she snatched up the lamp to run after him to the head of the flight of stairs to watch him go from her. At the last moment he paused in the dark well of the vestibule before going out into the street and looked up over her shoulder at where she stood, captured by the lamp's glow in an image that filled his whole heart. He did not know if he would ever see her again.

Slowly she went back into the room. She closed the door and leaned against it for a few minutes, torn by the parting. Then she sat down and removed the keeper to take off the gold band in preparation to wearing it on a chain around her neck until such time as he would come home again. The keeper went back onto her finger, the diamonds sparkling in the lamplight. She thought it aptly named. It would keep her for him alone. Most of all, it must be a talisman to keep him safe in all the dangers of the battlefield.

She did not see him leave Paris. She had hoped to ask Worth for time to see him ride away in the company of troops departing, but the shop was busy and customers were waiting in the dressmaking department, making such a request impossible. When the hands of the clock reached noon a terrible sense of desolation came upon her. She knew that the troop-train was bearing him away from Paris. To war. To Russian cannon. To the battlefield of the Crimea.

12

There were times when it seemed to Louise that Paris had forgotten that the tricolour was at war. Nothing stemmed its gaiety, its increasing opulence, its flamboyant imperial occasions. Crinolines were becoming wider and more elaborately ruffled and befrilled in keeping with the frivolity that prevailed. It was as if the whole city had become a brilliantly illuminated carousel that was beginning to rotate at an ever increasing speed created by the hedonistic mood of the Parisians and all who flocked to Paris to sample its abundance of pleasures.

More than a year had passed since Pierre had gone to the Crimea, and still the hostilities showed no sign of coming to an end. In contrast to the laughter and song and wine-flowing of Paris, French soldiers and their allies had endured the rigours of a terrible Russian winter with inadequate clothing and insufficient supplies. Louise wrote regularly to Pierre. He had been wounded in the Battle of Inkerman, but not severely enough to warrant being sent home, and although he assured her that he had quite recovered, she could tell that he was unable to throw off the depression that descended on him from time to time.

Now I know what the retreat from Moscow must have been like, he had written when the winter had been at its worst, *but thanks be to God the setbacks we have suffered are not in that category. There are times when it is hard to believe that there has ever been anything else but this war. Did I ever know Paris? Have I really breathed in the scent of flowers in the Champs-Elysées? Or was it all a dream from which I have awoken to reality? Then I remember loving you, and sanity returns with its own heartache.*

She longed to see him, and missed him desperately. It was a mercy to her that Worth never allowed her a moment's respite at the shop, and if one completed task left her with time on her hands he gave her another, unless she had already found more work for herself, which was what usually happened.

Yet it was not only she who was run off her feet. Worth and Marie worked as hard as anyone else, if not harder, taking no privileges because he happened to be the *premier commis* and she his wife. At times, due to the pressure of customers' demands, neither of them had any lunch until three o'clock or later in the afternoon, when the food in the staff dining-room would be warmed up for them. They were always first at the shop in the mornings in spite of having to travel some distance, Marie continuing her practice of rising very early in order to be dressed at the height of elegance, with her hair beautifully arranged, when she arrived at her counter by half past eight, after which she rarely sat down until the shop closed. Many of Worth's dresses were now displayed on lay figures in the dressmaking department, but she was called upon to change into garments for display purposes many times a day, and Louise often helped her in and out of them when not engaged in other work. Almost always Marie and her husband were the last to leave the premises, because there was ever one more matter to engage his attention, one more order to write down in readiness for the next day. Whether the proprietors realised it or not, Worth had gradually become the very heart of their business. He knew every piece of merchandise that came in and out of the shop, and had all the reins in his capable hands. Not only in Paris but in many districts of France his name was becoming known in commercial circles as an astute salesman who knew what he wanted, and it always had to be exactly right. Louise found it interesting that jet was now being produced for ornamentation on a lavish scale, due entirely to his lead, the very customers who had scorned it now wanting it to adorn their dresses. But already he was after something new, spurring on the makers of passementerie to produce a certain fringe that he had designed to give a shimmering effect, wanting a special plaiting in a ribbon binding, and ordering countless metres of gilt-threaded edging of his own creation that would give flounces the look of being dipped in liquid gold. There appeared to be no end to his inventiveness, and the passementerie makers found that by following him their sales increased enormously, the more alert among them having long since enlarged their workrooms and taken on a bigger workforce.

Louise often thought it a great shame that on the surface the credit for everything that Worth did went to his proprietors. Maison Gagelin was gaining a wide reputation for the elegance of its gowns and advanced ideas that had never stemmed from the bigoted confines of the proprietors' office. She wished she had the capital to invite Worth to go into business with her on their own, but her tiny investment, although it had grown, was not nearly enough yet to establish her with outlay in premises at a good address, which was essential. Sometimes she found the customers extraordinarily helpful when it came to financial matters. They were not aware of it, but as they chatted in the fitting-rooms, often to a female friend or relative who had accompanied them, scraps of information were dropped that referred indirectly to a rise or fall in financial spheres of commerce and industry. Louise hoarded them in her mind as she pinned and repinned a garment. On one occasion a particularly pleasant and friendly woman had remarked on her husband's interest in the concession granted for the building of a canal at Suez, saying what a marvellous project it would be, and Louise, plucking up her courage, asked if it would be a good proposition for investment when a company was formed. The lady, surprised and intrigued by such a knowledgeable enquiry from such an unexpected quarter, declared that it would be, some of her own finances being earmarked for it. At the next fitting she passed on another tip for investment in the meanwhile, which Louise found to be profitable. She often felt she was like a squirrel hoarding nuts for a winter that was still some distance away.

Pierre never came into her thoughts when she was considering the financial aspect of her future. She knew he did not approve of her wish to remain in dressmaking, although socially a successful wife could not harm him, and fame and fortune had been her aim from the start. It was something she had to achieve on her own, almost as if she needed to assert herself in the world to make up for never having known her father and little enough of her origins. All she did know about her mother's life as a silkweaver in Lyons she had recounted to Worth long ago in the early days of their acquaintanceship when he was newly come to Paris, telling him of the wonderful skills built up over the centuries that were in danger of being lost forever as the silk industry there showed signs of dying out, loom after loom falling silent even before she was born. She sometimes wondered if memories of those tales she had told him were in any way responsible for activating the intense interest he had been showing over past months in that almost destitute industry in Lyons. Alternatively, Worth being fascinated by silks of every kind, it was possible that while studying costumes in the portraits in the Louvre, which he still did whenever he had time, he had discovered some handsomely robed personage from the past flaunting Lyons silk woven in a design similar to that with the eyes and ears that he had first noticed years before in his own country.

In his capacity as *premier commis,* Worth had ordered a few lengths experimentally in traditional patterns that had not appeared for a century or more on the ordinary shop counter. Well pleased with the results, he had made a special trip to Lyons in order to investigate the situation for himself. He who loved the flow and texture of all beautiful fabrics had become like a man possessed in his passion for what he had found there. It seemed sacrilege to him that the Lyons weavers, who had once woven gloriously for the kings and queens of France, should be unemployed with their looms idle and almost no demand coming forth for some of the most wonderful materials that could be produced anywhere. He was determined to change that state of affairs. He ordered more lengths to be woven specially to his requirements, and was having dresses made up for display at Gagelin and Obigez's stand at the grand Exposition Universelle being held in Paris that summer, where visitors from all over the world would be able to view the spectacular marriage of his designs and Lyons silk.

Among the special orders delivered from Lyons was a length of pure white silk, flawless as new-fallen snow, which was to be made up as an underskirt for a dress about which there was some mystery. Designs for it had been ordered by one of the young ladies of the Empress's entourage, not for herself, but for a lady who could not spare the time to come herself. The lady wanted the dress to be simple and light and charming, much the sort of garment that Marie-Antoinette might have worn when playing at milkmaid with golden buckets at the Petit Trianon. If the name of the lady had been divulged to Worth, Louise did not know, but she imagined that it had. In any case, there was no difficulty in guessing the lady's identity, although as she checked and folded the precious layers of material needed for the garment, which was to be made up by the lady's own couturières, not by as much as the slightest glance did either reveal to the other that they knew the dress was destined for the Empress. Louise's only regret was that the very private ordering of it all meant that Worth could not expect his brilliant skills to receive acknowledgement publicly from Tuileries sources, which would be tantamount to an announcement of imperial patronage, and that was not given lightly, or on the strength of one design.

Stéphanie was responsible for the idea of approaching Maison Gagelin for designs. The Emperor had commissioned the artist Winterhalter to paint Eugénie with her most favoured ladies-in-waiting, and discussions about the dress she should wear had been endless, none of the ideas submitted by her own couturières quite pleasing her. Finally Stéphanie, remembering the artful simplicity of the dress she had seen worn by Madame Worth, suggested that the answer might be found at Maison Gagelin. Eugénie made a little face at the thought of deigning to allow a shop to compete for her requirements, but after another batch of sketches had disappointed her she agreed that as a last resort she would consider whatever could be shown her from that somewhat unusual source. After a preliminary visit to explain requirements, Stéphanie was surprised when she went back expecting to collect a selection of the couturier's designs drawn and painted by a professional artist for presentation. Instead she saw that only one design had been thus prepared between the thin vellum covers that protected it.

"Is this all, Monsieur Worth?" she questioned coolly.

His expression was bland. "That one sketch encompasses all that is desired," he replied with a sweep of his hand.

What insufferable arrogance! she thought to herself. She was quite sure that Eugénie would be equally put out, but that was not the case. Eugénie seemed thankful not to have to sort through another wide selection, and acclaimed the sketched dress as being exactly right for her. It struck Stéphanie that perhaps Monsieur Worth had guessed that the Empress had been sated with sketches to the point of rejecting everything when faced with a choice, which was why he had chosen to make a single offering. And what an offering! It was an enchanting creation, evocative of a summer's day, all frills and gathers of white tulle over silk, and threaded with ribbons of palest violet. It was to be worn with clusters of real violets on either side of the face. No wonder Winterhalter decided that the Empress should be painted handing a bunch of the same tiny blooms to one of her ladies-in-waiting. Again Stéphanie realised what an astute man Worth was. It was well known that violets were the Empress's favourite flower and that she loved all shades of their colour, which he had introduced so delicately into the filmy dress. Stéphanie made up her mind to patronise Monsieur Worth herself as soon as the forthcoming state visit of the English Queen was over, and the exposition with all its attendant imperial events closed, and she could concentrate on her own plans. She needed clothes that were warm and elegant and would travel well. Nobody else knew it yet, but she had made up her mind to visit Pierre in the Crimea.

She wrote to him often, bright and lively letters with news of people he knew, scraps of gossip that would entertain him, and accounts of anything amusing that had taken place. To judge from his replies, which came sporadically, he appreciated her correspondence, and although he did not use any endearments in his letters beyond sending his most affectionate regards, she understood that any unselfish man under constant threat of death or disablement through battle would not wish to tie a young woman with promises that could lead to heartache and disappointment.

The idea of going to see him had been in her mind for some time. She considered it grossly unfair that only the wives of a very few high-ranking officers were allowed to make the journey to visit their husbands, and then a paragraph in a newspaper caught her eye. She read that an Englishmen, a Mr. Thomas Cook, had organised a party of travellers into the Crimea, and they had actually witnessed one of the skirmishes from the hills. If all else failed she would contact him for escort, but she was hoping that her godfather would ease the way for her. From what he had said to her over recent months she had no doubt at all that he would favour Pierre as a husband for her. For herself, she knew she would want no other man until the end of her days.

By the end of June it became known that Eugénie was pregnant. After two miscarriages she had to receive the greatest care and attention, and every one of her ladies, Stéphanie included, was most anxious to ease all burdens from her and help her through a difficult period. There were speculative whispers as to how and when the baby had been conceived. It had happened sometime after the imperial couple had returned from a state visit to England, where it was known they had had a most happy time, striking up a genuine friendship with Queen Victoria and Prince Albert, and it was possible that the contentment had lingered long enough for Eugénie, who knew that she was still loved by her husband for all his infidelities, to believe for a little while that he had mended his ways.

When August came Eugénie was restricted by her condition in the part she could play in showing hospitality to the British Sovereign and her Consort, but nevertheless the visit was a huge success. All Paris turned out in the festooned streets and boulevards to greet Queen Victoria and Prince Albert, and cheered them wherever they went. Worth and Marie, who took a keen interest in all such events, managed to get a good viewing position to see them step from the train upon arrival at the gaily decorated railway station, the Union Jack and the tricolour waving merrily together. Walking home afterwards, Worth rolled up his eyes at the English Queen's atrocious clothes.

"It was not enough with that unflattering straw bonnet and that parasol of shrieking green," he exclaimed, striding along, "but she had a poodle embroidered on that hideously large handbag! A *poodle!*"

"But we heard her say with such pride to someone that her daughter had embroidered it," Marie pointed out charitably. "I think that was rather charming."

Worth groaned aloud. He had his own ideas as to how any first lady of a great nation should be dressed. Embroidered poodles were not included.

At the Exposition Universelle, which the royal couple visited several times, was a magnificent court mantle on the stand of Maison Gagelin, which Worth had created with queens and empresses and princesses in mind. Sumptuously embroidered in gold on white moiré antique watered silk, it was designed to hang gracefully from the shoulders instead of the waist, which was customary. From the number of heavily crested letters that had come with orders it was obvious already that he had set an established mode for all royal ladies now and in the future. It won a premier award for Messieurs Gagelin and Obigez. Worth was not even invited to be present at the imperial prize-giving when his employers, basking in the credit, received the honour from the hands of the Emperor himself.

With the summer and all its hectic activities over, Stéphanie felt able to relax and take time to work out what she would need for her journey to the Crimea. She was resolved that nothing should stop her from going to see the man she loved.

She did not disclose her destination to Worth, not wanting a whisper of her secret plans to leak out through a needlewoman's gossiping tongue or through being overheard by the alert ear of a servant. Nothing must reach the Emperor until she was ready to approach him herself. She simply said to the couturier that her travels would take her by sea and land, and she expected the climate to be bitterly cold.

Madame Worth paraded garments for a travelling wardrobe that delighted her. Warm, woollen dresses in glowing shades of cherry and plum and coral, evening gowns to shimmer magically over a practical interlining that would be inserted to keep out icy draughts, a sturdy and elegant riding habit to be protected by a weatherproof cape, and above all a handsome, fur-lined cloak with a hood.

"Start at once, Monsieur Worth," she ordered recklessly,

not considering that she would have a lot of unnecessary garments on her hands if her plans would come to naught.

Every fitting was spiced with excitement for her. Each garment was one in which Pierre would see and admire her, and the joyousness of her mood enhanced the natural friendliness of her nature, making her a welcome customer in the dressmaking department. Louise particularly enjoyed the fitting sessions. There was none of the petulance and impatience that many women showed, the exaggerated sighs of weariness, or the trivial complaints. Mademoiselle Stéphanie Casile arrived with a step as light as her heart seemed to be, quick to praise and appreciate, unable to stop giggling helplessly in a most infectious manner whenever anything went wrong, and all the time chatting away contentedly no matter how long she had to stand while Worth ripped out the sleeves or some other part of the garment, and the whole process of the fitting had to begin again.

Stéphanie liked Mademoiselle Louise and thought herself fortunate to have such pleasant company throughout the fittings. She found her intelligent and well-read, far more so than she was herself. Happily on a musical level they were equal, and once, during a discussion on an opera they both knew, burst into song simultaneously, which brought Worth back into the fitting-room with such an outraged expression that when he had gone again they both collapsed with mirth. If secrecy about her travelling plans had not been all-important, Stéphanie knew she would have confided in Mademoiselle Louise, there being the same close intimacy between a customer alone with a fitter as there was between a woman and her hairdresser, but she had to be cautious, and on that subject she gave nothing away. Yet they exchanged the circumstances of their lives, and each was aware of a certain empathy brought about through both being orphaned, and what it meant to be deprived of parental affection at an early age, no matter how hard others had tried to bridge the gap.

The day came when all the garments were finished. Impulsively Stéphanie took Louise's hands into hers. "Thank you for your part in making me these lovely clothes, Mademoiselle Louise. I hope that one day you will help in the preparation of my trousseau."

Louise smiled warmly. "I should be honoured, Mademoiselle Casile."

Stéphanie had not been idle in laying the rest of her plans

during the weeks when her clothes were being prepared. She had been making unobtrusive enquiries, questioned casually those with husbands in the Crimea, and finally located a widow who was to travel there in order to return with her husband's remains for burial in France, a special privilege granted to her by the Emperor himself in view of the late officer's extraordinary gallantry in the line of duty. The widow, Madame Hélène de Vincent, a fine-looking woman with dark eyes made darker by sadness, and a mass of soft brown hair worn in a chignon, was more than willing to chaperone Stéphanie should she be allowed to travel, saying that she would be exceedingly glad of her company.

"I will speak to the Emperor myself on your behalf if it proves necessary," Madame de Vincent offered. "In any case, you may tell him that your young company would be greatly comforting to me on my tragic mission."

The Emperor heard Stéphanie out before he spoke a word. "I love Pierre with all my heart, Sire," she concluded, her eyes filling up with tears on the force of her feelings. "I beg you to grant this favour, the only one I have ever asked of you in all my life. Let me go to him. Please!" She sank down to her knees beside his chair in the salon where he sat, her hands clasped in imploring supplication.

"Have you asked the Empress if she will allow you leave to embark on this romantic pilgrimage?" he enquired lazily, tilting his head back and looking towards the ceiling as he drew on his cigarette.

"No, Sire. I thought that as your goddaughter and your ward I should seek your permission first."

There was a long silence. She thought she would die of the suspense. Then she saw he was giving her a sideways look, an unmistakable twinkle in his eye. "What are you waiting for? You have my permission. I suggest you make your request to the Empress without further delay."

She gave a cry of joy, springing up and snatching his hand to kiss it, scattering cigarette ash everywhere. As the door closed after her he brushed the ash from his coat and trousers, smiling to himself. Madame de Vincent was a lady of the highest principles, who could be entrusted to look after the girl and keep her far from the battle lines and any unpleasant sights. Having lived a soldier's life in his younger days he knew well enough the effect it would have on the captain to see a young and beautiful Frenchwoman after months of the dirt and squalor and violence of war. He did not anticipate any more misplaced notions of marrying a mistress from that direction. Things could not have worked out better.

The Empress was harder to convince. She was anxious and concerned, and wrung her hands at the thought of Stéphanie venturing into a region thick with lustful soldiery. "But Madame de Vincent and I will be under the personal protection of General Bosquet the whole time we are there," Stéphanie protested. "We'll be escorted from the supply ship to our quarters and back again a few days later when we sail on the return voyage."

Eugénie finally agreed, but was unusually petulant, dabbing at the corner of her eye with a lace handkerchief. "Be sure you are back by the time I am brought to bed. I want all my ladies to be near me."

Left on her own, Eugénie closed her eyes wearily and leaned back against her cushions. She longed for the birth that was to come, yearning to hold her infant in her arms and to let forth all the pent-up maternal love that found its only outlet towards her ladies, all of whom were dear to her. If as a girl two cruel men had not broken her heart, the second beyond all hope of recovery, she would have been able to give back to her husband the passion he showed towards her, but the sensual side to her nature had been ruthlessly crushed to extinction through rejection by the two other men she had loved long before she had ever met him. Had Louis-Napoléon remained patiently faithful to her there was always the chance that she might have come by a long and tortuous route back to the ardent and expressive creature she had once been, but his sexual appetites were insatiable, his needs constant and demanding at all hours of the day and night, and when she was still little more than a bride he had had no compunction in seeking elsewhere the physical response that she had not been able to give him. Before they were married she had heard, but not believed, that he had once disappeared for an hour at a state gathering with a lady who was his mistress, announcing upon their flushed return that they had had a little rest. But she believed it now. Oddly, she still loved him, although he had finally made everything male abhorrent to her. If her baby was a boy she would be able to forgive the darling infant for being of the male sex, because with her duty done in bearing an heir to the imperial throne, her husband might lessen his visits to her bed.

Stéphanie sailed with Madame de Vincent early in November. The voyage proved to be particularly pleasant; not only was the weather relatively calm in the Mediterranean, but the captain and officers of the supply ship were extremely attentive and good company. They disembarked at a Black Sea port which was bustling and busy, where they were met by a Captain Desgranges. He offered his condolences to Madame de Vincent, spoke of her late husband's courage, which had been an inspiration to all, and then greeted Stéphanie conventionally, but with a look in his eyes of sheer appreciation that she was to see with variations in many another Frenchman's gaze before she left again.

"Is Captain de Gand not with you?" Stéphanie asked at once.

"No, but he has been sent for, and you will see him this evening."

"Does he know that I'm here?"

Captain Desgranges shook his head. "Official orders do not include personal explanations, mademoiselle. Word was sent that he should report to General Bosquet's headquarters, where he is to remain for three days." He compressed his lips in a smile. "I imagine he is quite mystified. I envy him his delightful surprise."

With an escort of mounted lancers, the widow and the girl on their entirely different missions, one at the end and the other at the beginning of love, travelled first in an ancient carriage obtained in readiness from some local source, and then by horseback, an army wagon trundling with their baggage in their wake. It was bitterly cold, and snow lay in drifts everywhere, the exposed ground appearing as grey as the sky. They passed French troops under canvas, camp-fires making red-gold flares of colour as smoke curled skywards, but few glanced in their direction, not realising that two women rode by, so bundled up were they against the icy air. Stéphanie was distressed to see how patched the men's uniforms were, some with blankets draped about them for extra warmth, their once smart gaiters dirty and mended. There was a good number who had added Russian greatcoats and other articles of clothing, some of it cossack, to their attire, and she did not care to think about where and how those garments had been acquired.

Once a party of British soldiers appeared ahead and passed them by at a brisk march, disciplined and crisply in step, but on the whole their appearance was no better than that of her own countrymen except for the whiteness of their pipe-clayed belts. From what she learned from Captain Desgranges, the British had fared worse than the French during that first terrible winter, and had it not been for Miss Nightingale, many more of the wounded would have died through lack of hospital facilities. Stéphanie thought that little advancement in welfare could have been made in the case of the Turkish soldiers whom she saw encamped, a gauntness to their faces telling of a shortage of rations along with every other kind of hardship.

She and Madame de Vincent were brought at last to a village that had suffered damage during some of the fighting, and General Bosquet's headquarters were in a large house that had changed hands twice before the French had taken the honours with the fall of Sebastopol. Evidence of a past grandeur was there in the painted ceilings and gilt ornamentation, but sconces had been ripped from the damask-panelled walls, and the heavy pieces of furniture that had not been looted bore scars inflicted by sabres and swords, some with musket balls buried deep in the wood. The change in atmosphere from outside was astonishing, the floor-to-ceiling stoves giving out a tremendous heat, flames flickering through the grilles, and both Stéphanie and Madame de Vincent were glad to shed their outer cloaks.

"I must apologise for a certain amount of disarray in the décor," Captain Desgranges said wryly, "but I trust you will be comfortable, and I assure you that when General Bosquet returns this evening he will be as honoured as the rest of us when you join us at dinner."

In their bedrooms, which were adjoined with communicating double doors, Madame de Vincent and Stéphanie found two maids ready to wait on them, both quiet peasant women with braid-trimmed, white kerchiefs tied about their foreheads and covering their hair, their whole appearance neat and clean. Hot tea was poured for the newly arrived travellers from a samovar, lemon slices floating in cups of a delicate china that must somehow have escaped all the marauders who had passed through the house, French and Russian alike, and there were sweet white rolls to eat, and tiny cakes flavoured with caraway.

No sooner had they finished their refreshment than the servants went to fetch pitchers of hot water for what was obviously an army tin bath, and both visitors were glad to take a turn in bathing away the tiredness of travel, the fragrance of the soap that each had brought with her drifting away on the steam. Their two maids warmed the large bath-towels by the stove to wrap about them when each was ready to step out of the water.

Madame de Vincent, who wished to spend a while alone in the chapel where her husband's coffin had been placed, was soon clad in a silk dress of the sombre black that accentuated the paleness of her features, and she went from her room, taking with her the tribute of evergreens for him that she had gathered herself on his own estate in France. Stéphanie was still in the process of getting dressed, shivering with nervous excitement as her maid brushed her hair and arranged it into clusters of curls. She had decided to wear the brightest dress that Monsieur Worth had made her, and after its unpacking every crease had been pressed out in readiness.

Wanting to make her entrance with as much impact as possible, she did not leave her quarters until she was sure that Madame de Vincent would have come from the chapel to join the company officers gathering with General Bosquet in the hour before dinner. At the head of the stairs she waited until she caught the widow's soft tones just once in the general rumble of male voices, and then she descended the stairs. The archway into the room was framed by brocade drapes slashed to ribbons in some foray, and there she paused on the threshold. All heads turned towards her, and a complete silence fell. Those present were used to the occasional visits of high-ranking officers' wives, ladies never younger than Madame de Vincent and invariably far less comely, but she caught the hard stare of every man present as she stood there in a shining dress of copper silk, her fair hair a gleaming aura, and the expanse of her smooth shoulders and the rounded swell of her breasts glowing white as alabaster. Her only jewellery was a pair of pearl and amber earrings, a gift from the Emperor, which sent small arrows of reflected light dancing in all directions. To see her appear so suddenly in all the elegance of a Paris half forgotten in the squalor and misery of war brought a sense of disbelief to every man present. The silence lasted only a matter of seconds, but momentarily she banished for each of them the black grimness that had permeated their existence in the Crimea from battle to battle and from bombardment to bombardment, punctuated by the screams of wounded men and dying horses, which had been the bitter price paid for the honour and prestige that they had won for their country and their Emperor.

One man was stepping forward to greet her. It was General Bosquet, squarely built and heavy with it, and with a flourish he stroked the ends of his bushy moustache with the back of his forefinger as he reached her and bowed.

"I bid you welcome, Mademoiselle Casile. I knew your father well. A fine man and a courageous soldier."

Stéphanie never knew what conventional answer she made amid the general conversation that had been resumed on all sides. With a sickening sense of disappointment she had thought that Pierre was not there, but when the general moved forward she had sighted him. He was staring over his shoulder at her as if he had not breathed from the moment she had appeared, his look compounded of incredulity and a terrible amusement as if he saw some joke turned against himself. She felt lost and afraid, unable to comprehend his reaction, and then he gave her a long, slow smile that changed his whole expression, leaving her in no doubt that he was pleased to see her. She could hardly tear her eyes from him to acknowledge others whom the general was presenting to her, only acutely aware that he had come to await his chance to claim her company. When eventually they stood face to face she was torn to see how much thinner he was, how strained about the mouth. She longed to press her own to those dear lips, but she was no longer the impulsive schoolgirl who had embraced him at Fontainebleau, and could not behave thus in a roomful of strangers. All she had been intending to say melted from her, and she became very still and quiet, her normally garrulous tongue seeming to have lost the power of speech. She lifted her hands to clasp and unclasp them once in a single expressive gesture of her silent joy in their meeting again. He gazed at her appreciatively.

"You are full of surprises, Stéphanie. I've never known quite what to expect of you since our very first meeting."

Her confidence returned, and with it her poise. A touch of mischief appeared in the corners of her lips. "I hope this is the best surprise of all."

He chuckled and leaned from the waist to bring his face close to hers. "The very best. Nobody else but you could have managed to appear in a theatre of war as if you had come from a magician's hat, and secure three days of furlough for me at the same time."

She laughed delightedly, taking the arm he offered her. Dinner had been announced, and General Bosquet was leading the way with Madame de Vincent into the dining hall. Throughout the meal Stéphanie was a centre of attraction, chattering away to all those around her, replying with smiles and flirtatious glances to those who raised their glass to her, and altogether thoroughly enjoying herself. She had her darling Pierre beside her, which was all that really mattered. Once when she slipped her hand into his under cover of the tablecloth he crushed her fingers so hard that she caught her breath on the pain of it, but he did not meet her eyes, appearing to be intent on a conversation elsewhere in which he was engaged. It was like the clasp of a drowning man, she thought. Then, with the new sophistication that she had acquired during her time at the Tuileries, she realised its significance. She felt a point of colour burn suddenly in her cheeks. He had conveyed a desperate need of her. Her heart began to thud against her ribs like a tolling bell.

Madame de Vincent performed her duties as chaperone diligently. She was responsible for the girl's well-being to the Emperor himself and she would not fail in her task, yet she would have preferred not to accompany them on walks through the village in the bitter cold, or to ride a little way across safe territory to explore an ancient fortress of considerable historical interest. Huddled in her fur cloak, which was as voluminous as Stéphanie's, she longed for the expeditions to be over and to return to the headquarters, but doggedly she remained with them at all times. To her relief there was no question of visiting the captured city of Sebastopol due to the unfortunate reason of an outbreak of cholera among the troops there, although they did ride up a hill slope to view at a distance what remained of that much-bombarded city that had finally fallen to the Allies a short while ago. Indoors she always kept at a tactful distance with a book or some embroidery whenever Stéphanie and her dangerously handsome beau sat talking together in the rosy glow of the flames flickering through a stove's grille, but at all times she kept them within her range of vision to ensure that no liberties were taken or condoned.

She supposed that for them the time flew past, but for herself it dragged tediously. All she wanted was to see the coffin safely onto the ship and to be gone from the dreadful part of the world where her beloved husband had met his untimely death. She welcomed the third and last day when it arrived, and was able quite to enjoy what amounted almost to a banquet given in honour of the two lady guests from France by the general and his officers.

That night she slept fitfully, thoughts of the morrow and the early start to be made on the return journey penetrating her sleep and making her stir restlessly on her pillow from time to time. Then abruptly her eyes flew open and she sat up in bed, her hair swirling about her shoulders. What had she heard? What sound had finally made her start from sleep?

Then she saw threads of candlelight touching the ridges of the floorboards under the communicating doors. Was Stéphanie ill? Talk of the cholera sprang into her mind. Flinging back the bedclothes she swung her feet to the floor with a feeling close to panic. She wanted to get away in the morning, and the prospect of having to remain with a sick girl for weeks on end was too dreadful to think about. Never had she longed more for her own country. Never had France seemed more safe and secure and civilised than in those seconds when she reached for her peignoir and thrust her arms into it. Scooping her long tresses free of the lace collar with one hand, she hurried across to the double doors and flung them wide.

"Stéphanie! Are you—" Her voice died in her throat. They were not naked. As she reminded herself over and over again later, they were not naked. Admittedly that could not be taken as to how far things had gone between them, but with her thoughts racing in the silence of shock she did not believe that Pierre de Gand with his fierce eyes and sensual mouth would tolerate modesty in a woman, or less than the ultimate in physical contact. Stéphanie, consternation and defiance in her face, sat against the pillows, her nipples showing high and shamelessly through the white cambric of her nightgown, her legs drawn under her. He was also on the bed, but sitting on the edge of it with hands in the pockets of his quilted dress-robe, one bare foot on the floor. His expression was one of controlled exasperation, and neither of them showed any surprise. Madame de Vincent did not doubt that the creaking of floorboards had given ample notice of her coming. A gush of despair revived her vocal chords, bringing forth her helpless exclamation on notes close to a shriek. "Whatever would the Emperor say?" Then she collapsed into a chair, covering her face with her hands, and burst into tears, the whole of her gentle nature at a loss. She heard Stéphanie begin to giggle hysterically between rage and humiliation.

At half past eight next morning General Bosquet, his officers, and all the soldiers attached to the headquarters stood to attention and saluted with full honours the departing coffin draped in the tricolour. As Madame de Vincent, already on horseback, inclined her head graciously and rode ahead, the mounted lancers moved forward in escort. Stéphanie on a chestnut mare followed beside Pierre, who was to see them to the ship and then rejoin his own unit.

Madame de Vincent stared unseeingly ahead as the barren landscape stretched out on either side with its wide snowdrifts in all the hollows. She was thinking that the whole expedition had been a nightmare and that that wretched girl, far from being consoling company to her now when she needed it most, had only added to her ordeal. If the Emperor should ever find out that she had failed in her chaperonage she would know herself to be disgraced in his sight and considered not worthy of the privilege he had granted her in the first place, which in turn would tarnish her husband's honoured memory. It was that aspect of the consequences that could follow the previous night's shameful episode. It had made her more willing to keep silent on the matter than she would otherwise have been. That in itself was another burden to bear, warring with her sense of duty. Admittedly, when her sobs had increased at the wild giggling, Stéphanie had brought herself under control and had appeared contrite at causing her such upset. But it had been the captain who had soothed her out of her tears, inadvertently giving her a sharp insight into that persuasive charm of his that her charge had found impossible to resist. Oh, yes, she could see how it had all come about, especially in such circumstances, but there was no excuse for either of them. She was resolved never to speak to Stéphanie again.

After a stop at a hostelry for refreshment she and the girl stepped once more into the hired carriage that had brought them to that place originally, and the journey continued in its final stage. When they reached the quayside it was dusk, and pathetic huddles of wounded were being assisted out of wagons or carried on stretchers up the gangway, taking the place of the supplies of food and clothing and ammunition that had come on the outward voyage. These were the men who had lost limbs or were too incapacitated to be patched up for battle again. Stéphanie felt a chill that had nothing to do with the freezing wind whirling snow in from the Black Sea, which had never been more aptly named, the waves as dark as the sky. She clung to Pierre in a last embrace before parting.

"Please take care. Don't let anything happen to you."

His expression was grim, his breath hanging with hers in the icy air. "The war can't last much longer. We have been through the worst of it, and you heard General Bosquet say that there was talk of peace moves on both sides. In any case, is it likely that I would let anything prevent me from going safely home to all that awaits me in France?" Then he kissed her without gentleness, almost with anger, leaving her lips bruised. The last she saw of him was as he rode away from the quayside, taking a different direction from the departing lancers.

On board she tried to converse a little with Madame de Vincent, with whom she was sharing a cabin, but she was met with a determined silence each time, and eventually gave up. The pleasant companionship that they had shared on the voyage out was quite gone. But there were plenty of others who were glad to talk to her. She offered her assistance to the ship's doctor, filled with pity at the plight of the wounded who were crammed in conditions of discomfort in every available corner of the ship, and he set her to feeding those unable to help themselves, which freed his orderlies for other tasks. When Madame de Vincent recovered from her seasickness she also gave what aid she could. When several of the patients died from their wounds, necessitating burials at sea, Stéphanie suffered great distress, but she hid it for the benefit of the rest, who looked to her to cheer them with her smiles and her chatter. With everything that had happened, as well as all that she had seen and heard throughout the expedition, she felt older and wiser, sadder and happier than before she had embarked for the Crimea, and was sure she would never be as frivolous or lighthearted again. She believed she had come to know herself as well as Pierre, and for that alone the journey would have been worthwhile, but to have achieved the true purpose for which she had gone in the first place was a precious bonus that she hugged to herself in secret and fearful exultation. If she had any regrets at all it was only that she had vented her anger on the last night of the sojourn at the headquarters against that poor, blundering woman whose untimely intrusion had been from the best of motives.

At Marseilles she was able to be of some comfort to Madame de Vincent, who had to be restrained when one of the coffin-bearers slipped on the gangway and for one macabre and terrible moment it seemed that their burden might plunge down into the sea. On the train Madame de Vincent thanked Stéphanie for her consideration shown at that particular time, and they did converse a little during the journey to Paris, the silence broken at last.

She found life at the Tuileries gayer and more extravagant than ever before, or else it appeared that way in contrast to the grim scenes of war that she had seen so recently. For a few days she felt strangely out of place, as if there were something unreal, almost magical, about the voluptuous settings unscarred by battle, and at the banquets, when exotic course after course was served, the wine flowing as if from a fountain, she recalled the gaunt faces of the Turkish troops, and the food almost choked her. But gradually she adapted again to her surroundings and once more felt at home, well pleased that so many people had welcomed her back. The Empress was particularly glad of her company and was eager that she should see all the dainty and intricately embroidered items that made up the forthcoming imperial baby's extensive layette, which, with the ornate cradle given by the City of Paris, was shortly to go on view to the public.

Among those who joined the long and never-ending queue to see the exquisite display was Marie Worth. She was expecting another baby herself and was sure that the Empress's joy equalled her own in anticipation of the event. The only difference was that the Empress faced the onerous prospect of disappointing a husband as well as a whole nation if she failed to produce a boy.

Louise, who had gone with her to view the layette, could not help contrasting Marie's daily routine with the leisurely time of rest and care that would be allotted to the Empress. In his enthusiasm for work Worth often forgot that his wife became more tired than before, and there were times when she looked dangerously pale and shadowed about the eyes. But she never complained, and although she must have found it difficult to face the heated-up food presented to her when she finally took a few minutes for a belated luncheon, she ate it stoically for the sake of her child and the necessity to keep up her strength.

Louise had herself returned from one of these snatched repasts one afternoon when she noticed that a visitor was waiting to see Worth, the circular package that he had with him proclaiming his mission. A never-ending stream of inventors of crinoline expanders made the rounds of the dressmakers, and their products were mostly ludicrous and impractical. The man's back was towards her, but as she approached there was something about the height and breadth of him that was vaguely familiar.

"You wish to see Monsieur Worth?" she questioned when she drew near.

His well-groomed head jerked round, and bright, twinkling eyes regarded her over his broad shoulder. "Louise! Well, I'll be damned!"

She gave a gasp of astonishment, clapping her fingertips to her cheeks. "Will Russell! Whenever did you come back to Paris?"

He laughed in pleasure at their reunion. "I arrived little more than an hour ago. It's good to see you again."

"I feel the same, seeing you after all this long time." She would hardly have known him, with his fair curls brushed into glossy order and his expensive clothes. He seemed to be equally intrigued by her appearance and he gripped her shoulders, holding her at arms' length while he scanned her from head to toe and back again.

"What finery! The black silk of a vendeuse and you wear it handsomely, my girl. You're a sight worth any amount of travelling to see." He caught up her hand, his eyebrows lifting at finding no wedding band. "Not married, then? Are the men of this country out of their minds?" The wide gold ring on the third finger of his left hand showed that he had taken the fateful step into matrimony.

"It should not be long now," she confided, her whole face aglow. "With the Peace Conference opening in Paris it should only be a matter of weeks or even days before an armistice is called in the Crimea."

Will grimaced sympathetically. "Your betrothed is involved in that mess, is he? At least the French fared better than the British. Some of the warm clothing my factory produced was earmarked for the Light Brigade, but few survived that terrible charge of the Russian cannons to need it. What's your betrothed's name? Which regiment is he serving with?" He raised his eyebrows again at hearing that the man she was to marry was of the Cent-Gardes, and whistled approvingly.

"Nothing but the cream of the regiments for you, eh? But he's the lucky one." He glanced about. "Where's Monsieur Worth? I'll get my business done, and then you and I will dine together and celebrate this meeting."

"I'll find him for you." She made to hurry away, and then paused to look back at Will. "It's just as if it were yesterday that we parted, except that you look so prosperous. I'm glad all appears to have gone well with you."

He smiled broadly in acknowledgement, following her with his eyes as she disappeared in the direction of the fitting-rooms. Financially things had gone well, but his marriage was another story. He had been deeply in love with Ellen Moncrieffe throughout the two years he had spent in Paris, and upon his return to England she had appeared as desirable as ever. Her father had made him wait another year until he had re-established himself in his own country once more. It had been a lavish wedding for the Moncrieffes' only child, with over four hundred guests and a tiered wedding cake three feet high. Ellen, ethereal in white satin and lace, had revelled in every minute, not wanting to leave the reception, and postponing their departure for as long as possible.

Later he had understood why. She had wanted to marry for the excitement of the day, to enjoy the status of being married, and to compete with her friends in the prestige of her home and mode of living. But to be a wife was a different matter. Their wedding night had been a disaster. Overprotected and cossetted by doting parents, naturally shy and retiring, she had come to the marriage bed in total ignorance, except that she had been warned by her mother that what took place there would be distasteful, degrading, and painful, but had to be endured for a husband's selfish pleasure. Encased to the throat, wrists, and ankles in her nightgown, she had huddled away from him, shivering with fright. He soon realised that her own body was a mystery to her, linked to all that was taboo and unknown, and even if he had not loved her he would have despaired that she had been brought up to believe her own nakedness to be shameful. He soothed, coaxed, and reassured, having resigned himself to sexual abstinence for a night or two, which was hard on a man of his strong passions, but the dismal honeymoon was over and they had been living in their own home for five weeks before the marriage was finally consummated. All the patient tenderness he had shown, the endless caresses that had brought her at long last to the point of surrender, were forgotten by her at the moment of possession. She had screamed out in pain and revulsion, reminding him horribly of a skewered butterfly, and ever after in their moments of intimacy she was rigid and resentful, sometimes tearful, making a mockery of their marriage, which by day she was careful to present as an ideal union. He had soon begun to see that she was one of those shallow women possessed of self-love, and his feelings towards her during their courtship had only fed her ego. She had thought to keep him on a string dancing after her for the rest of her life, but emotionally she would give nothing in return, her heart as barren as her body appeared to be. A child would have brought some joy into that house where every lace-curtain ruffle was starched and where every knob of coal for the fire would have been polished if it had been possible. Had he not wanted a son he would have taken her to him less than he did, and perhaps with it all he still hoped deep within the recesses of his mind that with time he would awaken love for love.

"Mr. Russell? I believe you wish to see me." Worth stood there, hands linked behind his back. He had spoken in French, but Will, knowing him to be a fellow countryman, answered him in English.

"How do you do, sir. I have come to Paris specially to show you my patented invention that nobody else has seen yet. I think you will find it of extreme interest."

Worth frowned with irritation, having been told by Louise that his visitor was fluent in the Gallic tongue, and he saw no compliment in Will Russell's choosing to speak English to him. As it happened, Worth no longer spoke English if it could be avoided. Like most converts to a new faith, which in his case was an overwhelming love for his adopted country, his zeal sometimes carried him away. Gradually he had come to see himself as being more at home in France than the French themselves. He thought and reckoned and even dreamed in French, which he now considered to be his first language. Always theatrical in his gestures, he had taken on Gallic mannerisms that had become quite natural to him in a deliberate shaking off of all that appertained to his Anglo-Saxon birth. He no longer had any real interest in anything that was not French. The materials he ordered for the shop and his own requirements in the dressmaking department were all woven in France. If he needed fine woollens he did not look to the British Isles, but sought them out from little-known French sources where he had located yarn and workmanship of equal quality. It went hard with him that only in Ireland was it possible to find a linen that could not be matched on French soil. He continued to import it because he had no alternative, but an English invention offered by an Englishman who chose not to speak French was a different affair altogether. He was prepared to reject it out of hand.

"I doubt it," he replied, continuing to speak in French. "I can tell you have a crinoline device to show me, and I have seen them all."

Will, weighing him up, was not going to switch languages until he was ready. As one Englishman dealing with another he saw no reason to use a foreign tongue in a bargaining matter. With easy arrogance which more than matched the flamboyance of Worth's own, Will stood solidly and looped a thumb in his waistcoat pocket.

"You're a confident man to make such a boast, Mr. Worth. My invention is not one of those wired concoctions or a variation on the heavy metal cages that almost pin a woman to the ground. Oh, no." He shook his head emphatically. "What I have designed is something entirely different. It is made up of fine steel hoops attached to each other by tapes and increasing in diameter from waist to hem. It is as light as a watch-spring." His broad shoulders shifted casually. "However, if you are not interested I'll take up no more of your time." He made to turn away.

"Wait!" Worth spoke in English, the richness of his Lincolnshire boyhood showing through. "Why did you come first to me?"

Will swung back, his glance and tone direct. "Gagelin and Obigez's has become renowned for its advanced ideas in fashion. I believe in going to the top."

Worth compressed his lips with some wryness. It was always the same. The shop took the credit for all his ingenuity and yet continued to offer him nothing but opposition every step of the way. He had had to fight for every innovation, every new idea, and every advancement, but the acknowledgement for success was never his. "Very well, Mr. Russell. I'll take a look at your watch-spring hoops."

Will grinned cockily and switched to French at last. "You've made a wise decision, Monsieur Worth."

As soon as Worth saw the model version of the invention

he knew all his problems with the crinoline were solved. Not only would it relieve women of the bulky weight of petticoats and padding, but he could make the crinoline even wider. From the current dome shape he could spread it out like a fan! What a framework for his dresses it would be! How the material would flow over it! He could scarcely wait to get it into the workrooms.

"I want the bottom hoop to be six yards in circumference," he declared, visualising the effect of at least ten yards of material over it, which with frills and flounces and loops and gathers would give a new and breathtaking dimension to the fashion.

"Six yards!" Will was surprised, but he did not question the order. "It shall be done."

Worth knew as well as Will that there was a fortune to be made out of launching the hoops quickly and capturing the market before imitators produced variations of it, which was inevitable, but in view of the high price Will was demanding for his product, which was quite within his rights, the proprietors of the shop had to be consulted. It was as Worth had feared. Instead of seeing what a golden opportunity had been put in their hands to hold exclusive rights to the invention in France, Messieurs Gagelin and Obigez held back from the outlay involved, and it was only with great difficulty that he finally managed to persuade them to invest enough to let him have a few weeks' headway in order to outstrip their competitors. He burned with frustration at their lack of foresight, thinking that if only he had the necessary funds he would have women buying diamond-studded hoops if he had decided that was how it should be.

Will was more than pleased. Not only would he flood Paris through Maison Gagelin with his hoops, but in the leeway that he had allowed them he would have time to build up tremendous stocks to launch himself in world-wide directions under their initial presentation, a true seal of approval. By arrangement he called at Louise's address for her that evening, and to meet Catherine again. He arrived with armfuls of gardenias for them both and a magnum of champagne which he insisted on opening at once. Afterwards he took them both out to dine at the Maison Dorée, which was a thrilling experience for Catherine, who had never been anywhere so grand before, and would have awakened poignant memories for Louise if Will had not been such totally different company from Pierre, exuberant, expansive, and in the highest spirits imaginable.

It had been his intention to complete his business as quickly as possible and leave Paris immediately, but since the next day was Sunday and Louise was free from work, he postponed his departure until that same evening. In the morning they joined the promenading crowds, he being interested to see at first hand the changes wrought by Baron Haussmann in the beautification of Paris. On a mundane level he had heard that the sewers of the city were now the envy of every capital in Europe, and on the way to Maison Gagelin the previous day he had had occasion to take note of the new street urinals that were as wildly ornate as small pavilions, rivalling the style of the gilded gas-lamps that by night banished the old darknesses where vice and crime had festered.

"What grandeur!" he exclaimed at the architecture. He found the spaciousness everywhere equally remarkable, and declared he would wager his last shilling that fifty carriages could be driven abreast down the avenue of the Champs-Elysées. He praised the abundance of newly laid-out parks and the open squares, and nowhere had the clearing away of mean buildings had more effect than in the vicinity of Notre-Dame, allowing it to soar alone in its magnificence. They went to take a look at the repaired and completed Louvre, and he stood in danger of being run down in the rue de Rivoli to observe the length to which it had been extended, remembering that once a dense mass of lofty houses with ragged roofs had blocked the view of the Tuileries.

In the afternoon he hired a coupé and drove her himself to join the wheeled cavalcade of fashionable folk that bowled through the Bois de Boulogne, which had now become the grandest park of all with its enlarged lakes fed by sparkling cascades, its arbours and shrubberies and well-planned drives shaded by the wide branches of the thousands of trees. Louise thought that nowhere in the world could more elegant traffic be seen. Here the élite of society, including the Empress herself, brushed wheels with the bold demi-monde, whose coachmen and footmen in powdered wigs and flamboyant liveries rivalled those of the imperial carriage itself. Louise noted that the most elegant women, whether courtesans or ladies, were wearing the new shade of blue called Cinders of Sebastopol in readiness to welcome home the victorious army from the Crimea. She had fitted customers into yards of the colour in every kind of fabric, and she never failed to marvel at Worth's ability to make each dress unique to the wearer.

That evening they dined quietly and at an early hour before the departure of his train. His mood was entirely different from the night before when he had been more than merry from the amount of champagne he had imbibed, the magnum having been only the start of it. Throughout that evening the conversation had been on a lighthearted level with news briefly exchanged and past times remembered among the three of them with much hilarity. Now, since the beginning of their Sunday together, they had filled in more details for each other. She had told him how she had first met Pierre, and he spoke of Ellen's loyal wait for him during those two years he had spent in Paris. He was as eager to know all about her advancement in the fashion world as she was to hear about his, although by the time they were being served the speciality of the house at Ledoyen's she realised that he had inveigled her into doing most of the talking, and there was still much more that she wanted to know about him.

"Tell me exactly how you started when you returned to England after we left Madame Camille's," she said while a waiter spooned onto their rosy slices of salmon a delicate green sauce made to a secret recipe known only to the restaurateur himself in the rivalry of the *cuisine classique* that existed among restaurants of renown. When the waiters had left them on their own again, Will answered her as they ate.

"First of all I opened a small factory in some run-down property in the East End of London, installing my own patented sewing-machines, and where—dare I say it to you?—I was able to get plenty of cheap labour, which was the only way to get launched. My garments were not run-of-the-mill, but had considerable cut and style. As a matter of fact I did all the cutting myself at first, working nearly twenty-four hours out of every day at times. Unfortunately things did not go well, and when the garments began to stockpile my finances were tottering on the brink, but I hit upon the idea of selecting four of the prettiest sewing-hands and getting them dressed up in the best of the outfits being made. I then travelled about with them, parading them before potential buyers." He glossed over the trouble he had had with those girls, who had fought and squabbled amongst themselves, jealous of each other and vindictive with it, but his imaginative presentation of his garments on their backs had brought him in a rush of orders, enabling him to take on many more hands and work the factory around the clock, and by the end of the year he was able to move into bigger and better premises. Since then he had gone from strength to strength in business and had secured an expanding market for his goods. It had been the complaints of the young women about the weight and bulkiness of their crinoline skirts, while fervently declaring it to be the fashion they wanted to stay forever, that had set him to inventing a means by which it could become easier to manipulate.

"The first of those hoops will be delivered to Maison Gagelin by the end of the week," he promised her confidently.

"I look forward to seeing them," she endorsed, full of admiration for his achievement.

He took a sip of wine, the crystal flashing points of light, and looked at her speculatively across the table. "You told me that you make your own clothes. Does Worth design them?"

"No, I do that. Naturally he must approve a sketch for a working dress, but he hasn't rejected one yet, although sometimes he suggests a small alteration. I always take his advice. I've learnt so much from him." Her eyes reflected her enthusiasm. "He is a genius. If he had been a sculptor he would have been another Michelangelo. If he had been a painter, the Louvre would have been filled with his masterpieces."

Will set down his glass. "Hmm. Lavish praise."

She caught his skeptic note and was determined to convince him. "Why should fabric be any less of an artist's material than marble or oils or water-colours? He can select a swatch of cloth and create what he will with it. It takes on life under his fingers. Many of his dresses are unquestionably works of art."

He was more interested in her talents than Worth's. "Your clothes have enough style for me. I noticed how women looked you over wherever we went today." His eyes narrowed. "I saw a similar reaction from the men, but that was for another reason."

She smiled, but made no comment. The waiters came to serve another course. It was duck à la Marengo de Joséphine and could not be faulted. Neither could the Bordeaux that shone ruby-red. Not until they had reached the coffee did he bring up the subject of fashion again.

"If you were not intending to marry I would ask you to come to England and work for me. You would give that Parisian touch to my garments that would set them apart from anything my competitors could produce."

She looked up from stirring her coffee. "Did you nearly ask me once before when you were leaving Paris?"

He glanced at her keenly. "Yes, I did, as a matter of fact. I felt we would have made a good partnership. Unfortunately I had nothing concrete to offer you then as I have now."

She raised her chin reminiscently. "Catherine was right, then. She asked me at the time if I would have gone with you."

"Would you have?"

She shook her head slowly. "I couldn't have left Paris then or now. I have a sense of destiny. I have always believed that the ultimate happiness of my life must be set from here."

He nodded. "I understand, but if circumstances should change, or if ever you have second thoughts about anything, there will always be a place for you in England."

She was surprised to hear a little catch in her voice. "Thank you, Will."

She went with him to the railway terminus. A porter found him a first-class seat and put his single piece of baggage on the rack. The steam from the engine billowed along the platform and enveloped them in misty swirls. He took her hands into his, smiling down into her face.

"I hope it won't be so long before we meet again, Louise. It's been a wonderful reunion for me."

"And for me, Will."

"Am I allowed to kiss the future bride farewell?"

Her eyes danced. "Everyone is allowed to kiss a bride."

But not as he kissed her. It was a repeat of the onslaught of his mouth that had taken place long before in a workroom by night, a deeply intimate and avid kiss, wildly passionate, and the force of it vibrated through his body into hers. The guard blew his whistle, and the last of the carriage doors began to slam. Will released her and sprang up the two high steps into the train, a porter banging the door shut for him. The window was open, and his expression was serious as he waved to her while the train carried him away and out of her sight.

She was thoughtful as she left the station and crossed the Place du Havre. It was foolish to think of what might have been, but she could not help wondering what would have happened and how things would have developed if a sharp-faced, vindictive woman had not chosen to intrude on those workroom premises so long ago.

In less than a week the first shipment of the Russell crinoline hoops was duly delivered at Maison Gagelin. Among them was one labelled as a gift for Louise. Worth was less than pleased at having to surrender one of the coveted number, but two days later there came the second of the many more shipments that were to arrive almost continually. He worked long hours, forgetting time for himself and everybody else in creating the largest and lightest crinoline dresses that had ever been seen. Marie was the first to wear one of them, her thickening waistline disguised with a clever use of fringe on jacket-tops. She declared that the inventor should be awarded a medal for freeing women from the cumbersome weight that had previously dogged the crinoline, and in her condition the lack of bulkiness was more than welcome. Louise was busy making a new dress in whatever free moments she had, wanting to have it ready to wear when Pierre returned, because none of her other dresses had skirts wide enough to cover the new hoops in the dimension of fashion that Worth had decreed.

Just two weeks after the armistice in the Crimea the Empress went into a difficult labour. Although Stéphanie was not among those in close attendance, she shared duties with others in the entourage in receiving the ministers of state and members of the family who would enter the bedchamber at the actual time of the birth, and she was in constant earshot of Eugénie's agony. All through the next day the terrible torment continued unabated. Everywhere in the palace people went about with strained and anxious faces. The Emperor himself was ashen, pacing about like a caged lion and unable to eat or sleep. Eugénie's screams became even more agonised. Stéphanie had been given permission to leave the vicinity several times, but she felt as if it would be deserting the Empress, who had only ever shown kindness to her, and so she remained, white to the lips and often feeling faint.

In the early hours of the third day it became a matter of life and death. The birth had to be induced by instruments without another moment's delay. The accoucheurs went to work, and Eugénie was delivered of a strong, lusty boy. The churchbells took up the rejoicing and cannon were fired, making windows shake.

Eugénie showed no emotion on the day the doctors told her that she must never have another child. She knew only a profound sense of relief. Her marital duties were at an end.

13

When Marie's second child was born it was another son. He was welcomed with great joy, and baptised Jean-Philippe, matching the infant Prince Imperial in being strong and healthy, a credit to his doting parents. As a thanksgiving Worth gave a charity donation to one of the Protestant churches in the city, and to be equally fair, he gave the same amount to a Catholic one. He was following a pattern he had set himself since his betrothal to Marie, always giving what he could as a practical expression of thankfulness for a blessing bestowed, and sharing it out as meticulously as Solomon. He still continued to snatch short periods of spiritual meditation whenever he could, taking no heed of whether it was cathedral, church, or chapel as long as the door opened and he could sit in solitary quietude without the disturbance of organised chanting or prayer. He knew his own failings and conceits, but wisely accepted that no man was perfect, and simply tried to do his best. He never swore or blasphemed, however incensed, and, still haunted by the childhood memory of his father's excesses, he had never so much as smoked a single cigarette or, although he appreciated good wine, ever had too much to drink. Loving Marie as he did, wholly and utterly with heart, body, and mind, he was spared the temptations of other women, and was content and faithful in his marriage.

His mother made the great adventure in travelling to France to see her new grandchild. Mrs. Worth's circumstances were now much improved. Worth made her an allowance, having always sent her anything he could spare even when struggling to make ends meet, and she was no longer beholden to her unpleasant relatives. In the past she had always cherished the hope that one day he would return to England and settle there, but she had come to realise that it would never be. He had made it clear in his correspondence that he thought of France as his home now, and intended never to set foot in England again. It was not that he bore his own country any animosity, but France had given him everything, a darling wife, the opportunity to excel in the profession he had chosen to follow in a way that would never have been possible in England, and more recently, his French-born sons.

"Do you ever hear from your father?" she ventured one evening when they were alone together while Marie was putting the baby to bed.

He strolled across to the window and stood looking out. "Yes," he replied with a coldness that was directed towards his absent parent. "He writes from time to time."

"To ask for money?"

"Always."

"Do you send it?"

"Yes, I do. I'm thankful not to have seen him all these years, and I never will, but I can't let him starve."

She came and stood beside him. "Can't you find it in your heart to forgive him? I forgave him long ago."

He turned and looked at her kindly. "I'm sure you did. On the very day he absconded, no doubt." His face hardened. "Well, I can't. I bear him no grudge on my part, but I can never forget the misery and suffering that he caused you, my dear mother. But he has gone from our lives. Let you and me never speak of him again." Deftly he changed the subject, putting an arm about her shoulders to draw her back into the room with him. "Incidentally, speaking of letters from England, I heard the other day from my old employer in London, Mr. Allenby of Lewis and Allenby. He learned a while ago of my advancement and wrote to congratulate me and wish me well. Since then we have corresponded from time to time."

"How very nice."

"He asked me recently if I would consider taking on the son of one of his business acquaintances. The young man in question is travelling at the present time to broaden his mind, and upon his return is to be thrust into his father's clothing shop with little if any knowledge of the trade, or feminine fashion either, for that matter. Mr. Allenby thinks that I should be the one to train the fellow, but he has not yet broached the suggestion to the father, wanting to ask first if I would be willing."

"What is the young man's name?"

"Robert Prestbury. He speaks French fluently, and has been educated at a good school. I've agreed to take him on when he returns home from Australia or America or wherever he is, sometime early next year. I believe I should find it interesting to have a protégé." He paused and tilted his head in a listening attitude. "It's very quiet in the nursery. Would you like to take a good-night look at your grandsons?"

Nothing could have pleased her more. They found Gaston already asleep, but when they reached the baby's nursery her infant grandson was not in his cot. Instead he was nestled in the crook of his mother's arm where she sat with him on a rug, his eyes appearing to follow the floating scarves of Indian silk that Marie was twirling and entwining about in the air with her free hand. From where she sat she looked blissfully over her shoulder at the two arrivals, much like a child herself in the radiance of her expression.

"We're playing such a lovely game. Jean-Philippe cried when I put him in his cot and I couldn't bear to see him unhappy."

Mrs. Worth observed the fond indulgence in her son's face as he regarded his wife. Marie and the baby certainly presented an enchanting picture, and it was typical of all she had seen since coming to their home. She considered her daughter-in-law to be a fine young woman and a capable housewife in true French style, but as a mother Marie was totally impractical, not having the least idea of how to deal with children. She only hoped that Worth would know how to discipline his sons when the need arose.

"He is just like you, Charles," Marie cooed, her rapt attention focused once more on the baby as she waved a drifting wisp of shaded blue silk before his gaze. "See! He loves beautiful colours already."

Worth went forward and dropped to one knee at his wife's

side, putting an arm about her shoulders as he joined her in looking at their child. "Exactly like me," he endorsed proudly.

Although Mrs. Worth did not suspect it, she was not alone in considering that Marie was not the most practical of mothers. Worth held privately to the same opinion, but he loved his wife too much to criticise her on that sweet fault. Louise also thought Marie was like a woman under a spell with regard to her offspring, but her own view was that Gaston and Jean-Philippe were the most fortunate of children to be born into a home with so much love in it. None could question the Worths' devotion to each other, and it still remained the case that the only cross words they exchanged were when Marie took a dislike to one of his designs. Then everybody around them knew about it.

Louise had had an anxious time over recent weeks. She had hoped that with the Armistice Pierre would soon be home, but it had taken until April before a treaty put a formal end to the war. Then a blow fell. She received a letter from one of his fellow officers to say that Pierre had succumbed to cholera, which was still filling the military hospitals, and he would keep her informed of the patient's progress. It seemed an eternity to her before word came of his slow recovery, and finally a letter from Pierre himself in a handwriting that spoke to her of the weakness that had not left him. He wrote that as soon as he was able to travel he would be transported to his home in the Loire Valley for a long convalescence. She would hear from him constantly. He loved her with all his heart.

Louise had taken Marie's place during the latter months prior to her confinement and since, during her postnatal absence, by wearing dresses for display to customers. For a while she enjoyed immensely the change of routine and then, although she did not show it, she often became bored with standing or walking around for inspection by customers, yearning to be back at more creative work again. Worth, however, was pleased with her. Being tall himself he found height in a woman attractive, and until he met Marie it had been the tall ones he had always noticed, so although he thought none could compare with his wife in setting off his clothes, Louise, being slightly above average height for a Frenchwoman, added a special grace of her own to them.

Throughout the last days of summer letters came regularly

from the Château de Gand. Louise, eagerly awaiting her reunion with Pierre, suffered deep disappointment when it had to be postponed indefinitely. He wrote that he had suffered a relapse, and on health grounds he had been given extended furlough to go south to the sun for full recuperation. She supposed there was anxiety about his lungs, and was thankful that he was receiving every care and privilege. She could bear his absence awhile longer when all that mattered was that he should be well again.

At work the autumn rush had given way to a mass of orders for the social events of the new year. Marie returned to the shop, leaving Jean-Philippe as with his brother before him to the charge of a reliable nursemaid, and her routine was soon as busy as before. When the day ended she was always anxious to get home to her little sons, and never had the distance between shop and home been more irksome than it was now. She wished, not for the first time, that she and her husband could live on the premises in one of the apartments located on the upper floors of the Gagelin building, but unfortunately all were tenanted.

In fashion the hooped crinoline was proving to be a great success. Only Messieurs Gagelin and Obigez had any doubt about the new dresses that their customers were flocking to buy. As they told each other, money was not the measure of everything. The trouble with Worth was that he had no compunction in sweeping aside the traditions and standards of their high-class shop whenever it suited him. Why they gave in to him they did not know. All too often they had allowed his verve and enthusiasm to overcome their better judgement, and the new crinoline was positively the last straw. The cause of their displeasure was that with hoops so light the skirts swayed and in swaying the *ankles* were revealed! In a high wind the most respectable of women revealed to perfect strangers their most intimate attire, giving rise to the bawdiest of jokes and lewd cartoons in the press. The owners of number 83, rue de Richelieu, suffered acutely in the knowledge that under their good and impeccable names Worth had launched the immoral fashion. They resolved that never again would they allow anything that reflected upon the dignity of their shop to go past them.

Worth himself was highly delighted with the popularity of his hooped crinolines, and had particularly beautiful petticoats made up in the workrooms that would ensure modesty and not billow out if the skirt swung unduly. Imitators were already producing similar hoops, and by coincidence whalebone hoops had also been marketed, but whatever was worn to support the skirt, one aim did not change, which was that crinolines should become wider and wider, a whim well matched to the expansive mood of a city bent frenetically on pleasure under the auspices of the most glittering court in Europe.

At the shop only Marie wore the extreme widths of crinoline, Worth limiting for convenience the circumference of those worn by his staff with the single exception of Louise, who as his premiere fitter was entitled to stand out from the rest of her fellow workers to a more moderate degree.

She always manipulated her skirt with care when she left the shop after dark, not wanting to brush against the rough walls of the narrow alleyway. One night when it was snowing thickly she had to concentrate on her hems as well, failing to notice the man who watched for her coming by a stationary fiacre. In her haste to get home out of the bitter cold she almost eluded him, darting away through the gaslamp's yellow aura of drifting snowflakes to be swallowed up in the darkness beyond. He went after her at a run to catch her about her waist and swing her into his arms and the warmth of his fur-lined cloak. Her cry was smothered by Pierre's rapturous kiss that banished all the time between and made it no more than yesterday when they had been last together.

"How I've missed you!" he gasped, his lips barely lifted from hers before he kissed her again.

She was in a state of delirious excitement, frantic as he for the renewal of the loving contact. "Are you really here? I can scarcely believe it."

"I thought this time would never come. Did ever two people have such misfortune as ours to be apart so long?"

"It's over now." She could not keep from touching his face and hair and shoulders with quick, fluttering caresses as if still having to reassure herself of his presence, and he kept her locked in his embrace as he hastened her back into the waiting fiacre.

"I'm starved for the sight of you." He pulled off her bonnet and took her face between his hands, his gaze echoing his words in the intoxication of his expression, her eyes letting him drown in their depths with all she felt for him. "But no more partings." His voice shook with the vehemence of his vow. "Tell me you still love me as I love you. Say to me what we have written to each other over and over again in our letters. I want to hear you speak those words."

She flung herself passionately across his chest. "I love you more than ever."

He gripped her by the arms, holding her there. "Enough to defy the whole world if needs be?"

"Yes, yes. What makes you ask that?" Uncertainty darkened the amber of her eyes almost to brown. "Is something wrong?"

"No," he answered in a deep whisper, enfolding her. "Not now. Not any more. You've told me all I want to know."

She had not asked where they were bound. They came to the apartment in the rue de Lenoir. Nobody else was there. Servants had made it ready for his Paris homecoming and then departed. Lamps glowed softly and flames flickered and danced in every grate.

In his arms she responded utterly to him, every nerve and pulse in her body having been quickened by his amorous play, and in the unrestrained elation of their lovemaking she was aware of some new element on his part that, even if she had wished it, she somehow could not have stemmed or brought to a halt. It was as if he were intent on plunging into the very soul of her, his mouth, hands, and body alive with a force and power that was making her feel possessed and claimed and conquered as never before. The ecstasy he broke forth in her was almost too great to be borne, and out of the throes of it she heard him groan erotically in long and total triumph.

He was sleeping when she slipped from the bed at dawn next morning. She bathed and dressed as quietly as possible. Before leaving to get to work she returned to the bedside and looked down at him where he lay barely covered by the tumbled sheet. She bent and put her lips softly to his forehead, half wanting him to stir, but he slept on. At the door, not knowing why, she felt compelled to turn and look once more at him. She felt that in sleep he had gone from her, and was seized with an acute sense of loneliness. Shaking her head at her own foolishness she closed the door silently behind her, and a few moments later was out of the apartment and descending the sun-streaked stairs.

All through the morning she felt as lightheaded and as lighthearted as if she had indulged in a champagne breakfast, which she did not doubt would have appeared if she had chosen to ignore her obligations to Worth and stayed on to miss appearing on time, but that was something she could not have done.

It was during the afternoon, when she was clearing up after a fitting, that she became aware of the electrified atmosphere that announced the arrival of an important customer. "Who is it?" she asked as she handed the dress over to one of the vendeuses who had been at the shop a long time.

"That old terror! Madame de Gand!"

Curiosity took her to the draped doorway that let into the dressmaking salon. Worth had received the customer from Monsieur Gagelin, who had escorted her there. Madame de Gand was glancing about impatiently.

"I am to meet my son's betrothed here! Where is she? Bring her to me."

Louise was dismayed at being caught so completely unawares. Surely Pierre should have warned her that his mother was in Paris and ready to meet her. No doubt he would have if she had woken him before leaving the apartment. During the night they certainly had not talked of anything beyond their immediate being together again. She drew in a deep breath, smoothed her collar, cuffs, and waist, and gave a final, unnecessary touch to her hair to ensure its neatness. She had taken a step forward into the salon when Madame de Gand happened to glance away in the opposite direction.

"There is Mademoiselle Casile now! Coming from the material department. Why didn't anyone say she hadn't arrived yet?"

Baffled, Louise followed the woman's glance and saw Stéphanie Casile approaching with some haste, obviously aware of being late. "Your pardon, Madame de Gand," the girl implored upon reaching the haughty woman. "I was early and decided to take a look at the latest fabrics on display. I quite forgot the time."

"Never make excuses. Not even to me. It's undignified. Now tell Monsieur Worth what you want."

Stéphanie turned shining eyes on him. "An evening dress for the official announcement of my betrothal, and afterwards a wedding gown and a trousseau, Monsieur Worth. The most beautiful you've ever created."

His expression was guarded. "I'm honoured, mademoiselle. Am I to understand that the fortunate groom-to-be is Captain de Gand?"

"Yes, that is right. We are to be married in early autumn."

Louise was not aware of having clutched at the fold of the drapes by which she was standing, but the room had begun to reel, and her one thought was to avoid collapsing in the view of those whose few words had held such dreadful import. She drew backwards out of the salon, and once out of sight she pressed her shoulders against the wall, her eyes shut as she fought for some control. She had known that shock made the teeth chatter, but she had never experienced the sensation before, and she put her shaking hands against her jawbone in a vain attempt to still the awful clicketing. Shivering racked her as if the temperature of her surroundings had dropped to subzero, and she could feel her strength ebbing from her. Two or three of her fellow workers came towards her with anxious enquiries, but she could not answer them. As her hands drifted limply to her sides she keeled over into blackness. If Worth had not happened to come through the draped archway in time to dart forward and catch her, she would have smashed her head into a cheval-glass.

Her faint lasted long. When she recovered consciousness she found herself alone with Marie and lying on a chaise-longue in the room set aside for those overcome by faintness. Memory returned, leaping into her eyes, dilating the pupils, and she jerked up from the pillow that had been placed under her head.

"Is it true?" she questioned frantically, her lips feeling curiously wooden.

Marie put aside the smelling-salts and supported her with one arm. "I'm afraid so, Louise. The two customers in question have gone now, but from what they said to Charles it appears that Mademoiselle Casile has been visiting the de Gand residence during the captain's convalescence. A few days ago a private party was held to celebrate their betrothal. Yesterday they returned to Paris, both of them to resume their duties in the imperial household. Madame de Gand came with them to be present at the official announcement next week during a ball at the Tuileries."

Louise rolled away, covering her face with an upraised arm, and the sobs that racked her were all the more terrible for being without a sound except for the rasping intake of breath. Marie's own eyes filled up in pity for such distress. It was what she had feared would happen all along, but Louise had been deaf to all friendly words of caution, and at times, away from the shop, had worn a diamond ring on her finger that was remarkably like an expensive keeper. Now Marie knew that it was. When she had opened Louise's dress to ease pressure around the throat, she had seen both the diamond ring and a plain gold band lying on a chain at the arrow of shadow between the girl's breasts. Marie did not doubt that Louise had been betrayed by the oldest trick that a man could play along the path of seduction.

"Is there anything I can do, Louise?" she implored, at a loss.

The answer came muffled with a shake of the head. "Nothing. Nothing."

Marie left her alone for a while, and when she went back later she found the room empty. To her amazement she discovered that Louise was once more at work, down on her knees adjusting the gathers of a dress under Worth's instructions. She was very pale, her eyes red-rimmed, but there was no faltering in her fingers, and she appeared to be in complete control of herself. It was as if by concentrating on work she was forcing herself away from the awful and enervating abyss of despair. Marie almost wept again at the staring look of unabated pain and anguish in Louise's tormented eyes.

Louise arrived home that night to find dark red roses delivered from Pierre, and a letter regretting that she had left him asleep when they had so much to talk about with regard to their future. His duties would prevent him seeing her that night, but he suggested that they meet the following evening at the apartment.

She let the letter fall into her lap where she sat. With her elbow on the table beside her she propped her brow in her hand. An hour and more went by. The roses lay wilting. Still she did not move. In her mind she was coming to terms with Pierre's betrayal and adjusting to the prospect of a life without him. It was the worst crisis that she had ever faced, but she would not go under. Not for her an orgy of self-pity and the indulgence of tears and more tears. She had shed enough. In her suffering she was paying the price of having boasted that no man should ever deceive her, and that she alone was in control of her destiny. Maybe it would teach her greater tolerance towards the failings of others in the future, if nothing else. And somehow—only God knew how!—she would survive.

The next evening she managed to get to the apartment early in order to arrive before Pierre. The servants installed there had been alerted to her coming, but she declined to remove her cape and bonnet, and went through to the salon to wait. Flames leapt in the fireplace, and the room was softly aglow. Through open doors she could see a table laid for two, champagne in an ice bucket, and amid the crystal and silver a floral centrepiece with candles. She understood now that the apartment had been planned all along for intimate tête-à-têtes, a place where he had thought to install her with his worthless promises and then to come to her whenever it suited him. She was thankful that Catherine's indecision had kept her from moving into the apartment before his departure to the Crimea, and she was astounded anew by her own gullibility at the time, her trusting belief in all he had said. His treachery and his deceit both before and since his return were of a magnitude almost impossible to comprehend, like the height of heaven or the distance to a star.

He had arrived! The sound of his voice as he spoke to a servant while divesting himself of his topcoat almost made her heart stop on the dagger of love and pain. Taking a deep breath, she braced herself and faced him as he came with a glad step into the room, closing the door swiftly behind him.

"Chérie! What a grand surprise to find you here already. Why are you still wearing your cape and bonnet? I'll take them from you."

She spoke before he could reach her. "I'm not staying. I've come to say goodbye. And to return these." She put the gold ring and the diamond keeper, which she had been holding in her ungloved hand, down on a small side table.

She had never seen a man look so shocked. He went ashen, his eyes taking on a look of such violent darkness that all doubt about his love was banished in her. But it was not the kind of love she had believed it to be. It was a love that could be slotted into second place, a self-indulgent love, a love that only understood sexual gratification and nothing of the tender and eternal fulfillment of a true loving link between a man and woman.

"You have heard!" he exclaimed hoarsely. "But how was that possible? There's been no announcement—"

"The future Madame de Gand has ordered her trousseau from Maison Gagelin."

Appalled, his cheeks hollowed. "God! I had no idea she ever went there. The prospect of such a catastrophe never occurred to me. My darling Louise—"

She shuddered involuntarily. "Please! No more endearments and no more deceit!"

He threw out his arms in the intensity of his appeal. "You must believe me when I say that I intended to tell you in the morning after our reunion."

She was suddenly seized with a terrible anger. "You should have told me before that night ever began!"

"No!" He grabbed her by the arms, ignoring her struggles, and hauled her close to him. "I wanted nothing to come between us that night. Not after being so long away from you. I thought to share a few last perfect hours with you before the time came for me to explain why I had asked if you loved me enough to defy all the world if need be."

For a few moments she ceased trying to jerk herself free, and stared at him in renewed anguish. "So it was then that you changed my role from bride to—"

"Don't say it!" He shook her violently in his stress to silence her, making her bonnet fall back from her head to dance upon its ribbons. Then, realising he was handling her roughly, his grip eased, and she snatched herself from him. He made no attempt to reach for her again, but his whole body was tense and poised as if he would ensnare her if she tried to leave. His speech came bitter and emphatic. "You and I would have been wed before I ever went away if there had been no delays. Like so many rare and marvellous chances in life, it was all left too late." Then he told her the whole story of his application to become betrothed, its outcome, and how he felt at having the course and pattern of his life and hers changed on the strength of the Emperor's whim. "I had hoped that Stéphanie would meet someone else in my absence, but this was not encouraged by either the Emperor or the Empress. They gave her permission to travel to the Crimea to see me, which in itself was a public showing of their approval of the relationship, forcing the issue. Nothing less than a betrothal could follow." No need to tell Louise that he had also inadvertently compromised the girl. By then he had accepted his fate and seen no reason why some advantage should not be gained from it. Any man would have done the same. Only the untimely interruption had thwarted what would otherwise have taken place. Faithfulness was never an important issue, although women were obsessed by it. Louise was no exception.

Her eyes were wells of desolation and bafflement. "So this

betrothal is not the result of a summer idyll during your convalescence, as I had supposed. Its origins are long-standing. You knew when you left for the war that there would be nothing for us when you returned."

"No, I disagree," he countered vehemently. "I had planned then that if I was lucky enough to come back unscathed we should make a life together. This marriage that has been arranged is simply one of convenience. Nothing more. It will make no difference to us."

Her face tautened. "No difference?" she echoed incredulously.

He sighed heavily. "If I had refused it I knew well enough what would have happened to me. My service in the Cent-Gardes would have been at an end. I would have been dismissed from the Army without honour and with ignominy for incurring the Emperor's displeasure on a matter of discipline." His haggard look deepened. "Can you begin to understand what that would have meant to me?"

She gave a bleak nod. "Yes," she said in little more than a whisper. Was she not now enduring a similar trauma for another reason?

Encouraged by what he believed to be the beginning of condonation on her part, he moved a pace nearer her. "You've already worn my ring, and it's on your finger that it rightly belongs. I'll always think of you as my true wife, the only woman I'll ever love, and you shall always have whatever your heart desires." He reached out and took up the gold band from where she had laid it with its keeper. His action went unnoticed by her, she having averted her face from him, her fingers pressed to her lips in her distress, her composure crumbling. He took another leisurely step, coming within touching distance of her. "If you tire of this apartment I'll have a house built just how you wish it, or buy any mansion you take a liking to, in the Faubourg St.-Germain, perhaps, or—"

Her hand was taken into his, and with screaming nerves she felt him single out her finger to replace the ring. Abhorrence of it engulfed her. "No! No! No!" She hurled her hand away with such force that the ring was knocked aside, gleaming as it spun through the air to drop and bounce and roll away out of sight. For a few awful seconds she thought he would strike her out of his wounded pride and vanity, waves of rage and temper flowing from him. The rigid gauntness of his staring-eyed expression reminded her of all the popular artists' impressions of her fellow countrymen rampaging in revolutionary attack, wild-eyed with nostrils flaring.

"Damnation!" he yelled at her, a pulse throbbing in his temple and in his jaw. "Does your love rely solely on a marriage certificate? It had not been spoken of when you first gave yourself to me. It was I"—he drove a thumb against his chest—"who could not endure the thought of not having you with me for the rest of my life. Do I mean so much less to you because through no fault of mine I lost the chance to secure a piece of paper that would legalise my bedding you? Was it only that certificate that you really wanted all along?"

She shook her head frantically, her fists clenched. "No! No! I would never have left you for any reason at all! I would have died first. You had only to tell me the truth. I wanted you forever."

He became calmer. His forehead cleared and his mouth actually relaxed into a faint smile of relief. "You have me forever. I love you. Only you. Nothing has changed between us."

She gave him a curiously pitying look as if she saw beyond the pride that would not accept defeat, and knew the suffering that must come. With effort she managed to continue as if he had not spoken. "If I had been told of the Emperor's decision against our marriage we could have talked about it together and found a way out. You could have resigned your commission with full honour and we could have left France to live abroad somewhere. In America or on the island of Martinique, or even followed French interests into Mexico." Then she saw by the fractional shift of expression in his eyes that he had considered the idea on his own and rejected it.

"I couldn't have left our country during the time of war," he answered stubbornly.

She gave a helpless little shrug, not denying his patriotic loyalty since none felt more for France than she, but because they had come to a point when they had nothing more to say to each other. He loved her, but not enough to give up everything for her as she would have done for him in that desperate situation. With a flash of insight she knew she had stumbled onto the very reason why he had concealed the truth from her. It would not have made a scrap of difference if there had been no war. Unbidden there came into her mind Catherine's oft-repeated adage that men always wanted to have their cake and eat it too. He was no exception. She picked up a glove she had dropped in readiness to leave, unable to endure any more, and feigned a strength she did not feel.

"I would have accepted your not being able to marry me. There have been many before us and there will be many after us who will love and be prevented from marrying through circumstances beyond their control, but I can't share you, Pierre. You underestimate the capacity of my feelings if you think that possible. Can't you see that I couldn't spend the rest of my life waiting and hoping for an hour or a day or a week or two granted now and again? I saw what that did to poor Catherine. In any case, by nature I could never endure second place."

"You'll always come first with me," he protested fiercely, unnerved at last by her determination to be free.

She could scarcely bear the stark anguish in his face, and bit into her lower lip as she struggled inwardly for calmness, but when she spoke it was with the tremulousness that reveals a fast-approaching breaking point. "For the sake of your marriage, and to enable me to start life afresh, we shall not meet again. Mademoiselle Casile will make you a fine wife, and you may rest assured that no word of our association will ever reach her ears either from me or from those few good friends of mine who have known of it." Her voice caught ominously in her throat, and she was frantic to get away. "Goodbye, Pierre."

Forcing her head to stay high she hastened from him. He did not attempt to stop her, but when she reached the door to tear it open, his desperate voice rang down the room to her. "You haven't finished with me. It can never be over between us. Remember how we met and parted and found each other again. I don't believe fate often plays tricks like that without good reason. You'll come back to me. You'll have to. And then I'll make up for all the wrong I've done you. You'll never be hurt again."

She emerged into the street in a tormented daze, and saw Catherine waiting for her. Never had she been more thankful to see that kindly face. Without a word Catherine put a comforting arm about her shoulders and led her away from the rue de Lenoir. Louise's face was agonised but dry-eyed. It was Catherine who had tears running down her cheeks. She was remembering the time when Henri Berrichon had gone from her life. She loved him still. She prayed that Louise would not be troubled for years to come by a love that would not fade.

14

Worth was in a dilemma. At Marie's request he had been prepared to spare Louise the fitting of the many dresses for the Casile trousseau, and work on the betrothal dress had been done by someone else, but now the bride-to-be had made objections. "I promised Mademoiselle Louise long ago that she should be the one to fit my wedding gown and trousseau," she declared firmly. "Please see to it, Monsieur Worth. I find her most agreeable, and always enjoy the chats we have. I'm sure you don't want me to find the fittings tiresome and a bore, particularly in view of the size of my order." It was a veiled threat that she might go elsewhere. He did not want to lose the order. The problem was solved for him by Louise herself, who caught word of it from someone who had overheard the customer's demand.

"But I had expected to fit Mademoiselle Casile's dresses," she said to him without emotion.

He studied her for a moment or two before replying. There was no denying that Louise had courage. At work she had continued as competently as if she had nothing on her mind, and there had been no tears, no unwarranted scenes, and no quarrels with fellow workers, which was the usual outcome when one or other of the female employees was going through the ordeal of heartbreak and desertion. She was just a little paler than before, with faint shadows under her eyes, which combined with some indefinable change in her features that he could not pinpoint. "Thank you, Louise. I appreciate your co-operation, and I fully understand what it means to you."

She gave a little nod, not wanting him to say any more, and returned to her work. At times of stress it was harder to bear kind words and sympathy than the rough edge of someone's tongue. How Worth would deal with her later on she did not know. To date nobody else suspected the secret that was hers, not even Catherine, and she had managed on several early-morning occasions to reach the outdoor privy without the undue haste that would have attracted attention. Her first thought after the initial shock of realising she was pregnant was to take flight, knowing at last what Pierre had meant when he said she would have to go back to him. During that night of their coming together again after over eighteen months apart he had woven her deeper into his own plot, determined that she should conceive. How cunningly he had met her from the shop, ensuring she had no access to the simple device she had always used after Catherine's sage advice to prevent pregnancy, and he had taken no precautions himself. By that means he had thought to bind her to him and thus ensure that when she learned there could be no marriage between them, all way of escape was barred to her.

She found it difficult to sleep, often pacing about her room as she tried to decide how best to cope with the new burden that had been laid upon her. She supposed Catherine would have suggested she visit an abortionist, but even if her baby had not been fathered by the man she loved, she could not destroy its life. Through no fault of its own it had come into being at a time of wild and heedless passion, and to reject the obligation put upon her would be to offend against herself as a woman, making her less than the humblest female animal that suckled its young, and leaving her without self-respect or dignity. Once again she made her resolve to survive, and this time her baby would survive with her. She would no longer be alone.

In the first day or two of panic she had considered packing her bags and going to Will Russell in England. He had offered her work, and she knew that he of all people would never turn her away. She had almost decided on that course of action when she remembered the way he had kissed her at the railway station, lustful, eager, and passionate. For his sake and her own it would be madness to risk another complicated involvement. Better to stay where she was and continue working for as long as she could conceal her state, and when that was no longer possible she would go into the country somewhere, have her baby, and find good foster parents to care for it until such time as she would be able to provide a proper home herself. At least she had some savings to see her through, although it went against the grain to have to touch a single sou of her careful investments towards the day when she would have a dressmaking salon of her own. At all costs Pierre must not know that he had been successful in his selfish impregnation of her, or he would give her no peace in his claim to her through their child.

The day came when Stéphanie arrived at the shop for the first fitting of one of the forty dresses that had been ordered from the sketches Worth had had done for her. The vendeuse in attendance took away her outdoor clothes and divested her of her dress. She was in her hooped petticoat when Louise entered the fitting-room, her reflection held in three floor-to-ceiling wall mirrors, and she spun around with a spontaneous exclamation of pleasure.

"How wonderful to see you again, Mademoiselle Louise. It's going to be just as I promised. You alone are going to fit me into all those marvellous clothes that Monsieur Worth has designed for me. How are you? Are you well? Are you glad to see me? I'm most happy to see you."

Louise compelled a smile to her lips, laying the dress she was carrying carefully along the length of a chaise-longue with the assistance of the vendeuse before answering. "I'm very well, thank you. I'm sure you will make a beautiful bride." She felt no personal enmity towards this amiable, exuberant girl, who was innocent of all the pain and turmoil that had come about, but it was proving far harder even than she had feared to be in her company.

"Look!" Stéphanie stretched out her arm and danced her fingers proudly to show off a large diamond set in gold. "It's the de Gand betrothal ring. Did you ever see anything so grand?" She giggled "Or so ostentatious! I much prefer a far prettier ring that Pierre chose himself for me, but I have to wear this one for the time being. We have all sorts of little jokes about it. He says he's marrying me because I'm always full of surprises and can make him laugh." She gave another infectious giggle. "That's only his jesting, of course."

"Of course," Louise agreed faintly.

"He is quite the handsomest man in Paris," Stéphanie said, taking up a stance of mock pride in her conquest, hands on her waist and chin uptilted. "Don't you think I've been extremely clever to ensnare him?" Her quip was merry. "Women flock after him, you know."

Louise busied herself in unhooking in readiness the dress that was to be fitted. "I'm sure they do. But then, as you say, he is extremely good-looking."

Stéphanie's eyebrows shot up. "Have you seen him, then?" she demanded excitedly.

"Yes. He came here once with Madame de Gand. It was quite a long time ago." Louise took up the dress. "Now if you care to stand still, Mademoiselle Michelle and I will help you on with this garment before Monsieur Worth comes in."

She and the vendeuse lifted up the layers of shot silk that shimmered from rose into lavender, and Stéphanie disappeared into it. Then Worth entered the fitting-room, and there followed his usual dissatisfaction with every part of the garment since perfection was nigh impossible at any first fitting, and he would settle for no less. Against her will, Stéphanie was slightly in awe of him. He was so imperious, lordly, and charming to her, and quite merciless to the dress, keeping up a flow of instructions to his fitter that surely nobody else could understand. It was a relief when he went from the fitting-room, leaving some final repinning to be completed, and she and Mademoiselle Louise were left on their own until the vendeuse should return to help her dress again. These were the times she liked best, when the two of them would laugh and chat together. On this day Stéphanie did most of the talking, not noticing that Louise was unusually quiet while being given an account of the trip to the Crimea and how Pierre had fallen ill with cholera when he had been due to come home, and then the bliss of sharing his convalescence at the Château de Gand.

"I was there when he arrived home. Nothing could have kept me away! I can't tell you how ill he looked—nothing but bones, and walking with a stick. But we all took such good care of him, and it wasn't long before he and I were able to go riding together, and for drives to visit neighbours, everyone wanting to entertain the returned warrior. I was so proud of him! Have you ever been to Tours? The Château de Gand lies not far from there. And such countryside! Hills and forests and vineyards as far as the eye can see. There is a dower house for Madame de Gand, and she is already preparing to move into it, but I don't suppose Pierre and I will spend much time at the château for a year or two, although it is not too tedious a journey from Paris." She went prattling on, revelling in having a listener who was about her own age. She was only a few years younger than the others in the Empress's entourage, but she had little in common with them and was often far lonelier in the social hubbub at the Tuileries than anyone could possibly suspect.

Louise was exhausted when at last she was able to leave Stéphanie to the attentions of the vendeuse and get away. She felt drained emotionally and did not know how she would be able to get through the innumerable fittings of the Casile garments that stretched ahead of her, but she must do it. The order had been given on that understanding, and there was no backing out now.

When the time came to work on the wedding gown she found it to be the greatest ordeal of all. Stéphanie was so full of palpitating excitement, so enraptured with the future ahead of her, that even in the early stages of the fittings she looked every inch the radiant bride, her pretty face shining out above the abundance of heavy white satin and Valenciennes lace that Worth had blended into a creation that far surpassed the gown that the Empress had worn on her wedding day.

It was after one of the many fittings that Worth was insisting upon that Louise found one of Stéphanie's earrings caught up in a frill of lace. Knowing that the girl could scarcely have left the shop's precincts, she hurried after her with it and reached her on the pavement.

"Thank you so much." Stéphanie took it gratefully and slipped its fine gold hook back into her ear. "It was my mother's. I would have hated to lose it."

Louise scarcely heard her. Too late she saw that Stéphanie had been met by Pierre at the shop's entrance. He was staring at her, raking her appearance from head to toe and back again. She knew his thoughts, knew what he was demanding of her in a silence that boomed against her ears, and quickly murmuring some vague reply about having been glad to have found the earring, she withdrew and hastened back into the shop. She slowed her pace as she returned to the dressmaking department, hand pressed to her side. How much longer could she go on lacing herself in so tightly? Since the baby had first quickened she had eased her stay-ribbons by a few centimetres, but was the present stricture still too much, endangering the baby's growth? She wished there was someone from whom she could seek advice. Catherine, who now knew about the baby, had never been pregnant herself, but was full of old wives' tales guaranteed to frighten a less clear-headed mother-to-be half out of her wits, and was not the one to consult. Contrary to what she had supposed, Catherine had been against an abortion, terrified of the physical danger involved.

"Don't you fret, my lamb," Catherine had exclaimed upon being told the news, too frantic to see that she herself was the one in a fret. "What's done can't be undone, except by risking your life to some backstreet crone, and we'll have none of that. I'll see you through it, and we'll manage to look after the little one between us."

"Calm yourself," Louise had urged patiently, capturing one of Catherine's agitated hands that were being waved about, and patting it reassuringly. "Nothing is going to part me from my baby before its birth and only afterwards for a short and temporary period. I have made my plans." And she had told her old friend what they were.

As Louise re-entered the dressmaking department Marie was parading in dress for a seated customer. By chance their eyes met, and Louise supposed herself to be pale from the encounter with Pierre when she saw concern sharpen Marie's glance. Then it came to her that Marie knew. Marie had guessed. It was like the lifting of a shadow from her. Now she knew who would be able to advise her about everything.

Marie did more than give advice. She donated a pile of baby clothes that Jean-Philippe had grown out of and told Worth the situation. With his permission Louise made herself short jackets with butterfly frills or with scallops of the same black silk as her working dresses, similar to those he had designed for Marie when she was at a similar stage of her pregnancy, which effectively disguised the relaxing of the lacing about her waist. As when Marie had worn them, these little jackets were much admired, and Worth received several orders for them from customers who were anything but *enceintes*.

As week followed week the dresses of the trousseau were completed, the bridal gown being the garment that required most attention. Louise was thankful that she felt fit and strong and could continue to do the work, suffering no discomfort since the morning sickness of the early days, although tiredness did overcome her at the end of the long day. When she took the last flight to the rooms where invariably she was home before Catherine, her steps became slower and slower, and at the top she always had to rest for a few moments, drawing breath. She was taking this much-needed pause late one evening in the shadows of the landing when she gradually became aware she was not alone there. She stiffened, knowing that the time had come for the confrontation with Pierre that she had dreaded, but which she had hoped against hope would never come about.

Pretending not to be aware of his presence she took her key from her purse, thinking to escape quickly behind her door before he could make a move. The key clicked in the lock, she shot through, and then with a great thud his fist blocked the closing door and he was inside with her. She saw at once that he had been drinking, his eyes very bright and angry, his handsome mouth set mulishly. With one hand he wrenched her cape from her and with the other jerked aside her black silk jacket with such force that it was half pulled from one shoulder. She was desperately afraid and did not dare to move. Slowly his gaze rose from her waist up to meet her face, his expression one of savage exultation and triumph.

"*Now* will you come back to me?"

She tugged the silk jacket from his grip and took a step away from him, frightened still and apprehensive. She swallowed deeply and found her voice. "No. You already belong to someone else. I will not take half a love from any man. When I said goodbye to you I meant it. Now will you please go."

He thrust his face towards her belligerently. "You're carrying my child. What can make us belong to each other more than that?"

She felt her self-control slipping away. All her nerves were much nearer the surface since the start of her pregnancy, and there was the gleam of unwanted tears in her eyes. "It's not your child. It's mine! You can never prove parenthood. No one can swear that I was the woman in your bed at the apartment that night. Nobody saw us arrive there and nobody saw me leave." She was seized by the rising tension that presages hysteria, and was powerless to stop it. "It's my baby! Mine! Stéphanie Casile will bear you all the legitimate children you could possibly want. Sons to grow up and be acknowledged by all the world as yours. And she the wife always at your side. She the one with whom you'll live your life and with time come to forget that you ever knew me." Sobs burst from her in a storm, and she flung her arms over her head in an agony of despair at all she had conjured up, thoughts too close to the heart to have ever been said to him of all people. Her torment increased beyond endurance as he seized her in a powerful embrace, pulling her arms away and covering her eyes, face, and throat with kisses.

"You love me still," he grated in his elation. Beside herself, hurt, humiliated, and degraded by his amorous violence and thoughtless insensitivity, she hit out at him, striking at his face and chest with hammering blows of her clenched fists. Caught off guard and struck painfully in the eye and across the nose, he released her from his arms.

"Get out!" she shrieked, the tears pouring down her face, completely hysterical and wanting only for him to be gone. "I warn you. If you ever dare to come near me again I'll kill myself. I'll throw myself in the Seine and my baby will die with me!"

He was shocked into sobriety, dismayed and horrified. "I'm deeply sorry. I let my feelings for you run away with me. Louise—"

She stumbled past him, pulled open the door and turned her face away, her cheek pressed against the rough surface as she waited for him to leave. His expression was stricken. He paused by the door, and unseen by her he half-reached out as if to make one last appeal, but then thought better of it. He took up his hat that he had earlier tossed aside, and left.

She slammed the door shut and shot the bolt home. Then she reeled away and fell to her knees, folding her hands over her enlarged waist, and bowed her head on the long stem of her neck as she whispered in the midst of her sobs to her unborn child.

"I didn't mean it. I'll never let anything happen to you. But I had to make him go, had to make him stay away. I can't spend the rest of my life being torn apart. I must salvage what is left. It has to be this way."

She slid one arm onto the seat of the chair beside her, and burying her face in the crook of her elbow she sobbed out all the tears she had refused to shed many weeks before.

In the days that followed she revised her plans. With Pierre aware of her condition there was no point in leaving Paris to escape his notice, and she was convinced her threat had checked completely any further advances. Not at all sure how Worth would react, she approached him with a request to take up work in the sewing-room where she would be gainfully employed and there would be no risk of offending customers with the sight of her condition when the little jackets could no longer conceal it. He had it in his power to dismiss her without references for being in her present state. After all, he had vouched for her moral character to secure her employment at Maison Gagelin and it could be said that she had let him down, but she felt that if he had intended to send her away, he would have done it earlier. She had not mentioned the identity of the father to Marie, who was too tactful to question on such a sensitive matter, but she knew Marie had guessed in the very first instant, just as her husband would have done.

"Hmm." Worth mulled over her request. "Very well, I've no objection. You had better work at the embroidery table, which could do with an extra hand. But I'll want you to finish the fittings on the Casile wedding gown."

"Yes, of course."

"One more thing. As you know, I do get customers ordering dresses for the advancing stages of the condition that you now share, and to date it has been impossible to show them how a finished garment will look or how great the extent of delicate concealment. Would you have any objection to wearing and showing these dresses for me? You would only appear in the small salon already set aside for ladies who are *encientes,* and you may be veiled to spare you any embarrassment. What do you say?"

She answered him without hesitation, a give-away huskiness in her throat. "I'll be glad to do it. And I'll be eternally grateful for being allowed to stay on."

He was, she thought, for one who discounted organised religion, the most truly Christian of men.

From then on her time was spent at the embroidery table in the workroom except when the Casile girl made a visit to the dressmaking department, or a pregnant customer came to order clothes, always by appointment to ensure both privacy and immediate attention. Then Louise, dressed ready in one of Worth's concealing creations, a throat-length veil over her hair and face, would wait seated in one of the salon's draped alcoves until at a quiet word from him she would rise and pace slowly around the floor for the customer's appraisal. This entirely new idea was greatly appreciated by the customers concerned, who found it encouraging to see that even in an advanced state of pregnancy it was possible to move with grace and to retain a fashionable mode of dress suited to their individual requirements. Word of Monsieur Worth's veiled lady spread like wildfire among those expecting a happy event, and the appointment book was filling up daily. But Worth did not escape the customary battle. Messieurs Gagelin and Obigez had to be persuaded once again that he had conceived a brilliant idea that was increasing business along a new line. After a great deal of deliberation and a study of the accounts the proprietors finally decided that since the whole process was being conducted with the good taste and discretion suited to their high-class emporium, they would concede on this point, but it was absolutely and indisputably also the final point of no return. In future the dressmaking department must keep to an even and conventional plane. It was fortunate that they did not ask the identity of the veiled lady amid all the hubbub of argument and decision. If they had known she was an unmarried employee in a state of shame, the whole innovation would have been crushed and obliterated.

Worth was left as always feeling taut and exasperated. More and more he resented the petty interference and bigoted views of his employers. He had always yearned to have his own exclusive premises, but never more than in the last two or three years, when he had begun to influence the whole range of fashion from his simple dressmaking department. His financial situation was naturally much improved since his earlier days, but he lacked the funds needed to set up on his own. Often, on Sunday walks with Marie pushing Jean-Philippe in the wicker perambulator and little Gaston's hand in his own, he would take note of suitable properties, and together they would discuss ways and means by which the dream they shared of a Worth establishment could come about, but always it remained a dream, and daily his frustration grew.

Stéphanie came for the final fitting of the bridal gown. The wedding was still three weeks distant, on the tenth day of September. Louise, well into her seventh month, wore a black silk overtop that fell from her shoulders to the curve of her crinoline, and a variation of these tops in all colours and fabrics formed part of some of the clothes that she displayed for those special customers. So elegant and cunningly designed were these tops that for a long time even Stéphanie had not been entirely sure that Mademoiselle Louise was in the state that she suspected, and since there was no marriage band on her finger it was not a subject that could be mentioned. But eventually the increased awkwardness of Louise's movements and the unguarded glimpses of her silhouette caught by the fitting-room mirrors dispelled all doubt.

"My wedding gown is surely your most beautiful creation, Monsieur Worth," Stéphanie enthused as he and Louise stood back to let her admire her reflection to the full, the layers of lace creating an effect that was light and ethereal, the gleam of satin complemented by the glow of flower clusters of pearls. She addressed the image of Louise in the mirror. "You will be with me on my wedding morning to help me dress, won't you?"

Worth spoke up. "We shall both be there." It was his custom to see that a bride of importance left for the church with his dress and veil in pristine condition and without any unnecessary or ill-chosen jewellery that could ruin the whole outfit. Since the Empress herself was to be among the important guests at the marriage, he was particularly anxious that his dress should be arrayed at its best. Privately he wished Stéphanie had more style to set it off. She was pretty enough and looked charming in it, but she lacked that rare quality of pure *chic* that caught the breath and stunned the eye. Marie had that air even in her nightgown.

Louise was dismayed that Worth had apparently quite forgotten the reason why she would not wish to help Stéphanie dress for the wedding. She had assumed that he would take the head vendeuse with him, which was usual, but he had granted Stéphanie's request without a second thought simply because he had become accustomed to the girl's expectation of her attendance. Any thought she had of evading the duty was dispelled when Stéphanie turned a half-frightened face to her the moment they were alone.

"I'm scared, Mademoiselle Louise. I love my betrothed so much, but I'm afraid that he's dreading the wedding day. When there's talk about it I see a certain look in his eyes, a kind of trapped look as if suddenly he hates everyone in the room, and me most of all."

"Hush! Hush!" Louise cried, wanting at all cost to silence her. "You must not say such things to me. You're nervous, as all brides are, but you can't confide your fears to a dress-maker's assistant."

"Why not? I've come to think of you as a friend over these many weeks. I arrived as a stranger at the Tuileries, naïve and out of place in that sophisticated company, and I still have no one who would listen to me kindly."

"Surely the Empress—"

"Not any more. I talked to her once when I was quite desperate and thought I had alienated Pierre, but although she is good and gentle in a thousand ways she is more impatient than ever when her ladies speak of love or romance, scoffing at whatever they say. Yet I don't understand why, because she has an eye for handsome men and makes it obvious, just as I've heard she has always done, teasing and flirting and turning their heads with her beauty. Then she becomes cold as ice and can be viciously cruel if a man dares to declare his amorous admiration, and at her request the Emperor will banish whoever it is from court. Men are nothing, she continually says, and that is how she would answer me if I went to her as I have turned to you."

"Then confide in the Duchess of Bassano. You have been staying with her since you came to Paris, and you are to marry from her house."

"No, she has never liked me very much. Once when I displeased her she called me a giggling little ninny, and that's what I am. No wonder Pierre regrets his promise to marry me. After all, I plotted and connived and trapped him into it—"

In desperation Louise put a hand over the girl's mouth. "Put all those foolish thoughts away. Think only of your love for the man you are to marry. Remember all those happy times you had together last summer. It will be like that for you again once you are wed. The period of a betrothment is always strained and often fraught with doubts. It is the same for him as it is for you, and it's up to you to banish whatever lies in the past in the new life that you'll create for him."

Stéphanie nodded, blinking back tears and wiping her lashes with the back of her hand in an unconsciously child-like way. "How sensible you are and how comforting. Yes, I will do as you say." Impulsively she reached out to hug

Louise. "If ever I had had a sister I should have wanted her to be just like you."

Then the vendeuse entered the fitting-room and there was no more intimate conversation. Louise suffered acutely from the ordeal of it for the rest of the day, her hands slow with the embroidery she was engaged in, and her anguish sharper than any physical pain.

On the eve of the wedding Louise with one of the junior vendeuses accompanied the huge circular bandboxes containing the bridal outfit to the Duke and Duchess of Bassano's residence, a grand edifice with gilded gates not far from the Elysée Palace. The trousseau had been delivered long since, but the bridal gown needed to have every frill and gather smoothed out at the last minute, and a lay figure of wicker supported the garment while this was done. Together Louise and her assistant completed their tasks, tucked the tissue paper back into the boxes, and were about to leave when a maidservant came to tell Louise that Mademoiselle Casile wished to see her. Somewhat apprehensive that another last-minute show of nerves was to take place, Louise followed the maidservant and was shown into the library.

Her first alarmed thought was that Stéphanie was ill. There was a thin look to her face, a bleakness to her eyes, but when the girl moved forward in greeting there was the same swift litheness to her step that belied any physical affliction. She bade Louise sit down, but remained standing herself, nervously drawing a lace-trimmed handkerchief through her hands. "May I call you Louise? I feel the time has come to dispense with formality between us."

"By all means."

"I should like to ask you an extremely personal question."

Louise's earlier apprehension gave way to a sick dread. She had no idea what might be coming, but she was certain it boded no good for either of them. "I'll answer it if I can."

"Who is the father of your unborn child?"

Louise blanched, thankful she was sitting down, and she clasped involuntarily the arm of the chair. "No one has dared to ask me that, and you have no right to do so."

"I think I have every right!"

Then Louise knew that something disastrous had happened or was about to happen. She tried not to show her inner qualms. "Perhaps you had better explain what you mean."

Stéphanie took a couple of paces in one direction and then

the other before she came to a standstill, plucking so hard at the handkerchief that there was the tiny sound of tearing lace in the quiet room. "Three days ago at the Tuileries I had reason to go to the Empress's apartment. The rooms of her suite open one into the other, and knowing that she would be in her bedroom I walked right through to reach it. I had come to her *cabinet de toilette,* a large room with looking-glasses and a frilled dressing-table and so forth, when I distinctly heard her speak my name in that clear, far-reaching voice of hers. Thinking I was being summoned to hurry forward I went without knocking into the anteroom that communicates with the bedroom. It has a gilded partition, and it is here that the Empress often hears mass and performs her devotions at her own private oratory. Before I could reach the bedroom door, which stood ajar, I heard my name again, but in connection with some mention of scandal. Two or three ladies of the entourage were with the Empress, so I stayed by the gilded screen and listened quite shamelessly. Do you want to know what I overheard?"

"No, no." Louise propelled herself up from the chair, shaking her head violently.

"I think you should. Apparently one of them had discovered that the woman with whom Pierre was seen everywhere before he went to the Crimea, and who was recognised by everyone to be his courtesan, has been fitting the garments of the bride he is to marry tomorrow. What do you say to that?"

Louise looked at her with tragic eyes. "I say that with all my heart I wish you had never heard that cruel talk."

"Do you deny that it is true?"

"The truth is that all was ended between Pierre and me before you and he were betrothed. In perfect honesty I will tell you that I have seen him once since, but that only made even more final what was already over and done with."

Stéphanie's face was full of conflicting emotions, hope, distrust, and fear intermingling. "Do you still love him?"

"He is no longer mine to love, and if he had truly loved me he would not be marrying you."

"But a gentleman never—" Stéphanie bit off the words, colouring.

Louise raised an eyebrow, finishing the sentence for her: "—never marries his mistress. Is that what you were about to say? Or was it that a gentleman, particularly an officer in the

Cent-Gardes, would never marry a woman of the working classes?"

Stéphanie was in a state of confusion. "I didn't intend to insult you."

Louise inclined her head. "I know that. But this is still the France of a Bonaparte where social gaps can be bridged, however grand the imperial trappings, and if a certain case is beyond the par, there are places elsewhere in the world where a man and woman of diverse backgrounds would be accepted. So basically Pierre had a free choice. You are the one he chose. I tell you again that it is over." A chill smile appeared quiveringly on her lips. "Don't think I'm being noble or self-sacrificing. I'm thinking more of myself than of you. I'll be frank in saying that in wishing you well, my motives are entirely selfish. The marriage between you and Pierre gives me back my freedom." She did not want Stéphanie to back out of the marriage at the last minute. It would do no good and only prolong matters, because if Pierre should not marry Stéphanie it would only be a question of time before he took as a bride someone else of whom the Emperor approved. Never her. Never the one who would have gone anywhere in the world with him if he had chosen to defy the threat of treason.

"But the baby? Is it his?"

Louise's face froze. "I have spoken the father's name only to one person. She is the woman who brought me up. I say once more that you have no right to ask such a question of me."

Stéphanie nodded helplessly. "I accept what you say. You have made me believe that I have nothing to fear from you, and the Empress forbade her ladies to mention the connection to anyone, but how am I going to face tomorrow, knowing how the scandal might have spread? First the civil ceremony at the Tuileries and then the church with ridicule and scorn repeated in everyone's eyes. And as if that were not enough, the hours of tittering and whispering at great wedding celebrations that will last four or five hours or more." The handkerchief she clutched had become shredded and she looked at it dazedly as if not knowing how it had come to be in that state.

Louise pitied her and out of that pity felt the strength of the bond that was friendship between them. "Who would dare to be scornful of you in the presence of the Emperor and Empress?" she encouraged stoutly. "In any case, I'm sure you have nothing to fear. The Empress's ladies would respect her wishes, and others forget whatever they might have heard when they see how happy and radiant you are. Tomorrow is the day you have been longing for. You've told me that many times. Don't let anybody or anything spoil it for you. You're going to marry the man you love."

To Stéphanie it was as if in the midst of her misery she had been cast a lifeline. She *was* going to marry Pierre, and nothing else mattered. All men had affairs before they married and settled down, and she had it in her power to make him forget Louise and all the others he must have known in his bachelor days. With a tilt of her chin she regarded Louise coolly.

"I think it would be best if you didn't come tomorrow. Let Monsieur Worth bring someone else."

Louise was engulfed with relief. "I'll tell him that."

"Goodbye, Louise."

Once outside in the evening air Louise was forced to stop twice before she reached the pavement beyond the gates, such a shaking in her limbs that she could hardly walk. Her emotions had been stretched to breaking point, and she could not take any more. Crossing the boulevard she was almost run down by a cab-horse, and only realised how close to danger she had been when the cabby yelled at her out of his own fright. On the recently opened Alma Bridge she slowed to a halt by the stone parapet and stared down into the lamp-splashed water, yearning for an end to the tearing heartache within her. Then the baby kicked strongly in her womb, reminding her of its lively presence. She drew sharply away from the parapet, and with straightened shoulders she continued her homeward way. A gendarme, who had been watching her, resumed his steady pacing across the bridge.

A month and a half later in the early hours of the last day of October when the sunrise was dousing the all-night lamps in the room with a pinkish light, Louise gave birth to a son in the presence of a sweating midwife and an anxious Catherine. It had not been an easy labour, but all that was forgotten when the baby was laid in Louise's arms. She looked at him and loved him and knew a pride in him that kept the smile on her lips even as she slept in exhaustion. He was to be baptised Paul-Michel for no other reason than that she liked the name. And perhaps in her heart of hearts she wanted to give him a link in the letter *P* with the father whom he would never know.

15

Robert Prestbury arrived with aplomb at Maison Gagelin. Not for him the employees' entrance or the cap-in-hand approach. He stepped out of a hired fiacre of some past grandeur, tipped the driver handsomely, and breezed through the door swung open by the doorman as if he had come to buy the shop. He snapped his fingers at an assistant.

"Where can I find Monsieur Worth?" He had spoken in French, starting as he meant to go on. No wily foreigner was going to get uppity with him through thinking he didn't speak the lingo as well as his own tongue. He had never achieved much scholastically, but he did have an ear for languages, and his extensive travels had given a final polish to his mastery of Italian, Spanish, and German that matched his command of the French *langage*.

"I'll show you, monsieur."

As the assistant led the way he followed at a swaggering saunter, twirling his cane and glancing about him. God! What a difference between this opulent edifice and the mean interior of his father's London shop, which had size, a few potted palms, a handful of display dummies, and little else. Not even a comely young shopgirl to squeeze, but sour-faced harridans who looked as thin as their own tape-measures and with lips as pinched as if permanently holding dressmaker pins. They would be the first to go when he took charge of the Prestbury Emporium. But before he could aspire to running that shop he had to prove to his father that he was capable, that he was ready to clip his wings and take life more soberly than in the past. Well, he had no choice in the matter. The legacy from his maternal grandmother, which had given him two years of independence and extravagance, had finally run out, and he was reduced to a trunkful of expensive clothes and little else. He knew Paris, which he had visited twice before, but he had been in the money then, able to enter freely the glittering, lascivious circles of the demimonde, throw a lavish party or two at the Maison Dorée, and on more than one occasion had widened his sexual experience luridly with *la belle* Castiglione, who had taken a fancy to his youth and vigour. This time circumstances would be entirely different, but nevertheless it was still Paris, and since an opening had been found for him through the kindly auspices of the silk merchant Allenby, an old friend of his father's, he had not ceased to congratulate himself on his good fortune. Nobody else could have persuaded his narrow-minded parent that a proper training in a renowned Parisian shop was what was needed to awaken a new and lasting interest in the Prestbury son and heir for the more humdrum family business. Robert had little time for foreigners himself, but he thought his father's bigoted attitude toward France could be likened to that of Lord Reglan, who throughout the Crimean campaign had persisted in referring to the opposing Russian forces as "the French," which was the ultimate stigma that he could apply. Considering that John Prestbury was in poor health and greatly in need of someone young and capable to take over, he had taken his time about agreeing to finance the Parisian venture instead of hastening it along. It was only the fact that the *premier commis* at Maison Gagelin was an Englishman known personally to Mr. Allenby that made John Prestbury finally agree to his son going there and not straight into his own emporium. He had remarked pontifically that a shop in the charge of a decent Englishman was guaranteed to be a respectable establishment, even in the sinful city of Paris. Robert grinned to himself. *More's the pity,* he had added succinctly to himself at the time, and he repeated the sentiment now.

He had arrived at the dressmaking department. It appeared that Monsieur Worth was engaged at the moment. Would he please take a seat. He would not be kept waiting long. Robert, still taking note of everything, sat down at ease in a gilded chair. The salon was remarkably busy. Customers were being attended to by smartly dressed vendeuses in black silk, or sitting to watch an afternoon dress being displayed by an eyeful of fine womanhood. A red-headed vendeuse was going past. Small breasts, but a pleasing profile. He liked that colour hair.

"Who's that parading in the blue dress?" he asked her with a twinkling glance.

"That's Madame Worth, monsieur."

"Oh, is it? Thank you." He followed the girl's departing back with his eyes. She had actually blushed. Good God! The shopgirls were prettier than at Prestbury's, but probably no less virtuous. What a crashing bore.

He saw a tall, slim man approaching him in a black frockcoat and trousers, the cravat folded immaculately and fastened with a pearl-headed pin, the waistcoat without a wrinkle. So this was Worth. Younger than he had expected. Early thirties. Distinguished and serious and very alert. Robert rose leisurely to his feet. Might as well impress the fellow from the start, and for good measure he would speak in French.

"This is indeed an honour, Monsieur Worth," he said with an easy, companionable air as if they were meeting quite socially, and extended his hand in readiness to shake the couturier's. "I'm Robert Prestbury. You're expecting me. Quite a tolerable place here, is it not?"

Worth ignored the outstretched hand. He had imagined that he had been summoned away from an important fitting to deal with some urgent matter, and upon hearing that the newcomer's name was Prestbury a wrathful look set his eyes blazing, and his whole expression became one of congested outrage.

"This is not a club, Prestbury! I do not greet my employees in the salon at the busiest time of the day as if they were customers of distinction. I replied to your father's most recent letter, giving the day and hour at which you were expected to report for work, and that was five days ago. You will remove yourself from these premises and arrive suitably dressed in sober black at the employees' entrance tomorrow morning at eight o'clock." His eyes had flicked contemptuously over the natty check in which Robert was attired. "A plain gold cravat-pin is permissible, but no fobs on the watch-chain. You will also shave your upper lip. Moustaches are not permitted in this establishment. That's all for the moment." He turned on his heel and strode away in the direction from which he had come.

Robert left the shop in high dudgeon. His reception had not been at all what he had anticipated, having assumed that from the start he would enjoy a privileged position due to the indirect association already established with Worth through Mr. Allenby, but it had been made clear to him that he could expect no favours. He was in two minds whether to go back there, but when he weighed up the alternative he decided he would be crazy to lose the time in Paris for the sake of his pride. That evening he took his cut-throat razor and shaved off the light-brown moustache that had adorned his face for a considerable time. Without it he looked younger than his twenty-four years and was not at all sure that was a good thing. His face was solidly boned with a square jaw, square forehead, and a well-shaped nose, long and jutting, with splendidly curved nostrils. His eyes were deep-set and a smoky blue, giving a deceptive softness to his glance as far as women were concerned. His shining hair had a tendency to fall forward silkily over his brow in a manner that a woman of his acquaintance had called "engaging," and he certainly found that female fingers always wanted to smooth it back for him. His mouth was wide, with indented laughter creases at the sides, the lips fleshy but firm, and his chin cleft with the eternal mark of the philanderer.

The following morning he arrived on time and was surprised to find not only Worth there before him, but also Madame Worth. She was dressed in black silk like the other women on the staff, but in the height of fashion, her dress most elaborately flounced as if composed of tulip petals, her hair immaculately coiffed, and it amused him to wonder if she slept in a tilted box at night like a doll in order to appear so exquisite at such an early hour.

No one appreciated Marie's appearance more than Worth himself. He loved her more than ever, and his sons were everything to him. Only one flaw remained in his life. He was still subject to the burdensome and unimaginative régime of Messieurs Gagelin and Obigez. His longing to burst free and establish his own business had been given a new impetus after the birth of his second child. It was his duty to provide a future where children could follow in a father's footsteps if need be. But nothing could be done without money. Considering the vast amounts he had made for his employers, a partnership was long overdue, but to his great disappointment it had become apparent that it was never to be. He was doomed by them never to have the scope he wanted, quite apart from the lack of real financial benefit that he had once anticipated.

Pondering these oft-considered thoughts, he made his usual morning survey of the shop to make sure that all was in order, every counter and shelf dusted, each display of goods perfectly arranged, and all the assistants, male and female, neat and tidy and at their places behind the counters in readiness for when the bolts would be drawn on the entrance doors and the commercial day could begin. He ended the tour of inspection, as he always did, in his own dressmaking department. There he found Robert Prestbury waiting by his office door for him in the workroom area.

Critically he looked his protégé up and down. The moustache had vanished, and Prestbury's appearance could not be faulted, the black frockcoat decidedly stylish and the correct amount of starched white cuff showing at the wrists. Worth, in spite of his bias towards all that was French, could not help admitting to himself that a certain type of well-dressed, personable Englishman did have the edge over a Frenchman, particularly in the matter of height, and he could see his lady customers succumbing to the accented French and polished manners.

"What do you know about materials, Prestbury?" he questioned abruptly. "After all, that's where fashion begins."

"I know a good piece of cloth when I see it. Scottish tweed, broadcloth, serge, drill, kerseymere, waistcoat silk, and velvet."

"Well, that's a good beginning. You've gained some sound knowledge from your own wardrobe, but on the whole, excepting silk and velvet, we deal with lighter fabrics here. Fashion is a living phenomenon, you know. Never scoff at it or belittle a trend. It reflects the mood and environs of a society, a new mode rising like a white horse on the sea to reach a spectacular peak before it subsides into the banal and the commonplace, finally breaking on the shore and vanishing altogether. I deal only with the rise and glory of the peaks, so you are being granted a unique opportunity to observe and learn all there is to know about fashion and the quality of workmanship that I have made synonymous with my own new sphere of *haute couture*."

"I'm conscious of the privilege, sir." Robert could not but admire the man's supreme self-assurance and total belief in his own talented achievements, all wonderfully laced with an unassailable and fully justifiable conceit.

"Good. I expect honesty, loyalty, punctuality, and unstinting hard work from all my assistants and sewing force. We take no note of the clock or our own tiredness when there are orders to be filled. I'm prepared to give you a month in which to prove yourself worthy of the training that you will receive here. Now!" Worth glanced about, looking for someone to whom he could entrust the newcomer for preliminary instruction, and he remembered that Louise was starting work again that day after the absence for her confinement. Such a light task would be well suited to her for the next two or three weeks. "You shall meet Mademoiselle Louise. She has climbed every rung in the fashion world from the first tacking of a garment to displaying my creations in this salon. Her own designs have considerable merit, and she is as authoritative on the quality of weave and design in a fabric as anyone could be. Ah! Here she is."

Louise never quite remembered her first impression of Robert, except that it registered with her that he was tall. It had quite flustered her, being called forward, because she thought for a few distraught moments that someone had seen her smuggle Paul-Michel into the building. He was not yet a month old and needed to be put to the breast regularly, making it impossible for her to leave him yet with anyone else. There were a number of small and inconvenient storerooms to the rear of the dressmaking department that had long since fallen into disuse, and she had made him a bed there in a drawer removed from a chest and set on a wide shelf out of any draughts. Tucked into his shawl he was good and contented, and if he did cry it was unlikely that anyone would hear him. She could count herself lucky that she was back in employment at Maison Gagelin, which was due entirely to her being in Worth's department and under his jurisdiction. Yet he never referred to the baby in any way. She could have been away sick with a heavy cold for that matter, because upon her return he merely expressed the hope that she was feeling well again, and left it at that. He had another pregnant woman showing the clothes to the appropriate customers, and this one had a wedding ring on her finger. Even if he had not chosen to ignore her having given birth to an illegitimate child, thus ensuring her continued employment, it would have been impossible to make the request that she should have the infant with her. His own wife had not returned to work until their babies could be left in other hands. She must only hope that neither he nor the proprietors would ever discover that a small infant was to come and go daily on the premises.

She was a good instructress, and Robert was intelligent and intuitive towards the trade, soon able to judge not only the quality, design, weight, nap, and strength of fabrics, but how they would drape or gather, loop or flounce. She taught him the differences between handmade laces, how to judge a Valenciennes or an Alençon, a Chantilly or a Brussels point, and how to distinguish the best of the machine-made products that had been revived at Worth's instigation, his use of it on many of his dresses having set a fashion that women everywhere had followed, resulting in a boom in the lace-making industry. It was the same with the manufacture of jet ornamentation, which in a very short while under his persistence had become extremely fashionable, taking a new turn in allowing those in mourning to add a discreet glitter to their garments. Had Robert not been basically lazy, more inclined to an easy existence than to a hardworking one, he could have kept up the good work that he did during his month on trial and come to excel at least in the selling side of the business, but his nature was against him, and all his life he had relied more on guile and the indulgence he could arouse in others to strew him a rosy and comfortable path.

Louise did not suspect this side of him during the period of instruction. She only became aware of his habit of standing a trifle too close to her, of putting his face no more than an inch or two away from hers in the study of a length of passementerie or some such goods, and always being quick to take her elbow, wrist, or support the back of her waist with his hand on stairs or steps or if passing through a crowded part of the shop. She discouraged it, and even if her state of mind had not been entirely maternal and withdrawn, she would not have wanted his or any other man's attentions at the present time. It was hard not to show impatience or irritation when he delayed her, wanting to keep her in conversation while the clock and her own milk-filled breasts made it necessary for her to slip away to Paul-Michel, but she managed somehow to maintain her equilibrium.

Her footsteps were always light as she hastened down the labyrinth of old passageways in the ancient rear of the shop to the tiny storeroom. A grated window high in the wall gave some illumination to the room, and on bright days sunshine penetrated, its warmth falling softly over her as she opened her dress and held her baby to her. Inevitably her thoughts went to Pierre sometimes, however hard she tried not to think of him. Naturally Stéphanie had not been back to the shop, and from the merest scrap of information that had come from somebody's chance remark, it would seem that recently the newly married de Gands were accompanying the Emperor and Empress on one of their tours to the provinces to make contact with the people. Often she sang softly to Paul-Michel as he lay at her breast, smoothing the black, downy hair on his fine-shaped head with her fingertips. Only one thing about his well-being saddened her. He must grow up deprived of a father's love and influence, something that had left a gap in her own early years, and she well remembered how she had envied other children in the alleys who had had a father to throw them merrily up in the air or even to box their ears if need be. If she as a girl had felt that loss, how much more would a boy miss a father?

When he had had his fill of milk, sometimes dropping off to sleep at the breast, she would return him to his bed, never leaving him without a last kiss on his brow. He was growing fast and putting on weight well. So far she had had no difficulty in smuggling him in and out of the shop, keeping him under her fastened cloak in a kind of sling that Catherine had made for her. Catherine adored him, and between the two of them he had more than a fair share of feminine devotion. But he mustn't be smothered. She wanted him to grow up strong and free and independent. Somehow that must be achieved. As she went from the storeroom several times a day and week after week, always closing the door soundlessly behind her, she had no idea that her presence in that part of the shop was beginning to be observed.

It had not taken long for Robert to hear from a couple of junior vendeuses willing to gossip with him that Louise was what was commonly known as a fallen woman. She had had a baby comparatively recently, and nobody knew who the father was. Louise was certainly not one to talk about her private life, and if the Worths knew, they had not given the slightest sign of it. This information about Louise made her still more intriguing in his eyes. It heartened him to know that she was in reality far more approachable than she appeared. He found her fascinating. There was something will-o'-the-wisp about her that drew and ever evaded. He thought he had never seen such lovely eyes, usually distant, calm, and quiet, but which positively sparkled with laughter whenever he happened to say something spontaneous that amused her, the long-lashed lids half closed as she threw her head back on the white stem of her neck, and for a few minutes he felt he had bridged the gap she kept between them. But such a time was always short-lived, and she would shake her head, still smiling, and bring him back to the more serious subject of the work in hand, becoming once more his strict mentor and teacher. He was sorry when her supervision of his training was at an end, because he saw less of her, she returning to the embroidery table and not to the fitting sessions she had hoped to take up again. He could only suppose that it was for her own good that she should remain prudently inconspicuous for a while longer as far as the proprietors were concerned.

Had he not taken such an interest in her and been alert for any glimpse of her at any time, he would not have noticed how frequently she either came or went along the corridor that led to some part of the shop where he had never been, and he supposed that stores of some kind needed for the embroidery- and sewing-tables were kept there. Now that he was serving in the dressmaking department, fetching and carrying bolts of material to ripple out in display to aid customers in their choosing, making appointments, showing trays of alternative trimmings to the dresses, and many other tasks, he was very mobile in his activities and often in and out of the workrooms. Although he took care to appear busy all the time and frequently was, he also managed to do as little as possible, often sliding his duties unobtrusively onto somebody else by being a second or two later in coming forward to a newly arrived customer, and always tried to avoid anything too arduous.

Taking advantage of a lull in the salon early one evening he slipped away into the corridor along which he had seen Louise disappear a little previously, intent on waylaying her. Here and there a gas-mantle flickered, giving a fitful light, but once broom cupboards and some locked doors had been passed, the gloom deepened into shadows. He drew back quickly as Louise suddenly emerged from them. As he watched, she paused to check her appearance in a dusty looking-glass on the wall, and seeing that her bodice was incorrectly fastened, she readjusted two buttons that were out of place. She gave an involuntary start of alarm as his reflection appeared behind hers, and spun about to face him, her eyes wide and scared.

"What are you doing here?" she demanded, her agitation out of all proportion to their meeting there.

"I just came looking for you. Don't you want company to and from the storeroom?"

"What do you mean?" she blurted out, looking to him even more frightened than before.

"Only that you must find it tedious running errands to and from the sewing-room on your own."

"Oh, I see." She relaxed visibly, ducking her head with a smile. "I don't mind it. Not at all."

He was watching her keenly. "I've missed our time together. When the shop closes this evening, let me take you out to supper. Don't refuse me again."

She shook her head at once. "No, thank you. I'll be going straight home."

He was piqued. Who did she think she was to turn him down? He was doing her a favour, and was prepared to do much more to please her once she dispensed with these artificial airs of virtuous aloofness. As she made to go on her way he stepped in front of her and spoke coaxingly.

"Come on, Louise. What do you want to go home for so early? I'm told there's nobody there but the old woman you live with, and that your protector, whoever he was, has deserted you. I'm a broad-minded fellow. It matters nothing to me. All I do care about is that a girl as pretty as you shouldn't hide herself away." He lowered his head to bring his eyes intently on a level with hers. "And yet you're more than pretty. I would call you beautiful." Unable to keep his hands from her any longer he pressed them to her wonderful breasts.

"Don't touch me!" She beat him away, but he closed in about her, trapping her in his arms, and angry with her.

"Don't play games with me. We both know you like a little fun, and you've teased me long enough." He sought to capture her mouth with his own, but she twisted wildly in his arms, and after a short tussle he let her go, glaring after her as she flew from him. He straightened his coat and smoothed his hair in preparation for returning to the salon. The bitch! The haughty bitch! Yet somehow he was more furious with himself than with her. Why hadn't he given her the benefit of a little finesse? There was no excuse for him since he was experienced enough with women not to have made such a ham-fisted mistake in letting his more basic feelings run away with him. But he wanted her violently. She had attracted him from the start, and because of what he had found out about her he had committed the folly of treating her like a whore.

Smitten by a regret unusual to him, he returned somewhat lugubriously to the showrooms. Custom was still slack, and the only lady present was being attended to by a vendeuse. With the talent he had developed for looking busy when he was not, he rearranged a few albums of Worth's designs that customers often browsed through, his mind concentrated entirely on Louise. It suddenly struck him that she had been empty-handed when she had gone to the storeroom, and empty-handed when she returned. Now he came to think about it, each time he had noticed her around that area it had been the same. How odd. How very odd.

* * *

Unbeknown to anyone else, Marie had been giving thought to that section of unused rooms, wondering if they could be turned into self-contained domestic quarters. More than ever she longed to live on the premises. She often felt anxious and exhausted with all she had to do, and had begun to wonder how much longer she could sustain such long working days that took her from home so early in the mornings and did not allow a return until late at night. It was sheer chance that she happened to glance out of the shop window one afternoon, and saw that a family who had long occupied the apartment at the top of the building was moving out.

Not even taking a moment to inform Worth, she went at once to the office of the proprietors, and she was convinced that good fortune was with her when they both happened to be there in consultation. They received her as always with pleasant courtesy, and as soon as she was seated she asked if the top flat had been relet yet.

"No, Madame Worth. It has not," Monsieur Obigez replied. "Why do you ask?"

She leaned forward eagerly in her chair, her hands clasped in her lap. "I'm asking because my husband and I would like to be the new tenants. For a long time we have wished to live on the spot. Not only would it make life much easier for him, but it would take away from me the burden of the daily distance from home, something that has taxed my strength greatly at times, my health not being what it was, as you know, messieurs. I should also be at hand if there happened to be any emergency involving my children, lifting another anxiety from my mind. In all I see it as the most convenient arrangement imaginable." She gave a happy sigh and awaited their reply, her face alight with anticipation. Then her expression began to fade as she saw they were looking at her aghast.

"Impossible! Out of the question!" they exclaimed in unison.

She could not believe her ears. "But why not? We would not expect a low rent or any special favours. Quite the contrary. We are well aware that property is valuable and sought after in this street. What possible objection could you have?"

They looked both grave and shocked, and although they were entirely different in stature, features, and build, the similarity in their expression gave them for the moment the look of brothers. Monsieur Gagelin spoke again and with equal vehemence.

"Madame Worth! Surely you can see that it is socially unacceptable for the *premier commis* and associate of so grand a shop as ours to live on the premises like a common concierge! Where would his dignity be? His present distinction? It would degrade his position and ours to allow such an unheard-of state of affairs."

She found their snobbery insufferable. That they should regard with contempt her simple request to live in all respectability five flights above the shop showed a complete lack of consideration for her and callously denied a means of easing the great burden of the business that her untiring husband carried for them without complaint and with constant enthusiasm, and for comparatively little reward. It was from his office and not theirs that every imaginative and profitable venture had stemmed. It was his intelligence and foresight that had established the dressmaking showrooms, revived industries to everyone's benefit, and created new lines that had given employment to hundreds of unknown workers while keeping Maison Gagelin to the forefront of the world's notice in fashion. She answered their pomposity with indignation and spirit.

"I fail completely to understand your attitude, messieurs. I had even been prepared to ask if we might rent the rooms to the rear of the dressmaking salon if the top flat happened to be let already." She tilted her head proudly and rose to her feet. "Charles Worth is a master and a genius. Nothing can touch or taint such an honourable man. He could live in a palace or a cellar or even above or behind a shop while continuing to command all respect. Good day to you."

She maintained her composure until she reached the dressmaking salon. There reaction set in, and once safely out of sight and hearing of the customers she took refuge in her husband's office and broke down. There Worth found her.

"What is it, my darling? Whatever is the matter?" He was deeply anxious, it being rare for her to show such womanly distress. And out it all came, her increasing concern for their children in her absence all day, the dread of her own physical weakness, and the insupportable disappointment of having her request for the tenancy of the apartment turned down. He listened in silence, holding her within the comfort of his arms, and made the decision that had long been in his mind. He had put up for years with his employers' bigoted opinions, overworked himself for the good of the firm, had to fight for every step of progress, and let the resulting glory go always to the shop's name. But they had gone too far in their callousness towards his dearest Marie. Her well-being and that of their children was at stake, and the proprietors had chosen to ignore her years of selfless service and the first small favour she had ever asked them by putting their own hideous snobbery first. It was the end of the road. The parting of the ways.

That evening after the shop was closed he called on a Swedish acquaintance whom he had known for a considerable time. He was welcomed with the offer of a Havana cigar, which he refused, and a superb glass of wine, which he accepted. Otto Gustave Bobergh had a similar background to Worth's. He had been trained in the drapery trade in Sweden before coming to France, and he had worked for a number of years in a fashionable shop. They had met socially and through business on many occasions, having much in common, and they had struck up, if not a friendship, then a very sound relationship built on mutual liking and a respect for each other's business acumen. Many times each had talked enthusiastically to the other of how he would handle an enterprise of his own, both always held back by lack of funds, Bobergh being only marginally better off than Worth. But recently Bobergh's financial position had improved somewhat, and Worth brought up the subject they had so often discussed, but with a new purpose.

"I'm leaving Gagelin's. I'm going to open up a grand salon of *haute couture,* and I need a partner. Why not pool your resources with mine and come in with me. Somehow we'll raise the rest that we'll need."

Bobergh, comfortably installed in a plush-upholstered wingchair, studied the perfect smoke-ring that he had just blown ceilingwards. "What premises did you have in mind?"

"There's a suite of rooms that takes up the whole of the first floor at number seven, rue de la Paix. I know that street is a quiet one and not a thriving commercial centre, but a couple of high-class milliners do good business there, Doucet sells the very best of linen and cravats at number seventeen, and there's a jeweller who sets gems for the court. Moreover, number seven has an imposing entrance flanked by pilastered walls, that cuts through the front of the building into an inner courtyard around which the floors are galleried. It's situated on the west side of the street only a short distance from the opening into the Place Vendôme with its exclusive properties. Well? What do you say? Are you interested?"

Bobergh sat forward, a slow smile spreading across his face. "Extremely interested. Let's discuss a few more details."

They talked far into the night.

It had taken a week for Louise to lose her fear of being followed again by Robert into the rear of the shop, but gradually she began to believe that his male ego had suffered sufficiently from her rebuff to keep him away from her. Her nervousness ebbed, and once more she went at intervals to her baby with as contented a mind as was possible in the difficult circumstances. Being at the embroidery-table meant that there were rarely any of the hindrances and delays in going to luncheon such as she had experienced during rushes of work in the fitting-rooms, and she was able to devote time to Paul-Michel regularly at the midday hour. Now that the winter weather had turned severely cold she was always anxious that he might have kicked the covers off during her absence, and she was deeply alarmed the day she entered the storeroom to see one of his extra blankets lying on the floor.

"How did you manage to do that, Paul-Michel?" she chided anxiously, hurrying across to the makeshift bed. Then her heart stopped. The baby was not there. As she whirled about in panic, Robert spoke to her tauntingly from the crate where he was seated against the wall in the gloom, holding Paul-Michel, wrapped in a shawl, to his shoulder. "Is this what you're looking for?"

She flew across with arms outstretched, fright still in her face. "Give me my baby!"

"Wait a minute!" He sprang up and dodged her, getting behind an ancient counter and fully enjoying his command of the situation. "I don't know that you're a fit person to have charge of this child. He was bawling his head off when I came in here, his pillow quite wet with tears. Think yourself lucky I happened to find him, and it was not anybody else."

"You were spying on me!"

"That's a harsh way of describing my interest in you. It'll do you no good to abuse me. What's to stop me revealing your little secret to all and sundry?"

She thumped both her fists down white-knuckled on the counter between them. "Nothing! But I'll not be blackmailed by you! Go and report me if you must, but give me my baby!"

He hesitated for a few moments and then held the child forward. Louise snatched Paul-Michel to her and rocked him in the crook of her arm, speaking lovingly to him and drying his still tear-wet face with a corner of his shawl. Robert regarded her with some embarrassment. He had thought upon discovering the child that a means of getting a hold over her had come his way, but he saw he was mistaken. This girl was too strong, too unbending to be coerced in that manner. More than ever he was drawn to her, even if she did have a snivelling brat to encumber her.

"Look here," he began stumblingly. "I didn't mean what I said. I admire you for taking such a chance with your employment in the way you are. I wouldn't think of telling anyone."

She raised her head and her eyes were almost dark gold in a dewiness of relief and gratitude. "Thank you, Monsieur Prestbury. I trust you to keep your word."

"Call me Robert."

She gave a quick nod. "Now if you would leave me alone with my baby, please, Robert?"

"Yes. Of course." He crimsoned, abhorred by the reminder of the link with motherhood that brought her there. Although he made for the door with some haste, he spoke again before turning the knob. "I'll keep guard for you, if you like."

She had already turned her back, unfastening her bodice, and she paused, looking over her shoulder at him, the whole of her serene face with its dawning smile of conciliation caught in a cameo of light that came from the grated window.

"That won't be necessary. In any case, I wouldn't let you risk trouble on my behalf. But it was good of you to offer."

He went from the storeroom much cheered by her smile. He had almost blundered the whole thing, but miraculously it had ended by putting him on a much better footing with her, giving him a clue as to how to go forward in the future. Stopping in front of the dusty looking-glass in the passageway he brushed a piece of fluff from the shawl away from his lapel, and there drifted from his hands the sweet milk-smell of baby, nauseating him. Hurriedly he made for the nearest washroom and used the carbolic soap that the firm provided, lathering the aroma away.

Worth was not entirely pleased with his protégé. For the first month Prestbury had acquitted himself well, and in the following weeks was never outwardly idle or in any way disagreeable. He had the polished manners and gave the kind of impeccable attention that rarely failed to win sales, praise from the customers often forthcoming. Yet the unease persisted, Worth unable to shake off the conviction that Prestbury expended more energy in appearing busy than in actually working. Just recently he had come across the fellow several times hanging about in the corridor entrance to the old storerooms, more like a gendarme on a street corner than a shop assistant who had serving to do. There was no doubt that Prestbury must be hauled over the coals. Sometimes a reprimand and a warning was enough to banish laziness. Worth made up his mind to do what he could to bring him to order, not only for Prestbury's own sake, but for Mr. Allenby, who had recommended him in good faith, and for whom Worth wanted to turn out a capable and competent businessman, far-sighted in the field of fashion and all appertaining to it.

Prestbury was not the only cause of irritation to Worth. Since Worth had given in his long notice to his employers, wanting to be fair in allowing them plenty of time for a replacement, his relationship with them had deteriorated sharply. He had fully expected them to relent about the apartment upon hearing that he was to part company with them, not that it would have made any difference to his decision, but they did not. On the contrary, they became if anything more snobbish and disdainful, treating him as if he were an ordinary employee whom they could well do without, instead of the *premier commis* who had made fortunes for them. Whether they imagined he would fail in the future without the vast commercial connections that flowed towards their renowned shop's name he did not know, but it seemed as if they thought he would come running back to them soon enough, having learnt his lesson, and were not in the least concerned about the matter. Perhaps it was for this reason they forbade him to mention his departure to anybody until they should announce it themselves, thus ensuring a minimum of disruption to customers and staff alike.

They had taken to stalking through the dressmaking department with an interfering and proprietory air as if to show him that he had already lost the independence of authority that they had chosen to allow him in countless matters which so often had clashed with their own judgement. But not any more. They no longer considered him important to them. What did he have to show the world that was his own? Every garment that he had ever designed had left the shop under the label of Maison Gagelin. Any reputation he had made had been lost in credit taken by them. In reports of the rare and magnificent materials used in dresses seen at the Tuileries and other glittering occasions there was never any mention of the *premier commis* who had instigated the retailing of them, only their esteemed names listed among the suppliers of such grandeur. It was their opinion that without them or their shop Worth could have achieved nothing and would become nothing again. It never occurred to either of those pompous gentlemen that they were losing the greatest couturier who had ever been born.

It was Marie's mention of the unused storerooms to the rear of the shop that made them decide to make an investigation. Monsieur Obigez remarked caustically to his partner that it was a pity that Worth had not spent some time finding a use for them instead of causing them so much annoyance on many occasions by bringing in another newfangled fashion notion that had made them money, but had personally displeased them.

Louise was putting Paul-Michel down again in his drawer-bed after feeding him one midday when Robert burst into the storeroom.

"Quick! Hide him! Get out of sight yourself! You mustn't be found here! The proprietors are poking their noses into all these rooms!"

For a single moment she stood paralysed with alarm, not knowing which way to turn. He gave her a shove towards the darkest corner, heaving some boxes aside with his shoulder, and pushed her against the wall. "Stay there and keep quiet."

"But Paul-Michel—"

"I'll see to him. Don't worry." He thrust the boxes back as far as they would go to conceal her, cursing the abundance of her crinoline that he crushed down as best he could, and then turned to the drawer where the baby lay, wide-eyed and content. Taking up the drawer-bed, he slid it back into the chest from which it had originally been taken, and closed it all but a fraction, allowing a passage of air. He had hardly drawn away from the chest when the door opened and both the proprietors appeared on the threshold, halting in their astonishment at seeing him there.

"Who are you? What the devil are you doing here?" Monsieur Gagelin demanded.

"I'm Prestbury, monsieur. From the dressmaking salon. I came to see if I could light the gas-mantle for you to see better."

"Gas-mantle? What gas-mantle? Nothing but lamplight has ever been used in this old part of the shop." The proprietor's eyes narrowed suspiciously. "Your cravat is awry, and there's dust on your sleeve. I don't believe you're up to any good. Have you appropriated some merchandise to which you have no right, and fear its discovery?"

"No, monsieur. Indeed not."

"I regret to say that I do not believe you." Monsieur Gagelin entered the room, peering around sharply. His partner followed him, and in turn came one of the junior apprentices carrying a lamp, the day being gloomy enough to allow little daylight to penetrate the cobweb-strewn windows of the various rooms. Where both gentlemen would merely have taken a cursory glance around, they now inspected everything closely. Monsieur Obigez noticed several triangular dust-free patches on some boxes stacked high, and promptly pulled some aside. The lamp's glow blended with a wintry thread of light to fall full on the harassed girl who stood with her back pressed to the wall.

"Mademoiselle—!" Her surname eluded him, for although she had been a considerable time in their employ he had had on the whole little contact with her or minor members of the staff of the dressmaking salon, leaving that side to Worth, but his voice thundered with the conclusion to which he jumped, his partner sharing it with him.

Louise had emerged hastily from her refuge, brushing the dust from her sleeves with tense fingers. "I'm Louise Vernet, and Monsieur Prestbury has nothing to do with my being here," she explained in a rush, wanting to save Robert. "I'm the one—"

"Silence! Lying will not help your case, mademoiselle," Monsieur Gagelin roared. "It is clear enough that our coming surprised you and this young scoundrel in a compromising situation. I will not ask how often these clandestine meetings have taken place during working hours, because I do not want to know. Once is enough for the immediate dismissal of both of you. You will both leave these premises immediately."

Her eyes flashed. "I'll go, but I'll not see an innocent person dismissed because of me." She went across to the drawer and pulled it out to scoop up Paul-Michel in all his blankets. "My son is the reason I sought privacy. I've been bringing him to the shop every day, unbeknown to everyone except Monsieur Prestbury, who kindly thought to save me from dismissal by warning me that you were on your way here. It was a kindly deed and well meant. I beg you not to penalise him for it."

"You are not married, young woman!" Monsieur Gagelin exclaimed as if it were a point she had overlooked, his face aghast. "You should have left the employment of this establishment in your disgrace long since. Go immediately!"

Still she stood her ground. "But not Monsieur Prestbury. The blame is all mine."

"He aided and abetted you in breaking all the rules of this respectable house of commerce. You will both go *now!*"

In exasperation she stamped her foot at Robert. "Speak up for yourself since no one will take notice of me."

He could see it was a lost cause, and with his flair for always salvaging the best of anything for himself, he looked at her with a steady, reassuring smile. "On principle, I wouldn't stay on here after the way you're being treated. We'll go together."

He put a protective arm about her shoulders, and they left the storeroom. She was overcome, unable to express how touched she was that he should have chosen to stand by her so resolutely. What she did not know was that Worth was leaving Maison Gagelin and had given Robert the chance to go with him when it was officially announced. As an honourable man Worth would not filch from the workforce of the dressmaking salon to establish his own staff at the new rue de la Paix premises when they opened early in the New Year, but as Robert was his protégé he was obliged through his word to Mr. Allenby to continue the young man's training, a point about which there could be no dispute should Robert choose to take advantage of the choice presented. Now Robert knew there was no choice. Getting chucked out prematurely by the proprietors meant several weeks of unemployment before Worth opened the new salon, but Robert quite welcomed the spell of liberty, particularly since his allowance from his father would bridge comfortably the interim period.

The whole incident took place out of Worth's sight and hearing, engaged as he was with a customer, and Monsieur Gagelin did not allow them a dignified departure. He stampeded them out through the staff doors and shot the bolts himself afterwards. It was the second time in her life that Louise had found herself dismissed on the spot, and on this occasion she no longer had only herself to think of, but had a baby dependent on her. She drew a shuddering breath of the frosty, outdoor air. At least neither of them would starve. Her small nest-egg would see them through until she found work of some kind again, even if it did mean that her cherished dream must lie a little further away in that far distant future.

"Let's go into a café and have a pot of coffee and talk," Robert suggested when they reached the street. "We've all the time in the world."

It was the first of the invitations she was to accept from him, feeling herself inextricably in his debt for his losing his employment through her, and thinking she would never forget the steadfastness he had shown. It made her forgive him completely for the earlier liberties he had tried to take with her.

They talked for a long while, learning about each other, and what they had done with their lives so far. She was enthralled with his account of all his travels, interested in the foreign places that he described, for he had the gift of easy talk and a knack of describing a scene vividly. She began to think him far more agreeable than she could have suspected from their first meetings, and after all he was neither the first nor the last man to try his hand at an easy seduction before realising the mistake he had made.

He walked her home and carried the baby up the flights to her door. She did not ask him in, and he did not expect it.

He would play the game by the rules from now on, having gained an advantage over her that she was unaware of.

"I hope you find other employment soon," she said, taking the baby from him.

"I'm sure we both will," he answered confidently, knowing that his optimistic attitude had cheered her greatly, "and we must keep in touch to know how things are going. Let's meet again soon."

She agreed and he left her, well pleased. Time enough in another few weeks to tell her that Worth would be needing sewing-hands and fitters at number 7, rue de la Paix. As she was no longer in the employ of Gagelin and Obigez she was free to apply. In the meantime, he would consolidate his relationship with her.

His plans did not quite work. Marie wrote at once upon learning of Louise's dismissal to tell her of the forthcoming openings in Worth's employment, but Robert was still in luck. Louise did not suspect that he had withheld this information from her.

16

In the rue Lepelletier the imperial coach taking the Emperor and Empress to a gala performance at the Grand Opéra was escorted by mounted lancers and followed by two other equipages bearing members of the entourage. Stéphanie, seated beside Pierre in the carriage immediately behind the imperial couple, looked out at the hundreds of people gathered in the light of the gas-lamps to thunder forth their cheers of loyalty and affection. She could guess that to the eager sight of the crowd Eugénie must look like a fairy queen in her diamonds and white lace, acknowledging their acclamation with her beautiful smile and a little wave of her hand. Probably many envied the Empress's seemingly perfect existence with her gallant husband and the son she adored, not knowing that the Emperor had taken as his mistress the wife of his own Foreign Minister, which Eugénie was more than aware of.

Were all husbands unfaithful? Stéphanie glanced sideways under her lashes at Pierre, who was gazing idly out of the other window, fully arrayed in his dress uniform, medals awarded for gallantry in the Crimea glinting on his chest, the purple trousers taut over his powerful horseman's thighs as he sat with his legs crossed. Never would she give him cause to stray. She loved him as fiercely and possessively after four months of marriage as she had done before, and had no reason to believe she had disappointed him in any way. On the contrary, he praised with affection her ability to surprise and pleasure him, a continuance of her earlier achievement on a different plane, and she was resolved never to lose the knack of being able to make him laugh, a whispered comment from her at some dull, official imperial function always bringing a dance of amusement to his eyes, his returning glance often holding her closer to him than at any time during their love-making. Why this should be she did not know. She was not sure if it meant that there was a gulf between them that she knew nothing about. At this point her thoughts always drifted to Louise with doubt and uncertainty. Perhaps he did still think about her, but that would fade with time. Whatever had been in his past was over and done with. Now she, Stéphanie de Gand, was the one to fill his present and his future.

The wheels were slowing down, and through the window she was able to see that the imperial carriage was coming to a halt at the steps of the Opéra. She looked towards Pierre with a sudden uprush of love, always delighting in appearing at his side, and reached out her white-gloved hand for him to take. Her impulsive gesture, causing her to turn away from the window, saved her from full facial injury as in the same instant there came an enormous explosion from that side of the street, the impact sending her tumbling against him, the glass shattering and showering over them.

She screamed, and he hurled her down onto the floor of the carriage, throwing himself over her as another bomb burst amid the terrified pandemonium of the crowds. Total darkness descended as every gas-light on the theatre and in the street went out, adding to the panic, the awning crashing down on those who had already fallen on the steps. Then the searing flash of the third bomb added to the carnage, the screams and shouts mingling with the maddened whinnying of injured horses, the bolting hooves of others charging away down the street.

The air was filled with the smell of smoke and explosive as Pierre removed his crushing weight from her and gathered her up onto the seat. "Are you all right?" he demanded.

She nodded, shocked and shaken, her lips colourless. "Yes, I think so." Then she raised her eyes and shrieked again at the sight of him. "What has happened to you?"

His face was streaming with blood from a cut by glass on his head, but he was not conscious of it. "Stay here and I'll come back to you," he ordered. "I must get to the Emperor."

If he is still alive, Pierre added grimly to himself as he swung out of the carriage. Lanterns were beginning to appear from the theatre, the beams of light showing the dead and injured lying about, the dying horses and those already still. Out of the smoke a man suddenly appeared from the direction of a narrow alley nearby, a pistol in his hand, and reached the imperial coach as Eugénie opened the door. Pierre gave a shout, hurling himself forward at the assassin, but gendarmes were before him, the man overpowered and brought down. Eugénie, icily brave, seemed almost unmoved by this final attempt to end the life of her and her husband, who had suffered no more than a scratched nose and, incongruously, a hole in his hat. She herself had a graze by her eye, and there was some blood on her skirt.

Pierre would have helped her alight, but she refused help from him and another who offered his hand. Drawing herself up, she looked every inch an empress, and her voice was chill. "We have more courage than any assassin. Let all see that." Louis-Napoléon followed her out of the coach, dazed with shock and moving like an automaton. He, who had never feared death for himself, was demoralised by the ultimate cowardice of the bomb-assassin who did not hesitate to destroy the lives of innocent bystanders. He moaned with distress at the sight of the wounded, his own lancers among them, and would have gone to them, but Eugénie, pausing abruptly on the opera-house steps that she was ascending, exerted her will over him.

"Stop being a blockhead!" she hissed with the harshness necessary to bring her husband to his senses. "Let's not make a farce of this incident!"

Obediently and with some return to dignity he went to her. Members of the entourage, most with minor cuts and bruises, gathered to follow them. Pierre was about to fetch Stéphanie when his attention was gripped in another direction. The beams of extra lanterns being brought from all sides by helpers for the wounded happened to play over some of those members of the crowd who had suffered minor injuries in the panic that had prevailed. He rushed to a young woman leaning weakly against the wall of the building that she had used for support in stumbling to her feet.

"Louise!"

He caught the unguarded look of love and relief at the sound of his voice, saw the instinctive reaching out to him, and then memory flooded back to her, taking her far from him again. The outstretched hands withdrew to fold agitatedly upon the edges of her cape.

"You've been wounded," she said in confusion.

"It's nothing." He pulled out a handkerchief and wiped away the blood from his brow. "What of you? What happened?"

"I was knocked to the ground when everybody took fright." She jerked with shock as a lancer's bullet put an end to a horse's agony, and stared towards the awful scene, her lips quivering uncontrollably. "Those poor people! Oh, those horses!"

He sidestepped to block her view with his body. "You must go home. I'll take you."

"No, no. It's not far and I'll be all right. Thank you for offering." She made a rapid move to go.

"One moment!" A single pace brought him close to her, looking down into her face. "Tell me. The child. What was it?"

Her eyes became stark, full of poignant shadows. "A boy."

"His name?"

"Paul-Michel."

His gaze followed her as she hastened away and was lost in the darkness. Then he turned and went to the carriage where Stéphanie waited at the open door. He supposed that she had witnessed the whole incident and would be curious about it.

"That young woman had been knocked down in the crush. I thought I would make sure that she wasn't injured."

"I recognised her. She is a dressmaking assistant."

"Oh?" He dismissed the subject purposefully. "Take my arm. The others have already gone in."

Obediently Stéphanie placed her narrow hand in the crook of his arm. He felt it trembling like a captured bird, and never thought there might be any other cause then the fright she had had from the bombs. As they entered the theatre they heard the burst of cheering and thunder of applause as all inside stood to acknowledge the safe appearance of the Emperor and Empress in the imperial box. Stéphanie saw nothing of the one act of *Guillaume Tell* or the ballet that followed. All that filled her eyes was the looks she had seen on the faces of her husband and the woman out of the crowd. Any doubt she might have had as to who was the father of Louise's baby had quite gone.

* * *

It took Louise quite a time to recover from the terrible night when she had gone with a lively and professional interest to see what dress the Empress would be wearing on the gala occasion that had turned to such tragedy. Over one hundred and fifty people had been killed and injured by the bombs of the Italian conspirator Orsini and his accomplices, who had been brought to justice. For herself, the shock of the experience had caused her to wean Paul-Michel before his time, although she was thankful that for the first eleven weeks of his life she had been able to care for him completely. At least she would be able to return to work freely when Worth opened his salon. One of the neighbours, a responsible woman who kept her own children clean and cared for, had agreed to look after Paul-Michel for a small payment when the time came. In the meanwhile Louise kept busy with some tasks of sewing that she managed to gather, and tried not to think of that chance, nightmare meeting with Pierre that had torn her apart all over again.

The day eventually came when Worth, wearing a new velvet-collared frockcoat of impeccable cut, surveyed his redecorated and refitted premises at number 7, rue de la Paix. He had never been happier, and to celebrate his new position as master in his own domain he had grown a large moustache, which Marie thought gave him an even more dashing air. She was equally delighted with her new home, the floor at number 7 being so large and spacious, circumferencing as it did the inner courtyard and having so many rooms that they were able to have their own comfortable apartment adjoining the salons. Otto Bobergh had kept his own accommodation elsewhere in Paris and was content to be a partner in the background, dealing in the more mundane aspects of the business, and he had proved to have aristocratic Swedish connections that had enabled him to raise the money needed without difficulty. An order for two dresses from the Queen of Sweden, gained through a good word from Bobergh's family, made an auspicious first entry in the order book.

There was a staff of twenty, all carefully selected. In the workrooms the best of skilled hands had been taken on, with ample space for increased numbers at the tables later on. Louise was made Worth's *première* fitter, and there was the usual complement of vendeuses to serve in the salons, all of whom had been chosen for their stately height and youth and attractive appearance. Robert and several other young men, all as tall as each other with a degree of good looks to match, were assigned to the material counters in one of the long salons where the display of fabrics could be at its best. It was not chance that over half the salon staff was English. Worth still held to his belief that his own countrymen and -women could contribute much in a sophisticated and striking presence to a well-run enterprise, and Mr. Allenby had been invaluable in sending him the right applicants, all outshining Robert Prestbury in an eagerness to excel.

The décor of the whole floor was designed to give an atmosphere both luxurious and opulent, with gilded pillars and plasterwork and grandly framed pier-glasses, the crystal chandeliers casting sparkling slivers of light over the ivory satin drapes, the gold fringes, and the Louis XV chairs and narrow sofas. An advertisement in the press kept the public notified that Worth and Bobergh had opened a high-class house for dresses and mantles, silks and the latest novelties, but apart from the regal order from Sweden there was no immediate wild rush of business, and it was obvious that the clientèle being aimed for would be built up slowly. Prices had to be kept at a modest level, or else even those customers who had followed Worth to his new address might be frightened away if asked to pay more than they had done at Gagelin and Obigez's.

Living on the premises was a great blessing to Marie. She was always practically within earshot of her children, whom she could attend to at will simply by slipping through a door. As before, a capable nurse had charge of them when their mother was otherwise occupied, although from the start both little boys were allowed to run at will in and out of the salons, where they were made a great fuss of by staff and customers alike. If Marie ever wasted any time it was in crimping Gaston's hair and curling Jean-Philippe's silky locks painstakingly about her fingers with a damp comb in an attempt to keep his baby ringlets beyond their original span, liking to see her boys with curls. Gaston put up with the crimping-papers stoicly, but Jean-Philippe was less submissive. When Marie was defeated by either the stubbornness of his hair or his wriggling impatience to be free of her ministrations, she often wept quite foolish tears. Yet the whole of her warm and loving nature, nurtured by her exceptionally happy marriage, made her an especially endearing mother in spite of her air of playing with dolls more than caring for two robust and sturdy young sons.

Like the Worth children, Paul-Michel also continued to thrive. He was a chuckling, good-humoured baby with his father's black hair and an unmistakable likeness across the eyes. He cut teeth, sat up vigorously, made the usual baby sounds that preceded speech, and began to show a determined urge to stand and crawl. Louise knew that she could have seen Pierre often in the Emperor's escort if she had gone to view any of the processions or parades, but she avoided all sight of imperial public occasions, wanting to give her heart a chance to heal. Yet in spite of all precaution she did see him again some months later. Robert, who never seemed to have enough of her company, had taken her to the Théâtre Français, where they had seats in the comfortable *fauteuils de galerie*, he always liking the best of everything whether he could afford it or not. She was using her opera glasses as the curtain went up on the second act, and distracted by the arrival of two latecomers in a box, she was drawn almost automatically to look in their direction. She felt her chest constrict. The woman with Pierre was a flame-haired demimondaine, her magnificent ivory bosom pouting out of its low décolletage. Louise lowered the glasses and kept her gaze rigidly on the stage, but it was impossible not to register the woman's bejewelled fingers plucking out *marrons glacés* from the frilled box resting on the plush-covered ledge, her small white teeth gleaming as she bit into them before feeding Pierre provocatively with the other halves. When the gaslights were raised in the auditorium for the interval, only the emptied box of confectionery remained. Pierre and his courtesan had gone. Louise was filled with compassion for Stéphanie, and felt herself to be safely forgotten at last. Perversely, although it was what she wanted, it only brought renewed pain.

It was that same night, out of her sadness and loneliness, that she responded for the first time to a kiss from Robert. Previously she had only received his kisses, her lips docile, her eyes unclosed. Her momentary yearning for comfort aroused him more than she had intended, inciting him to caresses that he had not attempted since she had fought him off in the storeroom corridor many months before. Against her will latent desires in her were stirred, reminding her that she was a young and passionate woman, long deprived of loving, but although she was fond of Robert she did not want to become amorously involved with him, and had made that clear from the start.

She thought she had come to know him fairly well. His failings were legion, but she showed him a tolerance she would never have shown towards anyone else, always remembering how he had tried to protect her at the cost of his own employment, standing by her when she had needed a friend. He was often great fun to be with, was generous to a fault when he had money, and was not above borrowing from her when he had none, sometimes forgetting to pay her back. Once, wanting to buy her flowers and having only a few centimes in his pocket, he bought country flowers from a gypsy child and arrived at her door with both arms full of blossoms. If he was in the mood he could sell a customer practically anything, but he was far too quickly bored, and frequently broke Worth's rule of no smoking on the premises by becoming expert at snatching time for a quiet cigar by the open window of a stockroom when he knew the couturier to be safely elsewhere. If he could get out of a chore he would, which made him less than popular with those he worked with, and he showed a decided preference for serving the younger and better-looking customers, particularly the married ones, while managing to leave the rest to his colleagues. Had he not been under the patronage of Mr. Allenby, about whom he boasted on occasion, it was unlikely he would have remained at number 7, rue de la Paix, for very long. Worth certainly showed patience, but whenever there were signs that it might be running out, Robert did endeavour to mend his ways, showing what he was capable of doing if he had a mind to. Then before long he was back to where he had been, taking life as if it owed him favours and needed nothing in return.

"It's all your fault," he answered Louise amiably when she tried to chide him into more conscientious behaviour. "How can I be alert and ambitious when you're ruining every day of my dreary existence by refusing to believe that I'm head over heels in love with you?"

It was always the same. He had a trick even in good humour of shifting the blame onto someone else, and such was his personality and disarming smile that he was far too easy to forgive.

* * *

In the matter of forgiveness Eugénie had shown herself amazingly merciful towards the conspirator Orsini before he had gone to the guillotine. She still felt that the man should have been allowed to live. He had been an Italian patriot who had sought to assassinate the Emperor in order to spur France into a revolution as an example for Italy to follow suit in throwing off the yoke of Austrian dominance. While condemning his methods, she could not but uphold the late man's dreams of liberty for his own country, and encouraged her husband that the time had come for him to fulfill his long-held yearning to liberate the country he had learned to love in his youth. Louis-Napoléon's mind was already made up on the point. He began to plan for war.

Louise felt desperate when she saw the preparations going on around her in the influx of marching men, the patriotic slogans pasted on walls, the newspaper reports that emphasised Austria's tyranny and bullying tactics. It was like hearing the sizzling of another Orsini bomb that was shortly to explode. Her feelings were entirely simple, bound to those who would be wounded or killed as well as to the ones who would be left widowed or fatherless. It brought Pierre constantly into her thoughts, making her particularly sensitive and emotional. She turned more than she would otherwise have done to Robert, who mistook her need for companionship for something deeper, and with renewed hope awaited the opportunity when he might lie with her.

War was declared at the end of April, and a few days later on a warm May day the Emperor left for the Italian front. Louise broke her rule of avoiding all imperial sights. The streets were crowded and she was jostled in the rush forward as the Emperor and his escort came into view, everyone cheering and shouting, patriotic fervour at its height. She saw Pierre. She was no more than an arm's length from him as he rode by, eyes a trifle cynical under the gleaming helmet, a faint smile on the handsome mouth. She was crushed out of his line of vision by those around her, but at the last second she heard herself cry out to him.

"Pierre! Good luck!"

Miraculously, he heard her. He turned in the saddle, his gaze sweeping the faces of those clustered close, but he failed to see her. Again and again he glanced back over his shoulder. It was in vain. Others blocked a view of her last wave to him.

It was destined to be a short and bloody war. In early June there was a great victory at Magenta. In Paris the cannons were fired in celebration, making clouds of birds flutter skywards in alarm. Within days the dyers were at work on a new shade, and before long Worth had bolts of a brilliant pinkish purple on display in every fabric from silk to brocade and wool. Orders flowed in for dresses in Magenta, and this was followed almost at once by a demand for a new shade of blue called Solferino after the victorious French Army routed the Austrians at a place in north Italy of that name. Even Robert was compelled by the rush of business to exert himself on the material counter, something he did not care to do. He was even more disgruntled when he received word to return home at once. His father, whose health had improved once the worry of his son's future and that of the Prestbury business had been removed through Mr. Allenby's kindly intervention, had suffered a relapse. Robert, knowing how easily his mother could fuss, did not suppose that it was nearly as bad as she made out, and he was doubly resentful since his unmarried sister lived at home and should have eased all responsibility from him. Nevertheless, he had to go.

"I've two months left of my training," he said to Worth, "and I'll be glad to return as soon as I possibly can and complete it when matters are settled at home."

Worth sighed inwardly. He had been looking forward to seeing the last of the young man, whom he considered to be a spoiled weakling continually dependent upon the strength of others to maintain even minor standards. He saw little hope for the Prestbury family business when Robert took over, but it would not be for the lack of instruction and training that he had given the young wastrel. "Very well, Prestbury. Give my kindest regards to Mr. Allenby."

Robert hesitated as if taken by surprise. "Er—yes, Monsieur Worth."

As he went from the office Worth sat back in his leather-buttoned desk chair and tossed down in exasperation a pen he happened to be holding. He had seen from Robert's reaction that it had not crossed the fellow's selfish, self-centred mind that he should consider paying his own respects to his worthy patron who twice a year had subsidised generously the meagre allowance that had been forthcoming from his father. Worth loathed ingratitude, particularly when a kindly man like Mr. Allenby was being taken for granted.

He turned to some of his latest sketches on the desk. The crinoline had never been wider, and he was heartily tired of it. Having reestablished himself securely under his own name he was once more guiding the reins of fashion, and recently he had invented a new type of skirt to do away with the bulk of gathers and pleats necessary to bring the vast amount of material in a crinoline into order about the waist. He called it a gored skirt, and although it used even more material in causing the bodice and skirt to be cut in one piece, often twenty or thirty metres, it gave a line that women had taken to with as much enthusiasm as if he were offering them eternal youth. But on the matter of the crinoline itself the whole female sex was obsessed with it, refusing to let it be dislodged. They did not seem to care that it had proved to be a life hazard, countless numbers all over the world having been burnt to death trapped in the cages of their hoops when their huge skirts had brushed against an open fire or knocked over a lamp or a candle. It had also become an absurdity long since in his opinion, making it necessary months before the present war for the numbers of guests to be reduced at the Tuileries to allow space for the enormous skirts. Onstage at theatre and opera house, whether the setting be that of mediaeval times or ancient Greece, all the women's costumes were crinolined, and he considered the effect quite ludicrous. He was left with no one to support his desire for change, least of all his darling Marie, who never liked a fashion until it had been around long enough for the humblest concierge to feel accustomed to it, and was as content as the rest of her sex that it should remain unaltered. His mind was alive with new ideas for other lines and different silhouettes, but for the first time female opinion had blocked solidly against him. How to break through? He flung himself out of the chair and went to stand by the window, staring down with unfocused gaze into the rue de la Paix, his hands thrust into his pockets. The problem would be solved if he could find a high-spirited woman, prominent in the public eye, who would be prepared to wear a dress that was different. Many of his customers moved in the highest social circles, but he wanted one who would be a leader of fashion, possessing the *chic* essential to such a launching. He smiled wryly to himself. Why didn't he admit it? The woman he wanted to wear his clothes was the Empress Eugénie herself. After the one design she had worn of his under the banner of Maison Gagelin for the Winterhalter painting, all Paris had been flooded with copies of that white-and-lilac creation. Wherever she led, the whole female world followed. But to the Empress, even if she had heard his name, he was just another couturier. He lifted his head sharply as the panes of the windows rattled a second before the boom of cannon resounded from the direction of Les Invalides. Another victory? He hastened out of his office and sent a junior member of staff to discover the news. The lad returned jubilant. The war was over! It had lasted less than eleven weeks. Staff and customers alike rejoiced. Louise crushed involuntarily the dress of Solferino blue that she happened to be holding, overwhelmed by thankfulness.

Several days later she was summoned to measure a customer making a first visit to number 7, rue de la Paix. To her consternation it was Pierre's wife who awaited her in the fitting-room.

"How are you, Louise?" The smile was tentative.

"I'm very well. Are you keeping so?"

Stéphanie inclined her head. "Particularly now that all anxiety about my husband's safe return from Italy has been removed from my mind. He has come through those great battles of the campaign quite unscathed."

Louise tried to preserve an impersonal show of the relief that engulfed her. She had scanned the tragically long casualty lists that had appeared, with a sickening dread that his name might be there, and to have it confirmed beyond all shadow of doubt that he was safe was the best news she could hear. "I'm thankful for your sake that he has been spared," she said quite evenly.

Stéphanie gave her a long, speculative look. "I appreciate your kind words. The reason I'm here is that I must look my best for my husband's return with the Emperor, and Monsieur Worth had promised me that six beautiful dresses will be ready in time."

"Then I will get to work without further delay." Louise took her tape-measure from around her neck and put ready the little notepad and pencil to write the measurements down.

"How old is Paul-Michel now?" Stéphanie enquired clearly.

Louise let slip the tape-measure she was putting around Stéphanie's bust, and hastily put it right again. "A year and eight months." She swallowed. "How did you know his name? Or even that my baby was a boy?"

"I heard in an indirect way." No need to say it had been through a terrible quarrel with Pierre after the night of the Orsini bombs. Unable to keep what she had witnessed to herself, she had let hurt and anger and jealousy run away with her. If only she had not seen them together everything would have gone along as before, she wallowing in blissful self-deception, imagining that she had the ability to eliminate all other women from his life. She would still have been happy, but now happiness in her marriage had slipped away from her. In retrospect she knew that if she had just kept silent as older and wiser wives would have done, she might still have some illusions intact. Instead, she had goaded him into making it plain that Louise still haunted him, and that it had been Louise's decision, not his, that his marriage should end what had been between them. Stéphanie bit the inside of her lip to keep it from trembling. He had been cruel in his frankness. But then, she had demanded honesty, and he had been honest, taking her at her word, not knowing that she wanted him to lie and lie and lie that she, his wife, was the one who meant most to him.

Obediently, at Louise's request, she bent her elbow to be measured for the sleeve length. Why had she come here today? Madame Palmyre had made her plenty of dresses only recently. Was it that she felt that Worth alone could give her that extra degree of elegance to look her best at a time when she had never needed it more? She was pinning all her hopes on her reunion with Pierre. For a while after their quarrel the breach had been wide, so wide that she began to fear for what she had done, but before he had left for Italy they had parted with a show of all having been patched up between them. On the eve of war she had reached for him in a heartaching yearning for reconciliation, and he had turned to her without restraint, making her believe that he did have some measure of deep-rooted feelings for her. She wanted to consolidate that state of affairs upon his return and make him truly glad to have come home to her.

She glanced sideways at Louise, who was jotting down on the notepad. She could see why any man would find it hard to forget such a woman. That profile, those extraordinarily fascinating eyes, the long, white throat, and the fine figure. But a wife was a wife, while a past mistress, even one with a child that was his, must eventually fade from his life. With a start she realised that Louise was speaking to her.

"All my measurements taken now, are they?" she managed to answer. "That's good." She touched her hair into place under her bonnet and took her green silk parasol that Louise handed to her. "I suppose you will be fitting my dresses as before at Gagelin's?"

Louise regarded her straightforwardly. "If you wish it, madame."

"I wish it. Good day."

Stéphanie left Worth's by way of the curving staircase. Her groom was waiting by the glass doors that led into the pilastered entrance, and opened them for her. The coachman, who had turned the horses in the inner courtyard, brought them trotting forward at the exact moment so that she could step directly into the open brougham. She snapped up her parasol as she was bowled out of the shade into the sun of the rue de la Paix. It had come to her why she had gone to Worth's. With Pierre's return imminent, she needed a friend to sustain her belief in herself and her ability to wipe out that estrangement as if it had never been. Louise had that inner strength, and had helped her before when she had needed good counsel. It was a piquant situation, but somehow she felt that she was being extremely sensible, and that Louise, if she had been informed, would have agreed with her. Much cheered, she faced the future with hope.

The scorching summer slipped on into August, bringing home the French troops from the victorious Italian campaign. Marie darted about getting ready to go and see the great parade. She chattered away to Jean-Philippe as she put on her fashionably shallow bonnet.

"Maman will hold you up to see the Emperor, and you are to have a posy of flowers to give to the bravest soldier that you see. Is it not a pity that poor Papa has to work hard and can't come with us?"

Jean-Philippe at three years old was gazing at her with rapt attention, not held by what she was saying, but by her appearance. He loved colour. It had surrounded him since birth in his father's sketches as well as in every kind of fabric under the sun, and when he painted pictures in his drawing-book he liked to use the brightest hues in the paintbox.

Today his mother was wearing a huge white crinoline covered with lace that floated and billowed like threads of soft clouds, but it was her long-ended sash that enchanted him, full of blues and reds and pinks and greens in a silk that he knew from his grown-up friends on the material counters came from a far-away place called India. The same marvellous silk that made up the sash lined the brim framing her bright, smiling face that descended towards him as she bent to pick him up in her arms. It was a moment of loving her that he was never to forget. It was as if fireworks were shooting those same magical colours in stars from his heart. He wrapped his arms around her neck and hugged her hard. She laughed protest, not at her own possible disarray, but that he should not crush his new clothes or untidy the curls she had given him with her own curling-tongs.

Before leaving she had a word with her husband. "Now you will let all the staff go out onto the balcony when the parade comes up the rue de la Paix, won't you?" she urged.

He chuckled indulgently. "Even if I had not wished to please you, my dove, I can't imagine that it would be possible to keep any woman on this floor, client or staff, from rushing to eye all that handsome soldiery."

She laughed as she took up the posies that lay waiting on the table for herself and her child, intending to kiss her husband and depart, but he stayed her with a loving embrace. She had returned only that morning from taking the waters for her health at a fashionable spa, and he wanted to adore her a little after the separation. He thought poetically that she could have sprung from the union of a butterfly and a rose, so enchanting was she, and as on many previous occasions he considered it a crime that her beautiful hair resting in coils on her pretty neck should be hidden by the conventional *bavolet* that adorned women's bonnets, often as the clumsiest of frills.

"Take off your bonnet," he coaxed. "I don't like that *bavolet.*"

"What's the matter with it?" she exclaimed anxiously, untying her bonnet ribbons.

"It exists," he replied cryptically. "That's all." As she handed him the bonnet he took up a pair of scissors, and she uttered a gasp of astonishment as he snipped away the stitches that held the frill of multi-coloured silk. With a twist of his clever fingers he fashioned the displaced material into a flat bow which he pinned high across the bonnet's crown. Holding up the re-adorned piece of millinery on his fingertip, he twirled it triumphantly. "*Voilà!* Now the Emperor himself will be able to admire my wife's crowning glory."

For once Marie approved. She tilted her head this way and that with the aid of a hand-glass, and thought the whole silhouette of the head much improved. And it *did* show off her hair, of which she was justly proud. Light-heartedly she departed with Jean-Philippe.

Outside in the pilastered entrance Gaston was waiting for them, full of what he had seen already. The rue de la Paix was like every other street in Paris in being cloaked in flags and banners, with triumphal arches, and every balcony hung with rich draperies, Worth having chosen gold brocade for those stretching the length of his floor at number 7. Marie's shadow danced behind her as she took her sons' hands in her own and led them through the gathering crowds into the vast sun-drenched square of the Place Vendôme and took the good viewing place reserved for them in one of the stands specially erected for thousands of spectators. Around her she heard women begin to whisper about her bonnet, as usually they did about her splendid dresses. She smiled to herself. Where Worth led, women followed. She did not doubt that many other bonnets would be shorn by this time tomorrow. Nearby, she noticed Stéphanie de Gand, and they acknowledged each other. Marie thought it most curious that Stéphanie and Louise seemed to have picked up the threads of their previous acquaintanceship during the fittings. Not that to her knowledge there was any reason why Stéphanie should not be friendly, but for Louise it must seem a strange state of affairs.

Jean-Philippe found it an extraordinary experience to be sitting in a stand in the Place Vendôme. Normally he walked through it with his parents and Gaston on Sundays, or trotted beside his nurse on daily outings to and from his home. While his brother chatted away excitedly to their mother, he was silent. His little mouth dropped open as he looked up and up and up to the statue at the top of the great column in the middle of the huge square. He knew it was another Bonaparte up there, the great Napoleon I, and not the Emperor he was to see today, but it seemed to him on this day of days and from this unusual angle that it had grown taller and was actually touching the palette blue of the sky.

"Look!" his maman said, diverting his attention towards

the gold-fringed canopied entrance of the Ministry of Justice where a grand lady had appeared against a backcloth of crimson velvet studded with the golden Napoleonic bee. "It's the Empress."

The whole square seemed to be filled with the music flooding from the regimental band preceding the parade as it moved up the rue de la Paix, the sun flashing fire from the instruments as they came into sight with a searing brilliance that dazzled the eye. Jean-Philippe held his breath with the wonder of it all.

On the long balcony of number 7 there was excitement among all those who had gathered from Worth's salons to wave and cheer and throw flowers from the baskets of blossoms that had been thoughtfully provided. The last row of bandsmen had passed, and after a suitable gap there came the Emperor with the gold of his cocked hat and his epaulettes gleaming, riding alone at the head of the marching column in his customary manner of eyes straight ahead, his face without expression, and his horse under perfect control. As the thrown blossoms were crushed under the deliberate hooves, Louise thought he must surely be overwhelmed by the rapturous reception being given him. In his wake came the mass of cavalry and the rest of the column that stretched away out of sight into the Boulevard des Capucines, having the appearance of a gigantic, undulating garland of incredible width, every officer and man bedecked with posies and blossoms that had been thrust into their hands and speared on their rifles. The shining helmets and flowing white plumes of the Cent-Garde were passing directly below, and although Louise scanned them she had no expectation of spotting Pierre, and was only thankful to know that he was among their number. She threw the last of the flowers she held in her own private tribute, and almost at once Robert brought her some more from another basket. He had come back to Paris after a short while in England, and when he put his arm familiarly about her waist he was only taking advantage of the few minor privileges that she allowed him.

"We'll be having our own celebration this evening, you and I," he reminded her, giving her waist a fond squeeze.

"I'm looking forward to it," she answered with perfect truth. Paris in jubilation was a sight not to be missed. She was glad that she and Robert were to be part of it.

At that moment there came from the Place Vendôme a tumultuous roar of approbation. Marie was as excited as everyone else. The Emperor, bringing his horse to a stately halt to take the salute of his loyal and victorious regiments, had taken up the little Prince Imperial from the Empress to sit before him on the saddle. The popularly acclaimed "Child of France" was dressed in a miniature Imperial Guard uniform complete with busby. Solemnly the small boy matched every action of his father's response to the homage of the parade, and the crowd loved it. Never had the imperial family been dearer to the people than on that day of days

When night came, all Paris danced in the streets. Every café and restaurant was crowded, extra tables put up everywhere and spread out on the pavements far beyond the protective awnings. It was as if the war had been a passing shadow, and now that it had gone the city was showing itself to be unchanged, still as wild and merry in the pursuit of pleasure as it had ever been. In some places the can-can dancers abandoned their bloomers in the spirit of the occasion, inciting men to an appreciative frenzy, and everywhere champagne corks popped unceasingly, chefs sweated over dish after dish to fill the orders of frantic waiters, and the whole city vibrated with music from countless thumping bands and grander orchestras swelling out the rhythms of Offenbach and Strauss into the balmy air. Robert had booked a restaurant table the day before, and it was a good one, comparatively secluded in spite of the crush, and they dined magnificently. When they had been served coffee, he moved closer to her on the banquette seat and took her hand into his.

"Do you realise that I have entered the last lap of my time at Worth's?" he began. "Before long I'll be thinking of going back to England for good."

She knew she would miss him. Their time together had not always been agreeable, often she had wanted to avoid him, and sometimes they had quarrelled, but always they had made it up again. "What is the latest news of your father?" she asked. "Is he still continuing to make good progress since your visit home?"

"Yes, he is, but the time has more or less come for him to give up completely." He paused, appearing to study her fingers, which he was stroking gently. "I care for you very much, Louise. So much that when I was in London I returned to Paris before I should have, simply because I couldn't wait to see you again. I'm asking you to marry me and to come back to England as my wife."

She was astounded. He had certainly pursued her, but she had never imagined that it was with any true depth of heart or feeling. "I wouldn't want to leave Paris, Robert. In any case, I have no thought of ever marrying."

"But you should. For your son's sake, if for no other reason. I'd be a good father to him. He'd go to the best of schools. Surely you should think of him, and in thinking of him also consider me."

She had to smile, and it was with sad amusement. Wily as ever, Robert sought to get his own way by the most powerful argument he could have put to her in the absence of love. "You don't particularly like children. To my knowledge, you have never once taken Paul-Michel onto your knee."

"Is that any fault of mine? He cries and hides behind your skirts as soon as I come near, and who could wonder at it when he is closeted in a world of women." He saw he had made his point, for she had lowered her lashes, looking quickly away from him. He pursued his advantage. "I know you don't love me as I love you, and there need be no pretence between us. I believe that with time I can make you love me, and that's all that matters now. You've long wanted a business of your own, and with me you shall have it. We'll be partners at Prestbury's. It needs to be reorganised, and you may make of it what you will. I know it's not the same as starting from scratch, but it will be no less of an achievement for you to create a place of Paris fashion in the heart of London."

She was shaking her head at all he was offering. "Please don't say any more. I can't marry—"

He moved hard against her and stopped what she was saying with a swift kiss. "I won't let you refuse me now. Think about all I've said. I love you. I need you. Don't make me leave Paris without you." Then he kissed her again with a change of mood, becoming merry and buoyant, and linked his fingers in hers. "Now we'll see what else this city can do to entertain us. You and I are going to dance the night away." He summoned the waiter for the bill, and a few moments later he had her helpless with laughter as he whirled her around and around down the length of the Champs-Elysées, pausing only to break away and swing like a boy from the branch of a tree and toss a coin to a flower-seller for a bunch of marguerites, one of which he plunged deep into her bosom and took another for a buttonhole before hurling the rest away like a shower of floating stars. It was dawn before they arrived at her door, and there he kissed her with a great ardour, her face held between his hands, his body pressed to hers. He lifted his lips away, still holding her, and spoke his plea in a whisper.

"Think about spending the rest of your life with me. This is how it could be between us always."

"The answer is no, my dear Robert," she protested gently, "and must remain no."

He shook his head, his smile determined. "I didn't catch what you said. I must have suddenly become deaf. My hearing will only return when you give me the right answer. You have some while yet to find it. Good night, sweetheart."

Her mind was so made up that during the next few days she merely worried as to how she should give him her final refusal without hurting him too much. Then she decided that she would simply play down any more talk in that direction until he came to realise sensibly and without pain that she had meant what she said. It was quite impossible to envisage any circumstances under the sun that could make her change her mind.

17

It was a client who told Louise of a small suite of rooms on an upper floor in some property that was owned by her family. Louise went to inspect it and found that the good address was deceiving, the entrance being through a side alley off the Boulevard des Capucines. Nevertheless, the rent was low for that reason, and she felt she could just afford to make a modest start on her own there. It would give her a small salon and a workroom for her seamstress, who would be Catherine, and she planned to do the cutting and fitting herself. The rest of the space would make cramped living accommodation, but it would be adequate. Robert was taken aback by the news and looked thoroughly disgruntled.

"I can't believe Worth would be prepared to let you go for any reason other than marriage."

"On the contrary, he has long known my aim and always encouraged me. Already he has offered to help me with reduced prices for material and passementerie and so forth, because I won't be able to carry any stock at first."

"That won't last. He could never stomach a rival."

She burst out laughing. "He has no rival, either now or in the future, but I can make a niche for myself in my own right."

His expression cleared. "Then make that niche in London. At Prestbury's. That's what you're going to decide in the end, you know."

His grin was confident and sure, making her heart sink. How was it possible to convince someone wholly used to getting his own way in life that in this matter he was not going to win? It was a great pity she did not have the keys already in her possession, which would surely convince him that she meant what she said, but she had to wait until the present occupier moved out.

The following Sunday started out much like any other. In the rue de la Paix the Worths set out with their children for a family stroll. From another direction Louise and Catherine were already wending their way into the heart of the city, Paul-Michel trotting between them. They always let him walk for a while, taking turns to carry him when he became tired. On this occasion Catherine was keeping up too swift a pace for him and he began to drag on her hand, not willing yet to be carried, but becoming fractious through the pace. She looked down at him with an extremely rare show of impatience. Whenever there was an event or a spectacular sight to see, a common enough occurrence, Catherine always knew about it, and on this occasion the venue was the Austrian Embassy in the rue de Grenelle.

"Come along, Paul-Michel. You'll make your maman and me late to see all the horses and carriages."

She was trying to interest him. He liked horses. For herself, all she wanted to view was the young wife of the new Austrian ambassador, Princess Pauline de Metternich, who that day was to attend her initial reception at the Palace of the Tuileries. Much had been written and gossiped about her.

Outspoken and unconventional, cast in the aura of the princely Metternichs, her own grandfather being her husband's father, which was in itself a pretty scandalous state of affairs, she was reputed to be as ugly as a monkey and as fascinating as a siren. Catherine could not wait to clap eyes on this extraordinary creature.

Obediently Paul-Michel toddled on for a little longer, but when he tripped and fell on his face, that was an end to it. Catherine almost hopped about with impatience. Louise bade her go ahead.

"We'll follow in a few minutes," she said, trying to quieten her son's sobs. "I know where the Embassy is."

Catherine needed no further encouragement. She hurried off, afraid that even now she would be too late to get to the forefront of those who would gather there. Louise found Paul-Michel more difficult to soothe than usual, and to distract him from the hurt he had suffered in his fall she carried him into a nearby park where children were playing. When his thumb went into his mouth she knew he would sleep, and holding him close to her she began to retrace her steps along a secluded, tree-lined path. She had failed to see one of the riders in the park dismount, hook the reins to a post, and cross a lawn towards her, but she froze to a halt as he drew level with her, overpowered by his totally unexpected presence. She forced herself to meet Pierre's eyes. What she saw there melted all the loneliness between, transporting her back in time, not to the agony of betrayal and parting, but to the early days of loving and being loved.

"I can't go on living without you," he said in the perfect understanding of thought that lovers share. Then his gaze lowered to the sleeping child. "Or without him." He bent his head and kissed his son's cheek. Then, as she stood there paralysed, he curved his arms around both of them and his mouth took hers with a passionate tenderness that seemed to settle all between them. It was as if she had no more will, and nothing else existed beyond their kissing and his embrace and the secluded grove. He had defeated her in a vulnerable moment with all guards down, and for the first time ever she was lost, and in being lost could turn only to him.

He drew her to a stone bench under the boughs. "A new beginning, my darling. Nothing that has gone before shall spoil the future. We must be together again, and it shall be only as you wish it and on your terms."

"I can scarcely believe this is happening." She was unable to regain her equilibrium.

"I have been watching out for you everywhere. Sooner or later I knew I'd find you. It was the only way to meet again. Not on any ground that was familiar to us before. There's so much to talk about, so much I want to hear. Where are you living now?"

"At the same address, but Catherine and I will be moving shortly." She told him of the rooms in the Boulevard des Capucines, and he expressed keen interest, praising her initiative and congratulating her on her aim at last to be achieved. He had learnt his lesson from the past, and was astute enough not to make offers of financial support or to help her by any other means. Instead, he sought to prepare the way for their lives ahead.

"I should like to view these premises. May we meet there soon?"

They both knew the outcome of a meeting alone. For her it would be a final and total commitment to loving him in a compromise that had brought him to accept her independence. She released a long-drawn breath.

"The keys will be mine in a short while now."

His expression slowly relaxed. "Tell me the day and the hour. I'll be there."

Their meeting was arranged. She rose from the bench, and he with her. He put both hands on her shoulders, keeping her mouth to his in a last kiss, and it was as if they were totally bound by the current of love flowing between them.

She met Catherine coming away from the rue de Grenelle, full of what she had seen. Her friend's prattle seemed to bounce about her ears like dropped pebbles, the sound just as meaningless. Catherine did not draw breath in her excitement.

"It's right what everybody says. The Princess is really ugly, with pop eyes, a yellowish skin, and a thick-lipped mouth like an ape's. But oh! She was something to see. Don't ask me why. It had nothing to do with her jewels, although she was loaded with them. I gaped at her. I really did. And I wasn't the only one." Catherine's voice trailed off at the lack of any comment, and she peered at Louise with realisation dawning in her eyes, her expression hardening sternly. "You've seen him, haven't you? Spoken to him as well, I dare say. I can tell by your face."

There was no doubt as to whom she meant. Catherine had

avoided saying Pierre's name from the time she first learned that Paul-Michel was on the way. Louise seemed to hear her own words coming from a distance.

"Be glad for me. All will be well now."

Catherine's own face congested. "How can it be? He has a wife, doesn't he? He'll tire of you as he's already tired of her. Can't you see farther than the end of your nose? The Holy Mother knows I never trusted him in the first place, and that's why I had no intention of moving into that fancy residence when you wanted me to, but kept you both on tenterhooks waiting for me to make up my mind. I knew if I held out long enough that it would fizzle out. I could tell he'd start to look elsewhere, and I was right then just as I'll be proved right again, you'll see!"

In all the years they had known each other Louise could never remember being as deeply and terribly angry with Catherine as she was now. "If you *had* moved when you were asked, there would have been a marriage. If you had not been jealous of my being in love you would not have hesitated for a moment. Instead, you procrastinated until the chance was lost. Not only did you prevent my becoming the true wife of the only man I'll ever love, but you denied Paul-Michel the right to be acknowledged by the world as his father's son!"

Catherine was struck dumb. It was not just because Louise had never spoken to her in such a burst of fury before, but because she knew that in her heart of hearts there had been jealousy and envy that had weighed as heavily as her doubts about Pierre de Gand. It was a terrible moment of truth for her. When Louise began to walk on she did not follow, but leaned against the wall by which she was standing, covering her eyes with her hand.

The gilded coaches that made up Princess de Metternich's procession were approaching the Tuileries. The Worths, catching sight of them, hurried forward and were lucky enough to get a position that gave a full view of the ambassador's wife as she alighted from the white satin-upholstered interior of her ornate coach, her jewels blazing. Both were struck by her tremendous personal mangetism that compelled the eye to her, making her extraordinary looks an asset rather than a disadvantage. When she had disappeared from sight the Worths continued their walk in silence, each contemplating what they had seen. They had gone no more than a few steps when each turned spontaneously to the other, both speaking at the same time.

"If only the Princess had been wearing one of your dresses today, Charles!"

"That is a woman who would do full justice to my clothes!"

They chuckled that they should have shared the same thought, but it lingered on long after that Sunday had come to a close. Marie, lying sleepless on the pillow, turned it over and over in her mind.

Louise's feelings when she went to work each day were buoyant and strangely unreal. It was as if the whole state of her emotions had lifted onto another plane that she did not quite comprehend and did not want to examine closely. It was enough to be fired through with the knowledge that she and Pierre were to be as one again. At home, the quarrel had been made up, and it was apparent that Catherine, chastened and conscience-stricken, would never again try to interfere in her life or raise any word against Pierre.

It all seemed in keeping to Louise in her elated mood when from a doorway on the landing of number 7, she sighted Worth and Marie near the head of the stairs, exchanging a most loving kiss. They had not seen her and she paused, not wanting to intrude, and yet unable to retreat. Marie was dressed for outdoors in a new outfit of bronze velvet, and in her arms she held a vellum-bound album.

"Good luck, my dearest," he said to her.

Marie smiled, putting her gloved hand against his cheek, her eyes bright with whatever secret it was they shared, and then she disappeared quickly down the stairs. Worth turned and went back into the main salon. Louise remained where she was for a few moments, feeling warmed by the harmony between them. It was akin to what she and Pierre had shared in their meeting again, but with one unbridgeable difference. No shadow of any kind lay between Marie and the man she loved.

Marie was bound for the rue de Grenelle. Her heart was beating against her ribs and seemed to increase its frantic fluttering with every step that brought her nearer the Austrian Embassy. Since the day she and Worth had seen the Princess de Metternich they had been unable to stop talking about her. If such a woman could be persuaded to wear just one of his dresses, it would be noticed wherever she went. With time others might discover where she had had it made, and it would bring him the special kind of client that he needed to give full rein to his creative genius, women to whom cost meant nothing, women whose aim in life was to wear the most beautiful clothes in the world. The decision had been made. His newest designs, as yet unseen by others, were put together in the special album she carried with such care, and she was going to approach the distinguished Princess as one woman of elegance to another. The gates of the Embassy loomed up before her. Marie braced herself and walked through.

Pauline de Metternich was not accustomed to receiving people she did not know. She dismissed out of hand the request of a certain Madame Worth to see her. It appeared that the young woman's husband wished to make her a dress, but she had never heard his name, and had her own dressmakers of distinction. What was more, it struck her as ludicrous that an Englishman should be presuming to teach the French to dress, and no less that through his wife he should dare to approach her since she could outshine any fashionable woman in Europe or anywhere else for that matter.

"Send her away," she instructed her lady-in-waiting, taking up again the book she had been reading before the interruption.

The lady-in-waiting hesitated, the album in her arms. Impressed by Madame Worth's own elegant attire, she had glanced through the sketches, and what she had seen had convinced her that she was justified in trying to gain an interview for the caller.

"May I suggest that Your Highness should just take a quick look at the designs. I've never seen anything quite like them myself."

Had the novel she was reading been more enthralling the Princess might never have agreed, but with her mind not fully drawn into it she took note of the unusual persistence of her lady-in-waiting, who was always at pains to preserve the much-cherished hours of privacy that could be rare enough to someone in her position. With the faintest of sighs she took the album onto her lap and without expectation opened the first page. The design that met her eyes was quite beautiful. She turned to the next page, and the next. Each appeared to be more ravishing than the last. Here was the hand of a true artist of *haute couture*!

"Show the caller in," she said decisively, not taking her eager eyes from the sketches, and did not look up until the Englishman's wife had entered modestly. "Sit down, Madame Worth," she invited, "and explain why you came to me."

"I was with my husband when we saw you arrive at the Palace of the Tuileries on the day of Your Highness's reception, and he has talked of nothing since but that he would like to make a dress for you." Briefly Marie explained how he had left Maison Gagelin to open his own house. The Princess displayed great interest, asking questions while all the time glancing again at the album on her lap. She was already making a selection, and although mightily rich, she was practical enough to expect value for money.

"Naturally my husband would wish you to set your own price," Marie concluded.

The Princess nodded. "I will have one day dress, and another for evening wear. Neither must cost me more than three hundred francs." It was a fair price to pay an unknown dressmaker, and if the dresses proved to be as well made as Madame Worth's appeared to be she would have secured a bargain for herself. She added a little incentive. "If the dresses please me I will wear the evening one to the State Ball next week."

Whn Marie arrived back at the rue de la Paix, one look at her face was enough to tell Worth that she had been successful. He caught her up and whirled her around in joyous triumph, and in the midst of laughter she told him that her success was beyond their wildest dreams.

"The Princess is to wear your dress to the next State Ball at the Tuileries!" she cried. "All the world will see it!"

Amid the flurry of excitement over the Princess's order, other customers had to receive the usual degree of attention, Worth never letting his standards slip for any reason at all. The day Stéphanie de Gand came for her appointment he was waiting to greet her. When he had transferred to his own premises he kept his innovation of having a veiled and pregnant woman in a salon set aside for those particular clients. It was there that Stéphanie took a seat, and Louise was sent for.

Louise knew she would never forget seeing Pierre's wife there. The sensation of champagne bubbles in her veins, which had sustained a delirious anticipation of the future, began to evaporate and subside with such a rush that it was as if all strength was ebbing from her. Perhaps Stéphanie, her own attitude that of exuberant nervousness, saw something of the hollowing of cheeks and eyes, because she made a request of Worth.

"I should like Mademoiselle Louise to sit by me," she said ingenuously, patting the seat of the chair next to her. "If you would allow it. I wish to consult her as one who has already been through the special experience that lies ahead of me."

With the exception of the pregnant woman, nobody on the staff was allowed to sit in the presence of customers. Worth was greatly put out that she had asked. He indicated to Louise that there was a footstool that would suffice in the salon where rules sometimes had to be bent a little to accommodate the quirks of customers who used the excuse of their pregnancy to be temperamental or tearful. He was thankful that Marie had never displayed any nonsensical whims.

As he signalled for the first dress to be shown, Stéphanie turned to Louise on the footstool with hands clasped together excitedly. "I can't tell you how happy I am that this good fortune has come to me. Pierre and I have had our little differences in the past, but that is all over now." She turned her head, her attention caught by the dress of grey lace with magenta ribbons being paraded in front of her. "La! That's pretty! Would that be comfortable to wear right through to the last days, do you think, Louise?"

Worth glowered. "All my dresses are designed to that end, madame."

Louise wished she could tell him that Stéphanie knew that perfectly well, but would be using each garment as a foil through which to engage the friendship that she feared to lose. It was easy to tell that Stéphanie felt frightened and alone, not nearly as sure of herself as she wanted to appear, and she wanted the comfort and support of the woman who had borne the half-brother of the baby in her womb.

The session dragged on. Louise felt the strain greater than anything she had ever known before. Stéphanie's garrulous comments on every dress shown were in reality a heart-cry that all the guileless hopes and dreams of everlasting love and happiness built on the forthcoming birth should come true.

And that could only be ensured if Louise undertook to remain in the past. How much did Stéphanie suspect? How much did she know? It was impossible to tell. Had all the high-primed instincts of being in love enabled Stéphanie to spot her husband's abstracted glance, perhaps? His preoccupation with thoughts not concentrated upon her? Or had he made the preparatory excuse for absence on a certain forthcoming evening that had not rung true?

As Louise sat there her own new world fell slowly apart. She had deceived herself for almost two days into thinking that loving Pierre was enough after all for everything to go well, but nothing had changed. He was still married to another woman who must make first claim on his time and affection, and soon the legitimate offspring of their marriage would supplant her own son. Later there would be other children in the dominant half of his life in which she would have no place, always the outsider, the other woman. How could she have forgotten the example set to her long since in Catherine's lonely waiting and watching for when a married lover would come, the endless disappointments, the constant humiliations? But there was still more than that. She had no right to cast a further blight over the life of her son. It stunned her to remorse to realise that she had not put him before all else during those days of feckless self-absorption. He had enough stigma to bear in being born illegitimate, and how could he grow up proud and strong and self-confident in the taint of scandal that came inevitably from any such affair? But it was not too late. There was still a path open to her, and she would take it and make a success of it. If she remained in Paris, Pierre would continue to pursue her. He had shown that he never meant to give in.

She cancelled her option on the premises in the Boulevard des Capucines the same day, and in the evening she accepted Robert's proposal of marriage. He was overjoyed, and with time running so short and many arrangements to be made, it was decided that they should marry on the morning he had been due to leave Paris, and they would catch the overnight Channel steamer to Dover. She did not write the news to Pierre, never having avoided the difficult assignments of life, and went instead to see him at the Tuileries. She had some delays before being allowed through, female visitors without known rank and distinction not being welcome on such illustrious ground. Eventually he received her in a small waiting-room in the military quarters, and she could tell at once that he was not entirely pleased to see her.

"Whatever brings you here, my darling?" he asked with a certain sharpness. "It's most unusual, you know. Not that it isn't wonderful to see you." He would have kissed her then, but she drew away, knowing she had just so much strength to carry out what she had to do, and no more. If she had needed confirmation that she had made the right decision about the future it was there in the unmistakable embarrassment she had inadvertently caused him by requesting an interview during hours of duty, when no wife would have appeared. But she had no choice. Time was fast running out.

"Since our meeting I've had time to think things over, and it was foolish of me to imagine that the situation was any different now from what it was before. There are many reasons why it would be an impossible position for you and for me, to say nothing of those to whom we are individually responsible."

He had gone quite white about the mouth. "My God! You came here to tell me that? Couldn't you have chosen a better time and place?" He glanced in fury at the clock on the wall. "In exactly seven minutes I have to be ready to escort the Emperor through the streets, and you decide to play the eternal coquette yet again for some ploy of your own. Heaven knows what you want of me, but you shall have it, even if it's my head on a platter. I'll do anything to please you, but it does not please me that you threaten to disrupt matters temporarily out of some headstrong whim of yours at such a damnably inopportune moment." He snatched up his helmet from where it was on the table and rammed it on, adjusting the chinstrap, the white plume falling silkily into place down the back of his uniform collar. "We are to meet Friday evening at the address you gave me, and then we'll talk out all our problems. There is nothing that can't be eradicated."

"I'll not be there. I've turned down those premises."

He was pulling on his white gauntlets. "A wise move. I thought at the time you told me that you could get something better. We'll go to the Café Anglais that evening. I'll book a private room. There's a special entrance and staircase that give secluded access, and—"

Already he was setting the pattern of subterfuge that would have moulded the rest of whatever time they would have had together. She wanted to clap her hands over her ears. "I won't be at those premises at the Boulevard des Capucines or anywhere else you suggest that evening," she burst out in interruption, wondering why it was her fate always to deal with self-centred men. Or was it simply a male trait that constantly predominated? "The reason is that I'll be packing. I'm leaving Paris. I'm going away."

His eyes narrowed. "Where? Lyons? Your mother came

from there, didn't she? Or are you opening your dressmaking business somewhere else in the provinces? You're determined to make things difficult for us, aren't you?"

She made a last attempt, spreading her hands out. "I came to tell you what I couldn't just write in a letter. I'm getting married. I'm going to England as the bride of a London man named Robert Prestbury."

He became very still. On the wall the clock ticked, and from outside in the courtyard there came the muffled clop of hooves and shouted orders and the marching footsteps of sentries changing guard. She had to turn away, stricken to tears by the starkness in his face. He spoke with controlled and quiet desperation, all harshness and anger gone.

"Don't match my folly with one of your own. You know that if ever two people were made for each other, we are. Let us salvage what we have left to us."

She was shaking her head and had reached breaking point, using effort to get her breath. "No good would come of it. We would have hurt ourselves and other people immeasurably. It has to end."

She went blindly from the room. She was twice stopped by guards and redirected as she tried to find her way out of the building through the cascading tears that filled her eyes. Later she could not remember walking home.

That same evening Princess Pauline de Metternich wore her first Worth gown. It was a masterpiece of simplicity in white tulle engaged with silver-threaded silk and adorned with a single cluster of marguerites on the huge skirt. She stood out in that vast assemblage of ornate *toilettes* as if some specially directed ray of illumination followed her alone wherever she moved, an illusion given strength by the constant rippling of heads that turned forever to her. The Empress, aglitter in her magnificent jewels where she sat beside the Emperor on the crimson-canopied dais, observed with considerable interest the beautiful dress being worn by the flamboyant newcomer to court. Before the evening was over she inquired of the Princess as to who had made it. Eugénie's arched brows lifted upon hearing that it was the creation of an Englishman named Worth, lavishly praised by the wearer as a new star glittering over all fashion. Amused, she nodded her head, the lights setting fire to her diadem.

"This star should be beset with satellites. I am prepared to be one of them."

The Princess de Metternich promised that Worth should

call upon Her Majesty next morning. She knew also that in future she would have to pay treble the figure and more for any dress from Worth. The Empress was also a star in her own firmament, and where she led, all her satellites would follow in her wake.

Worth was extremely busy when word came early for him to attend the Empress at ten o'clock. Whatever the time of day, it was customary for gentlemen to wear evening dress when being received by the Empress, but to Marie's dismay he refused to change out of his frockcoat.

"I'm an independent tradesman," he declared with pride. "Not a lackey."

She held both Jean-Philippe and Gaston up to the window to watch their papa leave for the palace. Perhaps he was right to wear his velvet-collared frockcoat. She did not think anything else suited him so well. It was also, she realised, a supreme arrogance. Worth, who believed himself to be so French, had never revealed himself more as an Englishman.

18

Louise saw the designs that the Empress had chosen, but that was all. Before the first pattern was cut, she and Robert were married, the day being the one booked for his departure from Paris. Catherine, the Worths, and a few other close friends attended the civil and religious ceremonies, after which they all ajourned to a restaurant for a wedding breakfast. Anybody could tell from the bride's face that it was not the happiest of days for her. Yet she was resolved to be a good wife to Robert, who had shown that he loved her enough in his own way to overlook what many men could not have ignored, and take another man's son as his own. She also intended to devote time and energy to doing whatever proved necessary to make Prestbury's prosperous, and Robert had promised that she should create a small part of her own Paris in the heart of London.

Everybody went to the railway station to see them off. She held Paul-Michel in her arms and waved from the compartment window until the beloved little group on the platform was lost from sight. Robert had already lounged back on the seat, having imbibed a considerable amount of champagne, and was waiting to take her onto his knee. But she remained looking out until the last spire and rooftop of Paris had disappeared from view.

Daylight had almost gone when they reached Calais, and it was cold and windy with a wild, rough sea that looked black in the pelting rain. Robert had booked a first-class cabin that was comfortable enough, but no sooner had the steamer left the harbour than it began to pitch against the huge waves. Robert ate a hearty supper, but Louise was queasy, as much from the tension of leaving France as from the movement of the ship, and she could eat nothing. She soon retired to the cabin, leaving her bridegroom to brandy and a cigar.

It was a relief to lie down in the narrow bunk. She closed her eyes wearily against the slow pendulum swing of her clothes on a peg and the constant onslaught of spray against the porthole. She had left the wick of the brass hanging lamp burning brightly, not wanting her little son, presently sleeping in the opposite bunk, to be scared if he stirred in such strange surroundings. When Robert came stumbling in he made such a clatter that Paul-Michel did awaken, setting up a terrified wail as the wick was turned out to plunge the cabin into inky blackness. She protested, but Robert took no notice, stripping off his clothes. She had expected him to take the spare upper bunk, but it was his wedding night. As she put her feet to the floor to find her way across to the frightened child, Robert seemed to fill the darkness around her with the warmth of his body. Her nightgown was yanked from her before he rolled her back under him into the hollow of the bunk. For a long while her son cried pitiably in terror at the creaking of the ship and the wild sea sounds before he finally fell into a whimpering sleep. At no time was she allowed respite to attend to him.

When morning came there was sun on the white cliffs of Dover, although the wind was still strong and rolling clouds scudded across the sky. On the train journey to London, Louise gazed out at her new land, appreciating the gentle views of the Kent countryside with its odd-shaped oasthouses and acres of orchards. Paul-Michel was good, kneeling beside her on the seat to watch the passing scenery with her, and later playing contentedly with a comical monkey-on-a-stick that Catherine had given him with her goodbye kiss.

The suburbs of London were beginning to appear, thick and sprawling under a forest of smoking chimneys, when Robert woke abruptly from the dozing that had made him silent company for most of the journey. He sat up, straightening his cravat and shooting his cuffs into place with a decidedly agitated air. He glanced quickly to one side and then the other at the passing landscape to locate exactly where they were, chewing his lower lip. To her he suddenly looked extraordinarily youthful and much like a schoolboy going home with a poor scholastic report in his pocket. It was a marked difference from the side of himself that he had revealed to her in the darkness of the night, but that was something she did not want to dwell on in her thoughts. He cleared his throat twice in preparation for speech. Since landing at Dover he had reverted completely to speaking only English to her, and in which she had replied. It was how it should be in whatever lay ahead, but she intended that Paul-Michel should never be allowed to forget his native tongue, and that they would always speak it when alone together.

"There's something I have to tell you, Louise. Something I suppose I should have told you before we left France."

She felt a quake of apprehension. "Yes?"

"Er—well, it's like this. My parents believe that Paul-Michel is my child."

She merely considered that to be kindly intentioned of him. From now on her son would be his to all intents and purposes, and they had agreed that his name should be changed from her single name to Prestbury. "That was gallant of you, but misguided. Surely you must have realised that your parents would be able to tell immediately that he is far older than he should be according to the length of time you've spent in Paris. He was about three weeks old when you arrived at Gagelin's just over two years ago. They'll be expecting an infant of little more than a year at most."

He cleared his throat again. "That's not the problem. I was in Paris before, you see. A couple of times, as a matter of fact. I've told them that we met then. The thing is, I couldn't say we were married all the time you were keeping me dangling on a string, although I did try to prepare them for a marriage when I was home for that short time. When I telegraphed to say that we were getting wed I added the lie that we already had a child from our union, which means they will assume that I have simply made an honest woman of you."

It was not a phrase she cared for, finding it patronising, but he was in such a state of growing agitation, constantly smoothing back the fall of hair that always swept one side of his brow, that all she wanted was to put him at his ease. "There's no harm in that," she said patiently.

"But my parents are so deucedly narrow-minded. I don't know what kind of reception you'll get. That's what I felt I had to warn you about."

So that was it. And she noticed that he had not aligned himself at her side for that reception, but had singled her out alone for it. "I must hope that they will like me enough to take charitable view. In any case, when they see Paul-Michel I can't believe they won't love him at once."

He did not share her maternal bias towards her offspring, and looked unconvinced. "Don't bank on it. My mother never had time for my sister Agnes or me, and we saw more of our nurse and our governess until I was eight. Then I was sent away to school, and that was more or less the end of my relationship with her. My father has always believed in children being seen and not heard, and took a cane to me at the least provocation. He won't be proud of a grandson conceived out of wedlock, and my mother would die if the truth should ever come out. After they've seen Paul-Michel I believe you'll find that everyone you meet will have been informed that we were married secretly about three years ago."

Th train began to slow down with a noisy hissing of steam that brought it alongside one of the platforms in the great arched London Bridge Station. He took his hat from the rack and gave instructions about the hand-baggage to the porter who jerked open the door. She was thoughtful as she alighted with Paul-Michel in her arms. She had been coerced into a false position and it went against her whole nature, but for Robert's sake she must go through with it.

A soberly dressed manservant from the Prestbury household had come to supervise the transportation of their trunks and boxes, enabling them to go straight through to the family equipage awaiting them in the forecourt of the railway station.

She found it exciting to see London for the first time. As they were driven across the bridge she pointed out to Paul-Michel the many barges and boats on the water, which made it as busy as the Seine. Again and again she asked Robert about the different grand edifices that they passed, the Houses of Parliament encased in the scaffolding of rebuilding, and the traffic-crowded streets and squares. In Piccadilly she looked for Swan and Edgar's, where Worth had served his apprenticeship, and spotted its fine frontage. She made up her mind to visit it at the first opportunity. On the whole it was hard to get much information out of Robert about the sights of the city around them, because although he knew it all, his answers were perfunctory as he sat slouched back in the corner seat, his mouth working so hard that she felt he must have gnawed through to blood in his lip. She found it consoling that he should be so concerned as to what kind of reception she would have at his parents' home, but his distracted mien was infectious, and against her will qualms began to flutter in her stomach.

They drew up in front of a large, gracious-looking terraced house with a railed area and stone steps scrubbed white, the brass bell-pull and boot-scraper ashine in the sun. It was situated in a square with a good-sized garden with trees and lawns and planted flowerbeds in the middle of it. Watch must have been kept for the carriage, because the front door was opened by a butler almost at once. Louise had a feeling of being observed from behind lace curtains on the first floor as she took the steps with Paul-Michel in her arms, Robert leading the way.

The interior of the house struck her as being very dark. It smelt of beeswax polish and blacklead and linseed oil. Everything gleamed. It was not an atmosphere that welcomed children. Robert addressed the butler as Merryfield, which she thought a singularly inappropriate name for such a dour-looking individual. Nevertheless, the man addressed her in almost perfect French.

"I trust you had a good journey, madame. It will be an honour to serve you in this house."

She was thanking him, appreciating the courtesy he had paid her, when a booming voice cut her short from the head of the flight of stairs. "None of that Bonaparte lingo under my roof! English is the language we use in this great country of ours, ma'am."

It was Robert's father, a thick-set, short-necked man with a balding head, abundant side-whiskers, and an apoplectic complexion, more purple than red. He was leaning heavily on a silver-handled walking stick, although he did not sound like an invalid. Robert greeted him with nervous abruptness, going up the stairs to shake his hand and leaving Louise to follow with her child on her own.

By the time she reached the carpeted landing, Robert had accompanied his father into a drawing-room, where he was kissing his mother, who was seated in a high-backed chair. Louise set Paul-Michel on his feet, took his small hand into her own, and crossed the threshold. The gaze of both Mr. and Mrs. John Prestbury went straight to her child with a look of frigid disapproval. They saw him as living proof of their son's lechery with an immoral young woman in the notorious capital of the country that every decent Englishman distrusted. Robert jerked his chin as he straightened his cravat unnecessarily. There was a fine beading of sweat on his brow and upper lip that gave him a curiously grey look.

"My dear parents," he said with a hardness of articulation that seemed closer to hatred than filial affection, "allow me to present my wife, Louise, and my son, Paul-Michel."

Verena Prestbury's thin lips compressed themselves still further as her eyes remained fixed on the child. She was in her mid-fifties, almost twenty years younger than her husband. She was not a plain woman, but the severity of her nature had combined with her dissatisfaction with life and had settled a permanent frown upon her visage, and dragged deep lines from her nose to the corners of her mouth. Her bronze-brown hair, much the colour of her son's, retained its youthful vitality, but was almost hidden by her lace cap.

"It will not do," she stated coldly. "It will not do at all, Robert. I forbid you to tell anyone that you were married only yesterday. That is why Agnes is not present at the moment. We had to spare her the knowledge of your disgrace."

"Whatever you say, Mother," he replied quickly, looking as if he wished himself anywhere but there.

Mrs. Prestbury deigned to switch her scrutiny to Louise, taking her in from her elegant Parisian bonnet to the hem of her travelling costume. "So you're Louise. I trust you are prepared to be a dutiful wife to my son. He has proved himself most honourable in marrying you. The least you can do is to show your gratitude until the end of your days."

Before Louise could reply, John Prestbury glanced towards his son in impatient inquiry. "She does speak English, I suppose?"

Louise answered for herself with personal dignity unassailed. "You need not fear that I won't understand anything you say. I hope I find you much improved in health since your illness, Mr. Prestbury, and that you, Mrs. Prestbury, are well."

"Nothing wrong with me, I'll thank you to know." John Prestbury thumped his cane twice in triumphant emphasis. "I 'ave stamina, the stuff that our brave Empire was built on. I'm a self-made man and proud of it."

That had been obvious. Mrs. Prestbury by her refined air surely came from better stock, even though her manners were singularly lacking. Louise was conscious of not one word of welcome having been uttered yet, and her own conventional phrases could have fallen on deaf ears for all the notice Robert's mother had taken of them.

"You have no *bavolet* on your bonnet, Louise."

"It is no longer the fashion." That was true. Since Marie Worth had appeared in her bow-trimmed bonnet it was fast disappearing as Parisian women wielded scissors on their millinery.

"It is in England." Mrs. Prestbury spoke of her country as if it were on a par with heaven. "You are showing your neck. It is not decent."

Louise thought that at this moment she might have received a warm and heartening glance from Robert in remembrance of amusement shared when Marie, after going to the races at Longchamps in a *bavolet*-less bonnet, had been criticised in the same way by a prim acquaintance, but no shared communication of the eyes was forthcoming from him. It made her wish that Worth were there. He had doubled up with laughter to hear that anyone should consider that showing the neck was immodest, declaring he would never get over it, and he would have laughed all over again to hear it once more from another source.

"I keep a remnant-box," Mrs. Prestbury continued, "and will find you a piece of stuff later for you to sew onto your bonnet and any others you may have brought with you."

Louise was wondering how much longer she could hold her tongue, her indignation rising to a whiter heat with every moment, and Robert's withholding of support made everything worse. John Prestbury was regarding Paul-Michel again, and addressed him with a wag of the end of the silver-topped stick.

"Your papa gave your name some fancy foreign pronunciation, but we'll have none of that nonsense here. Paul Michael is 'ow it's pronounced." He anglicised the name heavily. "But one good Christian name is enough for common use. You'll be known as Paul now, and Prestbury when you go to school. Understand?"

Paul-Michel's lower lip had begun to droop ominously from the beginning of the incomprehensible utterance barked at him in alarming tones. Since leaving the Channel packet even his maman had begun to talk away in gibberish when not speaking to him. He didn't like it, and he didn't like the cross man or the nasty lady, who had not smiled once or held out her arms to him as ladies usually did. He wanted his maman to take him home, away from this strange place, he wanted his aunt Catherine to lift him onto her wonderful cushion of a lap, and he wanted the chamberpot. He turned his face into his maman's skirt and wept as a warm trickle ran down his legs to form a little pool on the carpet.

In the bedroom allotted to them with a huge carved bed, wall-length wardrobe, and other furniture that matched in overpowering dimensions, Louise paced the floor while rocking her dry and reclad toddler in her arms. She upbraided Robert severely, not in English but in a flow of delicious French that released her tongue and her pent-up outrage.

"How could you let them speak thus to me! I wasn't even invited to sit down. I'll not stay a moment longer than necessary in this house. I want to move out into our own accommodation tomorrow."

Robert, who had stretched himself full length on the starched lace coverlet of the bed, defied the rules of the house that confined smoking to an allotted room and inhaled deeply on a cigarette, his gaze directed towards the ceiling as if a certain amount of shame kept him from facing her justifiable indignation. "I'm sorry. It was hell and I knew it would be, but there was nothing I could do about it then. Coming home has always had the same immediate effect upon me as when I used to get back from school. A kind of loathing for the whole process of it sets up in me, and I can do nothing but endure it for an hour or two before it passes."

She looked puzzled. "Do you mean you've never felt happy to come home?"

"Never. But then, it has always been the same as today, even when I was at prep school. Always a flood of disapproval about something. Unfortunately, this time you had to share in that reception." His lip curled cynically. "I believe my mother really enjoyed having a fresh target. It was much more diverting than having just me to aim at, and then Paul rounded it off superbly for her." He laughed quietly with satisfaction.

In her distress Louise was exasperated with him. "I don't know how you can think it funny. And stop shortening Paul-Michel's name."

He drew again on his cigarette. "Paul it is, and Paul it's going to be, so you had better get used to it. There's no point in stirring up unnecessary friction with my parents over it. There'll be enough without that, I can promise you. Don't think I want to remain in this house any more than you do, but I'm afraid for a while we'll have to."

"Why?"

"Financial reasons for a start. I'm broke."

"Then I'll pay a rent somewhere. You know I have savings."

He raised himself up on one elbow to stub out the cigarette in a Dresden dish for hairpins that he had taken from the dressing-table. "That's out of the question. For the present we must appear to be making our permanent home in this house. My father doesn't want my mother uprooted from it after he's gone, and expects me to look after her in it until the end of her days, to say nothing of my sister Agnes, who is hardly likely to marry. I simply have to seem to kow-tow to his every wish if I'm to get my hands on Prestbury's when he dies."

She drew in a deep breath to calm herself. "You told me in Paris that Prestbury's was already yours. You said we should be partners."

"So we shall. In time. Don't be taken in by Father's boasting. He's been given dire warning by his doctor to take life quietly, and to one of his irascible temperament that's virtually impossible."

She was outraged. "Don't dangle dead men's shoes at me! I want no part of that. Let's start up independently and on our own. We can both work hard and—"

"That won't do." He swung his long legs from the bed and

came across to put his arms about her. "It would take years to get going from the kind of small property that you are visualising. It would have been different in Paris, where you have connections. In any case," he added, choosing a line of argument that she would have to accept, "as you will hear Father remind me over and over again with his customary lack of tact, I'm committed by sheer filial duty to Prestbury's after the trust placed in the financing of my training with Worth." With satisfaction he saw he had won his point. He did not care a damn about principles, but he was not going to start from scratch with her in a back street somewhere when he had a ready-made business in his hands. In any event he was not going to jeopardise the rest of his share of inheritance when the old man kicked the bucket. "Half the cause of my father's ill health is concern over the business. If he had put in a good manager when he first started to ail it would have been different, but he is the type of man who never trusts anybody. He's also old-fashioned and out of date without realising it, advanced senility having drained him of the initiative that brought him from a market stall into a good-quality dress house. He can no longer cope with competition and won't admit it." He gave her waist a squecze. "Be patient for a little while, sweetheart. I want you to have full control of the shop. I know you have all the flair to influence its styles, and I admit that you've more business sense in your little finger than any that Worth was able to drive into my whole head. You have it in your power to relieve the entire burden of Prestbury's from my father, with all support from me. You can extend his days by it and more than benefit us, because once Prestbury's is prosperous enough, we'll be released from living in this morgue into a home of our own, with my mother's security under her present roof ensured, which is all my father really cares about." He began to fondle her persuasively, appearing to have dismissed without conscience the fact that he had given her an entirely false impression of how their lives were to be in England. "Everything will work out all right, you'll see."

There came a tap on the door. He heaved an exaggerated sigh at the interruption, and went with ill grace to answer it. Immediately his face took on an expression of genuine affability. "Agnes! How are you?"

Brother and sister embraced, and then Agnes came forward hesitantly. Her features were those of her father, but fined down and chiseled into a pleasing, almost delicate face as if somewhere in the forming of her bones her mother's better breeding had made itself substance and taken over. Her eyes were blue and her hair a slightly darker shade of Robert's brown, but lacking the bronze lights that still lingered in her mother's tresses.

Her smile was singularly sweet, matching her demeanour, her shyness so excessive that she stuttered when she spoke.

"I c-couldn't wait until teatime to m-meet you, dear sister, or to see my l-little nephew."

Louise could have wept tears of joy at this unexpected warmth in the chilliness of her new surroundings, and exchanged kisses on the cheek gladly.

Paul-Michel recognised the same deep friendliness in the tones of the newcomer and did not shrink away from her. When she held out her arms he knew all to be well and went to her with only a minimum of shyness that kept his chin doubled into his collar. Childlike herself, she sat on the bedroom carpet playing pat-a-cake and peep-bo with him, and made him a bunny-rabbit with long ears out of her handkerchief, all of which gave Louise the opportunity to bathe after her travels and change into an afternoon dress for tea.

It was her first experience of English afternoon tea. There was a beautiful lace cloth on the table, and tea was poured out of a silver teapot into cups of wafer-thin porcelain. There were cucumber sandwiches and hot, buttered muffins, and a rich plum cake. John Prestbury ate with such heartiness that Louise could not suppose he was to take dinner later, but that was not the case. To her relief Paul-Michel behaved perfectly, totally taken with Agnes, who sat on his other side. Robert's moroseness had not entirely dispersed, and Louise did not yet realise that his parents had a permanently dampening effect on his spirits whenever he was in their company, forcing him to a strained politeness that would on occasion crack disastrously, adding to the already difficult relationship. His sister did little more than smile now and again. Louise wondered if her quietness had originated as a defence, because it was plain from the normal flow of conversation that Agnes could rarely do anything right, coming in for as much criticism from her mother as the slovenly servants, the lack of flavour in the tea, and the poor service given by tradesmen.

Agnes came more out of her shell when dusk fell and she was able to introduce Louise and Paul-Michel to the nursery quarters. "It was h-here that Robert and I spent m-most of our early childhood," she explained, looking with affection around the day-room where firelight behind a stout guard played over the rocking-horse and battered toy-box and the Noah's ark. It was as if she welcomed a legitimate excuse to return to the domain that had been closed for many years until Robert's telegraphed communication had resulted in it being denuded of its dust-sheets and completely cleaned through. "I'm sure P-Paul will like it as much as we did, and Daisy can be t-trusted to take the greatest care of her charge."

Daisy was a pink-cheeked, smiling girl, who had been promoted to the new position of nursemaid after Agnes had learned that she had cared for several young brothers and sisters before coming into service. Paul-Michel, who was beginning to accept that things were not so bad after all, liked Daisy's red curls that danced all around the edge of her cap, and she had a big gap between her front teeth that he found fascinating. But he wanted his maman to bathe him and put him to bed on this first night, and it was done. He did not mind her leaving him to go downstairs when he discovered that Daisy was to stay in a chair by his cotside and the gas-mantle in the night-nursery was to be kept alight. He put his thumb in his mouth and slept.

Over dinner it became apparent to Louise that there had been a long discussion about her immediate future in the Prestbury business while she had been putting Paul-Michel to bed.

John Prestbury seemed impressed in spite of himself that her experience in the dressmaking business was so extensive and, being a man not to turn an advantage aside, he was fully prepared that she should take an active role.

"It sounds as if you're not afraid of a bit of honest toil, and that's in your favour," he conceded. "There's an elderly female on the staff who's done the measuring-up for years, but her eyesight is failing, and you can take over from 'er. All the sewing is done by outworkers who call for it daily, and you can check that in and out. We sell on the usual principle of supplying the material, and the customer 'as it made up to 'er own pattern. Nothing outlandish at Prestbury's, I can tell you. Always the most conservative of modes." He frowned down the table at her. "Nothing like the fancy garb I've seen you in since you arrived. I like my staff to wear plain black glacé silk. You do 'ave a respectable black dress or two to wear on the shop premises, I trust?"

"I have several."

Out of the corner of her eye Louise noticed Robert hastily taking a swallow of wine. He was as aware as she that what had suited Worth was going to prove startlingly elegant at Prestbury's, but Louise thought that this would be an encouragement to business, as once customers had asked for dresses to be made up like Marie's.

"Good." John Prestbury gave a nod, putting in a mouthful of rich roast duck. "Robert can make a start at the shop tomorrow. 'E learnt the ropes during the time 'e was 'ome during my short spell of illness. It'll be a real load off my mind not to have to get to Prestbury's every day. Not that I intend to retire all the time I've breath left in my body," he added hastily, glaring around as if he might be challenged.

Mrs. Prestbury spoke from the opposite end of the table. "I'm sure Robert will be glad of your guiding hand at all times, John."

Louise bit back the retort she longed to make. Why couldn't the woman encourage Robert instead of immediately undermining his father's statement with doubts that their son would be able to manage on his own. Mrs. Prestbury was like a great squid of depression, crushing down both her children with possessive tentacles, motherhood at its most virulent. Louise could feel the woman's constant disapproval directed towards herself like a blight that was impossible to shake off. Oh, to be out of this dreary house, and she hadn't been in it more than a few hours yet! It would not be her fault if Prestbury's didn't become a financial success in no time at all. With the incentive of gaining a home of her own, nothing should hold her back.

John Prestbury was pointing with his fork at Robert. "I expect 'ard work and a full sense of responsibility from now on. I didn't pay for you to train for two years in Paris without getting my just returns for it."

Robert looked decidedly strained. "I'll do my best, Father."

The dreadful meal dragged to its close. In the drawing-room afterwards Agnes proved to be an excellent pianist, but throughout the music John Prestbury grumbled over his coffee about political matters. Louise was glad to be turning the music sheets for Agnes on the other side of the room.

Later in the carved bed Robert proved anxious to make amends for his drunken usage of the previous night. He showed that he could be a considerate lover if so inclined, and she, momentarily lulled by the excuses she had made for him in her own mind for his weak acceptance of circumstances, sought to lose her own desperate unhappiness in the response he urged from her.

Three days later she went to see Prestbury's. Her unease about it had been growing. John Prestbury had gone there the first day with his son and had been greatly tired by the exertion, which had forced him to rest afterwards. She had offered to accompany Robert, but he dissuaded her, saying that there was no need to rush into things, which puzzled her since at the same time he obviously wanted her there. She felt a faint chill of premonition as he left her that morning. Was there still something that he had not told her or she had not heard? She knew from his time at Worth's that he could be devious, always evasive of difficulties, and she began to fear what she might find.

She walked to Prestbury's. It was no great distance away from the house in the square, and the street where it was situated was brisk and busy with any number of thriving businesses from high-class grocers to good boot-shops, cabinet-makers, and milliners. She came to Prestbury's from the opposite side of the road, and as she slowed to a halt all the apprehension that had been gathering in her caught sickeningly at her heart and dragged it down. The shop had a large frontage, was in need of a coat of paint, but nothing worse. The windows were crammed with cloaks, shawls, and mantles, showing that there was ample stock. But all the goods were black. Mourning black. Now she knew what Robert had not had the courage to tell her. Across the fascia of the shop the curly, gilded letters announced *Prestbury's Mourning Establishment.*

Robert saw her crossing the road. He opened the glass door to receive her, his face uncertain, and she entered without a glance at him. Inside, the blackness of the garments displayed and the draped lengths of crape against dark walls made her feel as if she had entered a dungeon. There was some dark purple for later stages of bereavement, and even a touch of white in the black-bordered handkerchiefs arranged in small pyramids on a stand, but otherwise the gloom was unrelieved. Without a word he led the way to his office. A cheerful fire burned in the grate and there was the scent of cigar smoke in the air. She did not doubt that a few minutes before he had had his feet up on the desk.

"Louise—"

She swung about and struck him hard across the face, her eyes blazing. "If ever you lie or cheat or deceive me again I'll leave you! I swear it!" As he stood there stunned into confusion, she jerked off her bonnet, cast off her cape, and removed her gloves. "But now we'll get to work. I want to examine every piece of merchandise in the place, check the stock, go through the books, see lists of wholesalers, meet the staff, and find out where the outworkers are located."

She kept him working with her at a pressure that showed no sign of easing off as one day followed another. At first he welcomed it, thankful that she had rallied in the face of what must have been a terrible blow to her, but then toleration began to give way to irritation. He had known that she would work hard, but he was not prepared to do the same for any longer than was necessary. He had had enough of being run off his feet at Worth's.

The whole idea of marrying her had replaced the aim of seducing her when he had had that short period at home during his father's slight heart attack. On the credit side, he had more than fancied her; she was stunning to look at with those strange, amber eyes and passionate mouth, and if anyone could get Prestbury's off the rocks and make a success of it she could, ensuring his future without the least effort on his own part. Against this move he had had to put his father's abhorrence of foreigners, particularly the French, since, like so many Englishmen, John Prestbury was able to remember Bonaparte's terrible threat to Europe, and the cost in lives to bring the tyrant down. There was also his mother, whose soured nature would move against any daughter-in-law, and finally there was Louise herself. Knowing that she did not love him as he would have wished, he had not dared to risk anything but the rosiest of promises as to how their lives would be in England. Then, upon arrival, he had decided it would be easier to withhold the nature of the shop's particular business until she should find out for herself. He would have thought she was punishing him for it if he hadn't known that even at the present pace she was allowing him to do less than she did herself. On one point he had to be particularly careful. It would ruin everything if she became pregnant. Moreover, childbirth and related hazards took too heavy a toll of women's lives, to say nothing of the high mortality rate among children, particularly those under five. No, he didn't want Louise to get in the family way with all its attendant distractions. He wanted her to keep to the grindstone of Prestbury's on his exclusive behalf.

"I'm going to visit the outworkers now," she said to him at the shop one morning. "Your father will be coming in later, and you can let him examine the books and inspect the resiting of stock for convenience, as well as pointing out the improvement in the general cleanliness of the place." One of her first actions had been to dismiss a slovenly charwoman and engage strong, young help for the polishing of floors and cleaning of windows, and she had chased the staff into more thorough dusting of shelves and counters. Yet all was done to Robert's credit. On the days when John Prestbury did not come into the shop for an hour or two Robert reported to him in full after dinner in the library, and never once was Louise mentioned. Robert had decided it should be that way, saying quite blatantly that his father would mistrust anything she did on her own initiative no matter how much good it did the business.

She had the addresses of the outworkers written down, and in order to cover the distances she took a hackney-cab, having it wait for her at each call. In the first house all seemed to be well. It was a pitiably poor home in a back alley, but there was a lamp with a good light over the table where the widow sat sewing with her three daughters, all under twelve, who worked with her. Their competent little fingers tacked marked seams or did the oversewing with remarkable neatness, while their mother showed herself to be an excellent seamstress on the advanced work. It was less reassuring to learn that they all worked twelve hours a day to earn the miserable coppers that John Prestbury paid for piece-work, and she intended to raise the rates of pay as soon as she could. From that house she went deeper and deeper into the slums, and the sights that met her were worse than anything she could remember from her own childhood. Innumerable small courts, all filthy, squalid, and insanitary, housed people like rabbit warrens, the streets between the dark, sooty tenements were narrow, the all-pervading stench that of the piled-up garbage and human ordure. She found twenty women in a cellar running with condensation, and understood why much of the delivered sewing often reeked unpleasantly and had to be hung on a line in the open air on the shop's premises before it could be taken inside. Word of her coming spread by some unknown grapevine, because as her tour extended, scuffling and running sent workers into hiding as if fear for the well-being of the goods might cause her to withdraw employment from the most overcrowded sweatshops.

She returned to Prestbury's cast down by what she had seen. It was appalling, and on the whole the standard of work was atrocious, but who could wonder at that when those unfortunate creatures laboured in those conditions. What she needed was two or three good, airy workrooms, properly equipped, where she could take on the best of the hands and give them a living wage. That poor widow for a start. She put the idea to Robert.

"There are a couple of stockrooms upstairs that could be turned out and tables installed. There I could supervise the work myself."

"Father would never agree to it." He had had a disagreeable morning. John Prestbury had taken exception to the resiting of stock, and there had been an unpleasant argument.

"Then it's up to you to persuade him," she insisted. "It's no wonder that custom is in the decline. Customers come here in grief and are fobbed off with ill-made rubbish that they're too distressed to take notice of until it's too late. They find themselves stuck with a wardrobe of badly fitting garments that have to last twelve months for the loss of a child or a parent, while it's particularly hard on widows of limited means with a full three years' mourning ahead of them." Glancing downwards at her skirt-hems she wrinkled her nose in distaste as she saw that they had been fouled by some of the places where she had had to walk. "I must find something else to change into immediately."

In the stockroom she had previously come across a single, ready-made garment in a shade of grey suitable for the later stages of mourning, and it appeared to be a sample of workmanship put out by a factory that had had no taker in John Prestbury. It was naturally of the cheapest cotton, but the style was pleasing, and she was not ashamed to wear it for the rest of that working day. She thought it would not have come amiss to have had a few such dresses on a stand in the shop, but she must not put forth such a suggestion yet awhile. Raising standards of workmanship was the first point at issue.

John Prestbury proved to be adamant about not having sewing-hands on the premises. "It would cost more in wages, to say nothing of the outlay in gas-light and a coal-fire in winter, and there's an end to it." He screwed his eyes up suspiciously at his son. "I suppose that was your French wife's 'ighfalutin idea? You keep 'er in 'er place at Prestbury's or you'll both be out. D'you 'ear?"

Louise fumed over the old man's short-sightedness, but it was to be the first of countless frustrations in the face of his stubborn opposition to change on all fronts. She did what she could with the garments that were sold, unpicking seams and resewing them herself to give customers a respectable fit, but there was a limit to what she could do. Trouble assailed her on other sides. Her refusal to retrim her bonnets had caused a wider rift with her mother-in-law. She felt that to give in for the sake of peace and quietness would be wrong. The point of issue was more than a *bavolet,* it was her whole attitude to life, her looking forward, her refusal to take a step back when the future always demanded new thought and fresh courage. Her working dresses displeased as well. They were labelled too ostentatious and far too *French*. Her nationality was used to condemn all that she did. She had to come to terms with the fact that her father-in-law despised her, while her mother-in-law loathed her, and there appeared little chance that there would ever be any change in that state of affairs. Only Agnes continued to show friendship to her, but the girl was curiously immature, happier to play with Paul-Michel than to be with adult company. It was impossible to hold anything but the lightest of conversations with her.

The Prestburys did occasionally entertain, and some invitations were forthcoming in turn for Robert and his wife. Louise was delighted to meet Mr. Allenby at a dinner party, and they had a long talk about Worth, of whom the gracious old gentleman was extremely proud. She and Robert were invited to a soirée at the Allenby house, and afterwards to card parties and musical evenings, making her wish for her own home where she could have returned at a personal level the hospitality she so enjoyed and appreciated.

The shop itself had become like a cage to her. With the conventions of mourning so strictly observed whole families were plunged into black upon a bereavement, and many did not emerge from it at the end of the twelve months' mourning period if another death occurred in the meanwhile. It meant that if Prestbury's could rebuild its reputation for good-quality clothing that would last, all its financial problems would be solved, and customers would come from far and wide. Louise saw that as her task, but it meant that all her skills in high fashion had to be shelved. Worth had often made dresses for those in mourning, but always with the elegance necessary to the women's particular role in society. Those who came to Prestbury's had an entirely different attitude of mind, and any who wanted something exceptionally stylish would never look for it there.

It had not taken her long to discover that the outworkers stole whatever they could, and must have tricked the shop out of any amount of stuff since the beginning of her father-in-law's physical and mental decline, and she was presently engaged in trying to sort the wheat from the chaff. As for the staff of the shop, they were honest beyond doubt, but she missed the community spirit of working together for the good of the business such as she had known under the direction of Worth. There were five females, all divided amongst themselves with petty jealousies and old feuds, yet quick enough to gang up together against the new Mrs. Prestbury, whose disciplined sense of order was considered irksome. She thought it an exceptional stroke of good luck when for various reasons of retirement, marriage, advancement, and moving, four of the women gave notice. It would leave her with the least disagreeable of the assistants, a somewhat silly creature easily led, and Louise looked forward to appointing four women on whom she could rely for loyalty and conscientious work. But Robert forestalled her one day when Paul-Michel was feverish, necessitating her staying at home with him. She returned to the shop to learn he had taken on staff of his choice, and she found herself with a different, but no better, selection than before.

"What's wrong with having young, presentable females?" he challenged sharply. "God knows enough gloomy faces come in and out of this place."

"People in misfortune need capable and sympathetic attention," she retorted, "and the bunch you've appointed look more fit to serve fancy satin garters and clock hosiery than mourning attire."

"You're getting pinched lips about everything at Prestbury's these days," he flung at her ill-temperedly. "You'll be saying I don't pull my weight next."

He half expected her to reply that he did not, which would have been the truth, but it was not so easy to make her quarrel with him any more, almost as if she had grown weary of the process, and she only turned her head away on a suppressed sigh. He admitted to himself that he was unreasonable towards her at times, blaming his general disappointment in his circumstances that needed an outlet, and she was a convenient butt for his grievances. He had believed quite genuinely that his father could not maintain the recovery made in his health, and his talk to Louise of her business acumen extending the old man's days had been to soft-soap her and not because it was what he had hoped himself. He had visualised himself lording it at Prestbury's after his father's speedy demise, able to spend his time there or anywhere else he pleased while Louise managed everything and built up the business in any way she chose, most surely chucking out the mourning wear and introducing her beloved Paris fashions as he had promised her she could do. But it was all proving to be very different. While John Prestbury continued to thrive and looked set to become a centenarian, Louise served at a counter, and measured garments that Worth would not have used as dust-rags. His own chief occupation in the office was finding means by which another slight alteration in the books could profitably reline an emptied pocket while escaping the eye of his wife and his father.

On the rare, busy occasions when he had to help serve in the shop, he loathed making himself agreeable to the customers. Occasionally there was the sprightly young widow merely observing the conventions of mourning upon the death of an older husband, and sometimes the more mature and comely ones who had probably buried two and were already on the lookout for a third, but on the whole the customers who came into Prestbury's adopted the long face deemed suitable to the nature of the purchases they were making, even in the latter stages of bereavement, and he missed the flirtations that had made life so agreeable at Worth's, as well as the interesting developments that had followed as a result of them. He had not spent all his time with Louise then any more than he did now. A married man in particular had to have some release from domestic routine. London, no less than Paris, had its wide variety of divertissements, but unlike the French capital, where the demi-monde was an accepted part of life, there was a prudish pretence that nothing existed beyond the excessive propriety of the domestic scene. Maybe that was why the gas-lit world of London catered extensively for every kind of vice while Paris, on the surface at least, proffered enjoyable sin. He had been in some rum places in his time and had a few narrow escapes. The danger of being attacked and robbed was common enough on any dark street at night, the dreaded London garrotters being a particular hazard in the shadows of the night dens, and he never went anywhere without his cane that had a blade concealed in it. He always told Louise he was spending the evening at his club. More often than not he did. But now and again he became a free night owl.

Louise brought the new members of staff into some order. The very atmosphere of the shop was not conducive to foolish giggling, and after a few days the four young females sobered down into being adequately helpful to customers if not entirely what she would have wished. On their behalf she tried to get her father-in-law to waive his rule of glacé silk as the material for the staff dresses, which the women had to supply themselves out of their own pockets. Unless it was of exceptionally good quality, which was beyond the low wages that he paid, glacé silk split and rotted easily, particularly under the arms, and the garments became shabby and unwearable in quite a short time, necessitating the often acute hardship of replacement. Her suggestion of a more durable material was turned down at once when she put it to her father-in-law.

"If they don't want to dress as I say, there's plenty more who'd put on sackcloth and ashes to get a job these days. It's glacé silk or nothing." His expression took on a faint sneer. "You don't understand a bit of class, that's the trouble with foreigners. Refinement and good taste, that's glacé silk. It gives the right tone to the business." There was no budging him. He later informed Robert that she was to keep to the simple duties allotted her of checking goods and serving at the counter, and he did not want to suffer her impertinence on a business matter of any kind again. What would the world come to if women ever tried to usurp the superiority of man?

"She's an uppity creature," he told his son. "I saw that from the first. Don't be afraid to beat 'er if you 'ave to. I 'ad to give your mother a lesson or two when we were first wed. Does 'em no 'arm and teaches respect where it's due."

Robert felt the hatred for his father seep through his veins like black glue. He felt both humiliated and frustrated by the whole situation, and inevitably, as soon as he was alone with Louise, he let his pent-up exasperation fly forth at her.

"In future keep your mouth shut about Prestbury's or anything else that's at all controversial in my father's house! Haven't I warned you enough about it? Wasn't that why I decided to appear to be the instigator of any improvement? Do you know what he advocated?" He shot his congested face close to hers. "That I beat you. And, by God! I will if you don't toe the line."

She became so still and pale and quiet under his abuse that he drew back from her, suddenly contrite and even more angry that he should be. For several days afterwards the atmosphere was painfully strained between them, but finally he decided to be magnanimous and bought her flowers as well as taking her to a play at Drury Lane and out to supper afterwards. All seemed to be well. He dismissed a faint twinge of misgiving as to whether everything would ever be quite the same again.

He took unobtrusive note of the shopgirls' dresses. It was as she had said. The seams stretched thin, the silk cracked in folds at the elbows, and there was much mending around the buttons of back-fastenings where the fabric had frayed. One of the girls looked particularly shabby, her dress having been purchased second-hand from a predecessor who had left. He had a word on his own with her in the office. She was a pretty little thing, very saucy and knowing, but all the ebullience went from her when she was told to buy herself new wear for the shop.

"I can't, sir," she wailed in despair. "My wages won't run to it. As you know, when you took me on here I'd been out of work for some time, and there's still arrears on the rent of my room, and I'm having to pinch and save at every turn."

He regarded her coolly, nothing in his expression to show that the tattiness of her attire contrasting with the neatness of her primped golden ringlets stirred him. There was a glint of white underwear at some seams, and the shimmer of flesh elsewhere. She was also sweating a little with fright, an intoxicant aroma in the close confines of the office. "That is nothing to do with Prestbury's, Miss Ashcroft. You were given the job on condition that you obeyed the rules of the establishment, which includes being properly attired."

Her expression was becoming increasingly anxious, and she twisted her hands frantically. "Please don't sack me, sir. I work hard and the customers like me, I know they do. Nobody has ever had cause to complain about me before. I swear I'll try to get another dress somehow. All I need is a little time."

He shook his head decisively. "That's out of the question. You're practically in rags now."

Her self-restraint gave way. She began to sob pathetically with open blue eyes spilling rolling tears, her whole frame shaking in her distress. "Maybe I could find one on Sunday at the market. Give me a chance, I beg you, sir!"

He rose from his chair behind the desk and came quite close to her, letting his gaze run over the upper half of the offending garment. "A market cast-off wouldn't do for Prestbury's. The seams would probably be no better than those here—and here." He had rested a hand on her shaking shoulder and he let it slide downwards to cup her ample breast in his hand. A shiver of understanding went through her. Under spiked wet lashes she met his narrowed eyes and swallowed convulsively.

"I dare say you're right, sir." Her voice was still throaty, but held the touch of a returning brazenness. "I'd be real grateful if you think of some other way by which I might replace my dress." He smiled slowly, and crossing to the door he turned the key. With Louise away visiting the outworkers there should be no interruption.

A week later Lily Ashcroft had her new dress, but she was discreet. What had happened was by no means uncommon. She had known others who had had to put their employment before their virtue, and it was not as though hers was exactly unsullied. But he was a greedy devil and she didn't like him much. Thank God she wasn't married to him.

Louise was suffering acutely from homesickness. It would not abate. She missed everything about France, from her dear Catherine and the Worths to the lively atmosphere of a Parisian Sunday, so different from the gloom and oppression of the British Sabbath with everything so sedate and solemn. Her marriage, viewed perspectively over many months, was far from what she had hoped it would be, and Robert, after having Paul-Michel's surname changed legally to his own, took little notice of the child, failing to give the father-son relationship that had been one of her reasons for marrying him.

The only brightness in her daily routine centred about

whatever time she could spend with her son, and it was also a joy to her whenever a letter came from France. Catherine wrote painstakingly once a month, giving news of friends and acquaintances, but mostly asking questions about Paul-Michel and wanting to be reassured that he had not forgotten her. Marie's letters were entirely different, transporting Louise back into that scintillating world of *haute couture* that she missed so much. Out of the written pages poured colour and excitement and the sheer beauty of the dresses that Worth was making, not only for the Empress, but for her ladies-in-waiting as well as every woman of importance in society. Sometimes Marie enclosed illustrations of Worth dresses that had appeared in fashion magazines, and Louise would pin them up on the office wall at Prestbury's, her fingers itching to be part of the process that made a few sketched lines by Worth into a marvellous gown. To keep her own hand in, anxious not to lose her touch on fashion, she made many sketches of dresses and jackets and bonnets, always seeking new ideas and variations on the current lines, and as she had always done, she cut out and sewed every new garment that she added to her wardrobe.

It was clear to her from all letters that came from Paris that Worth was making his fortune, and she rejoiced for him. A mere fifteen years had passed since the poverty-stricken young man on her childhood doorstep had become the *grand couturier* of Paris. Marie wrote of the complete redecoration of number 7, with the extension of the premises to other floors in the building with many more workrooms, a vastly increased number of sewing-hands and salon staff, and of the orders that had begun to come in from all over the world, particularly from the United States. But the de Gands were never mentioned, except once with the sad news that Stéphanie had miscarried and lost the baby.

Louise was folding away a letter from Marie one morning when Robert came late to the shop and found her in the office. "What's all that?" he enquired, nodding towards a neatly written sheet of foolscap that she had placed on his desk blotter.

"It's the outline I've worked out for Prestbury's. I believe that if your father could read it over quietly in his own time he would be more inclined to consider it. I notice he gets more and more confused over anything explained verbally to him, and it might well be anger with himself at not being able fully to comprehend that has made him refuse to consider anything else that has been put forward on any scale."

Robert was warily interested, and perched his weight on the desk to take up the paper and read it through. He knew she had already formed a nucleus of a few good outworkers at the home of the widow whose sewing had first impressed her. By keeping them all under one roof and raising the rates of payment from funds saved through dispensing with the rest, she was sure of a properly produced garment to meet any customer's requirements, but her plan was to introduce on stands and in the windows mourning clothes from factories that could be relied upon to supply consistently a high standard of goods. Prestbury's middle-class customers would have to be persuaded that a garment did not have to be hand-made in order to conform to ladylike apparel, but with a carefully chosen selection of ready-mades always abundantly on display, they should gradually be won over. On a purely practical point it would eliminate the mad rush to fill orders in a matter of days before a funeral, which in the past had allowed a lot of shoddy hand-sewing to slip through, and Robert could foresee a more clearly defined future for the shop as a retailer of high-class, ready-made mourning wear.

"This seems to be a splendid scheme," he endorsed cautiously. "Do you have any particular factory in mind?"

"I favour the one that supplied a sample dress for lighter mourning that was here when I first came. I've looked up the address." She pushed it across to him. "It's the Boston Street Factory in Southwark. If your father will give his consent to the scheme, I'll go there and see what else can be produced."

Robert thrust out his lower lip thoughtfully. His father was lower in health than Louise or his own mother realised. He had seen him convulsed with pain and doubled over in his chair when believing himself alone, and it was noticeable that he had given up coming to the shop. Louise imagined it was because John Prestbury was satisfied with the smooth running of it, and was taking life more quietly, but he knew it was more than that. At last his father had resumed the decline that had been temporarily halted.

"I'll choose a congenial moment to put this paper before him. Leave it to me. It shall be done."

A few days later he told her that his father had received the paper and agreed to read it. Agreement followed soon afterwards.

"It's all settled," Robert informed her jubilantly. "I had to take the credit for it all, so whatever happens you mustn't give the game away."

There was little chance of that. After what John Prestbury had said to her, she never spoke when business was being discussed, and did not intend to jeopardise the new venture by defying him now.

On the day she was set to take a hackney-cab to Southwark across the river she looked at the letter from the Boston Street Factory once again to try to decipher the signature of the manufacturer that had closed a clerk's neat writing of it. Suddenly it came to her what the name was. *William Russell.* She felt a quiver of excited surprise. Was it possible that he was the Will Russell that she had known?

The Boston Street Factory in an alleyway of the same name proved to be a large, red brick building five storeys high. At a reception desk she asked to see Mr. Russell, and after a few moments' wait she was escorted up a flight of stairs to the first floor. She saw him before he saw her. At the end of a long corridor a glass door stood open to his office, and he was in his shirt sleeves, dealing with someone unrolling a bolt of cloth. As she was led along she saw by his quick glance over his shoulder that he was somewhat impatient at being interrupted by a visitor. The man with the cloth was sent out, while Will Russell reached for his frockcoat and thrust his arms into it. She spoke to the clerk at her side.

"Leave me, please. Mr. Russell and I are old friends. I'd like to meet him on my own."

The clerk left her, and she continued on. The way between Will and her was clear of any other person. He had come to the doorway to await her, and as the distance diminished with her every step she saw his eyes first narrow with incredulity and then stretch wide, his eyebrows lifting. He gave a kind of half-shout of disbelief as he came darting forward with hands outstretched to catch hers in his own.

"My dear Louise! I can't believe it. You! Here! And the name I was given was a Mrs. Prestbury. Explain everything."

She thought she had never been so pleased to see anyone before in her whole life. Ridiculously, she had tears as well as joy at seeing him in her eyes. He swept her into his office, set her in a chair, and then flung forward another for himself. With elbows on his knees he leaned forward, still firing questions and shaking his head now and again in the sheer wonder of seeing her there. At first he seemed the same old Will, exuberant and enthusiastic, a trifle boisterous, and so quick to laugh, flinging his head back and showing every white tooth in his head, but gradually, as they went on talking after initial reminiscences that had caused their amusement, their mood changed to one of seriousness, and she saw, when the smiles went from his eyes and his mouth, that the years had made their mark on him. Inevitably he looked older, but his bones seemed harder and more pronounced, the fulness about the lips more ruthless, and an alert detachment seemed more natural to his gaze than the warmth that filled it at the sight of her.

He sent for a tray of tea, anxious that she should have some refreshment, and when the cups were poured he sat back with one long leg crossed over the other, his chin drawn into his dark silk cravat, watching her keenly under his brows. She told him all that had happened, holding back only what could never be shared with anyone else, and when she came to her marriage he was suddenly restless, flinging himself up out of the chair and thumping the cup and saucer that he held down on the tin tray with a little crash, making it vibrate on the desk.

"Why didn't you write to me?" he demanded almost angrily. "You went through that whole difficult period on your own when I could have helped you. One word from you and I'd have been on the next Channel steamer."

"I did think of contacting you when I was in the dilemma I mentioned," she admitted. "You had said there would always be work for me in your employ, but I decided otherwise."

"In my employ?" he echoed. "Good God! I would have married you and been father to your son!"

She was taken aback. "But you are married—"

He gave a kind of groan, running one hand through his thick, fair hair in a manner she well remembered. "Of course you didn't know. There was no way that you could have heard." He fixed her with a stare, his voice distant. "My wife died three years ago in childbirth, and a matter of six weeks later my infant daughter was buried in the same grave."

"Oh, Will." The cry of distress for his suffering broke from her.

"I loved Ellen dearly. We had our difficulties and our differences, but I loved her. The tragedy was that she hadn't wanted a baby. She was terrified of childbirth, but I failed to realise the extent of her fears. Selfishly I wanted a family and imagined that she would be happier and all would be well when children came. Her bouts of hysteria during her pregnancy were torture to me. After one screaming tirade against me she tried to throw herself from a window. From then on she had a nurse with her night and day. I suppose it is a miracle the baby lived at all, but when I lost her, all purpose in living seemed to go from me."

She had risen from her chair, her face full of compassion, and she stretched forth a hand to him in sympathy. "My heartfelt condolences, dear Will. What sad bereavements you have known. How did you come through?"

He held her hand in his. "There is always work." He gave a nod towards the litter of papers and swatches of cloth on his desk. "I went back to around-the-clock hours. Anything to avoid going home to that lonely house. Eighteen months ago I built this new factory, and I have over two hundred hands working for me. Recently I moved, but the greater part of my spare time is spent at my club." His lips compressed. "Friends often ask me why I don't marry again. I reply that I've drifted away from the domestic scene and feel more at home amid the whirl of wheels and the snipping of scissors."

"Yet you say you would have married me." Even as she spoke she saw his gaze deepen, compelling her eyes to remain locked with his.

"You have always lit fires in me, Louise," he admitted with wry tenderness. "As long ago as when you used to tease and flirt your skirts at me while I tried to concentrate on teaching you English." He looked down at her hand that he held, and felt the ring on her finger through the soft kid. "Last time we met I asked you why there was no wedding band. I would that it were the same again."

"If it were, then I should not be here, but still in Paris, and this meeting would never have come about."

"Of course." He smiled seriously, brought back by the careful pressure of her words to the bounds of their relationship through which they might not pass. "I will be thankful that our paths have crossed again. There is no reason why old friends should not meet often. You and your husband must dine with me soon. It will be agreeable to have good reason for a grand dinner party."

She smiled back at him. "We shall be delighted to come." Their hands still held. Both became aware of the retained contact at the same time, and he released his grip to let her slide her fingers away.

"I have been forgetting your purpose in coming to Boston Street in the first place," he said more casually, clasping his hands behind his back. "I should like to show you around the factory before you look at any of the garments we produce here. I think you will find much to gain your attention. I've been working on an invention to promote speed in the making of buttonholes, but it is still far from the stage of being patented."

Still talking, he walked at her side as they went from the office. She found the tour interesting. Unlike every factory she had ever heard about, the building was light and airy, Will explaining that he would not inflict working conditions that he had suffered himself in the past on fellow human beings. There was no crowding of those hand-sewing at the tables, while the workers at the cumbersome-looking sewing machines sat in long rows facing each other. Child labour was much in evidence, keeping the workers supplied from baskets of pieces cut to pattern on the cutting tables, the very young ones engaged in sorting scraps into sacks. Will told her that they were the offspring of women employees, whose decision it was whether to release them after the eight hours of work due, or keep them on for a further two hours to match their own day. She was glad to hear that gruel or a thick soup was served to the young ones daily from the factory kitchen.

"I'm accused by other factory owners of mollycoddling my workers," he remarked, "but my rules are strict. No drunkenness, no slacking, and no molesting of the women or any of the children by the men in charge. As you remember, I worked in a mill myself once, and so I know what misery can prevail if an employer cares nothing for the welfare of those who labour for him."

When they came to the stockroom Louise was very selective, choosing only those styles that she knew would be acceptable to Prestbury customers. The bulk of the order was for black, but she also included a range of purples and a variety of greys for those coming towards the end of a mourning period. They spoke of delivery dates, and then she was ready to leave, but not before the evening was settled when she and Robert would dine with him. At the last moment, when a hackney-cab had been hailed to the entrance for her, he stayed her on the factory steps.

"I should have extracted a promise from you long ago to turn to me in any time of trouble. I want your word that if ever you should be in need of help again, you would summon me."

She nodded, thinking that for the first time since coming to England she no longer felt alone. "I thank you, Will. And I promise."

He could not get her out of his thoughts for the rest of the day or in any day following. She had come back to haunt him as erotically and powerfully as she had done in the days gone by. He knew now she had always been a stronger force in his life than Ellen. Why he had loved Ellen as he had done was beyond comprehension, but the heart had its own rules and her delicate looks and small-boned body had always aroused his protectiveness and a desire to cherish her in spite of all she had done that would have destroyed any other man's feelings for her. With Louise his emotions were entirely different. Basic, perhaps, but more, too. In mind and body she was the only woman he had ever known whom he could visualise as the other half of himself. Alike in thought and attitude, ready to strive ahead through whatever life threw down, theirs would have been a love to shatter the universe. And in all the years he had known her he had kissed her only three times, yet he remembered those kisses where wilder lovemaking with other women had been long since forgotten.

On the evening of Will's dinner party Robert was at his most sociable, full of smiles, witty conversation, and flatteringly gallant to the ladies. Twenty guests sat down in the mahogany-panelled dining-room at the damask-covered table where Louise sat at her host's right hand. To Will it was as though his handsome house had come alive for the first time, and the reason was there in the sparkle of Louise's eyes and the pale gleam of her shoulders emerging from a dress of cream French satin that cast every other woman present into the shade. It was sheer waste that she should be married to Prestbury. In the interim period before this evening Will had made it his business to find out all he could about him and his family. Prestbury's origins were all right, but there was little else to commend him. Will took a sip of red wine. With the ruthlessness with which he had spared neither himself nor anyone else to get started on the rise to prosperity, he knew he would have no compunction in getting Louise away from her husband if he could. The hitch was the same now as it had been in the past: her affections being turned elsewhere. But he was not a man to give up, especially when it seemed as if fate had given him a second chance to gain what an untimely intrusion had snatched from him long ago during a midnight hour in a Paris workroom.

19

John Prestbury peered at the calendar, trying to remember when he had last visited his shop. He found it difficult to remember anything these days, but that didn't mean he had lost his wits, far from it. When Robert had first taken over Prestbury's he had made a point of calling in twice and sometimes thrice a week, always unannounced, intending to catch his son and staff alike on the hop. That's what kept people on their toes. But once he had crushed all possible interference from that French daughter-in-law of his and everything seemed to be running smoothly, it had been a welcome relief not to bestir himself and made the tedious drive more than very occasionally. The truth was that any small effort tired him, and with tiredness came those cramping pains in his chest that the doctor's physic could only lull. He recognized the symptoms that had dragged him down to that terrible fluttering of the heart last time, but now he was wiser and knew plenty of rest was all-important. And today, quite miraculously, he felt better. It followed a week quite free of pain, and the brightness of the sunshine outside was inviting. More than that, he longed to see the shop again. He missed the smell of new fabrics, the ping of the shop door, the paper rustle of goods being wrapped, and the conveying of expressions of sympathy that brought grateful looks from customers, many of whom he had seen through any number of bereavements. Business had gone down as older customers had themselves died off and other stores had opened up departments of mourning goods, but Prestbury's had never changed its personal attention to individual requirements, and that's what counted in the end.

"I'm going out," he said to his wife.

He grunted and puffed as he heaved himself into the brougham, wanting to shove aside the servant who assisted him, but having to accept the aid. Collapsing back into the seat he gave a sigh of relief, his knees spread wide to accommodate his huge belly, his hand shaking uncontrollably on the walking stick that he still gripped. With such a long span of time since he last ventured forth, he could be certain of surprising his son and staff alike with this visit. He deeply hoped that he would find Robert exerting himself as he made out he did during those evening reports on the shop's day and takings. Nothing would be more pleasing than to know that Allenby had been right in saying that proper training under the best master would set the lad on the right path. The trouble was that Robert was a sly kettle of fish and always had been. In truth, John Prestbury knew he had never liked his son. If Robert *was* his son. That niggling doubt had never been dispersed, and it was the root of his whole dislike. Verena with her haughty airs had been mighty quick to change her mind and marry him all of a sudden. Once he had tried in a fit of rage many years ago to choke the truth out of her, but already she was on the way with Agnes, and for the sake of the unborn child he had restrained himself. But never in looks or temperament had he ever seen anything of himself or his hardworking forebears in the boy. Robert was typical of Verena's whole family, with the same high-bred looks and superior mannerisms, typical too of the young gentlemen with whom she had been associating in the days when he, older than the rest, was trying to court her with nothing to commend him but a pocketful of brass sizeable enough to weigh against the stigma of being in trade.

He sighed again, blinking out through the window to see how far he had come on the way to the shop in Hampton Street, that had been such a source of pride to him for many years. It had been a bargain load of black bonnets selling like hot cakes on his market stall that had set him into mourning apparel. He was sharp enough to see where money was to be made. The war against Napoleon was in full force then, but even when peace came, people would still go on dying, and others would be forever wanting black to garb themselves in. He saw nothing macabre or morbid in it. Quite the contrary. In his first small shop he had found women thankful at a time of grief to be able to obtain all they needed in one place. It was in those early days that he became adept at the sympathetic word, the considerate attention that was remembered next time a bereavement came around. He went from strength to strength. He was thirty-five, with a thick gold watch-chain across his waistcoat, and could stand in the doorway of his new Hampton Street premises as a self-made man when he set his sights on Verena and resolved to have her. Fool that he was. He would have done better to find a sensible girl of his own class who would have given him sons he would have known as his own and never considered herself to be too high and mighty to be seen in the shop that supplied her with the comforts and luxuries she demanded. Not that anything had ever really pleased her. Marriage had blighted her, all that had attracted him to her soon withering away. But he was going to leave her well provided for, and since she did like the house they lived in, she should have it and all she needed until the end of her days. He had promised her once that she should never want for anything, and he'd keep his word beyond the grave.

One more corner and the next left turn would bring him to Prestbury's. Why Robert had to marry that French piece he'd never know. England was full of girls pretty as roses, and the young fool had to choose a foreigner. She was fine-looking enough to turn any man's head, none could dispute that, but he had the uncanny feeling that Robert had been tricked just as he had been duped years ago. That child of hers was a Frenchman through and through. Not an atom of Englishness revealed itself. The black hair, the handsome, black-lashed eyes that were a grey-green never seen to his knowledge in either his family or his wife's. Verena was of the same opinion, and they had discussed it together. Moreover, she had raked out some letters that Robert had written to Agnes on his travels, and at the time of the child's conception he had been touring Italy. John Prestbury snorted. His grandson? Bah! Never was and never would be.

As the brougham drew to a standstill he received such a shock that his mouth dropped open to a gape, his pendulous jaw aquiver. One window held a range of black goods draped in a manner that was not customary, but it was the other that outraged him, holding dresses in colours that Prestbury's had never carried before. Mauve! *Pale* grey! A particularly strong lilac!

He bounded out of the brougham with a power he had not known he possessed. Thumping on his stick, he charged into the shop. Customers were being served, making him hold back the bellow of wrath that was gathering in him, saliva already running from one corner of his mouth. He ripped aside the curtain at the back of the offending window and grabbed one of the garments from a stand. He felt his eyes bulge in their sockets. *Ready-made!* In *his* shop! Prestbury's, which from its humblest beginnings had prided itself on personal attention to all orders, was being shamed and disgraced by bloody factory rubbish only worn by the working classes and the poor!

He flung down the dress and glared about him. Louise was serving at a counter, but he could contain himself no longer. Lurching across, he brought up his stick and crashed it down on the counter in front of her. The customer squealed, and Louise stared quickly at him as if she thought he had lost his mind.

"Where's that 'usband of yours? In the office? Follow me!" With difficulty he raised his hat to the customer. "Your pardon, ma'am."

All in the shop stared after him as with Louise in his wake he stumped away in the direction of the office. He crashed the door open, and Robert, intent on the books, leapt up guiltily and slammed a ledger shut.

"Father! What are you doing here? I mean, are you well enough to come? Whatever is the matter?"

"I'll tell you what's the matter!" John Prestbury bunched a fist and shook it under his son's nose. "The goods in the window! 'Ow dare you tamper with Prestbury's!"

Robert looked completely baffled. Louise thought she knew what was amiss. "It must be those light colours. Miss Ashcroft and I dressed the window before the blind went up this morning."

Robert's reaction was as startling to her as his father's behaviour had been, his explosion of temper as virulent. "I told you never to put those goods of yours in the window. Damn you! Must you always override everybody else?"

John Prestbury rounded on her. "*Your* goods? What does 'e mean? What the 'ell is going on 'ere?"

It was then that Louise realized that Robert had never shown her father-in-law all she had written down for his perusal and consideration. John Prestbury knew nothing of the ready-mades that had come in from Will's factory. And the stockroom was full of them.

It all came out. John Prestbury ranted and raged. All the ready-mades must be returned. He'd have none of them in his shop. Nor would he have his daughter-in-law there either. He wagged a furious finger at her across the desk at which he sat.

"You get off 'ome! Don't you dare set your meddling foot on these premises again. I never did trust your French blood and I never will. Get out! Get—" He lost all breath as his chest suddenly exploded with pain. He felt himself slumping back in the chair, saw Louise's frantic face as she snatched his cravat free and ripped open his collar. There was a roaring in his head and a pounding behind his eyes. The last he ever knew was the cradling of the Frenchwoman's arms as if she sought to save him from slipping away with her own youth and strength.

The funeral was well attended. Many people came to pay their last respects to an honest tradesman. The horses pulling the draped hearse had black plumes two feet tall nodding from their heads, and the carriages stretched behind for a quarter of a mile. Afterwards the widow, her son, daughter, and daughter-in-law gathered in the library for the reading of the will. John Prestbury had no other relatives. The will was very straightforward. The house, the shop, and all else that he had possessed went to his wife, and after her demise to his daughter, Agnes. Robert was not mentioned. Verena heard her son's hollow groan of furious disappointment, but she did not turn her head. The will had not surprised her. It was what she had always expected. When it came to it, John could never have handed over his shop, the symbol of his own personal success, to a cuckoo in the nest. Through the will he had finally scored over her. He had shown that she had never really deceived him.

For two days Louise did not see Robert. He had flung himself out of the house and did not return. At her mother-in-law's request she opened the shop as usual. "Your husband did forbid me to go there again," she had pointed out.

"That was in his day," Verena had replied emphatically. "It is my business now."

Robert returned home during shop hours. Louise did not know how he had looked or what state he had been in, but he was pale, sober, and thoroughly ill-tempered when she came in from work. He greeted her with hostility.

"I hear you've been in charge during my absence. That suits you, doesn't it? If I hadn't agreed to all your suggestions we wouldn't be in this fix now. I should have known that by marrying a Frenchwoman my troubles would start. You stuck in my father's craw and you're the reason why he never got around to a codicil in his will, leaving the shop to me."

She controlled herself with difficulty. To quarrel with him would solve nothing. She knew him too well now to ask him to make a fresh start with her on their own as she had done once before. His excuse of commitment to Prestbury's had been the means of avoiding the individual effort of attainment, and he would always slide away from it. "I have suggested to your mother that she offer you a partnership. There is nothing to prevent her doing that, and it will give you equal status with her in the business and entitle you to a half share of the profits."

His eyes narrowed at her as his mood began to shift. "Is she agreeable to it?"

"Yes, I think she is. You will have to discuss it with her."

He could tell it was as good as settled. His mother might not like his wife, but she recognised her intelligence. No doubt pride had been swallowed to ask Louise how he might best be persuaded to carry on working at Prestbury's with some initiative and interest, and although he was gratified that his wife had used her wits on his behalf, he was not yet ready to show it, still blaming her for his having been omitted from the will. He answered her tauntingly and with a challenge. "It will be up to you to prove what you can do with the shop to make amends to me, won't it? I can't see Mother having any bigoted notions about factory wear if the sales of ready-mades continue to increase as they have done lately." He made a mocking flourish as if handing the whole project to her on his open palm. "Go ahead, my dear wife. Let's see how clever you really are. I'll remind you that I'm not removing from this house until we can afford a comparable establishment, so let's see how soon you can manage it."

She understood then exactly why he had married her. Love had not come into it, because he was incapable of loving anyone but himself. He had desired her and known that she would be useful to him. In trusting ignorance she had struggled to retain whatever had been good in their relationship, sought constantly to keep the fondness for him that she had known, but now nothing was left. The terrible consequence was that into that void there flooded a longing for Pierre that was sharper and more acute and more heart-tearing than at any time since their parting. Her lips began to tremble and she clapped her fingers over them, covering them with her other hand to still the choking sob that was threatening to burst forth from her throat.

Robert peered sardonically at her. "What's wrong? Why the tears in your eyes? Don't you think yourself capable of success after all?"

She could take no more of his goading. Suddenly she could take no more of him or the household or Prestbury's or any other part of their lives together. Her self-control broke on the great sob she could no longer hold back.

"Yes! Yes! Yes!" she hurled at him on a high-pitched note she scarcely recognized as her own. "I can and I will, but not as wife to you! I'm going back to Paris! I'm going home!"

He caught her before she was halfway up the stairs, grappling with her and forcing her back against the baluster rail, making her think her spine must crack. His livid face was bent over hers.

"If you go," he ground out through his teeth in raging temper, "you go alone. Paul is legally mine. He stays with me."

She closed her eyes tightly to shut out the sight of him and to beat down the vision of freedom that had filled her mind for those few wild and delirious moments. There was no escape. If she took Paul-Michel and fled he would have her hounded back to him. Women had no rights, least of all over their children.

He was releasing his hold on her, knowing that he had won. She continued on up the stairs, but at a slow pace. Her heart was as heavy as her dragging steps.

A pattern of days and weeks followed during which business improved and little else happened. Since the Prestburys were in mourning all social engagements were cancelled and none others forthcoming except from Will, who continued to invite Louise and her husband to his house, for which she was exceedingly grateful. There was always good company present, and her black evening dresses had such style, trimmed with Worth's glitter of jet, that she still caught every eye when she arrived, and had more than her fair share of male attention.

It was in the drawing-room at Will's house that the conversation took an unusually grave turn one evening as the guests gathered. For the past two or three mornings *The Times* had carried a report of the Prince Consort being confined to bed with what was first said to be a cold and then a slight fever, but one of the guests had associations with the palace and was able to give more specific details that he had learned only an hour before.

"He is suffering with severe head pains and much digestive disturbance."

"Is the cause known?" Louise asked.

"Could it be serious?" Will interposed.

"Typhoid is suspected. He has all the symptoms."

There was a general gasp of dismay. For someone young and strong it was a hard disease to fight, but for a man of forty-two, who was known to be no longer robust, it was extremely serious. A cloud of concern formed over the evening, nothing quite dispersing it.

The next morning when Louise left the shop to pay her weekly visit to the outworkers, she bought a newspaper purporting to have the latest news of Prince Albert's condition. It merely stated that the mild fever persisted, but as Louise continued on her way she contemplated with pity the Queen's desperate anxiety at such a time. As it happened, she had never seen the royal couple since coming to London, but she well remembered seeing them drive by with the Emperor and Empress on one of their state visits to Paris, looking pleased and happy at the tumultuous reception being given them by the crowds. She knew the Prince Consort to be greatly respected by the British people, and could imagine the depths of mourning into which the country and the Empire would be plunged if the seemingly inevitable happened.

As she walked along, her memory drifted to the first dress she had ever sewn at Madame Camille's, when she had asked why all the garments were in softly sombre colours. She had been told that the court was still in mourning for King Louis-Philippe's sister, but had it been the King himself they would have been up to their ears in black garments. She caught her breath suddenly and slowed her pace on the significance of the thought that had come to her. Swinging about with a speed that sent her hoops careening, she began to retrace her steps with haste, intent on sharing with Robert her extraordinary idea. To take a shortcut and re-enter the shop from the rear where the office was situated, she came through the wooden gates normally used only for the delivery of goods by wagon, and had to pass the window of it, glancing in to signal to Robert that she had returned on a matter of extreme importance. What she saw through the panes turned her ashen, and she jerked away from the sight to press herself back against the brick wall of the building, shocked and incredulous, the back of her hand across her mouth to stop from crying out. Her husband and Lily Ashcroft! Spread together on the office couch in lust and without dignity, and faintly, horribly ludicrous. She began to understand all manner of small incidents that had been without significance before. The smirks exchanged between the other shopgirls, and the whispering that had fallen silent at her approach. Lily's uppishness and increasing tendency to answer back. The black glacé silk dress of best quality that had been such a pleasant sight after the shabby garment previously worn. The girl's small extravagances that were not in keeping with her meagre wages. All clearly and devastatingly explained.

Louise propelled herself away from the wall and went back through the wooden gates, closing them behind her. In the alleyway she brushed the brick dust from her skirt, amazed at her own terrible calmness. Out in the street she hailed a cab. Not long afterwards she arrived at the Boston Street Factory. Will received her in his office. She put to him the scheme she no longer intended to share with Robert. He listened intently and assessingly.

"And you're willing to risk every penny of your savings on this gamble?" he questioned.

"Yes! More than that, I'm going to order on credit everywhere I can here and in France. But I'll need storage space and an outlet for selling afterwards, retail and wholesale. Will you help me there?"

He grinned slowly and appreciatively, leaning back in his

chair. "You have nerves of steel. I always suspected it. Naturally I'll help you, but before we settle that matter there is something I'd like to ask you."

"Yes?"

"Why have you come to me instead of sharing this venture with your husband? I should have thought, with the facilities of Prestbury's at his disposal—"

"No!" She flew up from her chair in an explosion of Gallic wrath, her fists clenched. "I will do nothing ever again in the name of Prestbury! That is at an end. All goods for this venture will be ordered under my maiden name."

He rubbed his chin thoughtfully. "I see. There's one suggestion I'd like to make."

"You'll not talk me out of anything!"

"I don't intend to." He got up leisurely and came around the desk to her. "I just wanted to say I'd like to come into this enterprise with you if you'd let me. The law doesn't recognise a woman's signature on a contract, but we'll have a private agreement of partnership drawn up, and then all can be conducted from these premises and through my labour force without any interference of any kind from outsiders, whoever they might be."

She was at a loss for words, overcome that he should be willing to share her reckless throw. "You would do this for me?"

He wanted to reply that he would do anything under the sun for her, but it was neither the time nor the place. "You're in agreement then?"

"Oh, yes!" The whole project had its roots in too grievous a matter for any jubilation, and each was aware of it. "Partners!" They shook hands seriously. Then they went to work.

Orders went forth to Manchester, Leeds, and Bradford. A telegraphed message went to Worth, who in turn contacted French mills, including those at Lyons, that could supply the goods needed. He himself despatched immediately all that he had available, and a shipment of jet trimming and black passementerie was sent off with the name of Worth stamped across the box. As day followed day the condition of the Prince Consort appeared to remain in abeyance, while into the Boston Street Factory there came bale after bale of funereal bunting for street and window draping, huge bolts of crape, and every kind of material from softest black velvet to strong broadcloth, including a special silk that the sewing-hands were turning into mourning cravats and armbands as fast as their needles could flash.

At home and at Prestbury's Louise went about her daily routine as normally as she could. The only significant action she took was to give Lily Ashcroft the sack. Hiring or firing staff was Robert's prerogative, but he only shrugged carelessly when she told him what she had done, pretending to be absorbed in the newspaper that he had brought to work with him.

"Insolent again, was she? You said last week that you were displeased with her." He rustled the printed pages to show the deliberate direction of his attention. "I see Prince Albert has failed to make the progress expected. That's not good, is it? I thought he was getting better."

When his wife did not answer he stole a sideways glance at her. She looked sad and grave and suddenly much wearied. He could scarcely expect her to concern herself over any member of the British Royal Family, so it must be worry over something else. Did she have any suspicions about Lily and him? Or was it just as it appeared, and she had lost patience with the girl's bold airs? Whatever it was, he was not going to run the gauntlet of trying to find out. Lily did not have to work at Prestbury's to be available whenever he wanted her.

The news of the Prince Consort's death stunned the nation. People could not believe it. His illness had been of such short duration, and although there had been much coming and going of doctors, the general mood promoted by the press had been one of optimism. It did not seem possible that the tall, serious man forever at the Queen's side was no more. Respect must be shown at once, and that meant the purchase of black clothes, black drapery for home and commercial premises, black bows for the family carriages and in the infants' perambulators, black veils for the nannies, black cravats and armbands for the servants and even for the smallest child. In a matter of hours it became known among London retailers that the Boston Street Factory of Southwark had seemingly unlimited stocks of all that could possibly be needed, and before the day was out orders began to flow in from other parts of the country. Will had had extra labour at the ready, but more had to be called in. Sweating in his shirt sleeves he dealt with orders as his packers toiled through the night hours wrapping and despatching, the wagons rolling continuously out of the factory yard to the railway station or off by road. Many shopkeepers came with their own horse-vans to collect goods, any number from far afield, and did not leave until nothing more could be crammed into the vehicles.

On a far more modest scale, Prestbury's was equally busy, Louise and the staff rushed off their feet. As stocks grew thin on the shelves Robert went to Will's factory to replenish, and was furious to find that he had to line up with other traders. He went elsewhere, only to discover a poor choice left and not half of what he wanted. As the day of the state funeral drew near the buying of black gained momentum. The whole of London shimmered with funereal drapery, as did every other large city and small town. Shops displayed mourning windows, much of the choice material swathing the huge pictures of the late Prince Consort having come from the Boston Street Factory, the truly elegant emporia boasting Lyons silk as an expensive mark of respect.

Louise did not see Will until the state funeral was over. It was the following evening at a dinner party held at the house of a mutual acquaintance. The host's wife and all the women present were in black. Louise with Robert at her side could only exchange the briefest of greetings with Will in the drawing-room, but during dinner his eyes, very bright and twinkling, met hers constantly down the length of table that divided them, and afterwards he seized the first available chance to draw her aside.

"What's your dearest ambition?" he asked her on a quiet chuckle. "Is it still to open your own dress salon?"

She held her breath. "You know it is. Are you telling me that it's become possible?"

He was enjoying himself. "Anything else?"

"To buy a house."

"Then you can start looking at both kinds of property tomorrow. The house must be your own choice, but I can advise you that there's a splendid little shop just going up for rent in a turning off Regent Street. This is the address." He handed her a card on which it was written down. "We're still selling as fast as we can, by the way. It will carry on for a long while yet. Orders are flooding in from all parts of the country. I've a notion that as partners we should remain in wholesale, particularly with choice materials from France.

Messrs. Marshall and Snelgrove of Oxford Street came themselves yesterday to buy all we had left of the heavy French satins and the Lyons brocade, reordering before they left. We must talk about it. How soon can we meet?"

"Tomorrow," she said, having dropped the address into her velvet reticule and drawn the strings tight. "After I have viewed the shop premises."

He glanced for a moment beyond her. "I think your husband is on his way over here. Maybe he thinks I've monopolised your company for long enough. As a matter of interest, how are you going to break the news to him that you have made yourself a tidy little fortune?"

Her lips twitched in a smile. "By announcing that I'm never setting foot inside Prestbury's again. I have gained my liberty on all points at last, and never shall I surrender it."

He chuckled again. "You're a formidable lady, my beautiful Louise. Already I see London conquered."

She tilted her chin merrily. "In my dresses, I trust!"

"Without a doubt."

Robert joined them then, some other people drawing forward as well, and she did not speak to Will on his own again that evening. She broke the news to Robert in the carriage on the way home. At first his reaction was mixed. That they had money at last, for instantly he mentally claimed all that she had to be equally his own, was a cause for riotous celebration, but weighed against it was the offence to his pride that she had done it without consulting him, and—nightmarish thought!—if the Prince Consort had survived she would have lost everything and plunged herself into debts that defied imagination. He ran a nervous finger around the inside of his high evening collar.

"Whew! You took a chance!" Then the full impact of what their change of circumstances would mean rushed home to him. He gave a triumphant laugh. "But you did it. You really did it. And it's only the beginning, I know it. Naturally you've finished with Prestbury's. I agree with you. From now on you must concentrate on what is ours, and I'll be with you all the way. Everything else can go to hell."

"No, Robert. You are a partner at Prestbury's, and if you follow the lines I laid down, you can make your own success there."

He gaped at her incredulously in the passing lamplight that filled the carriage. "You don't imagine I'm going to rot away there in a business that will never be mine, do you? Not when we can set up our own dress house—"

She interrupted him. "I should hope with time to purchase the business from your mother on your behalf, and then it would be yours. In the meantime I shall be setting up my dress house and running it by myself."

He could not believe what he was hearing. "Has the money turned your head already? You can't dictate to me. I'll remind you that you're still my wife and my chattel—"

She rounded on him in a fury. "Don't dare to speak of marital commitments to me! As far as I'm concerned they are severed. You will make a choice. You will either move into the new house with me that I intend to purchase, or you may stay with your mother and sister; it matters little to me either way."

"I have Paul—"

"Your mother has made it plain by bitter innuendo to me that she doesn't believe Paul-Michel to be your child. I have only to tell her the truth, and she will send my son packing to me wherever I am, glad to see the back of both of us. You could always prevent me from taking him back to France, I know that, but you would never persuade your mother to keep him any longer under her roof, and you would scarcely wish to care for him yourself elsewhere. Well? Which is it to be?"

He glowered and slunk back in the corner seat, gnawing his lip. "My father called you an uppity bitch, and he was right. Very well. For the time being it's agreed that I continue at Prestbury's, but I think that the whole situation should come up for review later. There's no question of my not living with you. No matter what you say, we're man and wife." A quirk of sardonic humour showed through. "For better and for richer in this case, I'd say, wouldn't you?"

She chose to ignore the jibe, giving a businesslike little nod. "That's settled then. You may rely on me to give you any advice on the running of Prestbury's that you need. I suggest you leave the ledgers to a qualified bookkeeper. We don't want any shades of doubt arising from them should the time come for purchasing the business. There's also the matter of the shopgirls' dresses that I forgot to mention to you. I arranged with your mother that each employee be given a ready-made dress of hard-wearing material from stock, to be replaced once every two years, or before if necessary. She agreed with me that the glacé silk has never been suitable for women in their humble financial position."

They rode on in silence. He felt as winded as if he had received a blow in the chest. How and when did Louise find out about the ledgers *and* Lily? She must have eyes in the back of that proud head of hers. It certainly explained why she had kept him at a distance these past three weeks or more, never letting him take her into his arms, and keeping him to his side of the wide bed. At first he had imagined she ailed, and then that she was tired and overworked during the rush at the shop, but now he understood it to be more than that. Much, much more. Well, he would let things stay as they were until the new house was purchased. Then there would be a new beginning. He would woo her all over again, and she was too forgiving by nature to harden her heart against him for long. Somehow or other he must get his hands on the purse-strings. He had always fancied a stable of good horses, two or three fast equipages, and membership of an exclusive club in St. James's. There was also everything else that an endless flow of money would give him. The future had never looked rosier. He had made a wise move in marrying his Frenchwoman.

Louise viewed several shop premises before she decided on the address that Will had given her. Without doubt it was the best, having a corner position with one window in Regent Street and the other with the entrance in a side street full of good properties. Workmen moved in and began the redecoration and the installation of fitting-rooms. She interviewed prospective employees, and as Worth had favoured English assistants in Paris, so she favoured those of her own nationality for the salon staff. She had soon discovered that to most Englishwomen a French accent was synonymous with elegance in a female and sexual passion in a male. She had sewing-hands hard at work in the rooms behind the salons long before the shop was due to open. They were making up the dresses of her own designs that she had sketched during the past weeks. Worth had recently decreed shorter skirts for daytime wear only, allowing boots and ankles to be seen, and Louise was following suit. She was dazzled by his brilliant stroke. It was his first move against the crinoline shape that had persisted far too long, his variation seemingly infinitesimal, but by its very subtlety lulling women into a sense of false security as he aimed for its ultimate banishment.

One of the dresses being made up in Louise's workroom was to particularly shapely measurements. Remembering how Marie had approached the Princess de Metternich, Louise went to see a striking young actress who was presently taking London by storm and reputed to be the Prince of Wales's latest mistress. The actress was impressed by the sketches Louise showed her, but, being entirely mercenary, would wear the dress only if she received it free of charge, although in return she would speak at every opportunity of the new Madame Louise of Paris, who was to be found in Little Argyll Street off Regent Street. Louise agreed, promising further dresses if custom resulted.

The new house was chosen, and the sale went through without delay. It was a well-built family residence, facing a park where Paul-Michel could play in charge of Daisy, who was promoted to nanny in her new employ, with a veiled cap and uniform of which she was inordinately proud. She had proved herself trustworthy, kind, and sensible, so that Louise had no qualms about her son being in her charge. Furniture was purchased, carpets laid, and domestic staff appointed. The move into the house was made a few days before the shop was due to open. Louise had been lucky enough to find a French cook, and the dinner on the first evening that she and Robert dined together in their new home made them feel they were back in Paris enjoying the cuisine of Magny's or the Café Riche.

"Excellent, my dear." Robert touched his napkin to a corner of his mouth. "What an evening this has been." He glanced with satisfaction around the room to convey his pleasure in what he saw as his house, in the repast they had shared and, as he returned his gaze to her with his glass raised, in his wife. She never failed to delight his eye apart from all else, and sitting there at the end of his dining-table with that creamy bloom upon her lovely skin, her hair dressed back in the new style of an elaborately coiled chignon, he felt justly proud of her. They had been on amiable terms again, he being obliging to her on all counts, and on this first night in their new abode he intended that they should be man and wife again in the true sense of the term.

He was well pleased to have his own suite of bedroom, dressing-room, and bathroom. It meant that he could return home at what hour he liked without questioning, not that Louise had ever remonstrated with him, but he appreciated the sense of freedom that it gave him, and the communicating doors of shining mahogany gave access to her own rooms. In a high state of amorous anticipation he tied the cord of his padded silk dressing robe, took up his silver-backed brush to give his hair a final smoothing, and then crossed the floor to press down the handles of the doors for both to open at his coming. They did not move. He exerted more force, and then dark colour gushed up his throat into his face as he realised they were securely locked. Earlier that evening they had not been. He had wandered in and out talking to her as they had both been getting ready to go downstairs and dine. He struggled to keep the choking rage from his voice.

"Louise! The doors appear to be jammed." He would give her a chance to redeem the situation. But no reply was forthcoming. No responding movement came from the other side. In any case the doors were thick and solid, designed originally perhaps to spare a wife her husband's snoring, and unless he kept his voice loud it would be impossible to converse through them. He tried to shake them, but they appeared as stout as the walls of Troy. His fist crashing on the panel must have echoed dully through her bedroom, but although he waited and listened, there came no click of key. Fuming, he flung himself out of the suite and went to her door that opened onto the landing. It was the same.

The next morning at breakfast she poured fragrant French coffee for him, talking about the grocer's where she had located it as if nothing untoward had occurred, seeming not to notice his sullen looks. As she handed him the cup he made no move to take it.

"I want tea," he grated, "and a decent English breakfast. Porridge, kippers, a cold collation, kidneys, bacon, eggs, haddock fricassé, scones, raisin bread, toast, and all the rest that an English gentleman may expect served to him at the morning hour. None of this foreign rubbish." His hand shot out and he sent flying from the table the dolly-lined basket of new-baked croissants and hot brioches that had smelt so appetising when he had entered the breakfast room. They bounded about, and crumbs scattered everywhere. She kept quite calm.

"Whatever you wish. I heard you say so many times in

your parents' house that you would have preferred the breakfasts that you used to have in France."

"Not any more."

She rang the little bell by her hand to summon the maidservant in attendance. "It will mean a slight wait while the dishes are prepared for you—"

"Never mind!" He sprang up out of his chair, pushing it back, and hurled aside his napkin. "I'll breakfast at my club. And you and I are going to talk later about a few other misunderstandings that have arisen. I tell you that I mean to be master in my own house!"

She sat alone at the breakfast-table, sipping the coffee that was the best she had had since coming to England. Robert's proprietory attitude towards everything did not disturb her. It fed his ego, which was essential to him, and he had suffered a sore blow over the locked door. But that was how it would remain. It was not just because of Lily. If every marriage foundered on the Lilys of the world there would be few couples left together, and a true relationship had to weather every kind of storm. If Robert had shown a trace of real affection for her over the past months she would have made the moving into this house a time of reconciliation, but he had never had any thought in his head except to use her for his own convenience in every possible way, and she had reached the limit of her sufferance. No man should manipulate her for his own ends again. It had been Pierre first and then Robert. Each equally selfish in his own way, but Pierre at least had loved her. And still loved her. She did not doubt that. What had been between them could not happen with such force of emotion to either ever again. They had both known it at the beginning and at the end. Except that there was never an end to such love. It was of the kind that survived all adversity, even that of betrayal and final parting.

She put down her emptied cup with a little sigh and passed her fingers lightly across her eyes. It was a rare indulgence to allow herself to think of Pierre, and she had been letting her thoughts run away with her. Lifting her head firmly, she glanced at the clock. She had many busy hours ahead of her, and it was time to start out. Will wanted her to see a new shipment of French velvets that had arrived, their venture in wholesale materials of top quality having become firmly established, and today she would deliver personally the actress's dress. It could not be compared with the deceptively simple concoction of white tulle and silvery silk that Worth had made the Princess de Metternich. She had had to judge a different scene where *toilettes* were less elaborate than those that had matched the effervescent mood of Paris, so that she had added where Worth had restrained, ornamented where he would have stripped free, and chosen for the material a rich taffeta in the latest of the new chemical dyes, a brilliant fuchsia with no fewer than a hundred frills to the skirt. The actress had adored it at the first fitting, and gone into raptures over the little silk butterflies that would adorn her hair. Long black gloves, totally new where wrist length was customary, and a black velvet sash, gave token tribute to court mourning. Fortunately the actress would be anything but solemn when she wore it, and had the kind of sparkling personality that commanded attention wherever she went. None would be able to ignore the dress made by Madame Louise.

Filled with hope for the future of it all she went upstairs to spend a little time with Paul-Michel before setting out. Although only four and a half years old he was already bilingual, sometimes confusing the odd word in either language when he spoke, but she knew that with time this would eliminate itself. Only in teaching him the alphabet and in the commencement of his reading did she keep to English since it would be through circumstances and habitat his first language. Entering the nursery she greeted him in French as she always did, and he ran to her for his morning kiss, still in his nightshirt and warm with sleep. She cuddled him to her, taking him onto her lap by the fire, and he chatted away about all he was going to do that day. His likeness to Pierre was becoming more and more marked, giving strength to the old wives' tale that a love-child always resembles the father.

That evening when Louise returned home, she entered her bedroom to find that Robert had had the lock removed from the communicating doors, which stood open. He was leaning a shoulder against the jamb, arms folded nonchalantly, a satisfied smirk on his face.

"How dare you!" she exclaimed furiously. "It will make no difference. I'll simply remove my possessions into another room."

"If you do, I'll send Paul, young as he is, away to school."

She was aghast, the colour draining from her face. "Are you mad? He's not yet out of the nursery!"

He was unmoved. "You have my ultimatum. I told you that I intend to be master in this house."

She could tell he was not bluffing. It seemed that fate intended to extract further sacrifice from her. She made him no reply, but turned her anguished face away. He knew he had won.

20

Louise's shop had been opened three years when she decided to take a trip to Paris. A certain Mademoiselle Brousseau, a middle-aged Frenchwoman originally from Chartres, had become her right-hand assistant, fully dedicated to the business, which allowed her more free time than she had had in the shop's early days. Madame Louise de Paris had opened with a window display of eye-catching dresses in the new aniline dyes of almost garish brilliance, all intricately banded with black, and in a matter of weeks not only were copies appearing for those unable to afford the Frenchwoman's gowns, but those who knew nothing of *haute couture* followed the mode that had been set by trimming up their wardrobes with yards of cheap black ribbon.

It did not take long for fashionable women to be drawn to the shop. The actress had kept her word, singing her French dressmaker's praises wherever she went, and was well rewarded with further dresses as more and more custom flowed in. Before the year was out Louise could have extended the premises along Little Argyll Street, but she had no intention of competing with the larger stores, and rented instead the floors above the shop, which enabled her to retain the look of having a small and exclusive premises, while having all the room she needed to expand her workshop and install extra fitting-rooms.

The royal wedding secured her success. The Prince of

Wales took as his bride the beautiful Princess Alexandra of Denmark, and the whole of London society was plunged into a furore of fashion. Louise produced a range of figure-hugging jackets that she called the "Alexandra" basquin, which sold as fast as they could be produced. Many of her dresses graced the innumerable balls and receptions and banquets held in honour of the royal couple, and if Worth's creations eclipsed hers she felt it to be an honourable rout, knowing that at least she came second to the master, and none could gainsay her there. Recently he had flooded the fashion world with looped-up top skirts and panniers, having been inspired by the sight of a simple working woman all unconsciously forming graceful folds in her skirt as she tucked it up over her petticoat to save its soiling before sweeping a floor. Nothing could have been further from the original than the sumptuous fabrics used in Worth's dresses and those that followed his lead, but the same classic draping was there.

Louise kept Marie in touch with her successful progress, receiving encouragement and congratulations with each reply. Although Worth had no time to read the letters that came from her, his wife passed on all the news. He himself had never been busier or more overworked or happier. The Midas touch had entered into her fingertips. Although his prices made even his wealthiest clients stretch their eyes, none went elsewhere, fawning on him for his attention, enraptured by his creations, and suffering his arrogance without complaint. He had been poor for too long not to know how to spend money now that it was his, his coffers ever filling up and overflowing no matter how deeply he dived into them for some lavish expenditure. Marie found herself with more jewels than she could wear. Her portrait was painted for the third time. Her slightest whim was instantly fulfilled. She had her own daumont lined with ivory satin to ride in, taking her place in the fashionable cavalcade through the Bois de Boulogne each afternoon, not even the imperial carriages drawn by thoroughbreds to better those driven by her liveried coachman. Leghorn hats were all the rage, and there had never been a prettier sight as the carriages bowled along, ostrich feathers and ribbons and wide-petalled flowers dancing on the dipping brims. Always whatever Marie wore seemed more flattering than all the rest, simply because it was known that her husband's magical skill had had a hand in its creation.

Although, by reason of being a tradesman, Worth could

not be accepted into society even if he had wished it, which he did not, he and Marie were both much fêted by many distinguished people. He still avoided social engagements wherever possible, but Marie was enjoying her new leisured life as much as her husband revelled in spending money, and she was to be seen at most of the grand social events of the season, frequently in the company of the Metternichs and many other such renowned and aristocratic personages. Never before had she been more of an advertisement for her husband's fashions, her appearance scrutinised from head to toe, ever the focus of attention wherever she went, only Worth aware that at heart she was still as shy and retiring as ever.

The domestic quarters at number 7, rue de la Paix, reflected their steadily increasing wealth. Worth had had all the furnishing fabrics woven at Lyons to his own designs. He proved to be quite secretive about the material he had ordered for the room that he and Marie liked best, smiling and looking teasingly mysterious whenever she questioned him about it. When it arrived there were many bolts of it, and he unrolled one much like a magician when they were on their own together, throwing the rich cloth forward in such a way that it billowed in huge ripples like a river of russet red and gold across the shining floor.

"See!" His great shout of triumph made the chandeliers vibrate.

She stared in amazement at the strange pattern of eyes and ears that winked and shimmered over each rise and fall of the glorious stuff, but she guessed instantly what it was. "It's the material you've always talked about!" she cried. "The one you saw in the portrait of Queen Elizabeth when you were just a boy!" It was a tale she had heard many times, it being a particular favourite with their own sons.

His face was vivid with pride. He stood with feet set apart, head thrown back, the silk velvet quiet now as he draped its fiery sheen from the grip of his hand.

"It's mine at last," he breathed.

He had always seen it as his talisman, and now the cloth of dreams had become a reality. Before long he would have variations of it adorning a grander residence than their present home, where they could spend the springs and summers. He had seen a plot of land just outside Paris at Suresnes where he planned to build a fine mansion that would be a fit setting for Marie and a man of genius. He had never been troubled by false modesty, and did not intend to start now. Why should he? He was as omnipotent in his own sphere as ever the great Elizabeth had been in hers. He was the one and only Worth, his the eyes and ears of the whole universe of *haute couture*.

Marie was more aware than her husband of the jealousy that his tremendous success had aroused, and she was deeply distressed when a scurrilous article appeared in a newspaper about the English couturier who took immoral liberties when closeted with half-naked clients. Worth read the piece and dismissed it with contempt. It was not the first time such slander had been levelled against him. He had seen women in their underclothes almost all of his commercial life, and had had any number of nippled breasts revealed to him by accident or design, but in the fitting-rooms he was concerned only with the dress in hand, and nothing else interested him. It had been different when he had first confronted Marie in a state of *déshabille* in the days of making her a shop dress. Her allure had stunned him into such a state of excitement that he had scarcely dared touch her, and to this day he was still stirred by the sight of her in a pretty disorder of stays and petticoats and gartered stockings.

"You know why this scandal has been purported," he said to her. "The Princess de Metternich publicly abused an audience at the Paris Opéra for failing to appreciate Wagner and his new opera. Therefore, since she is also my patroness as well as Wagner's, I must be tarred and feathered at the same time."

"But it's monstrously unfair!" Marie protested in tears.

He smiled and kissed her wet cheek. "When clients begin to stay away I'll find the time to worry, and not before."

Nobody stayed away. In fact, some new clients came along, intrigued by what they had read. If they were disappointed that no familiarities took place, they were not disappointed by the dresses made for them, and gave him their custom from that time forth. The article was soon forgotten, and before long the same newspaper was singing the praises of the magnificent fancy dresses that Worth was making for the masked balls that had become so popular in society.

Worth was as dictatorial with the fancy dresses as he was with everything else he made. No matter whom a client had made up her mind to represent, he would silence her with an imperious gesture, put a hand to his head as he called upon inspiration, perhaps walking slowly around the lady at the same time. Then he would tell her what he would make for her. The cost was always immensely high, but his sewing-hands were well remunerated for the long hours put into the work, and also he used only the best materials even if the costume was to be worn on one occasion only. He gowned the Empress as Marie-Antoinette in rose velvet with head plumes a full metre high; as the wife of the Doge of Venice in black velvet and scarlet satin so covered with her magnificent diamonds that she sparkled from top to toe, and in many other outfits of similar grandeur. The Princess de Sagan, a great giver of costume balls herself, was dressed by him as a peacock, the whole bird constructed in green and gold on her head, hundreds of peacock feathers in the train, and the front of the skirt pale blue as the sky, with trimmings of billowing clouds held up by a painted Cupid. There was no limit to the lavishness of his ideas, and every client knew that nobody else present would have anything like her own personal splendour. Worth went himself to one ball in silken robes of his "eyes and ears" pattern, causing his own sensation. Requests by others for the same pattern were firmly turned down.

After the draperies in the "eyes and ears" material had been made up for the walls of the favourite salon at number 7, rue de la Paix, Marie saved a left-over snippet and enclosed it in a letter to Louise, knowing that she would also be familiar with the origins of it. It slipped between the written pages as Louise opened the letter, and fell across her lap. She picked it up and smiled over it, her gaze reflective on the memory of Worth's halting French describing the pattern to her long ago in the rue du Fouarre. Later that same day she went to the National Gallery and stood before the portrait of the Virgin Queen for the first time. Holding the snippet of shining material up to the canvas, she thought it might well have been cut from a fold in the regal gown.

Now, some months later, Robert and Paul-Michel were going with her to Paris. Robert would never have let her take the boy without him, it being the one hold he had over her. She was presently negotiating to buy Prestbury's for him, but his mother was proving difficult, which did not help his sullen mood. Her own relationship with him had deteriorated to the point where he always spoke tersely to her and frequently with sarcasm. In temper he had used violence on her, jabbing her viciously in the ribs and once punching her in the stomach, but never where bruises might show to the outside world. With his sly and devious ways she sometimes felt that for all his superior physical strength and boasting assertiveness she had another child to look after, a feckless boy who would continue in his wayward role until the end of his days. How she could ever have imagined he would fulfill the role of father to Paul-Michel she did not know. He could be strict enough, demanding immediate obedience and dealing out punishment for the slightest misdemeanour, but he had no affection for the boy to balance matters. Not that he was always ill-tempered. There would be times when he was completely affable, and then Paul-Michel, having a warm and affectionate nature, would respond gladly, often with too much excitement, which frequently resulted in trouble and tears. It was Will who did most for the boy, taking him fishing and boating, teaching him to play cricket, and giving him his first riding lessons. Louise accompanied them on these expeditions from time to time, and the hours were always as happy for her as they were for her son. By necessity she saw Will frequently, their business partnership involving her in any number of joint decisions and discussions, and Robert made sneering innuendoes about the time they spent together, although she knew he did not seriously believe that there was anything untoward between them, or else his attitude would have been entirely savage.

She knew Will wanted her. It was an ever-present issue between them, not spoken of since the one occasion when he had admitted to the fires she ignited in him, but always there, sometimes charging the air so forcibly that it seemed to crackle about them, and these were the days when she was careful to avoid the slightest physical contact. To be kissed by Will was no mild experience as she knew from the past, and for his sake and hers she did not want to risk it occurring again. At first his approach was subtle, worldly, and totally assured, it being clear that he had no doubt that on the basis of their long, fond, and curiously binding comradeship, spiced as it had always been with a particular sexual rapport, she would accept him as a lover with little ado. When it began to dawn on him that it was not to be, he retreated into a kind of smouldering watchfulness. It had to be no more than a glance from her and he would see it. So she guarded her glances, having no such message to convey, and understood why at times he was unnecessarily impatient with her when they disagreed over some minor business matter.

There was a meeting with him at the factory on the eve of her departure for Paris. He had been to France himself several times during the past three years on business and now it was her turn, giving her a chance to view the fashion scene.

"I'm going to miss you, Louise. Don't have thoughts about going back to live in Paris once you have seen it again."

She smiled. "I can't pretend I haven't pictured a Madame Louise on the rue de Rivoli or the new Boulevard Haussmann, but for the present time that is out of the question."

"Pierre, of course?"

She shrugged a trifle ruefully in the manner he found so French and beguiling. "Can there ever be any other reason?"

"How do you know your paths won't cross again while you are there?"

"I queried that with Marie and learned that the de Gands will be at the Palace of St.-Cloud with the Emperor and Empress at that time. Stéphanie had ordered a host of new gowns because the imperial couple do not like to see their lady guests in the same dress for more than a few hours and never, never a second time." She gave a little laugh. "No wonder Worth is becoming such a wealthy man."

"Good luck to him." Will grinned approvingly. "Be sure and give him my compliments, by the way."

"Indeed I shall." She prepared to leave.

He hated to see her go. He was a rational man, not given to flights of fancy, but there gnawed in him a foreboding that one day Paris or Pierre de Gand, for it would be one or the other, would snatch her away from him for good. It was not her marriage that stood between them, her husband being a spineless, self-indulgent fellow with whom she had little in common, but all that was intrinsically French in her, bound up as it was with a love that held her still. Such a barrier was frustratingly unassailable, blocking him on all fronts. He cared for her deeply. Whether he loved her or not was an entirely different matter. He had not been lucky in that sphere, and it was best forgotten. In any case, he had lived long enough to know that love was not the important factor when a vital physical attraction prevailed. With Louise he simply hoped that with time she would choose to release towards him her own innate sensuality, to let forth her lush femininity that made her so desirable to him, and until then he could only wait, paving the way wherever he could.

"Try to be glad to come back to England when your trip is over," he advised seriously as he escorted her out of the building. "Don't break your heart all over again when it's time to leave France."

It had never mended, but he did not know that. She adopted a light tone. "You mustn't worry about me. I'll have my head too full of new ideas to think of anything but my designs for next season."

"I hope so."

"Wish me luck." Her golden-brown eyes were suddenly anxious.

"Always. *Bonne chance,* my dear Louise." He leaned forward and kissed her lightly on each cheek as it was done in France in greeting or farewell. To have touched her lips with his own would have released too much power in him.

"*Au revoir,* Will. I'll send you one of those new picture postcards that are becoming all the rage."

She kept her word. It was a patriotic picture of the Emperor and Empress with the young Prince Imperial, conjuring up an image of imperial domestic bliss. He would have preferred a letter, postcards allowing no space for anything except a signature beneath the picture, although she had signed it with affectionate greetings.

Paris was veiled in a mist when Louise saw it again, a sparkling mist of her own poignantly happy tears that she kept dashing away. As it was a workday Catherine could not be at the station to meet them, but Marie was there, waiting in the smoke-wreathed sunrays that poured down through the glass-domed roof, her sons with her. There was much laughter and talk and embracing, Robert hiding his boredom as both women exclaimed over how each other's offspring had grown, Paul-Michel being tall for his seven years while eleven-year-old Gaston and eight-year-old Jean-Philippe were equally strong and healthy in appearance, although inwardly much embarrassed by the curls that their maman had crimped into their hair for the occasion. They also envied Paul-Michel his conventional clothes. Their mamam designed special garments for them to wear on such auspicious days and they loathed their high-buttoned gaiters that made it agony to bend the knee, and the fancy blouses and tasselled caps in all the same monkey colour. In fact, Maman had once burst into tears when somebody had exclaimed with teasing laughter that they looked like a pair of little monkeys, but she had dried her tears, said that some people did not understand that the children of Worth should also be stylish, and they still had to wear the hateful garments. If Paul-Michel made a single derisive comment about them Jean-Philippe was resolved to do battle. But Paul-Michel did not seem to notice their clothes, only that they were fellow boys. He pulled a grubby twist of paper from his pocket and offered it.

"Have a piece of English liquorice," he invited in faultless French. "If you stick bits on your front teeth it looks as if they've been knocked out." The friendship was sealed.

Marie had insisted that the travellers go with her to number 7, rue de la Paix, where a luncheon had been made ready for them, so the Prestbury's baggage was despatched to the Grand Hôtel, where they were to stay, Louise's lady's maid, Robert's valet, and Nanny Daisy accompanying it. For Marie and her guests the satin-lined daumont was drawn up in the forecourt of the terminus. Louise noticed the gold monogram on the carriage door.

When they drove into the rue de la Paix Louise was amazed at its commercial growth. Other businesses, eager to benefit from Worth's success, had moved into every available property, and what had been a quiet street had become a place of thriving activity. Outside number 7 itself where the name *Worth* was emblazoned in gilt on the fascia of the entrance, was a throng of waiting carriages with liveried lackeys. The daumont swept through and drew up at the door. As she alighted, Louise saw that the gallery of the inner courtyard had been renewed and Worth's own monogram, gilded and gleaming, had been incorporated into the ironwork of all the supports. But that was nothing compared to the grandeur of the interior, all of which was new since she had last seen it. Floor upon floor in the tall building was now given over entirely to the business, and there was a richness of Aubusson carpet and damask panelling and ormolu and marble that caught the breath with each new vista, the whole set asparkle by crystal chandeliers. Worth was engaged with a client, and until he could join them, Marie took Louise and Robert on a tour, the three children being allowed to go thundering off at a run into the domestic quarters of the building, where Paul-Michel was to be shown a new batch of toy soldiers and a cannon that fired iron pellets.

Louise was barely able to judge her location as they went through the showrooms on the first floor, each given up to a particular range of fabric or colour, one devoted to black and white silks, every shade of green and blue in another, rose and coral in the next, and so on. She received friendly nods and smiles of recognition from those with whom she had once worked, all busy serving, the premises abustle with custom. A more restful atmosphere prevailed in a long salon where Worth's latest dresses were displayed like works of art, women studying them with a reverent air. Other clients sat in another handsome room where *mannequins*, as those who displayed dresses were now called, paraded in other beautiful garments. If any client wished to see exactly how she would look in a particular ballgown while waltzing around the floor of the Salle des Maréchaux at the Tuileries, she had only to step inside a room faced entirely with floor-to-ceiling looking-glass, the shaded lights simulating exactly the glow that came from the famous chandeliers. Louise declared it to be a most imaginative innovation, and so typical of Worth to think of it.

Marie nodded with a smile. "He has it here," she said, tapping her forehead proudly.

Luncheon was over in the private apartments when Worth appeared, full of apologies. "My dear Louise! To think I must snatch a greeting from you and rush back to work again." He had kissed her hand and now he twirled her around by it, looking her travelling costume up and down critically. "Yes, yes. The skirt nicely flat in front, with a half-hooped crinolette giving fullness at the back. Do you recall how it was once said that the full crinoline would never wane!"

"The whole world has followed your lead," she replied.

"Yes, it has," he agreed complacently. "You're still doing well in business, I hear. Congratulations. Always remember that women dress for their own pleasure and the still greater joy of snuffing out the others. It is in the 'snuffing out' that you as a couturière make your distinctive mark on fashion."

She smiled in agreement. "Women deliver themselves to me now with the confidence that they have ever shown in you, wanting my ideas and not their own. Any choice they have is between my creations."

He nodded approvingly. "Well done. That's how it should be, or else if they invented for themselves you and I would lose half our trade. Always decide for them. It makes them happy. If I tell them a dress suits them they need no further evidence. My signature to their gown suffices." He became aware that in talking on a subject dear to both of them he was spending more time than he could spare at the moment. "What are your plans in Paris?"

"Well, tomorrow—"

"Tomorrow you shall go with me to the Tuileries. I have a new dress for the Empress, and there may be some minor adjustments that you'll be able to carry out on the spot."

Louise was more startled by the news he had given her than by his casual appropriation of her time. "The Empress in Paris? I thought she and the Emperor had gone to St.-Cloud just now."

"That was cancelled at the last minute when the Emperor was indisposed. He's better again, I hear, but the man ails. It's my opinion that the doctors don't know what the matter is and won't admit it." He took out his gold pocket watch and glanced at it. "You had better be here by nine-thirty tomorrow morning. My appointment is always for ten o'clock."

Marie made a strong protest. "Charles! Louise isn't your *première* fitter any more. She is in Paris on business of her own."

He was not listening, having noticed Robert for the first time and extending his hand to him. "Good day. How are you?" Then he looked around. "Where's the boy?"

Marie answered. "With Jean-Philippe and Gaston. The three of them have become the best of friends."

"Have they? Then I'll get him an invitation to the Prince Imperial's party. They can go together. Now I must get back to work." He nodded to Louise and Robert, making his departure, but as he opened the double doors to leave he came to an abrupt halt, staring at the sight that met him on the threshold. Crammed side by side into a dress made ready for a very plump client were the three boys, Gaston with his monkey-bloused arm through one sleeve and Louise's son with his jacketed arm through the other, the skirt in thick ripples about their feet. In the middle, his merry face showing above the dip of the neckline, was Jean-Philippe, his eyes screwed up with suppressed laughter.

"Madame de Villemont to see you, Papa," he chortled.

Worth threw back his head in a sudden uninhibited roar of laughter. Behind him the others joined in, although Marie held up her hands at such unceremonious handling of the elaborately bejewelled gown. At that moment a vendeuse appeared through a door in the anteroom through which the boys had come.

"Madame de Villemont has arrived, Monsieur Worth," she announced innocently. Such gusts of fresh laughter followed that she stared in astonishment until she noticed what the boys were dressed up in. She clapped a hand over her mouth and dissolved into giggles. They had played similar harmless and amusing pranks before, but this was by far the funniest.

It was Louise and Marie who extricated the boys from the dress, all of them still laughing. Louise thought what a wonderfully happy atmosphere the Worth children had to grow up in, their presence accepted as naturally in the salons of the business as it was in their own home surroundings.

That evening she had a joyous reunion with Catherine, who made a great fuss of her and Paul-Michel. When the excitement had died down a little Louise noticed that her old friend had aged considerably in her absence. Taking the woman's needle-pitted fingers into her own she studied the swollen joints with concern.

"It's only a touch of rheumatism," Catherine said with a jolly air, pulling her hands away. Years of draughty workrooms and garret accommodation had taken their toll. She suffered with her chest as well, but so far she had managed to keep that secret, and she did not intend that Louise should discover it.

Louise wanted her to stay at the hotel with them, but she would not, too overawed by its sumptuousness, although she appreciated going home in a cab. Louise made up her mind that before leaving Paris she would buy Catherine her own comfortable apartment at a modest address where she would be settled until the end of her days.

Louise rode with Worth to the palace in his own monogrammed carriage, the huge box containing the dress packed by specially trained packers in the iron rack on the roof. They talked fashion all the way. He had begun introducing geometrical trimming, which seemed to him to express a new and as yet indefinable change in women's attitudes. At the Tuileries they walked in through the grand entrance, leaving the imperial servants to unload the box. Louise's heart contracted as she saw the familiar uniform of the Cent-Garde on duty everywhere, but as she took the marble staircase at Worth's side she reminded herself that there was faint chance that she would run into Pierre in that huge, gilded labyrinth. In the Empress's suite they came at last to the *cabinet de toilette* with its many mirrors. Eugénie, always punctual, appeared on the stroke of ten. Louise dipped into a deep curtsey as Worth bowed. They both received one of those bewitching smiles. At the age of thirty-eight Eugénie was still at the zenith of her beauty.

"Show me my new dress, Monsieur Worth."

"I have had it made up in a Lyons silk brocade, Your Majesty." He motioned to Louise, who was holding the unpacked gown, and she came forward to spread it out for inspection. "It has been specially woven, the unusual pattern only seen before in a precious antique shawl from ancient China."

Eugénie stared at it, her dislike apparent. The soft beige background with the spread of flowers in yellows and corals and palest greens did not appeal to her. "It's like an old curtain. I'll not wear that!"

There was more to her hostility than mere dislike of the undeniably exquisite brocade. Worth had met it before with her in anything to do with Lyons. It was a city that had never been loyal to the Emperor, and with a good deal of criticism currently being levelled throughout the country against both her husband and herself she was particularly sensitive about it. In many ways Worth found her as difficult to dress as Marie had ever been, because although she enjoyed being a leader of fashion, it was only along conservative lines, and unlike Pauline de Metternich, she always needed to be coaxed and charmed into wearing something entirely new. It had taken all his powers of persuasion to get her to adopt the new skirtline, and now she loved it. He was resolved to do battle once and for all over Lyons. He brought all his famous charm into play, the charm that made women melt and forgive his high-handed attitude towards them over and over again.

"On you this brocade will be shown to the splendour of its original design. It is unlike any other made during the past thousand years or more. I can't imagine a combination of colours more suited to your Titian hair. It will create interest everywhere and mean a full revival of the looms at Lyons almost overnight."

She was determined not to be won over this time. "I will not be seen in it. Take it away!"

He was undeterred. He had always got his own way with Marie in the end, and nobody could be more stubborn than she. The Empress was no different. "I think you should reconsider. After you have worn this dress, every fashionable woman in the world will want to possess a dress in Lyons brocade."

She was shaking her head again, her lips set, and Louise was astonished that Worth should argue with her where anyone else would have been all deference. Had she been an ordinary client in his showrooms he would probably have ordered her out, it being his policy never to be dictated to on any point. He had once sent away a highly important lady who had wanted him to make her an immodest fancy dress, saying that the goldsmith along the street would provide her with a string of jewels, which appeared to be all she needed.

In the midst of the argument, which soon became extremely lively, Worth smoothly determined and the Empress icily haughty, the Emperor came up the spiral staircase from his own rooms below, perhaps attracted by the sound of the wrangling, and bringing with him the aroma of the cigarette that he was smoking. With a master stroke, Worth immediately sought his support.

"I beg you, Sire, to help me persuade Her Majesty to wear this dress." He explained his reasons with enthusiasm. "As a small example, I can tell you that when I return to the rue de la Paix every woman of fashion on the premises will rush at me with a demand to know what colour and cloth the Empress will be wearing next, and if I mention this brocade I'll be up to my ears in orders for the same before the day is out."

Louis-Napoléon studied the dress, telling Louise to hold it up against herself. It was immediately enhanced by those lovely, amber eyes veiled in lashes black as jet. His most recent mistress had such expressive eyes. "Hmm. Very fine." He drew slowly on his cigarette and his lids narrowed against the smoke. "I think the dress is very fine." He gave his wife an encouraging nod. "It would be politic for you to wear it once, if never again. Renewed prosperity to any industry within the realm means greater benefit to France."

The battle was won. Eugénie tried on the dress and it fitted her perfectly. Afterwards Louise saw it placed on a wicker figure and set into a lift which had descended from the rosework in the ceiling. The lift was hoisted up again, the dress vanishing from sight into the rooms above where the Empress's garments were kept. In this way nothing was crushed by being carried up- or downstairs.

Filled with amazement at all she had seen, Louise left the palace with Worth, quite unaware that she had awakened surprise of another kind in someone else. Stéphanie, coming to take up her duties, had happened to see her leave with Worth, and was filled with apprehension. Surely Louise had not come back to stay! She must find out.

She did it by the simple means of going herself to the rue de la Paix that same evening. She had the perfect excuse, it being customary for clients of standing to go to number 7 on any evening before a social event of supreme importance. There they would have their hair dressed by expert *coiffeuses*, Worth himself seeing to the adornment of jewels or flowers or whatever else he had chosen for the elaborate arrangement of their tresses. Then, attired in their glorious gowns, they would be inspected by him for the minutest flaw in their appearance, which would be corrected by the flashing needle of a *première* seamstress, and not until he had pronounced each *toilette* to be perfect would they leave the building.

Stéphanie was somewhat disconcerted to find confusion reigning when she arrived. Worth was not well. He had been struck down by one of the severe headaches that plagued him from time to time, and the showrooms were full of princesses and duchesses and many other women of rank and distinction waiting for him to recover enough to complete the finishing touches to their attire. Neither was Madame Worth to be seen, being upstairs putting cold compresses on her husband's aching forehead. The Princess de Metternich, never a patient person, finally stamped her foot.

"If he cannot come down to us, then we must go up to him."

The élite cluster of clients filed up the stairs to be met by Marie, who begged them to keep very quiet and to let him rest after each viewing. In the midst of them Stéphanie waited until she should be admitted to his presence. All whispered out of consideration for him. When it was her turn, she found Worth lying on a brocade chaise-longue, a cold compress hiding his face, his wife hovering anxiously by him. With a finger and thumb he lifted the bandage by a corner, and his piercing eye raked Stéphanie up and down. He groaned loudly.

"Awful! Your sash is too tight. You look as dreadful as the rest."

Wordless, she passed on to join the others who had all been scathingly commented upon, each one dismayed and at a loss without him to put them to rights. Stéphanie alone had a dual purpose in lingering on.

The next to stand before the chaise-longue was Worth's own special patroness. The Princess de Metternich regularly sent him caskets of priceless jewels to be incorporated into a gown, as many of his other wealthy clients did, and she shone magnificently in dove-grey satin encrusted with rubies and black pearls, stunning in her glorious facial ugliness and her unassailable poise. Worth reacted as if she stood there in beggar's rags. He let the bandage drop back over his eye as if the sight were too terrible to be borne.

"Ghastly!" he moaned, his voice excessively weak.

Pauline de Metternich did not move meekly on. Her eyes twinkled and her mouth twitched with private amusement. "It seems to me, Monsieur Worth, that since we all look such frights you must have lost your touch. Your day is over, my good sir."

The effect of her words was immediate. Worth sat up and hurled aside the covering from his eyes that were lacklustre with the pain in his head, but his voice thundered forth. "Come, ladies! Downstairs!"

Stéphanie made a point of being the last for him to attend to, and as he retied her sash and adjusted the jasmine cluster in her hair, she brought up the subject for which she had come. "What a pity Madame Louise isn't here this evening to help you."

He was feeling nauseated by the pain that was threatening to split his head asunder, and for a moment it did not dawn on him why she should have brought up the name of someone long gone from his employ. Then he recalled the whole unfortunate episode that had involved Louise with the de Gand fellow. "I would have her back tomorrow if she wished it, but Paris has lost her to London. That's her home now."

Thankfully Stéphanie knew all was well after all.

The days in Paris flew past for Louise. She completed a lot of business, ordered the latest in passementerie and other ornamentation, including white jet, which Worth had recently introduced with great success, and in between she visited old friends with Catherine, spending as much time with her as she could. Paul-Michel could hardly be separated from his young companions, and during the second week moved out of the hotel to join the Worths when they went to take up their spring and summer sojourn at the mansion built at Suresnes. There the boys had ponies to ride, trees to climb, lakes to swim in, and the facilities of tennis courts, archery butts, croquet lawns, and many other pastimes to enjoy together. Louise and Robert were invited there to dine, sometimes in the vast conservatory that covered an acre, filled with exotic flowers and plants and rich foliage, or else in the house, which was steeped in luxury and extravagance, its windows giving fine views of Paris in the distance. There were whole salons panelled and draped in costly brocades, one given over entirely to the "eyes and ears" pattern of a fiery brilliance that gave it the look of being bathed in liquid copper, and the marble columns and floors and abundance of statuary ranged from mottled rose and ebony to the purest white of finest Carrara. Rarest porcelain filled every niche, jade and lapis lazuli and ivory dappled each salon with colour, blinds of oriental gauze diffusing the sunlight that touched eighteenth-century timepieces and the decorated furniture with its marquetry, and many wonderful bronzes. Most fascinating of all to many who came there were the specially constructed walls of glass wherein beautiful orchids made living tapestries, while fountains set in solid gold played in the vestibule below a vast chandelier that winked thousands of purely cut crystal pendants. Worth rode on horseback to the rue de la Paix each morning and home again in the evening, a dramatic figure in his tall top hat, his flying coat-tails of velvet, and his handsome face adorned by a moustache that had grown fuller with his increased importance on the Paris scene.

On the day of the Prince Imperial's party Paul-Michel would have preferred to have spent the time playing at Suresnes, but Jean-Philippe, who had been before, advised him that it would be fun. It was the Empress's custom to hold a large gathering of children once a year in the gardens of the Tuileries, inviting those born the same year as her son, and any others who came by one good reason or another onto the annual list. As there were organised games the Worth brothers were spared the leather gaiters, which would have hampered their running about, but they were dressed alike in another of their maman's designs in a light cream colour destined to be marred by grass stains and dust before half an hour was out. Their hair was also crimped. Paul-Michel pitied this last indignity, and once Marie had waved the three of them off in the carriage he used his spit to help the other two in a frantic dampening down of the loathsome curls.

The party was all he had been told it would be. There was a magician who produced rabbits from a hat and doves from out of the air, clowns who made him roll about with laughter, and tumblers who made a human pyramid that seemed high as the palace. There were races and a treasure hunt, and all the kinds of food that a boy liked best, with ices and chocolate choux buns that oozed cream in all directions when bitten into. There were other highlights to the day, and he told his mother about them at the Grand Hôtel when she was tucking him into bed. It was their last night in Paris. Tomorrow it was home again.

"Jean-Philippe and Gaston were presented to the Empress, and being with them I was too. She was all in white with a blue sash, and her hat had a wide brim to it." He was so used to hearing fashion talk that he knew these would be the details that his mother would want to hear. "After that one of the officers there came and talked to me. He had heard my English surname and wanted to know all about where I lived in England and about my parents and how long I'd been in Paris. I told him I liked to ride, and he had a groom saddle up his own cavalry horse for me to ride it around the courtyard. That was really exciting. Then it was time for the firework display." He frowned, tilting his head as he observed his mother. She looked upset. "What's the matter, Maman?"

"Did the officer tell you his name?" she questioned falteringly.

"Yes. Captain de Gand."

She turned so pale that he was alarmed, and pushed back the bedclothes to scramble forward on his knees and put his arms about her neck. "Are you not well, Maman?"

She hugged him to her, hiding her face in his small shoulder. "Yes, yes. A little tired, perhaps."

"I am, too. But I could stay in Paris forever. Well, not Paris, but Suresnes. I wish Jean-Philippe and Gaston were my brothers."

Still talking, listing all else he would miss when he was home again, he settled into his pillow as she drew the covers over him once more. Afterwards, leaving him in Nanny Daisy's charge, she took a cab and waited in it outside Catherine's place of work until she came out. They had arranged to have supper together on this last evening, Robert spending his nights in Paris in any way he wished. As soon as Catherine got into the cab she saw by Louise's eyes that something was wrong.

"Pierre and Paul-Michel have met."

Catherine listened to how it came about and tried to reassure. "Think no more about it. Paul-Michel will soon forget the whole incident."

Louise shook her head sadly. "For once I'm not thinking of Paul-Michel. He will forget, as you say. But Pierre won't. Marie told me that after a third miscarriage Stéphanie was informed that she would never be able to bear children."

Catherine lapsed into silence. There was nothing she could say to that. She could almost pity Louise's seducer. Fate certainly extracted its dues most cruelly.

21

Louise engaged a tutor for Paul-Michel upon their return from France, and the day nursery became a schoolroom. She returned to work with renewed zest, finally managed to purchase Prestbury's for Robert, and hoped that their domestic life would run more smoothly as a result of it. Will embraced her when they met again, but she drew away almost at once.

All went so well for her in business as the months slipped by that she felt some of Worth's luck must have rubbed off on her. She had become *the* couturière from whom mothers would order dresses for their debutante daughters to wear when presented at court. The Queen had virtually retired from public life after the death of Prince Albert, but Princess Alexandra of Wales deputised for her on this annual grand occasion, and it was still the highlight for every girl coming out. Hoops had now disappeared, the skirt gracefully straight in the front with an abundance of draped and gathered fulness to the rear that floated or swept or rippled, which enabled Louise to give every kind of variation to all the white dresses that were made ready for the debutantes' day of the year.

At times she had to suffer criticism of France. Since 1863 the British press had attacked the presence of French troops in Mexico, condemning the emperor's interference there, and now four years later the United States was demanding their immediate withdrawal. For herself, she found most worrying a leader in *The Times* that warned of a Prussian threat to the security of France. Since the short and bloody war executed by Prussia against Austria it had become obvious that the victorious Bismarck was now the power in Europe, and Louis-Napoléon, sick in health, was in decline. Yet, astonishing in the circumstances, Marie wrote with enthusiasm of the welcome that Bismarck had received upon his arrival at the great Exposition Universelle of 1867 recently opened. Worth had produced dresses in Bismarck brown, and instantly no woman of fashion would be seen in any other colour. Everything was in that hue, from hats to parasols. Louise frowned. She saw it as the colour of a shadow. Why should Bismarck be so lauded when so many other rulers and royal personages were also attending the exposition? Was it that her beloved Paris, all laughter and gaiety and flamboyance, was trying to seduce him away from all thoughts of war into an everlasting *affaire*?

She felt keenly homesick when Mr. Allenby came to dine after visiting the exposition as the guest of Worth. Will, who had also recently returned from Paris, was among the friends and acquaintances she had gathered about her table. Robert was absent. The dinner party was in honour of his birthday, but he had not been home the night before, and she had seen nothing of him all day. She had been sure he would turn up at the last minute before the guests arrived, but when he had failed to appear she had had to make a simple apology for his absence. She had no idea where he was or with whom, but more and more his behaviour left much to be desired. Her hopes that possession of his own business would give him some sense of responsibility had come to naught. He had simply installed a manager to do all the work, and only went to Prestbury's occasionally when it suited him, his shiftlessness more apparent than ever.

Over dinner both Mr. Allenby and Will were encouraged by the other guests to describe the Paris Exposition, which covered many acres and housed many wonders of the world, industrial and cultural, in the domes and pavilions and palaces that had been erected. One of the highlights for both men had been hearing a new Strauss waltz called "The Blue Danube" performed for the first time and conducted by the maestro himself. There was also talk on a more sombre note of the attempted assassination of the Tsar of Russia during his visit to Paris for the exposition. He had escaped unharmed, but it had been an incident of acute embarrassment to the Emperor and Empress. But even worse for them had been the news of the execution of Maximilian in Mexico, bringing personal grief and the end of the French influence in that part of the world. Mr. Allenby recounted how Worth had delivered a dress of palest yellow to the Empress shortly after the dreadful communication had been received.

"It was Alençon lace over heavy silk with a train yards long. I saw it myself before it left the rue de la Paix, and would have no hesitation in saying that it was surely the handsomest dress ever made. Worth said that in spite of her sadness the Empress gave a delighted exclamation at the sight of it, but she was too grief-stricken to think of wearing it to the distribution of the exposition prizes for which it had been designed. I doubt now if it will ever be worn. It would remind her too much of that terrible event in Mexico."

Louise could imagine that lovely gown disappearing up into the ceiling on the dressing-room lift, never to be seen again. Was nothing to go right for the Empress any more?

A little later in the drawing-room, when coffee was being served, Mr. Allenby, who was seated beside Louise on the sofa, took from his pocket a folded piece of tissue paper. Unwrapping it carefully he revealed a number of pressed violets.

"When Worth was checking the Empress's final appearance before she left for another exposition engagement," he said, "she dropped a few violets from a bunch she was fastening at her waist. He picked them up and asked if he might give them to me as a memento." His wrinkled face became wreathed in smiles. "That gracious lady then gave Worth the whole bouquet of her favourite flowers, bidding him give them to me with her compliments. I wanted to share some of them with you, my lady of France."

Louise was charmed by his kind thought and his old-fashioned gallantry. "I'll keep them always," she said, gazing at the violets with pleasure.

Not long afterwards the evening came to an end and all the guests departed except Will, who remained in the drawing-room. When she returned from seeing the rest out she felt deeply tired. He had poured some cognac into a glass, which he held out to her.

"Drink this. It will do you good. The evening has been a tremendous strain on you."

Obediently she took a sip from the glass and set it aside as she sank down onto the sofa, her moiré taffeta skirt rustling into azure folds. "I hope the guests did not feel uncomfortable. I tried to sustain an agreeable atmosphere."

"So you did. I'd say that after the first few minutes nobody missed that husband of yours. How much longer are you going to put up with him, Louise?"

She glanced up at him uncertainly. "I'm not sure that I understand you."

"I'm talking about divorce."

Her face was bleak. "Do you imagine I haven't considered it? But it is out of the question."

"Why? Do you fear you could not meet the tremendous costs involved? I can help you there."

She closed her eyes and shook her head. "Robert would never allow me to divorce him. You must remember that Paul-Michel is not his child. I would be branded a scarlet woman and a guilty party before I stepped into court. Moreover, Paul-Michel has been legally adopted by him, which means he would have no hesitation in depriving me of my son. It is that threat and nothing else that stops me." Her voice quavered and she rose quickly to her feet as if by action she might retain her self-control.

Will watched her closely. "Are you saying that Robert loves you? Is that why he would never let you go?"

The cognac glass was on a side table where she had placed it, and she ran a fingertip nervously around the rim. "No. He has never loved me. I'm his workhorse, his beast of burden, his hewer of wood and drawer of water. With me to provide for him, not only will he never starve, but he knows he can expect to live in considerable comfort until the end of his days."

Will reached out and closed his large hand firmly about her arm as though to stay her from any escape. "Is that all to your marriage these days?"

She looked away. "You have no right to ask me such questions."

"I have every right. Have I not known you for many years? Have I not loved you for as long?"

He had not known he loved her until this minute. The knowledge exploded within him, filling his brain and swamping his heart, and suddenly, out of the most illogical of human emotions, there was reason for all that had bound his life with hers since that long-ago day when he heard her clear voice mimicking him in a crowded, sweat-heated Paris workroom. The image he had of that pert young face turning towards him in laughter focused into the same visage that had become even lovelier in womanhood, the eyes alarmed at the words he had just spoken, defenceless and exposed. His grip on her arm tightened, and he drew her to him.

It was a long time since she had seen adoration burn in a man's gaze. Even longer since she had been held in an embrace of love. Out of the chill of her wounded loneliness she felt drawn by his warmth as if to a light, and as he cupped her face lightly with his palm and gently stroked her skin, a kind of sensual languor threatened to overwhelm her, taking the strength from her knees, so that she felt she might have fallen if he had not been holding her locked against him. A tremor ran through her as he bent his head to kiss her throat, her eyelids drooping, and when he took her lips with his own she clung to him, yielding her mouth to his as he kissed her with the hunger of years, with all the yearning that had been buried deep in him without his being aware of its true origins.

"My love, my love," he whispered against her ear.

Slowly she lifted her head from his shoulder where it had come to rest, and took his face between both her hands, a sadness for him in her eyes. "Will, my dear. It can't be. It can't be."

Robert's voice cracked like a whip from the direction of the door, where he had been standing for the past minute or two. "I'm mightily glad to hear it. A gentleman doesn't much care to share his wife with every Tom, Dick, and Harry, don't you know!"

She had started convulsively at the sound of his voice, not with any misplaced sense of guilt, but with revulsion at the insidious intrusion. Her hands slipped down to alight on Will's shoulders. He covered them with his own, not having taken his eyes from her.

"Leave with me now," he urged. "Fetch Paul-Michel and come in the clothes you stand up in. We'll sort the legal tangle out later."

Robert gave an incredulous snort. "Damn you, Russell! Get out of my house!"

Louise answered Will as if they were still alone. "What you're asking is impossible. I've told you why. Nothing can be changed."

Robert stamped across the room and struck Louise away from Will with such vicious force that she staggered back. "I've had enough of this!" he spluttered in rage. "If you don't leave this instant I'll summon the servants to throw you out!"

Behind them Louise gave a sharp cry. Her skirt had swept out over the whitehot coals in the fireplace as she had saved herself from falling, and flames were leaping up the moiré taffeta. Will lunged forward and threw her to the ground, snatching the hearthrug and smothering it over the flaring fabric. Robert tore off his coat, and on his knees used it to help extinguish the flames. It was all over in a matter of seconds. She was shocked, but virtually unharmed, a small burn on her palm where instinctively she had beaten at the flames. A thankfulness went through Will's mind that the crinoline had gone out of fashion. Had she been trapped in hoops nothing could have saved her. Still on one knee he helped her sit up, his arm about her shoulders, but when he would have assisted her to her feet Robert leaned across her and shook a clenched fist under his nose.

"Leave my wife alone!" Robert's face was congested with his undiminished temper.

In a gust of wrath Will grabbed him by the throat. "Due to you Louise could have suffered fatal burns!" His grip tightened. "If ever you use violence on her again I swear I'll thrash you within an inch of your miserable life!"

Louise pulled at his arm, frantic at the choking noises that Robert was emitting. "Will! Stop! You'll strangle him!"

He released his hold with a thrust that sent Robert back onto his elbows. Then he helped Louise to stand. There was a charred gap in her skirt, and scorched petticoats revealed. "I'll take you up to your room. You can direct me."

Will picked her up in his arms, ignoring her protests, and carried her up the flight and along a landing into her bedroom. There he laid her on the bed. She was still extremely white, and shaking from the whole ordeal. He would have jerked the bell-pull for her maid, but she raised herself from the pillow.

"No. Not yet. I'd rather lie here quietly for a little while on my own."

"But that burn on your hand. It must be attended to." He had wrapped his own clean handkerchief about it.

She smiled faintly. "It's far less than any number of burns I had from hot pressing irons in my sewing days." Her eyes held his. "Thank you, Will. You've always been so good to me."

There came a tap on the open door. One of the younger and burlier manservants stood there, another with him. They both looked extremely uncomfortable. "Begging your pardon, ma'am. We've had instructions from the master to escort this gentleman from the house."

Will took Louise's hand up from the coverlet where it was lying, and held it for a moment. "I'll enquire how you are to-morrow."

He left the bedroom with the two menservants in his wake. As he crossed the landing, Paul-Michel came from another direction in his nightshirt, rubbing his eyes sleepily. "Is Papa home yet?" Then he saw Will, and his whole face lit up. "Hello, Mr. Russell. Have you come to the birthday dinner party?"

Will smiled at him, ruffling his hair. "It's late, and the dinner party ended long ago. You'd better get back to bed. Good night to you."

"Good night, sir."

Downstairs, Robert had poured himself a whisky, and he took a mouthful of it as he stood in the open doorway of the drawing-room to watch Will depart. His face was still blotchy with temper, and he addressed his servants in a voice that throbbed with it.

"Never admit that man to my house again!"

Will paused on the threshold and looked back over his shoulder, his eyes flinty cold and contemptuous. "Remember my warning, Prestbury. I meant what I said."

As the door closed after him, Robert swore savagely under his breath, emptied his glass at a toss, and went to pour himself another. The decanter clinked in a dance against the rim of the glass, and two maids, who were rolling up the scorched hearthrug and brushing up scattered ashes, glanced towards him curiously. He rounded on them.

"Good God! What are you gaping at? Clear out of my sight!"

They hurried away, taking the hearthrug with them. He gulped the new measure of whisky, and when he had reached the dregs he slammed the glass down with a force that cracked it. The scene he had witnessed between his wife and Russell was going over and over in his mind. How much had gone before to bring them to the point of kissing under his roof? When he had opened the door and seen them locked together in embrace he had been totally dumbfounded. It had been that reaction which had kept him silent long enough to gather his wits and wait for the right moment to alert them to his presence. And he had begun to seethe with a kind of frenzy that Louise, his own wife, should indulge in such behaviour. That he had long since gone his own way was beside the point. There had always been one set of rules for a man and another for a woman. Damn her! His vanity and conceit had been assailed, making it impossible to subdue the aggravation of his mood. In spite of what he had overheard when the kiss had ended, he could not be sure that she had kept her marriage vows. But he would find out!

He flung himself out of the drawing-room and took the stairs two at a time. When he reached the landing he found his path blocked by Paul-Michel, who had appeared wraith-like in the glow of the single gas-light left burning.

"What the hell do you want?" he snapped impatiently. "Get out of my way."

"Happy birthday, Papa. This is my present. I hope you like it."

A cane with an ivory handle carved into the head of a unicorn was being held out to him, a paper birthday bow adorning it. Robert did not stop to think that all day the child had waited for the giving of the gift. All he was conscious of was that he was being frustratingly delayed when he had no time for anything but a confrontation with his wife.

"Don't come with such rubbish to me!" He seized the cane, broke it in two over his knee, and hurled the pieces away from him into the shadows, not caring where they fell. Bursting into his wife's room, he slammed the door after him with a force that vibrated through the house.

Louise had just removed her ruined dress and was in her petticoats, the upper one trailing a torn, scorched frill. She looked startled at his coming, and he was not surprised. It was a long time since he had been in her room. Her listless submission after the removal of the lock from the doors had proved to be an effective nullifier of passionate desire. It had made him hate her.

"You little whore," he ground out. "You worthless little whore."

She stiffened sharply, distaste for him in her clear gaze. "You have no cause to use such an ill-chosen term to me."

"I happen to think I have. You and Russell have known each other a long time. For all I know he may well be the father of your bastard."

She could never endure for him to speak thus of her son, perhaps afraid that one day it might be said in his hearing. It was the weapon he had used against her before, and with savage satisfaction he saw he had spurred her to a fierce anger that matched his own raw mood.

"Think whatever you wish," she retorted, casting aside the dress she had been folding, "but you are far from the truth. Who fathered my son is something you have never known and never shall know."

He was standing by her dressing-table, and with an enraged sweep of his arm he sent everything on it smashing to the floor. "Full of secrets, aren't you? Well, the past doesn't matter a damn to me, but the present and the future do. How many times before tonight has Russell asked you to go away with him?"

"Never!"

"I don't believe you." He began to advance slowly towards her, a measured pace at a time. "Do you know, he threatened to use violence on me if ever I laid a rough hand on you again. He doesn't want the goods spoiled, I suppose."

"Stop saying such things!"

"It's no use playing the innocent with me." Into his grating voice there seeped a salacious undertone. "You've been lovers from the start, haven't you?"

"No!"

"That's why he helped you with your first business venture, isn't it? I see it all now. How often does he pleasure you, my dear wife? Three times a week? Four? Or does it depend on how often you're able to meet? Sometimes six days out of the seven?"

"I won't listen to any more!" Her eyes were blazing, the ivory mounds of her breasts rising and falling quickly above the rim of lace. "Your accusations come from your own warped imagination."

"You'll listen to whatever I choose to say!" The air was heady with the sensuous fragrance of French perfume arising from the smashed bottles, seeming to blend with his mounting lust. He saw her take a step back, becoming fearful of his inexorable approach towards her, and a dark excitement seared through him. "I want to know what favours you preferred from him. Nothing I can't better, I can tell you that!"

He made a rush at her, seeing she was bent on a bid for escape. His arm caught her about the throat and he flung her backwards onto the bed. She gasped and struggled wildly, trying to fight him off, but he was like a man demented, and when the lace split, spilling out her breast, he bit her hard, making her scream out with the pain of it. Sobbing, she tried to claw his face, but he pinioned her down, tearing at his own clothes to free himself for her. Then suddenly they were no longer alone in the room.

"What the devil—?" Robert expostulated in a roar.

An ivory-handled piece of cane was beating at him. To her horror she saw her young son's contorted face and as if in a nightmare heard his terrified shrieking. "You're killing my maman! You're killing my maman!"

Robert half-lifted himself, and with the full force of his hand against the child's chest sent him hurtling out of her range of vision. But she heard the sickening thud of his head and body against the wall. Powerless to rise under the weight of Robert's palm pressed down across her mouth, her flailing arm touched the splintered end of the cane that had fallen onto the bed. Her fingers closed around it, and as he turned back to her with eyes slitted like a maniac's, a new rage adding to his strength, she hit him across the face with the ivory handle and saw the flesh part. He gave an awful yell, clapping his hand to the gashed wound, the blood already spurting, and she pushed him from her, scrambling free.

With a cry she saw Paul-Michel lying flat with his head still propped at an angle against the wall, one limp arm outflung. He was deathly white and his eyes were closed. For the worst few moments of her life she thought he was dead, but as she dropped to her knees and gathered him into her arms she saw he was breathing. Scrambling to her feet, she ran from the room with him, calling to the servants.

"Fetch Dr. Perkins at once! At once!"

For five days Paul-Michel lay in a coma. Louise was constantly at his bedside. She had what little food she could eat served to her there on a tray, and at night she would have continued her vigil without respite if the doctor had not insisted that she share it with Nanny Daisy. But she still stayed in the adjoining room, barely dozing, and was awake and on her feet long before she needed to be. She did not see Robert, but the doctor had told her that he had had to put seven stitches in her husband's forehead, and his eyes were black as a result of the bruising. How much Robert had told Dr. Perkins she did not know, but it must have been obvious to him that a domestic quarrel of extreme violence had caused the injuries to which he was attending. She sent instructions to the shop, where Mademoiselle Brousseau was carrying on competently in her absence, and wrote to Will, telling him that Paul-Michel had suffered a fall, promising to keep him informed. For herself, she assured him that he had no cause for anxiety.

When Paul-Michel at last opened his eyes and knew her, she discovered to her intense relief that he had no recollection of how he came to be in bed with his head bandaged, and she blessed nature's way of healing. Dr. Perkins assured her that from now on her son would recover quickly, and advised her to get some fresh air and exercise. She combined both by going to the shop, where any number of matters had accumulated in her absence. She had decided not to give Will any details of Paul-Michel's accident, thinking that no good could come of it in view of the disastrous encounter between her husband and him, and he made no probing questions, accepting that boyhood was subject to minor accidents, and remarked that he himself had cracked his head when he had been about the same age. As to the relationship between Will and herself she found that it had changed irrevocably. It was no longer possible, except when discussing business, to keep the distance that she had previously maintained. If anything, there was less physical contact than before, when he had taken her by the arm or hand at times in escort, but his eyes held a perpetual warmth that he made no attempt to conceal from her, and more than ever she saw him as a rock in her life that would never change.

Robert did not go out by day all the time half his face was wrapped in bandages, and where he went by night she did not know. He did not speak to her, passing her on the stairs as if he did not see her, and Paul-Michel was treated the same way. Memory had returned to the child within a few hours of the smashing of the birthday cane, and he believed distractedly that the hostile silence being maintained was his fault, until Louise reassured him that it was the accident to Robert's face that was the cause of it. Nevertheless Paul-

Michel remained subdued, and Dr. Perkins, making a check on the boy, suggested a month at the seaside would do him good. Louise could not leave the shop, having launched her clothes for the autumn, so he went in the charge of Nanny Daisy to Brighton. Shortly after their departure Robert did speak once to Louise. She was at her bureau in the drawing-room early one evening, writing a letter to Marie and another to Paul-Michel, when he entered and came across to stand by her chair without a word. Puzzled, she looked up over her shoulder and then sprang to her feet in distress, knocking back her chair. He had removed the bandage from his face, and it was a gruesome sight. The wound with the ugly puckering of the stitches was still red and sore, stretching from the left side of the brow to the right cheekbone, both his eyes dark as bruised plums, a yellowing of skin below where lighter bruises were fading. He gave her a mirthless grin.

"Dr. Perkins is here to change my dressings. I thought I would give you a sight of the damage you wrought on me before the fresh bandages are applied." He seized the back of her neck and wrenched her forward, bringing her face within a few inches of his. "Take a closer look. There'll be a scar, you know. But it's an ill wind that blows nobody any good. I have wondered many times how I should fare in a little more than twelve years' time when Paul comes of age and is beyond my jurisdiction. My guess was that you'd leave me. Go back to France, perhaps? Now my mind is at rest. I know you'll stay. You see, I'll carry forever the proof of your wild-cat manner of refusal of my conjugal rights, which in itself is a criminal offence by a woman in the eyes of the law. If ever you should take it into your head to up and go, I'll bring that charge against you." He moved his thumb and squeezed her neck cruelly. "The courts give harsh sentences to rebel wives who fail in their duties, particularly those already stamped by their own immoral behaviour. I think that for Paul's sake you will wish to keep at bay any scandal that might ruin his chances in life."

She jerked herself away and rubbed the red imprints left on her neck to ease the pain. "Is there no end to your selfishness?"

"Call it what you like. I see it as a means of keeping a marriage intact." He was about to turn from her when he paused, his glance hardening. "Incidentally, I've decided that it's time for Paul to be sent away to school. He'll go to Fountleigh in Berkshire, which is my old school. You had better prepare him. The autumn term starts in three weeks' time."

She went down to Brighton to spend the last few days of her son's holiday with him. She found him suntanned and happy, eager to show her where he fished from the pier, how well he could swim, and how high he could build a sand castle. He received the news of going away to school quite stoically. All the boys he knew at home were going off to schools in different parts of the country sooner or later. He did not want to leave his maman or Nanny Daisy, but he would not be sorry to leave the London house and the man who made it such a hateful place to live in. At least he knew Robert Prestbury was not his real father. Once in a temper Robert had called him a bastard, and when he had asked what the name meant he had been told. He had never talked to his maman about it, but he had to Mr. Russell. He was able to ask Mr. Russell anything. They always talked man to man, and all sorts of mysteries had been explained to him in a way that showed him that they were not mysteries at all, only human nature. He was well prepared to go to school, but there had to be one proviso.

"Let me go to school in France. The one that Jean-Philippe and Gaston go to in Paris. I can live with Aunt Catherine and come home to you in the holidays."

Louise would have gladly agreed, knowing he would be happy in Paris with a second home at Suresnes, but with regret she had to shake her head.

"Papa would never allow it. He has made up his mind that it shall be Fountleigh, and nothing will change him."

Louise's heart sank when she took Paul-Michel to begin the term at Fountleigh School for the Sons of Gentlemen. It was a large, bleak building, reminding her of the terrible children's prison in Paris, and she did not believe that in food and discipline and comfort it would be very much different. She found it impossible to understand why the well-to-do English considered it essential to send their sons away from home at the most tender age. The headmaster was a sour-faced man, and Louise averted her eyes from the birch kept handy by his desk, aware that Paul-Michel had seen it too.

Outside in the forecourt the new boys were saying good-bye to their parents. She thought of Worth, who had been turned out to earn his own living at the age of eleven, and there was her son, still only nine years old, also compelled to turn his back on all that was dear to him. She had kissed and embraced him before they had left the hackney-cab, which was still waiting at the gates to take her back to the railway station. She had known that he would not want a display of maternal affection at this moment of parting. He spoke to her in French.

"Be brave, Maman." His own lower lip was tremulous.

"I will. It won't be so many weeks until we're together again at Christmas."

She kept her smile bright. At the gates she turned and waved to him, thinking how little and forlorn he looked. He waved back. Then she saw no more, her own tears blinding her as she stepped quickly into the cab.

In a matter of weeks Robert's face had healed well, although the etched line of a scar remained, a daily reminder to Louise of the renewed bondage into which she had been enthralled. He spoke to her whenever it was necessary, but otherwise they had no conversation, and since his assault on her he never came near her. How long such a state of affairs between them would continue she had no idea, but she had work to absorb her, and when she entertained, her guests were no longer surprised by her husband's absence. If he should be there he was always the charming host, which led all but those who knew him well to suppose that it was merely business that caused his absence at times.

Paul-Michel wrote dutiful letters in painstaking copperplate, that she knew were checked by one of his schoolmasters before they were posted, but she could read between the lines, and it came as no surprise when the first words he burst out upon his return home for the holidays was that he hated the school and everyone in it. Later it emerged that he had made some friends, but it was a friendship that came from misery shared rather than a natural linking up through common interests. He looked thin and wretched and had a bad cold, which was not helped by the punishment meted out by Robert for his poor school report. He had to stay in his room for a week on water and gruel, which only allowed him out just in time for Christmas Eve. He and Louise then went Christmas shopping together.

To her relief Robert had decided to spend the festive season at his mother's house, which left her free to take her son with her after church to Will's home, where they were welcomed most warmly, Will with great restraint giving her a light kiss under the mistletoe. When the gentle exchange was over he held her hand hard in speechless expression of how much it had meant to him.

Paul-Michel jumped with joy at the sight of the tree that almost touched the ceiling. It was alive with lighted candles and atwinkle with glass baubles of every hue, a stack of presents beneath the branches. The child actually walked backwards for part of the way to the dining-room, unable to take his excited gaze from the coloured parcels being left behind, for he had spotted his name on several of them. At table they sat down to roast goose and plum pudding and mince pies and frothy trifle and shimmering jelly amid a host of other delicacies. Afterwards came the present-giving, Paul-Michel being allowed the privilege of handing out the gifts to Will's servants: a pretty dress-length of silk for the women, tobacco and leather gloves for the men, with an extra week's wages for all. Then the three of them were alone for their own exchange of gifts. Somewhat to Louise's consternation her son had insisted on buying a cane for Will, its handle not all that different from the one that Robert had smashed across his knee. And she came as near to loving Will as was possible when he exclaimed with pleasure over it, saying he would use it every day, and he knew none with a better one. It was all the more to his credit since he knew nothing of what had happened to that other cane, and she saw by the quiet expression on her son's face that much sorrow had been erased for him. Her own gift from Will proved to be an amber pendant set in gold filigree. She let him fasten it around her neck.

"It's beautiful," she breathed, looking down at it.

"It's the colour of your eyes," he said softly against her ear. She thought it the finest of compliments.

The day ended with the gas-light extinguished while they played snap-dragons together, picking out plump raisins from ignited brandy that illuminated their laughing faces with a blue glow. Paul-Michel dozed in the carriage on the way home, his head against his mother's shoulder.

She thought it sad that Will had not married again. The house he lived in should have been filled that day with the merriment of his own children, not just that of the son of the woman for whom he cherished an unrequited love. Yet if fate had not spun its devious webs, entangling him with Ellen and herself with Pierre, it might well have been that they would have come to love each other with the same measure of passion. Instead, Pierre was still the only man in her heart.

22

At the end of each holiday it became harder and harder for Paul-Michel to face going back to Fountleigh. He would not have found his lessons difficult if he had applied his mind to them, being highly intelligent and having inherited his mother's diligence, but from the first day the initiative and interest that had flourished under the teaching of his tutors at home seemed to drain from him as if the chill of the stone walls and the bleakness of the dormitories had entered into his very soul. Morever, he despised the injustices that he witnessed, the bullying that was rampant, the birching and the indignities. Most of all he resented not going to school in France. In spite of his English surname he felt as French as his mother and another term had hardly started when he fell into disgrace by bursting into uncontrollable giggles at the mispronunciations and lead-like accent of the master teaching French. The more he was shouted at to be silent, the cane slashing across his fingers each time, the more he giggled, no longer finding it funny, but unable to stop. He giggled on throughout the terrible birching inflicted by the headmaster, the relentless sound coming unbidden from his throat until he collapsed on the floor in a faint from the pain, blood seeping from his flesh. When he recovered he made up his mind to run away.

Louise had never been busier. The rush of orders for debutantes' presentation dresses had increased a hundredfold. She felt sometimes as if she were moving in an ocean of white silk and lace, the froth on the waves of it represented by the abundance of veiling, which would eventually be divided up to drift from many sets of soft white feathers, emblem of the Prince of Wales, with which each young head was adorned. By the same rules laid down by the court, all the bodices were low-cut with short sleeves and had to be of the same white silk as the skirt, the train no less than three and a half yards long and not more than four, but Louise found it an exciting challenge to design to these stipulations, knowing that each one of her clients could go off to the court of St. James's, where the presentations were still held, in the knowledge that her dress was not like another's. In Louise's opinion the new Paris line was the most graceful yet, with all the fulness concentrated over a pad at the back, owing its origins to Worth's gathering up of the overskirt in the folds inspired by the action of the peasant woman, and which now flowed to the rear like a peacock's tail. Equally new was the fashion for wearing curls on the forehead. Worth had persuaded Marie to cut a fringe and curl it one evening when she was going to the opera, and within days it was being copied in Paris, and had now spread to England and everywhere else in the Western world. Louise glanced in the looking-glass. She had adopted the style herself, and it suited her.

She often thought that the debutantes' fever of excitement and high-pitched delight over her dresses in the fitting-rooms would have powered a steam locomotive from John o' Groat's to Lands End. There were also heated squabbles between the debutantes and their mammas, who always came with them, tears and hysterics and frequently a swoon, which was inevitable when stays were tight enough to crack ribs and nothing on earth would have persuaded the wearer to loosen them. It often needed all Louise's tact and gentle persuasion to ease a fraught situation, and Mademoiselle Brousseau was equally adept, never without a bottle of smelling-salts in her pocket and a calming smile on her lips.

Those girls whose health was considered to be delicate were allowed on a doctor's letter to cover their arms and shoulders, but without exception this was only enforced by particularly anxious parents, while their daughters were willing to risk pneumonia to expose their shoulders and a discreet amount of bosom on such an auspicious occasion. Louise mediated by designing the prettiest sleeves and high necklines possible, which dried many a tear, but it was far more difficult to settle the debutante who was in mourning, which meant black from head to foot, even to the plumes. Frequently it was hard to tell at first if a listless, red-eyed girl arriving at the shop clad in black crape had suffered a close bereavement or was merely weeping for her own personal misfortune, while those who came with resentful mouths and high spots of angry colour in their cheeks were no less difficult to soothe, ready to reject everything out of hand because the demise of a distant cousin or a relative often unknown to them had thwarted their great day. Louise was dealing with a particularly tempestuous debutante in this state of mind when she was told that her husband was in her office and wished to see her most urgently.

"Tell Mr. Prestbury that I'll be there as soon as I can," she replied, not at all pleased. Robert had become exceptionally aggressive of late, and his habit of chewing his lip almost incessantly had returned, showing he had something on his mind, which was also confirmed by his frequent turning to the decanter to refill his glass. Being in his cups when he returned from a night out had always been common enough, but at home he had never done more than imbibe moderately, and was far from being a drunkard. When at last she was able to leave her client to the fitter, she hastened to her office. Robert, who was pacing the floor, turned on her in a fever of heated annoyance.

"My God! You took your time!"

"I'm extremely busy this morning. What has brought you here?"

He stubbed out a half-smoked cigarette, crushing it down. "I need some money urgently."

She thought that he looked anything but a man with empty pockets, his Savile Row frockcoat smoothly perfect over his broad shoulders, his waistcoat without a wrinkle, his tall silk hat, which he had not bothered to remove, agleam in its fine nap. Opening a drawer, she took out her purse.

"I have about fifteen pounds. Is that enough?"

He crashed a fist down on her desk, making the papers fly. "Dammit! No! I need five thousand now and more later!"

She stared at him incredulously. Many a time she had settled bills for him, usually for his clothes, sometimes for extravagant purchases beyond his own funds. Subsidising his income from Prestbury's was something she had been prepared to shoulder for the rest of their time together, knowing he would never be able to manage on his own, but as far as she knew, nothing had been oustanding, and five thousand pounds was an enormous sum.

"Whatever do you need so much for?" she exclaimed.

He continued his agitated pacing. "My creditors are dunning me. I owe money everywhere. I have just had a deucedly unpleasant encounter with someone I was unable to avoid. I tell you that you must help me out or I'll end up in prison for debt and you'll find the bailiffs moving into the house."

She was still bewildered. "How did you get in such a fix in the first place?"

He scowled at her, his mouth twisted unpleasantly. "That's it. Demand your pound of flesh before you let me see the colour of your money. All right, I'll tell you. I've been playing the horses. That's where fortunes are made these days. I had a run of good luck for a while, but during this past year it's been different. If you must know, I haven't enough to pay the wages at the shop next Friday, and the bank is threatening to foreclose there anyway."

"You have borrowed on Prestbury's?" She despaired at his improvidence. Always she had feared he would be swept into desperate straits, but had not imagined it would come so soon or without some warning through which he might be rescued.

"Yes, I've mortgaged it. Up to the hilt."

She passed a hand wearily across her forehead. So he faced his nemesis at last. "How much do you owe altogether?"

He did some reckoning and astounded her with the amount. As she shook her head, his expression became more belligerent. "Don't pretend you haven't got it or can't raise it, because I know you can. This business on its own is a goldmine with the prices that you charge."

She knew what the future would be if she gave in to his demands unconditionally. He would continue along his self-indulgent path, incurring further debts and liabilities until every penny was drained away even as it came in. All her hard work and long days would be for nothing until in the end she would be as bankrupt as he, unable to sustain any longer the creative business that she loved. She rested her spread fingers on the desk in front of her to steady their trembling. "Subject to your agreeing to a legal separation between us and forfeiting all control over Paul-Michel now and in the future you shall have your five thousand—"

"You're out of your mind! I'll never agree to that."

She continued as if he had not spoken. "To help bridge your debts our home and its contents shall be sold, together with the horses and carriages. I'll ask Will Russell to purchase Prestbury's at a fair price, no advantage being taken of its financial decline, which will clear you with the bank and leave something in hand."

He interrupted, maddened that she should continue to lay down terms. "I've no intention of letting either the house or Prestbury's be sold! You can draw on the business here to provide what I need."

She took a deep breath. "That's not possible."

"What do you mean? All London knows it's a roaring success."

"I mean that officially I'm not at liberty to dispose of its income, and I intend to invoke that protection. It was made against just such a contingency as you have created."

"I don't understand you."

"The business is mine by a certain arrangement, just as Prestbury's would be mine after Will purchases it out of my returns from the material import department at the factory. There again I have no agreement relating to our partnership, but on the surface I'm no part of it."

His mouth fell open. "You have entrusted your interests and your fortune to a complete outsider!"

She corrected him. "I have put Paul-Michel's future and my own into a trusted friend's hands. I have always known that one day you might try to sap my livelihood for your own ends, and also I had to be sure that if anything happened to me you wouldn't fritter away the dressmaking business to nothing before Paul-Michel came of age, leaving him penniless. It also meant security for him in another way, because you would not have kept him at Fountleigh or anywhere else for a single day once he became your sole responsibility. The only reason you sent him to your old school was that you were aware of its wretched conditions and wished to ensure Paul-Michel's misery as well as mine." She tossed her head. "All that shall end now. I want my son back. I'll put him into a good school of my own choice." Her palm slammed down on the bell on her desk with sustained pressure. "And at long last I will be free."

If she had not rung the bell when she did he would have used physical violence against her. She had seen it coming in the temper that consumed him, his jaw throbbing, his brows drawn savagely together, but the door opened almost instantly, keeping him at bay as the clerk from the outer office entered.

"I'm going to my lawyers with Mr. Prestbury," she informed the man, taking her cape from the cupboard. He darted forward to put it about her shoulders. "Tell Mademoiselle Brousseau that I expect to be gone for quite a while."

"Certainly, Madame Louise. I'll see that a cab is summoned right away."

She skewered on her little hat, which perched forward on her head, allowing fashionable display of the chignon. Robert, with nostrils flaring and hands clenched, accompanied her down the stairs and thrust himself first into the cab without assisting her.

At the lawyers' everything was put into motion. The separation should go through its legal formalities without undue delay. Had she pressed for a divorce it would have been a different matter, the ponderous and complicated procedure always exhausting time, money, and patience, although she agreed to give Robert his freedom if he should wish to marry again at any time in the future. For herself, she had no such plans. Robert undertook that upon the final settlement of his debts he would make no further claims against her. She drew up the draft on the bank for him to receive his five thousand pounds. He took it from her with ill grace, sullen and bitter-lipped, not meeting her eyes, and in spite of everything she found herself able to pity him, her capacity to forgive coming from the affection she had once felt for him.

As he hastened away to the bank he was already working out how to cushion matters to a certain extent. After the house was sold he would return to living at home, where at least he would have a comfortable standard of living without any financial outlay. His mother had begun to ail, keeping to her bedroom most of the day, and much of the sting had gone out of her. He thought her days numbered, and after she was gone his slow-witted sister would come to rely on him to manage her finances. Prospects were less disagreeable than had first appeared, but lust for vengeance against Louise was high in him. He had never thought she would slip from his fingers.

Left on her own with the lawyers, Louise was advised to do nothing that might prejudice her case when it came to court. Separation hearings were always extremely tricky, judges being particularly reluctant to set husband and wife legally apart, marriage vows having been taken for better or worse, and she must not act rashly. Her first thought of fetching Paul-Michel away from Fountleigh without delay could appear to be going against her husband's good intentions of having the boy suitably educated, and on no account must she move out of the house until it was sold; otherwise an interpretation of desertion and waywardness might be put upon it.

She felt enervated by the harrowing strain of it all as she returned to the shop, and also exasperated that every move any woman made was weighed against her husband's dominant rights. During the next few weeks she must tread the tightrope lightly. Although she longed to tell Paul-Michel of his forthcoming liberation, she dared not. One excited word from him to another, and there could be an inquiring letter to Robert from the headmaster. Never had she longed so for time to pass more quickly.

Robert was alone at home one afternoon when an anxious young junior master arrived from Fountleigh.

"I have the most serious news to impart, Mr. Prestbury," the young man began, twisting his hat round and round by the brim. "Your son has run away from school. He went in the night. His absence was not discovered until this morning. The police have been alerted and a search is going on." He thought the father seemed singularly unmoved. "There is every possibility that the boy will try to reach home, and if he should arrive here by some means, the headmaster wishes to be notified immediately."

"If he turns up on this doorstep," Robert answered coldly, "I'll see that he is returned to Fountleigh by the next train."

Louise was extremely tired when she arrived home. She was in the final throes of last fittings for the debutantes, whose excitement had risen at the news that the Queen herself would be there to receive a good number of them before leaving Princess Alexandra to take over. It meant great competition to be first there, and the line of carriages that always stretched up St. James's Street into Piccadilly would start to block the traffic earlier than ever when the day arrived. Robert called to her from the drawing-room as he refilled a glass.

"Your son has absconded from Fountleigh. God knows where the ungrateful little wretch is now."

She was shattered by the news, and outraged that Robert

had waited from early afternoon until this evening hour to let her know. She was further dismayed that he had asked no questions and discovered no details as to how it had come about.

"I'm going to Fountleigh myself!" she exclaimed. "I'll find out everything. There'll be an evening train."

She ran upstairs to her room, summoning her maid to her assistance. Within ten minutes she was being driven to the railway station. Robert, who planned to go out himself that evening, made his own leisurely way up the flight, and as he passed his wife's room he glanced into it. Her maid was hanging away the elegant black dress that Louise had worn that day at the shop, and her reticule lay on the dressing-table, the contents spread where she had caught up in haste whatever she had needed to take with her. He wondered if she had left any money. Casually he strolled into the room and cast his eye over what lay there. A lace-edged handkerchief, a ring of keys, a box of rouge, and a tortoiseshell comb. Her purse had gone with her, but half a dozen sovereigns had spilled out in her rush.

He did not touch anything then. Later, when the maid had left the room, he went back. The contents of the reticule had been tidily replaced, but he helped himself to the gold coins before turning to Louise's jewel-case. Ahead of him that evening lay the disagreeable prospect, somewhat faint-heartedly delayed, of informing his mistress that he could no longer afford her undivided favours, and a little sweetener in the shape of a piece of jewellery might help to diminish a scene. His mood was edgy and taut as it always was when he had to face something he would have preferred to avoid, and the amount of drink he had imbibed in the drawing-room had done nothing to lift his gloom. Lily Ashcroft would not be easy to handle. She had developed expensive tastes since he had first set her up in comfortable accommodation after Louise's dismissal of her from Prestbury's, a slight that she had never forgotten or forgiven. He did not have any affection for Lily, but her doll-like looks combined with her basic coarseness had appealed to him from the start. He would miss her along with everything else he was having to sacrifice, and Louise was entirely to blame.

Impatiently he raked about in the jewel-case. Louise preferred simple pieces to set off her clothes, nothing quite suited to Lily's more flamboyant taste, but he picked out a diamond brooch that he knew to have value, which should help to soothe his temperamental paramour. He wondered if there was anything else he could give her at no financial outlay to himself, and then he remembered the keys in Louise's reticule. Taking them out, he weighed them contemplatively in his palm for a moment or two before pocketing them quickly.

Lily was not in the best of moods when he arrived. She had thought he would be there earlier and had anticipated being taken to a recently opened music hall that she had heard about. It would not have been too late yet, but with Robert it was always bed first wherever they went, and invariably the same procedure afterwards if he was not too drunk. If she was tired or simply wanted to be rid of him for reasons of her own, she would encourage him to drink heavily, thankful enough when he remained slumped in the cab after she had alighted, and was driven off home. Her first impression had been of his avaricious nature and she had never had cause to change it, although he would spend lavishly when out to enjoy himself, and she could not complain of the standard of living at which she was maintained.

"You're late," she told him sulkily, spoiling for a fight.

He almost replied with the old adage that it was better to be late than never to appear, but it was not the time to tell her yet. "We've the whole night," he said instead, "and I have one or two surprises up my sleeve."

She was intrigued. She loved nice surprises. The first one came when he told her to close her eyes, and a moment later she was able to discern a play of light dazzling against her eyelids. Opening them, she saw him holding a diamond brooch to reflect the lamp-rays, and she gave a shriek of delight at the costliness of it if not at its delicate design.

"Ooo! It's lovely. Give it here!"

She wore it pinned to the bodice of her evening dress, and where she sat in the fancy place that he had taken her to, all smarming waiters and popping champagne corks, the sparkle of the diamonds was reflected in the silver cutlery, in the curve of the rose bowl on the table, and in a tall mirror on a distant wall. But it was not her birthday, and since he never gave something for nothing she wondered what was up, and her distrust of him returned, making her less amiable than appeared on the surface. Better to get him drunk and be on the safe side, because there was always the chance that he was plotting a surprise that wouldn't be to her liking. He was a bit strange in his desires at times.

"Let's have more champagne," she said, emptying her glass.

He complied, already far in his cups, and did not notice that she only sipped where he drank deeply. She had the uncanny feeling of being at a special occasion without knowing the origins of it. For once champagne was having a reverse effect on her, not inducing jollity, but allowing her mind to become clearer and colder and more detached, her suspicion of him alert and watchful. After a while he took a ring of keys out of his pocket and laid it on the damask cloth. His speech was getting slurred, his grin a trifle foolish.

"See those, my prett' Lily? They're keys to a wardrobe. A whole new wardrobe for you. I'm going to take you to it."

Out in the cool night air he reeled a little at its effect on all he had drunk, but her curious plane of thought persisted, giving her a kind of iron precision in all her movements. In Little Argyll Street he made her get out of the cab and dismissed it. She looked about nervously, seeing that they had arrived outside his wife's shop, which was closed and in darkness. She covered her brooch with her evening shawl. There were people about, but that did not always prevent attack by thugs and robbers, for which the streets at night were notorious. In the dark entrance he unlocked the door with one of the keys.

"What's all this about?" she questioned sharply.

He simply pushed her into the premises ahead of him and bolted the door after them. Lighting a match he led her up the stairs to the first floor, where he struck more matches and put flames to the gas-mantles in the fluted globes. As the showroom became lighter, all the dresses on display stands broke forth into combinations of the jewel colours for which Madame Louise had become known. Robert wheeled about and threw his arms wide expansively.

"Help yourself, Lily. Anythin' you like is yours."

She could not believe her good fortune. "D'you mean it? Really? What's your wife going to say?"

He replied pithily as to how much his wife's opinion mattered to him. "Louise and I are separatin.' I should nev' have married her. Damn bad mistake."

She shared his opinion. "What about this dress business?" she probed, thinking that if his wife was chucked out of it, she might get herself installed.

"It's hers and it'll stay hers." He made a derisive sweep of his arm that almost unbalanced him. "But until I throw back these keys at her you can empty the place of dresses as far as I'm concerned. It'll be her loss, not mine."

Unease still niggled at her. "Suppose she turns nasty and accuses me of stealing the stuff?"

"How can she? For one thing, she knows nothin' of wha's been 'tween you and me. As far as she's concerned, I haven't set eyes on you since the day she gave you the boot. I'll tell her I gave the dresses to a lady of my acquaintance, and she can do damn all about it. Nobody'll ever know you've been here."

"Cor! You're a one." Her tone did not support the levity of her exclamation, her assessing eyes directed with full interest at last towards the garments. Yet she was still wary as an alley cat, her light tread very similar as she approached the nearest dress, but as soon as she handled the rich fabric, excitement took complete possession of her. She began to fumble frantically with the hooks at the back of her waist. "Undo me! Give me a hand!"

For a while he helped her in and out of the dresses, but he was becoming increasingly clumsy, and finally he collapsed in one of the chairs, sprawling his long legs out in front of him. With the slow actions of the very drunk he took a cigar from its case and lit it. Letting his head head fall back to rest against the striped upholstery, he gave himself up to smoking it.

Lily darted hither and thither in her petticoats, leaving the dresses in glowing heaps on the floor where she had discarded them, only those of her choice being laid across a chair. She discovered more dresses in other showrooms upstairs, and continued to leave a trail of garments in her wake. Then she opened one door and gave a gasp at all that shimmered there. She put a match to the gas-mantle and then felt she had stumbled into the whiteness of a cloud. Dozens of exquisite white dresses on support figures lined the room, white linen spread under each, the handsome trains suspended by special hooks, and on a shelf above each a set of feathers wafted slightly in the draught that she had caused. Slowly she traversed the room, looking at them. There was nothing there for her, but even at such a time she was enthralled by the exquisite embroidery, the tiny flowerets of lace, the touch of swansdown, and the sheen of woven ribbons. All these dresses for the high and mighty on their special day had been created by that spiteful bitch who had kicked her out of Prestbury's just when she had been getting an upper hand over the other girls and had fancied being made a manageress. It wasn't all honey being tied to Robert's whims, and at times of misery and depression she was convinced she would have risen to important heights in a really big store like Swan and Edgar's or Marshall and Snelgrove's if only her chances hadn't been thwarted by that untimely dismissal. She would have liked to have gained a hold on this fine place, but that gutless Robert was letting the foreign woman get away with it. Under the force of her jealousy and self-pity, her fingers, which were handling the soft flow of a pearl-sewn skirt, began to needle sharp nails into the fabric. There was a satisfying rip, and a few pearls, released by the snapped thread, bounced off across the floor. She began to breathe deeply, and gripping the torn edges with both hands she split the length of the skirt down to the hem, then roughly she yanked at a sleeve, parting it from the bodice, and was impatient at the exertion needed to snap the tiny stitches until she remembered the scissors she had seen in a workroom on the same floor. Within moments she had returned with them, and she set to work swiftly and with devastating effect. A kind of sensual exultation accompanied the destruction, and she could not have stopped even if she had wished it until all was done.

Robert awoke blearily when she shook him by the shoulder. "Go and find a cab," she instructed. "I'm ready to leave."

He was beyond helping her with the dresses, and she had to make two trips from the shop to the cab after bundling him into a seat. It was she who turned out the lights and locked the shop door before getting in beside him. He pawed at her when she shoved the keys back in his pocket, but she pushed him away, wanting to gloat over her spoils, and he fell back helplessly.

"Tha's no way to show gratitude for a memento," he growled truculently, trying to heave himself up and failing, no strength in his legs. "I coulda left you with nothin'."

She glanced at him with a frown. "What do you mean?"

Still with limbs sprawled in disarray, he managed to wag a swerving finger at her. "Wha' I say. Can' pay your bills any more. I'm skint. Your pickin's t'night make final payment."

"Are you ditching me?" she demanded incredulously.

"No choice o' mine. Got to. In debt, y'see. Louise settlin' up." With effort he made to point at her brooch and lurched forward, propelled by the movement of the cab, his finger jabbing hard against it. "Tha's worth 'nough to bring you in a bit."

She shoved him back again, understanding at last what had been behind his odd attitude the whole evening, and she clutched the brooch protectively. "I'm not selling the best piece you've ever given me." A glint of realisation showed in her narrowed eyes. "But you didn't buy it, did you? I thought it too good to be true. Your wife's, wasn't it? My God, Robert! You're a miserable worm."

He was past responding to insults. "You'll have to sell it. Rent owin'."

"What?" She was horrified. He had slumped back and appeared to be on the point of slipping into a drunken stupor. She grabbed him by the silk lapels of his evening coat and shook him. "How much rent is owing? How long since you paid the landlord? One week? One month? Longer?"

"Long time," he muttered, chin sinking down onto his chest. "Long, long time."

She shook him again, beside herself. "What about the grocer? The butcher? My milliner?"

He blinked at her. "Sell th' brooch. Only way."

She screamed her outrage, pounding at him with her fists. "You sneaking bastard! I could kill you! I always knew you were a rotter through and through." She broke forth into the foulest terms that came into her head, sobbing dry tears of fury, he lying with his eyes closed, trying to wave aside her battering much as if he were being troubled by a fly. She became inflamed beyond endurance, her voice rising to a shriek as she fumbled at the cab door. "You get out! You get out of my sight and never come near me again!" The door swung wide. The horses were going at a moderate pace, but if they had been racing at full pelt she would have acted in the same way. Seizing him with all her strength, screaming at him as if demented, she dragged him to his feet, he somehow gathering it was time to alight. The cabby, hearing the commotion, hauled on the reins and jumped down from the box in time to break Robert's fall as she pushed him through the door. Staggering a step back under Robert's weight, the cabby set him away at arms' length, holding him until he regained some balance, swaying on his feet.

"Awright, guvnor?" the cabby queried. Then he looked up under bushy ehebrows at his female passenger, summing her up accurately enough. "You getting out too?"

"No, I'm not." She slammed the door shut. "Carry on."

As the cab drew away she glanced back once. Robert appeared to have gathered his wits and was stumbling in the wake of the wheels, shouting to her to come back. Then the cab turned the corner and he was swallowed up in the darkness. Something rolled against her foot. She saw it was his sword-stick, forgotten in the foray. Snatching it up, she hurled it out of the window and heard it strike against a wall somewhere far out of sight.

In spite of her seething anger she had not gone much farther before she recalled the enormity of the damage she had wreaked at the shop, and realised that by her impetuous treatment of Robert she could no longer rely on him not to denounce her. Rapping for the cabby's attention, she told him to return to pick up the gentleman after all. The route was retraced, but Robert was not to be seen, having most probably hailed another cab to take him home.

She knew then that she would have to dispose of the beautiful dresses. She dared not risk being found with them. They and the brooch would have to be sold in the right quarters as soon as it was dawn. Only then would she be able to deny any knowledge of them, or that she had ever set foot in the shop in Little Argyll Street.

Louise returned to London by an early milk-train. Paul-Michel had not been found, and at Fountleigh the headmaster had informed her that he was a difficult, rebellious child who had more than deserved the canings and the birching for insolence that he had recently received. It confirmed to her that it had been no other cause than sheer misery that had made her son run away, and when he was found he should never return to the brutal place.

Her hopes that by some miracle he would have come home in her absence were dispelled at once by the anxious inquiry of the servant who opened the door to her. She wrote a note to Will and despatched it by hand before going upstairs to bathe and change out of her travelling clothes. He arrived when she was putting the last hairpin into her re-dressed hair, and she hastened downstairs to intervene in the argument raised by the manservant forbidding him entrance on the orders that Robert had once laid down.

"How good of you to come," she exclaimed gratefully. "And at such an early hour."

Will gave her a smile. "You know I'll do whatever I can."

"You shall have breakfast first." She led the way into the morning-room, where the aroma of good French coffee awaited them. He ignored her protest that she could eat nothing, and set a brioche and apricot conserve in front of her, which he knew would tempt her appetite more than the array of English dishes set out on the sideboard.

"You had better tell me all that Paul-Michel ever said about the school," he said, helping himself substantially, "and if he had any friends with whom he might have taken refuge."

Her tired eyes widened. "But he would come home first."

Will seated himself opposite her and unfolded his linen napkin. "I'm sorry to have to say it, but I doubt that very much. He could not look for escape in this house. He would know what your husband's reaction would be."

She became so crestfallen that her head drooped. "I know no one who would not return him to the school or to this house immediately."

"Perhaps you are mistaken. I want you to talk about Paul-Michel. Just anything that comes into your head. Maybe I can slot it in with all he's ever said to me, and between us we might get some clue where to look for him."

It was a release for her and a genuine aid to him. Before he left the house he made no promises of any quick reappearance with Paul-Michel. He just bade her keep a good heart and go about her daily routine as best she could.

She could not find her keys when she was ready to leave for the shop, although her maid and Nanny Daisy helped her search high and low. Everything seemed destined to add to her present distress.

"When my husband wakes, ask him if he has seen them anywhere," she said to Nanny Daisy. Then she clutched the girl's hands in desperation. "And remember, send one of the grooms on the fastest horse to me if Paul-Michel should return."

"Never fear, ma'am," Nanny Daisy replied emotionally.

Mademoiselle Brousseau also had a set of keys, and she arrived first at the shop that morning, and opened up. Louise, having been delayed, arrived to find the shop in a turmoil, her trusted assistant full of the robbery of a number of dresses.

"What of the debutantes' dresses?" Louise demanded, cutting across the gasped account. "Have any of those been taken?"

"I haven't looked there yet, madame."

Louise rushed up each curving flight of stairs, fearful of

what she might find. The main bulk of the dresses had been delivered, but those that were left needed final fittings or minor adjustments. She was met by a sight worse than anything she could possibly have expected. In stunned silence she touched each ruined dress in turn, white beads and tiny pearls and little petals of white jet crunching underfoot. Behind her she heard Mademoiselle Brousseau arrive breathless from the stairs and begin to wail in lament. She addressed the woman without turning around, her voice toneless.

"How long since you sent for the police?"

"Just a second before you arrived, madame."

"Then we have a few minutes in which to remove all evidence of robbery on the other floors. On no account must the police be allowed in here." Louise spun about, full of action again. "If a newspaper should report my apparent neglect in allowing this to happen, I'd be ruined!"

Between them they rounded up every assistant and sewing-hand to tidy the place and get the dresses back onto the stands. As Louise worked with them she tried to think what kind of thief it was who would try on dresses before making a selection, and then slash a particular section of the most valuable. The last crumpled fold on a hem was being smoothed out when the police constable arrived with the girl who had been sent to fetch the law. Louise greeted him with a smile.

"I'm afraid you have been called in error," she said calmly. "There was rather a mess here this morning through somebody's carelessness. As you see, everything is in order again."

The constable's private opinion was that women were foolish enough to jump to any conclusion if not properly supervised, and it was not long before Louise was able to get rid of him. It was still not time to open the shop for the working day, and she gathered all her staff, assistants and sewing-hands alike, into one of the upper salons. She told them what she had found and stressed the need to keep it secret.

"Your livelihood is at stake, and so is mine," she informed them crisply. "If we fail to deliver these court dresses on time no debutante will ever come to this shop again, and it will damage the reputation of the business beyond repair. We have to replace those ruined dresses within fifteen days."

There was a chorus of protest. Mademoiselle Brousseau spoke for the staff. "Even if we all worked night and day it would be a physical impossibility, madame. All that embroidery! All that beadwork! It's such specialised work."

"It can be done," Louise replied, "with extra hands. And I know where to get the best of them to help us. I'm sending to France. In the meantime we'll start cutting from scratch again."

A frenzy of activity was set into motion. All in the business were used to long and hectic hours on the eve of the season and at other times of the year when fashion took a change, but it was a Herculean task that lay ahead of Louise and those she employed. After sending a fast postal despatch to both Worth and Catherine, Louise set to at the cutting-table, taking up the work side by side with those whom she had with time appointed to ease that task from her. As she worked, her mind was linked with Paul-Michel, her anxiety ever increasing as hour by hour went by with no word either from the house or from Will.

During the morning she had the locks changed. As there was no sign of a break-in, she was certain that somewhere she had dropped her keys, perhaps upon leaving the shop, and the mysterious thief had seen it happen, securing the keys to return later. By the close of the afternoon she had taken on a number of seamstresses presently unemployed and recommended by her own hands. Her work force was growing.

She went home for a short while after dusk. No word of her missing son awaited her, and she discovered that Robert had not returned home from the previous evening. It had happened so often before that she merely nodded at the information, and went back to the shop after snatching a bite to eat. She sent her workers home at midnight, and did manage some sleep in her own bed through sheer exhaustion. At five o'clock next morning she was back at the cutting-table when her sewing-hands began to reappear on the premises.

The day passed the same as before. Robert continued to stay away from the house. It was early in the morning of the third day that a diversion occurred in the arrival of the French sewing contingent in cabs from London Bridge Station. To Louise's delight and astonishment Catherine was among them. She threw herself into her old friend's ample arms, and knew the first comfort since the tearing anguish of Paul-Michel's disappearance had begun to rack her throughout every minute of every day.

"I never imagined that you'd come," Louise cried as they drew apart. "I just thought you would send me the best workers you could find."

"So I have, and so did Monsieur Worth," Catherine replied merrily, all eyes for the shop and full of approval. "He has spared you some of his own top embroiderers." Then she took another look at Louise, her expression changing. "You look dreadful. All to pieces."

Louise escaped any explanation about Paul-Michel at that time, organising the Frenchwomen into their various tasks and inviting them first to partake of a meal awaiting them in a kitchen where food was always prepared for her workers. Before long every new arrival was busy with a needle, Catherine's fingers not too stiff to make stitches as fine if not so speedy as in the old days.

A small hotel was accommodating the Frenchwomen, all except Catherine, who went home with Louise. Then, breaking down, Louise told her about Paul-Michel's disappearance. Catherine, who had been yearning to see the boy, found it hard to keep up her courage and cheer Louise, but she did her best. Nevetheless they were a distraught couple, and when Louise was informed that her husband was still absent, she began to feel concern. An inquiry sent to his mother's home drew a blank. He was not there. She waited one more day, and then informed the police. At the same time a manservant was sent to make a round of the hospitals, but no Robert Prestbury was listed as a patient.

Louise felt she would never have lived through those days if it had not been for the intense pressure of work that kept her and everyone else working like automata. Whenever she could spare time from the shop she was in the workroom, sewing side by side with Catherine as in the old days. To her it seemed that her life was taking a full circle, and she was coming back to where she started. It was almost as if she was being drawn to meeting Pierre all over again, but that she dismissed as a flight of fancy. Catherine said she had not seen him, her aches and pains preventing her from standing in crowds any more. In any case, Catherine had lost faith in the Emperor. She was among thousands condemning him for the Mexican fiasco that had kept French troops far away from their homeland at a time when a strong force would have kept Bismarck in his place and out of Austria, nipping the Prussian threat to Europe in the bud. Now it was common talk that Prussia was preparing for war with France, and what with political unrest and strikes and the hard winter that had sent the bread prices up again, there was a lot of ill feeling against the imperial couple, Eugénie blamed as well for her interference in government affairs. Louise shook her head sadly over the turn of events.

After a week had gone by a telegram came from Will. Louise opened it in hope and trepidation. "*Regret no news yet. Keep up your spirits. Will.*" She saw that it had been sent from Dover, and the significance of it struck home to her. Was Paul-Michel trying to get to France? Suddenly she saw her son as a little homing-pigeon, trying to reach the place he loved best. How was it that she, whose own heart had never left Paris, had not seen what Will must have guessed from the start?

It was decided that Catherine must return to Paris. They could not risk Paul-Michel arriving on her doorstep to find her absent. She and Louise made a fond farewell of each other. Louise waved her off, and then went back to the sewing in the frenzied climax that was growing.

She could no longer sleep at night. She would doze and then wake again, tension so high in her that she felt she must spring from the bed and run and run until she found her son somewhere. By day she moved from crisis to crisis, which ranged from a spool of special embroidery silk running out to reassuring a debutante who wanted delivery of a dress not yet sewn at the seams. On the eve of the last possible day for delivery the workrooms erupted in a final explosion of flashing needles and pressing irons. In the midst of that madness of white silk and beaded shimmering, Louise was told that a policeman wished to speak to her. Her husband had been found. She hurried to her office. One look at the constable's grave face told her that the news was bad.

"You'd best sit down, ma'am," he said. "It's my sad duty to inform you that your husband has been dead for several days. He was garrotted and his body thrown into the Thames."

She had to go with him to identify the body. It was a harrowing experience. The wire used by the garrotters as their foul murder weapon was imbedded in the swollen flesh of his neck, and she turned away from the sight in deepest distress. Poor unfortunate Robert! How ever had it happened that he, who had always boasted of his skill with a sword-stick, had been caught unawares and so brutally despatched? She was told that his pockets had been emptied of everything except a ring of keys which had been made rusty by immersion in the water. When they were handed to her she recognized them instantly.

It was late in the evening when she returned to the shop after closing hours. Robert's mother had received the sad news staunchly, but poor Agnes had needed to be comforted and consoled. Mademoiselle Brousseau, coming down from the busy sewing-rooms into the stillness of the deserted shop, saw Louise leaning against a shawl counter with her eyes closed in weariness, and was struck by how thin she had become over the past hectic weeks, how wan and strained her face was from all her trouble and ordeal.

"Madame," Mademoiselle Brousseau said gently, "I have news. Good news."

Louise bestirred herself, straightening her shoulders. "The dresses are done?"

"Almost to the last stitch. But it's better than that."

Louise's expression changed slowly to become suffused with hope. "My son?" she breathed, still half afraid that it could not be.

Her assistant nodded, brimming over with the pleasure of it. "Mr. Russell sent word that Paul-Michel is with him at his house."

Louise was already out of the shop. When the cab dropped her at the address, Will came hurrying down the stone steps to meet her, dark and tall in silhouette against the gas-light in the hall behind him. She threw herself against him, clutching him by the arms.

"Is Paul-Michel well? Is he unharmed?"

Will smiled down into her face. "He's footsore and weary and somewhat chastened by being brought home, but otherwise all is well. I picked up his trail after locating a cottage where he had been given a meal. I finally caught up with him on the northern outskirts of Calais."

"How did he get there?" she exclaimed in astonishment. "He had only a few pence in pocket money."

He led her into the house. "He stowed away on a French steam packet. Your son has spirit and initiative, Louise. Whatever you do, don't let Robert crush it once and for all by sending him back to that miserable school."

"Robert is dead," she replied huskily. She told him what had happened as they went up to the guest room where her son had been put to bed.

Paul-Michel was fast asleep, his face small against the vast pillows, his hair still damp from the bath that had washed away the dust and dirt of his travels. Louise sat down on the bed in the glow of the single lamp left alight, and leaned over to kiss his forehead. Then she took his hand up from the coverlet and held it between her own. Without being able to help herself she began to sob with bowed head, rocking primitively in the release of tension, unable to stem in any way the rasps and gulps that convulsed her. When Will began gently to stroke her hair she rose to her feet, reaching out blindly, and felt herself enfolded to the strength and height of him.

Her sobbing mouth was quietened by his kiss of tender purpose, none of his actions akin to the impatience and frustration he had shown during their brief, amorous encounters in the past. It was as if he had dispensed with time and all its attendant turmoil, able to lead her to him as never before. He eased her lips apart with his own, and then there was so much loving in his mouth that her hands, resting against his shoulders, slid up the nape of his neck to bury themselves in his thick curls. All her intense sensuality, long crushed down by circumstances, had burst forth out of her joy, her gratitude, her relief, and the old bond that had tied her to him over many years. She was fired through with desires that she had never thought to feel again for any man other than the one long gone from her life. Never had she wanted to be loved more. There was such a sweet aching in her breasts that the nipples were thrusting through their covering as if to seek in turn the caressing hand that explored their shape and form.

When he raised his lips fractionally from hers to whisper to her, she could not endure the passionate contact to be broken, and refastened her mouth to his, taking his words of love into her with kisses and causing him to crush her even closer to him. His thighs were like iron, and there was such power in him that her own soft contours seemed welded to him through their clothes. Such a trembling possessed her that when he swept her up into his arms and carried her from the room and the sleeping child, she supposed he had known that her knees could not have supported her much longer. She buried her face against him, her arms locked about his neck.

His bedroom was moonlit. It made the bed gleam palely, and touched with a silvery sheen the polished rim of bedhead and chair and the bowfront of a chest of drawers. He lowered her onto the turned-down sheet, but still she kept her arms around him as though unable to let him go. Kept within her embrace, he turned his head that he might kiss her throat and temple and ear as he unfastened the hooks down the back of her dress and loosened the silken ribbons of her stays that did no more than encase by whim of fashion a waist unchanged in slenderness since he had first seen her in girlhood. As he ran his fingertips down her spine she loosened her arms, and he lowered her back until her head came to rest on the pillow. She took his face between her hands, and they looked deeply into each other's eyes.

"I love you," he said softly, "and I've wanted you since the day we met."

A smile touched the corners of her lips. "My darling Will," she whispered. "I knew it then and I know it now."

If he had been given the choice of possessing her in those days gone by or during the hours opening up to him, he would have chosen to wait. Where she had been a lovely girl she was now an incredibly beautiful woman, ready to give and give and give out a generous heart and a fathomless well of passion, while he, shorn of the selfishness of youth, tempered by life to a full awareness of his love for her, wanted only to cherish and adore her into a fulfillment beyond anything she had ever known before.

He peeled the dress and her upper garments away from her, so that she lay naked to the waist of her petticoats. Then he removed his own clothes, and she watched the play of silver and shadow across his muscled body while she set free her coiled hair from its pins and drew it forward across her shoulders. When he came back to her he entwined both his hands in its glossy flow and pressed it to his lips like a man taking life-giving water. Letting it slip from his fingers again he lowered his head to kiss and caress her breasts, causing her to shudder sensuously, the gentle moistness of his mouth left upon them when he slid his hands down to her waist and onwards, taking the rippling waves of her petticoats down over her legs until her feet were free. As the moon passed behind a cloud the darkness that descended seemed at one with the engulfing sensations that sent tremors through her under the wonder of his stroking touch and ardent mouth and seeking tongue. Together they became all passion, nothing existing beyond the other, flesh against flesh, ardour meeting ardour, and in the return of moonlight he brought her with him to the fulness of ecstasy, no man having made an adored woman more his own.

Once in the night he lit the candle by the bed, no longer able to bear that so much of her should be shadowed from him, and amid her tousled hair she gazed blissfully at him, tracing his lips with a fingertip. He kissed her and made love to her all over again, their bodies ivory in the candleglow, and in the tint of dawn he took her deliciously half asleep, limp and sweetly amorous in his arms. He tried to extract a promise from her for the future then, but she only smiled, her eyes closed, and slept again before he could coax out of her what he wanted to hear.

23

Will would not tolerate Louise's refusal to marry him. As the weeks went by, it became a subject of many quarrels as heated as their nights were passionate.

"Why?" he demanded yet again. "What does it matter how long or how short a time you've been a widow? I say to hell with gossip, and let us be wed."

"You know it's nothing to do with that," she insisted, resolved this time to keep her patience. "I have told you that I'm never going to marry again."

"What about Paul-Michel? He and I like and respect each other. He needs to be part of a real family life."

"I married for that reason before, and I'm not doing it a second time." She drew in her breath. "In any case, he will not be at home much in the future. I promised him after he ran away that he should go to school in France as soon as he could read and write French as well as he can speak it. No boy could have worked harder. I've decided on a school in Paris where he will be a weekly boarder and can spend his Sundays with Catherine. He and I will have a little holiday there with her first. I plan to leave in a week or two."

He could not endure the thought of her going. It was as if he had come face to face at last with his long-held dread of her recapture by the past. "Don't think of it yet, I implore you. It would be nothing short of madness to take off for France now. Troops are mustering there, and the Prussian armies are gathering on the border in readiness for attack. War is likely to break out at any minute."

"I realise that, but the fighting would take place far away on Prussian soil. There would be no danger for Paul-Michel in Paris."

"Don't be so complacent!" he stormed, his rage fed on his fear of losing her forever. "Your Emperor is not fit to be a commander-in-chief. He's a desperately sick man, so pain-ridden that he can scarcely sit in a saddle. It's through his political blunders and international follies, much influenced by his imperious wife, that France has alienated herself from all her old allies. Do you think Bismarck would be trying to goad your country into war if she was as strong as she has been in the past? Wake up, Louise! Your glorious Second Empire is in its last days! One shot from a Prussian cannon, and the whole façade will crumble!"

She would not believe him. There was an image in her mind of the Paris she knew, bright and beautiful and rich and powerful, symbolic of an imperial age destined to shine like a lamp over duller régimes until the end of time. And nothing was going to stop her keeping her promise to her son, no matter that it was a great personal sacrifice to let him go so far from her.

France declared war on Prussia over an insurmountable insult shortly before Louise and Paul-Michel were due to depart. Will kept up his protests until the last minute, but Louise took his renewed warnings lightly, all else lost in the happy and exciting prospect of seeing Paris again. It was Paul-Michel who went to the root of the matter.

"I'm the one who's going to stay at school in France, sir. Not Maman. She'll be coming back to you soon."

Will watched the Channel steamer sail. He remained on the quayside long after her waving handkerchief and Paul-Michel's wildly flourished straw sailor-hat were lost from his sight.

Any doubt he might have implanted in Louise's mind vanished as soon as she saw again the city she loved basking in the hot summer sunshine. She was glad that she had huge trunks with her, accommodating a most splendid wardrobe of her own designs, that would do justice to a Paris endearingly unchanged in atmosphere, leafy with trees, glinting with gilt ornamentation, colourful with window boxes and imperial banners. The cafés still brimmed with life and merriment, the boulevards flowing with smartly turned out equipages and high-stepping horses. In front of the Madeleine the flower market blossomed riotously with roses and heliotrope, jasmine and pinks and verbena, the scent drifting on the warm air. Everywhere elegant women abounded, in tiny hats and sweeping dresses, watched in turn by the sauntering boulevardiers who twirled their moustaches in the manner popularised by the Emperor while hoping for a glimpse of ankle, their pleasure curtailed since the hooped crinoline had faded completely from the fashion scene. Many more buildings of grandeur, including the magnificent new opera house, had been erected or completed since her last visit to Paris, and splendid new stores offered a tempting array of fine goods in their windows. The Folies Bergères had opened to packed houses, and the can-can had reached still greater heights of popularity, its wild music crashing out everywhere. And on all sides there were soldiers marching, riding by on wagons, or strolling to see the sights before departing with the Emperor to the field of war. It gripped her unguarded heart to glimpse the sky-blue tunics of the Cent-Gardes when she and her son were driven past the Tuileries on their way to Catherine's comfortable little abode.

Once again there was an emotional reunion with her old friend, who was overjoyed to welcome Paul-Michel. This time it was Louise who showed immediate concern over Catherine's poorly appearance. "You don't look at all well. You've lost more weight. What's wrong?"

With some difficulty the truth was persuaded out of her. On the return voyage to France from England she had stayed on deck to avoid seasickness on a choppy swell, and had caught the kind of chill to which she had become vulnerable. Yes, it had gone to her chest. Yes, she had been off work, but thanks to the handsome little income that Louise allowed her she wanted for nothing. No, there was no cause for worry, and of course she could look after Paul-Michel on his Sundays out from school. That was cure enough in itself. Louise had to be satisfied with Catherine's assurances, but disquiet remained.

Louise's first call was on the Worths, and she took Paul-Michel with her, he eager to see the boys again. Her visiting dress was one of her most recent creations, one of which she was most proud. Made of striped blue-and-white Lyons silk, it was superbly bustled in the evolvement of the line with which Worth had wooed women away from the crinoline, showing them how it was possible to be curved and alluring as never before by the highlighting of the best aspects of the feminine figure. With the dress she wore a white straw hat with the brim turned up at one side, lavishly trimmed with flowerets and ribbons which were made of the same blue lace as her parasol. As she mounted the well-remembered staircase at number 7, her reflection held in an elaborately framed looking-glass, she thought how her childhood dream of wanting to dress as grandly as a queen of France had come true, and with it the wealth to maintain that fulfilled ambition. She and Worth had certainly come a long way since they had first met each other at a garret door.

She had not told Marie of her coming to Paris, planning a surprise, and it could not have been better received. She was embraced and kissed and made much of, Marie greatly excited to see her again. Jean-Philippe and Paul-Michel picked up their friendship as though they had never been apart, although the age difference with Gaston, now a handsome youth, tall like his father, set him apart from the younger ones. Both Gaston and Jean-Philippe, their straight hair and attire no longer subject to their mother's whim, were able to discuss fashion with Louise on equal terms, their knowledge of haute couture deep-rooted from childhood, and she could tell from the way they spoke that they already considered themselves part of their father's business and it was there that their future lay. Later Marie showed Louise some of Jean-Philippe's paintings. Not only had he inherited his father's artistic ability in the designing of clothes, but the talent had developed still further into making him an artist of considerable promise under the teaching of no less a painter than the famous Corot.

"Is Gaston an artist as well?" Louise inquired after admiring Jean-Philippe's work.

"He is the one with the business acumen," Marie answered with a smile, her maternal pride divided equally between her two sons. "I'm sure he'll be in full charge of the financial side of Maison Worth one day."

Worth's business now occupied the whole of the huge building of number 7. His partner, Otto Bobergh, who had ever kept in the background, had just retired on the tremendous fortune he had amassed as his share of the profits, and although they had always been on good terms, Worth was pleased that they had come to the parting of the ways. Recently Worth had taken the patient snail as his emblem, a creature that needed neither house nor dress, and ornamental snails had appeared everywhere at the Suresnes mansion, woven into tapestries, moulded in gold and silver, set in lapis lazuli, carved in marble, and even in support of a balcony on the new palatial extensions there. He now employed over a thousand people, and did not expect the war, which was bound to be of short duration, to make any difference to his business. Admittedly, many of his foreign clients were departing from Paris in some haste, but on the other hand, Frenchwomen were already ordering dresses for victory balls. Most of all he would miss his American clients. None spent more lavishly or were easier to manage. They came to him in the first place in awe, having heard tales and rumours that they had to be presented before he would consider designing anything for them, and it was true that over the years he had turned away any number of women who for one reason or another he had not wished to see in his creations. Yet he was equally willing to put himself to no end of trouble to help a client in distress. He had received one woman in his dressing-gown when she had arrived at six o'clock one morning, desperate for a special dress that evening, and Marie, still in bed, had poured the woman coffee from a tray while he had strolled around the bedroom seeking inspiration from the light of dawn. His flamboyant gestures and dramatic struttings while deciding what a watching client should wear all added to the aura about him, and he had taken to wearing a velvet beret and a flowing Rembrandt robe during hours of work, a genius in the garb of an earlier genius. It was all very fitting, and women loved it.

"Come to an Offenbach operetta with me this evening, Louise," Marie invited a few days after Louise's arrival. "I'm sure you will enjoy it."

It was a splendid moment for Louise when the operetta burst into light and colour on the stage, the merry music typifying all that made Paris the city that it was, and she applauded the songs and dancing with intense enjoyment. In the interval some of Marie's acquaintances came into the box to greet her, and it was a shock to Louise when Stéphanie was among them. Marie was compelled out of politeness to inquire after her husband even though it was within Louise's hearing.

"He left Paris today, Madame Worth. He has rejoined the Emperor at the Palace of St.-Cloud. It is from there that they will leave with the Prince Imperial for the theatre of war." She turned and took the seat beside Louise. "How well you look, and what a beautiful dress. Your own design, I suppose? I have asked for news of you from the Worths sometimes. You are the most successful couturière in London, I've been told. I was recently informed of your bereavement, and I offer my condolences. Are you on your own in Paris?"

Louise observed that Stéphanie had acquired a poise and aplomb that had never been there before. It was as if a soft gem had been polished into a hard and brittle brightness. "My son is with me," she replied.

"Indeed? He must be twelve years old now. Paul-Michel, isn't it? My memory hasn't failed me. I regret to say I have no children. Where are you staying in Paris? Yes, I know that street. I suppose you have been taking your son to see the sights?"

"We have had quite a few excursions already, and the day after tomorrow we shall take a drive to Versailles."

Stéphanie smoothed the feathers of her closed fan. "Why not take him to St.-Cloud instead and see the Emperor and the Prince Imperial go off to war?"

Louise stiffened slightly, not sure whether Stéphanie was taunting her. She kept to safe ground. "I have heard that the Emperor is far from well."

"He is a courageous man who ignores pain. No commander-in-chief could set a better example to his soldiers."

"It doesn't seem right to me that the Prince Imperial should go into danger." Louise was remembering that the boy was only a matter of months older than Jean-Philippe.

"He has been trained since infancy to be fearless. In any case, it is natural that the Emperor should want his young son at his side."

Louise had a feeling of being trapped. She tried to extricate herself. "I can't help but pity the Empress."

"Few would these days. She had made many enemies among those who do not know her as her friends do. Everything she has ever done has been in the interests of France, but that is no longer believed." She noticed that the rest of her party was drifting away to resume their seats before the curtain went up again, and as she made to go with them she looked back over her shoulder at Louise. "Remember what I said about St.-Cloud. It would be a sight for your son to remember all his life."

She went from the box. As the lights of the auditorium began to lower again Louise's carapace of calm gave way. "Stéphanie wants me to let Pierre see his son," she said shakily to Marie. "But how do I know that he would wish it? It could be a cruel whim on her part. I can't do it." Her clenched fists rose and fell on her lap. "I can't."

Marie sighed softly. "I think you should," she counselled sagely. "Madame de Gand would not have humbled herself to request it if she had not had her husband's good at heart. He is off to war, Louise. He may never come back."

It was a cloudy, sultry day when Louise and her son stood hand in hand by the entrance to the little thatched railway station that served the Palace of St.-Cloud. Wagonloads of baggage were being put on the waiting train, and officers and officials were milling about. Some of the local people had gathered, but there were no crowds. Louise had prepared Paul-Michel for seeing the Emperor and perhaps the Cent-Gardes officer who had let him ride the cavalry horse around the Tuileries stableyard, an occasion that he had never forgotten.

Just after half-past nine a line of equipages appeared from the direction of the palace. Along the route people raised the cry that had echoed so fiercely in Paris on the outbreak of war.

"To Berlin! To Berlin! *Vive l'Empereur!*"

Louise saw that the Empress was driving the Emperor herself in a pony chaise, and she was shocked to see the change in him. He looked sick and old, nothing left of the debonair figure that had always ridden so proudly in procession. She understood why the departure had been arranged quietly. It would have cast down the spirits of everyone to see him in such a state. In the carriage following there came the Prince Imperial, youthfully excited in his uniform, and with him were two officers. One was Pierre.

He saw her. His casual, sideways glance hardened into a stare of disbelief, and his head turned to keep his eyes on her as he was driven past. For a matter of minutes she lost sight of him, then he reappeared, coming towards her.

"Louise! I thought my eyes were playing me tricks!" he exclaimed as soon as the distance had narrowed between them. She saw he looked older, the clear-cut bones in his face a trifle blurred by indulgence, but he was no less handsome than he had ever been. How could she have forgotten that his eyes were the exact grey-green of her son's?

"I never thought we should meet again," she said huskily.

"Nor I, my dear." He kissed her cheek and they drew apart, each seeing memories of the past in each other's eyes. She had not been fully prepared for the effect of their meeting upon her. She felt overwhelmed, baffled to know how she had been able to carry on an existence without him, how her blood had been able to course in her veins, or her limbs move. She watched him stoop down to take Paul-Michel by the shoulders and look steadily at him. "You've grown a great deal since I saw you last. You're going to be tall, I can tell that. Do you remember me?"

The boy nodded. "Yes, Captain de Gand. Do you still have Sabre to ride?"

Pierre chuckled, much pleased. "Yes, I do. It's a pity he's already left for Metz, or else I'd have had him saddled up for you again."

"May I ride him when you come back from the war?"

"How long is your vacation? I'll try to make sure that we get the Prussians beaten before it's time for you to return to England." He smiled at what he had said, but Paul-Michel was intent on extracting a promise.

"I'm not going back to England, except for holidays. I'll be attending Collège St.-Nicholas in Paris."

"You will?" Pierre said slowly. "Then you shall have your chance to ride Sabre when the war is won. If you have your mother's permission."

She saw no reason to refuse. If Stéphanie was willing to condone meetings between father and son, she herself could not wish for anything more. There was no need to be involved in any way with any arrangements that they might make. She reassured them.

"Just as long as it's on a Sunday out from school and Catherine has made no other plans. I'm returning to London as soon as Paul-Michel starts school."

Pierre straightened up, keeping a hand protectively on the boy's shoulder, speaking to him again. "I expect you would like to have a closer look at the locomotive, wouldn't you? We'll exchange a few more words on the platform before I depart." Signalling to an official, he put Paul-Michel in his charge. Then he and Louise began to stroll along the grass under the trees. There was no place where they could be alone, and no spot where they would be unobserved. He told her that he had heard about her dress-house in London from Paul-Michel during their meeting at the Tuileries. "It's still a success, I'm sure," he commented, "but what of your marriage? Are you content?"

She kept her gaze ahead. I am widowed.

They took another pace or two in silence as he deliberated. "Then you really have no personal ties to take you back to England. Paul-Michel will be at school in Paris. All your old friends are there. I shall be there again myself when this war is over."

His meaning was clear. He was asking her to reconsider the situation between them. To remain in Paris in order that they might take up their life together again, but all the same problems still existed, and nothing had been solved. She shook her head slowly, and he stilled her action with his fingertips, bringing her face round to meet his eyes.

"I refuse to accept that everything is at an end," he said, almost breathing the words in order that none other than she should hear them. Then his gaze on her deepened. "Tell Paul-Michel who I am. I want him to know."

A discreet cough made an interruption. An equerry had followed them and was making his presence known. "The Emperor is about to board the train, Captain."

Time had run out. For another few seconds Pierre continued to hold her eyes compellingly. "Tell him! If you will promise me nothing else, grant me this one favour."

"I'll tell him," she answered emotionally, not at all sure that it was the right thing to do. Yet how to refuse a man on the eve of battle?

He nodded gravely, the stress showing, and taking a step backwards he saluted her. She watched him hurry away until he disappeared amid the clusters of officials that blocked all view of the Emperor's departure. With a tremendous hissing of steam the imperial train began to pull out of the little station. She saw the Emperor waving to those left behind on the platform, saw the Prince Imperial fluttering a white handkerchief, but she did not see Pierre. Not doubting that he could see her from somewhere in those passing carriages, she blew a kiss from her fingertips.

Paul-Michel was singularly quiet on the drive back to Paris. He sat in the opposite corner seat and looked out the window for a while. Then he said, "Captain de Gand is my father, isn't he?"

Louise was disconcerted by the unexpectedness of the question, although she did not let him see it. "Yes," she replied evenly. Since the truth had to come out it was probably as well now as later. "He is. How did you come to realise that?"

"Well, when I found out what being a bastard meant, I asked Mr. Russell if I was his son. He said that he wished I was, but I wasn't. My father was a courageous Frenchman, and I should be proud of that."

Louise closed her eyes for a moment. Dear Will. How like him to choose the right words at such an awkward questioning. She would be eternally grateful to him. "Yes, you should be proud," she endorsed. "Your father has been decorated more than once by the Emperor for gallantry in action. But I'm still not quite sure how you reached your conclusion."

Paul-Michel gave her a patient look as if her being a woman prevented her from understanding the intelligent male mind. "I worked it out from all you've ever said, and remarks that Aunt Catherine made when she thought I wasn't listening. Then there was that time after the children's party at the Tuileries when you were upset and I didn't know why. Later I just added it onto everything else. I think I almost knew when Mr. Russell also told me that my father was an army officer and that it was the Emperor who had prevented your marriage. He said there was no blame attached to you, Maman, or shame to me for being born out of wedlock. Then on the station platform, when Captain de Gand shook my hand, he said *'Au revoir, my son.'* The Empress kissed the Prince Imperial and told him to do his duty, but Captain de Gand called me *his son.*"

"Now you know almost everything," she said quietly. She indicated the seat beside her. "Come and sit by me. I'll tell you all I've ever heard about your father's home and his childhood, and all else I can remember that you should know." As the last kilometres to Paris were covered, Louise felt that she and her son had been drawn closer to each other than ever before.

Five days later the Emperor and his troops won a bloody battle on German soil. Champagne corks popped in Paris, and the whole city celebrated, but it was the last good news to come from the war. Almost at once the tide turned. French soldiers were mown down and scattered before the sweeping Russian advance. Word began to leak out in the press of blundering and a lack of preparation for such an onslaught. Resentment flared against the Emperor with the tidings of each new falling back, each ignominious rout. The mood of the people became ugly, and the Emperor's political enemies made themselves heard everywhere. Louise saw the whole city changing before her eyes, and the well-remembered smell of revolution seemed to hang in the air. The Empress as Regent returned to the Tuileries with her court and acted decisively, ordering martial law and making other moves to preserve the dynasty.

Louise received an urgent communication from Will telling her to return to England with Paul-Michel without delay, but she could not have left even if she had wished it. Catherine was not well. On the day that Paul-Michel started school, Catherine had waited in pouring rain for the latest casualty lists to be posted up outside the neighbouring police station. With so much grave news coming in she had wanted to spare Louise the shock of seeing the grim news in cold print if it should be there. Fortunately it did not appear, but the drenching in a cold wind had played havoc with Catherine's low state of health, and she was confined to bed with a fever.

Stéphanie was another who watched in dread for his name on any such communiqué received by the Empress. She had been at St.-Cloud with the rest of the Empress's ladies for the banquet that had been held on the eve of the Emperor's departure, but she had said nothing to Pierre of having seen Louise. It had been the same some long while ago when she had glimpsed her with Worth at the Tuileries, fearful then that Louise had returned to Paris to win Pierre back to her. How he had discovered his son at the Prince Imperial's party was still a mystery, although in his duties he sometimes checked the guest lists. Later she had known comfort in his telling her about the meeting, for at times they could be close in their relationship, and she had been thankful that he had only sought out the child and not the mother. It was then that she had realised that he would never subject her to the humiliation and scandal of being deserted by him, partly because he would have been ostracised himself, to say nothing of the woman involved and any children of the folly becoming social outcasts with him. It made his numerous infidelities no easier to bear; the anguish that his unfaithfulness caused her was still undiminished, but she did have a sense of security that had not been there before. Therefore she could be magnanimous in letting him see his son. It also alleviated her own sense of guilt. If she had not thrown herself into a rage of jealousy she might never have miscarried her first baby, which had made it impossible for her to carry subsequent babies, until it became apparent to the doctors that she would never bear a child. She loved Pierre. She knew what it meant to him not to have an heir. She was no longer jealous of Louise for having been loved by him, only because she had had his son.

Louise had no time to take notice of the growing unrest in the streets, although sometimes the strains of the "Marseillaise" reached her as another shouting swarm of people demonstrated somewhere in the distance. She was nursing Catherine night and day, fearful for her life, and all else had lost importance, even a natural concern about her business in London receding before the main issue. When Paul-Michel suddenly appeared one day with his school trunk being set down in the hall by a cabby, she could not think what he was doing there.

"What's wrong? Why are you here?"

"So many pupils have been taken home by their parents that the school is closing temporarily," he answered her, taking off his coat. Then, seeing she was still bewildered, he added incredulously, "Haven't you heard the news, Maman? The Emperor has surrendered. He and thousands of our troops have been taken prisoner by the Prussians."

She put her hand to her throat. "It can't be! It's little more than a month since the war started. We cannot be defeated!"

"It's true. The Prussians are said to be demanding the complete capitulation of France."

"No! No! Where did you hear all this?"

"The headmaster told us. I hope my father is safe. Is Aunt Catherine any better?"

In her heart Louise echoed his hope as she answered his query. "No, I'm afraid not. I'm glad you're with me. I need a helping hand. The doctor has not been to see her for two days because so many wounded have been brought from the fighting field into the hospitals, but physic for Catherine can be collected from his house. You shall fetch it for me." She gave him the address and told him to return as quickly as possible with any more news he might be able to gather at the same time.

He set off at once, not telling her that the streets were full of unruly mobs shouting and stampeding and tearing down the imperial eagle from gates and buildings. The cabby had had to take a roundabout route to reach the quiet cul-de-sac where the apartment was situated. Paul-Michel thought it exciting to get the chance to see all that was going on at first hand.

He had to go quite a long way to reach the doctor's house, but it took him far longer than was necessary, simply because on the way there he kept stopping to watch various skirmishes between rival revolutionary groups, and he lingered for a while on the outskirts of the dense crowd gathered in front of the colonnaded Hôtel de Ville, where a provisional government was being formed amid scenes of wildest confusion. He was almost home with the physic safely in his pocket when he heard a great shout go up like a clap of thunder, and there burst along the rue de Rivoli all those who had been waiting for the results, transformed now into a triumphant mob lusting for violence and blood, and bound for the gates of the Tuileries.

"Down with the Empress! Long live the Third Republic! Long live France!"

He understood what it meant: the Second Empire had fallen. France was a republic once again. He remembered the imperial lady with the beautiful face and the red-gold hair who had smiled at him when he had bowed to her at the children's party. He hoped that no harm would come to her.

At the Tuileries the noise of the approaching mob could be clearly heard, but still Eugénie refused to leave. Stéphanie, shaking with fear, was among those waiting in the Blue Salon while behind closed doors the Empress's loyal advisers begged her to take flight while there was still time. Previously they had wanted her to send for the Prince Imperial and to take command, but that would have meant civil war, and she would not agree. Neither would she allow a single shot to be fired to quell the disturbance or in her own defence. She remained adamant that no blood should be shed for her.

"Then you must leave at once," her old friend Count Metternich told her, "even though the safety of your own person means nothing to you. There is no telling what will happen to those remaining at your side when the mob breaks through into the palace."

She knew then that she no longer had any choice in the matter. The doors into the salon were opened for her and she came through to say goodbye to her ladies, the light playing on her rich Titian hair and on the silken folds of the beige dress that Worth had made for her, a shawl in the colour of her favorite violets about her shoulders. All wept, and many wanted to accompany her, but she refused them all except one, Madame Lebreton, who had no domestic ties. Stéphanie, obsessed by panic, fell to her knees and begged again to go with her.

"I don't know whether Pierre is dead or alive. I have no one but you, Your Majesty. Do not leave me on my own, I implore you."

Eugénie hesitated. Stéphanie was the Emperor's goddaughter, and as such was in greater peril than any of the others. "Very well, my child. Make haste and veil yourself. We must not be recognized."

Eugénie changed into black, and with a thick veil over her face rejoined the two who awaited her, similarly attired. With Metternich and his fellow ambassador, Count Nigra, in escort, they all hastened down to the courtyard. Before a plain carriage could be brought to the steps there came a deep roar as the mob broke through the railings, cutting off escape. They ran back up the long staircase and sped along galleries and corridors and through room after room to reach the communicating door at the opposite end of the palace that led into the Louvre. But luck was against them. The door was locked! Away behind them came the distant echoes of the mob forcing an entrance. Stéphanie gulped with fright. Again and again the ambassadors put their shoulders to the stout door in vain.

The sound of someone approaching at a run made them all spin about in alarm. To their intense relief it was a servant with a master key. He shot it into the lock and turned it, swinging it free. Eugénie paused to thank him before being hustled through by the others.

Their swift footsteps clacked at speed in the deserted Louvre, where all the greatest masterpieces had been removed to a place of safety at Eugénie's own orders, together with the crown jewels. Down the marble staircase they flew, the women's skirts whispering after them from stair to stair. At the doors out through the grand colonnade into the street St.-Germain-l'Auxerrois they had to wait to allow for a yelling crowd to go streaming by. "Death to the Empress! Death to the Spanish woman!"

Eugénie, pale and dignified, did not quail as she waited in the shadows of the doorway, although a nerve throbbed in her temple. As soon as the coast was clear Metternich hailed a cab, and as Eugénie was about to step into it a ragged urchin, hurrying to catch up with the rest of the crowd, slithered to a halt and gave an excited shout to those still within earshot.

"It's 'er! The Empress!"

Nigra sprang forward to clap a hand over his mouth and shake him into silence. The cabby pretended not to have heard, looking ahead as Metternich unceremoniously bundled the other two women in with Eugénie. As the door slammed and Metternich stepped back, the cabby's whip flicked and the horses bounded forward, bearing away the escapees. They were bound for the apartment of a loyal councillor on the Boulevard Haussmann, and were delayed time and time again by the boisterous mobs who jostled the cab and banged exuberant fists against it, never suspecting the identity of those within. Stéphanie was afraid her nerves would break under the strain, and she bit deeper and deeper into her lips to keep from screaming.

The Councillor was not at home, and their frantic ringing of the doorbell went unanswered. Down the long flights they went again, and Eugénie decided they would go to another friend on the Avenue de Wagram. Stéphanie was sent to fetch a cab, and in her near-hysterical state she misjudged the edge of the pavement, and her ankle clicked as she went down. But it was no time to think of herself, and she fought against fainting at the excruciating pain as she hauled herself into the fiacre after the others. Once again the man they sought was not at home, and they stood, a confused and disconcerted trio, on the pavement outside, Stéphanie leaning a hand against a wall to take the weight off her foot. Madame Lebreton suggested going to the American ambassador, but none of them could recall his private address. Nevertheless, it gave Eugénie another idea.

"My American dentist! We'll go there."

They had to walk, having no more money between them. Stéphanie limped along in agony at a distance behind the other two in order not to attract unwanted attention to them. It struck her as insanely incongruous that the Empress, lately lauded by all, should be reduced to banging in vain on doors and going on foot about Paris for the sake of a few francs.

For the third time they drew a blank. The dentist was at the hospital with the wounded, but they were invited into the waiting-room. Stéphanie fell half swooning with pain across a couch and did not move. When Dr. Evans returned home he was astounded to find the Empress there, her veil thrown back over her bonnet, and two other ladies with her.

"I have come to you in great trouble," she said quietly. "I have no one else to whom I can turn. Will you help me to get to England?"

He found his voice. "I will do everything in my power to see that you reach safety, ma'am."

During the night Stéphanie could not sleep for the pain. Dr. Evans himself had bound her ankle, pronouncing it a most severe sprain, and she was forced to come to terms with the fact that she must let the Empress go on without her. In no way must she hinder Eugénie's escape, and now that she could not put her foot to the floor she would be the most dreadful handicap. At dawn when the clock was striking five she and Eugénie said goodbye to each other. It was a most poignant moment. Stéphanie dragged herself to the window and held back the curtain to watch the carriage take away the woman who had borne so much for France, Eugénie of the violets, the imperial patroness of Worth, Empress of the French. Banished forever, and with her the glorious era that she had represented.

Louise was always to remember that particular night as the one in which Catherine took a turn for the better. She became less breathless, the fever eased, and she slept for longer and more peaceful periods. Louise, rising from the couch in Catherine's room where she took whatever rest she could, saw by the growing light that it was going to be a fine day. She had slipped on a robe when there came a jingling of the doorbell. Unable to think who could be at the door at such an early hour, she opened it to find Stéphanie held in the arms of a manservant, her foot showing bandages. Without a word Louise stepped aside to allow her to be carried in and put down on a sofa.

"That was Dr. Evans's coachman," Stéphanie began falteringly when Louise had seen him out again. "The dentist has taken the Empress to Deauville to see her safely onto a boat for England. I have so much to tell."

"I'll put on the coffee pot," Louise interrupted kindly. "I can see you have been through an ordeal."

Stéphanie stayed on with Louise while her ankle healed. Paul-Michel was wary at first of his father's wife, hostile and distant, but gradually, as Stéphanie became more herself, her spontaneous naturalness showing through, he found her downright good company when they played draughts and cards and backgammon to alleviate her boredom. He ran errands for her as well as for his mother, and every day

Stéphanie scanned the newspaper that he fetched for her, firstly for any glimpse of her husband's name, and secondly for news of the military situation. The Emperor may have surrendered to the Prussians, but the Third Republic had not, and the war was still on. Paris was being turned into a fortress, with troops streaming in the whole time to join their strength with the National Guard and the hodge-podge of untrained volunteers. Everywhere defences were being built up, thousands of men working around the clock, and cannon thrust barrels out of every great fort and from every strategic position. Armament factories had started up in every available premises, including part of the Louvre, and one railway station had become a foundry and another a factory making hot air balloons. In addition, droves of cattle and sheep came daily to swell the herds set to graze in the Bois de Boulogne, the Gardens of Luxembourg, and in every other park. All that was lighthearted and frivolous in the city had died away, leaving a grimness of determination that seemed reflected in the dull autumn skies.

Stéphanie contacted people she knew, and eventually received word that Pierre was a prisoner-of-war with the Emperor, both of them housed in considerable comfort with other imperial officers, although the same could not be said of the hundred thousand ordinary soldiers cooped up in miserable camps. Immediately Stéphanie became frantic to get out of Paris. She did not want to be besieged there if by some chance Pierre was released or escaped home to the Château de Gand. She sent a message to the Councillor to whose apartment the Empress had first gone in vain for aid. He came to see her the next day, and after he had gone again she told Louise that all arrangements had been made.

"I have to leave tomorrow or else it will be too late. I asked Monsieur Besson to bring papers to cover you and Catherine and Paul-Michel. I want you all to come with me."

Louise shook her head on a little sigh. "Catherine mustn't be moved from her bed. She couldn't possibly make such a journey. We must stay and face whatever comes."

"Then let Paul-Michel come with me. Monsieur Besson is convinced it will be a long, hard siege. Far away in the Loire countryside the boy will be safe. Surely this is what you would wish for him."

Louise could not refuse such a chance. She called her son to her and told him what she had decided, explaining that once the siege closed in nobody would be able to leave the city. He did not want to go, but she gave him no choice. He lost his temper, stamped and rampaged, but she remained adamant. When dawn came he said goodbye to Catherine, hugging her in the anguish of parting, and what she said to him Louise did not know, although it must have been a plea that he should make amends to his mother before departing. Just when it seemed to Louise he was about to stalk out without a word, he turned and embraced her fiercely.

"Au revoir, maman."

She held him tight and kissed him on the cheek. Then he broke from her and ran off down the stairs to where Stéphanie awaited him in the carriage. Louise leaned from the window and waved him out of sight, fighting hard to keep back her tears. Two days later the Prussians completed their encirclement of the city and the telegraph wires were cut. Paris was on its own.

Now that Catherine showed signs of being on the mend, Louise was able to leave her in charge of a neighbour, and it gave her the freedom to go and queue for bread and other necessities. Prices had already soared, and many food items had disappeared, stored away, it was said, until a still higher price could be demanded later on. Louise, who had kept Catherine's cupboards well stocked, decided that in future not a scrap of anything must be wasted, and there came back to her all the means by which she had scraped and connived and made do in the past. Shortages would not catch her unawares. She had been well schooled in fending for herself and those she loved a long time ago.

She went to number 7, rue de la Paix, the first chance she had had for some time, and saw how everything had changed. Custom had fallen off drastically, the downfall of the Empire and the prospect of the siege having put to flight like migrating birds an incalculable number of Worth's clients. Those who were left no longer wanted extravagant gowns. Sombre clothes had become the rule for women; nothing in the general attire must suggest the remotest link with the deposed Second Empire, and any elegantly dressed woman ran the risk of being attacked if she appeared in the streets. Poor Marie, who could not shed the *chic* with which she imbued her clothes, did not dare to venture out alone any more.

"I put on the plainest dress and cape one day last week," she moaned to Louise over a cup of coffee, "but I had gone no more than few paces when some rough folk began to shout at me. Fortunately Jean-Philippe came to my rescue and sent them off, but I was quite terrified." Some thumping on the floor above sent the chandeliers into a tinkling dance, and Marie glanced upwards. "We're turning all the other floors into an emergency hospital. Most of the seamstresses are making bandages and hemming bed-linen at the present time. Otherwise there's no work at all for most of them, and almost nothing for the rest. Yet Charles is going to continue paying wages to every one of his twelve hundred employees until we can all get back to normal again. He says he knows what it is to be penniless and hungry in Paris, and it's not going to happen to any of his staff."

Louise smiled to herself, thinking that her reminiscences about the past and Worth's had been running along the same lines. "I'd like to offer myself as a nurse," she said. "I've already bought myself a Geneva armband with a red cross and some aprons and a cap. In the meantime I'll do anything I can to help."

"That would be splendid," Marie declared.

The next day the first of many sorties by the National Guard went out to meet the Prussian lines. It did little more than show how strongly the Prussians were entrenched, and casualties were heavy. Number 7's first wounded were carried into the ornate premises and up the stairs. Those who were conscious blinked in disbelief from their stretchers at the gilt and glory surrounding them, and were lulled by the quietness of carpeted floors that muffled any sound, all of it somewhat incomprehensible after the stench and roar and mud of the dead-strewn battlefield. They were the first of many wounded to be treated, to recover, or to die where previously no thought had been given to anything beyond the perfection of a seam or the choice of a trimming.

Louise sent letters to Paul-Michel and Will by the postal balloons that took off at night, although due to the direction of the winds none could be returned by the same route, and the only news that came into the city was by pigeon. None of the tidings was good. More cities had fallen to the enemy. Other sorties took place out of Paris, all of them taking a heavy toll, and it was a terrible sight to see the wagons come rolling back up the Champs-Elysées filled with French wounded.

Louise, carrying out her nursing ceaselessly, had no time to follow the run of days as the weeks went by, bringing bitter winter weather. She could only tell it was Sunday if she happened to glance out at the number of people braving the low temperature to promenade in the old, traditional way. What a different sight it was from happier days gone by. The colour was now in the assorted and often tatty uniforms, and not in the hats and dresses. Women no longer lingered to look in shop windows, goods having fast diminished, and went instead on male arms to view the guns and the batteries, the young and the free following the same route to flirt with the soldiery. At night there was no street-lighting, the gas being conserved for arms factories and foundries, and the theatres had become hospitals as had the concert halls. As the stores of food dwindled everybody began to experience hunger, and the butchers offered meat of a kind never seen before, while the very poor were reduced to buying rats or trapping their own for a stewpot. The restaurants offered strange dishes on the menu that might be comprised of horseflesh or goat or a steak from one of the wild animals slaughtered for supply at the Zoological Gardens. Only wine was plentiful, the cellars of Paris having been the best in the world, and drunkenness was rife. All went about on foot, no horses to be seen any more in the shafts of a civilian vehicle, and dogs vanished mysteriously as did the cats, which reappeared as "gutter rabbits" on market stalls. Worth, who had the Englishman's passionate regard for good horses, kept a guard posted night and day on his favourite thoroughbreds, determined that they should not be stolen and end up on a butcher's slab. For himself, he declared he would starve before he would eat domestic meat.

"Yes, dear," Marie said reassuringly. The French housewife in her was certain that if such desperate straits were reached in the Worth household, she could disguise the contents of any cooking-pot with plenty of wine and herbs. And it might well come to that. The government had not allowed for the siege to last so long. Warehouses were getting low in grain, and almost all the cattle had gone. Not even the rich would be able to buy what was no longer there.

Louise was among those women who had to wait in long lines outside the boulangeries to buy bread, which had become black and hard with very little flour in it, and she took her turn with patience in other queues for the chance to buy a precious egg or some vegetables, which cost as many francs as they had centimes in peacetime. Her main problem was trying to keep at least one room in the apartment adequately heated for the convalescent Catherine, who must not catch a further chill. As if there were not enough hardships to endure, a winter colder than anyone could remember had descended, caking the windows with ice and making walking hazardous, many unfortunate people adding broken bones to their other miseries. The troops fared no better, sentries being found frozen to death at their posts, and in such weather no pigeons could fly, leaving the city bereft of outside news. To Louise, the sensation of being back at the beginning of everything had never been more upon her. She even found herself going to copses remembered from childhood, where the wood was protected by undergrowth, and drier than elsewhere. Gradually whole areas became bare of trees as the government allowed them to be felled and used for firewood, and not one remained along pavements where the previous summer the branches had given leafy shade.

The new year of 1871 was no more than eight hours old when Worth, ignoring the icy weather, set out for the Church of St.-Clotilde, taking Marie and his sons with him. Apart from his spontaneous moments of meditation snatched in any convenient place of worship, he had also created this annual pilgrimage for himself since he had first arrived in Paris, drawing in his wife and his children from babyhood as the years had gone by. He allowed three quarters of an hour by his gold watch, no more and no less, for sitting in the deserted church, absorbed in spiritual thought and thanksgiving. Much refreshed, he would rise up at the second that the time expired, and lead the way out of the church again. They were descending the steps outside when Jean-Philippe sighted a figure they knew, weighed down by a canvas sack of kindling.

"There's Madame Prestbury!" he exclaimed. Hurrying down the rest of the steps he darted across to her. The others viewed her surprise and gratitude as he heaved the sack from her onto his own broad young shoulders. Marie was the next to reach her.

"Have you been carrying out this heavy task every day before coming to nurse the wounded?" Marie exclaimed anxiously. Louise smiled and shrugged, explaining the necessity. Immediately Marie insisted that Catherine be moved to number 7, where there were still two or three rooms spare and at least there were adequate stocks of coal and logs to see the whole house through the rest of the cold weather.

That same day Catherine, unable to walk any distance, was transported by means of a stretcher borrowed from hospital supplies into the warm and comfortably furnished rooms that

Marie had offered. It made everything much easier for Louise, and Marie's thoughtfulness saved both her life and Catherine's, because when the Prussians at last began to bombard the city four days later, the house where they had lived was among the first buildings blasted into ruins.

All day the bombardment went on, and in the morning it began again. The German guns had now been trained on another section of the city, and it soon became obvious as the days went by that no part of Paris within range was to be spared. The shelling was indiscriminate, churches, hospitals, and schools among the buildings damaged or flattened. Huge craters appeared in the streets and pitted the parks, the boom of cannon and the whine of shells creating a horrible rhythm of sound that rarely ceased. In the midst of it all Communard agitators attempted to stir the population up against the government, trying to establish a Commune to take over, and Worth went out into the rue de la Paix to tear down the red placards that had been attached to the walls of his establishment.

"Bandits!" he raged. "Red bandits!" His loyalties and affections remained with the deposed Emperor, who was still a prisoner-of-war, and with the banished Empress. He had resolved that he would send a bouquet of French violets to Eugénie every year of her exile to the end of his days and hers.

Louise became more and more thankful that she had sent Paul-Michel to a place of safety. Due to conditions the mortality rate among children was appallingly high, and then the Collège St.-Nicholas, to which he would have returned upon the reopening of the schools some while since, received a direct hit during the night, killing some little boys asleep in the dormitory. She was deeply upset by the incident. On the whole the morale of the Parisians remained high. They joked about the change of diet and other deprivations that they had to bear, but gradually people began to look as pinched and bleak as the damaged city. Malnutrition and cold and disease took a deadly toll far higher than fatal casualties caused through the bombardment. Although the wealthy could still keep food on their tables, most of Paris existed on bread, wine, and coffee. Then bread began to get scarce, and a very real panic prevailed. Paris faced famine, but a last great sortie was to be made.

Louise stood with Marie at the window to watch the ragged array that marched off to meet the enemy. Hundreds of civilian volunteers, boys and elderly men amongst them, swelled the ranks of the National Guard, provisions being transported with them in a motley collection of hackney-cabs, omnibusses, and trade wagons. No contrast could have been more marked against the glitter and pomp of the imperial troops that had once dazzled the city, and yet at the same time it was a sight to stir Parisian pride and hope. The marchers were cheered all along the way. When the last of them had vanished from sight, Marie and Louise went to remake vacated beds on the emergency hospital floors and to see that many more were made up in every available space for the aftermath of battle.

It was a defeat on a scale almost impossible to comprehend, except that it spelt out the capitulation of Paris. The wounded, mud-caked and dazed, returned in a flood; those who survived unharmed staggered back in straggling groups, sickened and broken and in such a state of exhaustion that many collapsed in the streets and were cared for by shopkeepers and others near at hand. At number 7, Louise and all the other nurses were run off their feet. Even Catherine, poorly though she was, helped in her own way by giving comfort to the dying. Among them was Henri Berrichon. He did not know her, being too far gone in the throes of pain, but he gripped her hand at the moment of death, and it was she who kissed his brow and closed his eyes.

24

France surrendered. Bismarck, as if to grind her down still further in the hour of her defeat, demanded a token occupation of Paris. The government had no choice but to acquiesce. On the day the Prussians made their ceremonial entry into Paris to flaunt their victory, Marie and Louise drew down all the blinds at the windows of number 7. It was the same all over the city, the shops and cafés keeping their shutters up or displaying notices that Prussians would not be served. Six hundred German princes and other officers from distinguished families, resplendent in bright uniforms and shining helmets, rode at the head of the long column of cavalry and troops passing down the avenue of the Champs-Elysées. In a silence of hatred and hostility the crowds watched them go by. When the conquerors departed a few days later they left in their wake a bitter and festering sense of humiliation that did more to rouse certain sections of the people against the government than any of the blunders of the siege.

Louise, eager for a reunion with Paul-Michel, paid no heed to fresh clouds gathering, and sent off a letter to him, saying she was looking forward to his immediate return. Long-delayed mail came into the city along with its revictualling, and there was correspondence from Will, letting her know that her shop was still flourishing, he himself having promoted one of her protégées into looking after the designing aspect of the business in her absence. He missed her and he loved her and he was ever her devoted Will. She was touched, but slipped the letters back in the envelopes after only one reading, and in her reply she made no mention of returning to England. Having come through so much with Paris, how could she leave it now?

When a letter came from Paul-Michel she tore it open eagerly, expecting to read the time of his arrival, but it was not there. Instead, he wrote of the horses he rode, the school he attended daily, and of the friends he had made. She reached the final paragraph. *I do not want to return to Paris just yet, although I am longing to see you and Aunt Catherine again. Now that prisoners-of-war are being released and the Emperor has gone to England to join the Empress and the Prince Imperial in exile, my father is on his way home, and I should like to spend a few days with him before I leave. Please write and say that I may stay a little longer. Your affectionate and obedient son, Paul-Michel.*

She wrote at once and gave her permission, suppressing her own acute disappointment. Fortunately her time was fully occupied in finding another apartment for Catherine and herself, the idea of resettling in the city having taken such a hold on her, and with so many buildings damaged or destroyed, the search was not an easy one. Marie insisted that there was no rush to move out of number 7, for which Louise was grateful. The showrooms were in the process of being restored to their original state as the patients there either went home or were removed to hospitals outside Paris for further treatment. Worth had begun to shake out silks and satins that had been stored away. He knew women well enough to realise there was nothing like a new dress for restoring their spirits, and already he had received a visit from one client who had worn light summer clothes that he had made her throughout the siege, defying the merciless weather.

"I could not have been seen in winter garments that were not created by you, Monsieur Worth," she explained.

"Ah, madame," he replied with a gratified smile. "It is spirit such as yours that will make Paris herself again."

But that time was not yet. In a violent uprising the Communards seized power, the government was forced to flee to Versailles, and everywhere in Paris the red flag took the place of the tricolour, which was torn down and trampled underfoot. From Versailles the government sent in troops, and a civil war, which Eugénie had sacrificed the imperial dynasty to avoid, broke forth in the most bloody fighting that the city had ever seen. The Communards threw up barricades that blocked the streets, including the rue de la Paix, and the noise of rifle-shot and cannon-fire resounded night and day. Louise felt that her countrymen had gone mad. There was no other explanation for such butchery, which was making Frenchmen stain the whole city with fellow Frenchmen's blood. Worth would not allow her or any of the other womenfolk on his premises to go outside. Number 7 became a first-aid post once more when an orderly band of peacemakers, carrying banners appealing for the laying down of arms, was mown down by the Communards in front of Worth's building, and the wounded were carried in there and cared for until their own relatives took them away.

The incident directed the unwelcome attention of the Commune towards Worth and his family. A group of Communards came hammering for admittance. He would not have the huge street doors unbolted and unbarred to such rabble, and addressed them instead from the balcony, his own name gleaming in gilded letters above the closed entrance below.

"What is it you want?" he demanded haughtily, every inch the grand couturier in flowing bow-tie and velvet-collared frockcoat.

A burly Communard, bearded and sharp-eyed, was the spokesman for his comrades, and he stood with feet set apart, leaning back slightly from the waist as he looked up at Worth with a belligerent air.

"It's time you gave us some active support. We need every man we can get. I'll show you how to use one of these if you don't already know." He half tossed the rifle that he held, catching it within his grasp, and the bayonet flashed a reflection of grey light. "There's space for you at the guns in the Place Vendôme, no more than a stone's throw from your own doorstep."

For a moment or two Worth was speechless with outrage. That such a demand should be put to one whose unswerving loyalty to the Emperor and Empress would never wane! "I am an Englishman!" he retorted, his gaze sweeping the upturned faces of those below him with undisguised contempt. "Your revolutionary activities are no concern of mine."

He made to return indoors, but the Communard halted him with a harsh shout. "Wait! You've a grown son, Englishman. His name is Gaston, I believe."

Worth turned back to the balustrade. He knew that some Communards had been trying to persuade his seventeen-year-old son to join them. Only the previous day Gaston, white-faced and furious, had come storming into the house, declaring that he would die for France, but he would never take up arms for the loathesome Commune. "Well?" Worth snapped, his voice cold and contained.

The Communard showed his yellow teeth in a grin, a false amiability in his attitude. "Now Gaston can't profess to being an Englishman. Not with his mother being a Frenchwoman. There's enough good French blood in his veins to make him fit to stand at the barricades with us in the fight for freedom."

"Freedom to slaughter the innocent and the peacemakers!" Worth roared accusingly, the dreadful scene that he and his family had witnessed before their own home all too fresh in his mind. Below him the face of the Communard lost its superficial affability and became congested, sinews standing out in the thick neck.

"I recruit Gaston Worth in the name of the Commune!"

Worth crashed a fist down on the balustrade, making it ring. He was consumed by wrath. "You have no authority to commit him to your ranks!"

"You're mistaken there," the Communard snarled, his temper and that of those with him becoming dangerous. "As I said to you, we are in need of reinforcements in both men and arms, and your son is just the type of young fellow we're looking for. Now I come to think of it, you also have a younger son. I've seen him. He's a tall, strong lad. I'm recruiting him at the same time. Send them both down to us, Englishman!"

"Never!"

There came an ominous shake of the rifle. "I think you will. It would go hard on everyone else on your premises if we should have to break in and fetch out our two newest recruits."

It was a terrible threat. Worth knew of the rape and killings that had occurred in other cases where the Communards had rampaged through buildings where they had met resistance. He struggled in the paroxysm of his rage to give a coherent answer. "Very well," he forced out. "All I ask in return is that you allow them some minutes to gather together what they will need. The must have clothes and provisions."

"That's more like it," the Communard jeered, supported by the guffaws of his comrades. "Collect some extra food for us while you are about it, and include your best bottles from the cellar as well."

Worth withdrew immediately. Gathered in the room, where they had heard everything, were Marie with a restraining hand on the fuming Gaston's arm, her face very frightened, Jean-Philippe with her. Louise was also there, looking as pale as his wife. He drew breath and spoke quietly and decisively to them.

"Get your coats on. Stop for nothing. We must leave at once by the staff door out into the next street, going one at a time to avoid attracting attention." He turned to Louise. "You and Mademoiselle Allard must come with us. It would not be safe to remain here after the Communards discover we have gone."

"I can't take Catherine any distance on foot," Louise answered, "but I think I can walk her along the back street as far as the hotel. We'll go in by the kitchens and take a room there for the time being."

While Jean-Philippe and Gaston ran to alert those employees who happened to be on the premises, Worth filled his pockets from the safe, saw that Louise had the money she needed, and then shepherded all those in his charge through the expanse of number 7, which had no back door, to the way out in the adjoining building below the staff accommodation there. Jean-Philippe went first, followed a minute later by Marie and Gaston. The staff also melted away. When Worth had seen Louise and Catherine reach the kitchen entrance at the rear of the rue de la Paix hotel and vanish inside, he followed in the wake of his family. They met in a passageway on a flight of steps a safe distance away, and by a torturous route that avoided the worst of the fighting they eventually reached the northern outskirts of the city. They made their way by hired vehicle and train to Le Havre, ready for flight to England should the need arise. Accommodation proved difficult to find; many others with imperialist sympathies in similar situations had crowded into all the coastal towns to await events with the same thought in mind. Worth finally settled his family into an apartment facing the harbour, and wondered when he would see Paris again.

Louise and Catherine stayed on at the hotel. It offered a measure of safety and security to two women on their own, and they had no need to venture out-of-doors for anything. A number of foreign journalists were staying there, and through them Louise kept in touch with the latest developments. The government was throwing more and more troops into the fight to clear Paris. The Communards, facing defeat, put torches to some of the oldest and grandest buildings. The Cathedral of Notre-Dame escaped by sheer good fortune. Barrels of tar were set alight in the Salle des Maréchaux at the Tuileries where once the Princess de Metternich had displayed her first Worth gown to a glittering assemblage. The flames consumed the great palace, and the whole of the sky above the city glowed a terrible red.

The tricolour flew again in Paris as order was restored. Worth and his family returned to number 7 and found it relatively unharmed. The Communards had fired at the windows when the Worth boys had failed to appear, but the street doors had needed a battering ram both back and front to force an entrance, and when it became apparent that the quarry had fled, the Communards had had a fresh outbreak of fighting on their hands, which had put an end to the matter. Everywhere the city was coming to life again. Shopkeepers had taken down their bullet-pitted shutters, and café owners had set out tables and chairs under hastily patched awnings, the sound of music coming once more from cheerful little orchestras. Rubble was being cleared from the streets, and the long task of repairing buildings had begun. In the rue de Rivoli and other streets where whole areas had been destroyed by fire, architects were already about with new plans.

Louise found an apartment on the Champs-Elysées with a balcony from which Catherine could watch the world go by. A middle-aged widow who had lost her husband during the siege accepted thankfully the post of housekeeper and companion. She and Catherine had taken to each other, the widow having been a seamstress herself, and they had much in common. Louise, getting ready to take a train journey to Tours to get Paul-Michel, smiled at the sound of their happy chatter as she put on her little flowered hat. Worth had made her a hugely bustled dress for the occasion in mignonette, one of his tantalising shades that was neither grey nor green and continually appeared to be one or the other. She went to say adieu to Catherine.

"Paul-Michel and I will be home quite late tomorrow evening, so don't worry," she said, kissing her old friend on the cheek before she left. The smile still lingered in the corners of her lips as she stepped out into the ravishing June day to be driven to the railway station. She had written to Paul-Michel that she was coming to collect him, having decided that enough was enough, and it was time for him to be in her charge once again. She knew he would be pleased when she broke the news that she had made up her mind to open a dressmaking business in Paris comparable to the one in London, which she would continue to leave to Mademoiselle Brousseau's capable management. Worth had advised her to pay no attention to those gloomy individuals who predicted that Paris could not hope for a speedy economic recovery in view of its hedonistic past.

"That's the very reason why Paris will recover," he had insisted, "and our branch of commerce will be the first to soar. Women can't do without new clothes. Just see how my American clients have begun to return to me already with their faith, figures, and francs." He had smiled at her in the mirror, the conversation taking place during the first fitting of the mignonette dress. "They have *faith* that I will dress them as nobody else can, and they have on the whole splendid *figures* for me to put into shape, and finally there is no limit to the amount of *francs* that they will pay for the privilege. I tell you that people from every part of the globe will always flock to Paris for all that is joyous and unnecessary and frivolous. I thank God for it. An oasis in the desert of mediocrity.

Nobody ever has come or will come to the boulevards for anything but pleasure."

On such heartening advice she had looked around for suitable premises, and she had her eye on a little shop in rue Castiglione that was presently being restored after the fire. Later she might expand into the rue de Rivoli. She knew there would be plenty of competition to face. When Worth had launched himself there had been few such houses, but since then hundreds had sprung up and Paris had benefitted solidly by it. As Worth had said, fashion, with the beauty and happiness that was created through it, was as essential to the well-being of the world as anything more mundane and practical.

The train journey brought her to Tours. She stayed overnight in an hotel, and next morning set out again for the Château de Gand. If anything, the weather was even better than the previous day, and she rode shaded by her parasol in an open brougham, the warm breeze fluttering the petals on her hat and the frilled collar of her new dress. Such a longing to see Paul-Michel possessed her that she had no qualms about anything else that day. She did not expect to see Pierre. Stéphanie had been notified of her coming, and Louise did not doubt that on this occasion there would be no meeting with him. It was as it should be. The Château de Gand was Stéphanie's territory. No other woman had any rights there.

The château was mediaeval, large and turreted and set on a wooded slope that gave views of the surrounding countryside from every window. The drive was a full mile long, and Louise was driven past lush lawns and a wide lake to the forecourt and the huge entrance. She had expected Paul-Michel to come running down the steps to meet her, but he did not appear. A first twinge of misgiving assailed her. She was aware of an uncomfortable thumping of her heart as she was shown into a richly furnished room where Stéphanie awaited her. She was greeted courteously with all the warmth of their ambiguous friendship that had its extraordinary roots in loving the same man.

"How pleasant to see you again, Louise. My thoughts were with you all through that terrible siege and again through the ordeal of the Commune. Do sit down. I have ordered refreshment to be served upon your arrival. There was some fighting with the Prussians not far from here, but apart from hearing the distant noise of the gunfire we were undisturbed."

Louise sat on the edge of a chair. "How is Paul-Michel? Is he well?"

Stéphanie was quick to put her mind at rest. "He is bouncing with good health. And he has grown. I'm sure you'll be surprised by how much. He would have been here to meet you, but I wanted the opportunity to talk to you first, so he has taken his usual morning ride with Pierre."

"Paul-Michel rides well," Louise remarked with unconscious pride.

"Indeed he does. He's a born horseman." Stéphanie paused fractionally. "Just like Pierre. In fact, the likeness between them becomes more marked every day."

Louise could not quell her sense that all was not as it should be, although as yet she was unable to pinpoint what was wrong. "I trust Pierre has suffered no ill effects from his imprisonment by the Prussians."

"None at all. Being an imperial godson he received the same excellent treatment and respect as the Emperor himself. We are deeply saddened that those wonderful days of the Second Empire have gone forever. As you know, the Cent-Gardes were disbanded, and there's no question of Pierre going back into the Army. His loyalty was to the Emperor and there it remains. Now he has turned his mind and his energies to his lands and vineyards as well as the property he owns in this district and in Paris."

A tray of coffee and small almond cakes was brought in. The conversation did not resume until the coffee had been served. Louise heard the cup and saucer she held shiver slightly on the tremor of foreboding that went through her. What was wrong?

"When you see Paul-Michel," Stéphanie continued carefully, "he will make a request of you. I'm bound by a promise to him not to voice it on his behalf, but I implore you for his sake and for Pierre's to grant what it is that he will ask."

Now everything was clear. Louise knew beyond a shadow of doubt what would be requested, and the pain of it exploded within her. She put down her cup with deliberate care and clasped her hands tightly in her silken lap. She was afraid the shock would make her teeth chatter, but she was spared that embarrassment. Her lips seemed barely able to move. "I'll not give up my son."

Stéphanie came close to breaking point herself, and she leaned forward, her hands held out imploringly. "Don't make a decision yet," she begged emotionally. "Not until you hear what he has to say."

Louise could only stare at her. "I'll not give him up," she repeated tonelessly.

Stéphanie's voice throbbed. "He's Pierre's son too. I'll never be able to bear a child. There will never be another of Paul-Michel's generation in this house with the de Gand name. Let him grow up where he belongs. His roots are here. Don't take him away from Pierre." A sob broke in her throat and she covered her eyes with her hand.

Somewhere not far away a door banged hollowly, to be followed by the sound of running footsteps. Paul-Michel burst into the room. "Maman!" he shouted joyously.

They rushed to meet each other. They hugged, laughing and talking and questioning each other, she punctuating all she said by holding his face between her hands and kissing his brow before hugging him again. When they drew apart Stéphanie had gone from the room. Telling him about Catherine and her new home Louise did not sit down again, but remained standing to show she was ready for departure. She glanced at the clock on the mantel.

"There's a train for Paris that leaves Tours at three o'clock. If you will collect your belongings we can catch it easily."

He frowned, wandering across to the coffee tray. Absently he helped himself to a rose-coloured almond cake and bit into it. "I'd like to talk a bit first. Please sit down, Maman. It takes no more than three quarters of an hour to drive to the railway station. There's heaps of time."

"We can talk on the way—"

"Please!" he interrupted with a desperate glance of appeal.

She seated herself, trying to keep her expression bright and unconcerned. "Shall we talk about your school in Paris? The principal of the Collège St.-Nicholas is willing for you to start there again—"

"That's it," he stated flatly. "I don't want to leave my present school. I'm getting on well and I've made lots of friends there."

"That would mean staying on here," she replied faintly, "and I'm sure we can't impose any longer on the generous hospitality you have already received for so many months."

He rounded on her indignantly. "It's not hospitality. It's *home*. Madame Stéphanie told me that when I first came to the château with her. My grandmother at the dower house said the same when she told me all about my ancestors in the portraits in the gallery. I belong to this house."

Louise drew a shuddering breath. "What does your father say?"

He answered her in a quiet voice. "He wants me to stay. He would like to have my surname changed to his. He knows that I'll never like any other place in the world as much as I like it here." He heaved a heavy sigh. "But he insists it all depends on you. I must have your permission given willingly. He'll not have me kept against your wishes."

She looked down at her hands to hide her anguish from him. There was a tiny coffee stain on her white glove from the cup that had shaken in her grip, and she smoothed it with a fingertip. "I'm at a loss what to say. I can't seem to think for the moment."

He came and crouched down in front of her to look up into her face. "I'd come to see you in London. I'd spend vacations with you just as we planned when it was first decided I should go to school in Paris. You're always so busy that you wouldn't miss me in the meantime anyway."

She saw then what little time she had ever spent with him. If ever fate decreed that she should bear more children she would never make the same mistake again. She had sacrificed the very relationship that she treasured in her struggle to gain independence for herself and freedom for him. Now he had found his roots. He had cemented the filial tie between a son and father that she had always wished for him. He had come into his own, and she could not take it all from him. She had read once that courage was weakness that had prayed. Well, she was praying now to find the strength not to spoil anything for him. He must not go through life with any feeling of guilt towards her. She raised her head slowly and met his anxious eyes with a reassuring smile that reflected all her love for him.

"I give you permission to stay with your father. It will help me so much. As you say, I never seem to have time for anybody or anything when the rush of the season is on. But with your vacations to look forward to I'll make a point of arranging time off completely from business, which will give me much-needed holidays too." She became more animated. "We'll have such fun. We'll go wherever you want to go. To the seaside. To the Swiss Alps. To the Pyramids. To the moon!"

He burst out laughing, and she with him. "Yes, we'll do that, Maman."

For a little while, she thought. Then he would seek out those of his own age for holiday companionship, and rightly so. At the moment she must think only of keeping a smile for him.

"Let's say *au revoir* now. It really is time I was leaving, and after I've gone you may tell your father and his wife that between us we decided it would be much the best for both of us if you stayed on here."

He saw her off, riding in the brougham as far as the gates, and then waving to her until the turning road and woodland hid him from her sight. She had seen how deeply he felt this moment of parting, but her smile had remained intact. Only now did it quiver away. She leaned back against the crimson leather of the upholstery and saw nothing of the countryside passing by.

At Tours a porter found her a first-class compartment reserved for ladies, and since the train did not appear to be crowded, she had hopes of travelling alone. She took a corner seat and rested her head wearily, closing her eyes. When the door was suddenly jerked open with a rush of draught she opened her eyes, expecting to see a fellow passenger, and never dreaming it would be Pierre. She gasped, sitting forward, and he flung himself down into the seat at her side.

"I thought I should see you before you left the château! How could you leave without a word?" He pulled her into his arms and buried his face against her neck. "Louise, Louise. Do you think I don't know what a sacrifice you have made? I'll do everything in my power for our son." He raised his head to put one hand on the side of her face and fasten his mouth on hers, kissing her with a kind of adoring frenzy. Along the train there came the echo of doors slamming in preparation for departure. She fought for breath, freeing her lips.

"You mustn't come to Paris with me! Please get out while you can."

He drew his face away to look into her eyes, his own velvety in tenderness, his palm still against her cheek, his fingertips gentle and caressing. "There will be other times. Remember what I said to you at St.-Cloud? You are going to stay on in Paris, aren't you?"

The whole of her future hung in delicate balance. The full circle was complete. She was back to the point of being all over again. Deliberately she steeled herself against his sexual magnetism, the physical pull of their amorous past, and the utter yearning of her heart. Had they never met before it would have been as easy as it had ever been to love him.

"No," she said inexorably, her eyes lustrous in sadness and in the pain of parting. In a single word she had dismissed all the plans made over recent days, the property she had been considering, the completely new life she had anticipated. Paris was not for her. She had left it before at an emotional cost that had been terrible to her. Now she had to do it all over again. She measured her words, a throbbing in her throat. "I'm going home. To England."

The guard's whistle blew. The locomotive billowed forth steam. Pierre rose to his feet and stood staring at her, his mouth tightening, the bones standing out in his face. There was both threat and promise in his hard gaze on her. They both knew it was not over between them. It never would be. She had simply chosen to take another path.

Abruptly he swung the compartment door open and sprang out as the train began to move. She had a last glimpse of him through the window as he shut it again. His face bore the same expression as that of their son at the moment of good-bye. He could not bear to see her go.

A week later she was due to leave Paris. She had ensured that Catherine would want for nothing until the end of her days, and was being left in the best of care. She went by way of the rue de la Paix to the railway station, Worth having asked her if she would take a small parcel to England for him. In the Place Vendôme the column with the statue of Napoléon, which had been smashed down by the Communards in their rampage of destruction, had not yet been restored, and some of the debris still remained. As she was driven past, Louise remembered that it had become a popular saying at the time of the last exposition that the statue should never have been of Napoléon, but of Worth in solid gold for all he had done commercially for fashion as well as the rue de la Paix and the whole of Paris itself. She wished the replacement could be of her old friend in that precious metal and adorned by a cloak of lapis lazuli with the "eyes and ears" pattern picked out in precious jewels. The little fantasy enchanted her. And Worth himself would have seen it as no less than his due.

At number 7 the scene appeared to be just as it had always been. Clients were busy choosing materials, vendeuses went hither and thither, and on the upper floors the work-shops were in full swing once more. Yet as Louise went through the sumptuous showrooms she knew it was not the same. The Palace of the Tuileries was a burnt-out shell, and never again would Worth go there with wonderful dresses for the beautiful Eugénie to wear and dazzle the world. The age of the Second Empire had also been the age of Worth. Napoléon III had raised the lily of France to a glorious splendour never to be seen again, but it was Worth who had gilded it.

Although it was not yet midday Marie came to meet her in a vastly bustled dress of black-and-white satin floating with lace. Now more than ever she was to appear splendidly attired morning, noon, and night, accustomed at last to being forever noticed and acclaimed. Worth might have dropped into the habit of wearing comfortable old clothes in the garden at Suresnes, but Marie had come to a point when she would not have felt at ease in anything but the most extravagantly turned out *toilette* at any hour of the day. Worth had his way at last.

"So you're really going," she said, threading her arm though Louise's. "Don't let it be too long before you come and see us again."

Worth was busy on a dress for the President's elderly wife, who was following soberly and sombrely in Eugénie's wake as the First Lady of France, never appearing in anything but black. He broke away to bring Louise the small gilded box that he was to entrust into her care for personal delivery. Lifting the lid he showed her the bouquet of French violets on a bed of damp moss.

"For the Empress," he said with deep feeling, "from her loyal and devoted couturier."

The skies over the white cliffs were a soft English blue as the Channel steamer put in at Dover. Louise stood at the rails, a wisp of sea-breeze fanning a few tendrils of her hair, the sun casting diamonds on the lapping waves. Will was waiting on the quayside, a tall, broad figure with feet set squarely apart, hands clasped behind his back, a light-grey bowler at a jaunty angle on his head. He was eyeing her under his brows, his mouth compressed and smiling. An unmistakably triumphant smile. She could almost read his thoughts. He could have followed her to Paris and fetched her away under persuasion any number of times, but if he had, nothing would have been solved between them. He had had to wait until she returned of her own free will. He and Paris had done silent battle, and he had won.

She went down the gangway to him. Will had been as much a part of her life as Pierre had ever been. Yet there was no easy time ahead for him with her. How could there be when she was no more meek and pliable now than before she went away, and he was not one ever to be satisfied with second place in any woman's heart? She did not fear the struggle that lay ahead for them. It was what life and love were all about between a man and a woman. And Will was a man among men.

About the Author

Rosalind Laker and her husband live in Sussex, England, and have a second home in Norway: a four-hundred-year-old cottage in the mountains, overlooking a peaceful valley and pine forest. Mrs. Laker is also the author of novels of romantic suspense, THE SMUGGLER'S BRIDE and RIDE THE BLUE RIBAND. She has also written a trilogy which includes WARWYCK WOMAN, CLAUDINE'S DAUGHTER and WARWYCK'S CHOICE.